Fruit and Vegetable Preservation

Principles and Practices

Third Revised and Enlarged **Edition**

W0193385

Fruit and Vegetable Preservation

Principles and Practices

Third Revised and Enlarged Edition

RP Srivastava MSc PhD
Ex-Director
Horticulture and Food Processing
UP

Sanjeev Kumar MSc PhD
Scientific Officer (Horticulture)
UP Council of Agricultural Research
Lucknow, UP

CBSPD

CBS Publishers & Distributors Pvt Ltd

New Delhi • Bengaluru Chennai Kochi Kolkata Lucknow Mumbai
Hyderabad Jharkhand Nagpur Patna Pune Uttarakhand

Fruit and Vegetable Preservation

Principles and Practices
Third Revised and Enlarged Edition

ISBN: 978-81-239-2437-3

Copyright © Authors and Publisher

CBS Reprint: 2014
Reprint: 2015, 2016, 2017, 2019, 2020, 2022, 2023 **2024 2025**
First Edition: 1994
Second Revised and Enlarged Edition: 1998
Third Revised and Enlarged Edition: 2002
Reprint: 2003, 2005, 2006, 2007, 2009, 2010

Published by Satish Kumar Jain and Produced by Varun Jain for

CBS Publishers & Distributors Pvt Ltd
4819/XI Prahlad Street, 24 Ansari Road, Daryaganj, New Delhi 110 002, India.
Ph: 011-23289259, 23266861
Website: www.cbspd.com
e-mail: delhi@cbspd.com; cbspubs@airtelmail.in.

Corporate Office: 204 FIE, Industrial Area, Patparganj, Delhi 110 092
Ph: 011-4934 4934   Fax: 011-4934 4935   e-mail: publishing@cbspd.com; publicity@cbspd.com

Branches

- **Bengaluru:** Seema House 2975, 17th Cross, KR Road, Banasankari 2nd Stage, Bengaluru 560 070, Karnataka, India
  Ph: +91-80-26771678/79   Fax: +91-80-26771680   e-mail: bangalore@cbspd.com
- **Chennai:** 7, Subbaraya Street, Shenoy Nagar, Chennai 600 030, Tamil Nadu, India
  Ph: +91-44-26680620, 26681266   Fax: +91-44-42032115   e-mail: chennai@cbspd.com
- **Kochi:** 42/1325, 1326, Power House Road, Opp KSEB, Power House, Ernakulum Kochi 682 018, Kerala, India
  Ph: +91-484-4059061-65,67   Fax: +91-484-4059065   e-mail: kochi@cbspd.com
- **Kolkata:** 147, Hind Ceramics Compound, 1st Floor, Nilgunj Road, Belghoria, Kolkata-700056, West Bengal, India
  Ph: +033-25633055, 033-25633056   e-mail: kolkata@cbspd.com
- **Lucknow:** Basement, Khushnuma Complex, 7 Meerabai Marg (Behind Jawahar Bhawan),Lucknow-226001, UP, India
  Ph: +91-522-4000032   e-mail: tiwari.lucknow@cbspd.com
- **Mumbai:** PWD Shed, Gala no 25/26, Ramchandra Bhatt Marg, Next to JJ Hospital Gate no. 2, Opp. Union Bank of Ind Noorbaug, Mumbai-400009, Maharashtra, India
  Ph: 022-66661880/89   e-mail: mumbai@cbspd.com

Representatives

• Hyderabad	0-9885175004	• Jharkhand	0-9811541605	• Nagpur	0-9421945513
• Patna	0-9334159340	• Pune	0-9923910676	• Uttarakhand	0-9716462459

Printed at Glorious Printers, Jhilmil Industrial Area, Delhi, India

To
Beloved
Pooja

PREFACE TO THE THIRD EDITION

This book is now in its third edition. This book first revised in 1998 was well received by the readers including students of Horticulture, Food Technology and Home Science disciplines, manufacturers of preserved fruits and vegetables, amateurs, hobbysts and city dwellers. The stock of second revised edition was exhausted within a short time. This favourable response has encouraged us to adhere to the same basic format and objectives of the previous editions. Our goal is to provide readers with an introductory foundation in fruit and vegetable preservation technology upon which more advanced and specialized knowledge can be built. We are also aware that the book is widely used as basic reference outside the academic environment. The third revised and enlarged edition has been substantially updated and expanded where information was needed. Moreover, two new chapters have also been added in this edition. The suggestions received from various readers have also been incorporated.

The third edition continues to be aimed primarily at those with little or no previous instruction in fruit and vegetable processing technology. It is hoped that the edition in hand will continue to meet the day-to-day needs of students and others interested in fruit and vegetable preservation.We are confident that this edition will again receive your overwhelming response.

Lucknow (India)

December, 2001

PREFACE TO THE SECOND EDITION

This book "FRUIT AND VEGETABLE PRESERVATION-Principles and Practices" first published in 1994 was well received by the readers including students of Horticulture, Food Technology and Home Science disciplines, manufacturers of preserved fruits and vegetables, amateurs, hobbysts and city dwellers. The stock of first edition was exhausted within a short time. This has prompted us to bring out the second edition of the book by updating the information, making it more comprehensive by adding chapters on water for fruit and vegetable processing industries, quality charactertistics of fruits and vegetables for processing and quality control in food processing industry. The suggestions received from various readers have been incorporated.

It is hoped that the edition in hand will continue to meet the day-to-day needs of students and others interested in fruit and vegetable preservation. We are confident that this edition will again receive your overwhelming response.

Lucknow (India)   R.P. Srivastava
February 1998   Sanjeev Kumar

PREFACE TO THE FIRST EDITION

Fruits and vegetables are an important nutritional requirement of human beings as these foods not only meet the quantitiative needs to some extent but also supply vitamins and minerals which improve the quality of the diet and maintain health. It is, therefore, necessary make them available for consumption throughout the year in fresh or processed/preserved form.

India, though third largest producer of fruits after Brazil and U.S.A. and the second largest producer of vegetables after China, processes less than 0.5 per cent of the total production of fruits and vegetables. Most of the processed product consumed domestically. In order to improve the nutritional status of the people and also to exploit the export potential of processed products, there is need to increase the producitno of processed food in the country.

Fruit and vegetble preservation is one of the pillars of the food industry. Ever since we joined the U.P. Council of Agricultural Research we felt the need to encourage the fruit and vegetable preservation on massive scale. As a result, we thought of the idea of writing a book.

This book has been written from our experience of the past several years. It deals with the products prepared from various fruits and vegetablkes commercially as well as on home scale. Relevant information on enzymes, colours, additives, flavours, plastics, browning, toxins, adulteration, etc., has also been given. Each chapter has been presented to give additional theoretical information to understand the basic principles and methodology. Moreover, at the end of text, sixteen appendices have been given through which the readers can be benefited.

The present volume has been prepared primarily for the benefit of the disciplines of graduates and postgraduates in Horticulture, Food Technology and Home Science disciplines. It is also a ready reckoner for home scale preservation to any user. The authors believe that the readers wil get sufficient information connected with the frits and vegetables preservation. There may, however, be still some shortcomings in this book and the authors will be really grateful to receive suggestions from readers for incorporation in the next edition of this volume.

The authors gratefully acknolwedge the suggestions made by Dr. R.K. Pathak, Professor and Head, and Dr. I.S. Singh, Professor, Department of Horticulture, N.D. University of Agriculture and Technology, Faizabad, Uttar Pradesh.

We thank the International Book Distributing Co. (Publishing Division), Lucknow for publishing the book.

Lucknow (India)   R.P. Srivastava & Sanjeev Kumar
August, 1993

Contents

Introduction

The Green Revolution and subsequent efforts through the application of science and technology for increasing food production in India have brought self-reliance in food. The impetus given by the Government, State Agricultural Universities, State Departments of Agriculture and other organizations through the evolution and introduction of numerous hybrid varieties of cereals, legumes, fruits and vegetables and improved management practices have resulted in increased food production. However, the nation still faces the problem of the use of improper methods for the storage of food stuffs, leading to great wastage of the food produced. Such loses in the food front aggravate the existing syndromes of under nutrition and malnutrition.

Fruits and vegetables, which are among the perishable commodities, are important ingredients in the human dietaries. Due to their high nutritive value, they make significant nutritional contribution to human well-being. They are the cheaper and better source of the protective foods. If they can be supplied in fresh or preserved form throughout the year for human consumption, the national picture will improve greatly.

The perishable fruits and vegetables are available as seasonal surpluses during certain parts of the year in different regions and are wasted in large quantities due to absence of facilities and know-how for proper handling, distribution, marketing and storage. Furthermore, massive amounts of the perishable fruits and vegetables, produced during a particular season result in a glut in the market and become scarce during other seasons. Neither can they all be consumed in fresh condition nor sold at economically viable prices.

In developing countries agriculture is the mainstay of the economy. As such, it should be no surprise that agricultural industries and related activities can account for a considerable proportion of their output. Of the various types of activities that can be termed as agriculturally based, fruit and vegetable processing are among the most important. Therefore, fruit and vegetable processing has been engaging the attention of planners and policy makers as it can contribute to the economic development of rural population. The utilization of resources both material and human is one of the ways of improving the economic status of family.

In the post-green revolution era, eventhough food grains have been taken care of, fruits and vegetables for want of simple technologies of processing, preservation and transport to various places of need, have suffered post-harvest losses, estimated to be more than 25% and only about 1% of the total fruits and vegetables produced are processed. All forms of preserved fruits are in the reach of only the urban elite, and the rural masses who produce more than 90% of these fruits and vegetables are usually deprived of their usage.

India has made a fairly good progress on the Horticulture Map of the world with a total annual production of Fruits and Vegetables touching over 131 Million Tonnes during 1998-99. Today, India is the second largest producer of the Fruits (44 Million Tonnes) and Vegetables (87.5 Million Tonnes) as mentioned in Indian Horticulture Database-2000 published by National Horticulture Board. Our share in the world production is about 10.1 per cent in fruits and 14.4 per cent in vegetables. The Horticulture crops cover about 8 per cent of the total area contributing about 20 per cent of the gross agricultural output in the country. India produces 41.7% of the World mangoes, 25.7% of the bananas and 13.6 per cent of the world onion. However, the productivity of fruits and vegetables grown in the country is low as compared to the developed countries. The overall productivity of the fruits is 11.8 tonnes per hac. and vegetables is 14.9 tonnes per hac.

Major World Producers of Fruits and Vegetables (1998-1999)*

Fruits		Vegetables	
Country	Production ('000' MT)	Country	Production ('000' MT)
WORLD	434703	WORLD	606053
INDIA	44042	INDIA	87536
CHINA	53926	CHINA	237136
BRAZIL	37179	USA	34924
USA	31494	TURKEY	21743
ITALY	17676	ITALY	14501
SPAIN	13323	JAPAN	13629
MEXICO	12342	IRAN	12751
FRANCE	10863	EGYPT	12379
TURKEY	10263	RUSSIAN FED	12098
PHILIPPINES	10160	SPAIN	11496

* Source : Negi *et al.* (2000)

BOTTLING EQUIPMENTS

Cap Sealer

Cap Sealers

(Pneumatic)

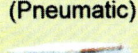
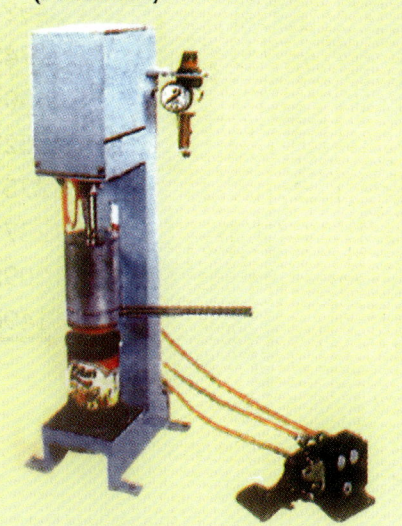

(Mechanical)

Photographs courtesy Bajaj Maschinen Private Limited
D-14, Lajpat Nagar-II, New Delhi-110 024

POTATO PEELER

Potato Slicer

Photographs courtesy Bajaj Maschinen Private Limited
D-14, Lajpat Nagar-II, New Delhi-110 024

JUICE EXTRACTION EQUIPMENTS

Fruit Mill

Pulper

Photographs courtesy Bajaj Maschinen Private Limited
D-14, Lajpat Nagar-II, New Delhi-110 024

BOTTLING EQUIPMENTS

Vacuum filling

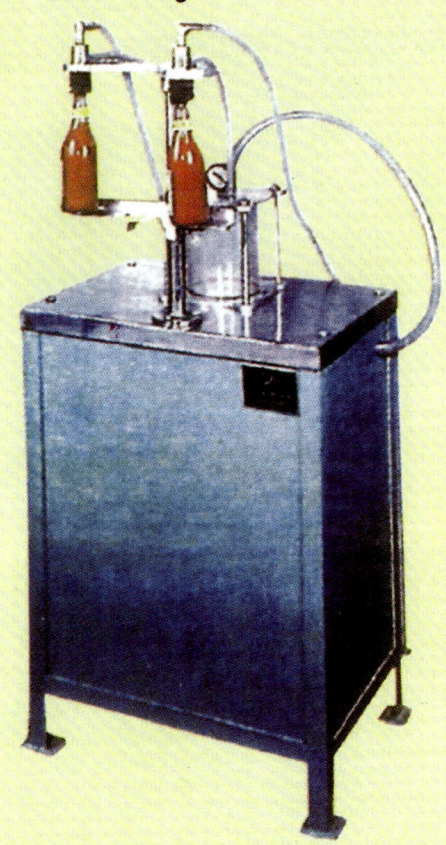

Crown
Corking
Machine

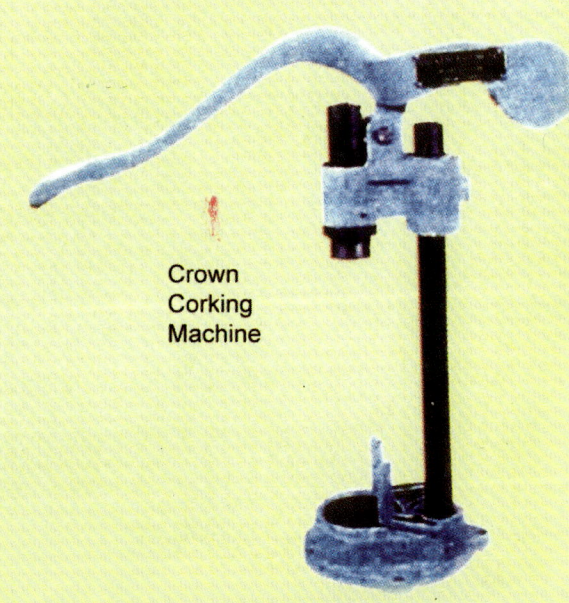

Photographs courtesy Bajaj Maschinen Private Limited
D-14, Lajpat Nagar-II, New Delhi-110 024

CANNING MACHINES

Double Seamer
(can still type)

Lid Embossing

Flanger

Double Seamer
(can rotary type)

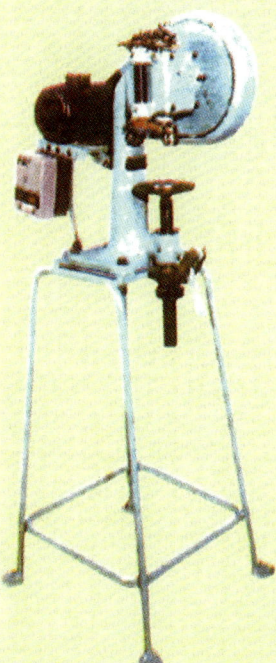

Rotary flat
(can body reformer)

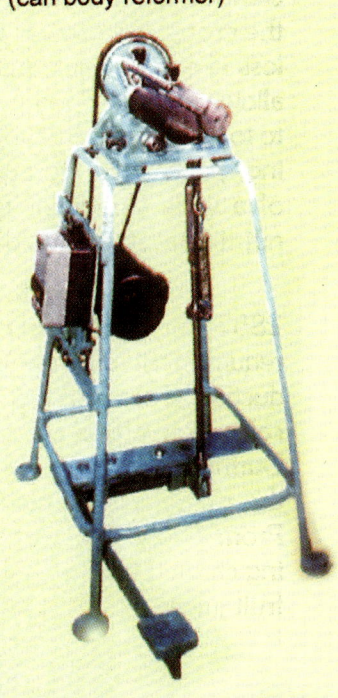

CANNING MACHINES

Exhaust Box

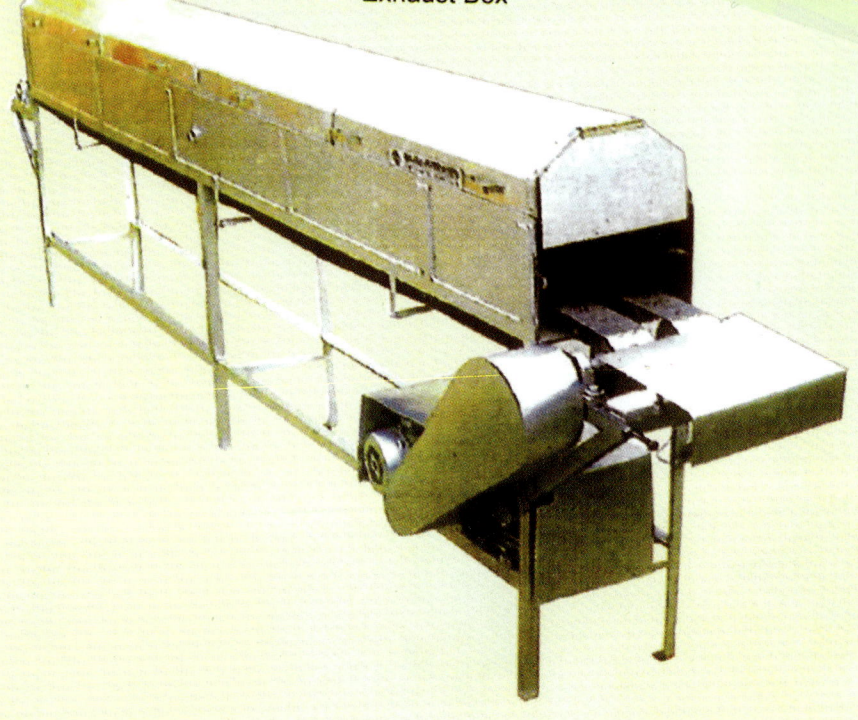

Canning Retort

STEAM JACKETED KETTLE

Photographs courtesy Bajaj Maschinen Private Limited
D-14, Lajpat Nagar-II, New Delhi-110 024

JUICE EXTRACTION EQUIPMENTS

Hydraulic
Juice Press

Rosing Machine

Screw type Juice Extractor

Introduction

Though the country is the second largest producer of fruits and vegetables in the World, our per capita consumption of fruits and vegetables for over one billion population is very low. More than 25 per cent of the fruits and vegetables production is unfortunately wasted due to inadequate facilities for processing. Despite such a large production, their processing is yet to be developed properly. The processing includes pre-processing of fruits and vegetables before these are fit to be used for final conversation into processed foods. Delay in the use of harvested food takes away its freshness, palatability, appeal and nutritive value. Tropical fruits are luscious, juicy and pulpy. They cannot be plucked early, cold-stored or subjected to controlled and long drawn out process as is possible in the case of fruits grown in temperate or cold regions. They are harvested at optimum maturity and processed or consumed promptly as they ripen because they require special attention and techniques.

The food preservation and processing industry has now become more of a necessity than being a luxury. It has an important role in the conservation and better utilization of fruits and vegetables. In order to avoid the glut and utilize the surplus during the season, it is necessary to employ modern methods to extend storage life for better distribution and also processing techniques to preserve them for utilization in the off season on both large scale and small scale.

Both established and planned fruit and vegetable processing projects aim at solving a very clearly identified development problem. This is that due to insufficient demand, weak infrastructure, poor transportation and perishable nature of the crops, the grower sustains substantial losses. During the post-harvest glut, the loss is considerable and often some of the produce has to be fed to animals or allowed to rot. Food processing, therefore, refers to the application of techniques to foods in a systematic manner for preventing losses through preservation, processing, packaging, storage and distribution, ultimately to ensure greater availability of a wide variety of foods which would help to improve the food intake and nutritional standards during the periods of low availability.

Fruit and vegetable processing was first started in an organized manner in 1857, mainly to make pickles and chutneys with a view to meeting the export requirement and canning of fruits and vegetables was started in 1927. The introduction of modern techniques of processing and preservation by addition of chemical preservatives could also be said to have been started from the same time. During the period 1927-1940, the processing and preservation was mainly in the manufacture of soft drinks like squashes, juices, cordials, barley water etc. From 1940 onwards the industry diversified the product mix and it started making canned fruits and vegetables, jams, jellies, and marmalades, tomato products, fruit juices, etc.

In the initial stages of development from 1927 onwards, the tendency was to locate the manufacturing units mainly in the consuming centres like Mumbai, Kolkata, Chennai, etc. Although this tendency, which is helpful for marketing finished products, still continues, the efforts made by various developmental agencies in the country have resulted in installation and commissioning of fruit and vegetable preservation units in the fruit growing areas in order to retain the maximum flavour and aroma of the raw materials. This is commendable development and it is likely that in the years to come more and more preservation and processing units will be set up in the growing areas in the rural parts of the country, opening up new avenues for rural employment. Even established fruit and vegetable canning factories or small/medium scale processing centres suffer huge loss due to erratic supplies of raw materials. As in most of the consuming city (centres), the manufacturers used to make purchase of raw materials from the markets of these centres, and as a result, direct link between the growers and processors was not established. Of late, this tendency has reversed and now the processors are trying to establish contacts with the growers directly so that they can get raw materials of adequate quality and the growers, in turn, can get a fair price for their produce. This has happened particularly with regard to pineapple, tomato, green pea and lime to the advantage of both growers and processors. In addition, there will be a gain also for the rural people resulting in all round rural development.

The main objective of fruit and vegetable processing is to supply wholesome, safe, nutritious and acceptable food to consumers throughout the year. Fruit and vegetable processing projects also aim to replace imported products like squash, jams, tomato sauces, pickles, etc., besides earning foreign exchange by exporting finished or semi-processed products. The fruit and vegetable processing activities have been set up, or have to be established in developing countries for one or other of the following reasons:

- diversification of the economy, in order to reduce present dependence on one export commodity;
- reduce fruit and vegetable losses;
- reduction of imports and meeting export demands;
- stimulate agricultural production by obtaining marketable products;
- generate both rural and urban employment;
- improve farmers' nutrition by allowing them to consume their own processed fruit and vegetables during the off-season;
- government industrialization policy;
- develop new value-added products.
- generate new sources of income for farmers/artisans.

Chapter 2

History of Food Preservation and Canning Industry

The art of preservation of food – meat, fish, vegetables and fruits — has been known since ancient times, the traditional methods, still in use, being drying in the sun, salting and smoking. In modern times, however, food preservation has become more of a science, based on the latest developments in science and technology, and food processing is an important and growing industry in many countries, including India.

The first recorded attempt to explain the cause of spoilage of stored food was by Needham in 1749. He observed that boiled mutton gravy, even if kept in a tightly corked bottle, became spoiled after some time, which he attributed to the spontaneous generation of microorganisms in the gravy. This theory was disputed by Spallanzani, who, in 1765, put forward the view that organisms are already present in the untreated air inside the vessel and these are responsible for the spoilage, which can be prevented by heating the food kept in an airtight container. This constitutes the basic principle of canning.

However, it took 40 years and a war for the canning industry to be actually born in France. During the Napoleonic war the French Government faced the difficulty of supplying food to its fighting forces at the front, since the food was often spoilt during transport over long distances. In 1795 the Government announced a reward of 12,000 Francs to the inventor who could develop a satisfactory method of preserving food for sea service and military stores. This award was won by M. Nicholas Appert who was the first to report the successful preservation of food in glass containers in 1804. He was awarded the prize in 1809 and the next year published a book on food preservation. In the English translation of the book entitled "The Art of preserving Animal and Vegetable Substances for Many Years" four important principles of food preservation were enunciated viz.,

1. Substances to be preserved should be enclosed in bottles;

2. The bottles should be corked with the greatest care, since the success of the process depends on this;

3. The bottles with the enclosed substance should be heated in a boiling

water bath, for a specific period depending on the substance; and

4.   The bottles should be removed from the water bath at the end of the specified period.

These principles of Appert are valid even now and are followed in every cannery. The method soon became very popular and in 1819 was introduced in U.S.A.

While Appert used only boiling water for sterilizing glass jars, others modified the method by adding common salt or calcium chloride to the water to raise its temperature of boiling so as to reduce the time required for sterilization.

Louis Pasteur, in 1864, demonstrated conclusively the role of microorganisms in food spoilage. He recommended heat treatment of food at sufficiently high temperature to kill the majority, though not all of the microorganisms, such as bacteria, moulds and yeasts present in food and preventing their access to the food inside the container by sealing the latter hermetically. This process of sterilization is called pasteurization.

In 1843, Winslow and Raymond Chevalien Appert reported that canned foods could be processed by steam and water under pressure. This led to the development of pressure cookers in 1852. Cooking of foods by means of pressure was first attempted by Papin in 1861. However, these pressure vessels were defective and frequently exploded.

An autoclave provided with an inlet for steam from an external source was used by Shriver in 1874. The use of pressure vessels marked a great advance in canning because less time was now required for processing of the can and packs of various shapes and sizes could be used.

In recent times it has been found that in case of liquids such as fruit juices, milk, etc., a shorter processing time with higher temperatures gives better quality products.

History of sanitary or open top cans

Soon after Appert received the award, in 1810 Augustus de Heine was granted a patent for the use of iron containers and Peter Durand for use of metallic containers for preserving food. About this period Donkin and Hall started a canning factory and the filled cans were tested by heating at 32°C to 45°C. Defective cans were detected by the bulging of their ends.

In early days, these containers were called "tinplate canisters" which was later shortened to "tin cans" or "tins" in England and "cans" in America. These cans were very crude in construction as compared to modern open top or sanitary cans. They were made entirely by hand from iron sheets with a heavy tin coating. Hand shears were used to cut the round ends and the blanks for bodies. The body blanks were shaped into cylinders whose overlapping edges were soldered to form the side seam. The end discs were cut slightly larger than the can diameter and their edges were turned over forming a flange. A hole was made in one of the ends and after filling the can it was closed by soldering on a small tinplate disc. Such cans, known as "hole-and-cap" cans, were in use as early as 1824 though a patent was granted to Fastier only in 1839.

Angilbert in 1833 used containers in which a full aperture could be used for filling, but his method of closing was very cumbersome. However, his method is similar to that now used for the ordinary type of can.

Hand making of cans continued till 1847 when a drop press machine was invented in America which made flanged ends from flat discs by dropping a heavy die on to the blank. This was followed by the invention of the pendulum press and the combination press which could cut the discs, flange them and punch the filler holes.

The above advances made possible the rapid production of can bodies. In 1876 a method of soldering was invented by Howe in which both the quantity of solder as well as the time for soldering the seams were reduced by rolling the cans at an angle and dipping them in molten solder.

The 'filler hole' cans remained in use for a very long time although opening them was very difficult and required a hammer and chisel. Moreover, only products of very small size could be filled due to the small size of hole. These difficulties led to the development of "open top" also called "open type" or "sanitary" cans which are still used. In these, the can ends are lined with a compound which produces a hermetic seal.

Lacquering of cans helps greatly to minimize the effect of corrosion and to protect the contents from metallic contamination. In 1868, Peltier and Paillard of Paris used varnish for internal coating and in 1882 Parry and Cobley suggested the use of sodium, potassium or calcium silicate and a serum made of proteinous materials.

The use of lacquer received greater attention when highly coloured products were found to become bleached or faded when kept in plain tinplate cans and blackening of cans and their contents was observed. However, the choice of lacquers suitable for coating is not an easy one. It must be nontoxic, odourless and not affect the flavour of the foodstuff in the can. At the same time the lacquer should adhere strongly to the can and not be affected by the high temperature of processing. In 1941, Farrow and Green classified lacquers into five groups:

1. Acid-resistant clear lacquers,
2. Sulphur-resistant lacquers,
3. Double-coated meat lacquers,
4. Phenolic meat lacquers,
5. Lacquers for deep drawing.

Recently a sulphur-resistant lacquer known as "corn enamel" has been introduced.

Preservation of fruits and vegetables using chemical preservatives has been practised in European countries since long. At present, only sulphur dioxide and sulphites and benzoic acid and some of its esters are permitted in foods. Sorbic acid and sorbates are permitted only in some cases. Antibiotics such as nisin, tylosin, etc., are still under consideration. A number of other chemicals, e.g., formaldehyde, salicylic acid and boric acid, which were earlier used as preservatives, have now been prohibited.

In India, the first fruit and vegetable processing factory was established in 1935 at Bombay which was followed by the setting up of units in Madras, Calcutta, Uttar Pradesh, and the Punjab. In 1950, the Central Food Technological Research Institute was established at Mysore, to promote the food processing industry and conduct research on various problems associated with foods. Its seven regional centres are located in Bangalore, Nagpur, Hyderabad, Lucknow, Ludhiana, Jammu and Trivandrum.

In order to control the quality of processed food the Government of India in 1955 passed the Fruit Products Order (F.P.O., 1955) according to which a licence is necessary for commercial manufacture of food products. Home scale processing does not require a licence. For licensing, a Food and Nutrition Board was established in 1973.

Government of India has also established a National Horticulture Board, Gurgaon (Haryana) for increasing the production of fruits and vegetables and their preservation to reduce post-harvest losses.

A Fruit Preservation and Canning Institute was established at Lucknow in 1949 by the Government of U.P. with the following objectives:

(i) To promote the development of fruit and vegetable processing industry.

(ii) To conduct research on problems associated with post-harvest and processing technology of fruits and vegetables.

(iii) To impart training in fruit and vegetable technology so as to create an infra-structure of trained personnel at supervisory and middle-management levels.

(iv) To popularize fruit and vegetable preservation on home scale.

Scope of Fruit and Vegetable Preservation in India

Preservation and processing of horticultural produce such as fruits, vegetables, spices, etc, assume a key position in the agro-industrial developmental plans of the country. Horticulture-based processing industries can stimulate the commercial growers to cultivate high quality crops for better economic returns to generate, in turn, enormous employment opportunities in production sphere of activities.

Fruits and vegetables are an important supplement to the human diet as they provide the essential minerals and vitamins and fibre (roughage) required for maintaining health. Fortunately, our country, with its wide range of soil and climatic conditions, is ideal for growing a large variety of fruits and vegetables, both indigenous and introduced. India has made a fairly good progress on the Horticulture map of the world with a total annual production of fruits and vegetables touching over 131 Million Tonnes during 1998-99. Today, India is the second largest producer of fruits (44 Million Tonnes) and vegetables (87.5 Million Tonnes).

However, for various reasons, this abundance of production is not fully utilized and about 20-30 per cent of it is wasted due to spoilage. Most fruits and vegetables are seasonal crops and perishable in nature. In a good season there may be a local glut, particularly of fruit, but because of insufficient transport facilities, lack of good roads and poor availability of packaging materials, the surplus cannot be taken quickly enough to the natural markets in urban areas. Moreover, the surplus often cannot be stored for sale in the off-season because of inadequate local cold storage facilities. Thus, the cultivators do not get a good price for their produce because of the glut, and some of it is spoilt resulting in complete loss.

High degree of perishability of certain fruits and vegetables, particularly those locally produced and grown in abundance in the remote and inaccessible centres/ pockets of the region, warrant scientific post-harvest management and processing to appreciate high value for the products. Experiences show that even proper marketing arrangement for fresh horticultural produce does not necessarily provide any practical solution for proper disposal of entire produce. To this, one may

Estimated Post-harvest losses of fruits and vegetables*

Fruit/Vegetable	% Loss
Apple	14
Banana	20-80
Grape	27
Lemon	20-85
Orange/Mandarin	20-95
Papaya	40-100
Cabbage	37
Cauliflower	49
Onion	16-35
Tomato	5-50
Potato	5-40

Source : Meena and Yadav (2001).

add the unmarketable surplus in the shape of low grade produce, overripe and underripe fruits, windfall and drops, bulky produce (for example, jackfruit), etc, which are considered for processing to avoid spoilage and concomitant economic loss.

Careless and improper handling of fruits and vegetables reduce the market value and keeping quality, ultimately causing enormous losses and depriving rightful benefits to both growers and consumers. Besides these quantitative losses, the loss suffered in quality before actual consumption can hardly be estimated. At present, more than 25 per cent of the fruits and vegetables valued at Rs. 67500 Million is reported to go waste annually. Although, the R & D efforts on the development of post-harvest handling has helped in reducing the spoilage, considerable losses continue to occur. Even if 10 per cent of the spoilage could be prevented during the glut season at the producing centres by converting them into new categories of processed products, there will be a saving of Rs. 6750 Million (Potty, 1988).

Two approaches are possible for solving this problem. One is the creation/expansion of cold storage facilities in the fruit and vegetable producing regions themselves, as also in the major urban consumption centres, to ensure supply of fresh fruits and vegetables throughout the year. Another approach is to process the fruits and vegetables into various products which could be preserved for a long time, and add to the value of the product. With increasing urbanisation, rise in middle class purchasing power, change in food habits and the dying out of the practice of making preserves in individual homes, there is increasing demand for factory-made jams, jellies, fruit beverages, dehydrated foods, pickles, etc., in the domestic market. Moreover, there is considerable demand for some of these products in foreign markets, e.g., mangoes both fresh and canned, fruit juices, salted cashew are good foreign exchange earners.

In spite of all this, the fruit and vegetable preservation industry at present is able to utilize less than 1 per cent of the total production for conversion into products like canned fruits, juices and their beverages, squashes, pulps, jams and jellies, pickles and chutneys, etc., as against 40-60% in developed countries. Thus, there is considerable scope for expansion of the industry, which in turn would give a fillip to development of horticulture specially in hill areas, and, through export of value-added products, earn more foreign exchange.

Preservation and processing of horticulture produce have multiple objectives, of which extending the consumption period, value addition and the possibility of diversification to range of products suiting to consumers' preference are the prime one. The basic preserving processes are canning, freezing, dehydration, salting, pickling and freeze-drying. Processing can help fresh produce to change into new or more usable forms and make it more convenient for preparation and consumption. Various preservation and processing techniques evolved, developed and now being gradually adapted for horticulture industries.

Advanced technology of processing has great potential to expand the farm produce markets beyond the region and country, because of conversion of perishable produce into stable forms that can be stored and shipped to distant market round the year, extending the availability of processed products and retaining their nutritive value and palatability. Processing can change horticulture produce into new and more usable forms which offer more convenience and linkings to the consumer at large. In essence, food processing industry takes care of mass production, downstream activities, quality control of raw produce and finished products and better processing techniques for desirable conversion into most acceptable forms. Recent advances in fruit and vegetable processing in horticulture sector include growing use of mechanical harvesting, bulk handling, automation, scientific canning, freezing, dehydration and application of modern biotechnologies to generate wide range of end products to cater for mass consumption at low price.

The rural homemakers who play a considerable role in food production have not been exposed to modern methods of preservation/processing. While disseminating a processing technology in the rural situation appropriateness of the technology should be assessed. The technology to be appropriate should meet the criteria of low cost, low input, low risk, rural bias, suitable for *small* scale application, use of local inputs and compatible with man's need for creativity. Therefore, appropriateness of the technology in the present context has been defined as one with low cost, low input, low risk type, rural bias, suitable for small scale application, use of local inputs and compatible with man's need for creativity. Constraints faced by rural families during processing of fruits and vegetables are :

(i)   Non-availability of modern processing technologies.

(ii)   Availability of machinery and equipments at a high cost.

(iii)   Lack of information about improved technologies.

(iv)   Lack of sufficient capital.

(v)   Lack of information about loaning schemes.

(vi)   Excessive burden of work and responsibility.

(vii)   Lack of recognition and appreciation in the family.

(viii) High cost and distant place for the availability of raw material.

(ix)   Difficulty in getting money from buyer after sale.

The various factors that have to be taken into consideration in setting up a fruit and vegetable processing industry are discussed briefly here.

1.   Product-mix

The product profile of the fruit and vegetable processing industry has remained static and is dependent only on a few fruits and vegetables like mango, pineapple, citrus, tomato and pea. The production of new products besides being necessary for the survival and growth of the processing industry, would also meet new taste and demand in home as well as export market.

A wide variety of products can be made from fruits and vegetables as shown in the table below. The choice of the products to be manufactured will depend on the readily availability of raw materials in the area where the processing unit is proposed to be set up and the consumer preference in the neighbouring markets.

14

Products prepared from fruits and vegetables

Sl. No.	Name of fruit/ vegetable	Product
	(A) Fruit	
1.	Mango	Juice, RTS, Nectar, Squash, Jam, Preserve, Toffee, Amchur, Pickle, Chutney, Canned mango, Mango powder, Mango concentrate
2.	Guava	Jelly, Cheese, Toffee, Nectar, Canned guava, Squash, Vinegar
3.	Aonla	Preserve, Jam, Candy, Syrup, Pickle, Chutney, Dried shreds, Triphla, Chyawanprash
4.	Pomegranate	Juice, Squash, Syrup, Anardana (dried product)
5.	Pineapple	Canned pineapple, Juice, Squash, Syrup, Jam
6.	Litchi	Juice, Syrup, Canned litchi
7.	Papaya	Jam, Candy, Nectar, Pickle, Sauce, Canned papaya, Papain
8.	Grape	Wine, Juice, Raisin, Munakka
9.	Karonda	Pickle, Jelly, Candy, Preserve
10.	Banana	Canned banana, Dried banana, Toffee
11.	Fig	Dried fig
12.	Loquat	Jam, Jelly, Canned loquat
13.	Ber	Candy, Preserve, Canned ber, Jam
14.	Bael	Preserve, Nectar, Squash, Canned bael, Cider
15.	Phalsa	Juice, Squash, Syrup
16.	Jackfruit	Pickle
17.	Citrus fruits	Juice, Pickle, Marmalade, Squash, Cordial, Barley water, Candy
18.	Jamun	Jelly, Syrup, Vinegar

19.	Strawberry	Jam, Juice
20.	Mulberry	Juice, Squash
21.	Apple	Jam, Preserve, Juice, Chutney, Cider
22.	Cherry	Jam, Candy, Canned cherry, Dried cherry
23.	Peach	Jam, Chutney, Canned and Dried peach
24.	Pear	Jam, Chutney, Pickle, Preserve, Canned pear
25.	Plum	Jam, Chutney, Sauce, Dried plum
26.	Apricot	Jam, Chutney, Canned and Dired apricot
27.	Date	Dried date
B. Vegetables		
1.	Tomato	Sauce, Chutney, Pickle, Puree, Paste, Canned tomato, Juice, Soup, Jam
2.	Cauliflower	Pickle, Dried and Canned cauliflower
3.	Carrot	Jam, Preserve, Pickle, Candy, Canned carrot
4.	Cabbage	Sauerkraut, Dried cabbage
5.	Peas	Canned peas, Dried peas, Pickle
6.	Brinjal	Pickle
7.	Green chilli	Pickle
8.	Beetroot	Pickle, Canned beetroot
9.	Radish	Pickle
10.	Turnip	Pickle, Canned and Dried turrnip
11.	Pointed gourd (Parwal)	Canned and Dried parwal
12.	Ash gourd (Petha)	Candy
13.	Bitter gourd (Karela)	Pickle, Dried bitter gourd
14.	Onion	Pickle, Dried onion
15.	Garlic	Pickle, Powder
16.	Beans	Canned and Dried beans
17.	Spinach	Canned spinach
18.	Ginger	Pickle, Preserve, Candy, Dried ginger, RTS, Syrup

19.	Cucumber	Pickle
20.	Water melon	Juice, Squash
21.	Musk melon	Juice, Squash
22.	Mushroom	Pickle, Sauce, Canned mushroom, Dried mushroom
23.	Potato	Chips, Papad, Starch, Canned potato

2. Availability of raw material

As stated earlier a wide variety of fruits and vegetables are cultivated in India and are available in abundance in the season. Some of these fruits like mango, guava, sapota, banana, cashewnut, jamun, pineapple, aonla and jackfruit do not grow in many countries and their products are likely to find a ready market in foreign countries. A contract between growers and the processing units would ensure the continued availability of good quality raw materials, at predetermined rates, to the industry.

3. Manpower

India is in an advantageous position, as compared to developed countries, in having a large reservoir of manpower, but skilled manpower in some trades is in short supply and productivity in general is low. Proper training, in-factory or institutional, good working conditions and reasonable wages would go a long way to increase productivity.

4. Capital

As in the case of any other industry, this is an important consideration for the food processing industry also. In recent years, with Government support, a number of big industries have diversified into the area of fruit and vegetable processing. There is, however, scope for small-scale units which require less capitals.

5. Lack of awareness

Most commercial fruit and vegetable growers are not aware of the market for preserved products and do not have the necessary technical knowledge to undertake processing themselves. The Central and State Governments have started a number of projects to impart different levels of training in canning and preservation, details of which are given later.

6. Marketing facilities

Although there is a demand for preserved products, which is likely to grow in future, these are not readily available in small towns due to reluctance of shop-keepers in stocking such items. The establishment of growers' cooperatives would help in the marketing of such products and it is the policy of the Government to encourage the establishment of such cooperatives.

7. Transport facilities

Earlier, the rapid transportation of fruits and vegetables in good condition from one part of the country to another for processing was a serious problem because of paucity of roads, their bad condition and shortage of trucks and rail wagons. There is now considerable improvement in both road and rail transport and the day is not far off when even remote rural fruit and vegetable producing areas will be connected to processing factories in distant parts of the country.

8. Availability of containers

Bottles and cans are the two major types of containers required by the food processing industry. Earlier these had to be entirely imported, but now the manu-facture of bottles of the required specifications has been taken up by a number of factories.

At present there is a great difficulty in the availability of cans since there are very few factories for their manufacture. Metal Box Company of India is the premier manufacturer, with factories in different parts of the country. There is need for setting up more factories to meet the demand for cans.

9. Publicity

Proper publicity is the only way to attract the consumer and give him infor-mation about the new products in the market. Publicity of the preserved food can create a good market even in backward areas as a majority of the population does not have knowledge of these products. These products can also be popularized by displaying in exhibitions and fairs, by practical demonstrations and distributing samples to the public.

10. Role of Government

Both the Central and the State Governments are giving encouragement to the fruit and vegetable preservation industry. In Uttar Pradesh, a Directorate of Horticulture and Food Processing has been established to promote the industry. Its functions are:

(a)   Establishment of community canning centres: These have been set up at every divisional headquarters in the State and in every important district. It is hoped that such centres will start functioning soon in other places also. These centres give technical advice regarding preservation and provide facilities to private individuals for canning and bottling of their raw material using latest equipment, not available in homes.

(b)   Training: Several types of training courses have been started. At every divisional headquarters and in important community canning centres there is a team of a lady instructor and assistant instructors to impart training exclusively to ladies. Such teams can also go to other places in the State on request. The duration of training, theoretical and practical, for preparing products for home consumption, is three weeks.

A post-graduate diploma course of 18 months duration (to be increased to 2 years) was started at the Government Fruit Preservation and Canning Institute, Lucknow. The course includes 3 months factory training.

The same type of training is also given at the Central Food Technological Research Institute, Mysore. Some agricultural universities have started departments of horticulture, with fruit technology as a major subject, to promote this discipline.

(c)   Research: At various research institutions all over the country attempts are being made to evolve better and more economic methods of preservation of fruits and vegetables under Indian conditions.

(d)   Commercial production : The U.P. Government has established food preservation and canning factories for commercial processing of fruits and vegetables on scientific lines. The products are sold at reasonable prices.

Fruit and vegetable processing is one of the most important agro-based industries. Owing to its seasonal and perishable nature, processing assumes a special significance. Fruit and vegetable processing play the role of siphoning off the seasonal gluts and surpluses of production and thereby help impart stability in prices. the industry is labour-intensive and offers high employment potential both at the farms and in the factories. The Government has already recognized fruit and vegetable products as one of the major thrust areas for augmenting the country's exports. Among fruits, mainly mango, pineapple, citrus and among vegetables, mainly tomato, onions, peas, okra and potatoes, are regularly processed. The fruit and vegetable processing industry in India in the organized sector is comparatively a recent phenomenon. The industry is highly decentralized with a majority of units being in the cottage/small sector. The majority of the units is in the private sector (95 per cent), the balance is among the public and cooperative folds. The capacity utilization of industry is around 45 to 50 per cent. More than 60 per cent production is of mango and mango-based products. About two-thirds of this production centres around fruit juices and fruit-based beverages. Indigenous products like pickles, chutneys, preserves and crystallized fruits constitute only 15 to 16 per cent of the total production. One of the major causes for low capacity utilization of the processing industry in the country has been the insignificant domestic market. Out of the total fruits and vegetables produced, only about 1 per cent of them are used for processing purposes. The Agricultural and Processed Food Export Development Authority (APEDA) is seized with the problem of increasing exports of fruits and vegetables, both in fresh as well as processed form.

Thus, food processing industries are concerned, though indirectly, with the welfare of the population, with special reference to health, nutrition and food safety.

Enzymes in the Food Industry

Enzymes are organic biocatalysts which govern, initiate and control biological reactions important for life processes'. Amylase found in saliva promotes digestion or breakdown of starch in the mouth. Pepsin found in gastric juice promotes digestion of protein. Lipase found in liver promotes breakdown of fats. There are thousands of different enzymes found in bacteria, yeasts, moulds, plants and animals. Even after a plant is harvested or an animal is killed, most of the enzymes continue to promote specific chemical reactions, and most foods contain a great number of active enzymes. Enzymes are large protein molecules which, like other catalysts, need to be present in only minute amounts to be effective. All enzymes are proteins but all proteins are not enzymes. Enzymes are exceptional as catalysts in the following respects:

(1) They are exceedingly efficient; under optimal conditions most enzymatic reactions proceed 10^8-10^{11} times faster than the corresponding non-enzymatic reactions.

(2) Most enzymatic reactions are specific in terms of the nature of the reaction and the structure of the substrate.

(3) The spectrum of reactions catalyzed by enzymes is very broad, e.g., hydrolytic, polymerization, oxidation, reduction, dehydration, etc.

(4) Enzymes themselves are subject to a variety of cellular controls. Even their biosynthesis is enzyme-catalyzed.

Many enzymes have been named by adding the suffix-ase to the name of the substrate catalyzed, e.g., urease, which catalyzes the hydrolysis of urea to ammonia and carbon dioxide.

Important properties of enzymes in fruit and vegetable technology

(i) Enzymes control the reactions associated with ripening of fruits and vegetables.

(ii) After harvest, unless destroyed by heat, chemicals or some other means, enzymes continue the ripening process, in many cases to the point of spoilage-such as soft melons or overripe bananas.

(iii) Because enzymes enter into a vast number of biochemical reactions in fruits and vegetables, they may be responsible for changes in flavour, colour, texture and nutritional properties.

(iv) The heating processes in fruits and vegetables processing are designed not only to destroy microrgranisms but also to deactivate enzymes and so improve the fruit and vegetables' storage stability.

(v) When microorganisms are added to foods for fermentation purposes, the important agents are the enzymes the microorganisms produce.

(vi) Enzymes also can be extracted from biological materials and purified to a high degree. Such commercial enzyme preparations may be added to foods to break down starch, tenderize meat, clarify wines, coagulate milk protein, and produce many other desirable changes.

Enzymes have an optimal temperature-around $+ 50^0C$ where their activity is at maximum. Heating beyond this optimal temperature deactivates the enzyme. Activity of each enzyme is also characterized by an optimal pH.

In fruit and vegetable storage and processing the most important roles are played by the enzymes classes of hydrolases (lipase, invertase, tannase, chlorophylase, amylase, cellulase), and oxidoreductases (peroxidase, tyrosinase, catalase, ascorbinase, polyphenoloxidase).

Enzymes used in the food industry

Enzymes are being increasingly used for the preservation and processing of a wide variety of foods and beverages. Some important enzymes are shown in the table below:

Enzyme	Class	Source	Application
Amylase	Hydrolases	Malt, fungi Malt, bacteria	Bread baking Mashing
		Malt, fungi	Precooked baby food, Breakfast food
		Bacteria, fungi	Syrups
		Fungi	Liquefying purees and soups
Cellulase	Hydrolases	Fungi, bacteria	Foods
Glucose isomerase	Isomerases	Fungi, actinomycetes	Sugar and starch

Glucose oxidase	Oxido-reductases	Fungi	Glucose removal
		Fungi	Oxygen removal
Invertase	Hydrolases	Yeast	Soft-centre candies
		Yeast	High-test molasses
Lactase	Hydrolases	Bacteria	Milk concentrate, ice-cream and frozen desserts
Pectinase	Hydrolases	Fungi	Pressing, clarification, filtration, concentration
		Fungi	Coffee bean fermentation, coffee concentrates
Protease	Hydrolases	Fungi	Bread baking
		Bacteria, fungi, pepsin, bromelin	Chill-proofing
		Bacteria, fungi, papain, bromelin	Meat tenderizing and condensed fish solubles
Rennin	Lyases	Fungi, animal	Cheese production
Takadiastase	Hydrolases	Fungi	Bread supplement, production of syrups

Immobilized enzymes

Although enzymes are useful as catalysts in food processing, they may not always be suitable for practical application. Conventionally, an enzymatic reaction is carried out in a batch process, by incubating the substrate with a soluble enzyme. But it is very difficult to recover the enzyme after the reaction, for recycling. Moreover, the presence of residual enzyme in the processed food may, in certain cases, cause allergy. To overcome these problems two approaches are possible. The first is the use of a synthetic polymer having enzyme-like activity (Synzyme). The second approach is the modification of the natural enzyme by immobilizing it.

Sometimes we wish to limit the degree of activity of an added enzyme but cannot readily inactivate the enzyme without adversely affecting the food. One way to accomplish this is to immobilize the enzyme by attaching it to the surface of a membrane or another inert object in contact with the food being processed. In this way reaction time can be regulated without the enzyme becoming part of the food.

Immobilized enzymes are defined as "enzymes physically confined or localized in a certain defined region of space with retention of their activity and which can be used repeatedly and continuously." The advantages of immobilized enzymes are :

(i)   recovery and reuse of enzyme is possible,

(ii) stability of enzyme is increased,

(iii) kinetic property of enzyme is enhanced,

(iv) product is enzyme-free,

(v)   permit continuous operation,

(vi) cost is lower, and

(vii) greater control of catalytic power is possible.

Immobilized enzymes are presently being used to hydrolyze the lactose of milk into glucose and galactose, to isomerize the glucose from corn starch into fructose, and in many other industrial food processes.

Plastics in Food Industry

P lastics form a very large, comprehensive family of materials with a wide range of properties that can meet almost every requirement of the packaging industry. Being man-made, plastics can be tailor-made to meet a specific requirement or achieve a combination of properties. As such, there will always be a polymer or a combination of polymers to meet almost every need. The British Standards Institution has defined plastics as "a wide group of solid composite materials which are largely organic, usually based on synthetic resins or upon modified polymers of natural origin and possessing appreciable mechanical strength". At a suitable stage in their manufacture most plastics can be cost, moulded or polymerized directly to shape.

Plastics can be divided into two main groups:

(A) Thermoplastics, and (B) Thermosets

(A) Thermoplastics

Thermoplastics are those materials which can be heated and cooled repeatedly without appreciable loss of mechanical and physical properties. Among the very wide range of thermoplastics which are used in large quantities in packaging are:

(1) Polyethylene

Polyethylene (PE) is produced by polymerization of ethylene. It is available in a range of densities with different properties as given below:

Properties of polyethylene

Type	Density (g/cc)	Gas-barrier	Water vapour barrier	Use temperature range ($^{\circ}$C)	Resistance to grease and oils	Uses
Ultra lowdensity polyethylene (ULDPE)	0.880-0.890	Poor	Good	-51 to 100	Good	Films, cross-linked foams

Linear lowdensity polyethylene (LLDPE)	0.900-0.940	Fair	Good	-51 to 100	Good	Pallets; thermoformed container films, coatings, nettings, foams
Low-density polyethylene (LDPE)	0.910-0.925	Fair	Good	-51 to 82	Good	Bottles, tubs, cups, tubing, closures, drums, pails
High-density polyethylene (HDPE)	0.941-0.965	Fair	Good	-40 to 100	Good	Bottles, films

Generally, PE refer to LDPE and HDPE. In addition to above, medium-density polyethylene (MDPE) with a density range of 0.926-0.940 is also available.

Polyethylenes are the most versatile of all thermoplastics and are widely used in the field of packaging. They are easy to process, economically priced and are used alone or in combination with other polymers to meet specific requirements. They are used in the form of single-layer or multilayer films, blow-moulded containers, tubes, moulded and extruded laminates, etc.

The major outlets for ULDPE are flexible packing in various forms and combination structures such as heavy-duty films made by blending with HDPE, LDPE, EVA (ethylene vinyl acetate) for cereals, crackers, etc., blown and cast monolayer films or cheese, frozen food, meat, beverages; coextruded and laminated film structures; coextruded shrink packages for poultry and meats; blow-moulded vacuum bags, multiwall bags, coextruded and laminated with various barrier layers.

LLDPE differs considerably in structure from LDPE. Its advantages include higher stiffness, improved environmental stress-cracking resistance (ESCR) and heat distortion resistance. The major outlet is in the form of films as in the case of LDPE.

HDPE has superior mechanical and physical properties and a higher heat distortion temperature. The major outlets are paper-like films of high molecular weight, woven sacks, blow-moulded containers, and injection-moulded containers like crates for transport and material handling.

Polyethylenes are widely accepted for the packaging of food products as well as chemical owing to their inert character, compatibility and safety in contact with most food products as well as resistance to almost all commercially used chemicals.

(2) Polypropylene

Polypropylene (PP) is a polymer having low density (0.90 g/cc) and is extremely versatile because of its excellent processability, physical and mechanical properties and high heat distortion resistance. The major outlets are in the form of biaxially oriented cans, moulded transport containers, box strappings, woven sacks and intermediate bulk containers for food grains, onions, potatoes, sugar, etc., metallized films as wrappers and laminates, closures, and thermoforming and blister packaging.

(3) Polystyrene

Polystyrene (PS) is one of the earliest commercially available commodity plastics. It is a very versatile material because of the ease with which it combines with other polymers to give the desired properties. General purpose polystyrene (GPPS) is rigid, easy to process, has a good surface finish and gives protection during transportation. High impact polystyrene (HIPS) has improved mechanical and physical properties. Expandable polystyrene is an excellent cushioning materials. The major outlets are injection blow-moulded bottles, injection-moulded containers, cushioning protection during transport, biaxially oriented films and thermoformed disposable products like coffee and ice-cream cups.

(4) Polyvinyl chloride

Polyvinyl chloride (PVC) is also a versatile packaging material. It can be formulated with such a variety of additives that the range of physical properties possible seems endless. It is readily available in thicknesses that range from 0.002 to more than 0.02 mm, as a semi-rigid barrier-type or highly flexible permeable film.

Of the variety of PVC packaging films available, unoriented, flexible types have the largest volume of use. Such films have dominated fresh meat packaging for over 15 years offering just the right combination of physical properties for such an application. These properties include abundant oxygen permeability (for maintaining red oxymyoglobin), excellent elastic memory (packages stay tight), outstanding optics (low haze, high gloss) and good sealability (for rapid in-store packaging). When properly formulated they are tough, extensible and will not fog when packages are placed in the cold supermarket meat display case.

PVC films that are uniaxially, preferentially or biaxially oriented are also available for food packaging.

(5) Nylon

Nylons, also known as polyamides (PA), are long chain molecules with amide functionalities as an integral part of the repeating unit. Nylon films can be produced by both the blown-film and the cast-film processes. The high strength and toughness of nylon are enhanced by biaxial orientation. Metallization of nylon films results in advantages such as improved barrier to moisture and oxygen properties, and good visual appeal. In addition, the films have excellent flexibility, flex-crack resistance and antistatic properties, and excellent printability.

Nylons are tough, have a high tensile strength and are very resistant to abrasion. They exhibit very little cold flow or 'creep'. Nylons are slightly hygroscopic and the granules must be dried by heating before extrusion or moulding. Chemically, nylons are inert to most inorganic reagents although they are attacked by oxidizing agents such as hydrogen peroxide and chlorine bleaches. Nylons are also attacked by concentrated mineral acids but dilute acids have no effect, except when hot. They are resistant to caustic alkalis even at concentrations up to 20%. The resistance of nylons to organic solvents is of particular interest. In general, they are unaffected by alcohols, ether, benzene, xylene, carbon tetrachloride, acetone and many mineral oils. Nylons are not particularly good barriers to water vapour but are very good gas barriers.

Some of the applications are vacuum and gas packaging of meats and cheeses; metallized nylon films are suitable for packaging of materials where retention of aroma is required. In coextrusion as a barrier layer, biaxially oriented films are used for food packaging and bag-in-box applications.

(6) Polyester

Polyethyleneterephthalate (PET), commonly known as polyester, is a homopolyer made from a dibasic acid, terephthalic acid, and ethylene glycol. The material has excellent clarity, rigidity, mechanical, physical and barrier properties, and can be used in contact with most food products. The major applications of PET are in the form of stretched or biaxially oriented bottles for beverages, including wines, biaxially oriented films and metallized films as one of the substrates in laminates for packing of foods, ovenable trays for frozen foods and PET copolymers for blister packaging.

(7) Ethylene-vinyl acetate

The polymerization process for ethylene-vinyl acetate (EVA) copolymers is similar to that for LDPE. EVA copolymers with a high vinyl acetate content (around 28-50%) are used as additives for waxes and adhesives, to improve strength, barrier properties, and processing characteristics. Of greater interest to packaging are the copolymers containing between 7% and 28% vinyl acetate. Those containing 7-8% may be considered as modified LDPE, whereas those in the range of 15-28% behave more like flexible i.e. plasticized, PVC. One advantage of EVA over flexible PVC is that its flexibility is inherent and does not depend on the presence of plasticizers which can be lost by migration or leaching.

In general, the properties of EVA compared with those of LDPE, are as follows:

(1)   More permeable to water vapour and gases;

(2)   Lower heat seal temperature;

(3)   Higher filler retention;

(4)   Greater flexural life;

(5)   Greater elasticity;

(6)   Higher impact strength;

(7)   Better low temperature properties; and

(8)   Greater resistance to environmental stress-cracking.

EVA films have low slip and a greater tendency to blocking so that a higher percentage of anti-blocking additives is necessary.

Uses of EVA include packaging of fresh meat, cling film for packaging of fruits, foodstuffs, nutritional pouches, snap-on caps, liners for bag-in-box containers and stretch wrapping.

(8)   Ethylene-vinyl alcohol

Films of ethylene-vinyl alcohol (EVOH) are characterized by outstanding gas barrier properties and excellent resistance to odour and flavour permeance as well as excellent processability.

These films are particularly suited for foods like pickles, soups, processed meats, condiments, coffee, tea, juices, sauces, jams, edible oils, beer, honey and salad dressings because of their special properties, such as:

(i)   They resist oils and organic solvents thus making them particularly suitable for packaging of oily foods and edible oils.

(ii)   With an OH-group in the molecular structure of the polymer, the film surface can be printed without pretreatment.

(iii) EVOH films maintain their superior barrier properties over a wide range of humidities.

(iv) Package made of EVOH is excellent for the retention of fragrance and aroma of the contents over a long shelf-life period.

(v) Coextruded films and sheets can be thermoformed, vacuum and pressure moulded.

(vi) They possess a high gloss and low haze resulting in outstanding clarity.

(vii) EVOH can be easily processed on conventional processing equipment.

(9) Polyvinylidene chloride

Polyvinylidene chloride (PVDC) resins are copolymers containing at least 50% vinylidene chloride. More than 90% of the world production is used in food and medical packaging.

The properties of PVDC film include low permeability to atmospheric gases, moisture and most flavour and aroma bodies, stress-crack resistance to a wide variety of agents, ability to withstand the rigours of hot filling and retorting. The major uses are for coating and film applications.

(10) Ionomers

The term ionomer was coined to describe a family of polymers in which there are ionic forces between the polymer chains, in addition to the normal covalent (chemical) bonds between the separate atoms in each chain. Ionomers are basically copolymers of ethylene and methacrylic acid, with some of the acid groups present in the form of a metal salt. The polymerization process is again similar to that of LDPE. Ionomers are made by Du Pont under the trade name 'Surlyn'.

At room temperature, ionomers have greater resistance to oils and greases than LDPE, although the differences are not so marked at elevated temperatures. Resistance to environmental stress cracking is good and is said to be higher than that of LDPE. Ionomers are resistant to weak and strong alkalis but are slowly attacked by acids. Other chemical properties of ionomers are similar to those of LDPE. Gas permeability is similar to that of LDPE but water vapour permeability is somewhat higher as is water absorption.

Ionomers also have exceptional toughness characteristics, as evidenced by their level of resistance to abrasion, puncture and tear. Film toughness is a key requirement for cavity-formed packaging as this property, along with adequate film thickness, imparts flex-crack resistance to package corners. Package sparkle and clarity, and adhesion to polar substrates in the presence of aggressive environments are additional properties offered by ionomers.

Flexible packaging is the largest and fastest growing market for ionomers. Since their invention in 1961, their unique combination of properties has earned ionmers a reputation as the ultimate in heat-seal layers for packaging structures. And, because the packaging industry's current trend is toward increased use of high speed, automatic, form-fill-seal equipment, the demand for ionomer heat seals is growing.

Another strong ionomer film area, previously dominated by PVC, is the skin-packaging of consumer carded display items. Ionomer film is widely used in skin packaging because of its high resistance to puncturing and its good adhesion to porous board surfaces.

Vacuum packaging of large cuts of fresh meat for box-beef shipment represents the most important area where nylon/ionomer coextruded film bags are used. The high grease resistance of ionomers has opened up markets in form-fill-seal pouches for convenience foods with a high added fat content. Soups, seasonings and spices are examples of products which use ionomer seal layers in form-fill-seal packaging constructions.

(11) Acidic copolymers of ethylene

Acrylic acid copolymers are offered by Dow Chemicals under the brand name PRIMACOR and methacrylic acid copolymers by Du Pont under the brand name NUCREL. The brand names of BASF (LUPOLEN), CDF (LOTADER) and Esso Germany (ESCORENE) are well known in Europe. As films, they have better clarity, toughness and stress-crack resistance than LDPE and have improved adhesion to aluminium foil and metallized films. In other properties such as tensile strength and rheological behaviour, they are quite similar to LDPE.

(12) Polycarbonate

Polycarbonate (PC) is an amorphous resin that can be processed by all the conventional processing techniques.

PC has excellent dimensional stability, rigidity, impact resistance and transparency over a wide temperature range. It makes an excellent structural layer in coextruded or laminated packaging for hot-fill at 80 to 99°C, retorting at 120°C, autoclaving at 138°C and frozen food packaging. PC can be sterilized with both gamma and electron-beam irradiation with good stability.

(13) Polyethylene based adhesive resin

Its very important use is in the bonding of two non-compatible materials in the coextrusion process. Some of the qualities of such resins are strong adhesion to thermoplastics, such as PE, PP, PS, PC, PET, EVOH, nylon, non-susceptibility to the effects of aging, hot-water treatment or retorting, hygienic safety in food contact, simple and easy to process by coextrusion blow-moulding, film coextrusion, tube coextrusion, etc. Typical applications are in the form of containers for vegetable, soups, juices and coextruded film pouches for meat and processed food such as spices, pickles, etc.

(14) Imide copolymers

The poly (glutarimide-acrylic) copolymers have been developed to meet the requirements of high temperature processing and end-use applications.

The unique qualities of these copolymers, such as high heat resistance, stiffness and good gas barrier properties, arise from the presence of the imide unit in the polymer.

The copolymers can be combined with other materials for multilayer composites. A major advantage is that they have good adhesion to many polymers, such as acrylics, PVC and polycarbonate.

Depending on the grade, the bottle design and the degree of orientation imparted by the process, it is possible for a filled and capped bottle to withstand over 160°C dry heat for two hours without distortion (not exceeding 1%). The ability of these copolymers to withstand retort temperatures coupled with moisture insensitivity of their gas barrier properties makes them ideally suited for retort applications.

(B) Thermosets

Thermosets are those materials which soften once on the application of sufficient heat, but harden on cooling. They are rarely used in the field of packaging except in a small way for threaded closures made out of phenol-formaldehyde and urea-formaldehyde. They mainly include alkyd resins (polyester), allyls, amino, epoxy, furan, ionomer, phenol-formaldehyde, urea-formaldehyde, polyamides, and silicones.

Flexible packaging

Plastics have been playing a vital role in the field of flexible packaging. In the form of laminates and multilayer coextruded films, they dominate the field because of some distinct advantages:

1. Meeting the exact performance requirement by selection of different types of layers of the composite structure.

2. Retailing in smaller unit packs gives protection from adulteration and is

convenient for the weaker sections of society.

3. Total prevention of repacking with spurious materials which are a major health hazard.

4. Ease of handling and storage.

The major outlets for such materials are the packaging of processed and convenience foods, dehydrated food products, dehydrated malted products like Bournvita, fruit juice concentrate like Rasna, edible oils, vanaspati and ghee, milk, tea, coffee, spices, and condiments, bag-in-box for non-carbonated fruit drinks, alcoholic beverages, mineral water, fruit juice concentrates, etc.

The materials most commonly used as substrates or layers for such applications are films of polyolefins, LDPE, LLDPE, HDPE, PP, polyester, PVC, metallized PET and PP. For coextruded multilayer films, LDPE, LLDPE, HDPE, PP, EVA, EVOH, primacor (bonding agent), nylon (barrier resin), ionomer (sealant layer), etc., polymers are used.

All these materials are printed on a gravure or flexo-multicolour printing machine and then cut into the required widths.

Plastic packaging applications in food industry

Plastics due to their versatility are making great inroads into the field of packaging of a variety of products, replacing conventional materials like paper, wood, glass, tin and aluminium. Being synthetic materials, they can be tailor-made to meet even the most demanding performance requirements of the product to be packed. Plastics can be converted to any desired shape or form by selecting one of the many processes available for conversion. From a simple poly bag to a sophisticated coextruded multilayer (up to 12 layers) structure for pouches, tubes and multilayer laminated tubes, laminates, biaxially oriented bottles, multilayers bottles, plastics have found easy entry into both urban and rural life-styles.

Plastics in the form of pouches, thermoformed tubs, bag-in-box, tetrapacks, etc., offer the advantages of convenience, freedom from pilferage and adulteration, ease of dispensing and disposal, safety in use and possibility of economical portion packs and are finding tremendous acceptance for the packaging of processed and convenience foods.

The products that are being packed in flexible packaging materials such as pouches made of laminates and multilayer films are edible oils, processed and convenience foods, snack foods, spices, tea, coffee, malted milk products, fruit juice concentrates, pan masala, betel nut powder, fruit juice based beverages, wine, country liquor, etc.

Thermoformed cups and tubs are extensively used for yogurt, ice-cream, shrikhand, jelly, fruit salads, etc., and portion packs for pickles, chutneys, ketchup, butter, jams, etc.

Stretched blow-moulded bottles of PET and PVC are being increasingly used for mineral water, beverages, edible oils, alcoholic beverages, etc. Tetrapacks and laminated pouches with variations such as built-in-straw are finding wide acceptance for the packaging of non-carbonated beverages and cold coffee, milk shakes, lassi, etc. Printed wrappers of laminates or BOPP (biaxially oriented polypropylene) films is another volume outlet for packaging biscuits and bakery products.

Suitability of major packaging materials for common food products under normal shelf-life

Product	Packaging materials				
	Low density polyethylene	High density polyethylene	Polypropy-lene	Polystyr-ene	Polyvinyl chloride
Alcoholic beverages	U	U	T	T	S
Cider	T	T	T	T	S
Cocoa	S	S	S	S	S
Coffee	S	S	S	T	S
Honey	S	S	S	S	S
Jams and jellies	S	S	S	S	S
Fruit juices	T	T	T	T	T
Pickles	S	S	S	T	S
Salt	S	S	S	S	S
Spices	T	T	T	T	S
Tea	S	S	S	S	S
Tomato ketchup	T	T	T	T	S
Vegetable Oils	T	S	S	T	S
Vinegar	S	S	S	S	S

S - Satisfactory
U - Unsatisfactory
T - Possibly satisfactory but further testing is required.

Advantages of plastics for packaging

1. Plastic packages are pilfer-proof, temper-proof, break-resistant, corrosion-resistant and leak proof.

2. Plastic can be processed into any desired shape or form, such as films, sheets, bottles, tubes, pouches, crates, etc.

3. Plastic packages do not pose any major disposal problem or environmental hazard, since almost all plastics can be recycled for reuse.

4. Plastics are light and less bulky than other packaging materials, which results in saving in cost of storage and transportation.

5. Some new plastics have excellent barrier properties to moisture, odour, oxygen and other gases so that the desired shelf-life of various products can be maintained.

6. They are resistant to most chemicals, non-toxic in nature and absolutely safe to use even in direct contact with food products, medicines, etc.

7. They can be sterilized by all conventional methods.

Hazards of plastic packaging

Packaging materials, packages and packaged products are liable to several hazards during storage and transportation, the most common ones being:

(A) **Static hazards:** These occur because of compression of goods due to stacking and are influenced by the nature of goods, duration of stacking, condition of floor such as evenness and stacking pattern.

(B) **Mechanical hazards :** Uneven lifting due to bad slinging, dropping of package and piercing, puncturing or tearing by hooks, straps, nails, etc., are the major examples.

(C) **Transport hazards :** These are vibration and bouncing particularly because of bad roads, shunting shocks, crushing by ropes used for tying, side impacts due to sudden braking and dropping of packages during loading or unloading.

(D) **Climatic hazards :** The major hazards are exposure to direct sunlight, rain water, temperature and humidity variations and environmental pollutant gases.

(E) **Miscellaneous hazards :** These are :

    (1) Some corrosive gases may cause stress-cracking.

    (2) Biological hazards, such as bacteria, fungi, rats, etc.

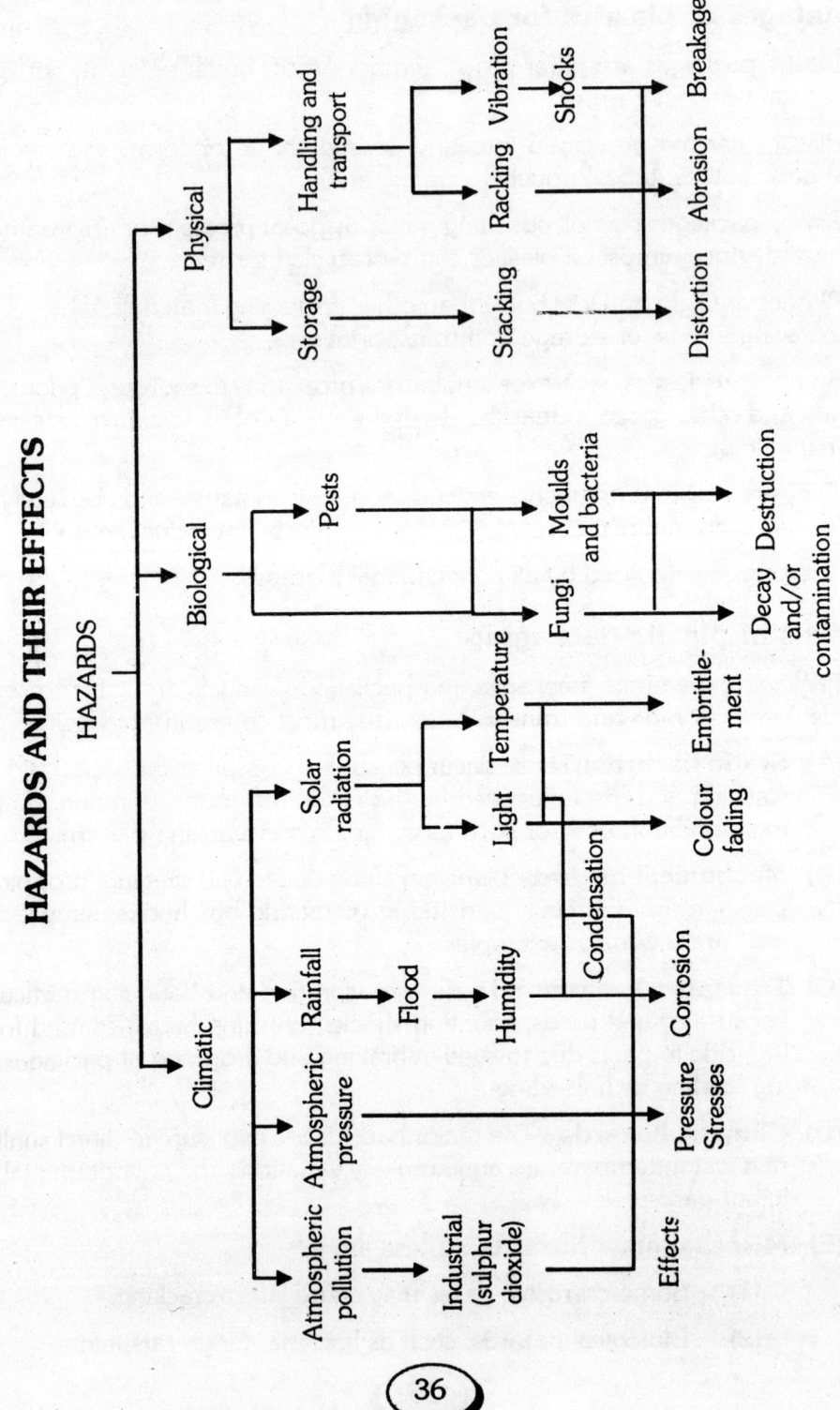

HAZARDS AND THEIR EFFECTS

(3) Contamination by other products stored alongside which may have leaked.

(4) Fire

Limitations

Plastic packages have certain limitations also, which are :

1. They are not a total barrier to gases and water vapour, although some new barrier plastics have greatly improved oxygen, gas and odour impermeability.

2. When stretched PVC/PET is used instead of glass for bottles, consumers may get the impression that there is less quantity of product because of reduced thickness.

3. Abrasion resistance is not always adequate.

4. Some chemicals do attack particular plastics.

Chapter 6

Food Colours

The acceptance of a food depends to a large extent upon its attractive colour. The characteristic colour of raw food is due to the pigments naturally present in it. Sometimes, artificial colour is added during the preparation and processing of foods to make them more attractive.

(A) Natural colouring matters

The natural colours (pigments) in vegetables and fruits can be classified on the basis of chemical structure as carotenoids (yellow-orange), chlorophylls (green), flavonoids and anthocyanins (red, blue and purple) and anthoxanthins (cream yellow).

The following pigments are present, singly or in combination, in plant-based foods.

1. **Chlorophylls :** These green coloured, fat-soluble pigments, involved in photosynthesis, are present in many plants specially in leafy vegetables such as cabbage and lettuce. There are two types of chlorophyll, a and b, which occur in plants in the ratio of 3:1. They are related to the porphyrins, an important group of biological pigments which includes haemoglobin. There is always some deterioration of chlorophylls on storage, whatever the processing method used.

2. **Carotenoids :** Carotenoids are fat-soluble, orange-yellow pigments that are present in many vegetables and fruits such as carrot, pumpkin, mango and orange. The first carotenoid isolated was from carrot and, therefore, was named carotene. Its concentration in a vegetable is indicated by the intensity of the colour.

The most widely distributed carotenoids are lutein, violaxanthin, and neoxanthin which found in green leaves. Carotene and zeaxanthin also occur widely but in small quantities. Some pigments predominate in certain plants like lycopene in tomato, capsanthin in red pepper and bixin in annatto.

Carotenoids are also present in most green leafy vegetables along with chlorophyll but their colour is masked by the green of chlorophyll. The fresh yellow-green colour of spring leaves is due to carotenoids together with a small amount of chlorophyll.

Carotenoids are extracted from annatto, saffron, paprika, tomato, etc., and used as natural food colourants. Extracts of carrot, butter fat and palm oil contains β-carotene the precursor of vitamin A and thus show vitamin A activity.

3. **Anthocyanins :** These are the red, blue and purple water-soluble compounds occurring in the cell sap of some fruits and vegetables, e.g., coloured grapes, red cabbage, cheery, apple and in most flowers. Anthocyanins are glycosides which on hydrolysis yield coloured aglycones known as anthocyanidins, which are phenylbenzopyran derivatives, and sugars. The sugar moities are glucose, galactose, rhamnose, arabinose, xylose, etc. A large number of anthocyanidins are known of which six are commonly present in foods. These are pelargonidin, cyanidin, delphinidin, peonidin, petunidin and malvidin. At low pH, the colour of anthocyanins is an intense red, which changes through orange and red to blue or purple as the pH value rises. Sulphite or sulphur dioxide rapidly bleaches the colour of anthocyanins. Removal of sulphite by boiling and acidification results in the regeneration of anthocyanins.

Sugars influence the stability of anthocyanins. Decolourization is not due to the sugar itself but is brought about by its degradation products, furfural and 5-hydroxymethylfurfural. Ascorbic acid reacts with anthocyanins resulting in the degradation of both the compounds. An intermediate peroxide is formed by the degradation of ascorbic acid and this reacts with anthocyanins. Oxidation of ascorbic acid is catalyzed by copper and iron and this results in further oxidation of anthocyanins. The effect of ascorbic acid is of particular importance in the preparation of fruit juices.

4. **Flavonoids :** These are very widely distributed in the plant kingdom. They are water-soluble, polyphenolic substances, similar in structure to anthocyanins, which also occur as glycosides, and include the sub-groups of flavones, flavonols, flavanones, chalcones, aurones and biflavanyls. Flavonoids may be the sole pigments in such vegetables as potato, cauliflower and yellow-skinned onion. The flavonoids most commonly found in the nature are the flavonols, kaempferol, quercetin and myricetin present in considerable amounts in tea. Less common are flavones such as apigenin, luteolin and tricetin. The other sub-groups occur to a limited extent. Flavones and anthoxanthins are responsible for the yellow-white or creamy white colour of potato and cauliflower. Flavanones occur mainly in citrus plants and can be used as synthetic sweeteners.

Flavonoids are usually more stable to heat and oxidation than the anthocyanins. The flavonoid, rutin (quercetin-3-rham-noglucoside), forms dark coloured complexes with iron which discolour canned foods (asparagus). The tin complex, in contrast, produces a desirable yellow colour.

5. **Anthoxanthins** : These are the creamy yellow, creamy white or yellow-white water soluble compounds occurring in the cell saps of some fruits and vegetables, e.g., potato, cauliflower.

   Anthoxanthins are glycosides which on boiling with dilute acid yield one or two molecules of monosaccharides and a flavone or a flavone derivative such as flavonal, flavanonal, or isoflavone.

6. **Tannins** : These are colourless or yellow substances which turn brown when fruits and vegetables containing them, e.g., brinjal, bottle gourd, apple, are cut and exposed to air. Thus tannins are responsible for enzymatic browning and also for the astringency of foods. Tannins are a complex mixture of polymeric polyphenols also known as tannic acid or gallotannic acid, and derivatives of flavones. They are divided into two major groups:

   (i)   condensed tannins, e.g., catechins and related compounds, and

   (ii) hydrolyzable tannins, e.g., gallic acid (gallotannins) and ellagic acid (ellagitannins).

7. **Quinones and Xanthones** : A large number of pigments found in the cell sap of flowering plants, fungi, bacteria and algae are derivatives of anthraquinone, naphthoquinone and benzoquinone and range in colour from pale yellow to almost black. Anthraquinone derivatives are the largest group of such pigments, followed by those of naphthoquinone and benzoquinone.

   Xanthones are a group of yellow pigments. One well-known member is mangiferin, which occurs as a glucoside in mangoes.

8. **Betalains** : Betalains are a group of red and yellow pigments found in red beet (*Beta vulgaris*) and, to some extent, in cactus fruits, pokeberries and a number of flowers (*Bougainvillea*).

   They resemble the anthocyanins and flavonoids in structure but unlike them, contain nitrogen. Betalains are stable in the pH range 4-6 but are degraded by thermal processing as in canning. Colour in the food may not always come from plant and animal pigments. It could be due to browning reactions that may be enzymatic or nonenzymatic. This aspect of food colouring has been discussed in a separate chapter entitled 'Browning Reactions'.

   A number of naturally occurring substances is used for colouring foods. According to the Fruit Products Order, India (1955), the following natural colouring matters, whether isolated from a natural source or synthesized, are permitted to be added to any article of food.

(i)   Cochineal or carmine

(ii) Carotene and carotenoids

(iii) Chlorophyll

(iv) Lactoflavin

(v)   Caramel

(vi) Annatto

(vii) Ratanjot

(viii) Saffron

(ix) Curcumin

Dehydrated beet powder, carrot oil and juices of fruits, e.g., strawberries and cherries, which impart a pink colour to ice-cream are also approved as natural colour additives.

(B) Synthetic colours

Only pigments from natural sources were available and used for colouring food till the coming of the first coal tar dye in 1857. Thereafter a large number of dyes were synthesized and some were used as food colourants.

However, gradually restrictions have been placed on their use as food additives in many countries. In India, no coal tar dyes or a mixture thereof, except the following are permitted to be used in food (F.P.O., 1955).

S.No.	Colour	Common name	Colour index	Chemical class
		Approved coal tar dyes		
1.	Red	Ponceau 4R	16255	Azo
		Carmoisine	14720	Azo
		Fast Red	16045	Azo
		Amaranth	16185	Azo
		Erythrosine	45430	Xanthene
2.	Yellow	Tartrazine	19140	Pyrazolone
		Sunset Yellow FCF	15985	Azo
3.	Blue	Indigo Carmine	73015	Indigoid
		Brilliant Blue FCF	42090	Triphenylmethane
4.	Green	Fast Green S	44090	Triphenylmethane
		Green FCF	42053	Triphenylmethane

Dyes used in food products should be pure and free from all harmful impurities. They should not contain more than 10 ppm of copper, 20 ppm of chromium, 1 ppm of arsenic and 10 ppm of lead and should satisfy Government regulations. In the selection of dyes, it is desirable to choose those which have high solubility in order to obtain a concentrated solution of a particular colour. Acid dyes are generally more stable in solution than alkaline ones. Strong sunlight, oxidation and reduction by metals like tin and zinc, and microorganisms affect the colour of dyes. Azodyes like Amaranth, Ponceau, Sunset Yellow, etc., fade quickly in the presence of tin, while triphenylmethane dyes like Fast Green, Light Green, etc., are less susceptible. The yellow Azodyes which are employed for colouring fruit squashes are not ordinarily decolorized by sulphur dioxide, which is added as preservative. Ponceau 2R and Erythrosine are stable to sulphur dioxide. Sunset Yellow and mixture of Tartrazine and Ponceau and Orange, generally used in orange squash, however, fade on prolonged storage in spite of all precautions. Since practically all dyes are adversely affected by prolonged heating, it is advisable to add them to the food towards the last stage of boiling.

Colours are generally available in the form of powders or ready-to-use solutions. The powder should first be made into a paste with a little cold water and the requisite quantity of almost boiling water added to the paste with constant stirring. The solution is allowed to stand till cool and any sediment formed is removed by filtration. To prevent sedimentation, glycerine is usually added to the solution to increase its density. About 10 per cent glycerine is sufficient for the purpose. Isopropyl alcohol also helps in increasing the solubility of the powder.

Dye solutions can be preserved by addition of 10 per cent alcohol (v/v), 25 per cent glycerine for short-period storage or 50 per cent glycerine for prolonged storage. Citric and tartaric acids added at the rate of 12.1 to 15.6 g per litre also act as preservatives. However, these acids cannot be used in case of dyes such as Erythrosine Orange I, Light Green, Guinea Green, etc., which get precipitated. Spoilage of solution can also be prevented by the addition of 0.1 per cent sodium benzoate as a preservative.

The amount of any permitted coal tar dye or mixture of permitted dyes which may be added to any fruit product should not exceed 0.2 g per kg of the final product.

Although colours add to the attractiveness of food products, it is better to avoid their use as far as possible and educate the consumer to use products not containing colourants. Colours can often be used to cover defects in the natural products.

Banned colours

According to the Public Health (Preservatives, etc., in Food) Regulations, 1925 (amended 1926 and 1927) of the Ministry of Health, U.K., the following colouring matters are not permitted to be added to articles of food.

1. **Metallic colours :** Compounds of any of the metals, antimony, arsenic, cadmium, chromium, copper, mercury, lead and zinc.

2. **Vegetable colouring matter :** Gamboge.

3. **Coal tar colours :** As mentioned in the table below :

Name	Synonyms
Picric acid	Carbazotic acid
Victoria Yellow	Saffron substitute, Di-nitrocresol
Manchester Yellow	Naphthol Yellow, Martius Yellow
Aurantia	Imperial Yellow
Aurine	Rosolic acid, Yellow coralline

Recently, the use of some colours in foods has been banned. In India, Acid Magenta II and Blue V.R.S., which were used in tomato ketchup and canned peas, respectively, have been deleted from the list of permitted colours. Both are triphenylmethane dyes. Instead of Blue V.R.S., Fast Green S and Green FCF have been recommended. Red 6B, Red FB and Brilliant Black have also been deleted as being harmful.

Chapter 7

Food Additives and Brominated Vegetable Oil (B.V.O.)

I n recent years more and more attention has been focussed on the safety of food particularly with respect to intentional and unitentional use of additives. No highly developed society can exist today without using food additives.

F.A.O. and W.H.O. in 1956 defined food additives as non-nutritive substances added intentionally to food, generally in small quantities, to improve its appearance, flavour, texture, or storage properties. The definition did not include vitamins and minerals.

The Food and Drug Administration of the United States in collaboration with the Food Protection Committee has defined food additive as a substance or a mixture of substances, other than a basic foodstuff, which is present in a food as a result of any aspect of production, processing, storage, or packaging. The term does not include chance contaminants. This definition includes *intentional* as well as *unintentional* additives. *Intentional additives* are substances deliberately added to perform specific functions, while *unintentional* (*non-intentional or incidental*) additives are substances, which have no intended function in the finished food but become part of the food product during some phase of production or subsequent handling. Both kinds of additives in excessive amounts can be detrimental to health.

Functions and uses of food additives

Food additives perform several functions such as drying, emulsifying, enhancing flavour, enriching, firming, flavouring, foam producing, glazing, leavening, lining food containers, maturing (flour), anticaking, antidrying, antifoaming, antihardening, antispattering, antisticking, bleaching, buffering, chillproofing, clarifying, colour retaining, colouring, conditioning (dough), creaming, curing, dispersing, dissolving, sweetening, texturizing, thickening, water-proofing, water-retaining, whipping, acidifying, making alkaline, neutralizing, peeling, plasticizing, preserving (including acting as antioxidant), pressure dispensing, refining, replacing air in food packages, sequestering unwanted metal ions, stabilizing, sterilizing and supplementing nutrients.

The major uses of food additives are as under :

(1) Enhancement of the attractiveness of foods by means of colouring and flavouring agents, emulsifiers, stabilizers, thickners clarifiers and bleaching agents;

(2) Maintenance of nutritional quality, such as by the use of antioxidants;

(3) Facilitating food processing by means of acids, alkalies, buffers, sequestrants and various other chemicals; and

(4) Enhancement of keeping quality or stability by the use of antioxidants, antimicrobial agents, inert gases, meat curers, etc.

Classification of food additives

The more than 3,000 different chemical compounds used as intentional food additives can be categorized into different groups. The important groups are given below:

(1) Antioxidants : An antioxidant is a substance which when added to fats and fat containing foods prevents their oxidation and thus prolongs their shelf-life, wholesomeness and palatability. Without them, fatty foods (e.g., potato chips, salted nuts, fat-containing dehydrated foods) cannot be stored for any length of time without becoming rancid.

Antioxidants function by interrupting the free radical chain reaction involved in lipid oxidation. An antioxidant should not have any harmful physiological effect and should not impart an objectionable flavour, odour or colour to the food in which it is present. It should be effective in low concentration (0.01 to 0.02 per cent) and be fat-soluble. Some antioxidants used in foods are butylated hydroxyanisole (BHA), butylated hydroxytoluene (BHT), tertiary-butylhydroquinone (TBHQ), propyl gallate (PG), thiodipropionic acid, dilauryl thiodipropionate, stannous chloride, tocopherols, more expensive naturally occurring vitamin E, sulphur dioxide, and ascorbic acid. Ascorbic acid prevents browning caused by enzymatic oxidation of phenolic compounds. Acids such as citric and phosphoric increase the effectiveness of ascorbic acid.

(2) Preservatives : Any substance which is capable of inhibiting, retarding or arresting the growth of microorganisms is known as a preservative. It may be a chemical or a natural substance (sugar, salt, acid). These have been discussed earlier in the chapter on 'Principles and Methods of Preservation'.

Sulphur dioxide and sodium benzoate, sodium and calcium propionate (as mould inhibitor in bread and cake), sorbic acid (as mould and yeast inhibitor in cheese and baked products, fruit juices, wines and pickies), and chlorine compounds (as a germicidal wash for fruits and vegetables) are also used as preservatives.

The term preservative includes fumigants, e.g., ethylene oxide and ethyl formate, used to control microorganisms on spices, nuts and dried fruits.

(3) Sequestrants : These are also known as *chelating agents* or *metal scavengers* since they combine with metals such as iron and copper and remove them from solution. Traces of metals catalyze oxidation and also cause discolouration, rancidity, turbidity and flavour changes in foods and must be removed by chelating agents such as ethylenediamine tetraacetic acid (EDTA), polyphosphates or citric acid. Calcium and sodium salts of organic acids, calcium chloride, calcium phosphate, tartaric acid, and citric acid, are also examples of sequestrants.

Sequestrants are used to suppress the action of some objectionable but practically unavoidable ingredients, e.g., in the manufacture of soft drinks iron in the water reacts with one of the flavouring substances to form an insoluble compound that makes the product cloudy. Citrates form a soluble complex with iron, whereas others render citric acid insoluble.

(4) Surface-active agents : These are also known as *emulsifiers* and are used to stabilize oil-in-water, water-in-oil, gas-in-liquid and gas-in-solid emulsions. Besides emulsifiers of natural origin such as lecithin and synthetic ones such as mono and diglycerides and their derivatives, certain fatty acids and their derivatives and bile acid can be used as emulsifying agents. Synthetic surface active agents, include defoaming compounds and detergents, e.g., propylene glycol monostearate and monosodium phosphate.

(5) Colouring agents : These are added to a large number of food items to make them attractive and appetizing. They may be of natural origin, e.g., extract of annatto, caramel, carotene and saffron, or synthetic. Synthetic dyes, besides providing a larger range of colours than natural substances, are generally superior to the latter in colouring power, uniformity and stability of colour and are cheaper. Food colours also include carbon black to impart blackness and titanium dioxide to intensify whiteness.

Further information on colours can be found in the chapter on 'Food Colours'.

(6) Buffers, acids and alkalies : These additives are primarily used to control or adjust the pH of foods and affect properties such as flavour, texture and cooking qualities. Acid in food may be a natural constituent as in case of fruits, or produced in it by fermentation. Certain chemicals are also added to adjust the pH, e.g., acetic acid, ammonium carbonate, ammonium hydroxide, calcium carbonate, calcium chloride, calcium citrate, citric acid, lactic

47

acid, malic acid, sodium acetate, sodium bicarbonate, succinic acid, tartaric acid, sulphuric acid, sodium hydroxide, etc.

(7) Stabilizers and thickeners : These substances help to improve the texture of foods, inhibit crystallization of sugar and formation of ice, stabilize emulsions and foams and reduce stickiness of icings on baked products. They combine with water to form gels and make the food viscous. Gum arabic, agar-agar, alginic acid, starch and its derivatives, gelatin, pectin, amylose, carboxymethylcellulose (CMC), carrageenan, hydrolyzed vegetable proteins are examples of such additives. Gravies, pie fillings, cake toppings, chocolate milk drinks, jellies, puddings and salad dressings are some foods that contain stabilizers and thickeners.

(8) Nutrient supplements : When foods are processed or stored there may be loss of some nutrients. In order to restore this loss or to provide more nutritional value than what nature may have provided nutrient supplements are added. These are mainly vitamins and minerals : vitamin D (added to milk), vitamin B, iron and calcium (to cereal products), iodine (to salt), vitamin A (to margarine), vitamin C (to fruit-juices and fruit-flavoured desserts).

Several essential amino acids are included in this group of which lysine is the only one absent in wheat flour. However, lysine is not permitted as an additive in wheat flour and white bread because sufficient lysine is available from other foods in a normal diet.

(9) Non-nutritive and special dietary sweeteners : Various sweetening agents have been used as substitutes for cane sugar (sucrose). Substances have been synthesized which are 10 to 3000 times as sweet as sucrose. Non-nutritive sweeteners are mainly used in the manufacture of low-calorie soft drinks. They are also added to low-calorie liquid foods, canned fruit, frozen desserts, salad dressings, gelatin desserts and some baked products.

Non-sugar sweeteners, besides helping to control weight, have made it possible for diabetics to enjoy foods they would otherwise not be able to eat. However, use of some of them has been restricted or banned because of their adverse effect on health.

The first synthetic sweetening agent was saccharin (sodium or calcium salt of orthobenzene-sulphonamide), which is 300 times sweeter than sucrose and is detectable in 10 ppm of water. It has a bitter and unpleasant after-taste. Because of its toxic effects on chronic use, its consumption has been restricted to 15 mg per kg of body weight (1 g per day for a 52 kg person). Recently, consumption of saccharin has been prohibited by the Government of India.

Cyclamates (sodium, magnesium, calcium and potassium salts of cyclohexylsulphamic acid) are 15 to 30 times as sweet as sucrose . F.D.A. of U.S.A. has banned their use on the basis of reports that they cause bladder cancer in experimental animals.

Aspartame, the methyl ester of L-aspartyl-L-phenylalanine, is about 180 times as sweet as sucrose and does not have any unpleasant after-taste. It is approved for use in chewing gum and as a dry base for beverages, etc., but not for baked and fried products because prolonged heating decomposes the compound.

Glycyrrhizic acid (obtained from licorice root) and neohespiridine, a dihydrochalcone isolated from citrus peel, are also used as sweeteners. 6-Chloro-D-tryptophan and thaumatin are also under trial as sweeteners.

(10) Flavouring agents and flavour enhancers : Flavouring agents and those substances, naturally occurring or synthetic, which are responsible for the characteristic flavours of almost all the foods in our diet. This is the largest group of food additives and includes about 2100 different substances.

Spices, herbs, plant extracts (root, leaves, stem, flower) and essential oils are widely used flavouring agents of natural origin. Since the preparation of extracts and essential oils is very costly natural flavouring substances are being replaced by synthetic ones.

Esters, aldehydes, ketones, alcohols and ethers having characteristic fruity odours can be easily synthesized and readily replace natural aromatic substances. Some examples of these are amyl acetate (banana), methyl anthranilate (grapes) and ethyl butyrate (pineapple). Generally, natural flavours can be reproduced by mixing a number of different synthetic substances.

Flavour enhancers do not possess any flavour themselves but they intensify the flavours of other substances through a synergistic effect. The best known, most widely used and somewhat controversial flavour enhancer is monosodium glutamate (MSG), the sodium salt of the naturally occurring glutamic acid, an amino acid extracted from seaweeds and soybean. Ribonucleotides (5- nucleotides) extracted from yeast possess ten times the flavour-enhancing property of MSG.

Further information on flavours can be found in the chapter on 'Food Flavours'.

(11) Anticaking agents and humectants : Anticaking agents prevent food particles from adhering to each other and becoming a solid lump in damp weather. These substance act by readily absorbing excess moisture, by coating the food particles to make them water repellent, and/or by diluting the mixture with insoluble particles. Calcium silicate is used to prevent caking of baking powder and table salt. Because it can absorb oils, calcium silicate is a useful anticaking agent in complex powdered mixtures and certain spices which contain essential oils. Calcium and magnesium salts of long-chain fatty acids (e.g. calcium stearate) are used as conditioning agents for dehydrated vegetables, salt and other food ingredients in powdered form. Other anticaking agents used are sodium silicoaluminate, tricalcium phosphate, magnesium silicate, magnesium carbonate, etc.

Humectants are moisture retention agents. Their functions include control of viscosity, texture, and bulking, retention of moisture, reduction of water activity, inhibition of crystallization and improvement or retention, softness. They also improve the rehydration of dehydrated food and solubilization of flavouring agents. Polyhydroxy alcohols such as propylene glycol, glycerol sorbitol and mannitol which are water-soluble, hygroscopic substance and moderately viscous in high concentrations in water are used as humectants in foods.

(12) Bleaching and maturing agents (flour improvers) and starch modifiers : Freshly milled flour has a yellowish tint and suboptimal baking qualities. Both the colour and baking properties improve slowly on normal storage. But this process can be accelerated in a controlled manner by the use of certain oxidizing agents. Benzoyl peroxide is such an agent which bleaches the yellow colour. Oxides of nitrogen, chlorine dioxide and other chlorine compounds both bleach the colour and mature the flour.

Oxidizing agents such as hydrogen peroxide are used to whiten the colour of milk for manufacture of certain kinds of cheese. Bromate and iodate are used in bread doughs for improving baking quality.

Starch modifiers, e.g., sodium hypochlorite, oxidize starches to increase their water-solubility.

(13) Other additives : There are a number of food additives whose functions are other than those mentioned above. These include the following types of substances:

(i) Firming agents : These are added to keep the tissues of fruits and vegetables crisp (firm), e.g., calcium chloride and aluminium sulphate.

(ii) Clarifying agents : These are used to remove haziness or sediment produced by oxidative deterioration in fruit juice, wines, beers, etc., e.g., bentonite, gelatin, synthetic resins (polyamides and polyvinylpyrrolidone).

(iii) Solvents : Suspended flavouring agents, dyes and other ingredients can be dissolved by adding solvents such as alcohol, acetone, hexane, propylene glycol, glycerine, etc.

(iv) Antisticking agents : e.g., hydrogenated sperm oil.

(v) Machinery lubricants : e.g., mineral oil.

(vi) Meat curing agents : e.g., sodium nitrite and sodium nitrate.

(vii) Crystallization inhibitors : e.g., Oxystearin.

(viii) Growth stimulants : e.g., gibberellic acid used for malting barley.

(ix) Leavening agents : e.g., ammonium sulphate used in yeast foods to promote the growth of baker's yeast.

(x) Freezing agents : e.g., liquid nitrogen for chilling foods.

(xi) Packing gases : e.g., inert gases for preventing oxidative and other changes in foods.

(xii) Enzymes : e.g., rennin for producing cheese and curd, papain for tenderizing meat and pectinase for clarifying beverages.

Miscellaneous additives are acetic acid, caramel, glycerine, nitrogen, phosphoric acid, sodium carbonate and bicarbonate, etc.

Brominated vegetable oils (B.V.O.)

Synthetic soft drinks, whether carbonated or not, are a mixture of various substances. Among these, flavouring agents (essential oils) are very important because they improve the flavour. Essential oils being water-insoluble remain in suspension which adversely affects the appearance of the beverage and reduces its consumer acceptability. It is, therefore, essential that flavouring agents should be stabilized. For this purpose dispersing agents or emulsifiers such as B.V.O., ester gum, sucrose acetate isobutyrate, glycerol tribenzoate, propylene dibenzoate, etc., are used.

Chemically, B.V.O. is a vegetable oil (olive, seasame, corn or cotton seed) whose density has been increased to that of water by bromination. It does not separate out in beverages and is extensively used for stabilizing flavouring oils in many synthetic beverages. It causes cloudiness in drinks and thus protects them from light-induced reactions.

However, according to W.H.O. reports, It causes cancer and skin diseases and damages or disrupts the cells of the human body. In U.S.A., B.V.O. is used in 15 ppm, while the Government of India has banned its use completely.

Substances prohibited as additives in foods

Brominated vegetable oil (B.V.O.)

Calamus and its derivatives

Chlorofluorocarbon propellants

Cobalt salts and their derivatives

Coumarin and dihydrocoumarin

Cyclamate and its derivatives

Diethylpyrocarbonate (DEPC)

Dulcin

Monochloroacetic acid

Nordihydroguaiaretic acid (NDGA)

Safrole

Thiourea

Colourants

Acid Magenta II

Blue VRS

Brilliant Black

Red FB

Red 6B

Source: Code of US Federal Regulations (1979); Prevention of Food Adulteration Act (India).

Not much work has been done in India on the toxicological evaluation of food additives. We, therefore, depend on work done in advanced countries as well as by the FAO, WHO and other international organizations.

There are situations where food additives are best avoided. Thus, additives should not be used:

1. in baby food and invalid food;

2. to mask spoilage or bad quality of food and thus deceive the consumer;

3. to cover up defects in handling and processing;

4. to make food attractive and appealing to consumers at the expense of its nutritional quality and safety;

5. to obtain a desired effect instead of adopting improved processing techniques; and

6. where the addition of, for example, an oxidizing agent may modify the nutrients in a food or in any other manner adversely affect the health of the consumer.

Caution is necessary even in using some of the permitted food additives. A list of such additives along with their uses and likely adverse effects is given below;

Additives to be used with Caution

Additive	Use	Possible adverse effects
Coal tar dyes	Colourant in vegetable and fruit products, soft drinks, candy, desserts, pastry, sausage, baked food, ice-cream, hot dogs, hamburgers, sweetmeats, snacks, confectionery, alcoholic and other beverages	Allergic reactions, cancer and pathological lesions in vital organs
Butylated hydroxytoluene (BHT)	Antioxidant in cereals, chewing gum, potato chips, edible oils, etc.	Cancer; allergic reactions; stored in body fat
Butylated hydroxyanisole (BHA)	Antioxidant in cereals, chewing gum, potato chips, edible oils, etc.	Appears to be safer than BHT but needs more testing
Caffeine	Sitmulant in soft drinks	Insomnia and other adverse effects at high levels of intake. Not recommended for children and pregnant mothers
Saccharin	Non-calorie sweetener in food products, also as adulterant	Bladder cancer reported in animals. Not recommended for normal people (not suffering from diabetes, obesity)
Sodium nitrite and nitrate	Preservative to prevent growth of bacillus, *Clostridium botulinum* and colourant for bacon, ham, meat, smoked fish, corned beef	Formation of small amounts of cancer-producing nitrosamines

Additive	Use	Possible adverse effects
Artificial flavourings	In soft drinks, breakfast cereals, baked goods, vegetable and fruit products, ice creams, custards, desserts, alcoholic beverages	Hyperactivity in some children; not adequately tested for safety
Monosodium glutamate	Flavour enhancer for soup, poultry, meat preparations, sauces, stews and cheese	Damages brain cells in infant mice, so not recommended for children; headache, tightness of head, neck and arms in sensitive adults (Chinese Restaurant Syndrome)
Sulphur dioxide and bisulphites	Preservative and bleach for sliced fruit, wine, grape juice, dried potatoes, dried fruit, vegetable and fruit products, etc.	Destroys vitamin B_1, but otherwise safe at prescribed levels
Phosphoric acid and phosphates	Acidifier, chelating agent, buffer, emulsifier, nutrient, discolouration inhibitor used in baked goods, cheese, cured meat, soft drinks, dried potatoes	Dietary imbalance that may cause bone thinning (osteoporosis) on prolonged use
Talc and Kaolin	Making dry powdery foods free-flowing and as dusting agent for rice, confectionery, chewing gum	Absorbed and stored in vital organs; cancer if asbestos is present.

Food Flavours

F lavour is a sensory phenomenon which is a combination of the sensations of taste, odour or aroma, heat and cold, and texture or "mouthfeel". Appearance of a food is important, but it is the flavour that ultimately determines its quality and acceptability. Natural flavouring materials such as spices, essential oils and fruit juices have been used for long in food preparations but as their supply has not kept up with the demand, with consequent rise in their cost, natural flavouring agents have been largely substituted by synthetic ones. Thousands of these synthetic compounds are now being used as food additives.

There are four basic tastes: salty, sweet, sour and bitter.

Sodium chloride is the only salt that has a pure salty taste. Besides imparting flavour to food, it is also an essential nutrient. Other salts have different tastes, e.g., some iodides and bromides are bitter while some salts of lead and beryllium are sweet.

Sugars are used more to impart sweetness than flavour to food. Fructose present in honey is the sweetest sugar followed by sucrose and glucose, whereas lactose in milk is slightly sweet and gives less flavour. Natural sweet compounds are generally polyhydroxy compounds with a straight chain structure, such as sugars, and the hexahydroxy cyclic alcohols, mannitol and sorbitol. Diverse compounds, such as saccharin, some peptides and cylcamates are also sweet.

Sourness of food is due to the presence of organic acids of which citric, tartaric and malic are the most common. Acetic acid produced by fermentation of alcohol is common in processed fruits. Ascorbic acid is abundantly present in fruits and vegetables. oxalic acid found in spinach and phosphoric acid and its salts are often used in the food industry. It is remarkable that the hydrogen ion is mainly responsible for sour taste. Except oxalic acid, all other acids are weak acids and the degree of sourness is not proportionately related to the hydrogen ion concentration.

Bitterness may be due to alkaloids, glycosides, other classes of organic compounds as well as inorganic salts. Naringin the bitter principle of grapefruit is a glycoside of rutinose and is not toxic, while amygdalin, a glycoside present in bitter almonds contains gentiobiose and a cyanide group, and is toxic. Mustard and horseradish contain the alkaloid sinigrin, which is harmful and gives an off-flavour. Quinine, strychine, nicotine, etc., are bitter alkaloids. Caffeine, a constituent of coffee and tea, is bitter. Phenolic compounds like tannin and some flavonoids combine bitterness with astringency.

Flavour compounds

The substances mainly responsible for the aroma of food products are volatile compounds. These may be aliphatic esters, aldehydes, or ketones and are present in fruit and other natural foods in very low concentration. Many thousands of natural flavouring compounds are known and in any one food there may be hundreds of these present. Some of the important groups of flavouring compounds are as under:

1. **Flavonoids:** Flavonoids are responsible for the flavour of many fruits, e.g., orange, lemon and grapefruit peels contain a number of flavanone glycosides. Among these, hesperidin (orange and lemon) and naringenin (grapefruit) are the most common. Hesperidin is quite tasteless, whereas naringenin has an extremely bitter taste.

2. **Terpenoids :** Terpenoids are ubiquitous in plant foods. They are the major components of citrus oils and contribute to the flavour of citrus fruits. Limonene, a monoterpene hydrocarbon, possessing a lemon-like odour constitutes approximately 90 per cent of most citrus oils. Naturally occurring oxygenated terpenes (mainly alcohols, aldehydes and ketones) provide the characteristic flavour of individual citrus species, e.g., neral and geranial of lemons and nootkatone (bicyclic sesquiterpene) of grapefruit.

    In the presence of air or dissolved oxygen terpenes undergo structural changes and hydration, hence citrus juice concentrates prepared by low-temperature vacuum evaporation are superior in flavour than those processed at high temperatures. Juices of certain varieties of orange and grapefruit become bitter when kept at room temperature for some time, due to the formation of the bitter limonin from its nonbitter precursor (limonin monolactone) by the action of the organic acids present in the juice. This can be prevented by removing the precursor by exposing the fruits to ethylene before juice extraction, or by the addition of a specific enzyme to the juice to degrade limonin.

3. **Sulphur compounds :** Certain volatile sulphur-containing compounds possess powerful and distinctive odours which contribute to both the pleasant and unpleasant aroma of many foods, e.g., vegetables belonging to the genus *Allium* (onion, garlic) and *Brassica* (cabbage, cauliflower, brussels sprouts, broccoli).

Vegetables of the Brassica family contain the sulphur compounds S-methylcysteine sulphoxide and thioglucosides. On cooking the vegetables, the former is converted into dimethyl sulphide which is partly responsible for odour. However, the predominant odour is that of the isothiocyanates formed from thioglucosides by enzymatic hydrolysis. This occurs only after rupture of the cells when enzymes convert the thioglucosides into the unstable thiohydroxamic-o-sulphate which too is unstable and undergoes spontaneous degradation to isothiocyanate.

The sulphur volatiles responsible for the odour of onion and garlic are not present as such in the intact vegetable tissue, but are formed rapidly when the tissue is ruptured by cutting or chewing, by the action of an enzyme on a precursor. The precursors and the enzyme are present in different cells of the tissue and come into contact only when the cells are ruptured. The precursors are cysteine sulphoxide derivatives which on enzymatic decomposition are converted into flavour compounds. The latter then undergo nonenzymatic degradation to more volatile compounds such as sulphides, disulphides and trisulphides.

The characteristic odour of garlic is due to allicin, which is formed from the odourless alliin (S-2-propenyl cysteine sulphoxide) by the action of the enzyme allinase. Allicin then undergoes nonenzymatic decomposition to disulphide and thiosulphinate. The disulphide further decomposes into a complex mixture of monosulphide and trisulphide.

The production of the volatile constituent of onion takes place similarly. Here the precursor S-1-propenyl cysteine sulphoxide is enzymatically cleaved to give propenyl sulphenic acid which is unstable and undergoes rearrangement to thiopropanal-S-oxide, the lachrymatory factor in onion.

4. **Other volatile components** : A number of other important volatile components contribute to the aroma of foods. In terms of aroma, foods can be classified into four groups, namely,

    (i)   those in which aroma is mainly due to one compound. e.g., banana (isopentyl acetate), orange (citral), almond (benzaldehyde);

    (ii) those in which aroma is due to a mixture of a few compounds, of which one is the major component, e.g., apple (2-methyl butyrate and four minor components);

    (iii) those in which aroma can be reproduced faithfully by the use of a large number of compounds, such as pineapple, walnut; and

    (iv) those in which aroma cannot be reasonably reproduced by a mixture of specific compounds, e.g., strawberries, chocolate.

These volatile compounds can be classified into the following important groups:

(A) Carbonyl compounds : Acetaldehyde contributes to the odour of butter, hexanal to that of apples, benzaldehyde is responsible for the aroma of almonds, cherries and peaches and geranial for that of lemon.

Amongst ketones. 2,3-butanedione contributes to the aroma of butter, celery and some other foods. Acetophenone is responsible for the flavour of many foods.

(B) Acids : Some acids have powerful odours. Acetic acid gives its characteristic odour to vinegar, and 2-methylbutyric acid to cranberries.

(C) Esters : The aroma of fruits is also due to esters, e.g., pentyl valerate (apple), methyl salicylate (grape), pentyl acetate (banana), octyl acetate (orange), ethyl butyrate (strawberry), butyl acetate (raspberry and strawberry).

(D) Hydroxy compounds : Amongst alcohols, cis-3-hexen-1-ol (tomato and raspberry), 1-octen-3-ol (mushroom) and geosmin (dry beans and beetroot) are important.

Amongst the phenols, phenol itself contributes to the aroma of some cheeses. Vinyl guaiacol is present in many foods, eugenol is an important component of oil of cloves but is also widely distributed and thymol is responsible for the odour of tangerine.

Moreover, a number of odoriferous amines, and oxygen, nitrogen and sulphur heterocyclics are components of various foods.

Types of flavour

The flavours of processed foods can be broadly classified into three types viz., Developed, Processed and Added.

1. Developed flavour : Flavour compounds that are formed during food processing may be either solids or volatiles and may originate from,

    (i)   fractionation, particularly during the manufacture of perfumes, and

    (ii)   decomposition or other reactions of food components.

2. Processed flavour : Heating changes the flavour of many foods profoundly, e.g., coffee beans, peanuts, meat.

3. Added flavour : These are added to confectionery, non-alcoholic beverages and other prepared foods, and are of two types.

    (i)   essential oils or oleoresins or other extracts of aromatic plants, e.g., peppermint oil, and

(ii) synthetic substances that may or may not occur in nature, e.g., benzal-dehyde (almond), acetylmethylcarbinol (butter), citral (orange), eugenol (clove), limonene (lemon), vanillin (vanilla).

Flavour additives

In case of certain flavours the substances responsible for them are difficult or impossible to isolate from natural sources such as strawberry, cherry and beans. These natural flavours have, therefore, to be imitated as far as possible by mixing a number of flavouring agents, natural and/or synthetic. The success of such an imitation is more a matter of art than of science and is judged by the consumers preference for the flavoured product. Both essential oils and synthetic flavouring agents must be used in accordance with good manufacturing practice the salient points of which are :

(i) The amount added shall not exceed that reasonably required to accom-plish the intended effect.

(ii) Substances that may become part of the food as a result of manufactur-ing shall be kept as low as possible.

(iii) The substance shall be of good grade.

Moreover, a flavouring agent may not be added to a food for which there is a standard, unless the standard includes it.

Food spoilage

 number of factors are responsible for spoilage of food. These are :

1. Infection by microorganisms,

2. Action of enzymes,

3. Damage by insects, parasites and rodents,

4. Characteristics and storage conditions of food,

5. Mechanical damage.

1. Microbial spoilage

Bacteria, yeasts and moulds may infect food after harvesting, during its handling, processing and storage. But not all microorganisms cause spoilage, e.g., lactic acid bacteria are used in the making of cheese and other fermented dairy products, yeasts for the production of wine and beer and *Acetobacter* bacteria for vinegar production. Spoilage organisms are present everywhere — in soil, air, water and even in the raw and processed food.

(i) Bacteria

These are unicellular microorganisms that are classed as plants though they do not contain chlorophyll. A bacteria cell is about 1 μm in length and somewhat smaller in diameter. Bacteria are classified according to their shape. Cocci are spherical, bacilli are cylindrical and spirilla and vibrios are spiral. Bacterial spores are more resistant than yeast or mould spores to most processing conditions. Bacteria, with a few exceptions, cannot grow in acid media in which yeasts and moulds thrive. They multiply by 'fission' or division of cells. When a bacterium becomes mature it divides into two, these two becomes four and so on. The growth of bacteria is very rapid and depends upon the nature of the food material, moisture, temperature and air. Some bacteria do not grow in air but temperature plays a major role in their growth, the optimum being generally 37°C.

Some bacteria produce spores which can be destroyed by heating at 121°C for 30-40 minutes. Bacteria are very sensitive to acids and are destroyed in their presence even at the temperature of boiling water. Hence, most fruits being acidic can be easily sterilized at 100°C whereas vegetables being non-acidic require a higher temperature of 116°C.

The important groups of bacteria are :

(a) **Bacillus** : rod-shaped;

(b) **Coccus** : spherical;

(c) **Coccobacillus** : oval-shaped;

(d) **Aerobes** : require atmospheric oxygen for growth, e.g., *Acetobacter aceti*;

(e) **Facultative anaerobes** : can grow with or without atmospheric oxygen;

(f) **Obligate anaerobes** : do not grow in atmospheric oxygen;

(g) **Mesophiles** : require a temperature below 38°C for growth;

(h) **Obligate thermophiles** : grow between 38 and 82°C;

(i) **Facultative thermophiles** : grow over the whole range of temperatures covered by mesophiles and obligate thermophiles and below;

(j) **Psychrotrophs** : grow fairly well at refrigeration temperatures and some can even grow slowly at temperatures below freezing.

Important food spoilage bacteria

Group	Genus
Acetics	*Acetobacter and Gluconobacter*
Lactics	*Lactobacillus, Leuconostoc, Pediococcus, Streptococcus*
Butyrics	*Clostridium*
Propionics	*Propionobacterium*
Proteol Gytics	*Bacillus, Pseudomonas, Clostridium, Proteus, etc.*

Some useful bacteria

The following bacteria are of great importance in the food processing industry.

Acetobacter sp.

These bacteria, also known as "vinegar bacteria", cause significant spoilage in the wine industry but are necessary for vinegar production. The important species are *Acetobacter aceti*, *A. orleansis* and *A. schutzenbachi*. They are very small, usually non-motile and generally do not form spores. These bacteria are aerobes and in the presence of oxygen convert ethyl alcohol to acetic acid. They are of two types- one type forms a tough shiny film on the surface of wine and the growth is known as "vinegar mother", while the other grows throughout the wine without forming "vinegar mother". These bacteria can be easily destroyed by heating to 65°C.

Lactobacillus sp.

Different organisms of this group, also known as "lactic acid bacteria", have different properties but all of them produce lactic acid from carbohydrates. Those which are used in distilling and brewing industries are facultative thermophiles (heat-tolerants) which grow abundantly at 50 to 55°C and produce much lactic acid. Mesophiles are used in the preparation of pickles. *Lactobacillus plantarum* is generally found in pickles and olives. The other important species are *Pediococcus cerevisiae*, *Leuconostoc mesenteroides*, *Streptococcus faecalis* and *Lactobacillus brevis*. These bacteria cause "lactic souring" and spoil wines, which can be easily prevented by maintaining a sulphur dioxide concentration of 0.007 per cent in wine.

(ii) Yeasts

Yeasts are unicellular fungi which are widely distributed in nature. They are somewhat larger than bacteria. The cell length is about 10 μm and the diameter is about a third of this. Most yeasts are spherical or ellipsoidal. Yeasts that multiply by means of 'budding' are known as 'true yeasts'. The bud when it becomes mature separates from the mother cell and functions like an independent organism. Yeasts grow luxuriantly at a moderate temperature in a solution of sugar in plenty of water. Under suitable conditions the sugar is converted into alcohol and carbon dioxide gas is evolved.

Yeast + Sugar → Alcohol + Carbon dioxide ↑

This is the reason that carbon dioxide is evolved from food materials spoiled by yeasts and pushes out corks from bottles with great force. Active fermentation can be easily recognized by the formation of carbon dioxide foams or bubbles. Yeasts prefer a low concentration of sugar for their growth. Most of them do not develop in media containing more then 66% sugar or 0.5% acetic acid. Boiling destroys the yeast cells and spores completely. Some of the yeasts which grow on fruits are *Saccharomyces*, *Candida* and *Brettanomyces*.

Pseudo-yeasts

These are like true yeasts but do not form spores. All the members of this group are particularly unsuitable for fermentation purposes as they produce off-flavours and cloudiness.

Yeasts causing food spoilage

Yeast	Product spoiled
Saccharomyces	Low-sugar products
Candida	High-acid foods, salty foods, butter
Brettanomyces	Beers, wines
Zygosaccharomyces (Osmophilic)	Honey, syrups, molasses, wines, soy sauce
Pichia	Wines
Hansenula	Beers
Debaryomyces	Meat brine, cheese, sausages, etc.
Hanseniospora	Fruit juices
Torulopsis	Milk products, fruit juices, acid foods
Rhodotorula	Meat, sauerkraut
Trichosporon	Chilled beer

(iii) Moulds

Moulds are multicellular, filamentous fungi belonging to the division Thallophyta but are devoid of chlorophyll. They are larger than yeasts. They are strict aerobes and require oxygen for growth and multiplication and tend to grow more slowly than bacteria.

The principal parts of a mould are a web-like structure known as mycelium and the spore. The mycelium is often white and cottony and penetrates into the attacked foodstuff. After fixing itself the mould produces viable spores which resist the unfavourable conditions after dispersal and germinate when they get favourable conditions. They thrive best in closed, damp and dark situations with an adequate supply or warm, moist air but require less free moisture than yeasts and bacteria. They prefer sugar-containing substances and may spoil jams, jellies, preserves and other sugar-based products. Acid medium favours their growth and, therefore, they grow well in pickles, juices, etc. This is the main reason that fruits and fruit products are attacked by moulds which not only consume nutrients

Common moulds, yeast and bacteria that cause food spoilage

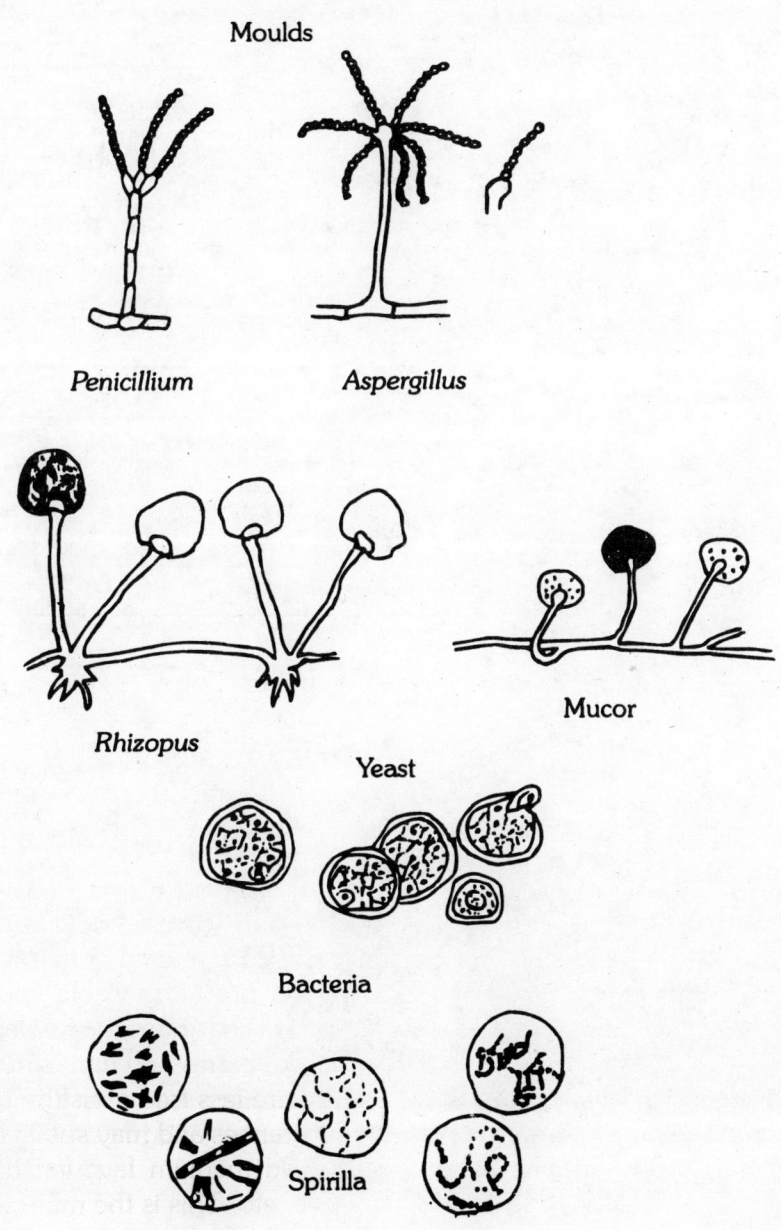

Moulds

Penicillium   Aspergillus

Rhizopus   Mucor

Yeast

Bacteria

Bacilli   Spirilla   Cocci

present in the food thereby lowering its food value but also spoil the flavour, texture and appearance of the product. They may grow even on moist leather but do not thrive in an alkaline medium. Moulds are sensitive to heat; boiling quickly destroys both moulds and their spores. The most important moulds are:

(a)   *Penicillium* sp.(Blue moulds)

(b)   *Aspergillus* sp. (Black moulds)

(c)   *Mucor* sp. (Gray moulds)

(d)   *Byssochlamys fulva*

(a)   *Penicillium* sp.

These are also known as blue moulds. In the initial stage of growth they have a cottony appearance but later when the spores or conidia are formed, their appearance becomes powdery and the colour becomes blue, brown or pink according to age. The spoiled materials have a 'mouldy' odour and flavour.

(b)   *Aspergillus* sp.

In the initial stages of growth it is white and cottony like *Penicillium* but later with the formation of spores, it becomes black and is hence known as "black mould". Unlike *Penicillium* it does not produce off-odour and flavour. They generally attacks grapes and bael.

(c)   *Mucor* sp.

It is gray in colour and hence is known as 'gray mould'. It is also known as 'pin mould' or 'bread mould' because it frequently grows on moist bread. Although *Mucor* attacks fruits, in the preservation of fruits and vegetables it does not pose a serious problem like blue and black moulds.

(d)   *Byssochlamys fulva*

This mould causes spoilage of canned fruits. The infected fruits disintegrate and sometimes carbon dioxide gas is also produced. It can grow under reduced oxygen tension and the ascospores possess high resistance to heat. For destroying spores heating of the cans at 88 to 90°C is essential.

Although the organism is not as resistant as some of the thermophiles, its control in canned foods is difficult. Canned products which cannot withstand prolonged heating without deterioration are ultimately spoiled. Association of this mould with fruit in the field has been observed. Hence the emphasis should be on eliminating the organism from the raw material itself instead of processing to destroy it in the can.

A small number of moulds produce toxic substances, known as mycotoxins, in food. *Aspergillus flavus* produces aflatoxins in harvested crops, such as ground-nut, which are stored in the field without drying properly'.

Two basic principles are followed in preventing microbial spoilage. the first principle is to destroy microorganisms in the food and prevent external microbial contaminations. This is the basis to canning technique. Second principle involves altering the environment in order to prevent or retard microbial activity. Water removal from microbial growth environment, for instance, can prevent microbial decay. Addition of sodium chloride or sugar used as preservative to jam, jellies, meat products, etc, is in essence an effective way for removal of water. Microbial growth can also be considerably avoided by lowering the temperature well below 32°F and bringing the pH level from acidic to highly acidic range. While the first principle applies to frozen food; the second, to pickled and fermented food. Acidification is used with a number of products, usually with ancillary heat treat-ment, known as pasteurization, to destroy yeasts and moulds. The common acids used are acetic, lactic, citric and tartaric. Of these, acetic acid is widely used in the manufacture of ketchup, pickles and similar products. Automicrobial agents such as sulphur dioxide, benzoic acid and benzoates. hydroxy-benzoic acid, sorbic acid, propionic acid, sodium diacetate, vitamin K_5, tannic acid, and anti-oxidants such as ascorbic acid (Vitamin C), ascorbyl palmitate, butylated hydroxy-anïsole and erythrobic acid can also be used for long-term preservation of fruits and vegeta-bles and some of the spices like ginger. onion, garlic, chillies, etc.

2. Enzymatic spoilage

Many reactions in plant and animal tissues are activated by enzymes. The changes in foods during storage can be produced both by enzymes present in the food or by enzymes from microorganisms that contaminate the food. A good example of the former is the ripening of banana due to the enzymes present which hasten the ripening process. After some time the fruit become too soft and unfit to eat. If there is a bruised spot on the fruit, yeasts can grow and produce enzymes which spoil the fruit.

Enzymes convert starch into sugars, protein into amino acids, and pectin into pectic acids and thus change the constituents of food. Some fruits and veg-etables turn brown when damaged or when their cut surfaces are exposed to air due to the presence of the enzymes phenolase, peroxidase and polyphenol oxi-dase. Their actions can be easily controlled by regulating the temperature and excluding moisture and air. Enzymes can act between zero and 60°C. The opti-mum temperature of reaction is usually 37°C, the rate varying directly with tem-perature. All enzymes are inactivated at 80°C.

3. Spoilage by insects parasites and rodents

Insects are particularly destructive to fruits and vegetables. The loss of food due to insects varies from 5 to 50 per cent depending upon the care taken in the field and during storage. Insect infestations in grains, dry fruits and spices are generally controlled by fumigation with methyl bromide, ethylene oxide or propylene oxide. Apart from the direct loss through consumption of the food, insects cause greater damage by the bruises and cuts they make in foods, thus exposing them to microbial attack resulting in total decay.

Certain parasites can spoil foods. A worm belonging to the genus *Anisakis* occurs in some fish and if such fish is eaten raw the worm can infect man. A common parasitic infection of foods is *Entamoeba histolytica* responsible for amoebic dysentery. This organism contaminates foods when raw human excrement is used as fertilizer for crops. Infected water and poor hygiene also spreads the parasite. Cooking kills most of these parasites.

Rats contribute substantially to destruction of food in countries where they are not controlled. Rats live up to 3 years and may have 3-8 litters. Apart from the fact that they consume large quantities of food, they contaminate it with their urine and droppings which harbour disease producing bacteria. Rats spread such human diseases as typhus, plague, typhoid, etc.

4. Characteristics and storage conditions of food

(A) Characteristics

The characteristics of a food influence the type of microorganisms that can grow in it and thus determine the changes in its appearance, flavour and other qualities.

(i) Composition : Proteins are degraded by proteolytic organisms. Many bacterial species, especially spore-formers, gram-negative bacilli such as *Pseudomonas* and *Proteus*, and a few cocci can degrade proteins. Moreover, spoilage by moulds is also common.

Fasts are digested by relatively few microorganisms, mainly moulds and a few gram-negative bacteria. Fats become rancid due to hydrolytic decomposition to malodorous fatty acids.

Carbohydrates are affected by carbohydrate-fermenting microorganisms, particularly yeasts and moulds. Bacterial species of the genera *Streptococcus, Leuconostoc* and *Micrococcus* are saccharolytic and can also attack carbohydrates. These degradation reactions are described below:

Protein + proteolytic microorganism → amino acids + amines + ammonia + hydrogen sulphide

Fat + lipolytic microorganism → fatty acids + glycerol

Carbohydrate + fermentative microorganism → acids + alcohols + gases

(ii) **Acidity :** The pH of nearly all foods is below 7.0. Foods are classified as acid or nonacid depending on whether the pH is below or above 4.5. Most fruits are acid foods, while nearly all vegetables, fish, meats and milk products are nonacid. The low pH of acid foods prevents the growth of most bacterial species. Such foods are spoiled mainly by yeast and moulds. Nonacid foods are particularly subject to bacterial spoilage, but also support growth of moulds under favourable conditions.

(iii) **Moisture :** Moisture is required for chemical reactions and microbial growth. Foods with a high percentage of water deteriorate fast. Variations in surface moisture due to changes in relative humidity can lead to lumping and caking, surface defects, crystallization and stickiness in foods. Condensation of even small amounts of moisture can result in the multiplication of bacteria and moulds.

Microorganisms require for their growth at least 13 per cent free water in foods. Moulds require the least free water and bacteria the most. Foods having high sugar or salt concentration do not support the growth of most microorganisms. Bacteria are generally inhibited by a salt concentration of 5 to 15 per cent, whereas many moulds and some yeasts can tolerate more than 15 per cent. A sugar concentration of 65 to 70 per cent is required to inhibit moulds but 50 per cent inhibits bacteria and most yeasts. Foods with high sugar or salt content are, therefore, most likely to be spoiled by moulds.

(B) Storage conditions

Temperature, aerial oxygen, light and duration of storage are the important factors that influence the type of microbial growth and spoilage of food during storage.

(i) **Temperature :** Heat and cold, though playing a role in food preservation, contribute to deterioration of food if not controlled. The rate of a chemical reaction doubles itself for *every* 10°C rise in temperature. Excessive heat brings about protein denaturation, destruction of vitamins, breaking of emulsions and desiccation of food by removing moisture. Several fruits and vegetables deteriorate on keeping even at the temperature of refrigeration (4°C). The deterioration includes off-colour development and surface biting. Banana, tomato, lemon and squash should be stored at about 10°C for retaining their quality.

Type of food and spoilage organism

Type	Predominant spoilage organism
Composition	
Protein	Bacteria, moulds
Fat	Moulds, a few bacteria
Carbohydrate	Yeasts, moulds
Acidity	
Acid (pH < 4.5)	Moulds, yeasts
Nonacid (pH > 4.5)	Bacteria

Minimum water activity (a_w) for growth of microorganisms

Microorganism	Minimum a_w
Bacteria	0.91
Yeasts	0.88
Moulds	0.80
Halophilic bacteria	0.75
Xerophilic fungi	0.65
Osmophilic yeasts	0.60

Low temperature retards spoilage but even a subfreezing temperature of about -7°C does not prevent multiplication of all microorganisms. Refrigerated foods are, therefore, subject to spoilage by moulds and by some yeasts and bacteria. Food stored at -18°C remains free from microbial growth and may even show a gradual decrease in the population of microorganisms. Foods and food products stored at room temperature or in warm locations are easily spoiled by mesophilic and thermophilic organisms.

(ii) Oxygen : Atmospheric oxygen may bring about undesirable changes in food such as destruction of food colour, flavour, and vitamins A and C. Oxygen is necessary for the growth of moulds and, therefore, it must be excluded from food in the course of processing, by deaeration, vacuum packing, or flushing containers with nitrogen or carbon dioxide and, in some cases, by the use of oxygen-absorbing chemicals.

(iii) Light : Light destroys vitamins B_2, A and C and also many food colours. Not all wavelengths of natural or artificial light are absorbed by food constituents or are equally destructive. Foods may be protected from light by impervious packing or keeping them in containers that screen out specific wavelengths.

(iv) Duration : All the above food deteriorating factors are time-dependent. The longer the storage time the greater the deterioration. Deterioration with time takes place with most foods except for cheese, wine and other fermented foods which improve up to a point with aging. For enjoying the best quality food it should be consumed before deterioration sets in.

Types of food spoilage and causative organisms

Food	Type of spoilage	Causative microorganism
Fresh fruits and vegetables	Gray mould rot	*Botrytis cinerea*
	Rhizopus soft rot	*Rhizopus nigricans*
	Blue mould rot	*Penicillium italicum*
	Black mould rot	*Aspergillus niger, Alternaria* sp.
	Sliminess or souring	Saprophytic bacteria
Pickles, Sauerkraut	Black pickles	*Bacillus nigricans*
	Soft pickles	*Bacillus* spp.
	Slimy kraut	*Lactobacillus plantarum, L. cucumeris*
	Pink kraut	*Rhodotorula* (asporogenous yeast)
Sugar products, Honey, Syrups	Ropy syrup	*Aerobacter aerogenes*
	Yeasty	*Saccharomyces* sp., *Taurula* sp., *Zygosaccharomyces* sp.
	Pink syrup	*Micrococcus roseus*
	Green syrup	*Pseudomonas fluorescens*
	Mouldy	*Aspergillus* sp., *Penicillium* sp.

Food	Type of spoilage	Causative microorganism
Bread	Mouldy	*Rhizopus* sp., *Aspergillus* sp.
	Ropy	*Penicillium* sp.
	Red bread	*Bacillus* spp., *Serratia marcescens*
Freash meat	Putrefaction	*Clostridium* sp., *Pseudomonas* sp., *Proteus* sp., *Alcaligenes* sp., *Chromobacterium* sp.
	Souring	*Chromobacterium* sp., *Lactobacillus* sp., *Pseudomonas* sp.
Cured meat	Mouldy	*Penicillium* sp., *Aspergillus* sp., *Rhizopus* sp.
	Souring	*Pseudomonas* sp., *Micrococcus* sp., *Bacillus* sp.
	Greening	*Lactobacillus* sp., *Streptococcus* sp., *Pediococcus* sp.
	Slimy	*Leuconostoc* sp.
Fish	Discolouration	*Pseudomonas* sp.
	Putrefaction	*Chromobacterium* sp., *Halobacterium* sp.
Poultry	Odour, slimy	*Pseudomonas* sp., *Alcaligenes*, *Xanthomonas* sp.
Eggs	Green rot	*Pseudomonas fluorescens.*
	Colourless rot	*Pseudomonas* sp., *Alcaligenes* sp., *Chromobacterium* sp., *Cloiformis* sp.
	Black rot	*Proteus* sp.
	Fungal rot	*Penicillium* sp., *Mucor* sp.
	Bacterial soft rot	*Erwinia carotovera, Pseudomonas* spp.

5. Mechanical damage

It is not possible to pick fruits from trees without some injury to them. Separating a fruit bruised from its stalk itself causes injury. Moreover, sometimes fruits are bruised or scratched during harvesting and handling. If precautions are not taken, the injured spots become the points of entrance of microorganisms which cause spoilage. Important examples of such spoilage are crown rot in banana, pedicel rot in pineapple, stem end rot in mango, green mould in citrus fruits and blue mould in apple.

Removal of diseased, damaged and scratched fruits during grading and post-harvest treatment of the fruits with fungicides like thiabendazole, benomyl, sodium orthophenylphenate (SOPP) are highly useful in reducing mechanical damage to fruits.

Classification of foods according to ease of spoilage

1. **Stable or non-perishable foods** : These do not spoil unless handled carelessly, e.g., sugar, flour and dry beans.

2. **Semi-perishable foods** : If these are properly handled and stored they will remain unspoiled for a fairly long period, e.g., potato and some varieties of apple.

3. **Perishable foods** : This group includes most of the important foods that spoil readily unless special preservation methods are used, e.g., most fruits and vegetables, meat, fish, poultry, eggs and milk.

Chapter 10

Browning Reactions

Browing reactions occur very widely in food materials. The colours produced range from pale yellow to dark brown or black, depending on the type of product and the extent of the reaction. In some foods browning is considered desirable, e.g., honey, chocolate, brown crust of baked products, etc., while in other foods it is detrimental, as in darkening of dehydrated fruits, vegetables, etc.

Browning reactions may be either enzymatic or nonenzymatic. Many of the enzymatic reactions are seen in fruits and vegetables, and involve the oxidation of polyphenolic compounds by oxidative enzymes in plant cells. The nonenzymatic browning reactions frequently involve sugars or sugar-related compounds.

(1) Enzymatic browning : Many fruits and vegetables have a tendency to turn brown when damaged or when cut surfaces are exposed to air, e.g., apples, bananas, potatoes, etc., and this is due to enzymatic reaction. The formation of brown colour is due to the action of the enzyme phenolase (also known as polyphenol oxidase, tyrosinase or catecholase) on phenolic substances. Normally, the phenolic substrates are separated from phenolase in intact tissues and browning does not occur. When foods containing such substrates are cut and exposed to air rapid browning of cut surface takes place.

$$\text{Polyphenols} + \text{Oxygen} \xrightarrow[\text{(in cells)}]{\text{oxidase}} \text{Brown}$$
(in cells) (air)

The enzymatic browning is due to the oxidation of phenols to orthoquinones, which in turn rapidly polymerize to form melanin (the brown pigment). When the substrate is a phenol, it is first converted by hydroxylation into orthodiphenol and then oxidized to orthoquinone. Tyrosine is the major phenolic substrate for phenolase action in foods. Other phenolic substances are caffeic acid, protocatechuic acid and chlorogenic acid. The reactions occur in several steps and are catalyzed by several enzymes, e.g., phenolases, peroxidases and others.

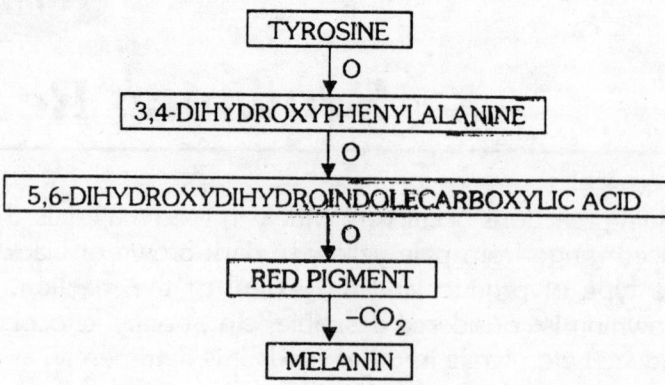

Some fruits do not contain these enzymes and do not darken on exposure of cut surfaces to air. Orange, lemon, grapefruit, strawberry, tomato, etc., seem to be free from these enzymes.

Melanin formation is undesirable during the processing of fruits and vegetables. Pigment formation can be eliminated by inhibiting enzyme action. Heat treatment, addition of sulphur dioxide or sulphites and ascorbic acid are the commonly used methods of inactivating these enzymes. Both sulphur dioxide and ascorbic acid are strong reducing agents. They consume oxygen and destroy the browning activity of enzymes and either of them may be added to products that tend to darken. The enzyme is irreversibly inactivated at pH values of 3 or less and this can be achieved by the addition of sufficient acidulants such as citric, malic or phosphoric acids. Browning can also be prevented by excluding oxygen from the reaction site or protecting the phenolic substrates. The exclusion of oxygen is achieved by immersing the tissues in brine or syrup, or by processing under vacuum and the phenolic substances are protected by the use of certain enzymes which modify orthophenolic substrates.

(2) Nonenzymatic browning: Nonenzymatic browning reactions are responsible for the colour and flavour of foods. Roasting of potatoes, like toasting of biscuits and baking of breads and cakes, produces a golden-brown colour. Sometimes this reaction produces a desirable flavour (the chocolate flavour of cocoa beans), at other times the reaction is undesirable (dark brown of potato chips). Because this does not involve enzymes, it is distinguished from enzymatic browning by being termed nonenzymatic browning. The presence of reactive reducing sugars is responsible for browning in foods. On heating the sugars undergo ring opening, enolisation, dehydration and fragmentation. The unsaturated carbonyl compounds that are formed react to produce brown polymers and flavour compounds. Heat-induced browning reactions can be divided into two groups: Maillard reaction and caramelization.

(a) Maillard reaction: Maillard reaction also known as Maillard browning is a colour, flavour, odour, and sometimes texture change which results from a chemical reaction between proteins and carbohydrates. It is named after the Frenchman Maillard who discovered it. The Maillard reaction denotes a group of many complex reactions between (i) nitrogenous compounds and sugars, (ii) nitrogenous compounds and organic acids, (iii) sugars and organic acids, and (iv) among organic acids themselves. The carbonyl group of acyclic sugars readily combines with the basic amino groups of proteins, peptides and amino acids, resulting in sugar-amines. The set of various reactions that sugar-amines undergo resulting in browning is known as the Maillard reaction. The sugar-amines have a brown colour at a low temperature. It has been found that histidine, threonine, phenylalanine, tryptophan and lysine are the most reactive aminoacids. The initial reaction is thought to be between the aldehyde group of the sugar and the amino group of the amino acid.

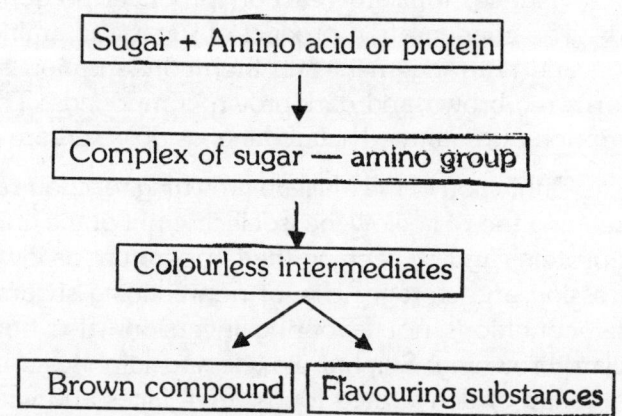

Maillard browning is responsible for the desirable browning of most heated foods such as bread crusts, roasted meats, and roasted coffee beans. This browning is accelerated by heat and occurs very quickly in ovens, slowly at room temperature, and very slowly at refrigerator temperatures. The browning that occurs during room temperature storage is a major cause of quality changes in preserved food. Very small amounts of the protein or carbohydrate substrates are needed for

Maillard browning to occur. The proteins of enzymes and those in the thin layer of cell membranes in fruits and vegetables is enough. In light-coloured foods such as dried apples the effects are particularly notice-able.

Maillard browning is also accelerated by low moisture content. Commercially dried milk and home dried foods which are both low moisture and stored at room temperature are frequently discarded due to this reaction. Maillard browning becomes more pronounced with increased storage time.

Light does not accelerate Maillard browning but does increase other colour changes. This problems is addressed commercially by packaging foods in opaque materials. Householders need to store their glass jars and plastic bags in dark places. Avoid a sunny window in the pantry or leaving a light on to decrease humidity or discourage pests.

Another nutrient which is affected is vitamin B_1 (thiamine). Because it has an amino group, it acts in the same way as an amino acid in combining readily with sugar in the browning reaction.

Hence, Maillard reaction products predominate in browned foods. The condensation product of sugar and amine undergoes enolization and rearrangement and then condensation and polymerization to form red-brown and dark-brown compounds. The brown to black, amorphous, unsaturated heterogeneous polymers are called "melanoids".

Inhibition of the Maillard browning reaction can be accomplished by keeping the pH below the isoelectric pH of the amino acids, peptides and proteins and by keeping the temperature as low as possible during processing and storage. Use of nonreducing sugars, such as sucrose, under conditions not favouring inversion, also helps to bring down Maillard browning. Sulphur dioxide and sulphites used in extending the storage life of dehydrated foods, fruit juices and wines also inhibit the reaction.

(b) Caramelization : Sugar in dry condition (or their syrups) when heated beyond their melting point decompose and form a brown mass known as caramel, which has a bitter, astringent taste. The process of caramelization occurs at a high temperature, while Maillard reactions develop brown colour at low temperature. With the use of suitable catalysts it is possible to carry out caramelization to provide either flavouring or colouring caramel for food use. For flavouring purposes, sucrose as concentrated syrup is caramelized. For the manufacture of caramel colours for use in beverages, glucose syrup is treated with dilute sulphuric acid and then partially neutralized with ammonia.

Besides reaction of sugars and amino acids, breakdown of ascorbic acid during storage of the products may be another possible reason for the development of browning.

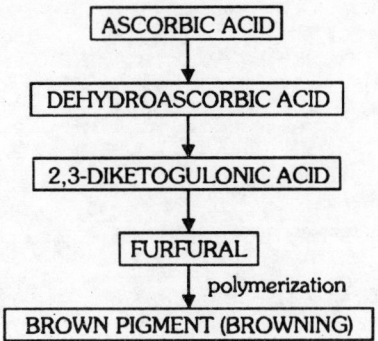

Browning may also be due to metallic contamination, mainly by iron and copper salts. The tannin in fruits and vegetables reacts with the iron of the tinplate to form ferric tannate, which is black in colour and spoils the appearance. Sometimes hydrogen sulphide gas is liberated (due to reaction between fruit acids and tinplate) from the canned product which, in turn, reacts with the iron of the can and forms black iron sulphide. Besides, browning is also caused by unsuitable vessels, e.g, traces of copper (1 ppm) coming in contact with hydrogen sulphide form black copper sulphide. Metallic contamination can be avoided by using glass containers, uniformly coating the interiors of cans with suitable lacquers of eliminating use or iron and copper vessels.

Chapter 11

Fermentation
(Acetic, Lactic and Alcoholic)

ecomposition of carbohydrates by microorganisms or enzymes is called fermentation. Fermentation of food results in the production of organic acids, alcohol, etc., which not only help in preserving the food but may also produce distinctive new food products.

The term fermentation has come to have somewhat different meanings as its underlying causes have become better understood. The derivation of the word fermentation signifies a gentle bubbling condition. The term was first applied to the production of wine more than a thousand years ago. The bubbling action was due to the conversion of sugar to carbon dioxide gas. When the reaction was defined following the studies of Gay-Lussac, fermentation came to mean the breakdown of sugar into alcohol and carbon dioxide. Pasteur later demonstrated the relationship of yeast to this reaction, and the word fermentation became associated with microorganisms, and still later with enzymes. The early research on fermentation dealt mostly with carbohydrates and reactions that liberated carbon dioxide. It was soon recognised, however, that microorganisms or enzymes acting on sugars did not always evolve gas. Further, many of the microorganisms and enzymes studied also had the ability to break down non-carbohydrate materials such as proteins and fats, which yielded carbon dioxide, other gases, and a wide range of additional materials.

Currently, the term fermentation is used in various ways which require clarification. When chemical change is discussed at the molecular level, in the context of comparative physiology and biochemistry, the term fermentation is correctly employed to describe the breakdown of carbohydrate materials under *anaerobic* conditions. In a somewhat broader and less precise usage, where primary interest is in describing the end products rather than the mechanisms of biochemical reactions, the term fermentation refers to breakdown of carbohydrate and carbohydratelike materials under either *anaerobic* or *aerobic* conditions. Conversion of lactose to lactic acid by *Streptococcus lactis* bacteria is favoured by anaerobic conditions and is true fermentation; conversion of ethyl alcohol to acetic acid by *Acetobacter aceti* bacteria is favoured by aerobic conditions and is more correctly termed an oxidation rather than a fermentation. Common usage frequently overlooks this distinction and considers both types of reactions to be fermentations.

But the word fermentation also is used in a still broader and less precise manner. The term *fermented foods* is used to describe a special class of food products characterized by various kinds of carbohydrate breakdown; but seldom is carbohydrate the only constituent acted upon. Most fermented foods contain a complex mixture of carbohydrates, proteins, fats, and so on, undergoing modification simultaneously, or in some sequence, under the action of variety of microorganisms and enzymes. This creates the need for additional terms to distinguish between major types of change. Those reactions involving carbohydrates and carbohydratelike materials (true fermentations) are referred to as "fermentative". Changes in proteinaceous materials are designated *proteolytic* or *putrefactive*. Breakdowns of fatty substances are described as *lipolytic*. When complex foods are "fermented" under natural conditions, they invariably undergo different degrees of each of these types of change. Whether fermentative, proteolytic, or lipolytic end products dominate will depend on the nature of the food, the types of microorganisms present, and environmental conditions affecting their growth and metabolic patterns. In specific food fermentations, control of the types of microorganisms and environmental conditions to produce desired product characteristics is necessary.

Fermentations occur when microorganisms consume susceptible organic substrates as part of their own metabolic processes. Such interactions are fundamental to the decomposition of natural materials, and to the ultimate return of chemical elements to the soil and air without which life could not be sustained. Natural fermentations have played a vital role in human development and are probably the oldest form of food preservation. Although the growth of microorganisms in many foods is undesirable and considered spoilage, some fermentations are highly desirable. Fruit and fruit juices left to the elements acquired an alcoholic flavour; milk on standing became mildly acidic and eventually became cheese; cabbage turned to sauerkraut. These changes tasted good and so early civilizations encouraged the conditions that permitted them to occur. Sometimes the desired results were obtained repeatedly, but this was not always so. It soon was also discovered that certain alcoholic fruit juices and sour milks would keep well, and so part of the food supply was converted into these ferms as a means of preservation.

Today, other methods of food preservation are superior to fermentation as means of preserving many foods. In technically advanced societies the major importance of fermented foods has come to be the variety they add to diets. In many less developed areas of the world, however, fermentation and natural drying are still the major food preservation methods, and, as such, are vital to survival of much of the world's population. The various preservation methods are based on the applications of heat, cold, radiation, removal of water, and other principles, all have the common objective of decreasing the numbers of living organisms in foods, or at least holding them in check against further multiplication. In contrast, fermentation, whether for preservation purposes or not, encourages the multiplication of microorganisms and their metabolic activities in foods. But only selected organisms are encouraged, and their metabolic activities and end products are highly desirable. The increasing application of biotechnology and genetic engineering techniques to food production is bringing added importance to food fermentations.

Acetic, lactic and alcoholic are the three important kinds of fermentation involved in fruit and vegetable preservation. The keeping quality of vinegar, fermented pickles and alcoholic beverages depends upon the presence of acetic acid, lactic acid and alcohol, respectively. Care should be taken to exclude air from the fermented products to avoid further unwanted or secondary fermentation. Wines, cider, vinegar, fermented pickles and other fermented beverage, etc., are prepared by these processes.

Some industrial fermentations in fruit and vegetable industries

---

(A) *Acetic acid* **fermentation (Acetic acid bacteria)**

Wine, cider, malt honey, or any alcoholic and sugary or starchy products may be converted to vinegar

(B) *Lactic acid* **fermentation (Lactic acid bacteria)**

Cucumbers → dill pickles, sour pickles, salt stock

Tomato → pickles

Lemon → pickles

Mango → pickles

Cauliflower → pickles

Olives → green olives, ripe olives

Cabbage → sauerkraut

Turnips → sauerruben

Lettuce → lettuce kraut

Mixed vegetables, turnips, radish, cabbage→Paw Tsay

Mixed vegetables in Chinese cabbage →Kimchi

Vegetables and milk → Tarhana

Vegetables and rice → Sajur asin

Coffee cherries → coffee beans

Vanilla beans → vanilla

> ***Lactic acid bacteria with other microorganisms***
> With yeasts—Nukamiso pickles
> With mould—tempeh, soy sauce
> **(C) Alcoholic fermentation (yeasts)**
> Fruit—wine, vermouth
> Malt—beer, ale, porter, stout, bock, Pilsner
> Wines—brandy
> Grain mash—whiskey
> ***Yeasts with lactic acid bacteria***
> *Ginger plant*—ginger beer
> Beans — vermicelli
> ***Yeasts with acetic acid bacteria***
> Cacao beans
> Citron

(A) Acetic acid fermentation

The production of vinegar (acetic acid) from fruit juices is perhaps one of the oldest organic acid fermetnations known. Acetic acid is produced by the oxidation of ethyl alcohol by bacteria such as *Acetobacter aceti*, *A. orleansis*, *A. schutzenbachi* and others. The biochemical reaction by which they form acetic acid from ethyl alcohol is as follows :

$$2CH_3CH_2OH + O_2 \rightarrow 2CH_3CHO + 2H_2O$$
$$2CH_3CHO + O_2 \rightarrow 2CH_3COOH$$

Some *Acetobacter* species do not stop at the stage of acid production but continue the oxidation to carbon dioxide.

$$CH_3COOH + 2O_2 \rightarrow 2CO_2 + 2H_2O$$

Theoretically, 100 parts of sugar (sucrose or maltose) should yield about 51 parts of ethyl alcohol or 67 parts of acetic acid. In actual practice, however, even under the most favourable conditions, 43 to 48 parts of alcohol and 49 to 56 parts of acetic acid only are produced. These losses in yield may be due to (i) the consumption of sugar in the solution by the yeast, (ii) loss of alcohol and acetic acid due to evaporation and oxidation, (iii) loss due to utilization by acetic acid bacteria for their growth, and (iv) small quantities of alcohol may also remain unconverted.

Hence, it is necessary to use a juice with at least 10 per cent sugar (maltose or sucrose) content for preparing a vinegar of about 5 per cent acetic acid strength. After conversion of alcohol into acetic acid the acetic acid bacteria attack the acid itself. This can be prevented by filling the containers up to the brim and sealing them airtight.

Further information on acetic acid fermentation can be found in the chapter on 'Vinegar'.

(B) Lactic acid fermentation

Lactic acid fermentation as a good method of preservation is another ancient art of unknown origin. It was investigated by Pasteur.

Lactic acid fermentation is an anaerobic intra-molecular oxidation-reduction process. Both homofermentative and heterofermentative lactic acid bacteria participate in food fermentation. In some cases, yeasts and moulds also participate along with lactic acid bacteria.

Important products prepared by lactic acid fermentation are given below along with predominant microorganisms concerned.

Raw material	Predominant organism	Product
Cabbage	*Leuconostoc mesenteroides, Lactobacillus plantarum, L. brevis*	Sauerkraut
Cucumber, tomato, lemon, mango, cauliflower, etc.	*Leuconostoc mesenteroides, Lactobacillus plantarum, L. brevis, Streptococcus faecalis, Pediococcus cerevisiae*	Pickles

In general, bacteria prefer low or no acid medium for their growth. The lactic acid bacteria, however, can grow in acid medium and can also produce acid through their action on the substrate. They can grow in the presence of 8 to 10 per cent salt. Advantage is taken of these two factors in pickling. The growth of undesirable organisms is inhibited by adding salt, while allowing the lactic acid fermentation to proceed.

Fermentation takes place fairly well in a brine containing approximately 5 per cent salt but proceeds somewhat slowly with 10 per cent salt. To some extent it continues up to 15 per cent, but at 20 per cent, all fermentation stops. It is, therefore, customary to place the vegetables in a 10 per cent salt solution to allow lactic acid fermentation to take place and then increase the concentration of salt gradually, so that by the time the pickle is ready, the concentration would have reached 15 per cent.

Temperature is another important factor in lactic acid fermentation. Lactic acid bacteria are most active at about 30°C. It is, therefore, essential that the temperature of the product undergoing lactic acid fermentation should be keep as close to 30°C as possible, especially in the beginning.

When vegetables are placed in brine, the soluble material present in them diffuses into the salt water due to osmosis and the liquid penetrates into the tissues. The soluble material contains, besides mineral matter, fermentable sugar also. The sugars serve as food for lactic acid bacteria, which convert them into lactic and other acids. In practice, 2-3 kg of salt is mixed with every 100 kg of material and the mixture allowed to stand for 12 to 24 hours, when sufficient juice comes out from the material to form the brine. If the vegetable does not contain sufficient amount of juice it is covered with brine containing 5 per cent salt. The soluble material extracted is fermented by the lactic acid-forming bacteria, which are generally present in large numbers on the surface of fresh vegetables.

When sufficient lactic acid is formed, the lactic acid bacteria cease to function, and any further change in the composition of the material is prevented.

Further information on lactic acid fermentation can be found in the chapter on 'Pickles'.

(C) Alcoholic fermentation

Ethyl alcohol can be produced by fermentation of any carbohydrate containing a fermentable sugar, or a polysaccharide that can be hydrolyzed to a fermentable sugar. Cider is one of the examples of alcoholic fermentation. It is brought about by yeasts.

The equation that describes the net result of alcoholic fermentation by yeast is given below:

$$C_6H_{12}O_6 + yeast \rightarrow 2C_2H_5OH + 2CO_2$$
$$\text{Ethyl alcohol}$$

Here a sugar is the substrate and the process is anaerobic. *Saccharomyces cerevisiae* is commonly employed for fermentation. It is imperative that the yeast must have a high tolerance for alcohol and must grow vigorously and produce a large quantity of alcohol.

100 g of a hexose sugar should yield 51.1 g of ethyl alcohol and 48.9 g of carbon dioxide. Besides alcohol, a number of other substances are also formed in small quantities. The alcohol content of wine is usually expressed as volume per cent, i.e., cc of alcohol per 100 cc of wine. The percentage of alcohol will be approximately equal to the Brix (total soluble solids) of the crushed material multiplied by a factor of 0.57, e.g., a crushed material containing 22 per cent total soluble solids should give theoretically a dry wine of about 22 x 0.57 = 12.5 volume per cent of alcohol (V%).

Further information on alcoholic fermentation can be found in the two chapters on 'Unfermented and Fermented Fruit Beverages and 'Vinegar'.

Chapter 12

Principles and Methods of Preservation

ood preservation can be defined as the science which deals with the methods of prevention of decay or spoilage of food, thus allowing it to be stored in a fit condition for future use. It is better if the following directions are kept in mind to control the spoilage.

1. Raw materials should be thoroughly examined and handled hygienic conditions to avoid microbial spoilage.

2. Equipments must be cleaned every time before use.

3. The cans should be carefully filled and exhausted sufficiently to produce a good vacuum.

4. Processing should take place as soon as possible after sealing of cans or bottles. The cooling process should also be done in such a manner that the cans are left sufficiently warm to dry off surplus moisture but not hot enough to cause "stack" burning.

5. Use of contaminated water should be avoided.

6. The finished products after canning or bottling should be stored in well-ventilated rooms in a cool and dry place. High storage temperature should be avoided.

Freshly prepared products are highly attractive in appearance and possess good taste and aroma, but deteriorate rapidly if kept for some time. This is on account of several reasons such as, (i) fermentation caused by moulds, yeasts and bacteria, (ii) enzymes present in the product may affect the colour and flavour adversely, e.g. apple juice turns brown due to the activity of oxidative enzymes in it, (iii) chemicals present in the pulp/juice may react with one another and spoil its taste and aroma, (iv) air coming in contact with the product, may react with the glucosidal materials present in it and render the product bitter, e.g., Navel orange and sweet lime juices often turn bitter when they are exposed to air even for a short time, and (v) traces of metal from the equipment may get into the product and spoil its taste and aroma.

In the preservation of foods by various methods, the following principles are involved:

1. Prevention or delay of microbial decomposition

(a) by keeping out microorganisms (asepsis);

(b) by removal of microorganisms, e.g., by filtration;

(c) by hindering the growth and activity of microorganisms, e.g., by low temperature, drying, anaerobic conditions, chemicals or antibiotics; and

(d) by killing the microorganisms, e.g., by heat or radiation.

2. Prevention or delay of self-decomposition of the food

(a) by destruction or inactivation of enzymes, e.g., by blanching;

(b) by prevention or delay of chemical reactions, e.g., prevention of oxidation by means of an antioxidant.

3. Prevention of damage by insects, animals, mechanical causes, etc.

To retain the natural taste and aroma of a product, it is necessary to preserve it soon after preparation, without allowing it to stand for any length of time. Various methods of preservation are employed and each has its own merits. The methods generally used are as under:

1. Asepsis (Absence of infection)

Asepsis means preventing the entry of microorganisms. Maintaining of general cleanliness while, picking, grading, packing and transporting of fruits and vegetables increases their keeping quality and the products prepared from them will be of superior quality.

Washing or wiping of the fruits and vegetables before processing should be strictly followed as dust particles adhering to the raw material contain microorganisms and by doing so the number of organisms can be reduced considerably.

2. Preservation by High Temperature

Coagulation of proteins and inactivation of their metabolic enzymes by the application of heat leads to the destruction of microorganisms present in foods. Further, heating can also inactivate the enzymes present in the food. Heating food to high temperatures can, therefore, help to preserve it. The specific treatment varies with:

(a)   the organism that has to be killed,

(b)   the nature of the food to be preserved, and

(c)   other means of preservation that may be used in addition to high temperature.

High temperatures used for preservation are usually: (i) pasteurization temperature (below 100°C), and (ii) sterilization temperature (100°C or above).

(i)   Pasteurization

Pasteurization frees the food from human pathogens and most of vegetative microorganisms. Heating of fruit juices, ready-to-serve (R.T.S.) and nectar is the most common method for their preservation. The process of heating at boiling temperature or slightly below it for a sufficient length of time to kill the microorganisms which cause spoilage, is called pasteurization.

Pasteurization does not kill all microorganisms present in the juice. Some spores and spore-forming bacteria like *Bacillus subtilis* and *B. mesentericus* can survive and multiply later. These survivor are, however, generally too small in number to cause any spoilage. Further, these organisms are highly sensitive to acid and cannot grow in the juice of acid fruits and acid vegetables.

Mould spores are destroyed by heating at 79°C for 5 to 10 minutes. Moulds require oxygen for their growth. Removal of air from the juice by filling the containers completely or deaerating the juice under vacuum or replacing the air with CO_2, therefore, facilitates the destruction of moulds even at a lower temperature.

Yeasts and acid-tolerant bacteria are readily killed if the juice is heated for a few minutes at about 66°C. Thermal death time (TDT) of bacteria given below in the table.

Thermal Death Time (TDT[1]) of bacteria

Bacteria	Time (min)	Temperature (°C)
Salmonella typhosa .	4.3	60
Staphylococcus aureus	18.8	60
E. coli	20-30	57.3
Streptococcus thermophilus	15	70-77
L. bulgaricus	30	71

---

1.   TDT is defined as the time required at a given temperature to kill a stated number of organisms under specified conditions.

The spore-forming bacteria found in tomato juice, however, require heating at a higher temperature of 88°C for a much longer duration. Heat resistance of bacterial spores are also given below in the Table.

Heat resistance of bacterial spores

Spore	Time (min) to kill at 100°C
B. anthracis	1.7
B. subtilis	15-30
C. botulinum	100-300
Flat sour bacteria	over 1000

Enzymes also require air (oxygen) at normal temperature for their action and can, therefore, be destroyed at a moderate temperature by removing air from the juice. Pectic enzymes which cause changes in flavour and also bring about the clotting of particles in the juice can be destroyed by heating the juice for about 4 minutes at 85°C, or for one minute at 88°C.

Usually juices, R.T.S. and nectar are pasteurized at about 85°C for 25 to 30 minutes according to the nature of the juice and the size of the container.

Acid fruit juices require a lower temperature and less time for pasteurization than the less acid ones. Juice can be pasteurized in two ways: (i) by heating it at a low temperature for a long period, or (ii) by heating at a high temperature for a short time only (HTST method). There are three methods of pasteurization.

(a) **Bottle or 'Holding' pasteurization :** This method is commonly used for the preservation of fruit juices at home. The extracted juice is strained or clarified as the case may be, and filled in bottles, leaving sufficient head space for the expansion of the juice during heating. The bottles are then sealed air-tight and pasteurized.

(b) **Overflow method :** Juice is heated to a temperature about 2.5°C higher than the pasteurization temperature, and then filled in hot sterilized bottles up to the brim, taking care that during filling and sealing the temperature of juice does not fall below the pasteurization temperature. The sealed bottles are pasteurized at a temperature 2.5°C lower than the filling and sealing temperature and then cooled. This method is very suitable for grape juice because it minimizes the adverse effect of air on the quality of the juice.

(c) **Flash pasteurization :** The juice is heated rapidly to a temperature of about 5.5°C higher than the pasteurization temperature and kept at this temperature for about a minute. The method has been developed specially for the canning of natural orange juice but can also be used for grape and apple juices. It has the following advantages:

(a)   loss of flavour is minimum,

(b)   vitamins are not destroyed

(c)   effects economy of time and space,

(d)   keeps the juice uniformly cloudy, and

(e)   juice is heated uniformly and thus its cooked taste is minimum.

(ii) Sterilization

Sterilization by definition, means the destruction of all viable microorganisms. Heat sterilization is the most effective process of food preservation. It has a severe effect on heat liable nutrients, particularly vitamins and mainly through Maillard reaction, the nutritional quality of proteins is reduced. By this method all microorganisms are completely destroyed due to high temperature. The time and temperature necessary for sterilization vary with the type of food. Fruit and tomato products should be heated at 100°C for 30 minutes so that the spore-forming bacteria which are sensitive to high acidity may be completely killed. Vegetables like green peas, okra, beans, etc., being non-acidic and containing more starch than sugar, require higher temperature to kill the spore-forming organisms. Continuous heating for 30 to 90 minutes at 116°C is essential for their sterilization. Before using, empty cans and bottles should also be sterilized for about 30 minutes by placing them in boiling water. Temperatures above 100°C can only be obtained by using steam pressure sterilizers such as pressure cookers and autoclaves.

The major differences between pasteurization and sterilization are as under:

S. No.	Pasteurization	Sterilization
1.	partial destruction of microorganisms	Complete destruction of microorganisms
2.	Temperature below 100°C	Temperature 100°C and abvoe
3.	Normally used for fruits	Normally used for vegetables

A quick technique of "Aseptic Canning", using high temperature, has also been developed which not only reduces the sterilization time but also improves the quality of the product markedly. Another methods is "Hot Pack or Hot Fill", generally used in homes for preparation of jam and other products. Both are discussed here in brief.

Aseptic Canning

Aseptic canning is a technique in which food is sterilized outside the can and then aseptically placed in previously sterilized cans which are subsequently sealed in an aseptic environment.

This process, also known as Martin aseptic canning, was first commercialized in 1950. The method is basically a short-time, high-temperature sterilization process. It combines flash pasteurization and cooling with aseptic packaging of fluid and semi-fluid products, thus eliminating the retorting and subsequent cooling phases.

This process consists of four separate operations, carried out one after another in a closed interconnected apparatus: (i) sterilization of product by appropriate quick heating, holding and cooling, (ii) sterilization of containers and covers with superheated steam, (iii) aseptic filling of cooled, sterile product into sterile containers, and (iv) aseptic sealing of the containers with sterile covers.

The temperature employed may be as high as 149°C and sterilization takes place in 1 or 2 seconds to yield products of the highest quality.

Details of process

Quick heating of liquid food may be done in a plate-type or in a tubular-scraped-surface-type heat exchanger. The latter consists essentially of a tube within a tube. Steam flows through the space between the tubes while food flows through the inner tube. The inner tube is also provided with a rotating shaft or mutator equipped with scraper blades to prevent the food from burning on the heat exchanger surface. In contact with the hot surface the thin layer of food is brought to sterilization temperature in a second or less. If it is desired to prolong the time beyond this, then a holding tube is added. Such rapid sterilization at extremely high temperatures, e.g., 1 or 2 seconds at 149°C, is sometimes referred to as ultra-high temperature (UHT) sterilization. The sterile food is now quickly cooled, since at these high temperatures product quality can be impaired in seconds. Quick cooling can be accomplished with the same types of plate or tubular-scraped-surface heat exchangers, by using refrigerants instead of steam.

The sterile cooled food now enters the aseptic canning line. This consists of a tunnel through which cans without their lids are conveyed and sterilized by superheated steam, a sterile filling zone also heated by steam where the cans enter a heated sterile can lid dispenser, and a closing machine which seals cans in a steam-heated sterile atmosphere. After the cans are sealed they are cooled by spraying water. Not only must the temperature of the food be accurately controlled before it enters the aseptic canning line, but can and lid sterilization temperatures must also be controlled since tinplate begins to melt at about 232°C and the temperature of superheated steam can be higher than this.

Aseptic packaging is not limited to metal containers. An aseptic system for bottling UHT sterilized cream has recently been introduced on a commercial basis. However, engineering problems related to breakage of glass due to thermal shock have not yet been completely solved.

Another form of aseptic packaging utilizes flexible packaging materials which are sterilized, formed, filled and sealed in a continuous operation. In some cases the disinfectant property of hydrogen peroxide is combined with heat to make it possible to use lower temperatures for sterilizing less heat-resistant packaging materials. Coffee cream is packaged in small single service paper packets in this way. Chlorine and other chemicals can be expected to find wider use in such applications in the future.

Hot Pack or Hot Fill

This term refers to the filling of previously pasteurized or sterilized food, while still hot, into clean but not necessarily sterile containers, under clean but not necessarily aseptic conditions. Such packaging is based on the fact that the heat of the food and some holding period before cooling the closed container render the container commercially sterile, e.g., in home when fruit pulp and sugar are boiled together to make jam and the hot jam is poured into jars that have been previously boiled, the principle of hot pack is being employed.

3. Preservation by Low Temperature

Microbial growth and enzyme reactions are retarded in foods stored at low temperatures. The lower the temperature, the greater the retardation. Low temperatures can be produced by (i) cellar storage (about 15°C), (ii) refrigeration or chilling (0 to 5°C), and (iii) freezing (-18 to -40°C).

(i) **Cellar storage (about 15°C) :** The temperature in cellars (underground rooms) where surplus food is stored in many villages is usually not much below that of the outside air and is seldom lower than 15°C. It is not low enough to prevent the action of many spoilage organisms or of plant enzymes. Decomposition is, however, slowed down considerably. Root crops, potatoes, onions, apples and similar foods can be stored for limited periods during the winter months.

(ii) **Refrigeration or chilling (0 to 5°C) :** Chilling temperatures are obtained and maintained by means of ice or mechanical refrigeration. Fruits, vegetables and their products can be preserved for a few days to many weeks when kept at this temperature. The best storage temperature for many foods is slightly above 0°C but his varies with the product and is fairly specific to it. Besides temperature, the relative humidity and the composition of the air can affect the preservation of the food. Commercial cold storages with proper ventilation and automatic control of temperature are now used throughout the country (mostly in cities) for the storage of semi-perishable foods such as potatoes and apples. This has made such foods available throughout the year and has also stabilized their prices.

(ii) **Freezing (-18 to -40°C) :** Freezing method is the most harmless method of food preservation. Microbial growth is inhibited and the rate of chemical reactions is slowed down at low temperatures. In commercial frozen storage the activity of meat enzymes is stopped while plant foods have to be blanched before freezing to avoid undesirable quality changes. At temperatures below the freezing point of water (-18 to -40°C) growth of microorganisms and enzyme activity are reduced to a minimum. Most perishable foods can be preserved for several months if the temperature is brought down quickly (quick freezing) and the food kept at these temperatures. Foods can be quick frozen in about 90 minutes or less by: (i) placing them in contact with the coil through which the refrigerant flows, (ii) blast freezing in which cold air is blown across the food, and (iii) dipping in liquid nitrogen.

Quick frozen foods maintain their quality and freshness when they are thawed (brought to room temperature) because only very small ice crystals are formed when foods are frozen in this manner. Many microorganisms can survive this treatment and become active and spoil the food if it is kept at higher temperatures. Frozen foods should, therefore, always be kept at temperatures, below -5°C. Enzymes in certain vegetables can continue to act even after being quick frozen and so such vegetables have to be given a mild heat treatment called blanching (above 80°C) before they are frozen to prevent development of off-flavours.

The best way of preserving pure fruit juice is by freezing. Properly frozen juice retains its freshness, colour and aroma for a long time. This method is particularly useful in the case of juices whose flavour is adversely affected by heating. The juice is first deaerated and the vacuum filled with nitrogen gas. It is then transferred into containers which are hermetically sealed and frozen. Moulds are sometimes not affected by this technique. Juice can be kept in good condition for a long time in frozen form at -12 to -17°C by excluding air. It is defrosted before consumption.

4. Preservation by Chemicals

Microbial spoilage of food products is also controlled by using chemical preservatives which do not include salt, sugar, acetic acid, oils, alcohols, etc., but only microbial antagonists.

The inhibitory action of preservatives is due to their interfering with the mechanism of cell division, permeability of cell membrane and activity of enzymes.

Pasteurized squashes, cordials and crushes have a cooked flavour. After the container is opened, they ferment and spoil within a short period, particularly in a tropical climate. To avoid this, it is necessary to use chemical preservatives. Chemically preserved squashes and crushes can be kept for a fairly long time even after opening the seal of the bottle. It is, however, essential that the use of chemicals is properly controlled, as their indiscriminate use is likely to be harmful. The preservative used should not be injurious to health and should be non-irritant. It should be easy to detect and estimate.

According to the British Food and Drug Act of 1928 a "preservative" is any substance which is capable of inhibiting, retarding or arresting the process of fermentation, acidification or other decomposition of food, but does not include common salt (sodium chloride), saltpetre (sodium or potassium nitrate), sugar, acetic acid or vinegar, alcohol or potable spirits, spices, essential oil or any other substance added to the food by the process of curing known as smoking.

The two important chemical preservatives permitted in many countries are :

(i)   sulphur dioxide (including sulphites), and

(ii)   benzoic acid (include benzoates)

These two are also allowed in India according to the Fruit Product Order (F.P.O.) of 1955.

(i)   Sulphur dioxide

It is widely used throughout the world in the preservation of juice, pulp, nectar, squash, crush, cordial and other products. It has good preserving action against bacteria and moulds and inhibits enzymes, etc. In addition, it acts as an antioxidant and bleaching agent. These properties help in the retention of ascorbic acid, carotene and other oxidizable compounds. It also retards the development of nonenzymatic browning or discolouration (after killing the enzyme) of the product. It is generally used in the form of its salts such as sulphite, bisulphite and metabisulphite.

Potassium metabisulphite ($K_2O.2SO_2$ or $K_2S_2O_5$) is commonly used as a stable source of sulphur dioxide. Being a solid, it is easier to use than liquid or gaseous sulphur dioxide. It is fairly stable in neutral or alkaline media but decomposed by weak acids like carbonic, citric, tartaric and malic acids. When added to fruit juice or squash it reacts with the acid in the juice forming the potassium salt and sulphur dioxide, which is liberated and forms sulphurous acid with the water of the juice. The reactions involved are as follows:

$$CH_2COOH \qquad\qquad CH_2COOK$$
$$3K_2O.2SO_2 + 2C(OH)COOH \rightarrow 2C(OH)COOK + 6SO_2 + 3H_2O$$
$$CH_2COOH \qquad\qquad CH_2COOK$$

| Potassium metabisulphite | + | citric acid | $\rightarrow$ | Potassium citrate | + | sulphur dioxide | + | water |

$$SO_2 + H_2O \rightarrow H_2SO_3$$
Sulphurous acid

Sulphur dioxide has a better preservative action than sodium benzoate against bacteria and moulds. It also retards the development of yeasts in juice, but cannot arrest their multiplication, once their number has reached a high value.

It is well known that fruit juices with high acidity do not undergo fermentation readily. The preservative action of the fruit acid is due to its hydrogen ion concentration. The pH for the growth of moulds ranges from 1.5 to 8.5, that of yeasts from 2.5 to 8.0 and of bacteria from 4.0 to 7.5. As fruit beverage like citrus squashes and cordials have generally a pH of 2.5 to 3.5, the growth of moulds and yeasts in them cannot be prevented by acidity alone. Bacteria, however, cannot grow. The pH is, therefore, of great importance in the preservation of food product and by regulating it, one or more kinds of microorganism in the beverage can be eliminated.

The concentration of Sulphur dioxide required to prevent the growth of microorganism at different pH levels are as under:

pH	Organisms and sulphur dioxide concentration (ppm)			
	Saccharomyces ellipsoideus (Yeast)	Mucor (Mould)	Penicillium (Mould)	Mixed bacteria
2.5	200	200	300	100
3.5	800	600	600	300
7.0	above 5000	above 5000	above 5000	above 1000

The toxicity of sulphur dioxide increases at high temperature. Hence its effectiveness depends on the acidity, pH, temperature and substances present in fruit juice.

According to Indian Fruit Product Order, the maximum amount of sulphur dioxide allowed in fruit juice is 700 ppm, in squash, crush and cordial 350 ppm and in RTS and nectar 100 ppm.

The advantages of using sulphur dioxide are : (a) it has a better preserving action than sodium benzoate against bacterial fermentation, (b) it helps to retain the colour of the beverage for a longer time than sodium benzoate, (c) being a gas, it helps in preserving the surface layer of juices also, (d) being highly soluble in juices and squashes, it ensures better mixing and hence their preservation, and (e) any excess of sulphur dioxide present can be removed either by heating the juice to about 71°C or by passing air through it or by subjecting the juice to vacuum. This causes some loss of the flavouring materials due to volatilization, which can be compensated by adding flavours.

The major limitations of sulphur dioxide are : (a) it cannot be used in the case of some naturally coloured juices like those of phalsa, jamun, pomegranate, strawberry, coloured grapes, plum, etc., on account of its bleaching action, (b) it cannot also be used for juices which are to be packed in tin containers, because it not only corrodes the tin causing pinholes, but also forms hydrogen sulphide which has a disagreeable smell and reacts with the iron of the tin container to form a black compound, both of which are highly undesirable, and (c) sulphur dioxide gives a slight taste and odour to freshly prepared beverages but these are not serious defects if the beverage is diluted before drinking.

(ii) Benzoic acid

It is only partially soluble in water hence its salt, sodium benzoate, is used. One part of sodium benzoate is soluble in 1.8 parts of water at ordinary temperature, whereas only 0.34 part of benzoic acid is soluble in 100 parts of water. Sodium benzoate is thus nearly 170 times as soluble as benzoic acid. Pure sodium benzoate is tasteless and odourless.

The antibacterial action of benzoic acid is increased in the presence of carbon dioxide and acid, e.g., *Bacillus subtilis* cannot survive in benzoic acid solution in the presence of carbon dioxide. Benzoic acid is more effective against yeasts than against moulds. It does not stop lactic acid and acetic acid fermentation.

The quantity of benzoic acid required depends on the nature of the product to be preserved, particularly its acidity. In case of juices having a pH of 3.5 to 4.0, which is the range of a majority of fruit juices, addition of 0.06 to 0.10 per cent of sodium benzoate has been found to be sufficient. In case of less acid juices such as grape juice at least 0.3 per cent is necessary. The action of benzoic acid is reduced considerably at pH 5.0. Sodium benzoate in excess of 0.1 per cent may produce a disagreeable burning taste. According to F.P.O. its permitted level in RTS and nectar is 100 ppm and in squash, crush and cordial 600 ppm.

In some European countries, especially Germany, generally methyl, ethyl and propyl esters of para-hydroxy benzoic acid are used. They are, however, not used in India.

In the long run benzoic acid may darken the product. It is, therefore, mostly used in coloured products of tomato, phalsa, jamun, pomegranate, plum, water-melon, strawberry, coloured grapes, etc.

The preservative should never be added in solid form but should be dissolved in a small quantity of juice or water, and the solution added to the bulk of the product. If this care is not taken, the solid may settle undissolved at the bottom of the container with the result that fermentation may start before the action of preservative can begin.

A number of chemicals such as hydrogen peroxide, formaldehyde, halogen-ated acetic acid, salicylic acid, etc., which were used as preservatives some years ago, have now been banned in many countries. In recent years, sorbic acid and tylosin, etc., are being tried.

5. Preservation by Drying

Microorganisms need moisture to grow so when the concentration of water in the food is brought down below a certain level, they are unable to grow. Moisture can be removed by the application of heat as in sun-drying or by mechanical drying (dehydration). Sun-drying is the most popular and oldest method of preservation. In these days, mechanical drying has replaced sun-drying. This is a more rapid process as artificial heat under controlled conditions of temperature, humidity and air flow is provided and fruits and vegetables, e.g., green peas, cauliflower, mango, mahua, etc., are dried to such an extent that the microorganisms present in them fail to survive.

In this method, juices are preserved in the form of powder. The juice is sprayed as a very fine mist into an evaporating chamber through which hot air is passed. The temperature of the chamber and the flow of air are so regulated that dried juice falls to the floor of the chamber in the form of a dry powder. The powder is collected and packed in dry containers which are then closed airtight. The powder when dissolved in water makes a fruit drink almost similar to the original fresh juice. Fruit juice powders are highly hygroscopic and require special care in packing. All juices cannot, however, be dried readily without special treatment. Mango juice powder is prepared by this technique but the method is very expensive and not popular in India.

6. Preservation by Filtration

In this method, the juices are clarified by settling or by using ordinary filters, and then passed through special filters which are capable of retaining yeasts and bacteria. Various types of germ-proof filters are used for this purpose. Recently this method has come into use in U.S.A., Germany, etc., for preserving apple and grape juices. It is not used in India. This method is used for soft drinks, fruit juices and wines.

7. Preservation by Carbonation

Carbonation is the process of dissolving sufficient carbon dioxide in water or beverage so that the product when served gives off the gas as fine bubbles and has a characteristic taste. Carbonation adds to the life of a beverage and contributes in some measure to its tang. Fruit juice beverages are generally bottled with carbon dioxide content varying from 1 to 8 g per litre. Though this concentration is much lower than that required for complete inhibition of microbial activity (14.6 g/litre), it is sufficient for supplementing the effect of acidity on pathogenic bacteria. Another advantage of carbonation is the removal of air thus creating an anaerobic condition, which reduces the oxidation of ascorbic acid and prevents browning.

Moulds and yeasts require oxygen for their growth and become inactive in the presence of carbon dioxide. In ordinary carbonated drinks, the oxygen which is normally present in solution in water in sufficient amount to bring about fermentation, is displaced by carbon dioxide. Although carbonated beverages contain sugar much below 66 per cent, the absence of air and the presence of carbon dioxide in them help to prevent the growth of moulds and yeasts.

High carbonation should, however, be avoided as it usually destroys the flavour of the juice. The keeping quality of carbonated fruit beverages is enhanced by adding about 0.005 per cent sodium benzoate. The level of carbonation required varies according to the type of fruit juice and type of flavour.

8. Preservation by Sugar

Syrups containing 66 per cent or more of sugar do not ferment. Sugar absorbs most of the available water with the result that there is very little water for the growth of microorganisms hence their multiplication is inhibited, and even those already present die out gradually. Dry sugar does not ferment.

Thus sugar acts as a preservative by osmosis and not as a true poison for microorganisms. Fruit syrup, jam, jelly, marmalade, preserve, candy, crystallized fruit and glazed fruit are preserved by sugar.

9. Preservation by Fermentation

Decomposition of carbohydrates by microorganisms or enzymes is called 'fermentation'. This is one of the oldest methods of preservation. By this method, foods are preserved by the alcohol or organic acid formed by microbial action. The keeping quality of alcoholic beverages, vinegars and fermented pickles depends upon the presence of alcohol, acetic acid and lactic acid, respectively. Care should be taken to seal the fermented products from air to avoid further unwanted or secondary fermentation. Wines, beers, vinegar, fermented drinks, fermented pickles, etc., are prepared by these processes.

Fourteen per cent alcohol acts as a preservative in wines because yeasts, etc., cannot grow at that concentration. About 2 per cent acetic acid prevents spoilage in many products.

10. Preservation by salt

Salt at a concentration of 15 to 25 per cent is sufficient to preserve most products. It inhibits enzymatic browning and discolouration and also acts as an antioxidant. Salt in the form of brine is used for canning and pickling of vegetables which contain very little sugar and hence sufficient lactic acid cannot be formed by fermentation to act as preservative. It exerts its preservative action by: (i) causing high osmotic pressure resulting in the plasmolysis of microbial cells, (ii) dehydrating food as well as microorganisms by drawing out and tying up the moisture by ion hydration, (iii) ionizing to yield the chloride ion which is harmful to microorganisms, (iv) reducing the solubility of oxygen in water, sensitizing the cells against carbon dioxide, and interfering with the action of proteolytic enzymes.

11. Preservation by Acids

Low acid foods are spoilt rapidly. Highly acidic environment inhibits the growth of food spoilage organisms. Lowering the protein of certain foods by anaerobic fermentation, action on carbohydrates producing lactic acid is one of the methods of food preservation. The same spoilage inhibitory effects can be produced by acidic additives such as vinegar or citric acid. Nutrient losses through fermentation are small. In fact, in certain cases, the nutrient levels are increased particularly through microbial vitamin and protein synthesis.

Acid conditions inhibit the growth of many microorganisms hence organic acids are added to or allowed to form in foods to preserve them. Acetic (vinegar), citric (lime juice) and lactic acids are commonly used for preservation. About 2 per cent acetic acid prevents spoilage of many products. Onions are bottled in vinegar with a little salt. Vinegar is also added to pickles, chutneys, sauces and ketchups. Citric acid is added to many fruit squashes, jams and jellies to increase the acidity and prevent mould growth.

12. Preservation by Oil and Spices

A layer of oil on the surface of any food produces anaerobic conditions which prevent the growth of moulds and yeasts. Thus pickles in which enough oil is added to form a layer at the top can be preserved for long periods. Spices like turmeric, pepper, and asafoetida have little bacteriostatic effect and their ability to prevent growth of other microorganism is questionable. Their primary function is to impart their characteristic flavour to the food.

13. Preservation by Antibiotics

Certain metabolic products of microorganisms have been found to have germicidal effect and are termed as antibiotics. Their use in medicine for controlling certain disease-producing organisms in the body is well known. Some antibiotics are also used to preserve fruits, vegetables and their products.

Nisin is an antibiotic produced by *Streptococcus lactis*, an organism commonly found in milk, curd, cheese and other fermented milk products. It is nontoxic and has no adverse effect on the sensory qualities of food. It is widely used in the food industry especially for preservation of acid foods in which it is more stable. It is commonly used in canning of mushrooms, tomatoes and milk products. Nisin suppresses the growth of spoilage organisms, mainly the gas-producing, spore-forming bacteria and toxin-producing *Clostridium botulinum*.

Subtilin, an antibiotic obtained from certain strains of *Bacillus subtilis*, is used in preservation of asparagus, corn and peas. It is most effective against gram-positive bacteria and spore-forming organisms. Canned peas and tomatoes containing 10 and 20 ppm of subtilin respectively were found to be free of microorganisms. Subtilin and nisin effectively reduce the thermal process requirements necessary to control the spoilage of several food products.

Pimaricin, an antifungal antibiotic, can be used for treating fruits and fruit juices.

At present the above three antibiotics are permitted only in such foods as are cooked prior to use and in the process of cooking the residual antibiotic is expected to be destroyed. Use of antibiotics along with other sterilizing agents including heat and radiation offer good promise.

14. Preservation by Irradiation

Sterilization of food by ionizing radiations is a recently developed method of preservation which has not yet gained general acceptance. The unacceptable flavour of some irradiated foods and the fear that radioactivity might be induced in such food has come in the way of its greater use. The harmful effects on the human body of radiation from nuclear explosions have given rise to such apprehension in the minds of many people.

When gamma rays or electron beams pass through foods there are collisions between the ionizing radiation and food particles at atomic and molecular levels, resulting in the production of ion pairs and free radicals. The reactions of these products among themselves and with other molecules result in physical and chemical phenomena which inactivate microorganisms in the food. Thus irradiation of food can be considered to be a method of "cold sterilization", i.e., food is free of microorganisms without high temperature treatment.

In the irradiation of foods for preservation, the radiation dose must be carefully controlled. It should be sufficient to destroy pathogenic and spoilage causing organisms and to inactivate food enzymes. Apart from the intensity of radiation, the amount of radiation absorbed and the period of irradiation are also to be controlled. The WHO and the International Atomic Energy Agency have recommended that radiation dose of up to 1 Mrad is not hazardous. The longer the food is exposed to radiation, the more radiation will it absorb. Radiation energy must be provided in such a manner that it reaches every particle of food to ensure adequate killing of all microorganisms.

Different organisms are sensitive to radiation to different extents, e.g., a dose of 10^3 to 10^7 rad kills microorganisms, 10^3 to 10^6 rad kill insects and 10^2 to 10^3 rad are lethal to humans. Sprouting of potatoes, onions, carrots, etc., are inhibited by 10^3 to 10^4 rad. In case of microorganisms, the approximate sterilizing dose for bacterial endospores is 3.0×10^6 rad, while that for yeasts and fungi is 5.0×10^4 rad.

Ionizing radiations can be used for sterilization of foods in hermetically sealed packs, reduction of the spoilage flora on perishable foods, elimination of pathogens in foods, control of infestation in stored cereals, prevention of sprouting of potatoes, onions, etc.

Chapter 13

Canning and Bottling of Fruits and Vegetables

T he process of sealing foodstuffs hermetically in containers and sterilizing them by heat for long storage is known as canning. The F.P.O. specifications for canned fruits and vegetables are given in Appendix IX.

In 1804, Appert in France invented a process of sealing foods hermetically in containers and sterilizing them by heat. Appert is known as the 'Father of Canning'. This work formed the foundation for modern canning procedure. In honour of the inventor, canning is also known as appertizing. Saddington in England was the first to describe a method of canning of foods in 1807. In 1810, Peter Durand, another Englishman, obtained the first British Patent on canning of foods in tin containers. In 1817, William Underwood introduced canning of fruits on a commercial scale in U.S.A.

Fruits and vegetables are canned in the season when the raw material is available in plenty. The canned products are sold in the off-season and give better returns to the grower.

Principle and Process of Canning

Principle : Destruction of spoilage organisms within the sealed container by means of heat.

Process

(1) Selection of fruits and vegetables

(i) Fruits and vegetables should be absolutely fresh.

(ii) Fruits should be ripe, but firm, and uniformly mature. Over-ripe fruits should be rejected because they are infected with microorganisms and give a poor quality product. Unripe fruits should be rejected because they generally shrivel and toughen on canning.

(iii) All vegetables except tomatoes should be tender.

(iv) Tomatoes should be firm, fully ripe and of deep red colour.

(v) Fruits and vegetables should be free from dirt.

(vi) They should be free from blemishes, insect damage or mechanical injury.

FLOW-SHEET FOR CANNING PROCESS

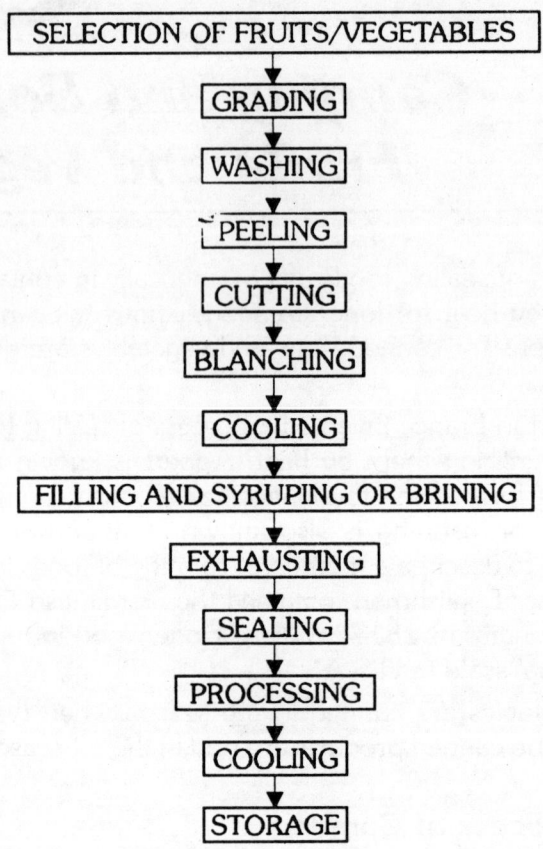

SELECTION OF FRUITS/VEGETABLES
↓
GRADING
↓
WASHING
↓
PEELING
↓
CUTTING
↓
BLANCHING
↓
COOLING
↓
FILLING AND SYRUPING OR BRINING
↓
EXHAUSTING
↓
SEALING
↓
PROCESSING
↓
COOLING
↓
STORAGE

(2) Grading

The selected fruits and vegetables are graded according to size and colour to obtain uniform quality. This is done by hand or by machines such as screw grader and roller grader. Fruits like berries, plums and cherries are graded whole, while peaches, pears, apricots, mangoes, pineapples, etc., are generally graded after cutting into pieces or slices.

(3) Washing

It is important to remove pesticide spray residue and dust from fruits and vegetables. One gram of soil contains 10^{12} spores of microorganisms. Therefore, removal of microorganisms by washing with water is essential. Fruits and vegetables can be washed in different ways. Root crops that loosen in soil are washed by soaking in water containing 25 to 50 ppm chlorine (as detergent). Other methods of washing are spray washing, steam washing, etc.

(4) Peeling

The objective of peeling is to remove the outer layer. Peeling may be done in various ways.

(i) Hand peeling : It is done mostly in case of fruits of irregular shape, e.g., mango and papaya, where mechanical peeling is not possible.

(ii) Steam peeling : Free-stone and clingstone peaches are steam peeled in different ways. The former are cut and steam washed. Potatoes and tomatoes are peeled by steam or boiling water.

(iii) Mechanical peeling : This is done in case of apples, peaches, pineapples and cherries and also for root vegetables like carrots, turnips and potatoes.

(iv) Lye peeling : Fruits like peaches, apricots, sweet oranges, mandarin oranges and vegetables like carrots and sweet potatoes are peeled by dipping them in 1 to 2 per cent boiling caustic soda solution (lye) for 30 seconds to 2 minutes depending on their nature and maturity. Hot lye loosens the skin from the flesh by dissolving the pectin. The peel is then removed easily by hand. Any trace of alkali is removed by washing the fruit or vegetable thoroughly in running cold water or dipping it for a few seconds in 0.5 per cent citric acid solution. This is a quick method where by cost and wastage in peeling is reduced.

(v) Flame peeling : It is used only for garlic and onion which have a papery outer covering. This is just burnt off.

Vegetables like peas are shelled, carrots are scraped, and beans are snipped or trimmed.

(5) Cutting

Pieces of the size required for canning are cut. Seed, stone and core are removed. Some fruits like plum from which the seeds cannot be taken out easily are canned whole.

(6) Blanching

It is also known as scalding, parboiling or precooking. Fruits are generally not blanched leaving the oxidizing enzyme system active. Sometimes fruit is plunged for a given time—from half to, say, five minutes, according to variety—into water at from 180°F to 200°F, and then immediately cooled by immersion in cold water. The object is to soften the texture and so enable a greater weight to be pressed into the container without damage to the individual fruit. Blanching is usually done in case of vegetables by exposing them to boiling water or steam for 2 to 5 minutes, followed by cooling. The extent of blanching varies with the food. This brief heat treatment accomplishes the following :

(i) Inactivates most of the plant enzymes which cause toughness, discolouration (polyphenol oxidase), mustiness, off-flavour (peroxidase), softening and loss of nutritive value.

(ii) Reduces the area of leafy vegetables such as spinach by shrinkage or wilting, making their packing easier.

(iii) Removes tissue gases which reduce sulphides.

(iv) Reduces the number of microorganisms by as much as 99%.

(v) Enhances the green colour of vegetables such as peas, broccoli and spinach.

(vi) Removes saponin in peas.

(vii) Removes undesirable acids and astringent taste of the peel, and thus improves flavour.

(viii) Removes the skin of vegetables such as beetroot and tomatoes which helps in their peeling.

Disadvantages

(i) Water-soluble materials like sugar and anthocyanin pigments are leached by boiling water.

(ii) Fruits lose their colour, flavour and sugar.

(7) Cooling

After blanching, the vegetables are dipped in cold water for better handling and keeping them in good condition.

(8) Filling

Before filling, cans are washed with hot water and sterilized but in developing countries these are subjected to a jet of steam to remove dust and foreign material. Automatic, large can-filling machines are used in advanced countries but choice grades of fruits are normally filled by hand to prevent bruising. In India, hand filling is the common practice. After filling, covering with syrup or brine is done and this process is called syruping or brining.

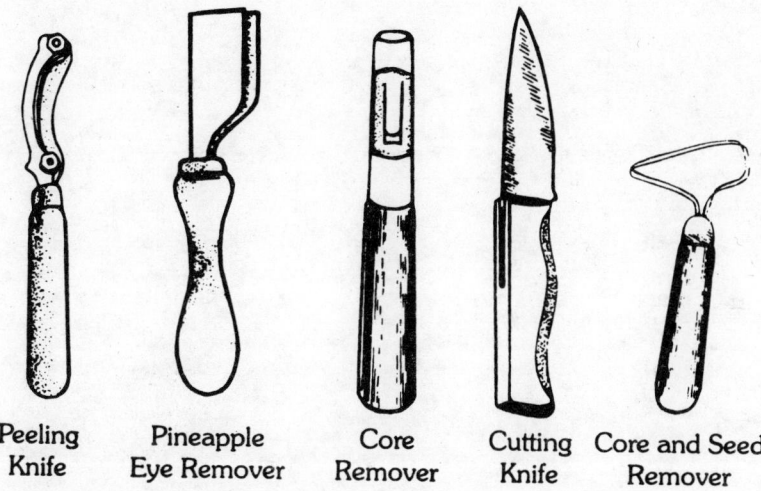

Peeling Knife

Pineapple Eye Remover

Core Remover

Cutting Knife

Core and Seed Remover

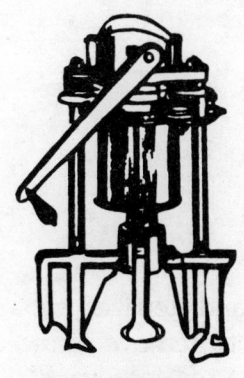

Can Sealer

Can Opener / Cork Remover

A 1-lb butter size can should hold 230 to 285 g of fruit slices and a A $2\frac{1}{2}$ size can 510 to 565 g.

The blanched vegetables are packed in sterilized cans which should hold the drained weight or vegetables as specified below:

1-lb butter size can   -   269-283 g

A $2^1/_2$ size can   -   538-566 g

pint size glass jar   -   283-311 g

(i) **Syruping :** A solution of sugar in water is called a syrup. White, refined sucrose is employed, either of cane or beet origin. Normally sucrose syrup is used in canning. Syrup is added to improve the flavour and to serve as a heat transfer medium for facilitating processing. Syruping is done only for fruits.

Strained, hot syrup of concentration 20 to 55° Brix is poured on the fruit. Fruits rich in acid require a more concentrated syrup than less acid ones. The syrup should be filled at about 79 to 82°C, leaving a head space of 0.3 to 0.5 cm. Sometimes citric acid and ascorbic acid are also mixed with the syrup to improve flavour and nutritional value, respectively.

The quantities of sugar to be dissolved in one litre of water to make syrups of different concentrations are given in the table below:

Sugar (kg)	Syrup concentration (%)
0.250	20
0.333	25
0.428	30
0.538	35
0.666	40
0.818	45
1.000	50
1.222	55

Syrups of various strength can be made by dissolving 1 kg of sugar in different volumes of water, as shown in the table on the next page :

Syrup strength	Water (litre)
Light	2.0
Medium	1.5
Heavy	1.0

(ii) Brining : A solution of salt in water is called brine. The objective of brining is similar to that of syruping. Only vegetables are brined. Common salt of good quality free from iron should be used. Hot brine of 1 to 3 per cent concentration is used for covering vegetables and is filled at 79 to 82°C, leaving a head space of 0.3 to 0.5 cm. The brine should be filtered through a thick cloth before filling.

Brines of different strengths are prepared by dissolving different amounts of salt in one litre of water, as shown in the table below:

Salt (g)	Brine concentration (%)
10.00	1
20.40	2
30.92	3
41.66	4
47.33	5
111.11	10
176.47	15

After syruping or brining the cans are loosely covered with lids and exhausted. Lidding has certain disadvantages such as spilling of the contents and toppling of the lids. Hence lidding has now been modernized by 'clinching' process in which the lid is partially seamed. The lid remains sufficiently loose to permit the escape of dissolved as well as free air from the can and also the vapour formed during the exhausting process.

Salt of high chemical and bacteriological purity only is used in vegetable canning.

(9) Exhausting

The process of removal of air from cans is known as exhausting. After filling and lidding or clinching, exhausting is essential. The major advantages of exhausting are as under:

(i) Corrosion of the tinplate and pinholing during storage is avoided.

(ii)   Minimizes discolouration by preventing oxidation.

(iii) Helps in better retention of vitamins particularly vitamin C.

(iv) Prevents building of cans when stored in hot climate or at high altitude.

(v)   Reduces chemical reaction between the container and the contents.

(vi) Prevents development of excessive pressure and strain during sterilization.

Containers are exhausted either by heating or mechanically. The heat treatment method is generally used. The cans are passed through a tank of hot water at 82 to 87°C or move on a belt through a covered steam box. In the water exhaust box , the cans are placed in such a manner that the level of water is 4-5 cm below their tops. The exhaust box is heated till the temperature of water reaches 82 to 100°C and the centre of the can shows a temperature of about 79°C. The time of exhausting varies from 6 to 10 minutes, depending on the nature of the product. In the case of glass jars or bottles, vacuum closing machines are generally used. The bottles or jars are placed in a closed chamber in which a high vacuum is maintained.

It is preferable to exhaust the cans at a lower temperature for a longer period to ensure uniform heating of the contents without softening them into pulp. Exhausting at high temperature should be avoided because the higher the temperature, the more is the volume of water vapour formed, and consequently the greater the vacuum produced in the can.

(10) Sealing

Immediately after exhausting the cans are sealed airtight by means of a can sealer. In case of glass jars a rubber ring should be placed between the mouth of the jar and the lid, so that it can be sealed airtight. During sealing the temperature should not fall below 74°C.

(11) Processing

Heating of foods for preserving is known as processing, however, in canning technology processing means heating or cooling of canned foods to inactivate bacteria. Many bacterial spores can be killed by either high or very low temperature. Such drastic treatment, however, affects the quality of food. Processing time and temperature should be adequate to eliminate all bacterial growth. Moreover, over-cooking should be avoided as it spoils the flavour as well as the appearance of the product.

Almost all fruits and acid vegetables can be processed satisfactorily at a temperature of 100°C, i.e., in boiling water. The presence of acid retards the growth of bacteria and their spores. Further, they do not thrive in heavy sugar syrup which is normally used for canning of fruits. Vegetables (except the more acid ones like tomato and rhubarb) which are non-acid in nature, have a hard texture, and proximity to soil which may infect them with spore-bearing organisms are processed at higher temperatures of 115 to 121°C.

The sourness of fruits and vegetables is due to their acid content (measured in pH) which has a great influence upon the destruction of microorganisms. The lower the pH the greater is the ease with which a product can be processed or sterilized. Fruits and vegetables can be classified into the following four groups according to their pH value.

Class	pH	Product
Low acid (called non-acid)	above 5.0	Vegetables such as peas, lima bean, asparagus, cauliflower, potato, spinach, beet, corn, french bean
Medium acid	4.5-5.0	Turnip, carrot, okra, cabbage, pumpkin, beet, green bean, etc., and products like soups and sauces
Acid	3.7-4.5	Tomato, pear, banana, mango, jackfruit, pineapple, sweet cherry, peach, apple and other fruits
High acid	below 3.7	Citrus juice, rhubarb, prune, sauerkraut, pickle, chutney, etc.

Bacterial spores can be more easily destroyed at pH 3.0 (fruits) than at pH 5.0 to 6.0 (vegetables, except tomato and rhubarb). Bacterial spores do not grow or germinate below pH 4.5. Thus, a canned product having pH less than 4.5 can be processed in boiling water but a product with pH above 4.5 requires processing at 115 at 121°C under a pressure of 0.70 to 1.05 kg/cm^2 (10 to 15 lb/sq inch). It is essential that the centre of the can should attain these high temperatures.

The temperature and time of processing vary with the size of the can and the nature of the food: the larger the can, the greater is the processing time. The processing time for different canned fruits and vegetables is given in the tables under 'Canning of Fruits' and 'Canning of Vegetables'. Fruits and acid vegetables are generally processed in open type cookers, continuous non-agitating cookers and continuous agitating cookers, while vegetables (non-acid) are processed under steam pressure in closed retorts known as automatic pressure cookers. In India, small vertical stationary retorts (frontispiece) are generally used for canned vegetable processing. The sealed cans are placed in the cookers, keeping the level of water 2.5 to 5.0 cm above the top of the cans. The cover of the cooker is then screwed down tightly and the cooker heated to the desired temperature. The period of sterilization (processing) should be counted from the time the water starts boiling. After heating for the required period the cooker is removed from the fire and the petcock is opened. When the pressure comes down to zero the cover is removed and the cans are taken out.

(12) Cooling

After processing, the cans are cooled rapidly to about 39°C to stop the cooking process and to prevent stack-burning. Cooling is done by the following methods:

(i)   dipping or immersing the hot cans in tanks containing cold water;

(ii) letting cold water into the pressure cooker specially in case of vegetables;

(iii) Spraying cans with jets of cold water; and

(iv) exposing the cans to air.

Generally the first method, i.e., dipping the cans in cold water, is used. If canned products are not cooled immediately after processing, peaches and pears become dark in colour, tomatoes turn brownish and bitter in taste, peas become pulpy with cooked taste and many vegetables develop flat sour (become sour).

(13) Storage

After labelling the cans, they should be packed in strong wooden cases or corrugated cardboard cartons and stored in a cool and dry place. The outer surface of the cans should be dry as even small traces of moisture sometimes induce rusting. Storage of cans at high temperature should be avoided, as it shortens the shelf-life of the product and often leads to the formation of hydrogen swell.

The marketable life of canned products varies according to the type of raw materials used. Canned peach, grapefruit, pineapple, beans, spinach, pea, celery, etc., can be stored for about two years, while pear, apricot, carrot, beetroot, tomato, etc., can be stored for a comparatively short period only.

Containers for packing of canned products

Both tin and glass containers are used in the canning industry, but tin containers are preferred.

(1) Tin containers

Tin cans are made of thin steel plate of low carbon content, lightly coated on both sides with tin metal. It is difficult to coat the steel plate uniformly and during the process of manufacture small microscopic spots are always left uncoated, although the coating may appear perfect to the eye. The contents of the can may react with these uncoated spots resulting in discolouration of the product or corrosion of the tin plate. When the corrosion is severe, black stains of iron sulphide are produced. It is necessary, therefore, to coat the inside of the can with some material (lacquer) which prevents discolouration but does not affect the flavour or wholesomeness of the contents. This process is known as "lacquering".

Two types of lacquers are used :

(i) **Acid-resistant :** Acid-resistant lacquer is a golden coloured enamel and cans coated with it are called R-enamel or A.R. cans. These cans are used for packing acid fruits which are of two kinds : (a) those whose colouring matter is insoluble in water, e.g., peach, pineapple, apricot, grapefruit, and (b) those in which it is water-soluble, e.g., raspberry, strawberry, red plum and coloured grape. Fruits of group (a) are packed in plaincans and those of group (b) in lacquered cans.

(ii) **Sulphur-resistant :** This lacquer is also of a golden colour and cans coated with it are called C-enamel or S.R. cans. They are meant for non-acid foods only and should not be used for any highly acid product as acid eats into the lacquer. These cans are used for pea, corn, lima bean, red kidney bean., etc.

Size of cans : The sizes of cans in general use are given below:

Trade name of can	Size (mm)
A 1	68 x 102
1-lb Jam	78 x 90
Al-T	78 x 119
A 2	87 x 114
1-lb Butter	103 x 70
A 2-lb Jam	103 x 102
A 2 ½	103 x 119
7-lb Jam	157 x 148
A 10	157 x 178

Recently, a midget can has become highly popular for fruit juices, mango nectar, etc. It holds about 165 ml of beverage and is a very popular picnic pack.

Tin containers are preferred to glass containers because of certain advantages:

(i)   ease of fabrication,

(ii)   strength to withstand processing,

(iii)   light weight,

(iv)   ease in handling,

(v)   cheapness, and

(vi)   can be handled by high speed machines.

(2)   Glass containers

Glass containers possess two distinct advantages over tin cans: (i) the contents being visible can be easily displayed, and (ii) they can be used over and over again. Moreover, glass of high quality does not contaminate the contents. Hence, such containers are preferred for packing baby food, but being fragile require extra care during handling and processing.

In recent years, plastic containers and heat-sealable pouches have been successfully tried in various research and development laboratories as possible substitutes for tin and glass containers.

Canning of fruits (and tomatoes)

The general process of canning has been discussed earlier. Large spoons, peeling and coring knives, aluminium or stainless steel pans of large size, sanitary cans, thermometer, hand refractometer, measuring cylinder and can sealing machine, etc., are generally required. The specific requirements of syrup strength, exhausting, processing temperature and time, and type of cans, etc., for canning of various fruits are given in the table entitled 'specific requirements for canning of fruits and tomatoes.'

Bottling of fruits

Bottles have proved to be very good containers for home preservation of fruits. Although their initial cost is high, they can be used several times and last for many years if carefully handled. The fruits look attractive through the glass and do not develop metallic flavour. Bottling does not need a sealing machine but is not suitable from the manufacturer's point of view as the initial capital required is high. Cans are cheaper, quite handy and lighter and loss due to breakage is less. Hence on commercial scale, tin cans are preferred to glass jars or bottles.

There are many types of glass containers of different shapes and sizes and with various types of hermetic seals. Jars fitted with wire clamps are considered to be the best. The products remain in a very hygienic condition and do not come into contact with rubber or metal.

Essential equipment and method of selection of the fruit, grading, sorting, washing, peeling, slicing and coring are the same as for canning of fruits (described under process of canning).

Filling and syruping : The bottles are thoroughly washed and sterilized. The fruit slices are filled leaving about 3 cm space at the top of the jar or bottle. The sugar syrup recommended for different fruits is filled boiling hot leaving a head space of 1-1.5 cm.

Exhausting and sterilization : Separate exhausting of bottles is not required and it is done simultaneously with sterilization by putting a pad of cloth (false bottom) under the bottles. The bottles should not be abruptly immersed in hot water, otherwise they may break because of sudden rise in temperature. The temperature of the water should be about the same as that of the contents and should be raised gradually and the bottles kept in the boiling water for the required time. At the start of sterilization the lids are left loose and the level of boiling water should come up to the neck of the bottle, but when sterilization is over the mouths of bottles and jars should be immediately closed or corked tightly.

Cooling and storage : These are done as for canning of fruits (described under process of canning). But products preserved in bottles requires more attractive lables.

Canning and bottling of vegetables

The general process of canning has been discussed earlier. A pressure cooker (autoclave, retort or sterilizer) is necessary, in addition to other equipment mentioned for the canning of fruits. Specific requirement regarding the brine strength, exhaust, processing temperature and time, and type of cans, etc., for canning of various vegetables are given separately in the table entitled 'specific requirements for canning of vegetables.'

Canning of curried vegetables

The vegetables selected should be mature, tender, free from blemishes and disease. They are graded suitably and after removal of the non-edible portion, washed thoroughly.

Preparation of vegetables: The vegetable is prepared according to its nature, e.g., the outer hard leaves of cabbage are removed, the leaves of cauliflower are removed before cutting it into small florets, peas are shelled, root vegetables are peeled and cut into pieces or slices of suitable size.

Specific requirements for canning of fruits and tomatoes

S. No.	Fruit	Preparation	Strength of syrup* (degrees Brix)	Exhaust	Processing time (min.) in boiling water for various sizes of containers			Type of can
					A2 (tin)	A 2 ½ (tin)	Pint jar (glass)	
1.	Apricot	Use whole or halve	55	Exhaust can at 82 to 100°C for 6-10 min or until temperature in centre of can reaches about 79°C	25	35	25	Plain
2	Banana	Peel, halve lengthwise or cut into slices 12 mm thick	30	-do-	-	20	-	Plain
3	Grapes	Remove stems	40	-do-	10	12	15	Plain, but for coloured grapes Lacquered AR
4.	Grape-fruit	Dip fruit in hot water at 93°C for 3-5 min, remove skin and peel individual segments	60	-do-	30	40	-	Plain
5	Guava	Peel, cut into pieces, remove seedy portion, treat with 2% brine and wash	40	-do-	20	20	25	Plain
6	Litchi	Peel by hand, remove pits	40	-do-	25	30	-	Plain
7	Loquat	Cut into halves	40	-do-	25	30	-	Plain
8	Mango	Peel. cut into slices	40	-do-	25	30	-	Plain

				Exhaust can at 82 to 100°C for 6-10 min or until temperature in centre of can reaches about 79°C				
9	Papaya	Peel, cut into slices, discard seeds	45		25	30	-	Plain
10	Peach	Soften by dipping in boiling water, cool quickly in cold water, remove skin, halve, pit and slice.	55	-do-	25	30	25	Plain
11	Pear	Peel, halve, remove cores	40	-do-	25	35	25	Plain
12	Pine-apple	Peel, cut into 1 cm slices, remove core and eyes	40	-do-	20	30	25	Plain
13	Plum	Prick	40	-do-	15	20	15	Lacquered AR
14	Straw-berry	Remove stem, add 0.25 kg sugar per 2 kg fruit, slowly boil, keep overnight, boil quickly before packing	50	-do-	10	15	15	Lacquered AR
15	Tomato	Place in loose muslin bag, dip in boiling water for a min then dip quickly in cold water to loosen skin, remove green, portions and stem, if present	Tomato juice is used instead of syrup	-do-	25	30	-	Plain

* For checking hydrogen swell and improving the flavour, about 0.5 per cent citric acid should be added to the syrup used for canning fruits of low acidity such as cherry, mango and papaya.

Specific requirements for canning of vegetables

S. No.	Vegetable	Preparation	Strength of brine (%)	Exhaust	Processing time (min.) at 115°C and 0.7 kg/cm2 or 10 lb/sq inch			Type of can
					A2 (tin)	A 2½ (tin)	Pint jar (glass)	
1	Asparagus	Wash, grade, cut lengthwise into pieces of desired size, blanch for 2 to 3 min	2	Exhaust can at 90 to 100°C for 6-10 min or until temperature in centre of can reaches about 79°C	20	25	30	Lacquered SR
2	Beans	Shell, grade, boil for 5 to 10 min, pack loose	2	-do-	40	40	35	Plain
3	Beet	Wash, steam boil for 15 min, add salt	2	-do-	30	30	25	Lacquered SR
4	Cabbage	Wash, boil 10 min, add salt	2	-do-	40	40	45	Plain
5	Carrot	Wash, scrape, boil for 5 min	2	-do-	20	25	35	Plain
6	Cauliflower	Soak in cold brine, boil for 3 min, add salt	2	-do-	20	20	25	Plain

7	Mushroom	Bleach with sodium sulphite and citric acid solution, wash, blanch for 4 to 5 min, then dip in cold water	2	Exhaust can at 90 to 100°C for 6-10 min or until temperature in centre of can reaches about 79°C	25	25	30	Plain
8	Okra (Bhindi)	Wash, remove cap, boil for 3 min, pack	2	-do-	25	35	35	Plain
9	Peas	Shell, grade, boil for 3 to 5 min	2 + 2.5% sugar solution	-do-	40	45	40	Lacquered
10	Potato	Peel, blanch for 3 min	2	-do-	40	45	45	Plain
11	Pumpkin	Wash, cut into pieces, cook until tender, mash	2	-do-	70	95	75	Lacquered SR
12	Spinach and other green leafy vegetables	Steam in covered vessel for 15 min, blanch with a little salt	2	-do-	50	55	55	Plain
13	Turnip	Peel, slice, blanch	2	-do-	30	35	35	Plain

The quantities of different spices that should be added to 1 Kg of vegetables are given below and the vegetable curry is prepared as usually done in homes. The quantity of water used should be little and the vegetable should not be tender after preparation.

Turmeric (powdered)	10 g
Red chillies (powdered)	10 g
Ghee or butter	160 g
Ginger (finely chopped)	10 g
Garlic (finely chopped)	20 g
Onion (finely chopped)	400 g
Tomato	350 g
Cardamom (major)	3 g
Cumin seed (powdered)	5 g
Coriander (powdered)	10 g
Salt (powdered)	60 g

Filling, exhausting and sealing : The hot curried vegetable is put in plain cans which are filled with 2% brine and then exhausted for 10 minutes (or till the temperature of the centre of the can reaches 77 to 82°C). The cans are then immediately sealed.

Processing: The sealed cans are placed in a pressure cooker at 115°C for 40 to 75 minutes, depending upon the size of container, kind and maturity of vegetable, etc.

Cooling and storage: The cans are removed from the pressure cooker and placed immediately under running water till they become fairly cool, then wiped dry and stored in a cool and dry place.

General considerations in establishing a commercial fruit and vegetable cannery

The following are the main factors which must be taken into consideration in establishing a commercial cannery.

(1) Availability of raw materials

Raw material is of primary importance. It should be of very high quality as has been described before in detail. Some fresh fruits and vegetables may be quite good for consumption as such or cooked, but are not suitable for canning.

The price of raw materials is one of the main factors which affect the cost of finished products. In India, the price of fruits and vegetables is quite high in the beginning of the season but later there is a glut when plenty of raw material of excellent quality can be purchased at a low cost. In U.S.A. and U.K., canners grow their own fruits and vegetables or supply quality seeds to farmers with whom they contract to buy their whole crop.

In our country, there are wide fluctuations in the availability of raw materials due to the maturing of different fruit and vegetable crops in different seasons. Hence, to ensure continuous functioning of the cannery, there should be provision for canning of alternative products during the off-season for the main products.

(2) Site and building

The site of the cannery dealing with fruits and vegetables should be in or near the growing area to ensure the ready availability of freshly picked raw material and to minimize the time taken for its transport.

The site should have adequate water supply and enough space should be available so that there is no congestion and there is scope for further expansion of the cannery. Sites having factories nearby which emit fumes that contaminate the air are not suitable.

After selecting the site the question of the type of building is to be considered. Existing old buildings are not suitable. The building should be designed for Indian conditions. Single-storied structures based on the requirement of working space, cost of the land, etc., are preferable as all equipment and heavy machinery can be erected without difficulty and can be shifted easily whenever necessary. Ventilation and lighting are also better in single-storied buildings. Generally fruit and vegetable canneries are single-storied.

The organisation of covered space in a cannery depends upon the type of product to be canned and scale of operation. The division of space should be done according to the steps of the canning process.

   (i)   **Receiving and storage section :** The area will depend on the nature of the raw materials. The receiving area should be as near to rail and road as possible specially where perishable products are concerned.

   (ii) **Preparation section :** The preparation section of a fruit and vegetable cannery requires a greater area than that of other products. It should be well sanitated so that the risk of spoilage is reduced. The section should be fitted with water and steam lines such that the spreading of hoses while washing is avoided. As far as possible floors should be (a) resistant to chemicals, (b) resistant to wear, (c) slip-proof, and (d) have proper slope with clean and well-placed drains. The area can also be subdivided into different compartments for washing, peeling or shelling, extraction of juice, etc.

(iii) **Filling, exhausting, sealing and processing section :** Care should be taken to control the humidity in this section where exhausting and sterilizing operations are mainly carried out. The floor should be quite sturdy to withstand heavy wear and tear.

(iv) **Finishing section :** This section where incubation, lacquering, labelling and packing are done should be scrupulously clean, cool and dry with good ventilation.

(v) **Laboratory :** Although a laboratory is expensive to set-up it is a very important unit of a cannery. Its functions are: (a) examination of raw materials, (b) control of processes, (c) quality control of finished products, (d) introduction of new processes and better products, and (e) development of new techniques.

Apart from the above sections, there should be suitable arrangement for storing cans, keeping machinery and other equipment and disposal of waste.

(3) Availability of labour

The problem of labour is not as acute in India as in developed countries as discussed in the chapter on "Scope of Fruit and Vegetable Preservation in India." The number of workers required depends upon the size of the cannery, type of products and degree of mechanization. Prior training of worker is essential.

(4) Duration of canning season

Canning operations will obviously be affected by seasonal fluctuations in the supply of fruits and vegetables. If the idle time is not utilized productively, unit cost of production goes up and the profitability goes down. Hence, for reducing the unit cost alternative products could be manufactured in the off-season.

(5) Water supply

Water plays an important role in the canning industry. It is used in substantial quantities for (a) cleaning of equipment, floors, walls, etc., (b) washing and preparation of raw materials, (c) preparation of brine, syrups, etc., (d) blanching, (e) cooling of processed cans, and (f) steam generation, etc.

The water should be free from contamination. If necessary, it should be chlorinated. Any good drinking water supply is suitable for canning, provided it is not unduly hard.

(6) Disposal of cannery waste

A large quantity of waste is produced by a cannery, containing a high percentage of solid matter, such as skins, peels and colloidal starchy material. Hence the cannery should be situated at such a place where waste could also be profitably utilized to make by-products.

(7) Transport facilities

The problems of transport in India has already been dealt with in the third chapter, i.e., "Scope of Fruit and Vegetable Preservation in India", and need not be discussed here. However, it is essential that the cannery should be situated near a road which connects it important towns in that area.

Causes of spoilage of canned foods

Spoilage of canned products may be due to two reasons:

(A)   Physical and chemical changes, and

(B)   Microorganisms.

(A)   Spoilage due to physical and chemical changes

(1)   Swell : When the ends of an apparently normal and perfect can with good vacuum become bulged it is termed as 'Swell' or 'Blower'. The bulge is due to the positive internal pressure of gases formed by microbial or chemical action.

(i)   Hydrogen swell : This type of bulging is due to the hydrogen gas produced by the action of food acids on the metal of the can. The bulging ranges from 'Flipping' to the 'Hard Swell'. The food generally remains free of harmful microorganisms and is fit for consumption.

(ii)   Flipper : The can appears normal, but when struck against a tabletop one or both ends become convex and springs or flips out, but can be pushed back to normal condition by a little pressure. Such a can is termed as "flipper" and may be an initial stage of swell or hydrogen swell. It may also be caused by overfilling, under-exhausting or gas pressure due to spoilage.

(iii)   Springer : A mild swell at one or both ends of a can is called a 'springer' which may be an initial stage of hydrogen swell or be due to insufficient exhausting or overfilling of the can. The bulged ends (or at least one end) can be pressed back to the original position, but will again become convex after some time.

(iv) Soft swell : At a more advanced stage, swell develops at both ends of the can which can be pressed and returned to normal position, but springs back when the pressure is removed. A swell of this type is termed as "soft swell" and is more or less similar to that of flipper.

(v) Hard swell : This is the final stage of swell. The bulged ends cannot be pressed back to normal position and the cans ultimately burst.

The following precautions are necessary to prevent the formation of hydrogen swells:

(a) Good quality tin plate should be used for making the cans. The quality is related to the porosity of the tin coating. The greater the porosity, the greater is the possibility of corrosion of the can. The porosity can, however, be decreased by increasing the thickness of the coating and making it more uniform. Plain cans are less susceptible to hydrogen swell formation than lacquered cans.

(b) About 0.5 per cent citric acid should be added to the syrup used for canning fruits of low acidity such as cherry, mango, papaya, etc. Citric acid checks the formation of hydrogen swell to a great extent.

(c) Before placing the lid a head space of 0.6 to 0.9 cm should be left in the can which is to be exhausted.

(d) The lid should be placed firmly or clinched before exhausting to ensure a high vacuum in the can.

(e) Cans should be exhausted for a fairly long time, but without affecting the quantity of the product unduly. The larger the quantity of oxygen remaining in the can, the greater would be the corrosion because oxygen combines with the nascent hydrogen formed by the action of acid on the tin container. In the absence of air, the rate of corrosion is low. Oxygen can be excluded from the can by filling it properly and exhausting it thoroughly.

(f) The sealing temperature should not be below 74°C.

(g) At high storage temperature hydrogen formation will be more, resulting finally in swell, hence canned products should be stored under cool and dry conditions.

(2) **Overfilling :** Spoilage due to overfilling is common. During retorting, over-filled cans become strained due to expansion of the contents, and in the absence of vacuum in them swelling takes place. If the cans are properly heat exhausted, the excess material overflows from it due to expansion and thus spoilage because of overfilling is avoided.

(3) **Faulty retort operation :** When the steam pressure is reduced rapidly at the end of processing, high pressure develops inside the cans resulting in their distortion and the cans when cooled look like "swells". Cans of very thin tin plate should not be used as they cannot withstand the pressure which develops in the cans while processing.

(4) **Under-exhausting :** Cans are exhausted to remove most of the air. This helps in the proper filling of fruits and vegetables and also creates a good vacuum, which is necessary to accommodate any pressure that might develop inside the can as a result of production of hydrogen due to corrosion.

Improperly exhausted cans may suffer severe strain during heat processing due to the large internal pressure of the gas present in it. Under-exhausted cans show strain ranging from slight flipping to distortion, depending upon the amount of gas evolved from the product and the size of the head space. All the gas must be removed by tilting the can and pressing its ends. Longer exhausting at a lower temperature of about 79°C gives better results than a short one at about 87°C, provided the cans are closed at the same temperature. The advantage of exhausting the cans is, however, quickly lost if they are allowed to cool down appreciably before closing. Any undue cooling of cans after exhausting and before closing should, therefore, be avoided.

(5) **Panelling :** It is generally seen in large sized cans that the body is pushed inward due to the high vacuum inside. This also occurs when the tin plate is thin or the cans are pressure cooled at very high pressure. In very severe cases, seam leakage may occur but normally this is not regarded as spoilage.

(6) **Rust :** Cans having external rust must be thoroughly examined after removing the rust and, if the walls show a pitted appearance, should be rejected as spoiled. Cans slightly affected by rust if not used immediately should be rejected. Rust is mostly seen under the label and subsequently affects the label as well. Rust formation can be checked if the cans are externally lacquered.

(7) **Foreign flavours :** During preparation, filling, storage or even transportation, conditions may become unhygienic and the products may develop for-

eign or "off-flavours". If unsuitable metallic containers are used, a "metallic flavour" develops. Flavour is an important characteristic for maintaining which packages must be examined at regular intervals.

(8) Damage : Rough handling of cans due to carelessness or ignorance may damage them. If any cans show signs of leakage or severe distortion they must be rejected.

(9) Undesirable texture : Texture is another important characteristic, like flavour and colour, which is detected easily by a consumer. In order to maintain the standard of a product its texture should be tested periodically. Although there are no precise parameters for measuring texture, an instrument like "Tenderometer", which measures the resistance to shearing and relative tenderness, can be used for peas and beans.

Calcium salts present in the water used for canning have a "toughening effect" on peas and beans, but such hardening is considered desirable for potatoes and tomatoes.

Care should be taken that the processing of soft fruits does not result in their becoming pulp.

(10) Corrosion of cans : Cans become corroded or perforated due to the acidity of the contents, specially highly acid fruits. In recent years, attempts have been made to reduce the spoilage by using improved lacquers for internal coating of cans.

(11) Leakage : A leaking can is known as a "Leaker". This may be due to: (i) defective seaming, (ii) nail holes caused by faulty nailing of cases while packing, (iii) excessive internal pressure due to microbial spoilage sufficient to burst the can, (iv) internal or external corrosion, and (v) mechanical damage during handling.

(12) Breathing : There may be a very tiny leak in the can through which air can pass in and destroy the vacuum. In such cases the food is damaged due to rusting of the can caused by oxygen in the air but still remains fit for consumption.

(13) Bursting : This may be caused by the excess pressure of gases produced by decomposition of the food by microorganisms, or by hydrogen gas formed by the chemical action of food acids on the tin plate. In such cases the canned product cannot be used.

(14) Buckling : Sometimes due to improper cooling, distortion of the can takes place resembling 'swell'. Although the distortion can be corrected by pressing, the cans are often badly strained and the contents become spoiled due to entry of microorganisms through the strained seams. This type of spoilage is known as "Buckling".Sometimes a peak or small ridge forms on the can which is known as "Peaking".

(15) Discolouration : This can be detected by visual examination of the can and its contents. Discolouration may be due to biological causes like enzymatic and non-enzymatic browning or metallic contamination. Enzymatic browning due to the enzyme polyphenol oxidase present in fruits and vegetables can be avoided by placing the peeled and cut pieces in 2 per cent salt solution. Non-enzymatic browning is caused by reactions between (i) nitrogenous compounds and sugars, (ii) nitrogenous compounds and organic acids, (iii) sugars and organic acids, and (iv) among organic acids themselves. These reactions are known as Maillard reactions.

Metallic contamination is mainly due to iron and copper salts. Some fruits and vegetables contain tannins which react with the iron of the tin plate to form black ferric tannate, which spoils the appearance of the contents. Sometimes hydrogen sulphide gas is produced by the reaction between fruit acids and the tin coating, which in turn reacts with the iron of the tin plate to form black iron sulphide. Discolouration is also caused by traces of copper (1 ppm) from the metal vessels used; in contact with hydrogen sulphide copper forms black copper sulphide. Metallic contamination can be avoided by using glass containers, coating the interiors of cans with lacquer and also eliminating the use of iron and copper vessels.

(16) Stack burning : If processed cans are not allowed to cool down sufficiently before storing, the contents remain hot for a long time. This is known as "stack burning" which results in discolouration, cooked flavour and very soft or pulpy product. Therefore, it is necessary to cool the cans quickly to about 39°C before storage.

(B) Microbial spoilage

(1) Pre-processing spoilage : This type of spoilage occurs because of the time gap between filling and heat processing of the containers. Although processing checks the growth of organisms the gas already present in the can causes swelling and flipping, so delay between filling and processing must be avoided, and also at all stages in the preparation of raw materials for canning.

(2) Under-processing spoilage: Under-processing of canned foods result in their spoilage by thermophilic bacteria and mesophilic organisms and this is termed as "under-processed" spoilage.

(a) Thermophilic bacteria : These bacteria can thrive at a high temperature of 100°C. If cans are stored without adequate cooling, the contents remain at a temperature favourable for incubation of such bacteria for a fairly long time, with the result that these bacteria multiply and spoil the product. It is, therefore, essential to ensure that cans are cooled to about 39°C before they are stored. Thermophilic bacteria grow by forming spores. Some species, called facultative , grow at 43°C while some others, called obligative, grow at 43 to 77°C. The latter are more difficult to kill than the former. Some thermophiles produce hydrogen, and some others hydrogen sulphide gas which blackens the contents. The only way to avoid bacterial contamination is to clean and wash the raw material thoroughly before canning. Sources of bacterial contamination are the plant, equipment, sugar, strach, soil, etc.

Three types of spoilage are caused by thermophiles:

(i) Flat sour : This occurs mostly in non-acid foods like vegetables and is caused by thermophilic species of *Bacillus* such as *B. coagulans* and *B. sterothermophilus*, which produce acid without formation of gas. It is, therefore, difficult to detect the spoilage from the external appearance of the can. It may be due almost entirely to under-processing. The product has a sour odour and its acidity is much higher than that of the normal product. It is not fit for consumption.

(ii) Thermophilic acid (T.A.) spoilage : In case of TA spoilage, the cans swell due to production of carbon dioxide and hydrogen by *Clostridium thermosaccharolyticum*. Spoilage mostly occur in low and medium acid foods. *C. thermosaccharolyticum* is an obligate thermophile and, therefore, develops in cans stored in hot condition.

(iii) Sulphide spoilage (Sulphur stinker) : It is caused by *Clostridium nigrificans* in low-acid foods. Spores of this bacterium are not very heat-resistant and their presence is an indication of under-processing.

(b) Mesophilic organisms : Spoilage by mesophilic organisms such as some species of *Clostridium, Bacillus*, yeast and fungi, is also indicative of under-processing.

Clostridium butyricum and *C. pasteurianum* cause a butyric acid type of fermentation in foods with swelling of the container due to the formation of carbon dioxide and hydrogen. Other species of *Clostridium* produce hydrogen sulphide and other undesirable gases. These putrefactive anaerobes generally grow in low-acid material such as vegetables, etc., but sometimes in medium-acid foods also.

Some gas-forming bacilli such as *Bacillus polymyxa* and *B. macerans* are also reported to cause spoilage of canned peas, spinach, peach and tomato.

The presence of non-spore forming bacteria in canned food indicates a leak or under-processing. Organisms which are thermoduric include enterococci and *Streptococcus thermophilus*. These heterofermentatives produce carbon dioxide which swells the can. Some other non-gas forming, non-spore forming bacteria which cause spoilage are species of *Pseudomonas, Micrococcus* and *Proteus*.

Moulds and yeasts and their spores are destroyed at pasteurisation temperature. Their presence in canned food indicates gross under-processing or leakage. Spoilage of canned products by yeasts results in carbon dioxide production and swelling of the cans. Film yeasts and fungi grow on the surface of the products and cause degradation. In the case of some fruits such as plums, sometimes the fruit breaks down and becomes pulpy in can due to the action of *Byssochlamys fulva*.

(3) After processing

(i) **Infection due to leakage through seams:** A large number of cans after processing show signs of microbial spoilage due to leakage of can seams. Cans which are water-cooled are more likely to leak than air-cooled ones. In such cases the cans may or may not swell depending upon the type of organism and if there is a defect in the seam it permits free passage of the gas formed in the can. For reducing this type of spoilage the bacterial level of the cooling water should be low and the cans should be properly exhausted to reduce seam strain. Moreover, buckling also allows the entry of microorganisms.

Chapter 14

Fruits and Vegetables Drying/ Dehydration and Concentration

The practice of drying of foodstuffs, specially fruits and vegetables, for preserving them is very old.

Both the terms 'drying' and 'dehydration' mean the removal of water. The former term is generally used for drying under the influence of non-conventional energy sources like sun and wind. If fruits or vegetables are to be sun-dried, they or their pieces should be evenly spread in single layer on trays or boards and exposed to the sun. In sun-drying, there is no possibility of temperature, and humidity control. The hottest days in summer are, therefore, chosen so that the foods dry very fast, thus preventing them from getting spoiled due to souring. Souring or turning acidic is usually due to growth of microorganisms which convert the carbohydrates in the food to acid. Quick removal of moisture prevents the growth of these microorganisms.

Dehydration means the process of removal of moisture by the application of artificial heat under controlled conditions of temperature, humidity and air flow, In this process a single layer of fruits or vegetables, whole or cut into pieces or slices are spread on trays which are placed inside the dehydrator. The initial temperature of the dehydrator is usually 43°C which is gradually increased to 60-66°C in the case of vegetables and 66-71°C for fruits.

The drying operation for fruits and vegetables is a complex one since this involves simultaneous exchange of moisture and heat. The relationship between the moisture content and temperature of air during drying process is referred to as 'psychometric' relation. Various factors that affect the rate of drying of horticulture produce include the following:

(i) Composition of raw materials

(ii) Size, shape and arrangement of stacking of produce

(iii) Temperature as well as humidity and velocity of air

(iv) Pressure (barometric or under-vacuum)

(v) Heat transfer to surface (conductive, convective or radiative)

Advantages of dehydration over sun-drying

1. The process of dehydration is much more rapid than sun-drying.

2. Dehydration requires less floor area and fewer trays.

3. Dehydration is done under very hygienic conditions.

4. Sun-drying is not possible in cloudy weather or during rains, whole dehydration or mechanical drying is not dependent on the weather.

5. The colour is dehydrated or mechanically dried fruits and vegetables remains uniform due to uniform drying temperature.

Drying/dehydration has some advantages compared to other methods of preservation:

1. The weight of a product is reduced to 1/4th to 1/9th its original or fresh weight and thus the cost of its transport is reduced.

2. Due to reduction in bulk of the product, it requires less storage space.

3. Cost of processing is very low, as less labour and no sugar is required.

The microorganisms require plenty of free water for their survival. Drying or dehydration removes biologically active water thus stopping the growth of microorganisms. This also results in reduced rate of enzyme activity and chemical reactions. The processing should be done in such a way that the food value, natural flavour and characteristic cooking quality of the fresh material are retained after drying. Fruits are considered to be dry when they show no signs of moisture or stickiness when held firmly in the hand. Vegetables are considered to be dry when they become brittle. At this stage, they should be removed from the dehydrator. The residual moisture in the vegetables should not be more than 6-8 per cent and in fruits 10-20 per cent. Dried fruits can be used as such or after soaking, while dried vegetables are usually soaked in water overnight and then cooked.

Drying/Dehydration Techniques

Several types of driers and drying methods, each better suited for a particular situation, are commercially used to remove moisture from a wide variety of food products including fruits and vegetables.

While sun drying of fruit crops is still practised for certain fruit such as prunes, figs, apricots, grapes and dates, atmospheric dehydration processes are used for apples, prunes, and several vegetables; continuous processes as tunnel, belt trough, fluidized bed and foam-mat drying are mainly used for vegetables.

Spray drying is suitable for fruit juice concentrates and vacuum dehydration processes are useful for low moisture/high sugar fruits like peaches, pears and apricots.

Factors on which the selection of a particular drier/drying method depends include:

- form of raw material and its properties;
- desired physical form and characteristics of dried product;
- necessary operating conditions;
- operation costs.

There are three basic types of drying process:

- Sun drying, solar drying;
- Atmospheric drying including batch (kiln, tower and cabinet driers) and continuous (tunnel, belt, belt-trough, fluidized bed, explosion puff, foam-mat, spray, drum and microwave);
- Sub-atmospheric dehydration (vacuum shelf/belt and freeze driers).

The scope has been expanded to include use of low temperature, low energy process like osmotic dehydration.

As far driers are concerned, one useful division of driers types separates them into air convection driers, drum or roller driers, and vacuum driers. Using this breakdown, following table indicates the applicability of the more common drier types to liquid and solid type foods.

Common driers types used for liquid and solid foods*

Drier type	Usual food type
Air convection driers	
kiln	pieces
cabinet, tray or pan	pieces, purees, liquids
tunnel	pieces
continuous conveyor belt	purees, liquids
belt trough	pieces

Drier type	Usual food type
air lift	small pieces, granules
fluidized bed	small pieces, granules
spray	liquid, purees
Drum or roller driers	
atmospheric	purees, liquids
vacuum	purees, liquids
Vacuum driers	
vacuum shelf	pieces, purees, liquids
vacuum belt	purees, liquids
freeze driers	pieces, liquids

*Source: Potter (1984)

In air convection driers, heated air is put into intimate contact with the food material and supplies a major source of the heat for evaporation. If liquid, the food may be sprayed or poured into pans or on belts. Pieces may be supported in any number of ways. Although heated moving air is common to this group of driers, additional heat also may be supplied by heated tray or belt supports. Drum or roller driers are limited to use with purees, mashes, and liquid foods that can be applied as thin films. Vacuum driers may employ any degree of vacuum to lower the boiling point of water. Freeze-driers are special kinds of vacuum driers generally operated at extremely low internal pressures so as to sublime water vapour directly from ice without going through the liquid phase. This classification is not rigid; since many driers are combinations. Thus, we can place a drum drier in a vacuum chamber or blow high-velocity heated air over the drum to speed drying; both practices are done commercially.

(A) Fruit and Vegetable Natural Drying-Sun and Solar Drying

Surplus production and specifically grown crops may be preserved by natural drying for use until the next crop can be grown and harvested. Natural dried products can also be transported cheaply for distribution to areas where there are permanent shortages of fruits and vegetables.

Home Drier

The methods of producing sun and solar dried fruits and vegetables described here are simple to carry out and inexpensive. They can be easily employed by grower, farmer, cooperative, etc. The best time to preserve fruits and vegetables is when there is a surplus of the product and when it is difficult to transport fresh materials to other markets. This is especially true for crops which are very easily damaged in transport and which stay in good condition for a very short time. Preservation extends the storage (shelf) life of perishable foods so that they can be available throughout the year despite their short harvesting season.

Sun and solar drying of fruits and vegetables is a cheap method of preservation because it uses the natural resource/source of heat: sunlight. This method can be used on a commercial scale as well at the village level provided that the climate is hot, relatively dry and free of rainfall during and immediately after the normal harvesting period. The fresh crop should be of good quality and as ripe (mature) as it would need to be if it was going to be used fresh. Poor quality produce cannot be used for natural drying.

Different lots at various stages of maturity (ripeness) must not be mixed together; this would result in a poor dried product. Some varieties of fruits and vegetables are better for natural drying than other; they must be able to withstand natural drying without their texture becoming tough so that they are not difficult to reconstitute. Some varieties are unsuitable because they have irregular shape and there is a lot of wastage in trimming and cutting such varieties.

Damaged parts which have been attacked by insects, rodents, diseases, etc. and parts which have been discoloured or have a bad appearance or colour, must be removed. Before trimming and cutting, most fruit and vegetables must be washed in clean water. Onions are washed after they have been peeled. Trimming includes the selection of the parts which are to be dried, cutting off and disposing of all unwanted material. After trimming, the greater part of the fruit and vegetables cut into even slices of about 3 to 7 mm thick or in halves/quarters, etc.

It is very important to have all slices/parts in one drying lot of the same thickness/size; the actual thickness will depend on the kind of material. Uneven slices or different sizes dry at different rates and this result in a poor quality end product. Onions and root crops are sliced with a hand slicer or vegetable cutter; bananas, tomatoes and other vegetables or fruits are sliced with stainless-steel knives. As a general rule plums, grapes, figs, dates are dried as whole fruits without cutting/slicing.

131

Some fruits and vegetables, in particular bananas, apples and potatoes, go brown very quickly when left in the air after peeling or slicing; this discolouration is due to an active enzyme called phenoloxidase. To prevent the slices from going brown they must be kept under water until drying can be started. Salt or sulphites in solution give better protection. However, whichever method is used, further processing should follow as soon as possible after cutting or slicing.

Dried fruits and vegetables have certain advantages over those preserved by other methods. They are lighter in weight than their corresponding fresh produce and, at the same time, they do not require refrigerated storage. However, if they are kept at high temperatures and have a high moisture content they will turn brown after relatively short periods of storage.

The main problems for sun drying are dust, rain and cloudy weather. Therefore, drying areas should be dust-free and whenever there is a threat of a dust storm or rain, the drying trays should be stacked together and placed under cover.

In order to produce dut-free and hygienically clean products, fruit and vegetable material should be dried well above ground level so that they are not contaminated by dust, insects, livestock or people. All materials should be dried on trays designed for the purpose; the most common drying trays have wooden frames with a fitted base of nylon mosquito netting. Mesh made of woven grass can also be used. Metal netting must not be used because it discolours the product.

The trays should be placed on a framework at table height from the ground. This allows the air to circulate freely around the drying material and it also keeps the food product well away from dirt. Ideally the area should be exposed to wind and this speed up drying, but this can only be done if the wind is free of dust.

With 80 cm x 50 cm trays, the approximate load for a tray is 3 kg; the material should be spread in even layers. During the first part of the drying period, the material should be stirred and turned over at least once an hour. This will help the material dry faster and more evenly, prevent it sticking together and improve the quality of the finished product. Products for sun drying should be prepared early in the day; this will ensure that the material enjoys the full effect of the sun during the early stages of drying.

At night the trays should be stacked in a ventilated room or covered with canvas. Plastic sheets should never be used for covering individual trays during sun drying.

Dry or nearly dry products can be blown out of the tray by the wind. However, this can be protected by covering the loaded tray with an empty one; this also gives protection against insects and birds.

In the selection of appropriate solar driers for commercial scale operation, it is imperative that economics be kept in view at all time. A total Energy System concept should be employed and due consideration be given to parasitic energy consumption.

The following features have been identified:

- large scale driers are more promising than small scale ones. However, small scale driers should not be neglected.

- the drier should be designed to maximize the utilization factor of the capital investment, i.e. multi-products (fruits, vegetables and other raw material) and multi-use (e.g. drying and heating water for domestic use).

- in general, an auxiliary heat source should be provided to assure reliability, to handle peak loads and also to provide continuous drying during periods of no sunshine.

- forced convection indirect driers are preferred because they offer better control, more uniform drying and because of their high heat collection efficiency result in smaller collector area. However, parasitic power should be kept to a minimum.

Two drier systems have been identified:

- a cabinet type drier with natural convection for internal air circulation for the processing of dried fruit such as mango, banana, pineapple, apricot, pear, apple, etc. and also for potato chips and other vegetables;

- a greenhouse type drier with forced air circulation.

Some of the barriers to the commercial development of solar driers have been attributed to:

- initial cost- poor farmers cannot afford them

- durability- constant breakdown due to using low cost building materials

- misuse- through lack of training and technical skills

- dependability and reliability- during the wet season when drying is critical there is not enough solar energy available

- the wider use of Solar Drying Systems has been limited by other factors which are not necessarily of a technical or technological nature. Among the most important are the lack of national policies directed to promoting the drying of produce at the production site, in order to reduce losses, improve quality and increase farmers' earnings.

Solar drier may be useful where-

- the cost of conventional energy is prohibitve and/or the supply is erratic, to supplement existing artificial drying systems and reduce fuel costs;

- the land is in short supply or expensive;

- the quality of existing sun dried products can be improved upon;

- the labour is in short supply;

- there is plenty of sunshine, but high humidity.

Solar drier may not be useful where-

- conventional energy sources are abundant and cheap;

- large amounts of combustible by-products or waste materials are freely available;

- there is insufficient sunshine;

- there is plenty of sunshine and arid conditions (sun drying may suffice);

- the quality of sun dried products already made cannot be improved upon;

- local operators are insufficiently trained;

- the ramifications of introducing a solar drier have not been completely thought out.

Shade Drying

Shade drying is carried out for products which can lose their colour and/or turn brown if put in direct sunlight. Products which have naturally vivid colours like herbs, green and red sweet peppers, chillies, green beans and okra give a more attractive end-product when they are dried in the shade.

The principles for the shade drying are the same as for sun drying. The material to be dried requires full air circulation. Therefore, shade drying is carried out under a roof or thatch which has open sides; it cannot be done either inside conventional buildings with side walls or in compounds sheltered from wind. Under dry conditions when there is a good circulation of air, shade drying takes little more time than is normally required for drying in full sunlight.

Osmotic Dehydration

In osmotic dehydration the prepared fresh material is soaked in a heavy (thick liquid sugar solution) and /or a strong salt solution and then the material is sun or solar dried. During osmotic treatment the material loses some of its moisture. The syrup or salt solution has a protective effect on colour, flavour and texture.

This protective effect remains throughout the drying process and makes it possible to produce dried products of high quality. This process makes little use of sulphur dioxide.

(B) Common Driers used for Drying/Dehydration

(a) Air Convection Driers

All air convection driers have some sort of insulated enclosure, a means of circulating air through the enclosure, and a means of heating this air. They also have various means of product support and special devices for collecting dried product; some have air driers to lower drying air humidity. Movement of air generally is controlled by fans, blowers, and baffles.

The air may be heated by direct or indirect methods. In direct heating the air is in direct contact with a flame or combustion gases. In indirect heating the air is in contact with a hot surface, such as pipes or fins heated by steam, flame, or electricity. The important point is that indirect heating leaves the air uncontaminated. On the other hand, in direct heating the fuel is seldom completely oxidized to carbon dioxide and water. Incomplete combustion leaves gases and traces of soot, which are picked up by the air and can be transferred to the food product. Direct heating of air also contributes small amounts of moisture to the air since moisture is a product of combustion, but this is usually insignificant except with very hygroscopic foods. These disadvantages are balanced by the generally lower cost of direct heating of air compared to indirect heating, and both methods are widely used in food dehydration.

(1) Kiln Drier: One of the simplest kinds of air convection drier is the kiln drier. Kiln driers of early design were two-story constructions. A furnace or burner on the lower floor generated heat, and warm air would rise through a slotted floor to the upper story. Foods such as apple slices would be spread out on the slotted floor and turned over periodically and a relatively long time is required for drying. This kind of drier will not reduce moisture to below about 10%. It is still in use for apple slices, hopps and occasionally for potatoes. These driers are generally used to dehydrate relatively large pieces of material. The rate of drying is effected by the properties of the drying air and the properties of the solid. The important properties of the air are temperature, humidity and velocity. The properties of the solid to consider are : the type of and variety of vegetable or fruit; the free moisture content, the method of preparation prior to drying, and the shape and size of the piece.

(2) Cabinet, Tray, and Pan Driers: A step more advanced is the cabinet drier in which food may be loaded on trays or pans in comparatively thin layers up to a few centimetres. Fresh air enters the cabinet (B), is drawn by the fan through the heater coils (C), and is then blown across the food trays to exhaust (H). In this case, the air is heated by the indirect method. Screens filter out any dust that may be in the air. The air passes across and between the trays in this design. Other designs have perforated trays and the air may be directed up through these. The air is exhausted to the atmosphere after one pass rather than being recirculated within the system. Recirculation is used to conserve heat energy by reusing part of the warm air. In recirculating designs, moist air, after evaporating water from the food, may have to be dried before being recirculated to prevent saturation and slowing down of subsequent drying. In such a case, this air could be dried by passing through a desiccant such as a bed of silica gel, or the moisture could be condensed out by passing the moist air over cold plates or coils. But when the exhaust air is not dried for recirculation, then the exhaust vent should not be close to the fresh air intake area, otherwise the moist exhaust air will be drawn back through the drier and drying efficiency will be lost.

Cabinet, tray, and pan driers are usually for small-scale operations. They are comparatively inexpensive and easy to set in terms of drying conditions. They may run up to 25 trays high and operate with air temperatures of about 95°C (dry bulb) and with air velocities of about 2.5-5 m/sec across the trays. They commonly are used to dry fruit and vegetable pieces, and depending on the food and the desired final moisture, drying time may be of the order of 10 or even 20 hours.

(3) Tunnel and Continuous Belt Driers: These driers are most commonly used for dehydrating fruits and vegetables. For larger operations, tunnel driers with elongated cabinets, through which trays on carts pass, are used. Hot air is blown across the trays. If drying time to the desired moisture is 10 hours, each wheeled cart of trays will take 10 hours to pass through the tunnel. When a dry cart emerges, it makes room to load another wet cart into the opposite end of the tunnel. Such an operation then becomes semicontinuous. Tunnel driers have been developed

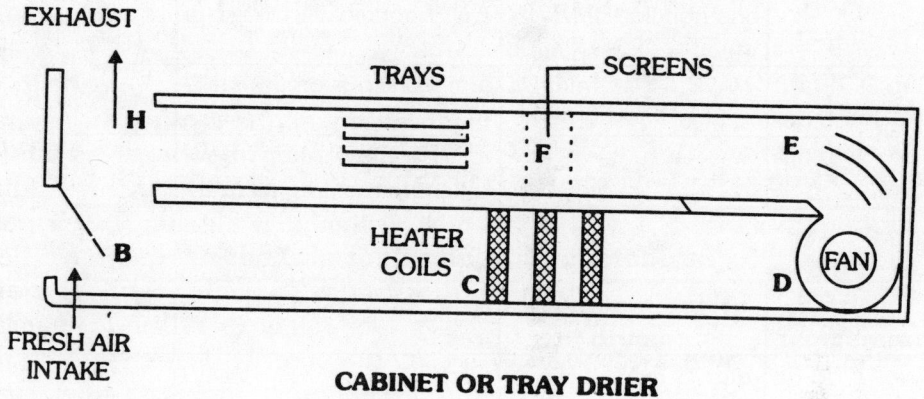

CABINET OR TRAY DRIER

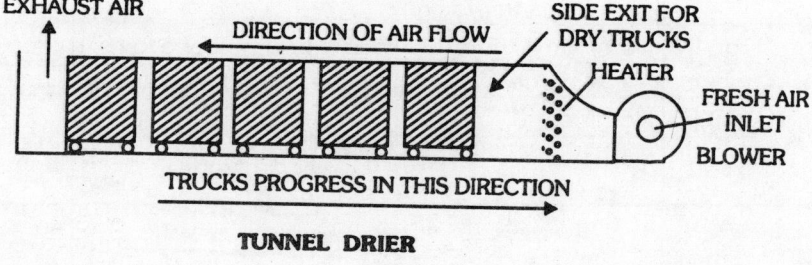

TUNNEL DRIER

to permit close control of the temperature and humidity of circulated air and the relative amount of new and recirculated air blended in the drying stream. A main construction feature by which tunnel driers differ has to do with the direction of airflow relative to tray movement. In the drier shown in Figure, wet food carts move from left to right. The drying air moves across the trays from right to left. This is a counterflow, or countercurrent, pattern in which the hottest and driest air contacts the nearly dry product, whereas the initial drying of entering carts gets cooler, moister air that has cooled and picked up moisture going through the tunnel. This means that initial product temperature and moisture gradients will not be as great, and the product is less likely to undergo case hardening or other surface shrinkage, leaving wet centers. Further, lower final moisture can be reached because the driest product encounters the driest air. In contrast, concurrent flow tunnels have the incoming trays and incoming hottest driest air travelling in the same direction. In this case, rapid initial drying and slow final drying can cause case hardening and internal splits and porosity as centers finally dry, which sometimes is desirable in special products.

Just as carts of trays can be moved through a heated tunnel, so a continuous belt may be driven through a tunnel or oven enclosure. This approach is used in a continuous belt or conveyor drier, and a great number of designs are possible. Some of the more common features are uniform automatic feeding of product to the belt in a controlled thin layer, zoned heat and airflow control in different sections, tumbling over of product onto a second strand of belt, automatic collection of dried product, and, of course, continuous operation. The drying capacity of such driers generally is stated in terms of weight of product dried from one moisture level to another per square meter of belt surface per hour. This also can be expressed in terms of kilograms of water removed per square meter of belt surface per hour under defined operating conditions.

(4) Belt Trough Drier: A special kind of air convection belt drier is the belt trough drier in which the belt forms a trough. The belt is usually of metal mesh, and heated air is blown up through the mesh. The belt moves continuously, keeping the food pieces in the trough in constant motion to continuously expose new surface. This speeds drying, and with air of about 135°C, vegetable pieces may be dried to 7-5% moisture in about 1 hour.

But not all products may be dried this way since certain sizes and shapes do not readily tumble. Fragile apple wedges may break. Onion slices tend to separate and become entangled. Fruit pieces that exude sugar on drying tend to stick together and clump with the tumbling motion. These are but a few additional factors that must be considered in selecting a drier for a particular food.

(5) **Air Lift Drier:** Several types of pneumatic conveyor driers go a step beyond tumbling to expose more surface area of food particles. These generally are used to finish-dry materials that have been partially dried by other methods, usually to about 25% moisture, or at least sufficiently low so that the material becomes granular rather than having a tendency to clump and mat. This might be used to finish-dry semimoist granules coming from a drum drier. Such granules at about 25% moisture can be brought to about 6% moisture more efficiently in a heated airstream than on the drum. This is because the more difficult moisture to remove in this falling rate period of dehydration is more easily evaporated from suspended particles in intimate contact with the heating medium. The suspended particles when dry are separated from the air and collected in a cyclone-type separator.

(6) **Fluidized-Bed Drier:** Another type of pneumatic conveyor drier is the fluidized-bed drier. In fluidized-bed drying, heated air is blown up through the food particles with just enough force to suspend the particles in a gentle boiling motion. Semidry particles such as potato granules enter at the left and gradually migrate to the right, where they are discharged dry. Heated air is introduced through a porous plate that supports the bed of granules. The moist air is exhausted at the top. The process is continuous and the length of time particles remain in the drier can be regulated by the depth of the bed and other means. This type of drying can be used to dehydrate grains, peas, and other particulates.

(7) **Spray Driers:** By far the most important kind of air convection drier is the spray drier. Spray driers turn out a greater tonnage of dehydrated food products than all other kinds of driers combined. There are various types of spray driers designed for specific food products. Spray driers are limited to foods that can be atomized, such as liquids and low-viscosity pastes and purees. Atomization into minute droplets results in drying in a matter of seconds with common inlet air temperatures of about 200°C. Since evaporative cooling seldom permits particles to get warmer than about 80°C and properly designed systems quickly remove the dried particles from heated zones, this method of dehydration can produce exceptionally high quality with many highly heat-sensitive materials, including milk, eggs, and coffee.

In typical spray drying, the liquid food is introduced as a fine spray or mist into a tower or chamber along with heated air. As the small droplets make intimate contact with the heated air, they flash off their moisture, become small particles, and drop to the bottom of the tower from where they are removed. The heated air, which has now become moist, is withdrawn from the tower by a blower or fan. The process is continuous in that liquid food continues to be pumped into the chamber and atomized, along with dry heated air to replace the moist air that is withdrawn, and the dried product is removed from the chamber as it descends.

One type of spray drying foams liquid food, such as milk or coffee, before spraying it into the drier. The result is a faster drying rate from the expanded foamed-droplet surface area and lighter-density dried product. This is known as foam-spraying drying.

It was stated that when particles are dry, they do not stick to the drier wall. An exception, is thermoplastic substances such as juices high in sugar. Even when dry, these melt, stick, and build up on the wall. One kind of spray drier has a double wall and circulates cold water or cool air so as to chill the lower portion of the inner wall where dried juice particles would accumulate. Thus prevented from melting and fusing, these juices too may be spray dried and collected in particulate form.

Another type of spray drier has been developed especially to handle thermoplastic materials and other highly heat-sensitive foods. This is known as the BIRS spray drier. The BIRS drier uses countercurrent cool, dry air of about 30°C and 3% RH. To give the droplets sprayed in at the top of the tower sufficient time to dry at this relatively low temperature, the drying tower is built exceptionally tall. It may be 67 m high and 15 m in diameter. As droplets descend, they dry in about 90 sec. Products like orange, lemon, and tomato juices, otherwise difficult to spray dry because of thermoplasticity, can be dried this way. Because there is not rapid escape of steam from particles in this cool process, such particles are less puffed and more dense than many conventionally spray-dried products. Low temperature also favours retention.

(b) Drum or Roller Driers

In drum or roller drying, liquid foods, purees, pastes, and mashes are applied in a thin layer onto the surface of a revolving heated drum. The drum generally is heated from within by steam. Driers may have a single drum or a pair of drums. The food may be applied between the nip where two drums come together, and then the clearance between the drums determines the thickness of the applied food layer; or the food can be applied to other areas of the drum. Food is applied continuously and the thin layer loses moisture. At a point on the drum or drums a scraper blade is positioned to peel the thin dried layer of food from the drums. The speed of the drums is so regulated that the layer of food will be dry when it reaches the scraper blade. which also is referred to as a doctor blade. The layer of food is dried in one revolution of the drum and is scraped from the drum before that position of the drum returns to the point where more wet food is applied. Using steam under pressure in the drum, the temperature of the drum surface may be well above 100°C, and often is held at about 150°C. With a food layer thickness commonly less than 2 mm, drying can be completed in 1 min or less, depending on the food material.

Typical products dried on drums include milk, potato mash, heat-tolerant purees such as tomato paste, and animal feeds. But drum drying has some inherent limitations that restrict the kinds of foods to which it is applicable. To achieve rapid drying, drum surface temperature must be high, usually above 120°C. This gives products a more cooked flavour and colour than when they are dried at a lower temperature. Drying temperature can, of course, be lowered by constructing the drums within a vacuum chamber, but this increases equipment and operating costs over atmospheric drum or spray drying.

For relatively heat-resistant food products, drum drying is one of the least expensive dehydration methods. Drum dried foods generally have a somewhat more "cooked" character than the same materials spray dried.

(c) Vacuum Driers

Vacuum dehydration methods are capable of producing the highest quality dried products, but costs of vacuum drying generally also are higher than other methods which do not employ vacuum. In vacuum drying, the temperature of the food and the rate of water removal are controlled by regulating the degree of vacuum and the intensity of heat input. Heat transfer to the food is largely by conduction and radiation. Vacuum drying methods usually can be controlled with a higher degree of accuracy than methods depending on air convection heating.

All vacuum drying systems have four essential elements: a vacuum chamber of heavy construction to withstand outside air pressures that may exceed internal pressure by as much as 9800 kg/m^2; a heat supply; a device for producing and maintaining the vacuum; and components to collect water vapour as it is evaporated from the food.

(1) Vacuum Shelf Driers: One of the simplest kinds of vaccum driers is the batch-type vacuum shelf drier. If liquids such as concentrated fruit juices are dried above about 5 mm Hg, the juice boils and splatters, but in the range of about 3 mm Hg and below, the concentrated juice puffs as it loses water vapour. The dehydrated juice then retains the puffed spongy structure. Since temperatures well below 40°C can be used, in addition to quick solubility there is minimum flavour change or other kinds of heat damage. A vacuum shelf drier is also suitable for the dehydration of food pieces. In this case, the rigidity of the solid food prevents major puffing, although there also is a tendency to minimize shrinkage.

(2) Continuous Vacuum Belt Drier: Vacuum driers can be engineered for continuous operation. This drier is used commercially to dehydrate high quality citrus juice crystals, instant tea and other delicate liquid foods.

The drier consists of a horizontal tanklike chamber connected to a vacuum-producing, moisture-condensing system. Two revolving hollow drums are mounted within the chamber. A stainless steel belt is connected around the drums which moves in a counterclockwise direction. The drum on the right is heated with steam confined within it. This drum heats the belt passing over it by conduction. As the belt moves, it is further heated by infrared radiant elements. The drum to the left is cooled with cold water circulated within it and cools the belt passing over it. The liquid food in the form of a concentrate is pumped into a feed pan under the lower belt strand. An applicator roller dipping into the liquid continuously applies a thin coating of the food onto the lower surface of the moving belt. As the belt moves over the heating drum and past the radiant heaters, the food rapidly dries in the vacuum equivalent to about 2 mm Hg. When the food reaches the cooling drum, it is down to about 2% moisture. At the bottom of the cooling drum is a doctor blade which scrapes the cooled, embrittled product into the collection vessel. The belt scraped free of product receives additional liquid food as it passes the applicator roller and the process repeats in continuous fashion. Products dried with this equipment have a slightly puffed structure.

(3) Freeze-Drying: Freeze-drying has been developed to a highly advanced state. Much of the development work has been aimed at optimizing the process and equipment to reduce drying costs, which still may be two to five times greater per weight of water removed than other common drying methods. Freeze-drying can be used to dehydrate sensitive, high-value liquid foods such as coffee and juices, but it is especially suited to drying solid foods of high value such as strawberries, whole shrimp, chicken dice, mushroom slices, and sometimes food pieces as large as steaks and chops. These types of food, in addition to having delicate flavours and colours, have textural and appearance attributes that cannot be well preserved by any current drying method except freeze-drying.

In this method, the material such as fruit juice concentrate, is first frozen on trays in the lower chamber of a freeze drier and the frozen material dried in the upper chamber under high vacuum. The material dries directly by sublimation of ice without passing through the intermediate liquid stage. The dried product is highly hygroscopic. It reconstitutes readily. Mango pulp, orange juice concentrate and guava pulp have been found to give freeze-dried powders of excellent quality in regard to taste, flavour, reconstitution property etc.

Today, food companies wishing to install freeze-drying equipment on a major scale. It also is sometimes advantageous to combine freeze-drying with air drying. Vegetable pieces may be air dried to about 50% moisture and then freeze-dried down to 2-3% moisture, as in the "Aire Freeze" process of the California Vegetable Concentrates Company. This combination gives a high quality product at lower cost than with freeze-drying alone.

Differences between Conventional and Freeze Drying

S.No.	Conventional Drying	Freeze Drying
1.	Successful for easily dried foods such as seeds, fruits and vegetables.	Successful for most foods but usually limited to those not successfully dried by other methods.
2.	Generally it is not satisfactory for meat products.	Successful for cooked and raw animal products.
3.	Conventional drying is a continuous processing.	Freeze drying is a batch processing.
4.	Temperature between 37 and 93°C generally used.	Sufficiently low temperature is used to prevent thawing.
5.	Drying usually at atmospheric pressure.	Drying usually below 4mm Hg pressure.
6.	Drying time may be short, usually less than 12 hours.	Drying time generally between 12 and 24 hours.
7.	Evaporation of water from food surface.	Moisture loss by sublimation of ice without passing through the intermediate liquid stage.

S.No.	Conventional Drying	Freeze Drying
8.	Solid dried particles.	Porous dried, highly hygroscopic particles, reconstitute readily.
9.	Higher density than the original food.	Lower density than the original food.
10.	Odour frequently abnormal.	Odour usually natural.
11.	Slow rehydration, usually incomplete.	Rapid, complete rehydration possible.
12	Colour usually darker.	Colour usually natural.
13.	Flavour may be abnormal.	Flavour generally natural.
14.	Storage stability good, tendency to darken.	Storage stability excellent.
15.	Costs generally low.	Costs generally high.

Atmospheric Drying of Foams

Vacuum drying methods, and freeze-drying in particular, can produce dehydrated foods of exceptional quality. With liquids and purees, nearly the same quality can be obtained at atmospheric pressure with less expensive equipment and operating costs. This has been done in some instances by drying prefoamed liquid foods. Foaming is done to expose enormous surface area for quick moisture escape. This, in turn, can permit rapid atmospheric drying at somewhat reduced temperatures. In this type of drying, naturally foaming foods such as egg white are mechanically whipped to a foam density of about 0.3 g/cm^3. Foods that do no whip as readily, such as concentrated citrus juices, fruit purees, and tomato paste, are supplemented with low levels of an edible whipping agent belonging to such groups of materials as vegetable proteins, carbohydrate gums, or monogylceride emulsifiers prior to being whipped. Stable foams are then cast in thin layers onto trays or belts and are dried by various heating schemes. One such dehydration method is known as foam-mat drying.

Foam-mat Driers are used primarily for liquids which are prefoamed by whipping, adding a low level of an edible whipping agent to liquids that do not whip readily. Foaming a liquid exposes enormous surface areas for quick moisture removal which also permits use of lower drying temperatures. Foam is deposited in a uniform layer on a perforated tray or belt through which hot air is blown. Foam layers of many foods can be dried to about 2 to 3% moisture in approximately 12 min.

FLOW-SHEET FOR DRYING/DEHYDRATION OF FRUITS AND VEGETABLES

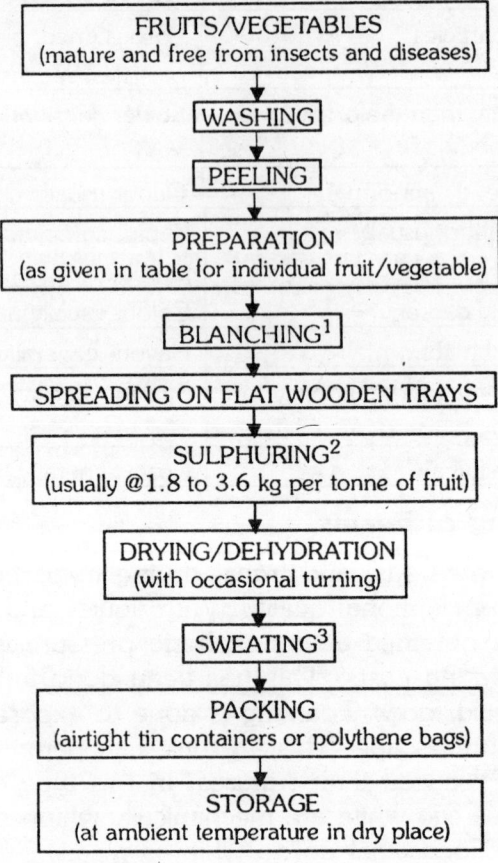

```
          ┌──────────────────────────────────────────┐
          │           FRUITS/VEGETABLES              │
          │ (mature and free from insects and diseases)│
          └──────────────────────────────────────────┘
                             │
                       ┌──────────┐
                       │ WASHING  │
                       └──────────┘
                             │
                       ┌──────────┐
                       │ PEELING  │
                       └──────────┘
                             │
          ┌──────────────────────────────────────────┐
          │              PREPARATION                 │
          │ (as given in table for individual fruit/vegetable)│
          └──────────────────────────────────────────┘
                             │
                      ┌─────────────┐
                      │ BLANCHING¹  │
                      └─────────────┘
                             │
          ┌──────────────────────────────────────────┐
          │   SPREADING ON FLAT WOODEN TRAYS         │
          └──────────────────────────────────────────┘
                             │
          ┌──────────────────────────────────────────┐
          │              SULPHURING²                 │
          │ (usually @1.8 to 3.6 kg per tonne of fruit)│
          └──────────────────────────────────────────┘
                             │
          ┌──────────────────────────────────────────┐
          │            DRYING/DEHYDRATION            │
          │        (with occasional turning)         │
          └──────────────────────────────────────────┘
                             │
                     ┌──────────────┐
                     │  SWEATING³   │
                     └──────────────┘
                             │
          ┌──────────────────────────────────────────┐
          │                PACKING                   │
          │ (airtight tin containers or polythene bags)│
          └──────────────────────────────────────────┘
                             │
          ┌──────────────────────────────────────────┐
          │                STORAGE                   │
          │ (at ambient temperature in dry place)    │
          └──────────────────────────────────────────┘
```

1. **Blanching:** Exposing fruit and vegetable to hot or boiling water-as a pre-treatment before drying has the following advantages:

   - it helps clean the material and reduce the amount of microorganisms present on the surface;

   - it preserves the natural colour in the dried products; for example, the carotenoid (orange and yellow) pigments dissolve in small intracellular oil drops during blanching and in this way they are protected from oxidative breakdown during drying;

   - it shortens the soaking and/or cooking time during reconstitution.

   During hot water blanching, some soluble constituents are leached out: water-soluble flavours, vitamins (vitamin C) and sugars. With potatoes this may be an advantage as leaching out of sugars makes the potatoes less prone to turning brown. Blanching is a delicate processing step; time, temperature and the other conditions must be carefully monitored. A suitable water-blanching method in traditional processing is as follows:

- the sliced material is placed on a square piece of clean cloth; the corners of the cloth are tied together;

- a stick is put through the tied corners of the cloth;

- the cloth is dipped into a pan containing boiling water and the stick rests across the top of the pan thus providing support for the cloth bag.

The average blanching time is 6 minutes. The start of blanching has to be timed from the moment the water starts to boil again after the cloth bag has been dipped into the pan. While the material is being blanched the cloth bag should be raised and lowered in the water so that the material is heated evenly. When the blanching time is completed the cloth bag and its content should be dipped into cold water to prevent over-blanching. If products are over-blanched (boiled for two long) they will stick together on the drying trays and they are likely to have a poor flavour.

Green beans, carrots, okra, turnip and cabbage should always be blanched. Sodium bicarbonate is added to the blanching water when okra, green peas and some other green vegetables are blanched. The chemical raises the pH of the blanching water and prevents the fresh green colour of chlorophyll being changed into pheophytin which is unattractive brownish-green. The producer can choose whether or not potatoes need blanching. Blanching is not needed for onions, leeks, garlic, tomatoes and sweet peppers. Tomatoes are dipped into hot water for one minute when they need to be peeled but this is not blanching.

As a rule fruit is not blanched but thick skinned fruits are sometimes lye-peeled to 'check' the skin or to remove the peel to facilitate drying, e.g., peaches.

Use of preservatives : Preservatives are used to improve the colour and keeping qualities of the final product for some fruits and vegetables. Preservatives include items such as sulphur dioxide, ascorbic acid, citric acid, salt and sugar and can either be simple or compound solutions.

Treatment with preservatives takes place after blanching or, when blanching is not needed, after slicing. In traditional, simple processing the method recommended is:

- put enough preservative solution to cover the cloth bag into a container/pan;

- dip the bag containing the product into the preservative solution for the amount of time specified;

- remove the bag and put it on a clean tray while the liquid drains out. The liquid which drains out must not go back into the preservative solution because it would weaken the solution.

Care must be taken after each dip to refill the container to the original level with fresh preservative solution of correct strength. After five lots of material have been dipped, the remaining solution is thrown away; i.e. a fresh lot of preservative solution is needed for every 5 lots of material. The composition and strength of the preservative solution vary for different fruit and vegetables.

The strength of sulphur dioxide is expressed as "parts per million" (ppm). 1.5 grams of sodium metabisulphite in one litre of water gives 1000 ppm of sulphur dioxide. Details for solutions of different strengths are given in the following table.

Dilutions of sodium metabisulphite with water to obtain ppm of sulphur dioxide (SO_2)

ppm SO_2	Sodium metabisulphite	
	Grams per litre of water	Grams per 20 litres of water
1000	1.5	30.0
2000	3.0	60.0
3000	4.5	90.0
4000	6.0	120.0
5000	7.5	150.0
6000	9.0	180.0
7000	10.5	210.0

The preservatives solutions in the fruit and vegetable pre-treatment can only be used in enamelled, plastic or stainless-steel containers; never use ordinary metal because solutions will corrode this type of container.

As a general rule, preservatives are not used for treating onions, garlic, leeks, chillies and herbs.

2. **Sulphuring:** Sulphur dioxide fumes act as a disinfectant and prevent the oxidation and darkening of fruits on exposure and thus improves their colour. This phenomenon is generally seen in sliced fruits which darken due to oxidation of the colouring matter. Sulphur fumes also act as a preservative, check the growth of moulds, etc., and prevent cut fruit pieces from fermenting while drying in the sun. Vitamins in sulphured fruits are protected but not in unsulphured ones. Vegetables are not generally sulphured.

The whole fruits, slices or pieces are exposed to the fumes of burning sulphur inside a closed chamber known as 'sulphur box' for 30-60 minutes or in small airtight rooms.

'Sulphur box' is a closed airtight chamber of galvanized iron sheet. It is fitted in a wooden framework having runways on both sides to hold the trays. For small scale sulphuring, a box of size of 90 x 60 x 90 cm which can hold 11 trays, each of 80 x 60 x 5 cm size, is suitable. A box holding 10 trays will require burning of about 3 g of sulphur in one charge.

3. Keeping dried products in boxes or bins to equalize moisture content.

Spoilage of dried products

Dried fruits and vegetables are subject to insect attack even when properly dried and stored. Insects not only consume foodstuff, but also leave much debris which spoils the appearance of the product. These insects can be killed either by heating or by fumigation. In heat treatment, dried fruits are dipped in boiling water or in a dilute solution of salt and then re-dried at 54-65°C. Dried vegetables may be heated directly without preliminary dipping. Fumigation with ethylene oxide inside the storage chamber also reduces attack by insects.

Dried fruits become musty or mouldy and dried vegetables soft of slimy if kept in a damp atmosphere in unsealed containers. Proper sealing and storing of containers at ambient temperature and in a dry place is important.

Dehydrated fruit and vegetable potential defects and means to prevent them are given below:

Defects	Causes	Prevention
Moulding	High product moisture, above equilibrium relative humidity corresponding to water activity $a_w=0.70$	Reduce water content down to optimum values. Pack in hermetic airtight packages.
Infestation	Presence in dried products of larvae or insects.	Storage room disinfection with toxic gases. Fumigation of packed products and of packages. Disinfection by heat (60-65°C) of products before packing.

Defects	Causes	Prevention
Browning	Chemical reaction (Maillard. etc.)	Reduce as much as possible water content. Store at low temperature.
	Enzyme catalyzed reactions	Enzyme inactivation by blanching or steaming before drying.
Reduced rehydration ratio	Too high temperature in final stage of drying	Operate inside final temperatures as recommended.

Source : Dauthy (1995)

Schedule for drying of fruits

S. No.	Fruit	Preparation and pretreatment	Sulphuring time	Drying temperature
1.	Banana	Wash, peel, halve lengthwise or slice crosswise 12 mm thick	30 min	55-60°C or sun dry
2.	Date	Wash, dip in boiling 0.5% caustic soda solution, then rinse	-	45-50°C or sun dry
3.	Fig	Wash	1 hour (only Adriatic variety)	55-60°C or sun dry
4.	Grape (Muscat and wine variety)	Dip in boiling 0.5% caustic soda solution, then rinse	1 hour	55-60°C or sun dry
5.	Mango	Wash, peel, cut into 12 mm thick slices	2 hours	45-50°C or sun dry
6.	Papaya	Wash, peel remove seeds and cut into 6 mm thick slices	2 hours	60-65°C or sun dry
7.	Apple	Wash, peel, core trim and cut into 5 mm thick slices	30 min or immerse in 1-2% KMS solution for 30 min and drain	60-65°C or sun dry
8.	Apricot	Wash, halve, destone	30 min	50-60°C or sun dry

S. No.	Fruit	Preparation and pretreatment	Sulphuring time	Drying temperature
9.	Pear	Wash, peel, cut into halves, remove core, keep in 1-2% salt solution	30 min or immerse for 20-30 min in 1-2% KMS solution and drain	60-65°C or sun dry
10.	Peach	Wash, remove pits cut into halves	30 min	60-65°C or sun dry
11.	Aonla	Wash, grate, add salt (@ 40 g/kg grated material)	-	sun dry

Schedule for drying of vegetables

S. No.	Vegetable	Preparation	Treatment before drying	Drying temperature
1.	Cauliflower	Wash, remove stalks covering leaves and stems break flowers apart into pieces of suitable size	Blanch 4-5 min, immerse for 1 hour in 1% KMS solution and drain	55-60°C or sun dry
2.	Cabbage	Wash, remove outer leaves and core, cut into fine shreds	Blanch 5-6 min, immerse for 10 min in 0.5% KMS solution and drain	55-60°C or sun dry
3.	Chillies (red)	String mature dark red pods and hang in sun	No treatment	50-60°C or sun dry
4.	Green peas	Wash, remove shell and collect the grains	Blanch or steam for 3-4 min, immerse in 0.5% KMS solution and drain	60-65°C or sun dry
5.	Onion	Remove outer dry scales, cut into 5 mm thick slices	Dip for 10 min in 5% salt solution drain	60-65°C or sun dry
6.	Garlic	Peel the clove, use as such or cut into 5 mm thick slices	Dip for 10 min in 5% salt solution and drain	60-65°C or sun dry
7.	Palak, methi, other leafy green vegetables	Sort, wash. trim off rough stems and stalks, shred	Blanch for 2 min in boiling water or steam	60-65°C or sun dry

S. No.	Vegetable	Preparation	Treatment before drying	Drying temperature
8.	Potato	Wash, peel and cut into 10 mm thick slices	Blanch in boiling water or steam for 3-4 min and immerse in 0.5% KMS solution	60-65°C or sun dry
9.	Tomato	Wash	Blanch for 30-60 seconds, peel and slice 10 mm thick	60-65°C or sun dry
10.	Turnip	Wash, remove stalks, peel and cut into 5 mm thick slices	Blanch for 2-4 min in boiling water and then immerse for 1-2 hour in 1% KMS solution	50-55°C or sun dry
11.	Beans	Wash and remove strings, split pods lengthwise	Blanch for 4-5 min	60-65°C or sun dry
12.	Beet	Wash, peel and cut into 10 mm thick slices	Steam for 10 min	60-65°C or sun dry
13.	Bitter gourd	Wash, remove both ends and cut into 10 mm thick slices	Blanch for 7-8 min	65-70°C or sun dry
14.	Brinjal	Wash, cut lengthwise into 10 mm thick slices	Blanch for 4-5 min and then immerse for 1 hour in 1% KMS solution	50-52°C or sun dry
15.	Carrot	Wash, scrape stalks and tips, cut into 10 mm thick slices	Blanch for 2-4 min in boiling 2% common salt solution	60-65°C or sun dry

Reconstitution test for dried/dehydrated products

In reconstitution water is added to the product which is restored to a condition similar to that when it was fresh. This enables the food product to be cooked as if the person was using fresh fruit or vegetable.

All vegetables are cooked but many of the dried fruits can be used for eating after they have been soaked in water. The following reconstitution test is used to find out the quality of the dried products.

Reconstitution test

1. Weigh out a sample of 35 grams from the bulked and packed final product of the previous day's production.

2. Put the sample into a small container (beaker) and add 275 ml of cold water (and 3.5 g salt).

3. Cover the container (with a watch-glass) and bring the water to the boil.

4. Boil gently for 30 minutes.

5. Turn out the sample onto a white dish.

6. At least two people should then examine the sample for palatability, toughness, flavour and presence or absence of bad flavours. The testers should record their results independently.

7. The liquid left in the container should be examined for traces of sand/soil and other foreign matter.

This test can be used also to examine dried products after they have been stored for some time. Evaluation of rehydration ratio may be performed according to the following calculations.

Rehydration ratio : If the weight of the dehydrated sample (a) used for the test is 5 g and the drained weight of the rehydrated sample (b) 30g, then

$$\text{Rehydration ratio} = \frac{b}{a} = \frac{30}{5} = 6 : 1$$

Rehydration Coefficient : If the drained weight of 10g of dried sample containing 5% moisture after rehydration is 70g, and the fresh sample before drying contained 90% moisture, then

$$\text{Rehydration Coefficient} = \frac{\text{Drained wt of de-hydrated sample} \times \left[100 - \begin{array}{c}\text{Moisture content}\\ \text{of sample before}\\ \text{drying}\end{array}\right]}{\left[\begin{array}{c}\text{Wt. of dried} \\ \text{sample taken} \\ \text{for rehydration}\end{array} - \begin{array}{c}\text{Amount of moisture} \\ \text{present in the dried} \\ \text{sample taken for} \\ \text{rehydration}\end{array}\right] \times 100}$$

$$= \frac{70 \times (100 - 90)}{(10 - 0.5) \times 100} = 0.74$$

Per cent water in the rehydrated material : The drained weight of the rehydrated sample being known, the per cent water content in the rehydrated material is calculated by-

$$\frac{\text{Drained wt of rehydrated material} - \text{Dry matter content in the sample taken for rehydration}}{\text{Drained wt of rehydrated material}} \times 100$$

Following the values given under "coefficient of rehydration", the moisture content in the rehydrated sample is $\dfrac{70 - 9.5}{70} \times 100 = 86.43\%$

A simpler test for eating quality can be carried out without weighing and measuring. The material is placed in a cooking pot with water (and a little salt). The pot is then covered and boiled as described above. Except for a few products which are eaten in the dry state, most dried fruit and all dried vegetables are prepared by soaking and cooking. Often this preparation is carried out incorrectly and dried products get a bad reputation. Good quality dried products, after cooking and if properly treated should be similar to cooked fresh produce. In order to get good results, the following methods are recommended:

(i) **Quick method :** Cold water, ten times the weight of the dry product, is added to the dried product. The container is covered, brought to the boil and simmered until the product is tender. The cooking time may be 15 to 45 minutes after the boiling point has been reached.

(ii) **Slow method :** This gives better results than the quick method. Cold water is added to the dry food and is left to soak for 1 to 2 hours before cooking. The product is then cooked in the same water as that in which it was soaked. The actual cooking time will probably be shorter than that for the quick method.

Besides above, following points should also be kept in mind while reconstituting and cooking the dehydrated fruits and vegetables-

(i) If too much water is added the cooked product will have little flavour. However, if too little water is added the product may dry and burn. This can be avoided by adding small quantities of water during cooking.

(ii) Always cook with a lid on the container.

(iii) Salt, if required, should be added when the cooking is almost complete.

    (iv)   Partly used packages of dry products should be reclosed tightly or kept in containers with good fitting lids.

Food Concentration

Foods are concentrated for many of the same reasons that they are dehydrated. Concentration can be a form of preservation, but only for some foods. Concentration reduces weight and volume and results in immediate economic advantages. Nearly all liquid foods to be dehydrated are concentrated before they are dried because in the early stages of water removal, moisture can be more economically removed in highly efficient evaporators than in dehydration equipment. Further, increased viscosity from concentration often is needed to prevent liquids from running off drying surfaces or to facilitate foaming or puffing. Also, some concentrated foods are desirable components of diet in their own right. For example concentration of fruit juices plus sugar yields jelly. Many concentrated foods, such as frozen orange juice concentrate and canned soups, are easily recognized because of the need to add water before they are consumed.

The more common concentrated foods include evaporated and sweetened condensed milks, fruit and vegetable juices and nectars, sugar syrups and flavoured syrups, jams and jellies, tomato paste, many types of fruit purees used by bakers, candy makers, other food manufacturers, and many more.

Methods of Concentration

(i) Solar Concentration

As in food dehydration, one of the simplest methods of evaporating water is with solar energy. This was done to derive salt from sea water from earliest times and is still practiced today in the United States in man-made lagoons. However, solar evaporation is very slow and is suitable only for concentrating salt solutions.

(ii) Open Kettles

Some foods can be satisfactorily concentrated in open kettles that are heated by steam. This is the case for some jellies and jams and for certain types of soups. However, high temperatures and long concentration times damage most foods. In addition, thickening and burn-on of product to the kettle wall gradually lower the efficiency of heat transfer and slow the concentration process. Kettles and pans are still widely used in the manufacture of maple syrup, but here high heat is desirable to produce colour from caramelized sugar and to develop typical flavour.

(iii) Flash Evaporators

Subdividing the food material and bringing it into direct contact with the heating medium can markedly speed concentration. This is done in flash evaporators. Clean steam superheated at about 150^0C is injected into food which is pumped into an evaporation tube where boiling occurs. The boiling mixture then enters a separator vessel in which the concentrated food is drawn off at the bottom and the steam plus water vapour from the food is evacuated through a separate outlet. Because temperatures are high, foods that lose volatile flavour constituents will yield these to the exiting steam and water vapour. These can be separated from the vapour by essence-recovery equipment on the basis of different boiling points between the essences and water.

(iv) Thin-Film Evaporators

In thin-film evaporators, food is pumped into a vertical cylinder which has a rotating element that spreads the food into a thin layer on the cylinder wall. The cylinder wall of double jacket construction usually is heated by steam. Water is quickly flashed from the thin food layer and the concentrated food is simultaneously wiped from the cylinder wall. The concentrated food and water vapour are continuously discharged to an external separator, from which product is removed at the bottom and water vapour passes to a condenser. In some systems the water vapour temperature is raised by mechanical vapour recompression to yield steam for reuse to save energy. Product temperature may reach 85^0C or higher, but since residence time of the concentrating food in the heated cylinder may be less than a minute, heat damage is minimal.

(v) Vacuum Evaporators

Heat-sensitive foods are most commonly concentrated in low-temperature vacuum evaporators. Thin-film evaporators frequently are operated under vacuum by connecting a vacuum pump or steam ejector to the condenser.

It is common to construct several vacuum vessels in series so that the food product moves from one vacuum chamber to the next and thereby becomes progressively more concentrated in stages. The successive stages are maintained at progressively higher degrees of vacuum, and the hot water vapour arising from the first stage is used to heat the second stage, the vapour from the second stage heats the third stage, and so on. In this way, maximum use of heat energy is obtained. Such a system, called a multiple effect vacuum evaporator. Systems employed in the grape juice industry continuously concentrate juice from an initial solids content of 15% to a final solids concentration of 72% at rates of 4500 gal of single strength juice per hour. Similar systems concentrate tomato juice from 6% solids to 30% solids at rates of 15,000 gal or more of single strength juice per hour. Use of energy-saving mechanical vapour recompression is common.

Even with efficient vacuum evaporators where water may boil at 30^0C or slightly lower, some volatile flavour compounds are lost with the evaporating water vapour. These volatile essences can be recovered, or "stripped", from the water vapour and returned to the cool concentrated food as has been mentioned earlier. However, it is possible to concentrate foods at still lower temperatures and further minimize heat damage and volatile flavour loss; one method of doing so is known as freeze concentration.

(vi) Freeze Concentration

When a solid or liquid food is frozen, all of its components do not freeze at once. First to freeze is some of the water which forms ice crystals in the mixture. The remaining unfrozen food solution is now higher in solids concentration.

It is possible, before the entire mixture freezes, to separate the initially formed ice crystals. One way of doing this is to centrifuge the partially frozen slush through a fine-mesh screen. The concentrated unfrozen food solution passes through the screen while the frozen water crystals are retained and can be discarded. Repeating this process several times on the concentrated unfrozen food solution can increase its final concentration several-fold. Freeze concentration has been known for many years and has been applied commercially to orange juice.

(vii) Ultrafiltration and Reverse Osmosis/Hyperfiltration

Low-temperature separation and concentration processes employing perm-selective membranes are increasingly being used in the food industry. These applications are largely dependent on membrane properties such as water permeability rate, solute and macromolecule rejection rates, and length of useful membrane life. Different membranes are required for different liquid foods.

There are two types of pressure-driven membrane separation processes: (a) reverse osmosis/hyperfiltration, and (b) ultrafiltration. In the former, micromolecular solutes are selectively removed, whereas the latter separates out relatively larger solute molecules or colloids. Ultrafiltration membranes are generally "less tight" than reverse osmosis membranes; that is, they restrict macromolecules such as proteins but with moderate pressure allow smaller molecules such as sugars and salts to pass through. Reverse osmosis membranes are "tighter", and with greater pressure will permit the passage of water but hold back various sugars, salts, and larger molecules. In nature, osmosis involves the movement of water through a perm-selective membrane from a region of higher concentration to a region of lower concentration. The region of lower concentration generally contains solutes in solution and has associated with it an osmotic pressure. It is possible to reverse the normal flow of water through the membrane by applying pressure on the solute side of the membrane in excess of the osmotic pressure. This is reverse osmosis.

Various polymers are used for reverse osmosis membranes; these are cellulosic esters, mixed esters of cellulose with acetate/propionate/butyrate, cellulose triacetate, polyacrylonitrile and its copolymers, polyurethanes, etc. Polymers used for ultrafiltration membranes should be rigid/glassy, should not be detectably softened or plasticized by water, and be relatively insensitive to hydrolytic and/or oxidative degradation in aqueous environments. Examples are polymethyl methacrylate, polyvinyl-chloride, polystyrene, poly acrylonitrile, rigid cellulosic esters. These synthetic membranes are manufactured with considerable control over their physical and chemical properties.

Applied to food concentration, ultrafiltration and reverse osmosis processes involve pumping liquid foods under pressure against perm-selective membranes in a suitable support. Equipment may be similar to pressure filters in design. Filtrates passing through one membrane may be further modified by passing through a second tighter membrane. These membrane permeation processes are being used in concentration of beverages and fruit juices, coffee and tea extracts, emulsions, dairy products; concentration and purification of macro-molecules like proteins and enzymes; desalting of protein solutions; treatment of processing wastes, etc.

Changes during Concentration

Concentration processes that expose food to 100°C or higher temperatures for prolonged periods can cause major changes in organoleptic and nutritional properties. Cooked flavours and darkening of colour are two of the more common results. With most foods the lower the concentration temperature the better, since the reconstituted concentrated food should resemble as closely as possible the natural product. Even at the lowest temperatures, however, concentration can cause other changes that are undesirable. Two such changes involve sugars and proteins.

All sugars have an upper limit of concentration in water beyond which they are not soluble. For example, at room temperature, sucrose is soluble to the extent of about 2 parts sugar in 1 part water. If water is removed beyond this concentration level, the sugar crystallizes out. This can result in gritty, sugary jellies or jams. It also results in a condition knows as "sandiness" in certain milk products when lactose crystallizes due to overconcentration.

As for effects on proteins, it has been pointed out that proteins can be easily denatured and precipitated from solution. One cause of denaturation can be high concentration of salts and minerals in solution with the protein. As protein-containing foods such as milk are concentrated, the levels of milk salts and minerals can become sufficiently high to partially denature the milk protein and cause it to slowly gel.

Microbial destruction, another type of change that may occur during concentration, will be largely dependent on temperature. Concentration at a temperature of 100^0C or slightly above will kill many microorganisms but cannot be depended on to destroy bacterial spores. When the food contains acid, such as fruit juices, the kill will be greater, but again sterility is unlikely. On the other hand, when concentration is done under vacuum, many bacterial species not only survive the low temperatures but multiply in the concentrating equipment. It, therefore, is necessary to stop frequently and sanitize low-temperature evaporators, and where sterile concentrated foods are required, to resort to an additional preservation treatment.

INTERMEDIATE-MOISTURE FOODS (IMF)

Adjustment and control of water activity to preserve semimoist foods has attracted increasing attention. Intermediate-moisture foods or semimoist foods, in one form or another, have been important items of diet for a very long time. Generally, they contain moderate levels of moisture, of the order of 20-50% by weight, which is less than is normally present in natural fruits and vegetables, but more than is left in conventionally dehydrated products. In addition, intermediate-moisture foods contain sufficient dissolved solutes to decrease water activity below that required to support microbial growth. As a consequence, intermediate-moisture foods do not require refrigeration to prevent microbial deterioration. There are various kinds of intermediate-moisture foods: natural products such as honey; manufactured confectionery products high in sugar, jellies, jams, and bakery items such as fruit cakes; and partially dried products including figs, dates etc. In all of these products, preservation is partially from high osmotic pressure associated with the high concentration of solutes; in some, additional preservative effect is contributed by salt, acid, and other specific solutes.

Chapter 15

Freezing of Fruits and Vegetables

F reezing as a preservation method probably was observed by prehistoric people during cold weather; and, until frozen storage cabinets were developed in the late 1800s, naturally occurring snow and ice were used to freeze foods outside. Clarence Birdseye was one of the first to experiment with quick freezing as a way to retain fresh taste and texture. In the 1930s, his products were introduced to U.S. consumers.

With the development of mechanical refrigeration and of quick-freezing techniques, the frozen food industry has expanded rapidly. Even in homes, freezing of foods has now become common because home deep-freezers are readily available. Under the usual conditions of storage of frozen foods microbial growth is prevented completely and the action of food enzymes greatly retarded. The lower the storage temperature the slower will be the rate of a chemical or enzymatic reaction, but most of them will still continue at any temperature. Therefore, it is a common practice to inactivate the enzymes in vegetables by scalding or blanching the latter before freezing, when practicable. Blanching has been discussed in the chapter on "Canning and Bottling of Fruits and Vegetables". The rate of freezing of food depends upon a number of factors such as the method employed, the temperature, circulation of air or refrigerant, size and shape of package, kind of food, etc.

When compared to most other food preservation methods, freezing requires the least amount of food preparation before storage and under optimum conditions it has the best nutrient, flavour, and texture retention. Since food remains microbiologically safe during freezing, its shelf life is determined by chemical and physical changes that occur during storage. Rancidity-oxidative with and without enzyme involvement and tissue damage from ice formation are responsible for most of the quality deterioration in frozen foods. At 0°F (-18°C) fruits can usually retain good quality for 12 months and vegetables for 8-12 months. Increasing storage temperature results in shorter shelf lives. For each 18°F (10°C) increase in temperature, the storage time is approximately cut in half. Sliced foods (increased surface areas), cured foods (low a_w), and fatty foods (rancidity) lose quality more rapidly.

Freezing is cheaper than canning and frozen products are of better quality than canned products, but for storage of frozen products uninterrupted supply of electricity if essential, which is a problem at least in homes.

TECHNOLOGICAL FLOWSHEET FOR PREPARATION OF FRUITS/ VEGETABLES FOR FREEZING

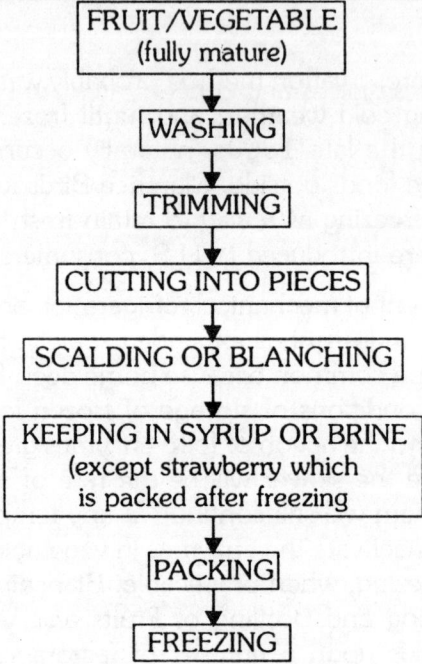

Methods of freezing

There are various methods of freezing:

(1) Sharp freezing (Slow freezing)

This technique, first used in 1861, involves freezing by circulation of air, either naturally or with the aid of fans. The temperature may vary from -15 to −29°C and freezing may take from 3 to 72 hours. The ice crystals formed are large and rupture the cells. The thawed tissue cannot regain its original water content. The first products to be sharp frozen were meat and butter. Nowadays freezer rooms are maintained at -23 to −29°C or even lower, in contrast to the earlier temperature of -18°C.

(2) Quick freezing

In this process the food attains the temperature of maximum ice crystal formation (0 to -4°C) in 30 minutes or less. Such a speed results in formation of very small ice crystals and hence minimum disturbance of cell structure. Most foods are quick frozen by one of the following three methods :

(A) By direct immersion

Since liquids are good heat conductors, food can be frozen rapidly by direct immersion in a liquid such as brine or sugar solution at low temperature. Berries in sugar solution, packed fruit juices and concentrates are frozen in this manner. The refrigeration medium must be edible and capable of remaining unfrozen at −18°C and slightly below. Direct immersion equipments such as Ottesen Brine Freezer, Zarotschenzeff "Fog" Freezer, T.V.A. Freezer, Bartlett Freezer, etc., of commercial importance earlier, are not used today.

Advantages

(i) There is perfect contact between the refrigerating medium and the product, hence the rate of heat transfer is very high.

(ii) Fruits are frozen with a coating of syrup which preserves the colour and flavour during storage.

(iii) The frozen product is not a solid block because each piece is separate.

Disadvantages

(i) Brine is a good refrigerating medium but it cannot be used for fruits.

(ii) It is difficult to make a syrup that will not become viscous at low temperature.

(iii) The refrigeration temperature must be carefully controlled, as at high temperature the medium will enter the product by osmosis and at low temperature the medium may freeze solid.

(iv) It is very difficult to maintain the medium at a definite concentration and also to keep it free from dirt and contamination.

(B) By indirect contact with refrigerant

Indirect freezing may be defined as freezing by contact of the product with a metal surface which is it self cooled by freezing brine or other refrigerating media. This is an old method of freezing in which the food or package is kept in contact with the passage through which the refrigerant at -18 to -46°C flows. Knowles Automatic Package Freezer, Patterson Continuous Plate Freezer, FMC Continuous Can Freezer and Birdseye Freezers are based on this principle.

(C) By air blast (Air blast freezing)

This refers to vigorous circulation of cold air in order to freeze the product. Freezing is done by placing the foodstuffs on trays or on a belt which are then passed slowly through an insulated tunnel containing air in it. Here the air temperature is approximately -18 to -34°C or even lower. This process is economical and a variety of sizes and shapes can be accommodated.

Rapid freezing rates are achieved commercially in a variety of ways. Individually quick frozen vegetables are frozen by blowing cold air (air blast freezing) as vegetables pass through the freezer on a belt or by "tossing" the vegetables with cold air as they pass through the freezer on a mesh screen (fluidized bed freezing). Plate freezing is also used. In this method packaged vegetables are placed on a metal surface that is cooled by refrigerants and another plate may be placed on top of the package. Vegetables frozen by blast methods are in discrete pieces and usually cooked without thawing but solid masses of foods such as pureed squash may be thawed before cooking.

(a) Fluidized bed freeing

This is a modification of air blast freezing. The foodstuff is fluidized to form a bed of particles, and then frozen. Air is forced upward through the belt to partially lift or suspend the particles. If the air is appropriately cooled, drying can be done quite speedily. The depth of the bed of particles varies with the product. Solid food particles of the size of peas upto strawberries can be frozen with a depth of 1 to 5". Peas and whole kernel corn are easily fluidized particles and the bed depth used is slightly more than one inch. Green beans/french beans are partially fluidizable products, and the depth is 8 to 10 inches.

Fluidized bed freezing has certain advantages :

- it gives more sufficient heat transfer and more rapid rates of freezing;
- extent to which the product gets dehydrated is less, and
- defrosting of equipment is required less frequently.

(b) Plate freezing

In this method, food products are placed in contact with a cold surface. The cooling temperature of the metal surface is accomplished by using cold brine or vaporizing refrigerants. This process is suitable for packaged food products which may rest on/slide against or be pressed between cold metal plates. The process is also suitable for unpacked foodstuffs, e.g., shrimps, which can be frozen by freeze-adhesion to a slowly rotating cold drum. Fruit juices can also be frozen in cylindriçal scraped-surface heat exchangers.

Contact-plate freezing is quite economical. It minimizes problems of dehydration, defrosting of equipment and packet bulging.

The advantages claimed for quick freezing over slow freezing (sharp freezing) are : (i) smaller ice crystals are formed, hence there is less mechanical destruction of intact cells of the food, (ii) period for ice formation is shorter, therefore, there is less time for diffusion of soluble material and for separation of ice, (iii) more rapid prevention of microbial growth, and (iv) more rapid slowing down of enzyme action.

(3) Cryogenic freezing

Although most foods retain their quality when quick frozen by the above methods, a few (mushrooms, sliced tomatoes, whole strawberries and raspberries) require ultrafast freezing. Such materials are subjected to cryogenic freezing which is defined as freezing at very low temperature (below -60°C). The refrigerants used at present in cryogenic freezing are liquid nitrogen and liquid carbon dioxide. In the former case, freezing may be achieved by (i) immersion in the liquid, (ii) spraying of liquid, or (iii) circulation of its vapour over the product to be frozen.

(4) Dehydro-freezing

This is a process where freezing is preceded by partial dehydration. In case of some fruits and vegetables about 50 per cent of the moisture is removed by dehydration prior to freezing. This has been found to improve the quality of the food. Dehydration does not cause deterioration and dehydro-frozen foods are relatively more stable.

(5) Freeze-drying

In this process food is first frozen at -18°C on trays in the lower chamber of a freeze drier and the frozen material dried (initially at 30°C for 24 hours and then at 20°C) under high vacuum (0.1 mm Hg) in the upper chamber. Direct sublimation of the ice takes place without passing through the intermediate liquid stage. The product is highly hygroscopic, excellent in taste and flavour and can be reconstituted readily. Mango pulp, orange juice concentrate, passion fruit juice and guava pulp are dehydrated by this method.

Changes during freezing

Quick-freezing rapidly slows down chemical and enzymatic reactions in foods

163

and stops microbial growth. A similar effect is produced by sharp freezing, but less rapidly. The physical effects of freezing are of great importance. There is an expansion in volume of the frozen food and ice crystals form and grow in size. These crystals are larger in slow freezing than in quick freezing and more ice accumulates between tissue cells and may crush the cells. During freezing, water is redistributed in food by the formation of ice crystals. This alters the characteristics of a food upon thawing since separated water usually does not return to its original position. Ice crystals themselves do not preserve the food but in fact damage it. When water changes state from liquid to solid, there is a 9% increase in volume that is responsible for many of the inferior textural characteristics of frozen food. Undesirable texture changes in thawed tomatoes and potatoes are extreme examples. It is claimed that ice crystals rupture fruit and vegetable tissue cells and even microorganisms. The increased concentration of solutes in the cells hastens their salting out, dehydration and denaturation of proteins and causes irreversible changes in colloidal systems, such as the syneresis of hydrophilic coloids. Further, freezing is considered to be responsible for killing microorganisms. The vegetative cells of yeasts and moulds and many Gram-negative bacteria are susceptible, while Gram-positive bacteria including staphylococci and enterococci are moderately resistant, while spores of bacilli and clostridia are insensitive to freezing.

Changes during storage

Chemical and physical reactions that decrease overall quality continue even in foods stored at 0°F (-18°C). The losses that occur during a normal storage period usually exceed any damage that occurs to the food during the initial freezing or thawing.

(A) Physical changes

Fluctuation in storage temperature results in an increase in the size of ice crystals resulting in physical damage to the food.

(i) Recrystallization

Recrystallization is a physical change in which many small ice crystals combine to form a smaller number of large crystals. Temperature fluctuations during storage and longer storage times enhance recrystallization. Recrystallization also occurs in the early stages of thawing where it often damages plant cells that were left intact during the initial freezing process. The end result is decreased quality of products that had been properly frozen. Recrystallization frequently spoils ice cream. Large molecular weight compounds such as gums and modified cellulose may physically inhibit the growth of ice crystals and are added commercially for this reason. Householders add gelatin and fat-cream instead of milk — to reduce recrystallization.

(2) Sublimation

Desiccation of the food at its surface is likely to take place during storage. When water goes from the solid to the gaseous state without passing through the liquid phase as opposed to the way ice would normally melt if placed in a glass of water, it is called sublimation. Freezer burn is caused by sublimation of ice from the surface of the food into the air inside the freezer. Freezer burn can affect the quality so adversely that the food is discarded. Sublimation is possible when the water vapour pressure of the ice is higher than the vapour pressure of the surrounding air. This vapour pressure difference occurs between all frozen foods and the air. The surface of freezer burned food usually appears as dry, grainy and brownish spots where the chemical changes take place and the tissues become dry and tough.

Wrapping to form moisture-proof barriers is the most effective preventive measure for freezer burn. Vapour-resistant materials and tape and containers without excess space reduce the amount of air-to-surface exposure. Foods wrapped in single layers with larger surface area : volume ratios are more susceptible to freezer burn and the accompanying quality loss, though single layers freeze more rapidly so ice crystal size is smaller and more evenly distributed, which is desirable. Perhaps package shape should be determined by expected storage time since ice crystal damage can occur immediately. Freezer burn is more likely to occur with increased lengths of time, so labelling packages with storage dates and keeping a list on the outside of the freezer to aid inventory control reduces the chance of freezer burn.

(3) Denaturation

Protein alterations responsible for a decrease in solubility are collectively known as denaturation. As the ionic concentration increases in freezing, through a reduction in water content, the proteins form bonds with each other instead of water, and insoluble complexes result. This change (protein denaturation) may be responsible for increased toughness in frozen foods.

(B) Chemical changes

Microbial growth ceases at temperatures below 28°F (-2°C) for most foods, but chemical reactions continue in foods even at 0°F (-18°C). Such reactions include lipid oxidation, Maillard and enzymatic browning, flavour deterioration, protein insolubilization, and degradation of chlorophyll and vitamins. Quality changes, not safety (microbial) changes, are the reason for frozen food discard.

When food is placed in the freezer for storage the rates of nonenzyme catalyzed reactions decrease as the temperature is lowered to about 28°F (-2°C). During this time much of the water in the food is in a super cooled state-cooled below freezing, but not yet crystalline ice. As the temperature continues to decrease the reaction rates actually increase until reaching a maximum-often 21 to 18°F (-6 to -8°C). The increased concentration of solutes in the unfrozen portions may be responsible for this occurrence as they are closer to each other for reactions. The rates then decline again with further cooling. Oxidation, including loss of vitamin C and E, goes through such as freeze-induced reaction rate increase. When household freezers fluctuate, they often go from 0°F (-18°C) to 21°F (-6°C) to 28°F (-2°C). With each fluctuation, the quality deteriorates and shelf life is shortened significantly.

Off-odours that develop in frozen foods routinely cause consumer discards. Volatile compounds can accumulate in the tissues during storage which are related to off-odours in thawed raw and cooked vegetables. Off-odours may also be the result of oxidation of lipids. Those due to chemical changes in the food have been described as alfalfalike in green beans and peas, as composted grass in spinach and asparagus, as stale cabbage in brussels sprouts, as cardboard in ice cream (not related to the storage container), and oxidized oil in lima beans.

In unblanched or underblanched vegetables, enzymes remain active during the freezing process, frozen storage itself, and thawing to catalyze reactions that produce off-flavours and off-odours. Enzyme activity may increase or decrease depending on the enzyme as the food chills from 32 to -14°F (0 to -10°C); however temperatures below this result in greatly decreased enzyme activity.

Colour retention in frozen foods is more easily achieved than with canning, but problems still occur. Some colour-degrading reactions are catalyzed by enzymes and some are nonenzymatic. Blanching green vegetables slows the enzyme-catalyzed conversion of chlorophylls a and b (green pigments) to pheophytins (olive green) during frozen storage. This is not, however, a perfect treatment since during blanching heat and acid from the plant tissues also cause a significant amount of this conversion. Blanching at a high temperature, 199-212°F (93-100°C), for a short time of 1-2 minutes causes less chlorophyll conversion than blanching at lower temperatures, 189-194°F (87-90°C), for a longer time of 3-5 minutes. The recommendation to add vegetables to water (or steam) only after it has reached a full rolling boil addresses this phenomenon. Chlorophyll conversion can also occur during frozen storage. The rate is slowed with lower temperatures. Broken plant tissue (cut, bruised) accelerates chlorophyll degradation, thus frozen chopped spinach has poorer quality colour than the whole leaves. When green vegetables are stored for periods longer than 1 year, nonenzymatic oxidation of chloropylls to pheophytin usually occurs. Blanching does not have an affect on this reaction. When dry white sugar is added to strawberries prior to freezing, the anthocyanin pigment (red) becomes more stable and browning reactions are also diminished.

Enzyme-catalyzed oxidative browning also decreases the appearance of frozen food. Raw plant foods such as apples, peaches, pears, yellow cherries, mushrooms potatoes, cauliflower, and beets are particularly affected since their colour shows the defects well. When ice crystals disrupt the cell's natural barriers, the browning enzymes and substrates are free to react. Oxidative browning is most severe near the surface where oxygen is readily available; however, in foods with many intercellular air spaces such as apples, the browning throughout. This oxidative browning can be retarded by heat inactivation of the enzymes, adding antibrowning agents such as ascorbic acid and sulphite to packing syrup, and excluding oxygen.

Ascorbic acid is the most difficult nutrient to preserve in frozen storage because it can be oxidized at low temperatures. This reaction requires oxygen, is catalyzed by enzymes, and its rate is temperature related. The enzymes which catalyze ascorbic acid oxidation can be heat inactivated, but some ascorbic acid continues to be lost with storage. If fruits and vegetables are packaged in oxygen permeable containers such as plastic coated card-board boxes, there is significant loss of ascorbic acid. Foods with lower pH (fruits as opposed to vegetables) and those containing less copper lose less ascorbic acid during storage.

Unfrozen concentrated solution of sugars, salts, etc., may ooz out from fruits or concentrates during storage as a viscous material called "metacryotic liquid."

Chemical changes such as insolubilization or gelation of proteins, lipid oxidation, and degradation of vitamins and pigments occur fairly slowly at 0°F (-18°C), but at faster rates as storage temperature is increased.

Frozen food does not deteriorate from a safety (microbial) standpoint, but the freezing process cannot be counted on to render the food safe to eat if it contained viable microorganisms that can cause foodborne illness. As a general rule, the food should be considered as safe to consume after freezing as it was before freezing. The microbial flora of frozen prepared foods depends upon the microorganisms in the raw ingredients, microorganisms, introduced during manufacturing from equipment surfaces and personnel, the amount of heat treatment before freezing, extent of recontamination before packaging and the conditions of the frozen storage. The occurrence of organisms which can cause foodborne illness in frozen foods that will be consumed without further heating is of special concern. It is variable depending upon all of these factors. Commercial manufacturers that prepare frozen food are subjected to periodic government inspections for sanitation and food safety. Freezing, whether at the commercial or household level, cannot be relied upon to render unsafe food safe; proper handling before and after frozen storage is still needed.

Thawing

Plant and animal tissues and gels-this encompasses most foods-thaw more slowly than they freeze. It takes longer to thaw a food than to freeze it because the heat transfer is by conduction. During freezing, the outer surfaces contain ice crystals first, followed by the center portions. In thawing, the outer portions first change from solid ice to liquid water followed by melting of the central portions. Initially the temperature rise is rapid, but this only occurs before much of the outer surface has changed to the liquid state; most foods remain solid until 23°F. Nonflowable water is a better insulator than ice. A plateau stage follows which is the result of this unflowering water impairing heat transfer. When thawing is done with microwaves, conduction is not the major method of heat transfer and this scenario does not apply.

During thawing, the food passes slowly through temperatures near the melting point where chemical reactions and recrystallization can occur. Thus, there is more opportunity for the quality of the food to be decreased during thawing than freezing. This is particularly the case when householders exercise little care in thawing the food they so carefully blanched, wrapped, and quickly froze. Rapid thawing minimizes recrystallization and limits the time cells are exposed to detrimental concentrations of solutes at high subfreezing temperatures.

Rapid and safe thawing at the household level requires some judgement decisions. A single method is not best for all situations. Thawing cooked foods at room temperature may be more rapid than in the refrigerator, but it may pose a health hazard when the outer portions are warmed beyond safe temperatures. Thawing with microwaves is efficient but often uneven and, because parts may become warm, it should be done just before cooking or serving. Thawing wrapped foods under cool running water is a rapid and safe method, but due to high water waste, it is not commonly used. Placing wrapped foods in still water may not be safe if forgotten. Cooking vegetables directly from the frozen state minimizes thawing changes, but will increase the cooking time. For solid blocks of food, this may result in over-cooking outer layers.

Freezing process for fruits and vegetables

Suitable vegetables : Beans, cauliflower, peas, carrot, etc.

Suitable fruits : Pineapple slices, mango slices or pulp, guava slices and orange segments, etc.

(i) FLOW-SHEET FOR FREEZING OF BEANS

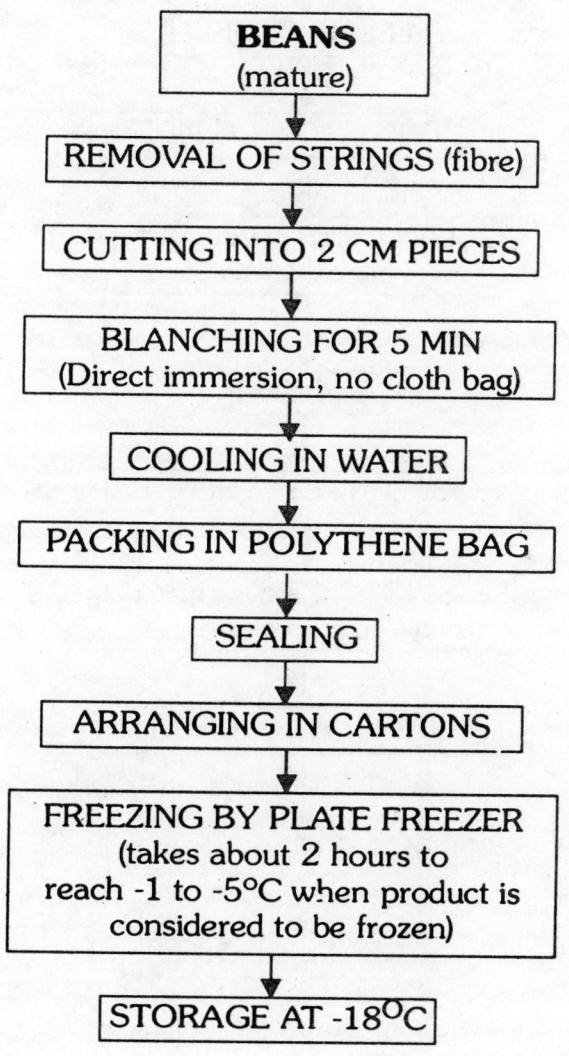

BEANS
(mature)

↓

REMOVAL OF STRINGS (fibre)

↓

CUTTING INTO 2 CM PIECES

↓

BLANCHING FOR 5 MIN
(Direct immersion, no cloth bag)

↓

COOLING IN WATER

↓

PACKING IN POLYTHENE BAG

↓

SEALING

↓

ARRANGING IN CARTONS

↓

FREEZING BY PLATE FREEZER
(takes about 2 hours to
reach -1 to -5°C when product is
considered to be frozen)

↓

STORAGE AT -18°C

(ii) FLOW-SHEET FOR FREEZING OF CARROT

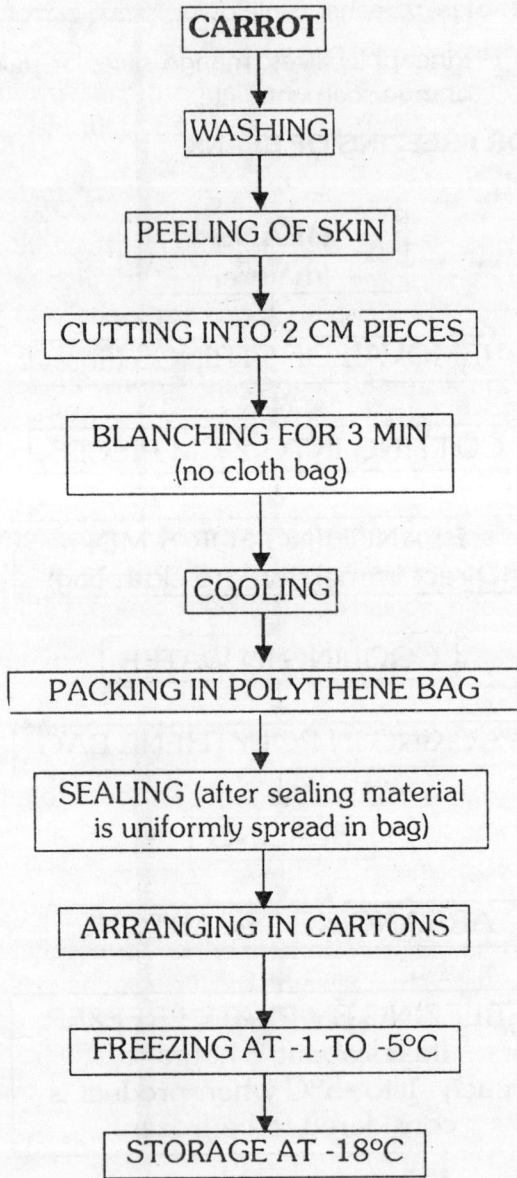

CARROT
↓
WASHING
↓
PEELING OF SKIN
↓
CUTTING INTO 2 CM PIECES
↓
BLANCHING FOR 3 MIN
(no cloth bag)
↓
COOLING
↓
PACKING IN POLYTHENE BAG
↓
SEALING (after sealing material
is uniformly spread in bag)
↓
ARRANGING IN CARTONS
↓
FREEZING AT -1 TO -5°C
↓
STORAGE AT -18°C

(iii) FLOW-SHEET FOR FREEZING OF PEAS

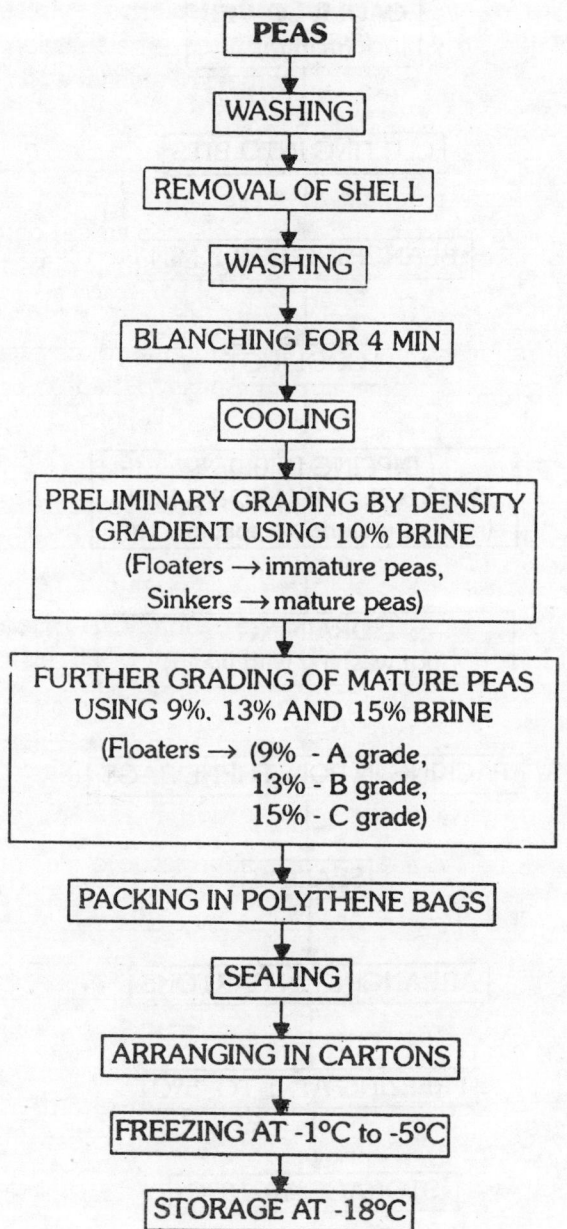

(iv) FLOW-SHEET FOR FREEZING OF CAULIFLOWER

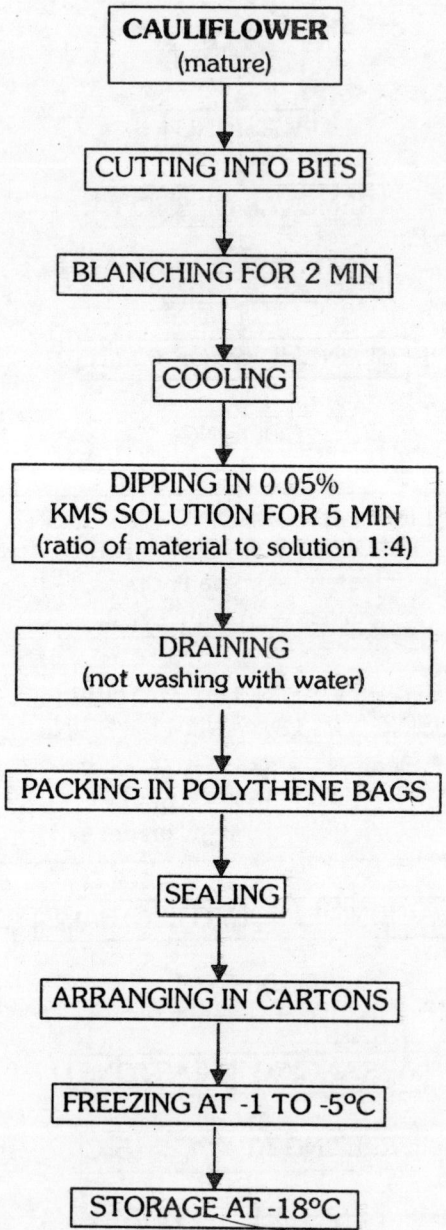

CAULIFLOWER
(mature)

↓

CUTTING INTO BITS

↓

BLANCHING FOR 2 MIN

↓

COOLING

↓

DIPPING IN 0.05%
KMS SOLUTION FOR 5 MIN
(ratio of material to solution 1:4)

↓

DRAINING
(not washing with water)

↓

PACKING IN POLYTHENE BAGS

↓

SEALING

↓

ARRANGING IN CARTONS

↓

FREEZING AT -1 TO -5°C

↓

STORAGE AT -18°C

(v)   FLOW-SHEET FOR GUAVA FREEZING

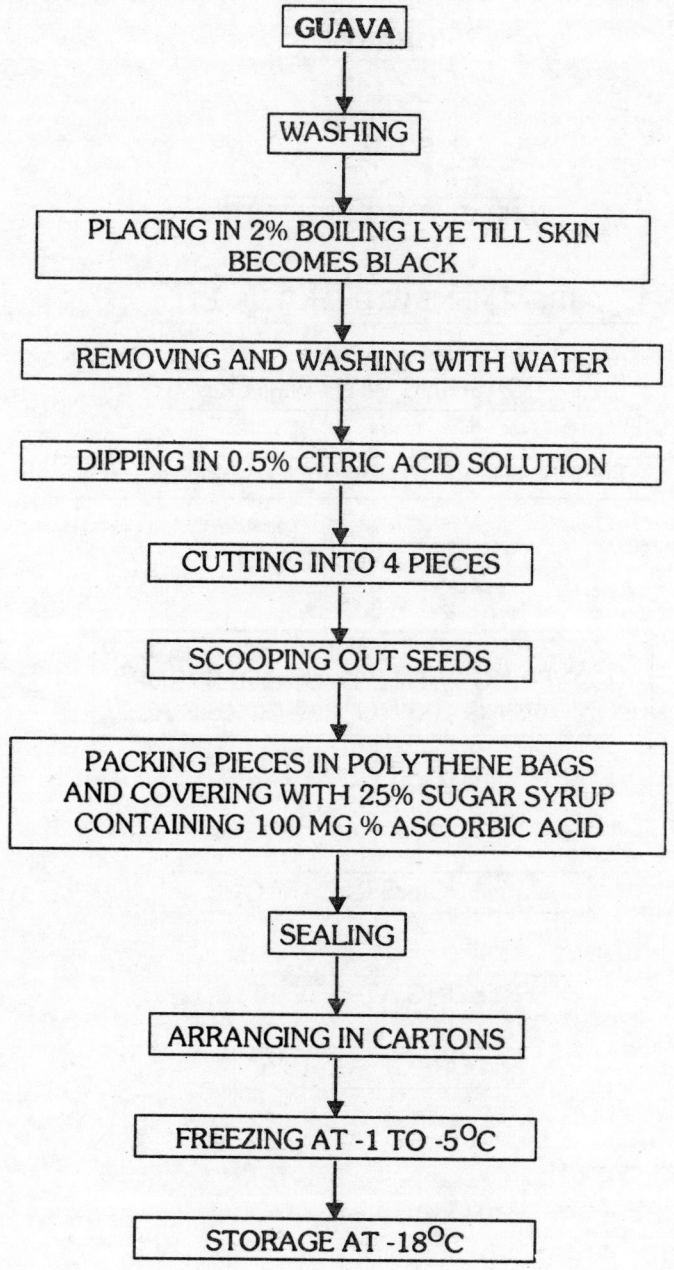

GUAVA

↓

WASHING

↓

PLACING IN 2% BOILING LYE TILL SKIN BECOMES BLACK

↓

REMOVING AND WASHING WITH WATER

↓

DIPPING IN 0.5% CITRIC ACID SOLUTION

↓

CUTTING INTO 4 PIECES

↓

SCOOPING OUT SEEDS

↓

PACKING PIECES IN POLYTHENE BAGS AND COVERING WITH 25% SUGAR SYRUP CONTAINING 100 MG % ASCORBIC ACID

↓

SEALING

↓

ARRANGING IN CARTONS

↓

FREEZING AT -1 TO -5°C

↓

STORAGE AT -18°C

(VI) FLOW-SHEET FOR ORANGE FREEZING

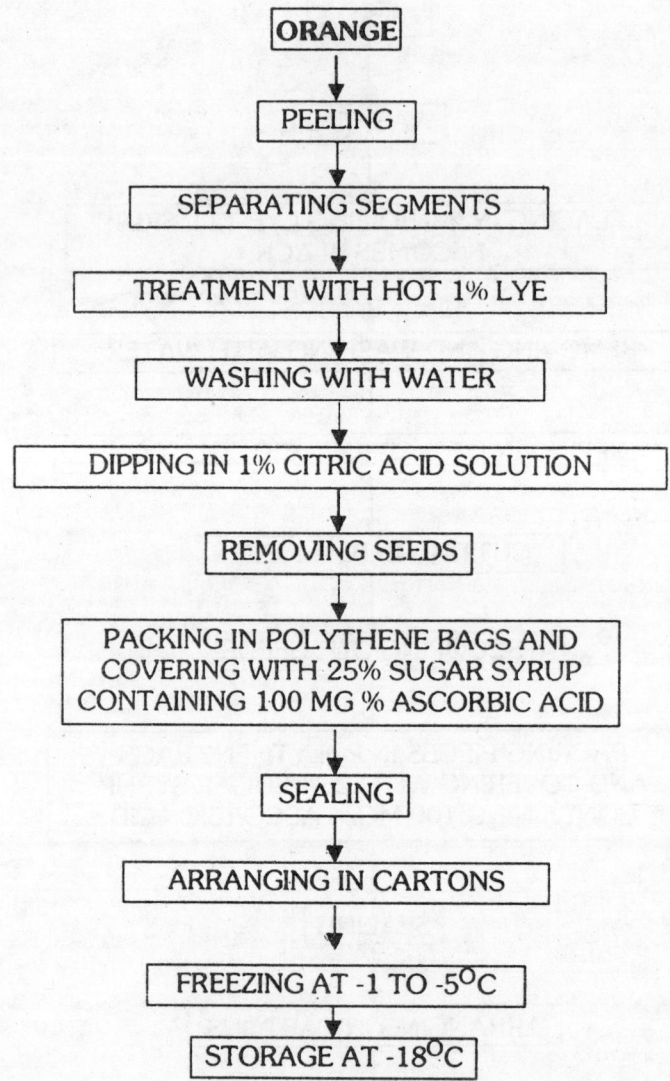

ORANGE

↓

PEELING

↓

SEPARATING SEGMENTS

↓

TREATMENT WITH HOT 1% LYE

↓

WASHING WITH WATER

↓

DIPPING IN 1% CITRIC ACID SOLUTION

↓

REMOVING SEEDS

↓

PACKING IN POLYTHENE BAGS AND
COVERING WITH 25% SUGAR SYRUP
CONTAINING 100 MG % ASCORBIC ACID

↓

SEALING

↓

ARRANGING IN CARTONS

↓

FREEZING AT -1 TO -5°C

↓

STORAGE AT -18°C

Chapter 16

Unfermented and Fermented Fruit Beverages

P roduction of fruit beverages on a commercial scale was practically unknown till about 1930, but since then it has gradually become an important industry. In tropical countries like India, fruit beverages provide delicious cold drinks during the hot summer. Due to their nutritive value they are becoming more popular than synthetic drinks which at present have a very large market in our country.

Synthetic drinks contain only water (about 88%) and total carbohydrates (about 12%) and provide about 48 K-cal, whereas fruit based drinks contain vitamins (A, B and C) and minerals (iron, calcium, etc.) and provide more calories. Thus, fruit-based drinks are far superior to many synthetic drinks. If synthetic preparations are replaced by fruit beverages, it would be a boon to the consumers as well as to the fruit growers.

Fruit beverages

Fruit beverages are easily digestible, highly refreshing, thirst-quenching, appetizing and nutritionally far superior to many synthetic and aerated drinks. They can be classified into two groups:

(A) Unfermented beverages : Fruit juices which do not undergo alcoholic fermentation are termed as Unfermented beverages. They include natural and sweetened juices, RTS (ready-to-serve), nectar, cordial, squash, crush, syrup, fruit juice concentrate and fruit juice powder. Barley waters and carbonated beverages are also included in this group.

(B) Fermented beverages : Fruit juices which have undergone alcoholic fermentation by yeasts include wine, champaigne, port, sherry, tokay, muscat, perry, orange wine, berry wine, nira, and cider.

Preparation and preservation of unfermented fruit beverages

The general process for the preparation and preservation of unfermented fruit beverages is as under:

(i) **Selection of fruit :** All fruits are not suitable because of difficulties in extracting the juice or because the juice is of poor quality. The variety and maturity of the fruit and locality of cultivation influence the flavour and keeping quality of its juice. Only fully ripe fruits are selected. Over-ripe and green fruits, if used, adversely affect the quality of the juice.

(ii) **Sorting and washing :** Diseased, damaged or decayed fruits are re-jected or trimmed. Dirt and spray residues of arsenic, lead, etc., are removed by washing with water or dilute hydrochloric acid (1 part acid: 20 parts water).

(iii) **Juice extraction :** Generally juice is extracted from fresh fruit by crush-ing and pressing them. Screw-type juice extractors, basket presses or fruit pulpers are mostly used.

The method of extraction differs from fruit to fruit because of differences in their structure and composition. Before pressing, most fruits are crushed to facilitate the extraction. Some require heat processing for breaking up the juice-containing tissues. In case of citrus fruits, the fruit is cut into halves and the juice extracted by light pressure in a juice extractor or by pressing the halves in a small wooden juice extractor. Care should be taken to remove the rind of citrus fruits completely otherwise it makes the juice bitter. Finally, the juice is strained through a thick cloth or a sieve to remove seeds. All equipment used in the preparation of fruit juices and squashes should be rust and acid proof. Copper and iron vessels should be strictly avoided as these metals react with fruit acids and cause blackening of the product. Machines and equipments made of aluminium, stainless steel, etc., can be used. Dur-ing extraction juices should not be unnecessarily exposed to air as it will spoil the colour, taste and aroma and also reduce the vitamin content.

(iv) **Deaeration :** Fruit juices contain some air, most of which is present on the surface of the juice and some is dissolved in it. Most of the air as well as other gases are removed by subjecting the fresh juice to a high vacuum. This process is called deaeration and the equipment used for the pur-pose is called a deaerator. Being a very expensive method, it is not used in India at present.

(v) **Straining or filtration :** Fruit juices always contain varying amounts of suspended matter consisting of broken fruit tissue, seed, skin, gums, pectic substances and protein in colloidal suspension. Seeds and pieces of pulp and skin which adversely affect the quality of juice, are removed by straining through a thick cloth or sieve. Removal of all suspended matter improves the appearance but often results in disappearance of fruity character and flavour. The present practice is to let fruit juices and

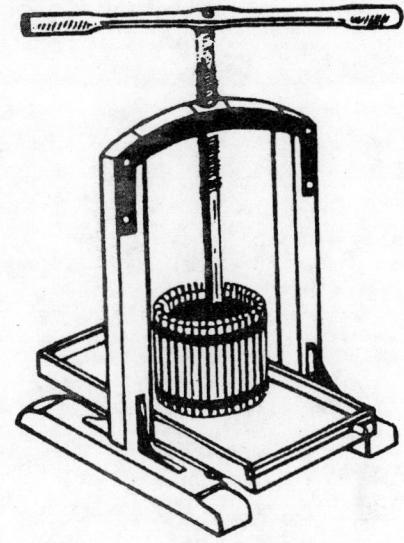

Basket Press

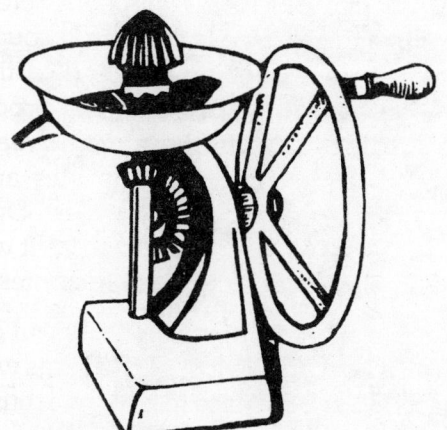

Lime Juice Extractor

Lime Juice Squeezer

beverages retain a cloudy or pulpy appearance to some extent. In case or grape juice, apple juice and lime juice cordial, however, a brilliantly clear appearance is preferred.

(vi) **Clarification :** Complete removal of all suspended material from juice, as in lime juice cordial, is known as clarification which is closely related to the quality, appearance and flavour of the juice. The following methods of clarification are used:

(A) **Settling :** The juice is stored in a carboy or barrel, after adding a chemical preservative to ensure that it does not undergo fermentation, e.g., lime juice is stored for 3 to 6 months for settling with the addition of 700 ppm sulphur dioxide. Colloidal pectins, gums, proteins, mucilaginous solids settle down and the juice is syphoned off for further treatment. However, the process is very slow.

(B) **Filtration :** Filtration is necessary to remove completely all fine and colloidal suspensions. In this process, the juice, after straining, is forced through a filtering medium which may be cotton pulp, wood pulp, woven fibre cloth, etc. The colloidal suspension tends to clog the filter, hence a filter aid is used to reduce clogging. The most important filter aids are supercel, kieselguhr, spanish clay and bentonite, which are added to the extent of 0.1-0.2 per cent. However, a filter aid may impart an unpleasant taste to the juice, therefore, these should be used with caution. Recently, china clay has been demonstrated to be a good filter aid.

(C) **Freezing :** The pasteurized juice kept in a carboy is frozen at -18°C and thereafter stored for 4 to 7 days at room temperature. This is a costly method and is used to some extent only for clarification of grape juice.

(D) **Cold storage :** This is generally used for grape juice. The juice is stored at -2 to -3°C for one month during which the suspended matter settles down and clear juice can then be taken out.

(E) **High temperature :** The juice is heated at 82°C for about a minute when the colloidal material coagulates and settles down. After cooling rapidly, the juice is mixed with a filter aid and passed through a filter press. Pomegranate juice is prepared by this method.

(F) **Chemicals :** Fining agents such as gelatin, albumen, casein, and a mixture of tannin and gelatin, are also used for clarification.

(a) **Gelatin :** It is used for apple and cashew apple juices. On addition of gelatin solution, the colloids present in the juice coagulate and form a flocculent precipitate which settles down. The precipitation is due to electrostatic action between the positively charged gelatin particles and negatively charged colloids (pectins, gums, proteins and mucilaginous substances) in the juice. Recent work indicates that a hydrogen bond is formed between the phenolic group of juice and the peptide group of the gelatin molecule.

(b) Albumen : Solid albumen available in the market is dissolved in warm water to make a 2 per cent solution. A solution of egg-white may also be used. The albumen solution is mixed with the juice, which is heated to about 91°C to ensure complete coagulation of albumen.

(c) Casein : Addition of hydrochloric acid to skimmed milk precipitates casein which is thoroughly washed with water to remove traces of acid, dried and powdered. It is then dissolved in a little liquor ammonia and the solution diluted 10 to 20 times with water and then boiled to remove all traces of ammonia. It is again diluted with water to give a 2 per cent solution which is mixed with the juice. In 24 hours the acids in the juice precipitate the casein which settles down along with other colloidal particles.

(d) Mixture of tannin and gelatin : The tannin-gelatin method is very widely used for clarifying fruit juices. The quality of gelatin to be added is determined by carrying out a preliminary laboratory test. Sufficient tannin is added to minimize the bleaching action of gelatin. About 42 g of tannin and 85 g of gelatin are generally required for every 455 litres of juice. The juice is well stirred, the tannin solution is added to it with stirring and the gelatin solution is then added. The treated juice is allowed to stand undisturbed for 18 to 24 hours to let the suspended matter coagulate and settle down. The clear juice is then syphoned off carefully without disturbing the sediment. In case of lime juice addition of 213 g of tannin and 283 g of gelatin per 2500 litres of juice, preserved by the addition of about 350 ppm of sulphur dioxide, immediately after extraction, gives a sparkling clear product. The colloidal matter settles down completely in 4 to 6 days and the clear supernatant juice can be syphoned off and used for preparation of cordial.

(G) Enzymes : Soluble pectins in the juice are responsible for keeping in suspension other materials such as hemicellulose. When the pectin is destroyed by adding pectic enzyme preparations, e.g., Pectinol and Filtragol, it settles down and during this process also carries down other materials. After filtering, the clear juice is heated to about 77°C for 30 minutes to stop the enzymatic action otherwise the juice becomes cloudy again.

(vii) Addition of sugar : All juices are sweetened by adding sugar, except those of grape and apple. Sugar also acts as preservative for the flavour and colour and prolongs the keeping quality. Sugar-based products can be divided into three groups on the basis of sugar content:

(a) Low Sugar - 30 per cent sugar or below,

(b) Medium sugar - Sugar above 30 and below 50 per cent,

(c) High Sugar - 50 per cent sugar and above.

Sugar can be added directly to the juice or as a syrup made by dissolving it in hot water, clarifying by addition of a small quantity of citric acid or few drops of lime juice and filtering.

(viii) Fortification : Juices, squashes, syrups, etc., are sometimes fortified with vitamins to enhance their nutritive value, to improve taste, texture or colour and to replace nutrients lost in processing. Usually ascorbic acid and beta-carotene (water-soluble form) are added at the rate of 250 to 500 mg and 7 to 10 mg per litre, respectively. Ascorbic acid acts as an antioxidant and beta-carotene imparts an attractive orange colour. For a balanced taste some acids are added. Citric acid is often used for all types of beverages and phosphoric acid for cola type of drinks.

(ix) Preservation : Fruit juices, RTS and nectars are preserved by pasteurization but sometimes chemical preservatives are used. Squashes, crushes and cordials are preserved only by adding chemicals. In the case of syrup, the sugar concentration is sufficient to prevent spoilage. Fruit juice concentrates are preserved by heating, freezing or adding chemicals. The details regarding methods or preservation are given in the chapter on 'Principles and Methods of Preservation'.

(x) Bottling : Bottles are thoroughly washed with hot water and filled leaving 1.5-2.5 cm head space. They are then sealed either with crown corks (by crown corking machine) or with caps (by capping machine).

Unfermented Beverages

(1) Juices : Juices are of two types -

(a) Natural juice (pure juice) : It is the juice, as extracted from ripe fruits, and contains only natural sugars.

(b) Sweetened juice : It is a liquid product which contains at least 85 per cent juice and 10 per cent total soluble solids.

Pure fruit juices, such as apple juice and orange juice are commercially manufactured in several countries. Apple juice is generally bottled while other juices are canned. The techniques for preparation of various fruit juices are given as follows:

179

(i) Apple juice

FLOW-SHEET FOR PROCESSING OF APPLE JUICE

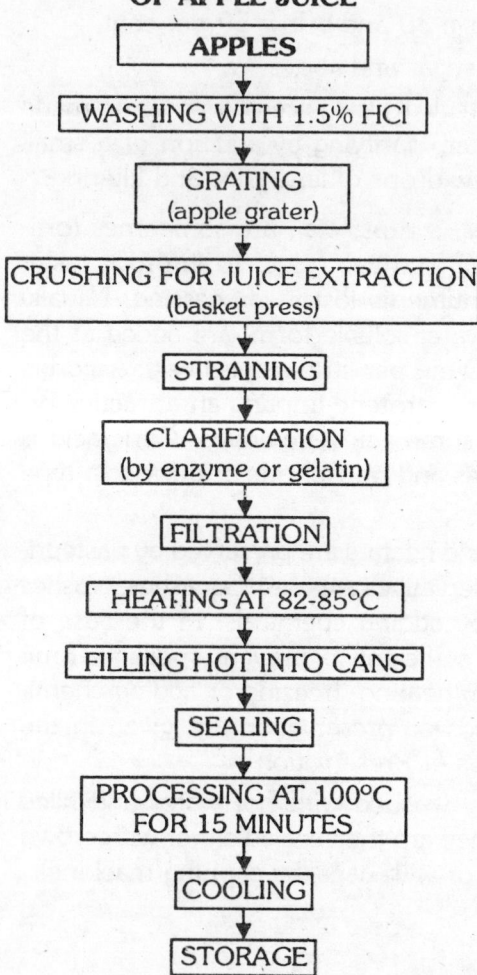

APPLES

↓

WASHING WITH 1.5% HCl

↓

GRATING
(apple grater)

↓

CRUSHING FOR JUICE EXTRACTION
(basket press)

↓

STRAINING

↓

CLARIFICATION
(by enzyme or gelatin)

↓

FILTRATION

↓

HEATING AT 82-85°C

↓

FILLING HOT INTO CANS

↓

SEALING

↓

PROCESSING AT 100°C
FOR 15 MINUTES

↓

COOLING

↓

STORAGE

(ii) Grape juice

FLOW-SHEET FOR PROCESSING OF GRAPE JUICE

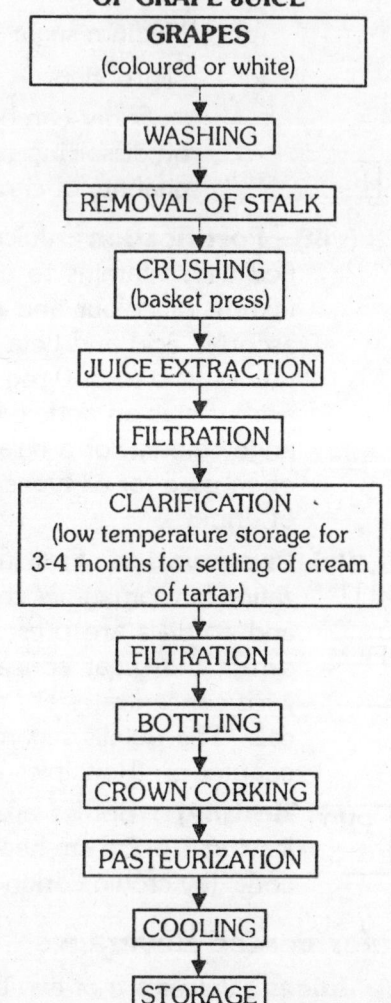

GRAPES
(coloured or white)

↓

WASHING

↓

REMOVAL OF STALK

↓

CRUSHING
(basket press)

↓

JUICE EXTRACTION

↓

FILTRATION

↓

CLARIFICATION
(low temperature storage for
3-4 months for settling of cream
of tartar)

↓

FILTRATION

↓

BOTTLING

↓

CROWN CORKING

↓

PASTEURIZATION

↓

COOLING

↓

STORAGE

Note : *In case of coloured grapes, it is necessary to heat the crushed fruit at 60-65°C for 10 to 15 minutes to extract the colouring matter. The juice can also be preserved by adding sodium benzoate. Addition of sulphur dioxide is not recommended as it imparts a bitter taste to the juice.*

(iii) Pineapple juice

**FLOW-SHEET FOR
PROCESSING OF
PINEAPPLE JUICE**

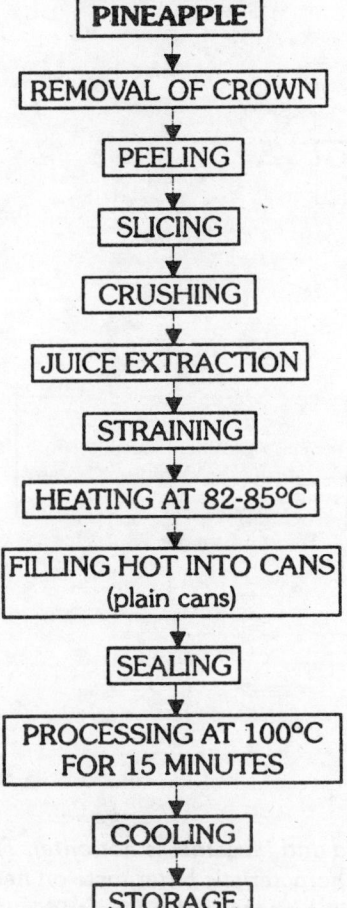

| PINEAPPLE |
| REMOVAL OF CROWN |
| PEELING |
| SLICING |
| CRUSHING |
| JUICE EXTRACTION |
| STRAINING |
| HEATING AT 82-85°C |
| FILLING HOT INTO CANS (plain cans) |
| SEALING |
| PROCESSING AT 100°C FOR 15 MINUTES |
| COOLING |
| STORAGE |

(iv) Pomegranate juice

**FLOW-SHEET FOR
PROCESSING OF
POMEGRANATE JUICE**

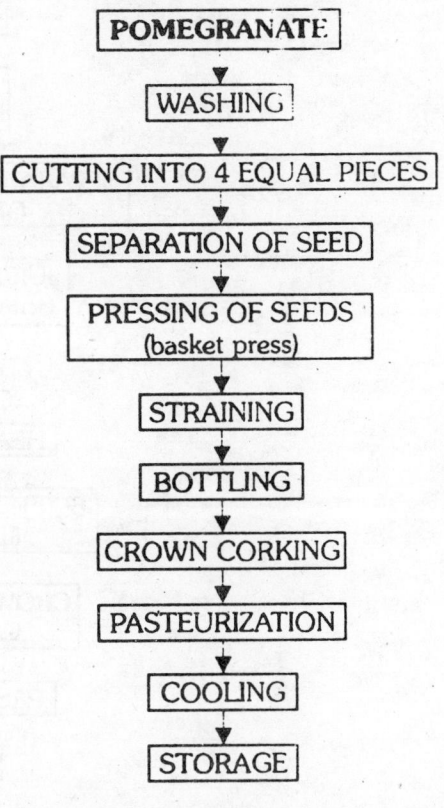

| POMEGRANATE |
| WASHING |
| CUTTING INTO 4 EQUAL PIECES |
| SEPARATION OF SEED |
| PRESSING OF SEEDS (basket press) |
| STRAINING |
| BOTTLING |
| CROWN CORKING |
| PASTEURIZATION |
| COOLING |
| STORAGE |

Note : *Pomegranate juice can also be preserved by addition of sodium benzoate.*

(v) Citrus juice

FLOW-SHEET FOR PROCESSING OF CITRUS JUICE

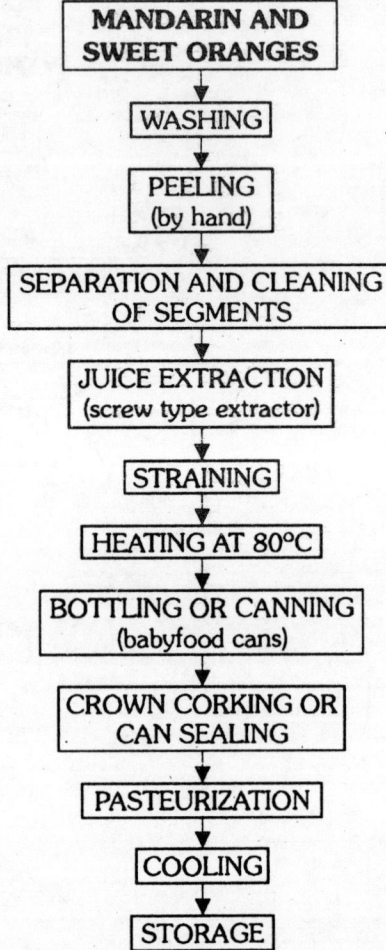

Note : *Canned juice of sweet oranges such as Malta and Mosambi is not bitter. The juice from mandarin orange, however, often develops a characteristic bitter taste on heating the can or bottle. This bitterness is due to the limonin present in the juice and is not acceptable.*

The bitterness can be reduced considerably by dipping the segments in 2% boiling NaOH for 2-3 minutes to remove their adhering outer covering and fibrous material which cause bitterness, before extraction of juice. Addition of 5-6 per cent sugar also helps in reducing the bitter taste. Other important precautions for reducing the bitterness are (i) selection of fully ripe fruits only, (ii) hot water treatment prior to peeling or cutting of fruits, and (iii) avoiding excess pressure during extraction.

To improve its quality and preserve the vitamin C content, the juice is generally deaerated and flash pasteurized. Preservation of pure orange juice with all its natural flavour is still a technical problem.

(vi) Mango juice

FLOW-SHEET FOR PROCESSING OF MANGO JUICE

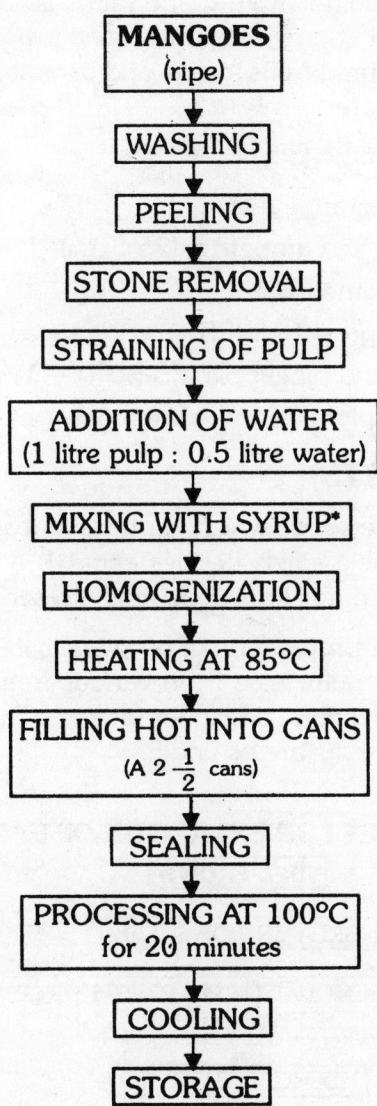

MANGOES
(ripe)

↓

WASHING

↓

PEELING

↓

STONE REMOVAL

↓

STRAINING OF PULP

↓

ADDITION OF WATER
(1 litre pulp : 0.5 litre water)

↓

MIXING WITH SYRUP*

↓

HOMOGENIZATION

↓

HEATING AT 85°C

↓

FILLING HOT INTO CANS
(A 2 $\frac{1}{2}$ cans)

↓

SEALING

↓

PROCESSING AT 100°C
for 20 minutes

↓

COOLING

↓

STORAGE

*Note : Syrup is prepared by dissolving 200 g of sugar and 1 g of citric acid in 800 ml of water (for 1 kg pulp). Commercially the juice is adjusted to 15% TSS and 0.3% acidity. Prepared juice can also be bottled and crown corked before pasteurization.

(vii) Blended juices

Sometimes two or more juices are mixed to yield a well-balanced, rightly flavoured, highly palatable and refreshing drink. Juices are blended so as to utilize a too sweet fruit (grape), a bitter fruit (grapefruit), too acidic or tart fruits (sour lime, sour plum, galgal, sour cherry, etc.), bland and insipid tasting fruits like pear or apple, and strongly flavoured fruits (guava and banana). Some of the common commercial blends of juice are:

(1) Grape (97%) and lime (3%)

(2) Grape (50%) and orange (50%)

(3) Orange (50-75%) and grapefruit (25-50%)

(4) ·Apple (97%) and lime (3%)

(5) Apple (74%) and grapefruit (25%) + 1% sugar

(6) Apple (50-75%) and pineapple (25-50%) + 1% sugar

(7) Apple (37%) and plum (62%) + 1% sugar

(2) Ready-to-serve (RTS)

This is a type of fruit beverage which contains at least 10 per cent fruit juice and 10 per cent total soluble solids besides about 0.3 per cent acid. It is not diluted before serving, hence it is known as ready-to-serve (RTS).

Before undertaking the preparation of beverages, it is necessary to know the techniques of extraction of pulp/juice from various fruits used for RTS, nectar, squash, syrup, etc. The extraction techniques for some fruits have been described earlier and for some other fruits are as under.

(i) Bael

FLOW-SHEET FOR EXTRACTIN OF BAEL PULP

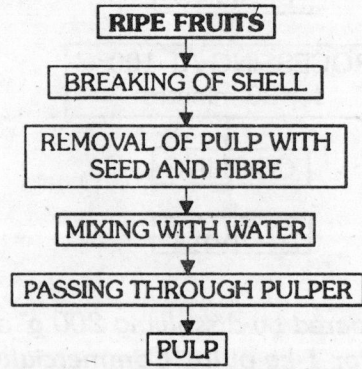

RIPE FRUITS
↓
BREAKING OF SHELL
↓
REMOVAL OF PULP WITH SEED AND FIBRE
↓
MIXING WITH WATER
↓
PASSING THROUGH PULPER
↓
PULP

Note : *Pulp can also be obtained by heating the mixture of pulp and water a little, followed by straining through a thick cloth.*

184

(ii) Guava

FLOW-SHEET FOR EXTRACTIN OF GUAVA PULP

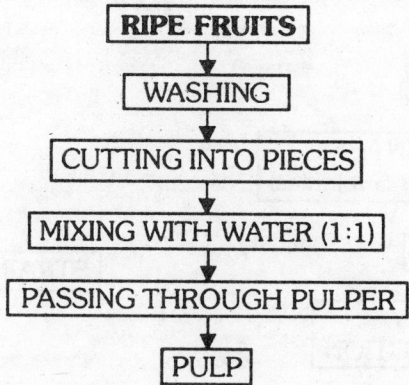

```
RIPE FRUITS
    ↓
  WASHING
    ↓
CUTTING INTO PIECES
    ↓
MIXING WITH WATER (1:1)
    ↓
PASSING THROUGH PULPER
    ↓
   PULP
```

Note: *Pulp can also be obtained by grinding the pieces finely with water in a grinder followed by straining through thick cloth.*

(iii) Jamun

FLOW-SHEET FOR EXTRACTION OF JAMUN JUICE

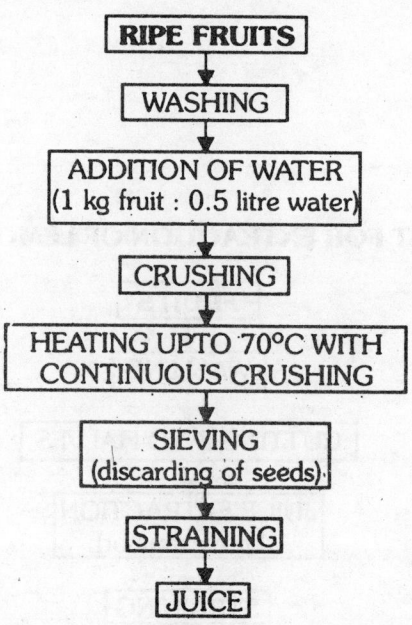

```
RIPE FRUITS
    ↓
  WASHING
    ↓
ADDITION OF WATER
(1 kg fruit : 0.5 litre water)
    ↓
  CRUSHING
    ↓
HEATING UPTO 70°C WITH
CONTINUOUS CRUSHING
    ↓
   SIEVING
(discarding of seeds)
    ↓
  STRAINING
    ↓
   JUICE
```

(iv) Aonla

FLOW-SHEET FOR EXTRACTION OF AONLA PULP AND JUICE

(a)   **(b)**

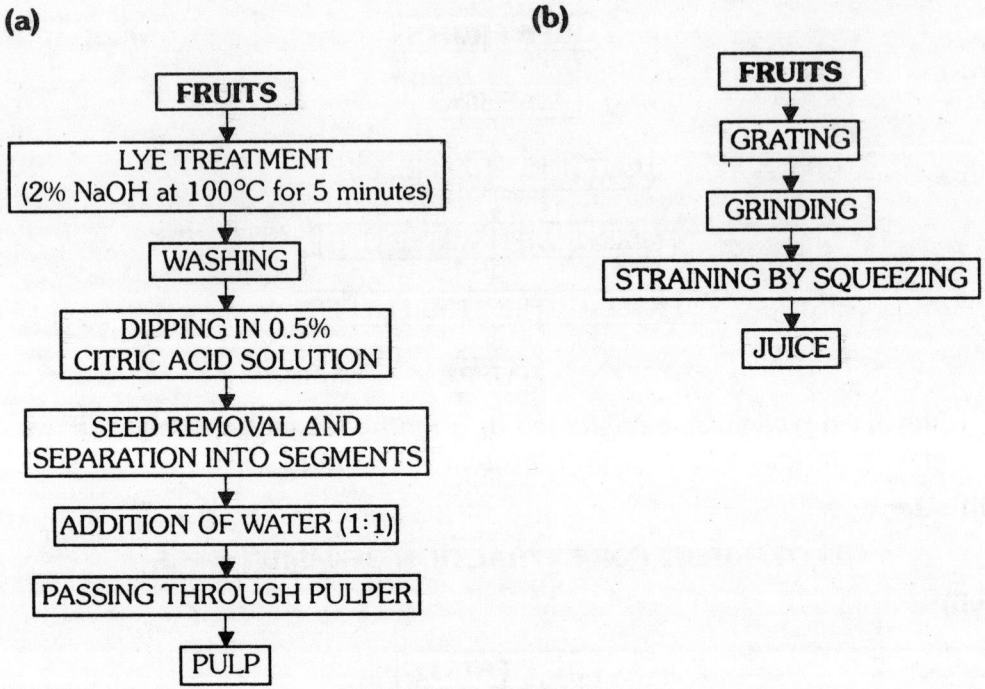

(v) Lemon / Lime

FLOW-SHEET FOR EXTRACTION OF LEMON/LIME JUICE

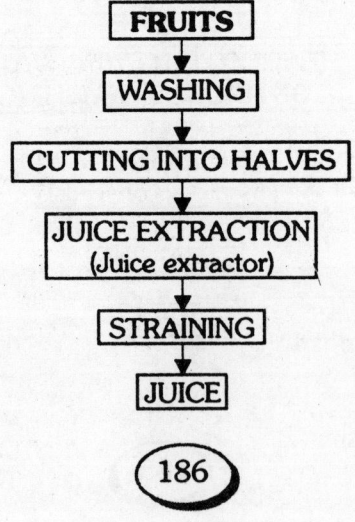

(vi) Karonda, Phalsa and Plum

FLOW-SHEET FOR EXTRACTION OF KARONDA, PHALSA AND PLUM JUICE

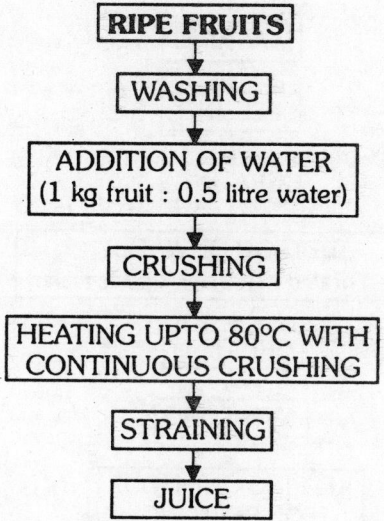

RIPE FRUITS
↓
WASHING
↓
ADDITION OF WATER
(1 kg fruit : 0.5 litre water)
↓
CRUSHING
↓
HEATING UPTO 80°C WITH CONTINUOUS CRUSHING
↓
STRAINING
↓
JUICE

(vii) Papaya

FLOW-SHEET FOR EXTRACTION OF PAPAYA PULP

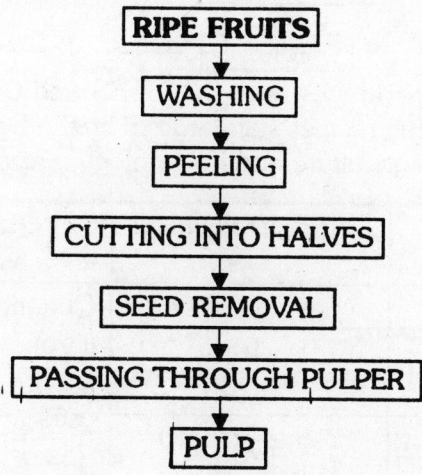

RIPE FRUITS
↓
WASHING
↓
PEELING
↓
CUTTING INTO HALVES
↓
SEED REMOVAL
↓
PASSING THROUGH PULPER
↓
PULP

Note : *Papaya pulp can also be obtained by crushing finely and straining.*

(viii) Ginger

FLOW-SHEET FOR EXTRACTION OF GINGER JUICE

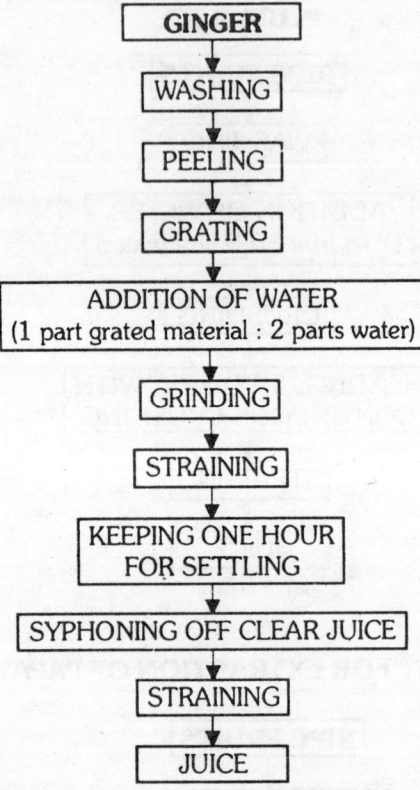

```
        ┌─────────────────┐
        │     GINGER      │
        └─────────────────┘
                 ↓
        ┌─────────────────┐
        │    WASHING      │
        └─────────────────┘
                 ↓
        ┌─────────────────┐
        │    PEELING      │
        └─────────────────┘
                 ↓
        ┌─────────────────┐
        │    GRATING      │
        └─────────────────┘
                 ↓
   ┌──────────────────────────────┐
   │      ADDITION OF WATER       │
   │(1 part grated material : 2 parts water)│
   └──────────────────────────────┘
                 ↓
        ┌─────────────────┐
        │    GRINDING     │
        └─────────────────┘
                 ↓
        ┌─────────────────┐
        │    STRAINING    │
        └─────────────────┘
                 ↓
   ┌──────────────────────────────┐
   │      KEEPING ONE HOUR        │
   │        FOR SETTLING          │
   └──────────────────────────────┘
                 ↓
   ┌──────────────────────────────┐
   │  SYPHONING OFF CLEAR JUICE   │
   └──────────────────────────────┘
                 ↓
        ┌─────────────────┐
        │    STRAINING    │
        └─────────────────┘
                 ↓
        ┌─────────────────┐
        │     JUICE       │
        └─────────────────┘
```

Commercially RTS beverages (with 13% TSS and 0.3% acid) can be prepared by using the following recipes standardized by the Department of Horticulture, N.D. University of Agriculture and Technology, Faizabad.

S. No.	Fruit	Juice/Pulp (%)	Quantity of water required (litre)
1	Bael	10	Quantity of finished product (litre) - Quantity of [Juice (litre) + sugar (kg) + acid (kg)] used
2	Lemon/Lime	10	
3	Guava	10	
4	Aonla (blend)	Aonla pulp 10 Lime juice 2 Ginger juice 1	
5	Mango	10	
6	Ginger	2.5	

For preparing the beverages the total soluble solids in the pulp/juice and its acidity are first determined and then requisite amounts of sugar and citric acid dissolved in water are added for adjustment of TSS and acidity.

In homes, RTS can be prepared by using the following recipes:

S. No.	Fruit	Juice (litre)	Sugar (kg)	Citric acid (g)	Water (litre)
1	Bael	1.0	1.20	28	7.7
2	Lemon/Lime	0.5	1.30		8.2
3.	Guava	1.0	1.25	28	7.7
4.	Aonla blend (10 part aonla juice : 2 part lime juice : 1 part ginger juice)	1.3	1.60	22	10.0
5	Mango	1.0	1.25	28	7.7
6	Ginger	0.25	1.30	30	8.4

FLOW-SHEET FOR PROCESSING OF RTS BEVERAGES

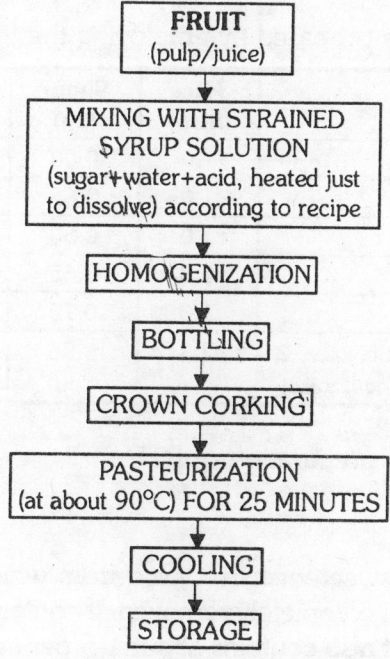

FRUIT
(pulp/juice)

↓

MIXING WITH STRAINED SYRUP SOLUTION
(sugar+water+acid, heated just to dissolve) according to recipe

↓

HOMOGENIZATION

↓

BOTTLING

↓

CROWN CORKING

↓

PASTEURIZATION
(at about 90°C) FOR 25 MINUTES

↓

COOLING

↓

STORAGE

(3) Nectar

This type of fruit beverage contains at least 20 per cent fruit juice/pulp and 15 per cent total soluble solids and also about 0.3 per cent acid. It is not diluted before serving.

Commercially, nectar (with 13% TSS and 0.3% acid) can be prepared by using the following recipes standardized by Department of Horticulture, N.D. University of Agriculture and Technology, Faizabad.

S. No.	Fruit	Juice/Pulp (%)	Quantity of water required (litre)
1	Mango	20	Quantity of finished product (litre)–Quantity of [juice (litre) + sugar (kg) + acid (kg)] used
2	Papaya	20	
3	Guava	20	
4	Bael	20	
5	Jamun	20	
6	Aonla (blend)	Aonla pulp 20 Lime juice 2 Ginger juice 1	

For preparing the above beverages the total soluble solids and total acid present in the pulp/juice are first determined and then the requisite amounts of sugar and citric acid dissolved in water are added for adjustment of TSS and acidity.

In homes, nectar can be prepared by employing the following recipes:

S. No.	Fruit	Juice (litre)	Sugar (kg)	Citric acid (g)	Water (litre)
1	Mango	1.0	0.60	13	3.3
2	Papaya	1.0	0.65	13	3.3
3	Guava	1.0	0.60	13	3.3
4	Bael	1.0	0.65	15	3.3
5	Jamun	1.0	0.70	7	3.3
6	Aonla blend (20 part aonla juice, 2 part lime juice, 1 part ginger juice)	2.3	1.35	4	7.8

Process : Similar to that of preparation of RTS.

(4) Cordial

It is a sparkling, clear, sweetened fruit juice from which pulp and other in-soluble substances have been completely removed. It contains at least 25 per cent juice and 30 per cent TSS. It also contains about 1.5 per cent acid and 350 ppm of sulphur dioxide. This is very suitable for blending with wines.

Lime and lemon are suitable for making cordial. In homes, cordial can be prepared using the following recipe:

Lime/Lemon juice	- 1.0 litre
Sugar	- 1.25 kg
Water	- 1.0 litre
Potassium metabisulphite	- 2.0 g

FLOW-SHEET FOR PROCESSING OF CORDIAL

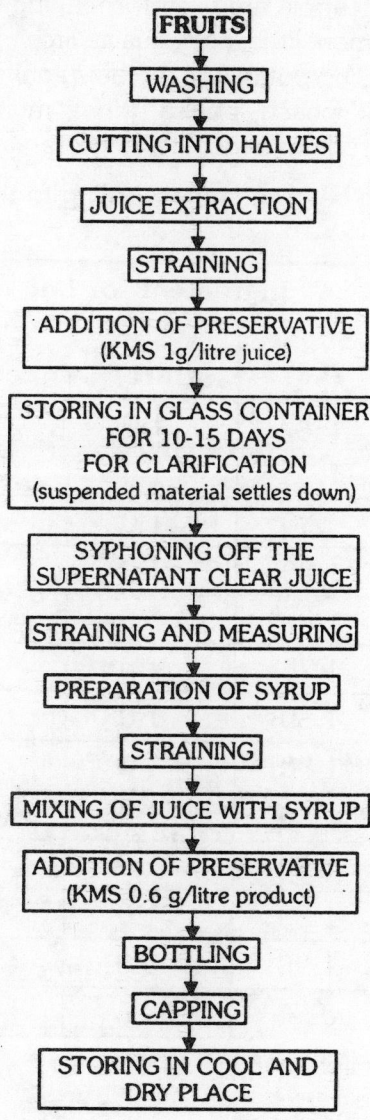

FRUITS
↓
WASHING
↓
CUTTING INTO HALVES
↓
JUICE EXTRACTION
↓
STRAINING
↓
ADDITION OF PRESERVATIVE
(KMS 1g/litre juice)
↓
STORING IN GLASS CONTAINER
FOR 10-15 DAYS
FOR CLARIFICATION
(suspended material settles down)
↓
SYPHONING OFF THE
SUPERNATANT CLEAR JUICE
↓
STRAINING AND MEASURING
↓
PREPARATION OF SYRUP
↓
STRAINING
↓
MIXING OF JUICE WITH SYRUP
↓
ADDITION OF PRESERVATIVE
(KMS 0.6 g/litre product)
↓
BOTTLING
↓
CAPPING
↓
STORING IN COOL AND
DRY PLACE

Note : *Juice can also be clarified by tannin-gelatin mixture. This process has been discussed earlier under 'Clarification of juices'.*

191

5. Squash

This is a type of fruit beverage containing at least 25 per cent fruit juice or pulp and 40 to 50 per cent total soluble solids, commercially. It also contains about 1.0 per cent acid and 350 ppm sulphur dioxide or 600 ppm sodium benzoate. It is diluted before serving.

Mango, orange and pineapple are used for making squash commercially. It can also be prepared from lemon, lime, bael, guava, litchi, pear, apricot, pummelo, musk melon, papaya, etc., using potassium metabisulphite (KMS) as preservative, or from jamun, passion-fruit, peach, phalsa, plum, mulberry, raspberry, strawberry, grapefruit, etc., with sodium benzoate as preservative.

In homes, squashes can be prepared according to the following recipes:

S. No.	Fruit	Ingredient for one litre pulp/juice			
		Sugar (kg)	Water (litre)	Citric acid (g)	Preservative (g)
1	Orange*	1.75	1.0	20	2.5 KMS
2	Mango	1.75	1.0	20	2.5 KMS
3	Lime, Lemon	2.0	1.0	-	2.5 KMS
4	Bael	1.80	1.0	25	2.5 KMS
5	Litchi	1.80	1.0	25	2.25 KMS
6	Pineapple	1.75	1.0	20	1.9 KMS
7	Guava	1.80	1.0	20	2.0 KMS
8	Papaya	1.80	1.0	25	2.5 KMS
9	Karonda	1.80	1.0	5	4.0 SB
10	Phalsa	1.80	1.0	5	4.0 SB
11	Jamun	1.80	1.0	15	3.0 SB
12	Plum	1.90	1.0	10	4.0 SB
13	Water melon	0.50	0.25	10	1.5 SB
KMS= Potassium metabisulphite					
SB= Sodium benzoate					

* TECHNOLOGICAL FLOW-SHEET FOR REMOVAL OF ASTRINGENCY FROM ORANGE JUICE

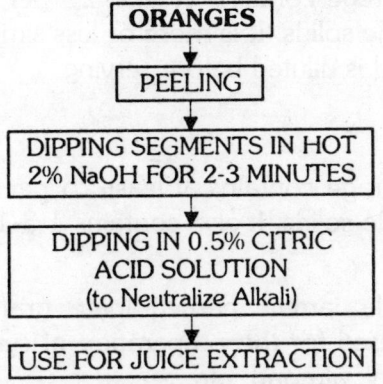

```
ORANGES
   ↓
PEELING
   ↓
DIPPING SEGMENTS IN HOT
2% NaOH FOR 2-3 MINUTES
   ↓
DIPPING IN 0.5% CITRIC
ACID SOLUTION
(to Neutralize Alkali)
   ↓
USE FOR JUICE EXTRACTION
```

FLOW-SHEET FOR PROCESSING OF SQUASH

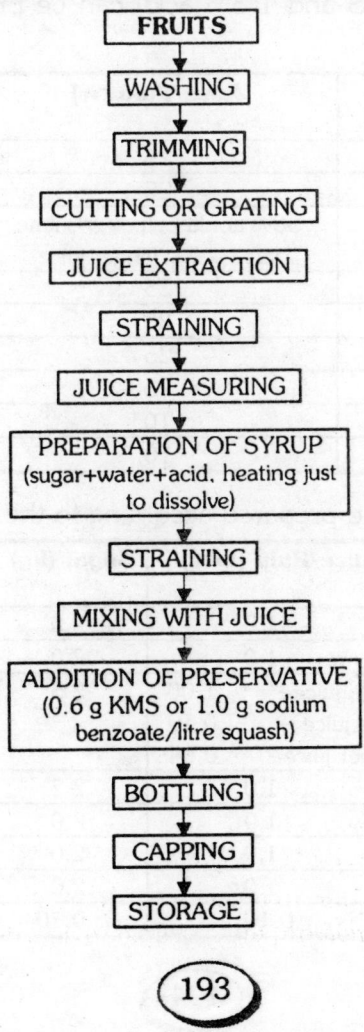

```
FRUITS
   ↓
WASHING
   ↓
TRIMMING
   ↓
CUTTING OR GRATING
   ↓
JUICE EXTRACTION
   ↓
STRAINING
   ↓
JUICE MEASURING
   ↓
PREPARATION OF SYRUP
(sugar+water+acid, heating just
to dissolve)
   ↓
STRAINING
   ↓
MIXING WITH JUICE
   ↓
ADDITION OF PRESERVATIVE
(0.6 g KMS or 1.0 g sodium
benzoate/litre squash)
   ↓
BOTTLING
   ↓
CAPPING
   ↓
STORAGE
```

(6) Crush

This type of fruit beverage contains at least 25 per cent fruit juice or pulp and 55 per cent total soluble solids. It is more or less similar to squash, contains about 1.0 per cent acid and is diluted before serving.

(7) Syrup

This type of fruit beverage contains at least 25 per cent fruit juice or pulp and 65 per cent total soluble solids. It also contains 1.3-1.5 per cent acid and is diluted before serving.

Fruits like phalsa, aonla, jamun, pomegranate, grape, lemon, orange and sometimes ginger can be used for the preparation of syrup. It is also prepared from extracts of rose, sandal, almond, etc.

Syrups (with 68% TSS and 1.3% acid) can be prepared commercially by using the following recipes:

S. No.	Fruit	Juice/Pulp (%)	Quantity of water required (litre)
1	Phalsa	25	Quantity of finished product (litre) − Quantity of [Juice (litre) + sugar (kg) + acid (kg)] used
2	Jamun	25	
3	Aonla (blend)	50% aonla pulp + 5% lime juice + 2% ginger juice	
4	Grape	25	
5	Pomegranate	25	
6	Lemon	25	
7	Orange	25	
8	Ginger	10	
9	Rose extract	10	

In homes, syrup can be prepared according to the following recipes:

S. No.	Fruit	Juice/Pulp (litre)		Sugar (kg)	Water (litre)	Citric acid (g)
1	Phalsa	1.0		2.0	0.50	10
2	Jamun	1.0		2.0	0.50	15
3	Aonla (blend)	Aonla juice -	1.00	2.5	0.50	5
		Lime juice -	0.10			
		Ginger juice -	0.04			
4	Grape	1.0		2.2	0.50	5
5	Pomegranate	1.0		2.0	0.50	5
6	Lemon	1.0		2.0	0.50	-
7	Orange	1.0		2.0	0.50	10
8	Ginger	0.10		0.70	0.20	15

Syrup from extracts

Syrups containing extracts of rose, sandal, kewra, mint, khus, almond, etc.. are very popular. The preparation of some of these syrups is described below·

(i) **Rose syrup :** Clean rose petals (100 g) are soaked overnight in about 200 ml. of water, then well rubbed, heated for about 5 minutes and strained. The syrup is prepared by using 100 ml of rose extract, 700 g of sugar, 10 g of citric acid and 250 ml of water. Sometimes raspberry red colour and rose water are also added.

(ii) **Sandal syrup:** Sandalwood powder (50 g) is soaked overnight in about 250 ml of water, then heated for about 5 minutes and strained. The syrup is prepared by using the extract, 1.3 kg of sugar, 400 ml of water, and 10 g of citric acid. Sometimes Kewra essence is also added.

(iii) **Almond syrup:** Almond kernels (50 g) are soaked in 200 ml of hot water for some time, the loosened skin is removed and the kernels are ground with 10 g of cardamom (small) and the juice is strained. Syrup is prepared by using above extract, 1.3 kg of sugar, 10 g of citric acid and 350 ml of water. Sometimes kewra or rose essence is added as required.

Synthetic syrups

Heavy sugar syrup of 70-75 per cent strength is used as the base of all synthetic syrups and they are flavoured and coloured with artificial essence/flavours and colours. They never contain fruit pulp/juice. A large proportion of these syrups can, however, be replaced by real fruit juices, squashes and syrups which are more nutritious.

Large quantities of synthetic syrups (orange, lemon, pineapple, raspberry, strawberry, khus, kewra, etc.) are manufactured and sold in various countries. These can be prepared by using 1.5 kg of sugar, 500 ml of water and 15 g of citric acid. Different colours and flavours are added as required. Among colours, orange red, lemon yellow, green, raspberry red, etc., are mostly used, while artificial essence/flavours of rose, kewra, orange, pineapple, strawberry, lemon, etc.. are added as flavouring substances.

TECHNOLOGICAL FLOW-SHEET FOR SYRUP PROCESSING

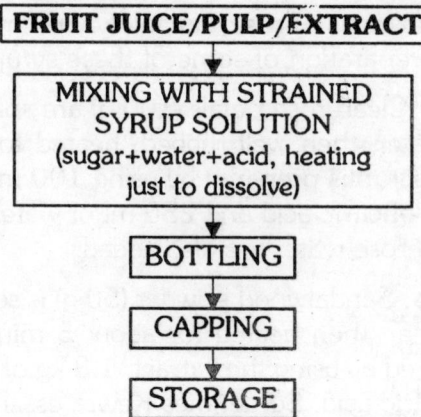

Note : *Fruit-based syrups do not need preservatives, but for longer shelf-life 350 ppm sulphur dioxide or 600 ppm benzoic acid (as required) may be added before bottling. In case of synthetic syrups, the syrup is strained before adding essence and colour.*

(8) Fruit juice concentrate

A fruit juice from which water has been mostly removed by heating or freezing is known as concentrate. Carbonated beverages are prepared from this. They contain pure juice with at least 32 per cent total soluble solids. The major advantages of concentrates are :

(i) Reduced weight and bulk compared to juice result in economy in packaging, storage and transport.

(ii) The whole crop of fruits is fully utilized during peak season, thus helping to stabilize the price.

(iii) The product can be used as base material for making various food and beverage formulations.

Problems with concentrates

(i) Fermentation is not prevented,

(ii) Non-enzymatic browning occurs, and

(iii) Gel formation takes place.

In some countries, concentrates of pure fruit juices particularly of orange, apple, pineapple and grape are highly popular. The major methods deployed for production of fruit and vegetable concentrates are : (i) freezing and mechanical evaporation: (ii) low-temperature vacuum evaporation; and (iii) high-speed high-temperature evaporation.

(9) Fruit juice powder

Fruit juice can be converted into a free-flowing, highly hygroscopic powder by puff-drying, freeze drying, vacuum drying, spray drying or drum drying. The powder has the advantage of long shelf-life and is soluble in cold water. But during the drying process much of the characteristic fresh flavour is lost, which is compensated for by adding to the juice powder natural fruit flavour in powder form. Reconstitution of the powder mixture yields full strength fruit juice drink. Techniques have been standardized by Central Food Technological Research Institute, Mysore, for preparation of powder from mango, orange, lemon, guava, passion-fruit, banana, avocado, tomato, etc.

(10) Barley water

Fruit beverage which contains at least 25 per cent fruit juice, 30 per cent total soluble solids and 0.25 per cent barley starch is known as barley water. It also contains about 1.0 per cent acid.

Barley water is prepared from citrus fruits such as lime, lemon, grapefruit and orange and of these lime and lemon are mostly used.

It is prepared by using about 1 litre of fruit juice, 2.0 kg of sugar, 15 g of barley flour and 1.3 litre of water. Essence and potassium metabisulphite (as in case of cordial) may be added if desired.

(11) Carbonated beverages

The use of fruit juices in the preparation of carbonated drinks is practically unknown in India. Mostly, artificially flavoured drinks which have no nutritive value are prepared by this method. The use of fruit juices would increase the nutritive value of carbonated beverages.

The juice can be directly carbonated, or can be stored as such, or in the form of concentrate for carbonation whenever necessary. Carbonated beverages can keep well for about a week without addition of any preservative. If the products are to be kept for a longer period, 0.05 per cent sodium benzoate must be added. For example, while preparing carbonated orange syrup; juice, sugar and citric acid in the ratio of 1:1.55:0.044 should be used. For carbonation, 42 to 56 g of this prepared syrup is filled in 285 to 340 g bottles. In the same manner syrups of pineapple, lime, lemon, etc. can be prepared. Lemonade, orangeade, ginger, strawberry, lime juice, are examples of carbonated beverages.

FLOW-SHEET FOR PROCESSING OF BARLEY WATER

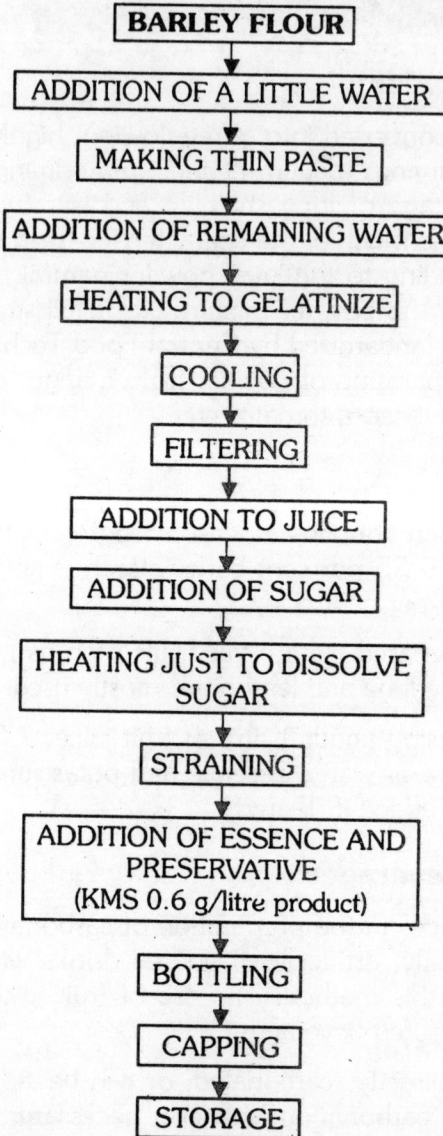

BARLEY FLOUR

↓

ADDITION OF A LITTLE WATER

↓

MAKING THIN PASTE

↓

ADDITION OF REMAINING WATER

↓

HEATING TO GELATINIZE

↓

COOLING

↓

FILTERING

↓

ADDITION TO JUICE

↓

ADDITION OF SUGAR

↓

HEATING JUST TO DISSOLVE SUGAR

↓

STRAINING

↓

ADDITION OF ESSENCE AND PRESERVATIVE
(KMS 0.6 g/litre product)

↓

BOTTLING

↓

CAPPING

↓

STORAGE

Fermented Beverages

These have been known to mankind from time immemorial. But the development of biochemical principles of fermentation was originated by Lavoisier in France in 1789 by way of analyzing the chemical composition of sugar and its fermentation products such as ethanol, carbon dioxide and a trace of acetic acid. Much later in 1860, the fellow countryman Louis Pasteur carefully analyzed the fermentation products and showed that in addition to ethanol and carbon dioxide, other compounds such as glycerol and succinic acids are also produced.

Fermentation process in beverage preparation is mediated through yeast and in the process it produces a range of products such as organic acids, alcohols, esters and sulphurous compounds. Grape wine is the oldest example of a fermented beverage.

(1) Wine

Wine is defined differently in the laws of different countries, e.g., in China wine is considered to be an alcoholic beverage and the Chinese word for it may be translated as *appetite wine*. In California, it is defined as the fermented juice of various fruits. But wine generally denotes the product produced by fermentation of grape juice. The most satisfactory definition seems to be "wine is a beverage resulting from the fermentation by yeasts of the grape juice with proper processing and addition."

In other words, wine strictly signifies the fermented alcoholic beverage produced from grape juice without distillation.

Grapes have been historically associated with wine-making because of following advantages:

(i)   Juice is extremely rich in natural sugar.

(ii)   Natural association of fermentative yeasts with berries.

(iii) High content of nitrogenous matters in promoting growth of yeast and hence fermentation.

(iv)   High acidity of juice favouring yeasts and protecting against other bacterial fermentation.

(v)   High alcohol and acid content in the fermented wine keep it stable and safe for prolonged storage.

The varieties of wines are endless and they differ in so many attributes that it is difficult to classify them. According to colour, there are two types, *red* and *white*. In making *red wines*, the grapes are crushed and stemmed but the skin and seeds are left in the must. *White wines* are made from white or greenish grapes or from the juice of grapes from which the skin have been removed.

Grape wines are of two kinds, *dry* and *sweet*. *Dry wines* are those which contain very little or no sugar that can be detected by testing. In *sweet wines*, the sugar content is high enough to be detected by taste. The alcohol content of these two kinds of wines ranges from 7 to 20 per cent. Wines with 7 to 9 per cent alcohol are known as "*light*", those with 9 to 16 per cent "*medium*", and those with 16 to 21 per cent "*strong*".

Sparkling wines contain carbon dioxide. They are made effervescent by secondary fermentation in closed containers, generally in the bottle itself. *Still wines* are those which do not contain carbon dioxide. *Fortified wines* contain added alcohol in the form of brandy. Generally wines with more than 12 per cent alcohol are fortified with fruit brandy (alcohol) prepared by distilling grape wine.

Equipments used for wine making

(i) **For crushing and pressing :** Roller crusher or basket press.

(ii) **Primary fermentation vessel :** Open-ended cylindrical vessels of suitable size made of plastic or wood.

(iii) **Secondary fermentation vessel :** Narrow mouthed containers of wood, plastic or glass.

Thermometer, hydrometer, hand refractometer, measuring cylinder, syphon tube, filter, bottles, crown corks and corking machine, etc., are also required.

(i) **Selection of fruit :** The grape berries should be ripe and fresh. Blemished ones should be rejected. White wine is produced from varieties having greenish or yellowish skin. Red wines derive their colour from red pigment present in the skin or flesh of coloured varieties. The different species and varieties of grapes suitable for wine making are given in the following table.

S.No.	Botanical name	English name	Variety
1	*Vitis vinifera*	European grape	Beauty Seedless, Arka Shyam
2	*V. labrusca*	American grape	Concord, Catawea, Niagara
3	*V. rotundifolia*	Muscadine grape	Jems, Scupper

(ii) **Crushing :** It is done with the help of a basket press. Before crushing the grapes their stems and stalks are removed. Crushed material (must) is put in jars which should not be filled more than three-fourths.

(iii) **Addition of sugar :** Cane sugar is added to maintain at least 20 per cent total soluble solids but not more than 24 per cent. If the grapes are sour, 70 g of sugar are added for each kg of grapes.

(iv) **Adjustment of pH:** If necessary, pH of juice has to be adjusted. If it is too low, the juice is diluted with water; if too high, tartaric acid is added to lower it. If water is added more sugar has also to be added to raise the percentage of total soluble solids. Usually an acid content of 0.6 to 0.8

TECHNOLOGICAL FLOW-SHEET FOR PROCESSING OF GRAPE WINE

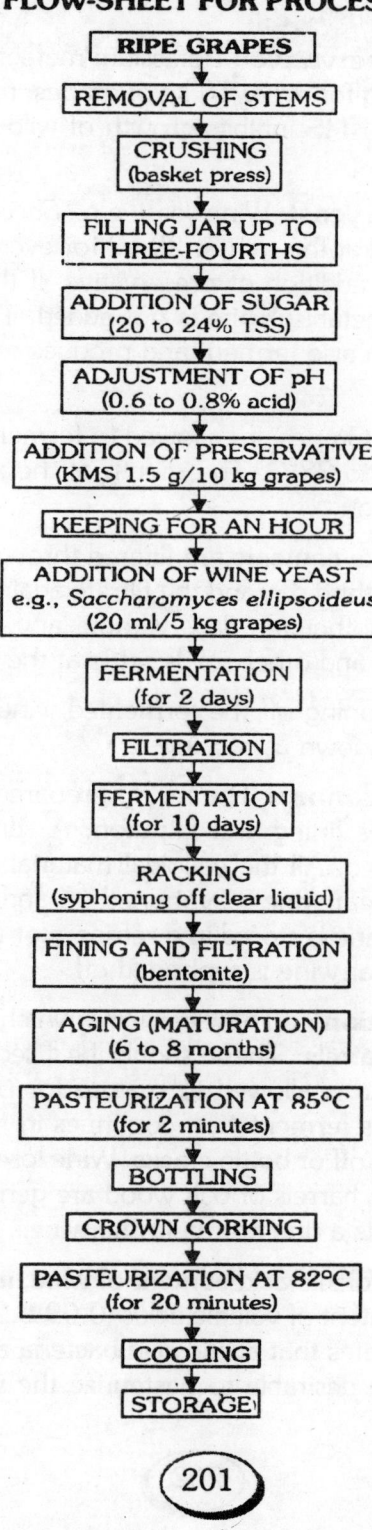

RIPE GRAPES

↓

REMOVAL OF STEMS

↓

CRUSHING
(basket press)

↓

FILLING JAR UP TO
THREE-FOURTHS

↓

ADDITION OF SUGAR
(20 to 24% TSS)

↓

ADJUSTMENT OF pH
(0.6 to 0.8% acid)

↓

ADDITION OF PRESERVATIVE
(KMS 1.5 g/10 kg grapes)

↓

KEEPING FOR AN HOUR

↓

ADDITION OF WINE YEAST
e.g., *Saccharomyces ellipsoideus*
(20 ml/5 kg grapes)

↓

FERMENTATION
(for 2 days)

↓

FILTRATION

↓

FERMENTATION
(for 10 days)

↓

RACKING
(syphoning off clear liquid)

↓

FINING AND FILTRATION
(bentonite)

↓

AGING (MATURATION)
(6 to 8 months)

↓

PASTEURIZATION AT 85°C
(for 2 minutes)

↓

BOTTLING

↓

CROWN CORKING

↓

PASTEURIZATION AT 82°C
(for 20 minutes)

↓

COOLING

↓

STORAGE

per cent is maintained.

(v) **Addition of preservative :** Potassium metabisulphite (KMS) is added at the rate of 1.5 g for every 10 kg of grapes, mixed and allow to stand for 2 to 4 hours. KMS inhibits growth of wild yeasts and spoilage organisms.

(vi) **Addition of wine yeast:** Wine yeast, e.g., *Saccharomyces ellipsoideus* inoculum is added at the rate of 20 ml for every 5 kg of grapes, about an hour after the addition of preservative. If the yeast is not available then potassium metabisulphite is not added. The yeast present in the skin of grapes can also ferment and produce wine but it is not of good quality.

(vii) **Fermentation :** Grapes are allowed to ferment for two days in a cool place, i.e., at 22 to 28°C. The mouth of the jar is covered with cloth during fermentation.

(viii) **Filtration :** The contents are filtered through a thin muslin cloth or a filter aid on the third day and the filtrate again allowed to ferment in a cool place for another ten days without any disturbance. During this period yeast cells and other solids settle at the bottom.

(ix) **Racking :** Syphoning off the fermented wine to separate it from the solid deposits is known as racking.

(x) **Fining and Filtration :** The newly prepared wine is sometimes not clear and requires fining and filtration. A suitable fining agent, e.g., bentonite, is added. All the colloidal material settles down along with bentonite. The clear wine is syphoned off and filtered if necessary. Alternatively, the wine is stored in a refrigerator for about two weeks and thereafter the clear wine is syphoned off.

(xi) **Aging (Maturation) :** The clear wine which is syphoned off is filled into bottles or barrels. These should be filled completely and sealed airtight. The wine is allowed to mature for 6 to 8 months in a cool place. Sometimes fermentation continues in the bottle with the result that the cork flies off or bottle cracks. Wine loses its flavour during aging because of which barrels of oak wood are generally used for storing it. The wood imparts a fine aroma to the wine.

(xii) **Packing :** The volatile acid content of wine, mainly acetic acid, should be low. High content of volatile acids (0.09-0.20 g/100 ml. in terms of acetic acid) indicates that acetic acid bacteria are active during fermentation. It is often desirable to pasteurize the wine to destroy spoilage organisms and coagulate the colloids that cause cloudiness. Generally wines are pasteurized at 82 to 88°C for 1-2 minutes and then bottled. The bottles are closed with crown corks of good quality, pasteurized at 65°C for about 20 minutes, then cooled and stored.

The following are the well-known wines produced in various countries:

(2) Champaigne

It is a sparkling wine, made chiefly in France, from certain varieties of grapes such as Chardonay and Pinot Noir. It is made in other countries as well. The fermentation is allowed to proceed to completion in bottles which are specially made to withstand high pressure of gas produced during fermentation.

(3) Port

It is a fortified, sweet red wine made originally in Portugal, but now in other countries also.

(4) Sherry

A Spanish wine, matured by placing the barrels for 3 to 4 months in sun-light, where the temperature is as high as 54 to 60°C.

(5) Tokay

This is a very famous fortified wine made in Hungary.

(6) Muscat

It is prepared from Muscat grapes in Italy, California, Spain and Australia.

(7) Perry

Wine made from pears is known as *perry*. Its method of preparation is similar to that of apple cider. Wastes, culled fruits and trimmings left over from canning may also be used for making perry.

(8) Orange wine

Orange juice is sweetened by adding sugar and then allowed to ferment. The method of preparation is similar to that of grape wine. Orange oil should not be added to the juice as it hinders and sometimes stops fermentation.

(9) Berry wine

Wines prepared from berries like strawberry, blackberry and elderberrys are known as 'Berry wines'. These products are generally popular in other countries but are not common in India.

(10) Nira

It is prepared from the juice of the palm tree.

(11) Feni

This is a fermented wine made from cashew apple in Goa.

(12) Cider

It is mostly prepared by fermentation of special grade of apples which have a high tannin content of 0.1-0.3 per cent. However, a great deal of confusion exists as far as the apple cider is concerned. In the U.S.A., apple cider means non-clarified apple juice, whereas apple juice is the clarified and treated sparkling juice. On the contrary in the Europe and in India, apple cider pertains to the fermented apple juice. In the U.K., special varieties of apples known as cider apples are used. For cider preparation apples may be graded on the basis of tannin and organic acid contents as 'bitter-sweet', 'bitter-sharp', 'sweet' and 'sharp'. Nearly 60 per cent of full-flavoured cider is prepared using bitter-sweet and bitter-sharp apple. Cider apples are so chosen that their juice contain higher percentage of sugar (i.e., 12.5 per cent) than normal apple juice (10.5 per cent) with higher proportion of sugar in the form of fructose. In India, cider apples are not available in sufficient quantity, hence dessert varieties which are easily available, are used. There are two types of apple cider, dry and sweet.

Fruits such as bael, jamun, phalsa and aonla can also be used for preparation of cider. The technique of preparation which is more or less similar to that of grape wine is summarized on the next page.

To attract wider clientele for the cider consumers, most cider preparations are carbonated nowadays. This is done by refermentation of cider by repeating the process of sugar and yeast additions in a pressure tank or sometimes by chilling cider prior to subjecting carbon dioxide injection under controlled pressure. Cider, thus carbonated, is protected from microbial attack by sulphitation and pasteurization.

TECHNOLOGICAL FLOW-SHEET FOR PROCESSING OF CIDER

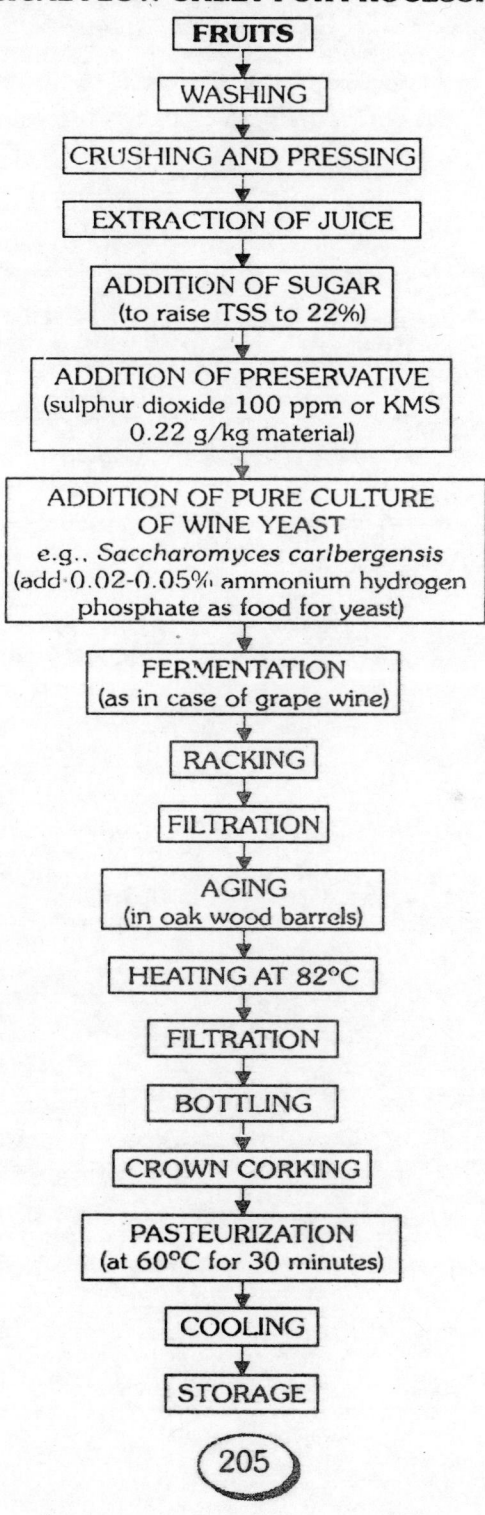

FRUITS
↓
WASHING
↓
CRUSHING AND PRESSING
↓
EXTRACTION OF JUICE
↓
ADDITION OF SUGAR
(to raise TSS to 22%)
↓
ADDITION OF PRESERVATIVE
(sulphur dioxide 100 ppm or KMS
0.22 g/kg material)
↓
ADDITION OF PURE CULTURE
OF WINE YEAST
e.g., *Saccharomyces carlbergensis*
(add 0.02-0.05% ammonium hydrogen
phosphate as food for yeast)
↓
FERMENTATION
(as in case of grape wine)
↓
RACKING
↓
FILTRATION
↓
AGING
(in oak wood barrels)
↓
HEATING AT 82°C
↓
FILTRATION
↓
BOTTLING
↓
CROWN CORKING
↓
PASTEURIZATION
(at 60°C for 30 minutes)
↓
COOLING
↓
STORAGE

Chapter 17

Vinegar

 **V**inegar is perhaps the oldest known product or fermentation. The word is derived from French 'vinaigre' meaning sour wine (vin = wine, aigre= sour).

Vinegar is a liquid obtained by alcoholic and acetic fermentation of suitable materials containing sugar and starch (at least 10 per cent fermentable sugar). It contains about 5 per cent acetic acid and has germicidal and antiseptic properties. In the trade, vinegar is labelled according to the material used in its manufacture, e.g., malt vinegar (from malt) and cider vinegar (from apple juice).

The amount of acid in vinegar is expressed as 'grain strength' which is ten times the percentage of the acetic acid present in it, e.g., vinegar having 5 per cent acetic acid is termed as vinegar of '50 grain strength'.

Types of vinegar

Vinegars are of two types-

(A) Brewed vinegars, and (B) Artificial vinegars

(A) Brewed vinegars : Brewed vinegars are made from various fruits, starchy materials (potato) and sugar containing substances (molasses, honey) by alcoholic and subsequent acetic fermentation.

(1) Fruit vinegar : Generally apple, grape, orange, jamun, peach, pear, pineapple, apricot and banana are used. Vinegar made from apple juice is known as cider or apple cider vinegar, while that from grapes as wine or grape vinegar.

(2) Potato vinegar : In this case starch is extracted from potato and hydrolyzed by the enzyme diastase before fermentation.

(3) Malt vinegar : Malt vinegar is derived wholly from malted barley, with or without the addition of the cereal grain, malted or otherwise, the starch of which is saccharified by the diastase of the malt before fermentation. Distilled malt vinegar is prepared by distilling the malt vinegar. The product merely contains the volatile constituents of the vinegar from which it is derived. It is colourless and is generally used in the manufacture of pickled onions.

(4) Molasses vinegar : In this case molasses is diluted to 16 per cent total soluble solids, neutralized with citric acid and then fermented.

(5) Honey vinegar : It is prepared from low grade honey.

(6) Spirit vinegar : Spirit vinegar is the product prepared by acetous fermentation of a distilled alcoholic fluid which in turn is produced by fermentation. It is usually made by alcoholic fermentation of molasses and then distilled prior to acetic fermentation. It is also called as grain vinegar, distilled vinegar, white vinegar or alcohol vinegar.

(7) Spiced vinegar : Spiced vinegars are prepared by steeping the leaves or spices in an ordinary vinegar.

(B) Artificial vinegars : Artificial vinegars are prepared by diluting synthetic acetic acid or glacial acetic acid to a legal standard of 4 per cent and are coloured with caramel. Artificial vinegars are also called as synthetic vinegar or non-brewed vinegar.

Steps involved in vinegar production

Two distinct steps are involved in its preparation.

(i) Conversion of the sugar in fruits, etc., into alcohol by yeast (alcoholic fermentation) : The most efficient yeasts for fermentation of sugary substances and fruit juices into alcohol are *Saccharomyces ellipsoideus*, *S. malei* and *S. cerevisiae*. For starchy substances, *S. cerevisiae* is the best. In order to obtain quality vinegar, it is essential to first destroy wild (naturally occurring) yeasts and other microorganisms by pasteurization, and then to inoculate pure yeast. The nutrients for the growth of yeast such as phosphates, ammonium and potassium salts and sugars are naturally present in fruit juices and in honey and molasses. The most favourable temperature for the growth of yeast is 25-27°C. Fermentation becomes abnormal at 38°C and ceases altogether at 41°C and below 7°C. The chemical reaction involved in alcoholic fermentation is as under:

$$\underset{\substack{\text{Glucose or Fructose} \\ \text{(Fermentable sugar)}}}{C_6H_{12}O_6} \xrightarrow[\substack{\text{Anaerobic} \\ \text{condition}}]{\text{Yeast}} \underset{\substack{\text{Ethyl} \\ \text{alcohol}}}{2C_2H_5OH} + \underset{\substack{\text{Carbon} \\ \text{dioxide}}}{2CO_2}$$

(ii) Conversion of alcohol into vinegar by acetic acid bacteria (acetification) : Acetic acid fermentation is brought about by acetic acid bacteria (*Acetobacter* spp.) which are strongly aerobic but whose activity is greatly reduced by light. Acetic acid fermentation should, therefore, be carried out in the dark. The nutrients required for bacterial growth are generally present in the alcoholic liquor itself, but in the case of distilled alcohol, malt sprouts, phosphoric acid, potassium carbonate, trisodium phosphate and ammonium hydroxide are added as nutrients. For acetic acid fermentation, the alcohol content of the fermented mash is adjusted to 7-8 per cent by dilution with water, because acetic acid bacteria do not grow well at higher concentrations of alcohol. After this adjustment, mother vinegar containing acetic acid bacteria is added at the rate of one part to ten parts of fermented mash in order to check the growth of undesirable microorganisms and to hasten the fermentation process. The chemical reaction involved is as under:

$$C_2H_5OH + O_2 \xrightarrow[\substack{\text{Aerobic} \\ \text{dark} \\ \text{conditions}}]{\substack{\text{Acetic acid} \\ \text{bacteria}}} CH_3COOH + H_2O$$

Ethyl alcohol   Oxygen   Acetic acid   Water

Outline scheme of vinegar production

Fruit, Grain, Root crops
(Starch)

$$(C_6H_{10}O_5)_n\ H_2O \xrightarrow{\substack{\text{Enzymes} \\ \text{(acid)}}} x\ C_6H_{12}O_6 + y\ C_{12}H_{22}O_{11}$$

Starch   Glucose   Maltose

Fermentable mono and disaccharides
(Alcoholic fermentation)

$$C_6H_{12}O_6 \xrightarrow[\substack{\text{Anaerobic} \\ \text{conditions}}]{\text{Yeast}} 2C_2H_5OH + 2\ CO_2$$

Glucose or Fructose   Ethyl alcohol   Carbon dioxide

Ethyl alcohol (Acetification)

$$C_2H_5OH + O_2 \xrightarrow[\substack{\text{Aerobic} \\ \text{dark} \\ \text{conditions}}]{\substack{\text{Acetic acid} \\ \text{bacteria}}} CH_3COOH + H_2O$$

Ethyl alcohol   Acetic acid   water

Acetic acid

Preparation of vinegar

Vinegar is prepared by the following methods:

(A)   Slow process

(B)   Orleans slow process

(C)   Quick process (Generator or German process)

(A)   Slow process

This process is generally used in India. The fruit juice or sugar solution, filled in earthen pots or wooden barrels, is kept for at least 5-6 months in a warm, damp room to undergo spontaneous alcoholic and acetic fermentations. No special care is taken, but the mouth of the container is covered with cloth to keep out insects, dirt, etc. The main defects of this method are:

(i)   Incomplete alcoholic fermentation;

(ii)   Slow acetic fermentation;

(iii) Low yield; and

(iv)   Inferior quality of vinegar.

(B)   Orleans slow process

The vinegar prepared by this process is clear and of superior quality. The steps of the process are:

1. **Selection of fruit:** Grapes, apples, oranges, mangoes, dates, jamun, or any other sweet fruit of third grade having about 10 per cent sugar in the juice are taken. Cores and peels of certain fruits discarded during canning and jam making can also be used.

2   **Extraction of juice :** The fruits or vegetables are cut into small pieces and then crushed or pressed through a thick muslin cloth. Fruits which do not yield juice readily are heated with a small quantity of water before pressing.

3. **Adjustment of sugar :** Only juice containing low percentage of sugar is suitable for the growth of yeast. The concentration of sugar is determined by means of a hand refractometer and adjusted to about 10 per cent either by diluting the juice with water (if the sugar content is high) or by adding additional sugar.

4. **Fermentation :** The juice is heated (pasteurized) to destroy the microorganisms and then filled in glass carboys, earthen pots or wooden barrels (Fig.A) to three-fourths of their capacity. The two important steps in the preparation of vinegar are:

    a.   Alcoholic fermentation

    b.   Vinegar fermentation.

    a.   *Alcoholic fermentation :* Pure wine yeast, obtained from a winery or

210

a chemist's shop, is well powdered and dissolved in a little warm juice and then added at the rate of 1.5 g per litre to the whole lot of juice with frequent stirring. The mouth of the carboy or barrel is loosely plugged with cotton wool to allow carbon dioxide gas to escape. The gas should be completely removed otherwise it hinders the yeast fermentation. Initially there is continuous frothing which indicates the progress of fermentation, but it ceases after 3 weeks when the fermentation is complete. All the sugar is converted into alcohol as can be seen by testing with a hand refractometer which indicates 0-1 per cent total soluble solids.

During the fermentation the temperature is maintained at 22 to 27°C as fermentation ceases above 41°C and below 7°C. The fermented juice is stored for 1 to 2 weeks for sedimentation and then strained through a cloth, or the clear supernatant is syphoned off into a clean container which is filled up to three-fourths its capacity (Fig. B). Vinegar fermentation should be taken up only after ascertaining that the alcoholic fermentation is complete, otherwise yeast will retard the fermentation. For vinegar fermentation the alcohol content of the fermented liquid is adjusted to 7-8 per cent by dilution with water, because acetic acid bacteria do not grow at a higher concentration of alcohol.

b. **Vinegar (acetic) fermentation :** This is brought about by acetic acid bacteria. Unpasteurized vinegar or "mother" vinegar is added to the product of alcoholic fermentation in the ratio of 1:10, and mixed well. Thereafter the liquid should not be disturbed otherwise the film of vinegar bacteria will break and sink to the bottom and consume the nutrients in the liquid without producing vinegar. The mouth of the container is closed with a cork having two holes for proper aeration. The temperature of this liquid is maintained at 21 to 27°C and the fermentation is completed in 10 to 15 weeks when the acetic acid content reaches a maximum.

Then the vinegar is syphoned off or strained through a thick cloth leaving at the bottom of the container a turbid liquid, which is used as "mother" vinegar for fresh fermentation.

5. **Aging :** Vinegar prepared by the above method is turbid and does not possess a good taste. It is stored in containers for 4 to 8 months during which the vinegar develops a good aroma and flavour and becomes mellow.

6. **Clarification :** The clear aged liquid should be syphoned out and filtered.

7. **Colouring :** Caramel colour is added for colouring.

8. Pasteurization : The vinegar is poured into previously sterilized bottles, corked airtight and the bottles heated (pasteurized) in hot water at 71 to 77°C for 15 to 20 minutes, so that further growth of bacteria is stopped and the strength of vinegar maintained during storage.

Note: An ideal vinegar should contain only about 0.3 per cent sugar. A higher percentage denotes incomplete fermentation due to excess of acetic acid during yeast fermentation.

(C) Quick process (Generator or German process)

In this process additional oxygen is supplied for the growth of bacteria and the surface of the bacterial culture is also increased resulting in rapid fermentation. The equipment, used known as "Upright Generator", is a cylinder of height 3.66 to 4.2 m and diameter 1.2 to 1.5 m which is divided into three compartments:

(i) Distributing (ii) Central, and (iii) Receiving.

(i) Distributing compartment : This is the upper compartment and is about 30 cm above the central one. It is separated from the central compartment by a partition having small perforations. In the distributing compartment there is fitted a W-shaped tilting trough or revolving sprinkler which distributes the liquid by trickling slowly over the material filled in the central compartment.

(ii) Central compartment : This is filled with pumice stone, straw, corn cobs, rattan or beech wood shavings to increase the surface area. Beech wood shavings are preferred as they remain tightly coiled even when wet with vinegar. This compartment is fitted with an adjustable opening near the bottom for admission of air.

(iii) Receiving compartment : This is the lowest compartment of the generator and is separated from the central one by a perforated partition placed about 1.5 m above the bottom of the generator. Here the vinegar is collected.

Method of Preparation : The material in the central compartment is sprinkled and wetted with unpasteurized vinegar containing acetic bacteria. Then a mixture of the alcoholic fermentation product and vinegar (2:1) is slowly trickled through the generator to promote the growth of vinegar bacteria. Within a few days the bacterial growth is enough for efficient functioning of the generator. The alcoholic fermentation liquid is now mixed with mother vinegar in the ratio of 1:2 to increase its acidity from 3 to 3.5 per cent and passed through the generator

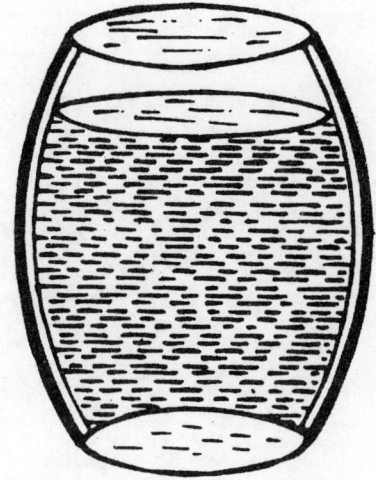

Fig. A.
Wooden Barrel placed vertically
for Alcoholic Fermentation

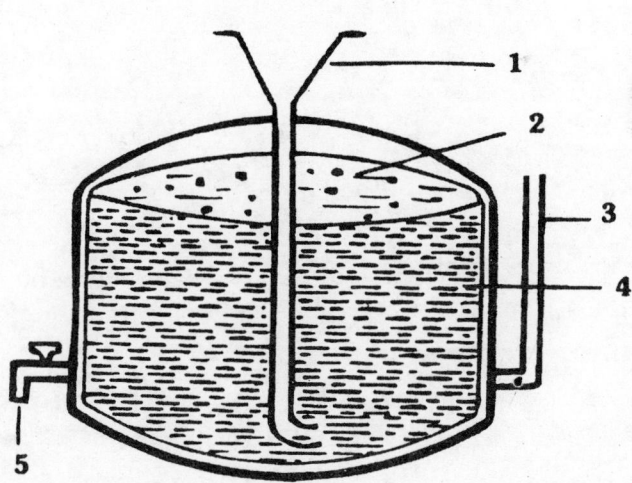

Fig. B.
By Vinegar Bacteria

1. Funnel, 2. Disc with hole,
3. Level indicator, 4. Liquid
5. Outlet

where it is converted into acetic acid in a single passage. This process is repeated till all the alcohol is converted.

Precautions

1. To eliminate contaminating microorganisms, the copartments and air passage are cleaned regularly.

2. The optimum temperature of 27 to 30°C required for the activity of vinegar bacteria should be maintained by regulating the air intake in the generator and the rate of flow of the liquid. If the temperature increases, the rate of flow of alcohol should be increases and the intake of air decreased. If there is a decrease in temperature, the intake of air is increased and the rate of the flow of the liquid reduced.

3. For proper functioning in all seasons, the generator is fitted with coils through which steam or cold water can be passed to maintain the desired temperature.

Problems in vinegar production

(1) **Wine flower :** When unfermented juice is exposed to air a film of yeast called wine flower forms on the surface of the liquid. The film causes cloudiness and also destroys alcohol. The growth of wine flower can be prevented by (i) filling the carboys or barrels up to the brim, (ii) addition of 20-25 per cent unpasteurized vinegar, and (iii) spreading liquid paraffin on the surface of the fermented liquid.

(2) **Lactic acid bacteria :** Presence of lactic acid bacteria is very common in fermented juice. These bacteria interfere with acetification, cause cloudiness, produce lactic and other acids which have disagreeable mousy flavours and thus spoil the quality of vinegar. This can be avoided by using 20-25 per cent unpasteurized mother vinegar or a pure culture of yeast.

(3) **Insects and worms :** Among insects, vinegar flies (*Drosophila cellaris*), vinegar louse and vinegar mites are important. These can only be avoided by maintaining proper sanitary conditions. Vinegar eels (*Anguillula*) are thread-like worms found in vinegar, which destroy the acid and can be killed by heating the vinegar to about 60°C or removed by filtration. Vinegar eels are strongly aerobic and do not grow if the container is filled up to the brim.

Chapter 18

Jam, Jelly and Marmalade

T hese constitute an important group of preserved forms of fruits which are made extensively in homes as well as produced commercially. Their production can be increased many fold by making use of culled-fruits that are unsuitable for canning and dehydration.

Jam

Jam is a product made by boiling fruit pulp with sufficient sugar to a reasonably thick consistency, firm enough to hold the fruit tissues in position. Apple, pear, sapota (chiku), apricot, loquat, peach, papaya, karonda, carrot, plum, strawberry, raspberry, mango, tomato, grapes and muskmelon are used for preparation of jams. It can be prepared from one kind of fruit or from two or more kinds. Commercial jams such as tutti-frutti can be prepared from pieces of fruit, fruit scraping and pulp adhering to cores of fruits which are available in plenty in canning factories.

Jam contains 0.5-0.6 per cent acid and invert sugar should not be more than 40 per cent. F.P.O. specifications for jam are given in Appendix IX. In the home it can be prepared by using the recipes as given in the table.

Fruit/Vegetable	Ingredient for one kg pulp		
	Sugar (kg)	Citric acid (g)	Water (ml)
Aonla	0.75	-	150
Apple	0.75	2.0	100
Apricot	0.60	1.0	100
Carrot	0.75	2.5	200
Grapes	0.70	1.0	50
Guava	0.75	2.5	150
Karonda	0.80	-	100
Loquat	0.75	1.0	100
Mango	0.75	1.5	50
Musk melon	0.75	2.5	50
Plum	0.80	-	150
Peach	0.80	3.0	100
Pear	0.75	1.5	100

Papaya	0.70	3.0	100
Raspberry	0.75	2.0	100
Strawberry	0.75	2.0	100
Sapota	0.75	3.0	150
Mixed jam (papaya and pineapple pulp in equal amounts or pineapple, guava and mango pulp in equal amounts)	0.80	2.5	100
Tutti-frutti jam (pineapple, apple. pear and mango pieces in equal amounts)	0.80	2.5	100

TECHNOLOGICAL FLOW-SHEET FOR PROCESSING OF JAM

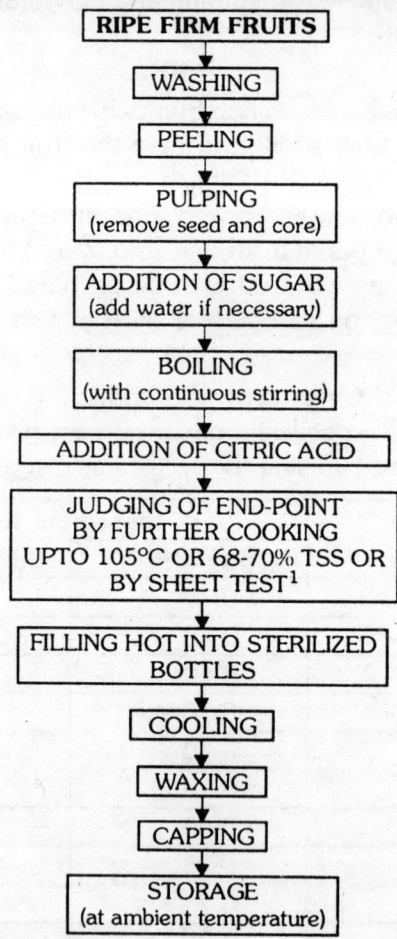

RIPE FIRM FRUITS

↓

WASHING

↓

PEELING

↓

PULPING
(remove seed and core)

↓

ADDITION OF SUGAR
(add water if necessary)

↓

BOILING
(with continuous stirring)

↓

ADDITION OF CITRIC ACID

↓

JUDGING OF END-POINT
BY FURTHER COOKING
UPTO 105°C OR 68-70% TSS OR
BY SHEET TEST[1]

↓

FILLING HOT INTO STERILIZED
BOTTLES

↓

COOLING

↓

WAXING

↓

CAPPING

↓

STORAGE
(at ambient temperature)

1. **Sheet or flake test:** A small portion of jam is taken out during boiling, in a spoon or wooden ladle and cooled slightly. It is then allowed to drop. If the product falls off in the form of a sheet or flakes instead of flowing in a continuous stream or syrup, it means that the end-point has been reached and the product is ready, otherwise, boiling is continued till the sheet test is positive.

Problems in jam production

(i) Crystallization : The final product should contain 30 to 50 per cent invert sugar. If the percentage is less than 30, cane sugar may crystallize out on storage and if it is more than 50 the jam will become a honey-like mass due to the formation of small crystals of glucose. Corn syrup or glucose may be added along with cane sugar to avoid crystallization.

(ii) Sticky or gummy jam: Because of high percentage of total soluble solids, jams tend to become gummy or sticky. This problem can be solved by addition of pectin or citric acid, or both.

(iii) Premature setting : This is due to low total soluble solids and high pectin content in the jam and can be prevented by adding more sugar. If this cannot be done a small quantity of sodium bicarbonate is added to reduce the acidity and thus prevent pre-coagulation.

(iv) Surface graining and shrinkage : This is caused by evaporation of moisture during storage of jam. Storing in a cool place can reduce it.

(v) Microbial spoilage : Sometimes moulds may spoil the jam during storage but they are destroyed if exposed to less than 90 per cent humidity. Hence, jams should be stored at 80 per cent humidity. Mould growth can also prevented by not sealing the filled jar and covering the surface of jam with a disc of waxed paper because mould does not grow under open conditions as rapidly as in a closed space. It is also advisable to add 40 ppm sulphur dioxide in the form of KMS. In the case of cans, sulphur dioxide should not be added to the jam as it causes blackening of the internal surface of the can.

Yeasts are not a serious problem due to the high concentration of sugar.

Jelly

A jelly is a semi-solid product prepared by boiling a clear, strained solution of pectin-containing fruit extract, free from pulp, after the addition of sugar and acid. A perfect jelly should be transparent, well-set, but not too stiff, and should have the original flavour of the fruit. It should be of attractive colour and keep its shape when removed from the mould. It should be firm enough to retain a sharp edge but tender enough to quiver when pressed. It should not be gummy, sticky or syrupy or have crystallized sugar. The product should be free from dullness, with little or no syneresis (weeping), and neither tough nor rubbery.

Guava, sour apple, plum, karonda, wood apple, loquat, papaya, and gooseberry are generally used for preparation of jelly. Apricot, pineapple, strawberry, raspberry, etc., can be used but only after addition of pectin powder, because these fruits have low pectin content. Fruits can be divided into four groups according to their pectin and acid contents:

1. ***Rich in pectin and acid*** : Sour and crab apple, grape, sour guavas, lemon, oranges (sour), plum (sour), jamum.

2. ***Rich in pectin but low in acid*** : Apple (low acid varieties), unripe banana, sour cherry, fig (unripe), pear, ripe guava, peel of orange and grapefruit.

3. ***Low in pectin but rich in acid*** : Apricot (sour), sweet cherry, sour peach, pineapple and strawberry.

4. ***Low in pectin and acid*** : Ripe apricot, peach (ripe), pomegranate, raspberry, strawberry and any other over-ripe fruit.

F.P.O. specifications for jelly are given in Appendix IX. Its acid content should be 0.5-0.75 per cent. In the home it can be prepared by using following recipes:

Fruit	Ingredients for one litre extract	
	Sugar (kg)	**Citric acid (g)**
Guava	0.75	3.0
Sour apple	0.75-1.00	2.0
Gooseberry	0.80	-
Karonda	0.75	-
Jamun	0.75	1.0
Wood apple	1.00	-
Plum	0.75	2.5
Loquat	0.80	2.0
Papaya	0.75	3.0

Important considerations in jelly making

Pectin, acid, sugar (65%), and water are the four essential ingredients. Pectin test and determination of end-point of jelly formation are very important for the quality of the jelly.

(A) Pectin

Pectin substances present in the form of calcium pectate are responsible for the firmness of fruits. Pectin is the most important constituent of jelly. It is a commercial term for water-soluble pectinic acid which under suitable conditions forms a gel with sugar and acid. In the early stage of development of fruits, the pectic substance is a water-insoluble protopectin which is converted into pectin by the enzyme protopectinase during ripening of fruit. In over-ripe fruits, due to the presence of pectic methyl esterase (PME) enzyme, the pectin gets largely converted to pectic acid which is water-insoluble. This is one of the reasons that both immature and over-ripe fruits are not suitable for making jelly and only ripe fruits are used.

The setting of pectin is also dependent upon the pH and sugar concentration. Stiffness of the gel increases with increasing concentration of pectin up to a certain point beyond which the addition of more pectin has little effect. Too little pectin gives a soft syrup instead of gel. Pectin tends to keep the sugar from crystallizing by acting as a protective colloid, but is not effective when the concentration of sugar is 70 per cent or more. The jellying power of fruit pectin depends upon the amount of pectin used as well as its degree of polymerization and acetyl content.

The amount of pectin extracted varies with the method of extraction, the ripeness of the fruit, the quantity of water added for extracting the juice and the kind of fruit. Usually about 0.5-1.0 per cent of pectin of good quality in the extract is sufficient to produce good jelly. If the pectin content is higher a firm and tough jelly is formed and if it is less the jelly may fail to set.

Determination of pectin content : The pectin content of the strained extract is usually determined by one of the following two methods.

(i) Alcohol test : This method, involving precipitation of pectin with alcohol, is outlined below:

One teaspoonful of strained extract is taken in a beaker and cooled, and 3 teaspoonfuls of methylated spirit are poured gently down the side of the beaker which is rotated for mixing and allowed to stand for a few minutes.

(a)   If extract is rich in pectin, a *single, transparent lump or clot will form*. An equal amount of sugar is to be added to the extract for preparation of jelly.

(b)   If extract contains a moderate amount of pectin, *the clot will be less firm and fragmented*. Three-fourths the amount of sugar is to be added.

(c)   It extract is poor in pectin, *numerous small granular clots will be seen*. One-half the amount of sugar is added.

(ii) Jelmeter test : The jelmeter is held in the left hand with the thumb and forefinger. The bottom of the jelmeter tube is closed with the little finger. The strained extract is poured into the jelmeter with a spoon, held in the right hand, till it is filled to the brim. While still holding the jelmeter, the little finger is removed from the bottom end and the extract is allowed to flow or drip for exactly one minute, at the end of which the finger is replaced. The reading of the level of extract in the jelmeter is noted. This figure indicates how many parts of sugar are to be added to one part of juice.

(B) Acid

The jellying of extract depends on the amount of acid and pectin present in the fruit. Of the three acids citric, malic and tartaric found in fruits, tartaric acid gives the best results. The final jelly should contain at least 0.5 per cent (preferably 0.75%) but not more than 1 per cent total acids because a larger quantity of acid may cause syneresis.

pH of extract : Jelly strength increases with the increase in pH until optimum is reached. Further addition of acid decreases the jelly strength. The optimum pH for a jelly containing 1 per cent pectin is approximately 3.0, 3.2 and 3.4 for 60, 65 and 70 per cent TSS, respectively. The pH of the jelly can be controlled by (i) adjusting pH of extract with acid/alkali, and (ii) adding a suitable buffer. Fruits also contain salts like sodium citrate, sodium potassium tartrate, etc., which have buffering action and help to control pH. In general, the optimum pH value for jelly is 3.2.

(C) Sugar

This essential constituent of jelly imparts to it sweetness as well as body. If the concentration of sugar is high, the jelly retains less water resulting in a stiff jelly, probably because of dehydration.

Inversion of sugar : When sugar (sucrose) is boiled with an acid, it is hydrolyzed into dextrose and fructose, the degree of inversion depending on the pH and duration of boiling. Because of partial inversion of the sucrose, a mixture of sucrose, glucose and fructose are found in the jelly. This mixture is more soluble in water than sucrose alone and hence the jelly can hold more sugar in solution without crystallization.

(D) Judging of end-point

Boiling of jelly should not be prolonged, because excessive boiling results in a greater inversion of sugar and destruction of pectin. The important point to remember is that it is the fruit extract which requires boiling and not the added sugar. If a jelly is cooked for a prolonged period, it may become gummy, sticky, syrupy and deteriorate in colour and flavour. The end-point of boiling can be judged in the following way:

   (i) **Sheet or flake test:** As described under jam.

   (ii) **Drop test :** A drop of the concentrated mass is poured into a glass containing water. Settling down of the drop without disintegration denotes the end-point.

Page 220

Jelmeter

(iii) Temperature test : A solution containing 65 per cent total soluble solids boils at 105°C. Heating of the jelly to this temperature would automatically bring the concentration of solids to 65 per cent. This is the easiest way to ascertain the end-point.

TECHNOLOGICAL FLOW-SHEET FOR PROCESSING OF JELLY

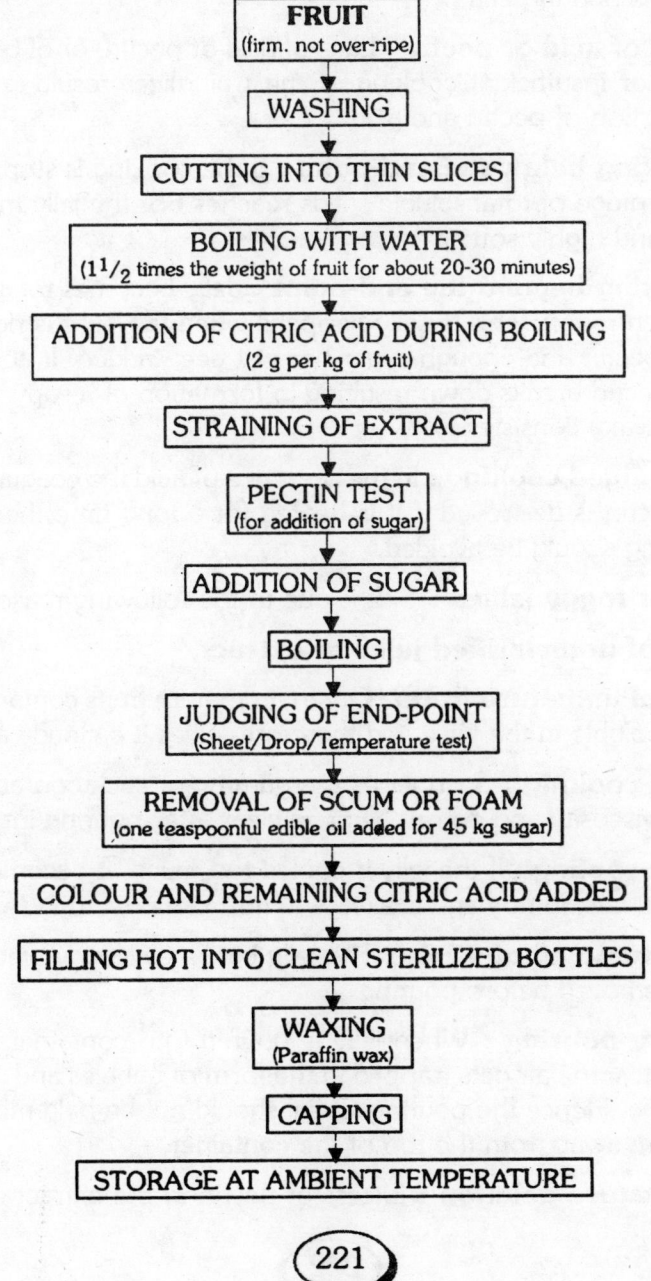

FRUIT
(firm. not over-ripe)

WASHING

CUTTING INTO THIN SLICES

BOILING WITH WATER
($1\frac{1}{2}$ times the weight of fruit for about 20-30 minutes)

ADDITION OF CITRIC ACID DURING BOILING
(2 g per kg of fruit)

STRAINING OF EXTRACT

PECTIN TEST
(for addition of sugar)

ADDITION OF SUGAR

BOILING

JUDGING OF END-POINT
(Sheet/Drop/Temperature test)

REMOVAL OF SCUM OR FOAM
(one teaspoonful edible oil added for 45 kg sugar)

COLOUR AND REMAINING CITRIC ACID ADDED

FILLING HOT INTO CLEAN STERILIZED BOTTLES

WAXING
(Paraffin wax)

CAPPING

STORAGE AT AMBIENT TEMPERATURE

Problems in jelly making : The most important difficulties that are experienced are as follows:

1. **Failure to set :** This may be due to :

    (i)   **Addition of too much sugar :** It results in a syrupy or highly soft jelly which can be corrected by addition of sufficient quantity of fresh, strained extract rich in pectin.

    (ii) **Lack of acid or pectin :** Lack of acid or pectin, or of both, in the fruit used or insufficient cooking of the fruit slices resulting in inadequate extraction of pectin and acid.

    (iii) **Cooking below the end-point :** If the cooking is stopped before the percentage of total soluble solids reaches 65, the jelly may remain syrupy and highly soft.

    (iv) **Cooking beyond the end-point :** Jelly becomes tough due to over-concentration. This usually happens when the juice is rich in both acid and pectin and enough sugar has not been added. If acid is in excess, the pectin breaks down resulting in formation of a ropy syrup or a jelly with waxy consistency.

    (v)   **Prolonged cooking :** In the presence of acid the coagulating property of pectin is destroyed if it is heated for a long time, hence prolonged heating should be avoided.

2. **Cloudy or foggy jellies :**   It is due to the following reasons:

    (i)   **Use of non-clarified juice or extract.**

    (ii) **Use of immature fruits :** Green, immature fruits contain starch which is insoluble in the juice and therefore, gives it a cloudy appearance.

    (iii) **Over-cooking :** Such jellies are gummy or sticky on account of their high viscosity and do not become clear after pouring into containers.

    (iv) **Over-cooling :** If the jelly is cooled too much, it becomes viscous and sometimes, lumpy and is always almost cloudy.

    (v)   **Non-removal of scum :** The jelly becomes cloudy when the scum is not removed before pouring.

    (vi) **Faulty pouring :** When jelly is poured into containers from a grea height, some air gets trapped in the form of bubbles and makes the jelly opaque. Hence the pouring vessel should not be held more than about 2.5 cm away from the top of the container.

    (vii) **Premature gelation :** Excess of pectin in the extract causes premature gelation with the result that air may get trapped in the jelly and thus make it opaque. It can be avoided by :

(a) Heating the solution to the boiling point and immediately pouring it into containers so as to reduce the time of contact between pectin, acid and boiling sugar;

(b) Using low concentration of sugar;

(c) Using a slow-setting pectin; and

(d) Not using acid during cooking and instead putting a concentrated solution of acid in the container prior to pouring the cooked juice.

3. **Formation of crystals** : It is due to addition of excess sugar and also to over-concentration of jelly.

4. **Syneresis or weeping of jelly** : The phenomenon of spontaneous exudation of fluid from a gel is called syneresis or weeping and is caused by several factors: ·

(i) **Excess of acid** : It causes breakdown of the jelly structure by hydrolysis or decomposition of pectin. It occurs more in tender jellies and can be prevented by mixing either some quantity of juice low in acid or more of pectin, so that a larger quantity of sugar can be added which helps in reducing the acidity and increasing the volume of jelly.

(ii) **Too low concentration of sugar** : This causes the network of pectin to hold more liquid than it possibly can do under normal conditions.

(iii) **Insufficient pectin** : This results in the formation of a pectin network which is not sufficiently dense and rigid to hold the sugar syrup.

(iv) **Premature gelation** : This causes breaking of the pectin network during the pouring of jelly into containers and thus the jelly becomes weak and remains broken.

(v) **Fermentation** : Though a high percentage of sugar (65%) prevents ordinary fermentation, it can takes place in jelly if syneresis occurs. Storage of jelly in a damp place, even if covered with a seal of paraffin wax, favours the growth of mould. The growth may be due to several reasons: (a) not covering the jelly properly, (b) not pouring sufficiently hot paraffin wax so as to kill the moulds and bacteria present on the surface of jelly, and (c) breaking of paraffin wax seal. Hermetically sealable glass jars and cans are used to avoid this problem.

Marmalade

This is a fruit jelly in which slices of the fruit or its peel are suspended. The term is generally used for products made from citrus fruits like oranges and lemons in which shredded peel is used as the suspended material. Citrus marmalades are classified into (i) jelly marmalade, and (ii) jam marmalade.

F.P.O. specifications for marmalade are given in Appendix IX. In the home it can be prepared by using the following recipe:

Sweet orange (Malta)	-	1 kg
Khatta or lime	-	0.5 kg

After pectin extraction

Pectin extract	-	1 litre
Sugar	-	750 g
Shredded peel	-	62 g

(1) Jelly marmalade : The following combinations give good quality of jelly marmalade:

(i) Sweet orange (Malta) and khatta or sour orange (*Citrus aurantium*) in the ratio of 2:1 by weight. Shreds of Malta orange peel are used.

(ii) Mandarin orange and khatta in the ratio of 2:1 by weight. Shreds of Malta orange peel are used.

(iii) Sweet orange (Malta) and galgal (*Citrus limonia*) in the ratio of 2:1 by weight. Shreds of Malta orange peel are used.

(2) Jam marmalade : The method of preparation is practically the same as that for jelly marmalade. In this case the pectin extract of fruit is not clarified and the whole pulp is used. Sugar is added according to the weight of fruit, generally in the proportion of 1:1. The pulp-sugar mixture is cooked till the TSS content reaches 65 per cent.

Problems in marmalade making

Browning during storage is very common which can be prevented by addition of 0.09 g of KMS per kg of marmalade and not using tin containers. KMS dissolved in a small quantity of water is added to the marmalade while it is cooling. KMS also eliminates the possibility of spoilage due to moulds.

TECHNOLOGICAL FLOW-SHEET FOR PROCESSING OF MARMALADE

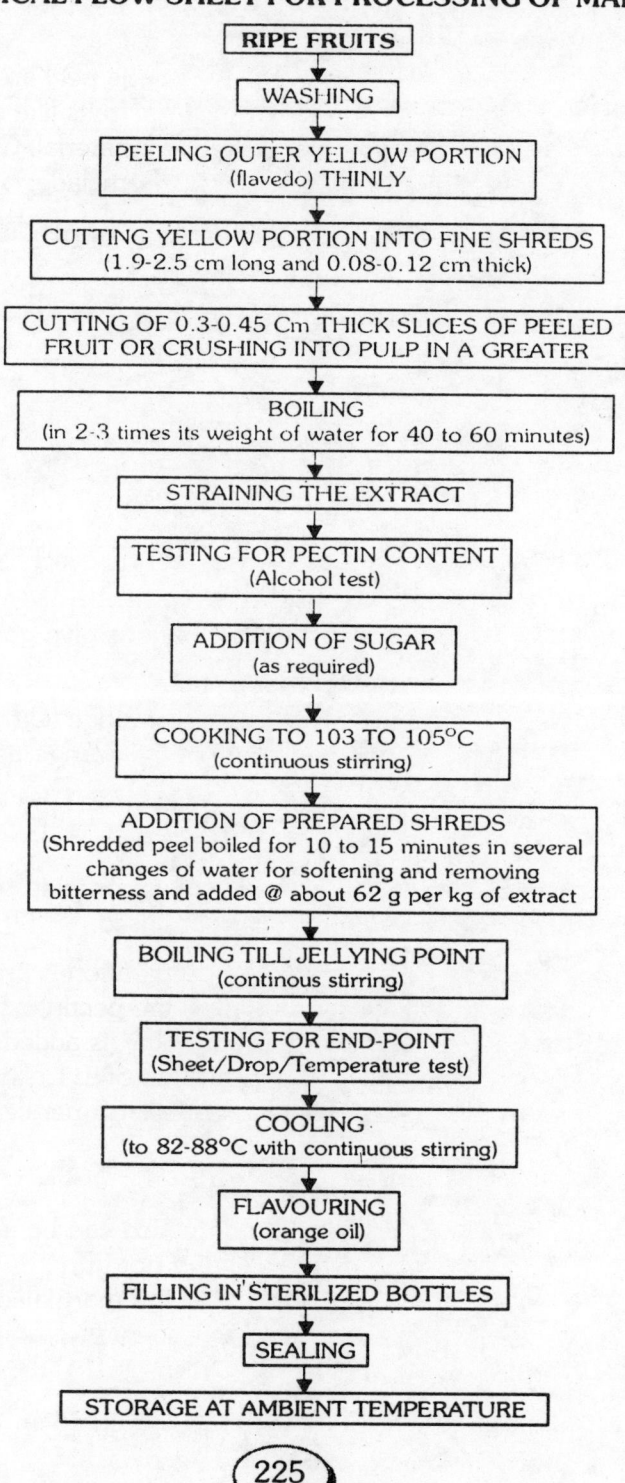

RIPE FRUITS

WASHING

PEELING OUTER YELLOW PORTION
(flavedo) THINLY

CUTTING YELLOW PORTION INTO FINE SHREDS
(1.9-2.5 cm long and 0.08-0.12 cm thick)

CUTTING OF 0.3-0.45 Cm THICK SLICES OF PEELED
FRUIT OR CRUSHING INTO PULP IN A GREATER

BOILING
(in 2-3 times its weight of water for 40 to 60 minutes)

STRAINING THE EXTRACT

TESTING FOR PECTIN CONTENT
(Alcohol test)

ADDITION OF SUGAR
(as required)

COOKING TO 103 TO 105°C
(continuous stirring)

ADDITION OF PREPARED SHREDS
(Shredded peel boiled for 10 to 15 minutes in several
changes of water for softening and removing
bitterness and added @ about 62 g per kg of extract

BOILING TILL JELLYING POINT
(continous stirring)

TESTING FOR END-POINT
(Sheet/Drop/Temperature test)

COOLING
(to 82-88°C with continuous stirring)

FLAVOURING
(orange oil)

FILLING IN STERILIZED BOTTLES

SEALING

STORAGE AT AMBIENT TEMPERATURE

Chapter 19

Preserve, Candied and Crystallized Fruits and Vegetables

Preserve

A mature fruit/vegetable or its pieces impregnated with heavy sugar syrup till it becomes tender and transparent is known as a preserve. Aonla, bael, apple, pear, mango, cherry, karonda, strawberry, pineapple, papaya, etc., can be used for making preserves.

F.P.O. specifications for preserves are given in Appendix IX. In the home they can be prepared using 1 kg of fruit, 1 litre of water and 1 kg of sugar. A little quantity of acid (citric or tartaric) is added during the preparation to prevent crystallization of the syrup.

General considerations

Cooking of fruit in syrup is difficult because the syrup has to be maintained at a proper consistency so that it can permeate the whole fruit without causing it to shrink or toughen. Cooking directly in syrup causes shrinking of fruit and reduces absorption of sugar. Therefore, the fruit should be blanched first to make it soft enough to absorb water, before steeping in syrup. However, highly juicy fruits may be cooked directly.

Fruits may be cooked in syrup by three processes as given below:

(i) **Rapid process :** Fruits are cooked in a low-sugar syrup. Boiling is continued with gentle heating until the syrup becomes sufficiently thick. Soft fruits such as strawberries and raspberries, which require very little boiling for softening, unlike hard fruits like apples, pears, and peaches, which require prolonged heating, can be safely cooked in heavy syrup. Rapid boiling should, however, be avoided as it makes the fruit tough, especially when heating is done in a large shallow pan with only a small quantity of syrup. The final concentration of sugar should not be less than 68 per cent which corresponds to a boiling point of 106°C. This is a simple and cheap process but the flavour and colour of the product are lost considerably during boiling.

(ii) **Slow process :** The fruit is blanched until it becomes tender. Sugar, equal to the weight of fruit, is then added to the fruit in alternate layers and the mixture allowed to stand for 24 hours. During this period, the fruit gives out water and the sugar goes into solution, resulting in a syrup containing 37-38 per cent total soluble solids. Next day the syrup is boiled after removal of fruits to raise its strength to about 60 per cent total soluble solids. A small quantity of citric or tartaric acid (1 to 1.5 g per kg sugar) is also added to invert a portion of the cane sugar and thus prevent crystallization. The whole mass is then boiled for 4-5 minutes and kept for 24 hours. On the third day, the strength of syrup is raised to about 65 per cent total soluble solids by boiling. The fruit is then left in the syrup for a day. Finally, the strength of the syrup is raised to 70 per cent total soluble solids and the fruits are left in it for a week. The preserve is now ready and is packed in containers. In practice, the number of steps may be varied.

(iii) **Vacuum process :** The fruit is first softened by boiling and then placed in the syrup which should have 30-35 per cent total soluble solids. The fruit-syrup blend is then transferred to a vacuum pan and concentrated under reduced pressure to 70 per cent total soluble solids. Preserves made by this process retain the flavour and colour of the fruit better than by the other two methods.

In all these processes, the fruit is kept covered with syrup during cooking as well as afterwards otherwise it will dry up and the quality of the product would be affected.

The product should be cooled quickly after the final boiling to prevent discolouration during storage.

The fruits are drained free of syrup and filled in dry containers or glass jars. Freshly prepared boiling syrup containing 68 per cent total soluble solids is then poured into the jars/containers which are then sealed airtight. In commercial scale production, however, it is better to sterilize the cans to eliminate any possibility of spoilage of product during storage.

Candied fruits/vegetables

A fruit/vegetable impregnated with cane sugar or glucose syrup, and subsequently drained free of syrup and dried, is known as candied fruit/vegetable. The most suitable fruits for candying are aonla, karonda, pineapple, cherry, papaya, apple, peach, and peels of orange, lemon, grapefruit and citron, ginger, etc. Pineapple cores, which are a waste product in the canning of pineapples, can be candied directly without any preliminary treatment. There is scope for developing this useful by-product. F.P.O. specifications for candied fruits are given in Appendix IX.

The process for making candied fruit is practically similar to that for preserves. The only difference is that the fruit is impregnated with syrup having a higher percentage of sugar or glucose. A certain amount (25-30 per cent) of invert sugar or glucose, viz. confectioners glucose (corn syrup, crystal syrup or commercial glucose), dextrose or invert sugar is substituted for cane sugar. The total sugar content of the impregnated fruit is kept at about 75 per cent to prevent fermentation. The syrup left over from the candying process can be used for candying another batch of the same kind of fruit after suitable dilution, for sweetening chutneys, sauces and pickles, and in vinegar making.

PROCESSING FLOW-SHEET FOR MANUFACTURING OF PRESERVE AND CANDY

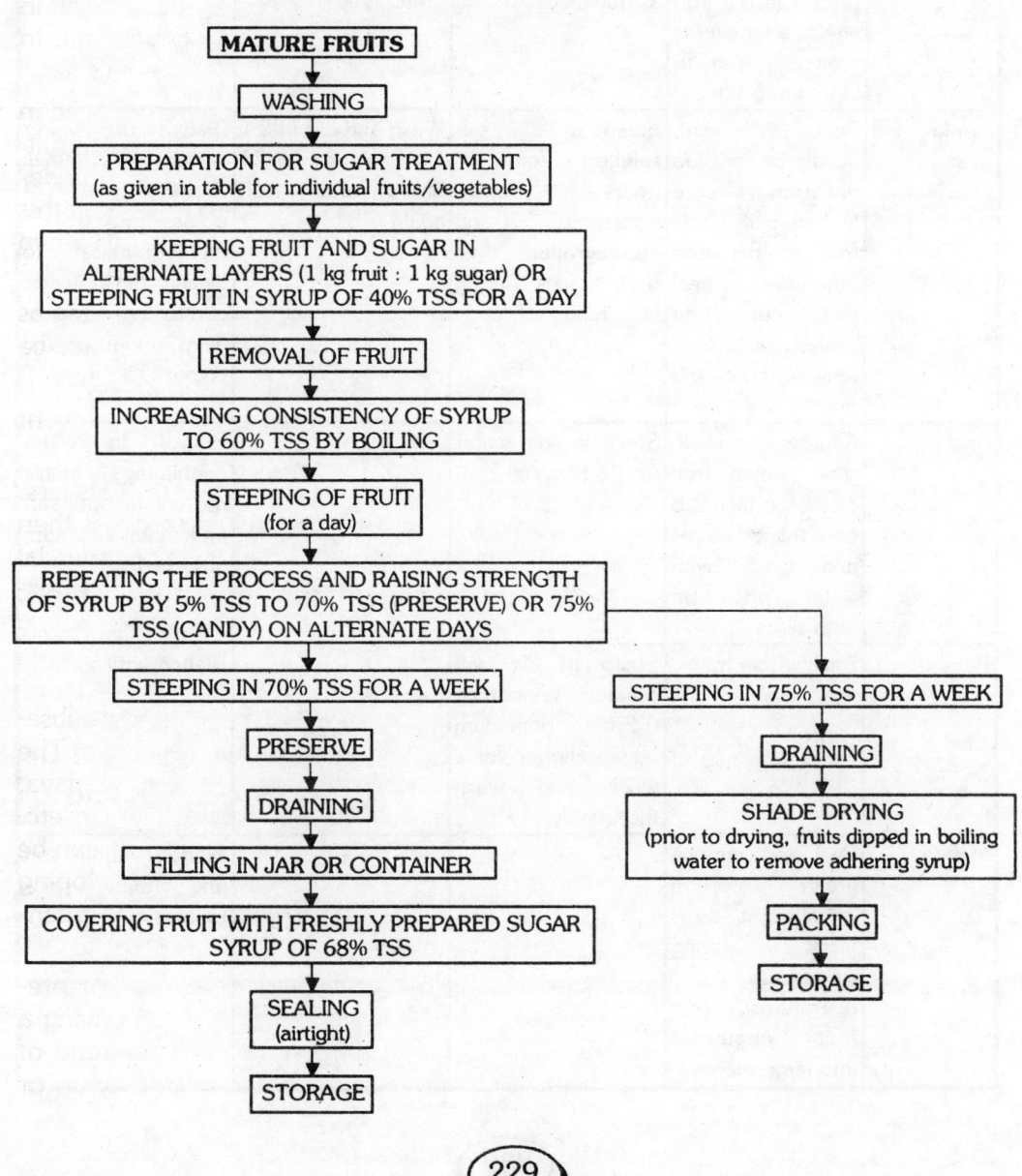

Preparation of fruits/vegetables making for preserve and candy

Fruit/vegetable	Steps of Process			
	Step I	Step II	Step III	Step IV
1	2	3	4	5
Aonla	Prick with fork, needle or gooseberry pricker (avoid iron needle as it causes browning due to tannin in fruit)	Steep in 2% salt solution for 24 hours to remove astringency	Wash and dip in 2% alum solution for 24 hours then wash thoroughly	Blanch until soft but segments do not break or crack
Apple and pear	Peel, prick with needle or fork (do not remove core and stem if whole fruit to be used otherwise peel and cut into halves or quarters, remove core and prick)	Steep in 2% salt solution for 24 hours to prevent browning and disintegration of fruit tissues during blanching	Wash and dip in 2% alum solution for 24 hours and wash again	Blanch in water containing small quantity of potassium metabisulphite to bleach or in water containing edible deep green or red colour
Bael	Remove shell, slice peeled fruit crosswise into 2.5 cm thick pieces and wash with water, prick on both sides	Steep in cold water for 24 hours	–	Blanch in water containing edible red colour until soft and sufficient colour absorbed
Ber	Prick whole fruit	Steep in 2% salt solution containing 0.2% potassium metabisulphite for a week and wash thoroughly	–	Blanch until soft
Mango	Peel and remove green portion (because it turns black during subsequent operations), cut fruit lengthwise into large pieces	–	–	Blanch until soft and then prick pieces

1	2	3	4	5
Karonda and Cherry	Cut into two pieces and remove seeds	Steep in 2% salt solution containing 600 ppm sulphur dioxide (in form of potassium metabisulphite) for 24 hours to bleach, thereafter wash and prick with fork		Blanch in water containing 0.05% erythrosine and 0.25% citric acid to soften sufficiently and fix the artificial colour
Pineapple	Peel, cut into 1 cm slices, remove core and eyes, prick slices on both sides	Steep in 2% salt solution for 24 hours	Wash and steep in cold water for 12 hours	Blanch until soft
Papaya	Peel, cut into rectangular pieces 4 cm long and 0.5-1.0 cm thick, remove seeds and prick	Steep in 2% salt soultion for 24 hours	Wash thoroughly	Blanch until soft
Strawberry and Raspberry	Remove stems	-	-	Blanch for a minute
Petha (Ash gourd)	Cut lengthwise into large pieces, remove fluffy portion, peel, prick and cut into pieces of suitable size	Soak in dilute lime water for 24 hours to harden texture	Wash and soak in 2% alum solution for 24 hours and wash again	Blanch (until tender) in water containing a little potassium metabisulphite to bleach
Ginger	Scrape off skin from tender, fibreless, large sized rhizomes, and cut into pieces	-	-	Boil for an hour with 0.5% citric acid solution (to improve colour) in pressure cooker, then prick and wash
Carrot	From tender carrot having soft pith, scrape off thin peel and green leafy portion, prick and cut into suitable sized pieces	-	-	Blanch until soft
Citrus peel	Remove the rags from thick rind orange, citron, pummelo, etc.	Dip in 2% hot sodium bicarbonate solution for 30 minutes, then wash and prick	-	Blanch until tender and to remove bitterness

231

Glazed fruits/vegetables

Covering of candied fruits/vegetables with a thin transparent coating of sugar, which imparts them a glossy appearance, is known as glazing. F.P.O. specifications for glazed fruits are given in Appendix IX. The preparation of glazed fruits has been described by Cruess as under:

Cane sugar and water (2:1 by weight) are boiled in a steam pan at 113-114°C and the scum is removed as it comes up. Thereafter the syrup is cooled to 93°C and rubbed with a wooden ladle on the side of the pan when granulated sugar is obtained. Dried candied fruits are passed through this granulated portion of the sugar solution, one by one, by means of a fork, and then placed on trays in a warm dry room. They may also be dried in a drier at 49°C for 2-3 hours. When they become crisp, they are packed in airtight containers for storage.

Crystallized fruits/vegetables

Candied fruits/vegetables when covered or coated with crystals of sugar, either by rolling in finely powdered sugar or by allowing sugar crystals to deposit on them from a dense syrup are called crystallized fruits. F.P.O. specifications for crystallized fruits are given in Appendix IX. The candied fruits are placed on a wire mesh tray which is placed in a deep vessel. Cooled syrup (70 per cent total soluble solids) is gently poured over the fruit so as to cover it entirely. The whole mass is left undisturbed for 12 to 18 hours during which a thin coating of crystallized sugar is formed. The tray is then taken out carefully from the vessel and the surplus syrup drained off. The fruits are then placed in a single layer on wire mesh trays and dried at room temperature or at about 49°C in driers.

Problems in preparation of preserves and candied fruits

(i) **Fermentation :** It is due to low concentration of sugar used in the initial stages of preparation of preserves. Sometimes fermentation also occurs during storage due to low concentration of sugar and insufficient cooking. This can be prevented by boiling the product at suitable intervals, by adding the required quantity of sugar and by storage in a cool and dry place.

(ii) **Floating of fruits in jar :** It is mainly due to filling the preserve without cooling and can be avoided by cooling the preserve prior to filling.

(iii) **Toughening of fruit skin or peel :** It may be due to inadequate blanching or cooking of fruits hence blanching till tender is necessary. Toughness may develop when cooking is done in a large shallow pan with only a small quantity of syrup.

(iv) Fruit shrinkage : Cooking of fruits in heavy syrup greatly reduces absorption of sugar and causes shrinkage. Therefore, fruits should be blanched first or cooked in low-sugar syrup.

(v) Stickiness : It may develop after drying or during storage due to insufficient consistency of the syrup, poor quality packing and damp storage conditions.

If candied and crystallized fruits are stored under humid conditions, they lose some of their sugar due to absorption of moisture from the air. Further, they become mouldy if they are not sufficiently dried and are packed in wet containers.

There is considerable scope for exporting preserves and candies. Since these products are hygroscopic, water-proof packaging like metal and glass containers which are impermeable to water vapour should be used. Newer flexible plastic films would be cheap and highly effective. There is need for exploring the possibilities of utilizing various types of plastics for packaging of such products.

Chapter 20

Pickles

T he preservation of food in common salt or in vinegar is known as pickling. It is one of the most ancient methods of preserving fruits and vegetables. Pickles are good appetizers and add to the palatability of a meal. They stimulate the flow of gastric juice and thus help in digestion.

Several kinds of pickles are sold in the Indian market. Mango pickle ranks first followed by cauliflower, onion, turnip and lime pickles. These are commonly made in homes as well as commercially manufactured and exported. Fruits are generally preserved in sweetened and spiced vinegar, while vegetables are preserved in salt.

Pickling is the result of fermentation by lactic acid-forming bacteria, which are generally present in large numbers on the surface of fresh vegetables and fruits. These bacteria can grow in acid medium and in the presence of 8-10 per cent salt solution, whereas the growth of a majority of undesirable organisms is inhibited. Lactic acid bacteria are most active at 30°C, so this temperature must be maintained as far as possible in the early stage of pickle making. When vegetables are placed in brine, it penetrates into the tissues of the former and soluble material present in them diffuses into the brine by osmosis. The soluble material includes fermentable sugars and minerals. The sugars serve as food for lactic acid bacteria which convert them into lactic and other acids. The acid brine thus formed acts upon vegetable tissues to produce the characteristic taste and aroma of pickle.

In the dry salting method several alternate layers of vegetables and salt (20-30 g of drysalt per kg vegetables) are kept in a vessel which is covered with a cloth and a wooden board and allowed to stand for about 24 hours. During this period, due to osmosis, sufficient juice comes out from the vegetables to form brine. Vegetables which do not contain enough juice (e.g., cucumber) to dissolve the added salt are covered with brine (steeping in a concentrated salt solution is known as brining). The amount of brine required is usually equal to half the volume of vegetables. Brining is the most important step in pickling. The growth of a majority of spoilage organisms is inhibited by brine containing 15 per cent salt. Lactic acid bacteria, which are salt-tolerant, can thrive in brine of 8-10 per cent strength though fermentation takes place fairly well even in 5 per cent brine. In a brine containing 10 per cent salt fermentation proceeds somewhat slowly. Fermentation takes place to some extent up to 15 per cent but stops at 20 per cent strength. It is, therefore, advisable to place the vegetables in 10 per cent salt solution for vigorous lactic acid fermentation.

As soon as the brine is formed, the fermentation process starts and carbon dioxide begins to evolve. The salt content is now increased gradually, so that by the time the pickle is ready, salt concentration reaches 15 per cent. When fermentation is over, gas formation ceases. Under favourable conditions fermentation is completed in 7 to 10 days. When sufficient lactic acid has been formed, lactic acid bacteria cease to grow and no further change takes place in the vegetables. However, precautions should be taken against spoilage by aerobic microorganisms, because in the presence of air pickle scum is formed which brings about putrefaction and destroys the lactic acid. Properly brined vegetables keep well in vinegar for a long time.

At present, pickles are prepared with salt, vinegar, oil or with a mixture of salt, oil, spices and vinegar. These methods are discussed below :

(1) Preservation with salt

Salt improves the taste and flavour and hardness the tissues of vegetables and controls fermentation. Salt content of 15 per cent or above prevents microbial spoilage. This method of preservation is generally used only for vegetables which contain very little sugar and hence sufficient lactic acid cannot be formed by fermentation to act as preservative. However, some fruits like lime, mango, etc., are also preserved with salt. The preparation of some pickles is described below :

(i) **Lime pickle :** Lime 1 kg, salt 200 g, red chilli powder 15 g, cinnamon, cumin , cardamom (large) and black pepper (powdered) each 10 g, clove (headless) 5 numbers.

PROCESSING FLOW-SHEET FOR LIME PICKLE

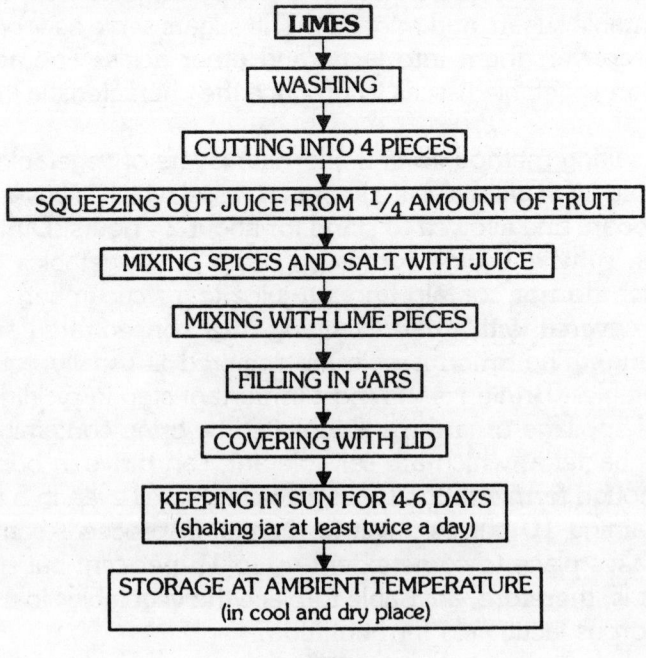

LIMES

↓

WASHING

↓

CUTTING INTO 4 PIECES

↓

SQUEEZING OUT JUICE FROM $1/4$ AMOUNT OF FRUIT

↓

MIXING SPICES AND SALT WITH JUICE

↓

MIXING WITH LIME PIECES

↓

FILLING IN JARS

↓

COVERING WITH LID

↓

KEEPING IN SUN FOR 4-6 DAYS
(shaking jar at least twice a day)

↓

STORAGE AT AMBIENT TEMPERATURE
(in cool and dry place)

(ii) **Lime and green chillies pickle :** Lime 750 g, green chillies 250 g, salt 200 g, cinnamon, cumin, cardamom (large) and black pepper (powdered) each 10 g, clove (headless) 8 numbers.

PROCESS : Similar to that for lime pickle.

(iii) **Mango pickle :** Mango peeled and sliced 1 kg, salt 200 g, red chilli powder 10 g, asafoetida 5 g, fenugreek, black pepper, cardamom (large), cumin and cinnamon (powdered) each 10 g, clove (headless) 6 numbers.

PROCESSING FLOW-SHEET FOR MANGO PICKLE

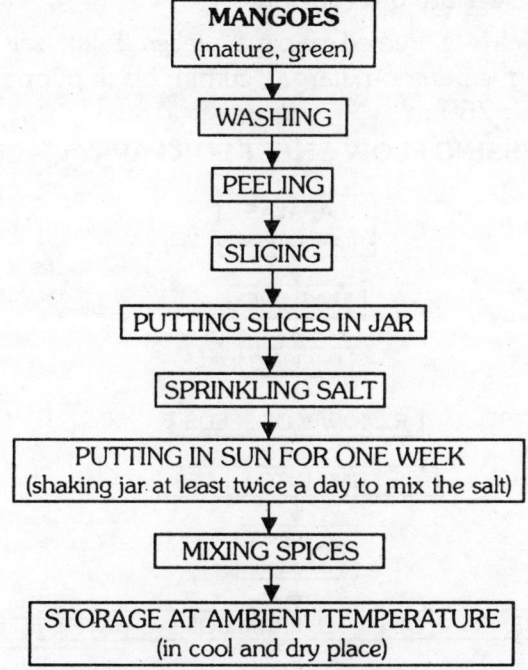

(iv) **Sweet mango pickle :** Mango slices 1 kg, salt 120 g, red chilli, cumin, cardamom (large), aniseed, cinnamon, black pepper, coriander (powdered) each 10 g, clove (headless) 6 numbers, jaggery or sugar 500 g.

PROCESS : Similar to that for mango pickle.

(v) **Sweet lime pickle :** Lime 1 kg, salt 100 g, ginger (chopped) 50 g, turmeric, black pepper, cardamom (large), aniseed, red chilli (powdered) each 15 g, clove (headless) 5 numbers, jaggery 700 g.

PROCESS : Similar to that for lime pickle.

(2) Preservation with vinegar

A number of fruits and vegetables are preserved in vinegar whose final concentration, in terms of acetic acid, in the finished pickle should not be less than 2 per cent. To prevent dilution of vinegar below this strength by the water liberated from the tissues, the vegetables or fruits are generally placed in strong vinegar of about 10 per cent strength for several days before pickling. This treatment helps to expel the gases present in the intercellular speces of vegetable tissue.

Vinegar pickles are the most important pickles consumed in other countries. Mango, garlic, chillies, etc., are preserved as such in vinegar. Some common recipes for vinegar pickles are given below :

(i) **Papaya pickle :** Peeled papaya pieces 1 kg, salt 100 g, red chilli powder 10 g, cardamom (large), cumin, black pepper (powdered) each 10 g, vinegar 750 ml.

PROCESSING FLOW-SHEET FOR PAPAYA PICKLE

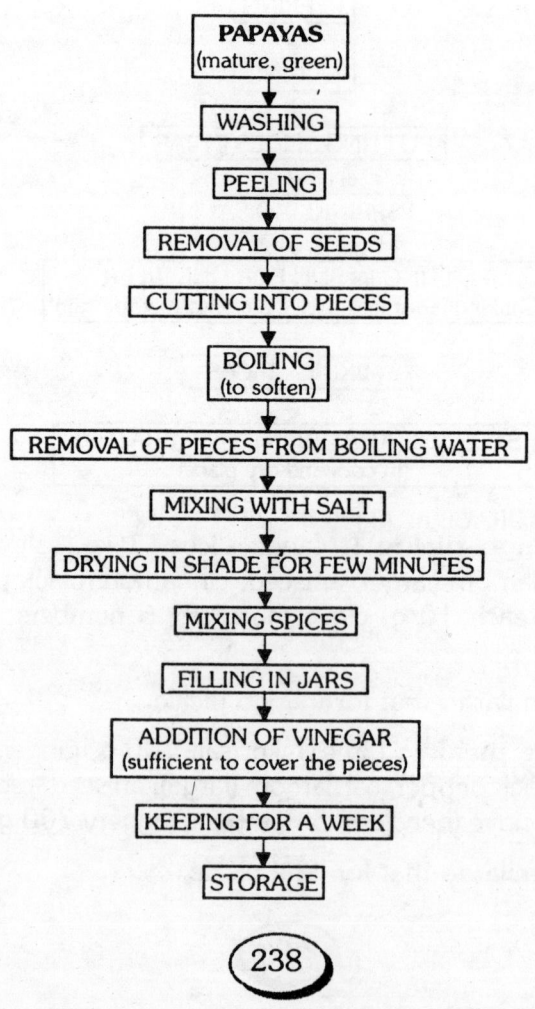

```
        PAPAYAS
     (mature, green)
           ↓
        WASHING
           ↓
        PEELING
           ↓
    REMOVAL OF SEEDS
           ↓
   CUTTING INTO PIECES
           ↓
        BOILING
       (to soften)
           ↓
REMOVAL OF PIECES FROM BOILING WATER
           ↓
     MIXING WITH SALT
           ↓
DRYING IN SHADE FOR FEW MINUTES
           ↓
      MIXING SPICES
           ↓
     FILLING IN JARS
           ↓
   ADDITION OF VINEGAR
(sufficient to cover the pieces)
           ↓
   KEEPING FOR A WEEK
           ↓
        STORAGE
```

(ii) **Pear pickle :** Pear 1 kg, cinnamon, cardamom (large), black pepper, cumin (powdered) each 10 g, sugar 250 g, clove (headless) 5 numbers, vinegar 250 ml.

PROCESSING FLOW-SHEET FOR PEAR PICKLE

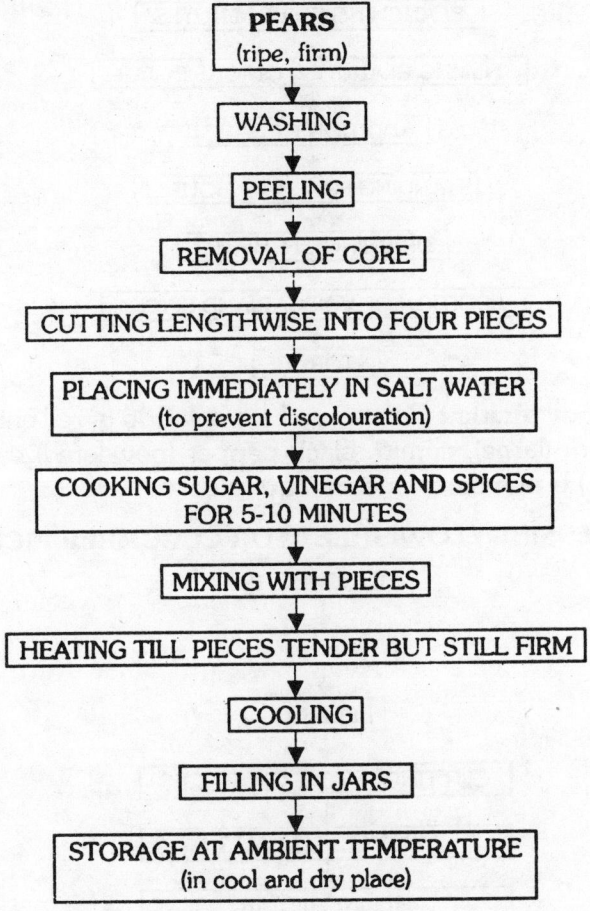

Similarly, pickles can be prepared from apple, peach, plum, etc. Plums and peaches are peeled by blanching in boiling water.

(iii) **Onion pickle :** Onions 1 kg, vinegar 1 litre, salt 250 g, red chilli powder 10 g, cardamom (large), black pepper, cumin (powdered) each 10 g, clove (headless) 5 numbers.

PROCESSING FLOW-SHEET FOR ONION PICKLE

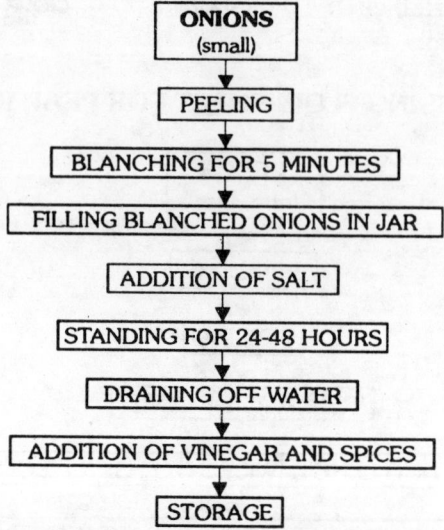

```
        ONIONS
        (small)
          │
        PEELING
          │
  BLANCHING FOR 5 MINUTES
          │
 FILLING BLANCHED ONIONS IN JAR
          │
     ADDITION OF SALT
          │
 STANDING FOR 24-48 HOURS
          │
   DRAINING OFF WATER
          │
 ADDITION OF VINEGAR AND SPICES
          │
        STORAGE
```

(iv) **Cucumber pickle :** Cucumber 1 kg, salt 200 g, red chilli powder 15 g, cardamom (large), cumin, black pepper (powdered) each 10 g, clove (headless) 6 numbers, vinegar 750 ml.

PROCESSING FLOW-SHEET FOR CUCUMBER PICKLE

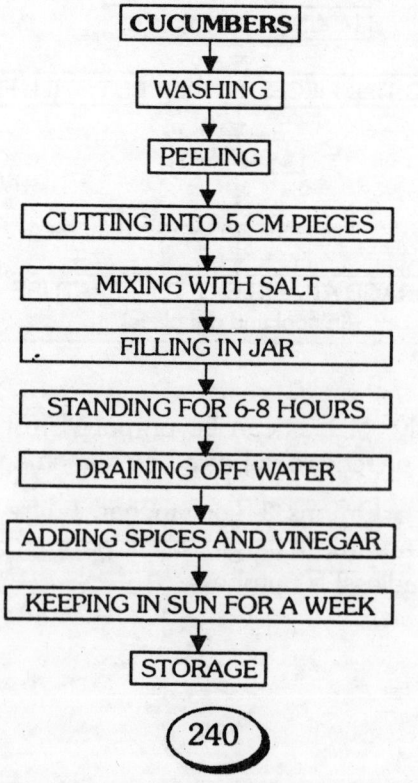

```
       CUCUMBERS
          │
        WASHING
          │
        PEELING
          │
  CUTTING INTO 5 CM PIECES
          │
    MIXING WITH SALT
          │
     FILLING IN JAR
          │
  STANDING FOR 6-8 HOURS
          │
   DRAINING OFF WATER
          │
 ADDING SPICES AND VINEGAR
          │
 KEEPING IN SUN FOR A WEEK
          │
        STORAGE
```

(3) Preservation with oil

The fruits or vegetables should be completely immersed in the edible oil. Cauliflower, lime, mango and turnip pickles are the most important oil pickles. Methods of preparation of some oil pickles are given below :

(i) **Mango pickle :** Mango pieces 1 kg, salt 150 g, fenugreek (powdered) 25 g, turmeric (powdered) 15 g, nigella seeds 15 g, red chilli powder 10 g, clove (headless) 8 numbers, black pepper, cumin, cardamom (large), aniseed (powdered) each 15 g, asafoetida 2 g, mustard oil 350 ml (just sufficient to cover pieces).

PROCESSING FLOW-SHEET FOR MANGO PICKLE

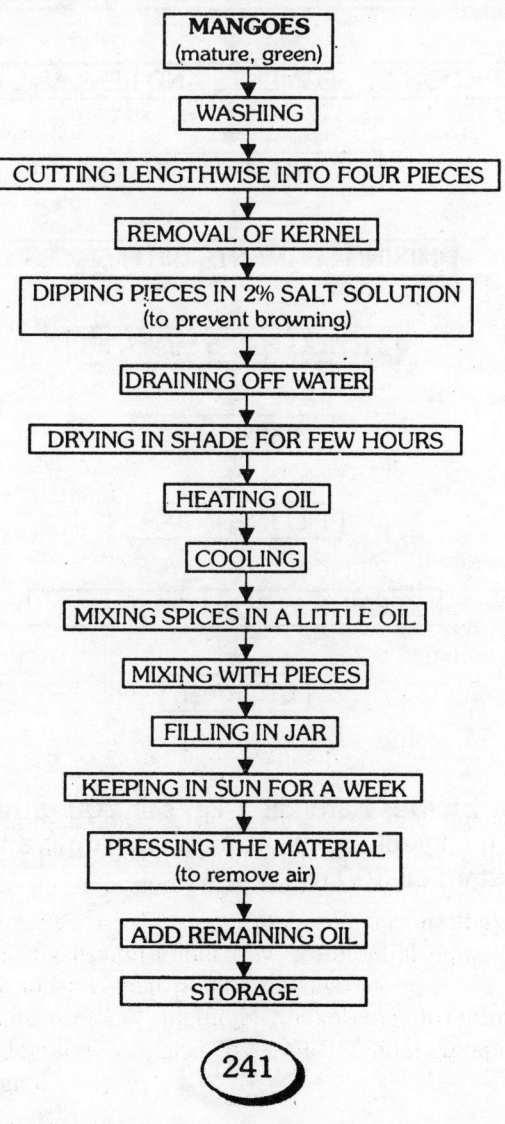

```
        MANGOES
      (mature, green)
           ↓
        WASHING
           ↓
  CUTTING LENGTHWISE INTO FOUR PIECES
           ↓
     REMOVAL OF KERNEL
           ↓
  DIPPING PIECES IN 2% SALT SOLUTION
       (to prevent browning)
           ↓
    DRAINING OFF WATER
           ↓
  DRYING IN SHADE FOR FEW HOURS
           ↓
      HEATING OIL
           ↓
       COOLING
           ↓
  MIXING SPICES IN A LITTLE OIL
           ↓
    MIXING WITH PIECES
           ↓
     FILLING IN JAR
           ↓
  KEEPING IN SUN FOR A WEEK
           ↓
   PRESSING THE MATERIAL
      (to remove air)
           ↓
    ADD REMAINING OIL
           ↓
       STORAGE
```

(ii) **Aonla pickle :** Aonla 1 kg, salt 150 g, turmeric (powdered) 10 g, nigella seeds 10 g, red chilli powder 10 g, fenugreek 30 g, clove (headless) 5 numbers, oil 350 ml.

PROCESSING FLOW-SHEET FOR AONLA PICKLE

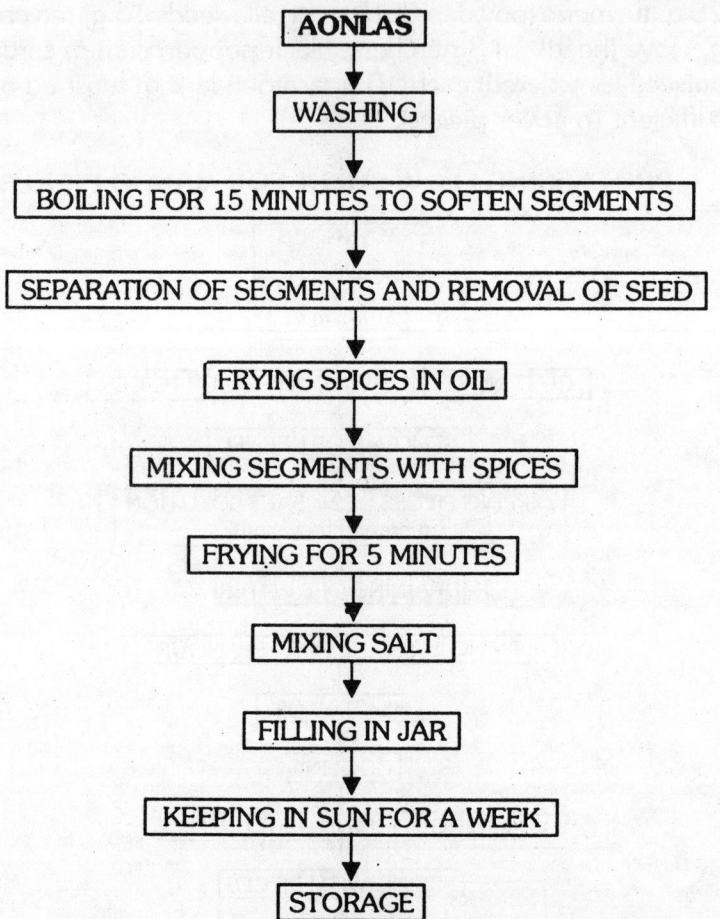

AONLAS

↓

WASHING

↓

BOILING FOR 15 MINUTES TO SOFTEN SEGMENTS

↓

SEPARATION OF SEGMENTS AND REMOVAL OF SEED

↓

FRYING SPICES IN OIL

↓

MIXING SEGMENTS WITH SPICES

↓

FRYING FOR 5 MINUTES

↓

MIXING SALT

↓

FILLING IN JAR

↓

KEEPING IN SUN FOR A WEEK

↓

STORAGE

(iii) **Karonda pickle:** Karonda 1 kg, salt 200 g, red chilli powder 15 g, turmeric, fenugreek, cumin, cardamom (large), aniseed (powdered) each 10 g, mustard oil 300 ml.

PROCESSING FLOW-SHEET FOR KARONDA PICKLE

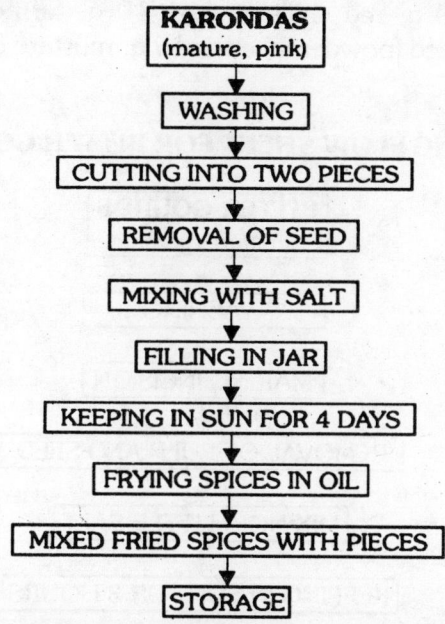

KARONDAS
(mature, pink)
↓
WASHING
↓
CUTTING INTO TWO PIECES
↓
REMOVAL OF SEED
↓
MIXING WITH SALT
↓
FILLING IN JAR
↓
KEEPING IN SUN FOR 4 DAYS
↓
FRYING SPICES IN OIL
↓
MIXED FRIED SPICES WITH PIECES
↓
STORAGE

(iv) **Lime pickle** : Lime 1 kg, salt 120 g, turmeric, cardamom (large), red Chilli, cumin, aniseed, black pepper (powdered) each 10 g, asafoetida 2 g, mustard oil 500 ml.

PROCESSING FLOW-SHEET FOR LIME PICKLE

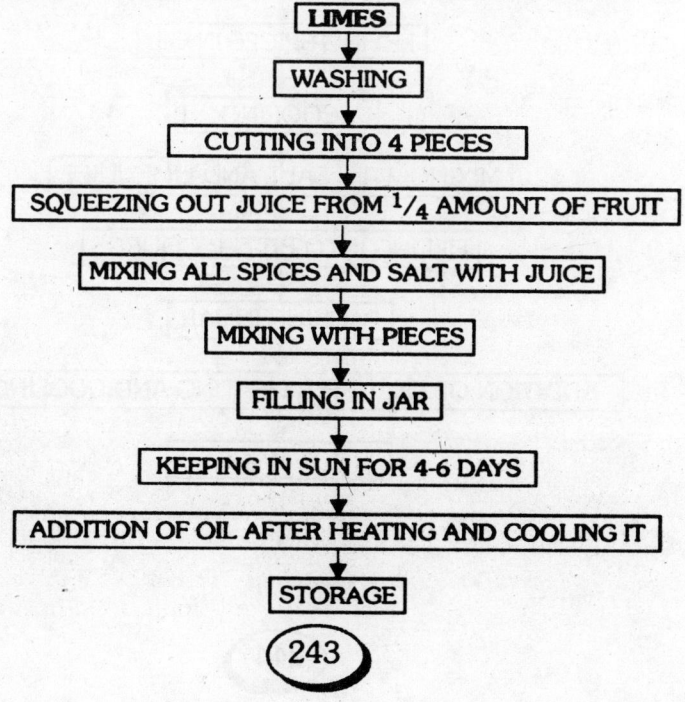

LIMES
↓
WASHING
↓
CUTTING INTO 4 PIECES
↓
SQUEEZING OUT JUICE FROM 1/4 AMOUNT OF FRUIT
↓
MIXING ALL SPICES AND SALT WITH JUICE
↓
MIXING WITH PIECES
↓
FILLING IN JAR
↓
KEEPING IN SUN FOR 4-6 DAYS
↓
ADDITION OF OIL AFTER HEATING AND COOLING IT
↓
STORAGE

(v) **Bitter gourd pickle :** Bitter gourds 1 kg, salt 150 g, tamarind pulp or amchur 250 g, red chilli powder 10 g, turmeric, cardamom (large), cumin, aniseed (powdered) each 10 g, mustard (ground) 100 g, mustard oil 500 ml.

PROCESSING FLOW-SHEET FOR BITTER GOURD PICKLE

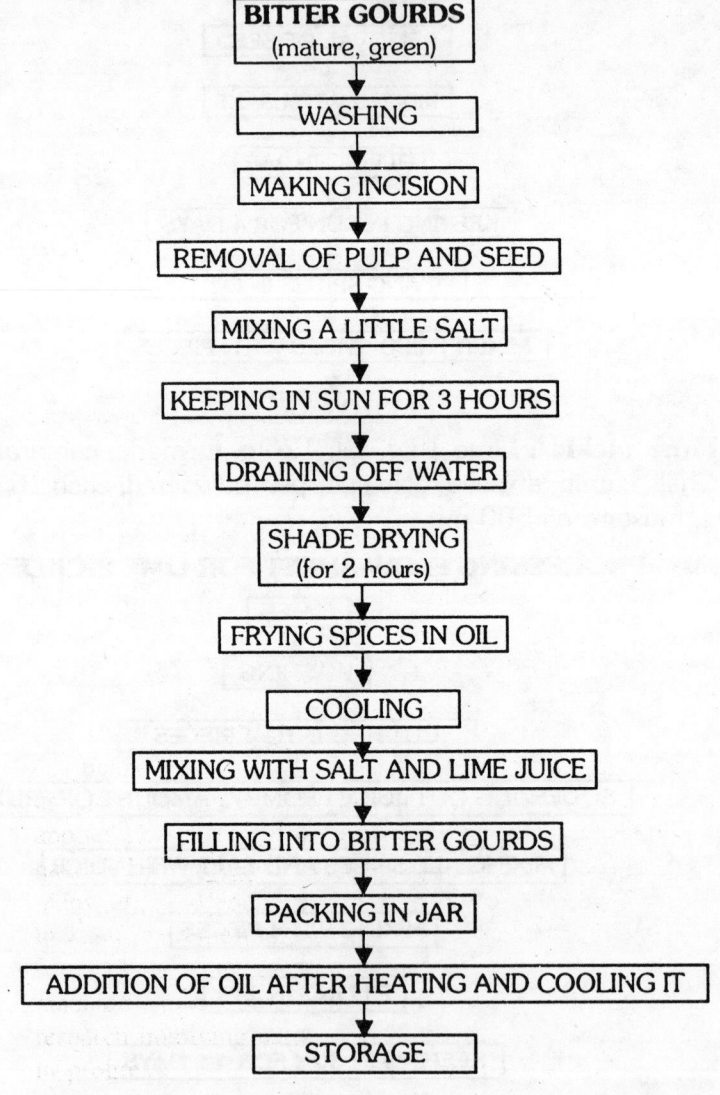

BITTER GOURDS (mature, green)
↓
WASHING
↓
MAKING INCISION
↓
REMOVAL OF PULP AND SEED
↓
MIXING A LITTLE SALT
↓
KEEPING IN SUN FOR 3 HOURS
↓
DRAINING OFF WATER
↓
SHADE DRYING (for 2 hours)
↓
FRYING SPICES IN OIL
↓
COOLING
↓
MIXING WITH SALT AND LIME JUICE
↓
FILLING INTO BITTER GOURDS
↓
PACKING IN JAR
↓
ADDITION OF OIL AFTER HEATING AND COOLING IT
↓
STORAGE

(vi) **Brinjal pickle** : Brinjal 1 kg, salt 100 g, red chilli, turmeric, black pepper, cardamom (large), cumin, aniseed (powdered) each 10 g, mustard (ground) 50 g, mustard oil 350 ml.

PROCESSING FLOW-SHEET FOR BRINJAL PICKLE

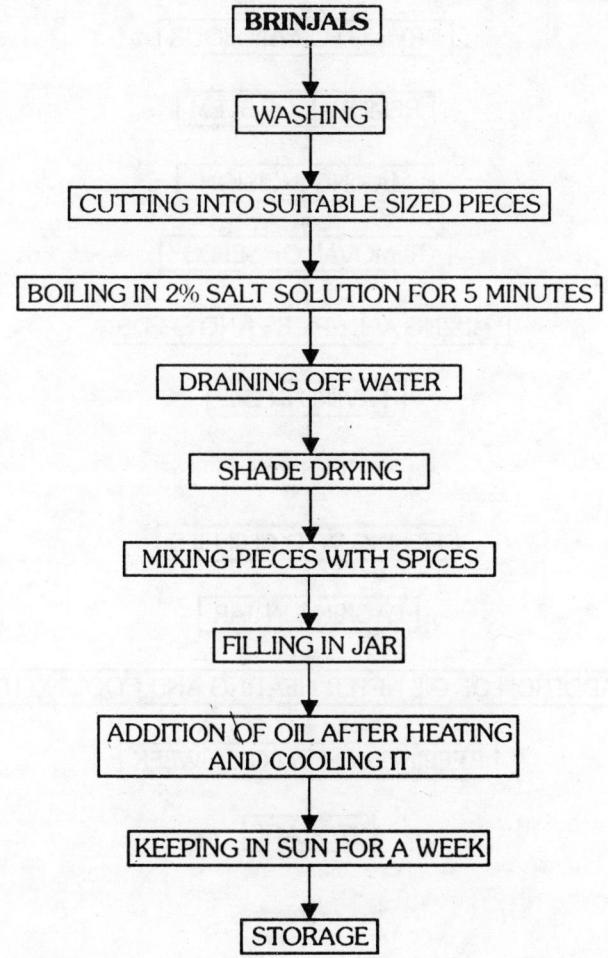

BRINJALS

↓

WASHING

↓

CUTTING INTO SUITABLE SIZED PIECES

↓

BOILING IN 2% SALT SOLUTION FOR 5 MINUTES

↓

DRAINING OFF WATER

↓

SHADE DRYING

↓

MIXING PIECES WITH SPICES

↓

FILLING IN JAR

↓

ADDITION OF OIL AFTER HEATING AND COOLING IT

↓

KEEPING IN SUN FOR A WEEK

↓

STORAGE

(vii) **Red chilli pickle :** Red chillies 1 kg, salt 100 g, amchur 250 g, cardamom (large), black pepper, cumin, aniseed (powdered) each 15 g, clove (headless) 6 numbers, mustard (ground) 100 g, mustard oil 700 ml.

PROCESSING FLOW-SHEET FOR RED CHILLI PICKLE

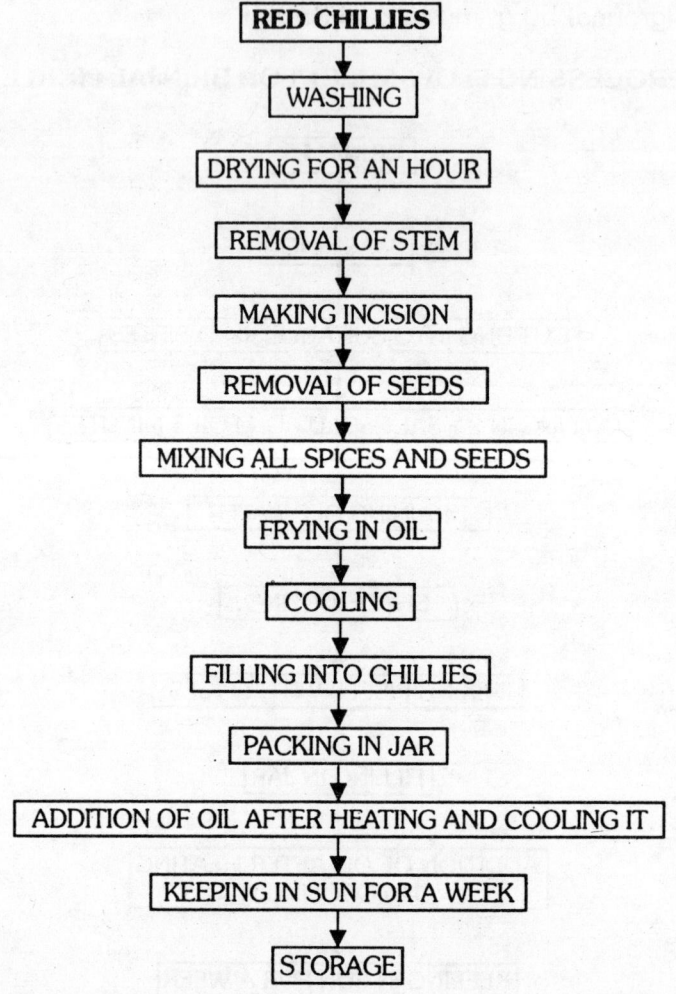

RED CHILLIES

↓

WASHING

↓

DRYING FOR AN HOUR

↓

REMOVAL OF STEM

↓

MAKING INCISION

↓

REMOVAL OF SEEDS

↓

MIXING ALL SPICES AND SEEDS

↓

FRYING IN OIL

↓

COOLING

↓

FILLING INTO CHILLIES

↓

PACKING IN JAR

↓

ADDITION OF OIL AFTER HEATING AND COOLING IT

↓

KEEPING IN SUN FOR A WEEK

↓

STORAGE

(viii) **Green chilli pickle :** Green chillies 1 kg, salt 150 g, mustard (ground) 100 g, lime juice 200 ml or amchur 200 g, fenugreek, aniseed, cardamom (large), tuRmeric, cumin (powdered) each 15 g, mustard oil 400 ml.

PROCESSING FLOW-SHEET FOR GREEN CHILLI PICKLE

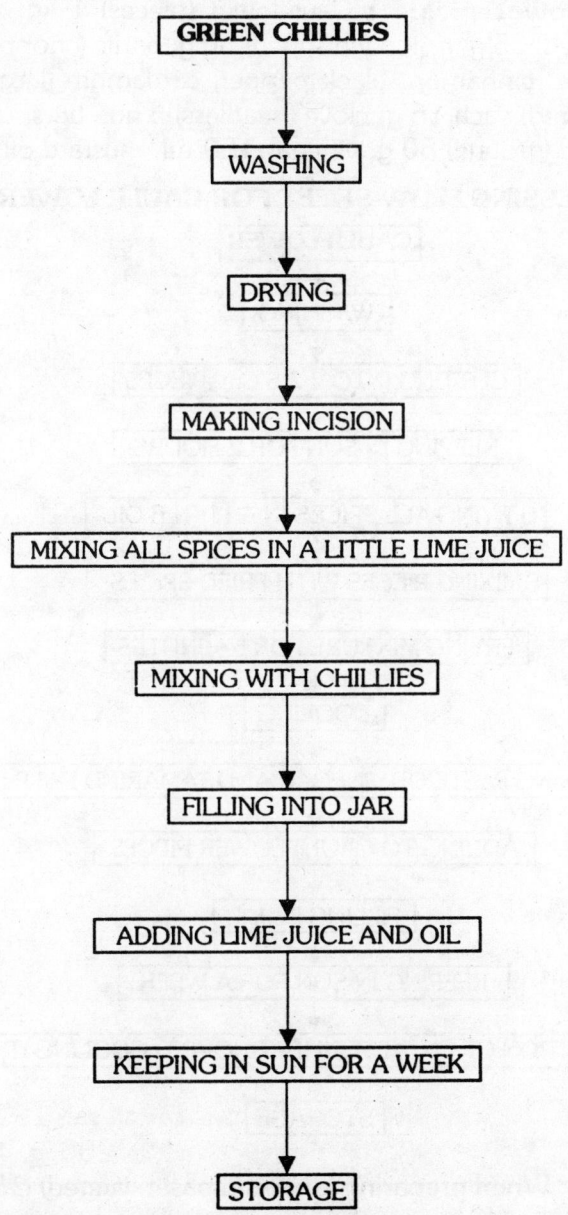

GREEN CHILLIES

↓

WASHING

↓

DRYING

↓

MAKING INCISION

↓

MIXING ALL SPICES IN A LITTLE LIME JUICE

↓

MIXING WITH CHILLIES

↓

FILLING INTO JAR

↓

ADDING LIME JUICE AND OIL

↓

KEEPING IN SUN FOR A WEEK

↓

STORAGE

(4) Preservation with mixture of salt, oil, spices and vinegar

(i) **Cauliflower pickle :** Cauliflower (pieces) 1 kg, salt 150 g, ginger (chopped) 25 g, onion (chopped) 50 g, garlic (chopped) 10 g, red chilli, turmeric, cinnamon, black pepper, cardamom (large), cumin, aniseed (powdered) each 15 g, clove (headless) 6 numbers, tamarind pulp 50 g, mustard (ground) 50 g, vinegar 150 ml, mustard oil 400 ml.

PROCESSING FLOW-SHEET FOR CAULIFLOWER PICKLE

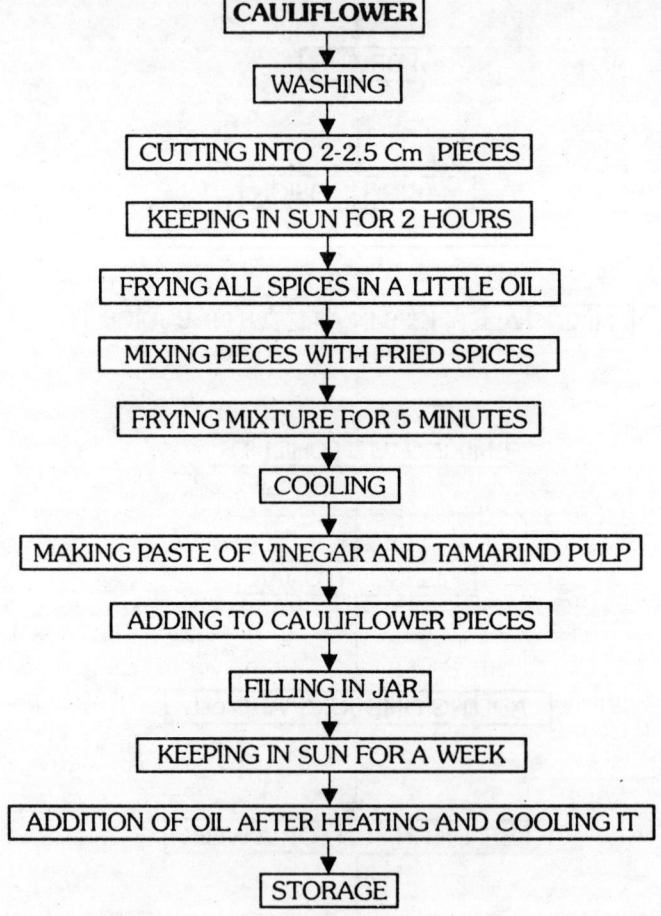

```
            CAULIFLOWER
                 ↓
             WASHING
                 ↓
    CUTTING INTO 2-2.5 Cm PIECES
                 ↓
     KEEPING IN SUN FOR 2 HOURS
                 ↓
   FRYING ALL SPICES IN A LITTLE OIL
                 ↓
   MIXING PIECES WITH FRIED SPICES
                 ↓
    FRYING MIXTURE FOR 5 MINUTES
                 ↓
             COOLING
                 ↓
 MAKING PASTE OF VINEGAR AND TAMARIND PULP
                 ↓
    ADDING TO CAULIFLOWER PIECES
                 ↓
          FILLING IN JAR
                 ↓
    KEEPING IN SUN FOR A WEEK
                 ↓
 ADDITION OF OIL AFTER HEATING AND COOLING IT
                 ↓
             STORAGE
```

When preparing tamarind paste, jaggery (150 g,) can be mixed for sweetening.

(ii) **Carrot pickle :** Recipe and process for carrot pickle is similar to that for cauliflower pickle.

(iii) **Sweet turnip pickle :** Turnip 1 kg, salt 100 g, onion (chopped) 50 g, garlic (chopped) 10 g, ginger (chopped) 20 g, cumin, cardamom (large) red chilli, aniseed, cinnamon, black pepper (powdered) each 10 g, mustard (ground) 20 g, tamarind pulp 100 g, jaggery 200 g, vinegar 100 ml., mustard oil 200 ml.

PROCESSING FLOW-SHEET FOR SWEET TURNIP PICKLE

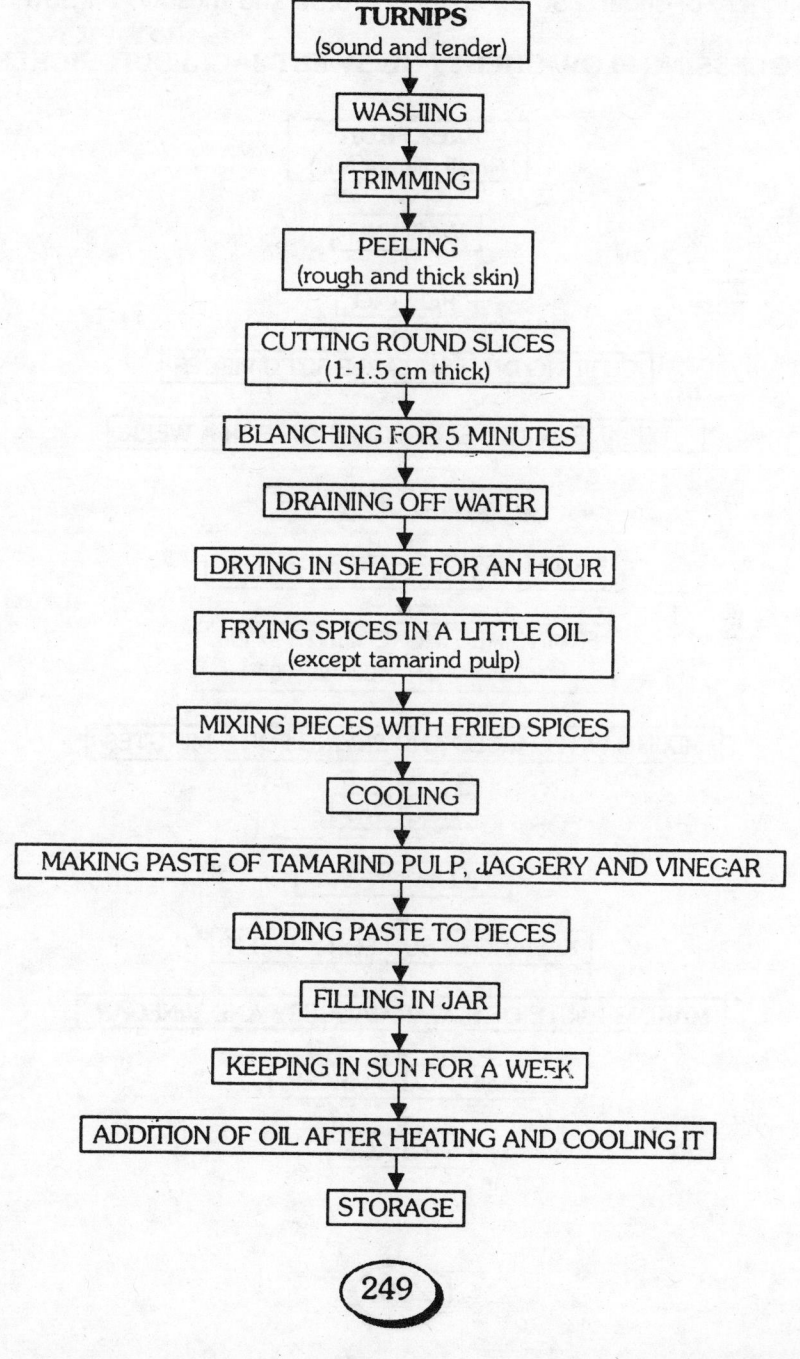

TURNIPS
(sound and tender)

WASHING

TRIMMING

PEELING
(rough and thick skin)

CUTTING ROUND SLICES
(1-1.5 cm thick)

BLANCHING FOR 5 MINUTES

DRAINING OFF WATER

DRYING IN SHADE FOR AN HOUR

FRYING SPICES IN A LITTLE OIL
(except tamarind pulp)

MIXING PIECES WITH FRIED SPICES

COOLING

MAKING PASTE OF TAMARIND PULP, JAGGERY AND VINEGAR

ADDING PASTE TO PIECES

FILLING IN JAR

KEEPING IN SUN FOR A WEEK

ADDITION OF OIL AFTER HEATING AND COOLING IT

STORAGE

(iv) **Red chilli pickle :** Recipe and process are similar to that described for pickles preserved in oil except that 300 ml of oil is used per kg chillies.

(v) **Sweet jackfruit pickle :** Jackfruit pieces 1 kg, salt 100 g, red chilli powder 15 g, cumin, cardamom (large), black pepper, aniseed (powdered) each 10 g, onion (chopped) 50 g, clove (headless) 8 numbers, jaggery or sugar 250 g, vinegar 150 ml and mustard oil 350 ml.

PROCESSING FLOW-SHEET FOR SWEET JACKFRUIT PICKLE

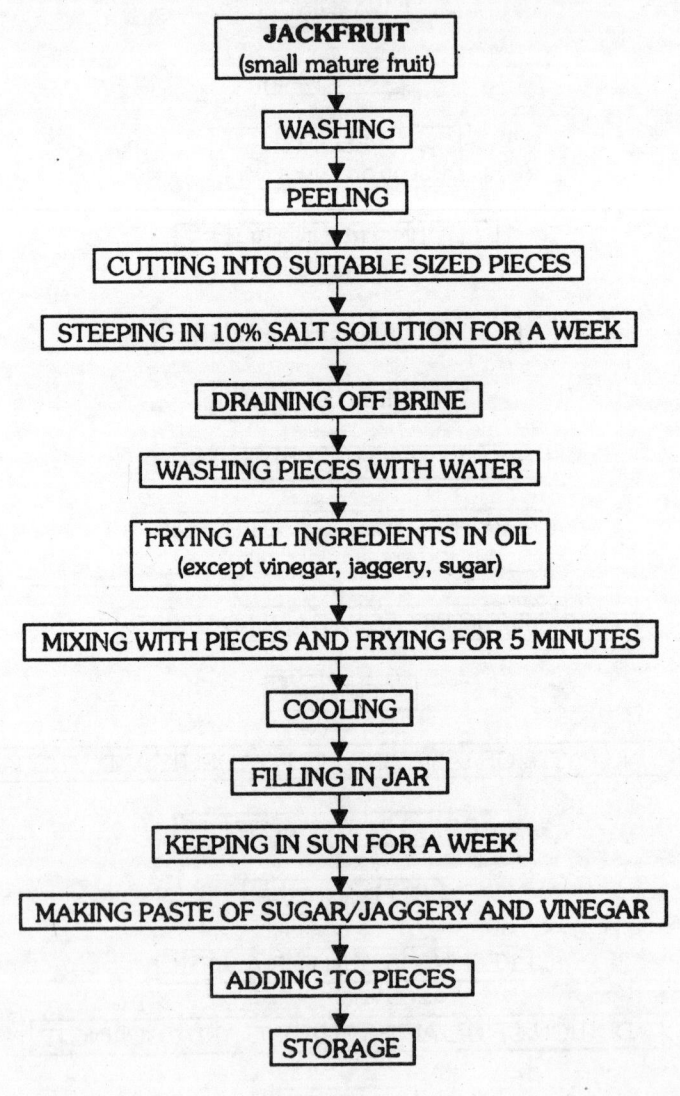

(vi) **Tomato pickle :** Tomatoes 1 kg, salt 75 g, garlic (chopped) 10 g, ginger (chopped) 50 g, red chilli, cumin, cardamom (large), cinnamon, turmeric, fenugreek, aniseed (powdered) each 10 g, clove (headless) 5 numbers, vinegar 250 ml, mustard oil 300 ml.

PROCESSING FLOW-SHEET FOR TOMATO PICKLE

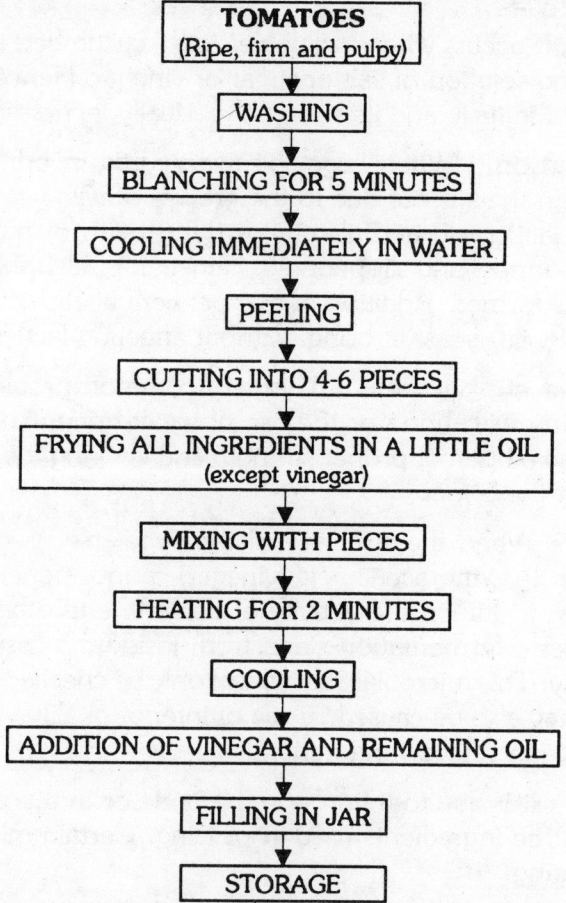

```
          TOMATOES
      (Ripe, firm and pulpy)
              ↓
           WASHING
              ↓
    BLANCHING FOR 5 MINUTES
              ↓
   COOLING IMMEDIATELY IN WATER
              ↓
           PEELING
              ↓
    CUTTING INTO 4-6 PIECES
              ↓
 FRYING ALL INGREDIENTS IN A LITTLE OIL
          (except vinegar)
              ↓
      MIXING WITH PIECES
              ↓
    HEATING FOR 2 MINUTES
              ↓
           COOLING
              ↓
 ADDITION OF VINEGAR AND REMAINING OIL
              ↓
        FILLING IN JAR
              ↓
           STORAGE
```

(vii) **Mixed vegetable pickle :** Cauliflower pieces + diced carrot + turnip slices + peas (in equal amounts) 1 kg, salt 100 g, ginger (chopped) 20 g, onion (chopped) 50 g, garlic (chopped) 10 g. red chilli, black pepper, turmeric, cardamom (large), aniseed, cumin, fenugreek (powdered) each 10 g, cloves (headless) 5 numbers, mustard (ground) 50 g, vinegar 200 ml, mustard oil 450 ml.

Process : Similar to that for sweet turnip pickle. Jaggery or sugar (200 g) may be added by making into a paste with vinegar, if sweetness is desired.

Problems in pickle making

(1) **Bitter taste :** Use of strong vinegar or excess spice or prolonged cooking of spices imparts a bitter taste to the pickle.

(2) **Dull and faded product :** This is due to use of inferior quality materials or insufficient curing.

(3) **Shrivelling :** It occurs when vegetables (e.g., cucumber) are placed directly in a very strong solution of salt or sugar or vinegar. Hence, a dilute solution should be used initially and its strength gradually increased.

(4) **Scum formation :** When vegetables are cured in brine, a white scum always form on the surface due to the growth of wild yeast. This delays the formation of lactic acid and also helps the growth of putrefactive bacteria which cause softness and slipperiness. Hence, it is advisable to remove scum as soon as it is formed. Addition of one per cent acetic acid helps to prevent the growth of wild yeast in brine, without affecting lactic acid formation.

(5) **Softness and slipperiness :** This very common problem is due to inadequate covering with brine or the use of weak brine. The problem can be solved by using a brine of proper strength and keeping the pickles well below the surface of the brine.

(6) **Cloudiness :** When the structure of the vegetable used in pickling, e.g., onion, is such that the acetic acid (vinegar) cannot penetrate deep enough into its tissues to inhibit the activity of bacteria and other microorganisms present in them, fermentation starts from inside the tissues, rendering the vinegar cloudy. This microbial activity can only be checked by proper brining. Cloudiness may also be caused by use of inferior quality vinegar or chemical reaction between vinegar and minerals.

(7) **Blackening :** It is due to the iron in the brine or in the process equipment reacting with the ingredients used in pickling. Certain microorganisms also cause blackening.

Chapter 21

Chutneys and Sauces/Ketchups

C hutneys and sauces are important food products prepared both in homes as well as commercially in India. They improve the digestion and are good appetizers. F.P.O. specifications for chutneys and sauces are given in Appendix IX. Fruits such as mango, apple, plum, apricot, and peach, and vegetables like tomato, cauliflower, turnip, and carrot are the raw materials used. Ginger, garlic, onion, herbs, spices, etc., are added for flavour. Sometimes powdered cloves are added. Since the flower-head of clove contains tannin which causes browning, black neck ring formation takes place in sauces /ketchups if whole cloves are used. Hence cloves should be used only after removing the flower-head. Vinegar, tamarind pulp, and pomegranate seeds (anardana) impart acidity. Sweetness is provided by sugar and jaggery, and salty taste by common salt. Chutneys and sauces do not get spoilt due to the presence of vinegar, salt, sugar and some spices. Chemical preservatives are sometimes added to prevent spoilage.

Iron and copper equipments should not be used in the preparation of chutneys and sauces as these metals are acted upon by vinegar. Further, traces of these metals, dissolved in oil, catalyze the development of rancidity in the products. They also form black compounds with the tannin of fruits and spices and thereby adversely affect the colour, taste and flavour of the product. The vessels used should be glass-lined, or made of nickel or stainless steel.

Chutneys

A good quality chutney should be palatable and appetizing. Mango chutney is an important food product exported from India to many countries. Apple and apricot chutneys are also very popular in the country.

The method of preparation of chutney is similar to that for jam except that spices, vinegar and salt are added. The fruits/vegetables are peeled, sliced or grated, or cut into small pieces and cooked in water until they become sufficiently soft. The quality of a chutney depends to a large extent on its cooking which should be done for a long time at a temperature below the boiling point. To ensure proper thickening, cooking is done without a lid even though this results in some loss of volatile oils from the spices. Chopped onion and garlic are added at the start to mellow their strong flavours. Spices are coarsely powdered before adding. Vinegar extract of spices may be used instead of whole spices. Spice and vinegar are added just before the final stage of cooking, because prolonged boiling causes loss of some of the essential oils of spices and of vinegar by volatilization.

In mango and apricot sweet chutneys, where vinegar is used in large quantity, the amount of sugar added may be reduced, because vinegar itself acts as a preservative. These chutneys are cooked to the consistency of jam to avoid fermentation.

Recipes for chutneys

Some common recipes for preparation of chutney are given below. However, it is always possible to go beyond a recipe, ignoring conventional tastes and creating something new.

1.   Sweet mango chutney

Mango slices or shreds 1 kg, sugar or gur 1 kg, salt 45 g, onions (chopped) 50 g, garlic (chopped) 15 g, ginger (chopped) 15 g, red chilli powder 10 g, black pepper, cardamom (large), cinnamon, cumin, aniseed (powdered) 10 g each, clove (headless) 5 numbers and vinegar 170 ml.

PROCESSING FLOW-SHEET FOR SWEET MANGO CHUTNEY

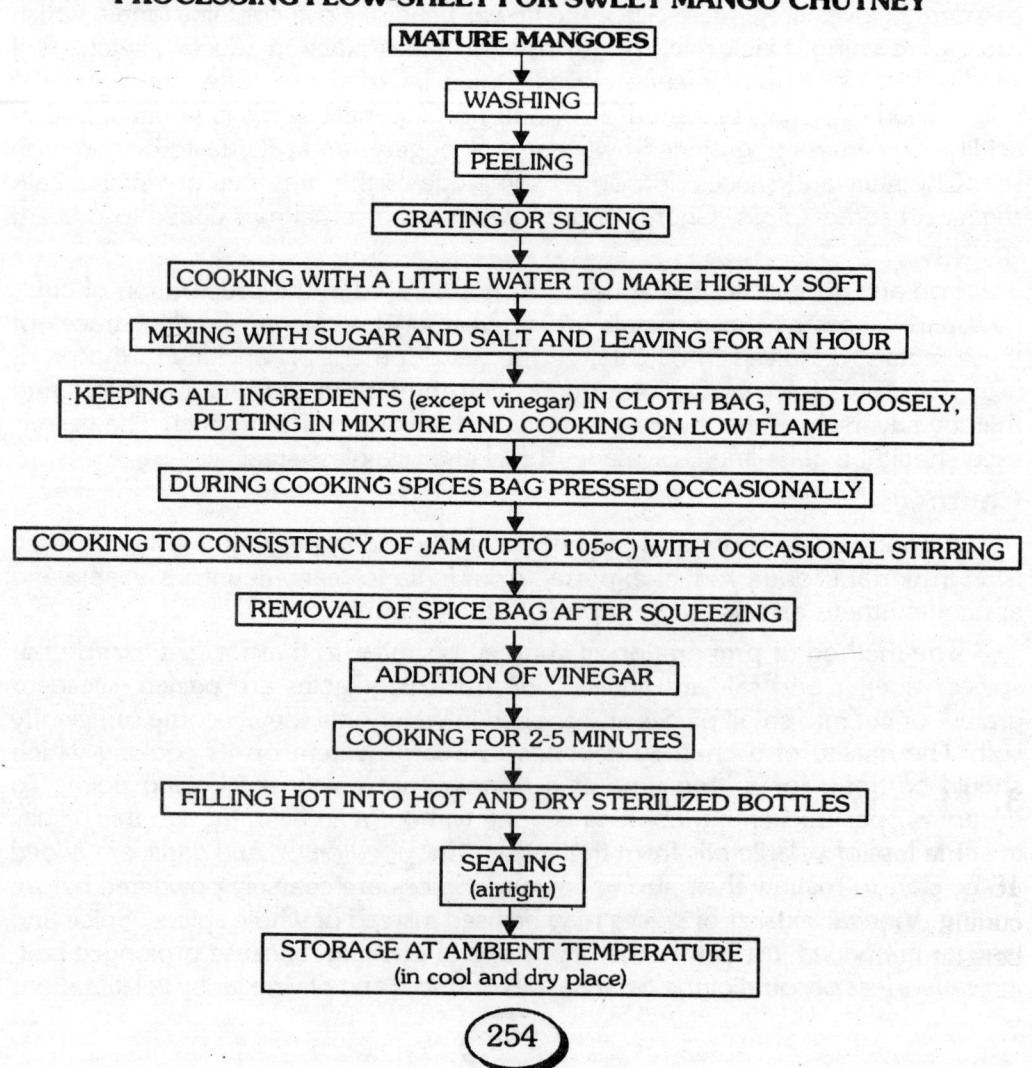

MATURE MANGOES
↓
WASHING
↓
PEELING
↓
GRATING OR SLICING
↓
COOKING WITH A LITTLE WATER TO MAKE HIGHLY SOFT
↓
MIXING WITH SUGAR AND SALT AND LEAVING FOR AN HOUR
↓
KEEPING ALL INGREDIENTS (except vinegar) IN CLOTH BAG, TIED LOOSELY, PUTTING IN MIXTURE AND COOKING ON LOW FLAME
↓
DURING COOKING SPICES BAG PRESSED OCCASIONALLY
↓
COOKING TO CONSISTENCY OF JAM (UPTO 105°C) WITH OCCASIONAL STIRRING
↓
REMOVAL OF SPICE BAG AFTER SQUEEZING
↓
ADDITION OF VINEGAR
↓
COOKING FOR 2-5 MINUTES
↓
FILLING HOT INTO HOT AND DRY STERILIZED BOTTLES
↓
SEALING
(airtight)
↓
STORAGE AT AMBIENT TEMPERATURE
(in cool and dry place)

254

2. Apple chutney

Apples slices 1 kg, sugar 750 g, salt 45 g, dried dates (chopped) 100 g, raisins 50 g, ginger 50 g, red chilli powder 10 g, black pepper, cardamom (large), cinnamon, cumin, aniseed (powdered) 10 g each, clove (headless) 5 numbers, onion (chopped) 250 g, garlic (chopped) 15 g and vinegar 200 ml.

PROCESSING FLOW-SHEET FOR APPLE CHUTNEY

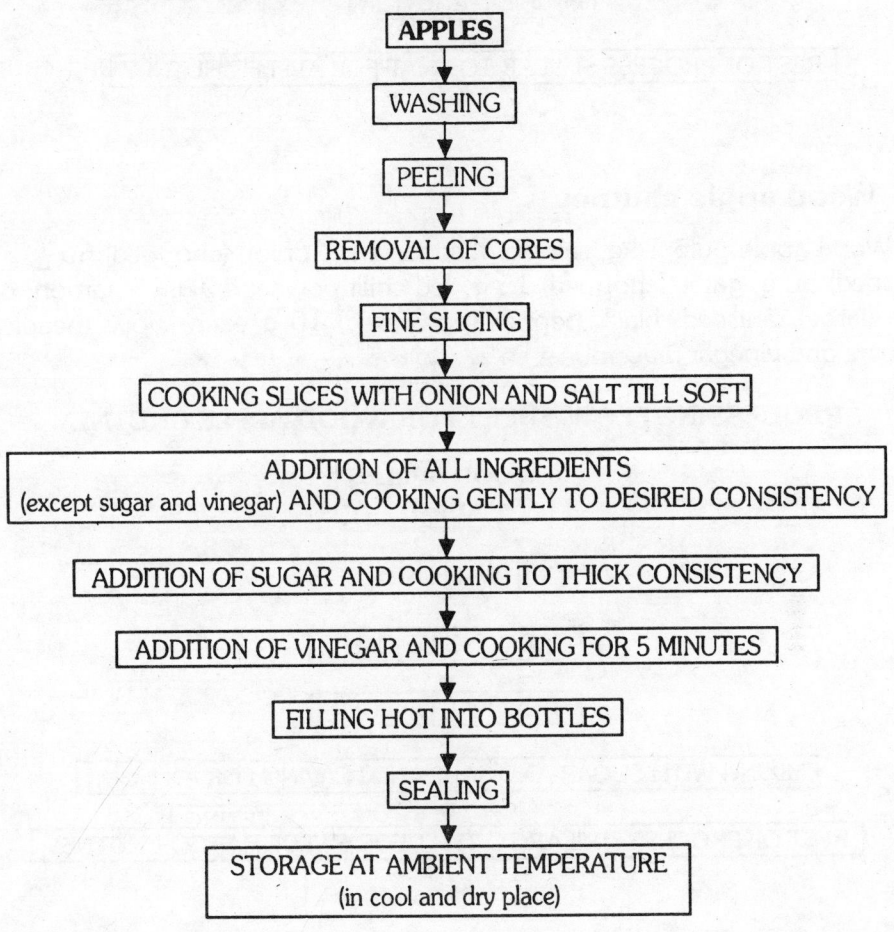

APPLES

↓

WASHING

↓

PEELING

↓

REMOVAL OF CORES

↓

FINE SLICING

↓

COOKING SLICES WITH ONION AND SALT TILL SOFT

↓

ADDITION OF ALL INGREDIENTS
(except sugar and vinegar) AND COOKING GENTLY TO DESIRED CONSISTENCY

↓

ADDITION OF SUGAR AND COOKING TO THICK CONSISTENCY

↓

ADDITION OF VINEGAR AND COOKING FOR 5 MINUTES

↓

FILLING HOT INTO BOTTLES

↓

SEALING

↓

STORAGE AT AMBIENT TEMPERATURE
(in cool and dry place)

3. Plum chutney

Plum pulp 1 kg, sugar 750 g, salt 45 g, onion (chopped) 50 g, garlic (chopped) 15 g, ginger (chopped) 25 g, red chilli powder 10 g, black pepper, cinnamon, cumin, cardamom (large), aniseed (powdered) 10 g each, clove (headless) 5 numbers and vinegar 175 ml.

PROCESSING FLOW-SHEET FOR PLUM CHUTNEY

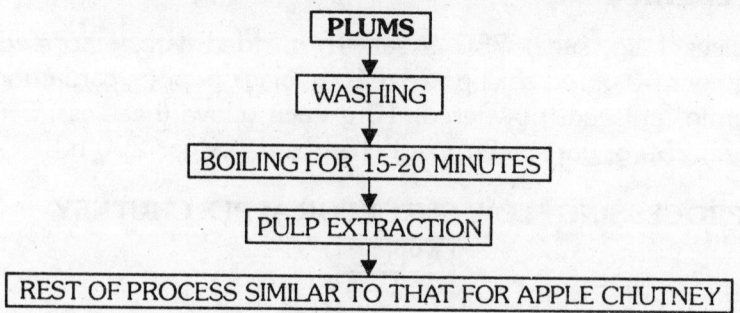

4. Wood apple chutney

Wood apple pulp 1 kg, salt 45 g, sugar 1 kg, onion (chopped) 50 g, ginger (chopped) 50 g, garlic (chopped) 15 g, red chilli powder 10 g, cinnamon, cardamom (large), aniseed, black pepper (powdered) 10 g each, clove (headless) 5 numbers and vinegar 100 ml.

PROCESSING FLOW-SHEET FOR WOOD APPLE CHUTNEY

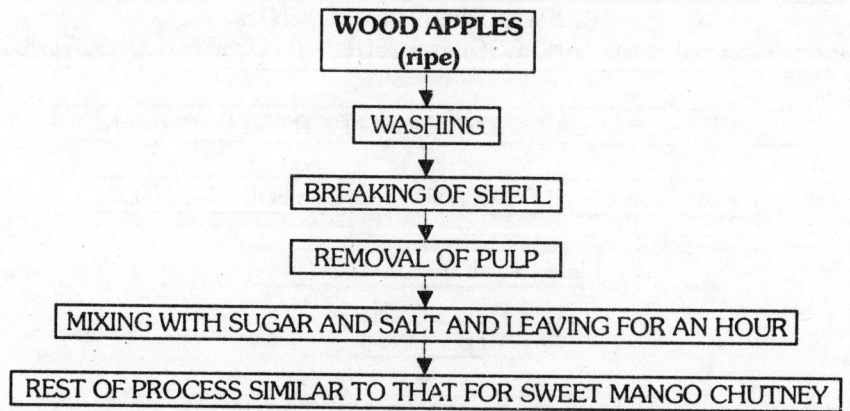

5. Apricot chutney

Apricot slices 1 kg, sugar 1 kg, salt 45 g, onion (chopped) 50 g, ginger (chopped) 20 g, garlic (chopped) 10 g, red chilli powder 10 g, black pepper, cinnamon, cardamom (large), aniseed, cumin (powdered) 10 g each, clove (headless) 5 numbers and vinegar 150 ml.

PROCESSING FLOW-SHEET FOR APRICOT CHUTNEY

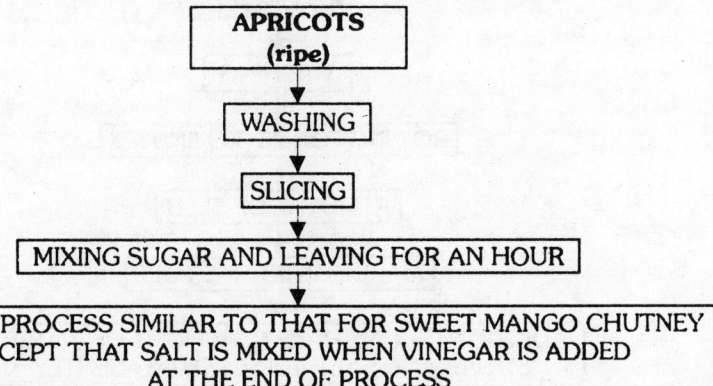

```
          ┌──────────────┐
          │  APRICOTS    │
          │   (ripe)     │
          └──────┬───────┘
                 ▼
          ┌──────────────┐
          │   WASHING    │
          └──────┬───────┘
                 ▼
          ┌──────────────┐
          │   SLICING    │
          └──────┬───────┘
                 ▼
┌──────────────────────────────────────────┐
│ MIXING SUGAR AND LEAVING FOR AN HOUR      │
└──────────────────┬───────────────────────┘
                   ▼
┌──────────────────────────────────────────┐
│ REST OF PROCESS SIMILAR TO THAT FOR SWEET │
│ MANGO CHUTNEY EXCEPT THAT SALT IS MIXED   │
│ WHEN VINEGAR IS ADDED AT THE END OF       │
│ PROCESS                                    │
└──────────────────────────────────────────┘
```

6.   Papaya chutney

Papaya halves 1 kg, sugar 750 g, salt 45 g, onion (chopped) 100 g, ginger (chopped) 50 g, garlic (chopped) 15 g, red chilli powder 10 g, cumin, cardamom (large), cinnamon, aniseed and black pepper (powdered) 10 g each, clove (headless) 5 numbers and vinegar 200 ml.

PROCESSING FLOW-SHEET FOR PAPAYA CHUTNEY

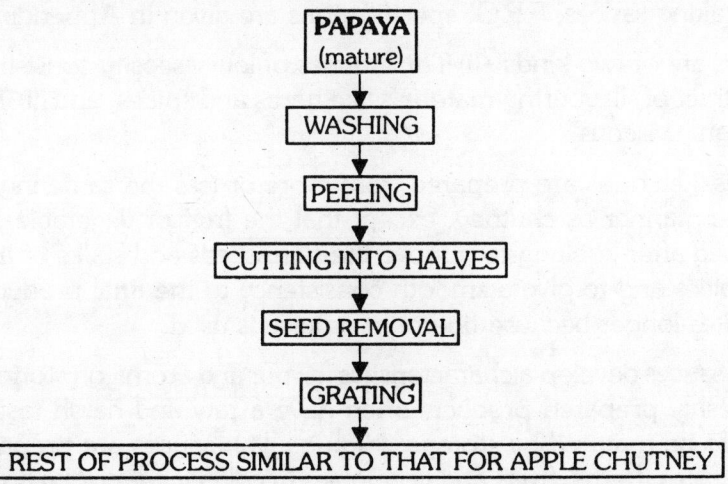

```
          ┌──────────────┐
          │   PAPAYA     │
          │  (mature)    │
          └──────┬───────┘
                 ▼
          ┌──────────────┐
          │   WASHING    │
          └──────┬───────┘
                 ▼
          ┌──────────────┐
          │   PEELING    │
          └──────┬───────┘
                 ▼
     ┌────────────────────┐
     │ CUTTING INTO HALVES│
     └──────────┬─────────┘
                ▼
     ┌────────────────────┐
     │   SEED REMOVAL     │
     └──────────┬─────────┘
                ▼
          ┌──────────────┐
          │   GRATING    │
          └──────┬───────┘
                 ▼
┌──────────────────────────────────────────┐
│ REST OF PROCESS SIMILAR TO THAT FOR       │
│ APPLE CHUTNEY                              │
└──────────────────────────────────────────┘
```

7.   Tomato chutney : See chapter on 'Tomato Processing'

8.   Aonla chutney

Aonla 1.25 kg, sugar 1 kg, salt 50 g, onion (chopped) 50 g, ginger (chopped) 15 g, garlic (chopped) 15 g, red chilli powder 10 g, black pepper, cinnamon, cardamom (large), aniseed, cumin (powdered) 10 g each and vinegar 100 ml.

PROCESSING FLOW-SHEET FOR AONLA CHUTNEY

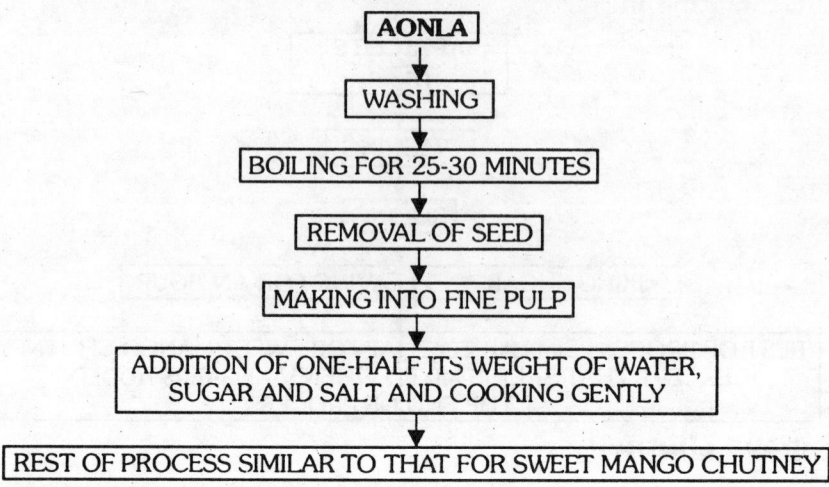

AONLA
↓
WASHING
↓
BOILING FOR 25-30 MINUTES
↓
REMOVAL OF SEED
↓
MAKING INTO FINE PULP
↓
ADDITION OF ONE-HALF ITS WEIGHT OF WATER, SUGAR AND SALT AND COOKING GENTLY
↓
REST OF PROCESS SIMILAR TO THAT FOR SWEET MANGO CHUTNEY

Sauces (Ketchups)

There is no essential difference between sauce and ketchup. However, sauces are generally thinner and contain more total solids (minimum 30%) than ketchups (minimum 28%). Tomato, apple, papaya, walnut, soybean, mushroom, etc., are used for making sauces, F.P.O. specifications are given in Appendix IX.

Sauces are of two kinds : (i) *Thin sauces* of low viscosity consisting mainly of vinegar extract of flavouring materials like herbs and spices, and (ii) *Thick sauces* that are highly viscous.

Sauces/ketchups are prepared from more or less the same ingredients and in the same manner as chutney, except that the fruit or vegetable pulp or juice used is sieved after cooking to remove the skin, seeds and stalks of fruits, vegetables and spices and to give a smooth consistency to the final product. However, cooking takes longer because fine pulp or juice is used.

Some sauces develop a characteristics flavour and aroma on storing in wooden barrels. Freshly prepared products often have a raw and harsh taste and have, therefore, to be matured by storage. High quality sauces are prepared by maceration of spices, herbs, fruits and vegetables in cold vinegar or by boiling them in vinegar. The usual commercial practice is to prepare cold or hot vinegar extracts of each kind of spice and fruit separately, and then blend these extracts suitably to obtain the sauces which are then matured. Thickening agents are also added to the sauce to prevent sedimentation of solid particles. Apple pulp is commonly used for this purpose in India but starch from potato, maize, arrowroot (cassava) and sago are also used.

A fruit sauce should be cooked to such a consistency that it can be freely poured without the fruit tissues separating out in the bottle. The colour of the sauce should be bright. Sauces usually thicken slightly on cooling. By using a funnel hot ketchup is filled in bottles leaving a 2 cm head space at the top and the bottles are sealed or corked at once. The necks of the bottles, when cold, are dipped in paraffin wax for airtight sealing. It is advisable to pasteurize sauces after bottling since there is always a danger of fermentation, especially in tomato and mushroom-based sauces. Other sauces are more acidic and less likely to ferment but should be pasteurized all the same. For this the bottles are kept in boiling water for about 30 minutes.

Recipes for sauces (ketchups)

(1)   Tomato sauce : See chapter on 'Tomato Processing'.

(2)   Apple sauce

Apple pulp 1 kg, sugar 250 g, salt 10 g, onion (chopped) 200 g, ginger (chopped) 100 g, garlic (chopped) 50 g, red chilli powder 10 g, clove (headless) 5 numbers, cinnamon, cardamom (large), aniseed (powdered) 15 g each, vinegar/ acetic acid 50 ml and sodium benzoate 0.7 g per kg finished product.

(3)   Plum sauce

Plum pulp 1 kg, sugar 100 g, salt 20 g, onion (chopped) 50 g, ginger (chopped) 25 g, garlic (chopped) 10 g, red chilli powder 10 g, clove (headless) 5 numbers, black pepper, cardamom (large), cinnamon (powdered) 10 g, each, vinegar 40 ml and sodium benzoate 0.7 g per kg sauce.

PROCESSING FLOW-SHEET FOR PLUM SAUCE

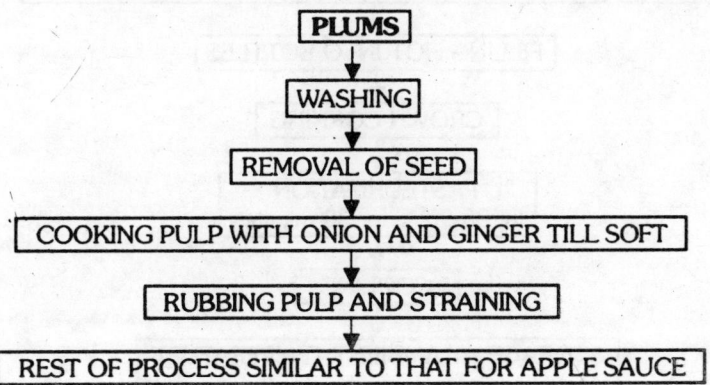

PROCESSING FLOW-SHEET FOR APPLE SAUCE

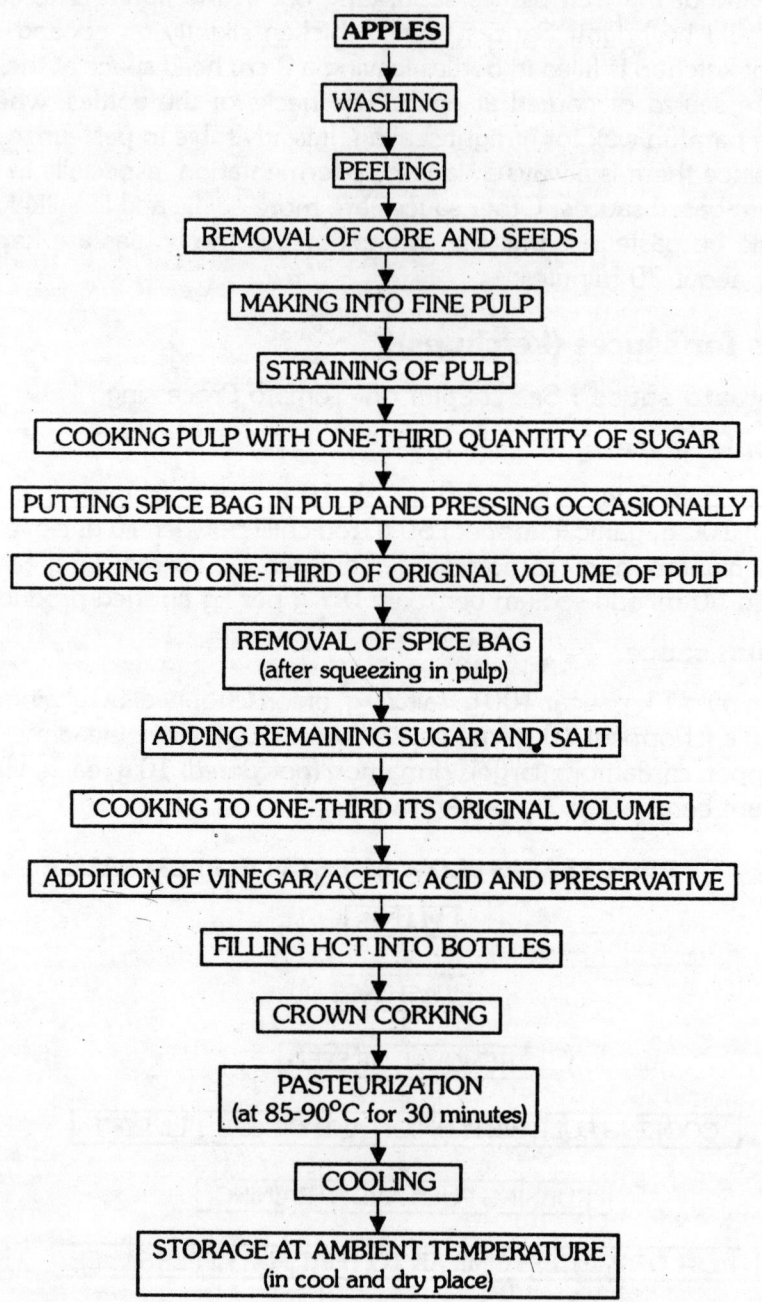

APPLES

↓

WASHING

↓

PEELING

↓

REMOVAL OF CORE AND SEEDS

↓

MAKING INTO FINE PULP

↓

STRAINING OF PULP

↓

COOKING PULP WITH ONE-THIRD QUANTITY OF SUGAR

↓

PUTTING SPICE BAG IN PULP AND PRESSING OCCASIONALLY

↓

COOKING TO ONE-THIRD OF ORIGINAL VOLUME OF PULP

↓

REMOVAL OF SPICE BAG
(after squeezing in pulp)

↓

ADDING REMAINING SUGAR AND SALT

↓

COOKING TO ONE-THIRD ITS ORIGINAL VOLUME

↓

ADDITION OF VINEGAR/ACETIC ACID AND PRESERVATIVE

↓

FILLING HOT INTO BOTTLES

↓

CROWN CORKING

↓

PASTEURIZATION
(at 85-90°C for 30 minutes)

↓

COOLING

↓

STORAGE AT AMBIENT TEMPERATURE
(in cool and dry place)

(4) Papaya sauce

Papaya pulp 1 kg, sugar 50 g, salt 14 g, onion (chopped) 50 g, garlic (chopped) 5 g, ginger (chopped) 10 g, red chilli powder 5 g, hot spices 10 g, vinegar 40 ml and sodium benzoate 0.7 g per kg sauce.

PROCESSING FLOW-SHEET FOR PAPAYA SAUCE

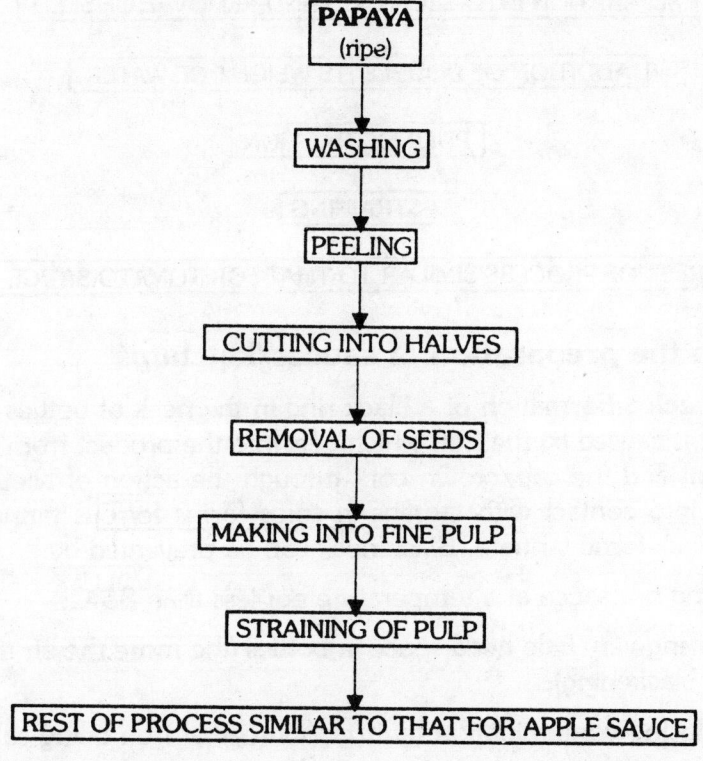

```
        PAPAYA
        (ripe)
          │
          ▼
       WASHING
          │
          ▼
       PEELING
          │
          ▼
  CUTTING INTO HALVES
          │
          ▼
  REMOVAL OF SEEDS
          │
          ▼
  MAKING INTO FINE PULP
          │
          ▼
  STRAINING OF PULP
          │
          ▼
REST OF PROCESS SIMILAR TO THAT FOR APPLE SAUCE
```

(5) Mushroom sauce : See chapter on 'Mushroom Processing'.

(6) Aonla sauce

After extraction of pulp, the recipe and procedure for preparation of aonla sauce are similar to that for tomato sauce. Tomato pulp of high lycopene content may be mixed with aonla pulp to give a better colour to the sauce.

PROCESSING FLOW-SHEET FOR AONLA SAUCE

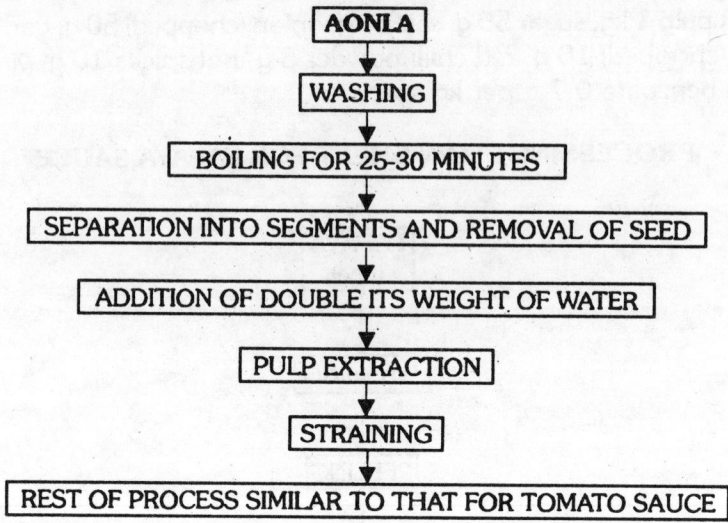

AONLA

↓

WASHING

↓

BOILING FOR 25-30 MINUTES

↓

SEPARATION INTO SEGMENTS AND REMOVAL OF SEED

↓

ADDITION OF DOUBLE ITS WEIGHT OF WATER

↓

PULP EXTRACTION

↓

STRAINING

↓

REST OF PROCESS SIMILAR TO THAT FOR TOMATO SAUCE

Problem in the preparation of sauces/ketchups

Black neck : Formation of a black ring in the neck of bottles is known as black neck. It is caused by the iron which gets into the product from the metal of the equipment and the cap/crown cork through the action of acetic acid. This iron coming into contact with tannins in spice forms ferrous tannate which is oxidized to black ferric tannate. Black neck can be prevented by:

(i)   Filling hot sauce at a temperature not less than 85°C;

(ii) Leaving very little head space in bottles (the more the air the greater is the blackening);

(iii) Reducing contamination by iron, sources of iron being salt and metal equipment;

(iv) Partial replacement of sugar by corn syrup or glucose syrup which contain sulphur and prevent blackening;

(v)   Addition of 100 ppm sulphur dioxide or 100 mg% ascorbic acid;

(vi) Storing bottles in horizontal or inverted position to diffuse the entrapped air (O_2) throughout the bottle thus reducing its concentration in the neck sufficiently to prevent blackening;

(vii) Using cloves only after removing the flower/head.

There is considerable scope for developing a variety of thin as well as thick sauces, using indigenous materials and making suitable changes in the recipes. Apple sauce and tomato sauce are quite popular in India. These are sometimes adulterated with other fruits and starchy vegetables like papaya, ash gourd and pumpkin. Besides red colour is added to a sauce not containing tomato and the cheap product passed off as expensive tomato sauce. Recently addition of colour to tomato sauce has been banned in India.

Chapter 22

Tomato Processing

Tomato is grown in our country in abundance, both in summer and winter seasons, but those grown in winter are superior in quality because they contain more total solids. They are a good source of vitamin C. Fresh tomatoes are very refreshing and appetizing but cannot be stored for a long period. Often they are sold at distress prices during the peak harvest season and nearly 25 per cent of the produce is spoiled due to mishandling. Such losses can be avoided by converting tomatoes into delicious products. In U.S.A., Canada, Australia, etc., large quantities of tomatoes are canned or made into paste, puree, juice, ketchup and sauce. In India, tomato sauce and ketchup are very popular and are being manufactured on an increasingly large scale, mostly in small units. As tomatoes are available practically throughout the year there is scope for setting up large-scale processing units.

The quality of a tomato product is judged by its colour, which is dependent on the redness of the tomatoes used. In fact, the red pigment (lycopene) can be used as an index of the amount of tomato actually present in a product. High quality tomato products can be prepared only by : (i) using plant-ripened uniformly red tomatoes as the yellow and greenish portions not only mask the red colour but also cause browning due to oxidation; (ii) avoiding prolonged heating, and cooling the product quickly after preparation; and (iii) not using iron and copper equipments at any stage of processing. Lycopene (self-oxidizing isomer of carotene) turns brown when it comes into contact with iron. Iron also forms black compounds with the tannin in the tomatoes and the spices used. Equipment used should be glass-lined or made of stainless steel.

Tomatoes can be processed into a number of products:

(1) Tomato juice : Plant-ripened, fully red fruits are selected, discarding all green, blemished and over-ripe fruits. A good quality juice should be of deep red colour, possess the characteristic taste and flavour of tomato, contain about 0.4 per cent acid (in terms of citric acid), be uniform in appearance and have high nutritive value.

F.P.O. specifications for tomato juice are given in Appendix IX. In addition the juice should contain 0.5% salt, 1% sugar and 0.4% acids. In the home it is prepared by using 1 litre of juice, 10 g of sugar, 5 g of salt, 1 g of citric acid and 1 g of sodium benzoate. Tomato juice/pulp can be extracted by hot or cold pulping. Hot pulping is superior to cold pulping because in the latter case, extraction of juice is somewhat difficult and its yield is less, vitamin C is oxidized more rapidly, the juice is lighter in colour and there are chances of microbial spoilage. On commercial scale, a pulper or continuous spiral press is used for juice extraction but in homes tomatoes are strained through a steel sieve.

PROCESSING FLOW-SHEET FOR TOMATO JUICE

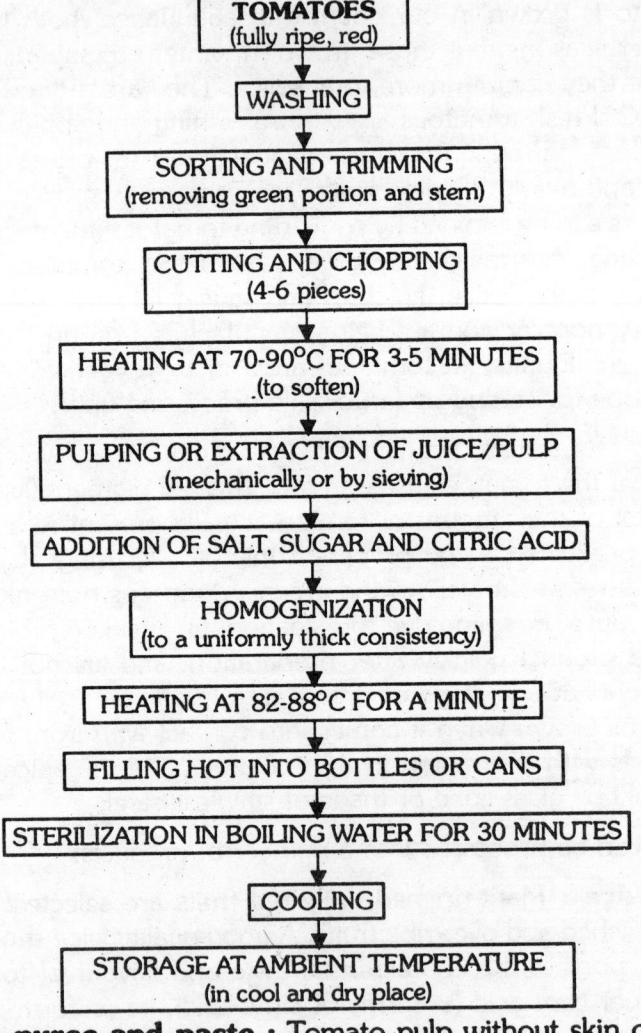

TOMATOES
(fully ripe, red)

WASHING

SORTING AND TRIMMING
(removing green portion and stem)

CUTTING AND CHOPPING
(4-6 pieces)

HEATING AT 70-90°C FOR 3-5 MINUTES
(to soften)

PULPING OR EXTRACTION OF JUICE/PULP
(mechanically or by sieving)

ADDITION OF SALT, SUGAR AND CITRIC ACID

HOMOGENIZATION
(to a uniformly thick consistency)

HEATING AT 82-88°C FOR A MINUTE

FILLING HOT INTO BOTTLES OR CANS

STERILIZATION IN BOILING WATER FOR 30 MINUTES

COOLING

STORAGE AT AMBIENT TEMPERATURE
(in cool and dry place)

(2) Tomato puree and paste : Tomato pulp without skin or seeds, with or without added salt, and containing not less than 9.0 per cent of salt-free tomato solids, is known as 'medium tomato puree'. It can be concentrated further to 'heavy tomato puree' which contains not less than 12 per cent solids. If this is further concentrated so that it contains not less than 25 per cent tomato solids, it is known as tomato paste. On further concentration to 33 per cent or more of solids, it is called concentrated tomato paste. F.P.O. specifications for tomato puree and paste are given in Appendix IX.

Tomato pulp is prepared from ripe tomatoes in the same manner as tomato juice. Cooking for concentration of the pulp can be done either in an open cooker or a vacuum pan. In the former most of the vitamins are destroyed and the product become brown. On the other hand, use of vacuum pans, which are expensive, help to preserve the nutrients and also reduce the browning to a great extent. In vacuum pans the juice is boiled at about 71°C only. Ordinarily tomato juice can be concentrated to 14-15 per cent solids in an open cooker, but for obtaining higher concentrations a vacuum pan is required. Moreover, sterilization of the product is also possible in a vacuum pan. While cooking in an open cooker, a little butter or edible oil is added to prevent foaming, burning and sticking.

If, after cooking, the total solids content of the juice is higher than required, more juice is added to lower it, if it is lower, cooking is continued till the desired concentration is reached. The end-point of cooking puree and paste can be determined either with a hand refractometer or by measuring the volume (a known volume of juice is concentrated to a known volume of final product) with the help of a measuring stick.

PROCESSING FLOW-SHEET FOR TOMATO PUREE/PASTE

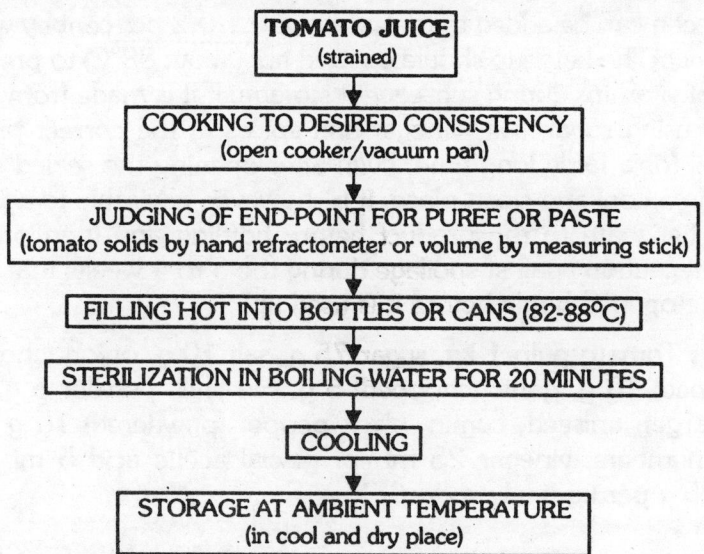

TOMATO JUICE
(strained)

COOKING TO DESIRED CONSISTENCY
(open cooker/vacuum pan)

JUDGING OF END-POINT FOR PUREE OR PASTE
(tomato solids by hand refractometer or volume by measuring stick)

FILLING HOT INTO BOTTLES OR CANS (82-88°C)

STERILIZATION IN BOILING WATER FOR 20 MINUTES

COOLING

STORAGE AT AMBIENT TEMPERATURE
(in cool and dry place)

(3) Tomato sauce/ketchup: It is made from strained tomato juice or pulp and spices, salt, sugar and vinegar, with or without onion and garlic, and contains not less than 12 per cent tomato solids and 25 per cent total solids.

F.P.O. specifications for tomato sauce/ketchup are given in Appendix IX.

General considerations: About one-third of the sugar required is added at the time of commencement of boiling to intensify and fix the red tomato colour. If the whole quantity of sugar is added initially, the cooking time will be longer and the quality of pulp will be adversely affected. Generally, the sugar content in ketchups/sauces varies from 10-26 per cent. On the other hand, salt bleaches the colour of the tomato product; it is, therefore, desirable to add it towards the end of the cooking process. Spices are generally added in powdered form to the product by spice bag method. Instead of whole spices, essential oils of spices oleoresins and spice extract can also be used. Essential oils, however, do not give the characteristic true aroma of whole spice but oleoresins provide true aroma. At present, spice extract is used in many industries for sauce/ketchup preparations. These do not adversely affect the colour of the product and are generally added a few minutes before the end of cooking.

The salt content of the product should be 1.3-3.4 per cent. Good quality vinegar is essential for the preparation of high quality sauce/ketchup. It should contain 5.0-5.5 per cent acetic acid and should be added when the product has thickened sufficiently, so that the acid is not lost by volatilization. Tomato sauce/ketchup generally contains 1.25-1.5 per cent acetic acid. Sometimes glacial acetic acid (100 per cent acetic acid) is used which is colourless and cheaper than vinegar. In order to increase the viscosity and prevent the separation of pulp form clear juice, pectin can be added to the extent of 0.1-0.2 per cent by weight of the finished product. The ketchup should be filled hot (about 88°C) to prevent browning and loss of vitamins during subsequent storage. If it is made from tomatoes of good quality, using sugar, salt, vinegar and spices in the correct proportion, it does not spoil for a fairly long time, even after opening the sealed bottle, if the latter is kept in a cool and clean place. It is, however, advisable to add 0.025 per cent sodium benzoate to the product before bottling and then pasteurize the bottles as a precaution against spoilage during the 3 to 4 weeks that the ketchup remains in the opened bottle before it is used up.

Recipe : Tomato pulp 1 kg, sugar 75 g, salt 10 g, onion (chopped) 50 g, ginger (chopped) 10 g, garlic (chopped) 5 g, red chilli powder 5 g, cinnamon, cardamom (large), aniseed, cumin, black pepper (powdered) 10 g each, clove (headless) 5 numbers, vinegar 25 ml or glacial acetic acid 5 ml and sodium benzoate 0.25 g per kg final product.

PROCESSING FLOW-SHEET FOR TOMATO SAUCE/KETCHUP

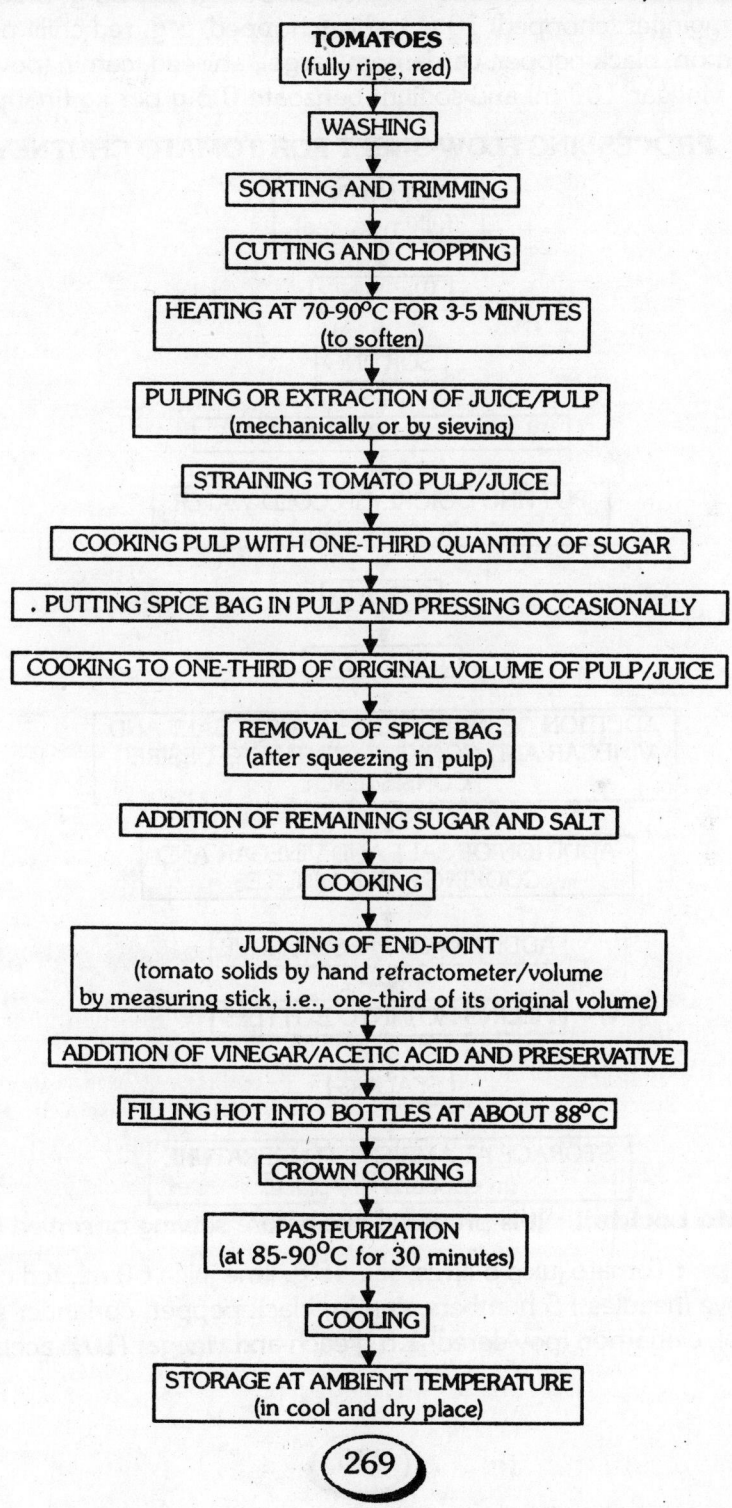

TOMATOES
(fully ripe, red)

WASHING

SORTING AND TRIMMING

CUTTING AND CHOPPING

HEATING AT 70-90°C FOR 3-5 MINUTES
(to soften)

PULPING OR EXTRACTION OF JUICE/PULP
(mechanically or by sieving)

STRAINING TOMATO PULP/JUICE

COOKING PULP WITH ONE-THIRD QUANTITY OF SUGAR

. PUTTING SPICE BAG IN PULP AND PRESSING OCCASIONALLY

COOKING TO ONE-THIRD OF ORIGINAL VOLUME OF PULP/JUICE

REMOVAL OF SPICE BAG
(after squeezing in pulp)

ADDITION OF REMAINING SUGAR AND SALT

COOKING

JUDGING OF END-POINT
(tomato solids by hand refractometer/volume
by measuring stick, i.e., one-third of its original volume)

ADDITION OF VINEGAR/ACETIC ACID AND PRESERVATIVE

FILLING HOT INTO BOTTLES AT ABOUT 88°C

CROWN CORKING

PASTEURIZATION
(at 85-90°C for 30 minutes)

COOLING

STORAGE AT AMBIENT TEMPERATURE
(in cool and dry place)

(4) Tomato chutney : Tomato 1 kg, sugar 500 g, salt 25 g, onion (chopped) 100 g, ginger (chopped) 10 g, garlic (chopped) 5 g, red chilli powder 10 g, cinnamon, black pepper, cardamom (large), aniseed, cumin (powdered) 10 g each, vinegar 100 ml and sodium benzoate 0.5 g per kg final product.

PROCESSING FLOW-SHEET FOR TOMATO CHUTNEY

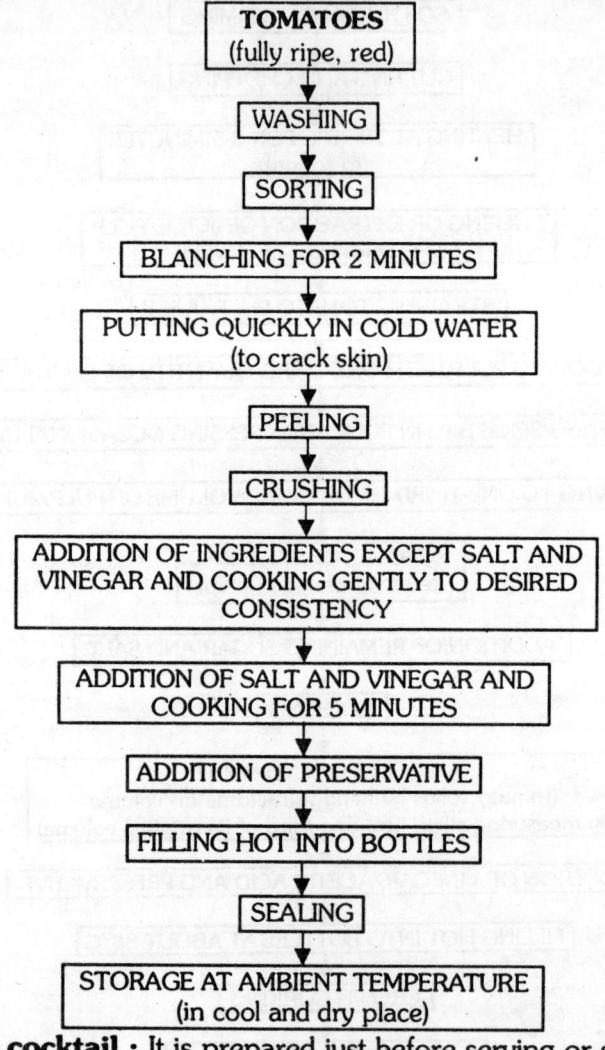

TOMATOES
(fully ripe, red)
↓
WASHING
↓
SORTING
↓
BLANCHING FOR 2 MINUTES
↓
PUTTING QUICKLY IN COLD WATER
(to crack skin)
↓
PEELING
↓
CRUSHING
↓
ADDITION OF INGREDIENTS EXCEPT SALT AND VINEGAR AND COOKING GENTLY TO DESIRED CONSISTENCY
↓
ADDITION OF SALT AND VINEGAR AND COOKING FOR 5 MINUTES
↓
ADDITION OF PRESERVATIVE
↓
FILLING HOT INTO BOTTLES
↓
SEALING
↓
STORAGE AT AMBIENT TEMPERATURE
(in cool and dry place)

(5) Tomato cocktail : It is prepared just before serving or served from stock.

Recipe : Tomato juice 5 litres, salt 45 g, lime juice 60 ml, red chilli powder 0.25 g, clove (headless) 5 numbers, cumin, black pepper, coriander seed, cardamom (large), cinnamon (powdered) 1.5 g each and vinegar (10% acetic acid) 300 ml.

PROCESSING FLOW-SHEET FOR TOMATO COCKTAIL

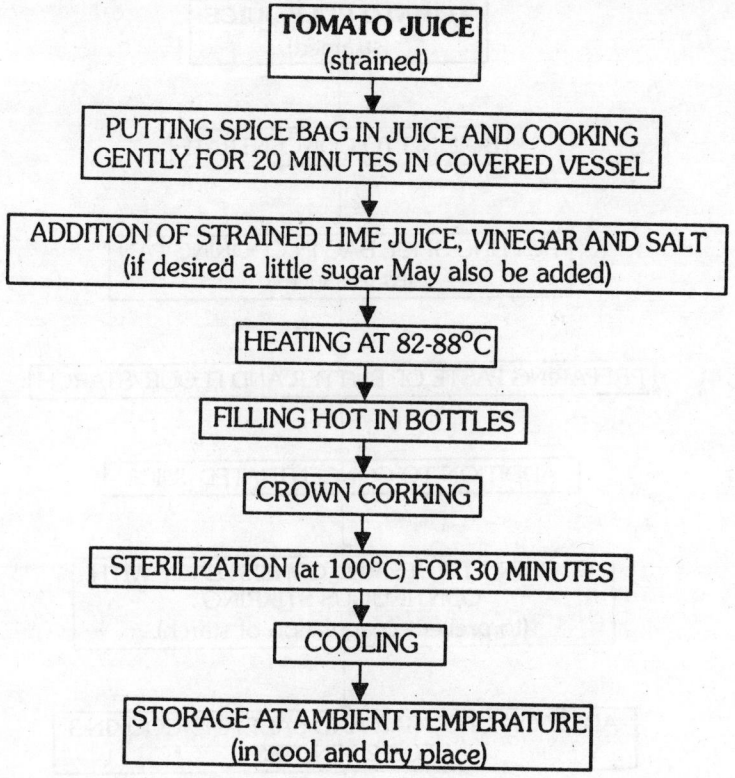

TOMATO JUICE
(strained)

↓

PUTTING SPICE BAG IN JUICE AND COOKING
GENTLY FOR 20 MINUTES IN COVERED VESSEL

↓

ADDITION OF STRAINED LIME JUICE, VINEGAR AND SALT
(if desired a little sugar May also be added)

↓

HEATING AT 82-88°C

↓

FILLING HOT IN BOTTLES

↓

CROWN CORKING

↓

STERILIZATION (at 100°C) FOR 30 MINUTES

↓

COOLING

↓

STORAGE AT AMBIENT TEMPERATURE
(in cool and dry place)

(6) Tomato soup: Soup is becoming very popular in homes. Stored soup is warmed at the time of serving. F.P.O. specifications are given in Appendix IX.

Recipe : Tomato pulp 1 kg, salt 20 g, sugar 20 g, butter or cream 20 g, flour/starch 10 g, onion (chopped) 20 g, garlic (chopped) 5 g, clove (headless) 5 numbers, cumin, cardamom (large), black pepper, cinnamon (powdered) 1 g each and water 350 ml.

(7) Canned tomatoes : See chapter on "Canning and Bottling of Fruits and Vegetables."

(8) Tomato pickle : See chapter on "Pickles."

(9) Tomato chilli sauce : It is highly spiced product made from ripe, peeled and crushed tomatoes and salt, sugar, spices, vinegar, with or without onion and garlic. The method of preparation is similar to that for tomato sauce

PROCESSING FLOW-SHEET FOR TOMATO SOUP

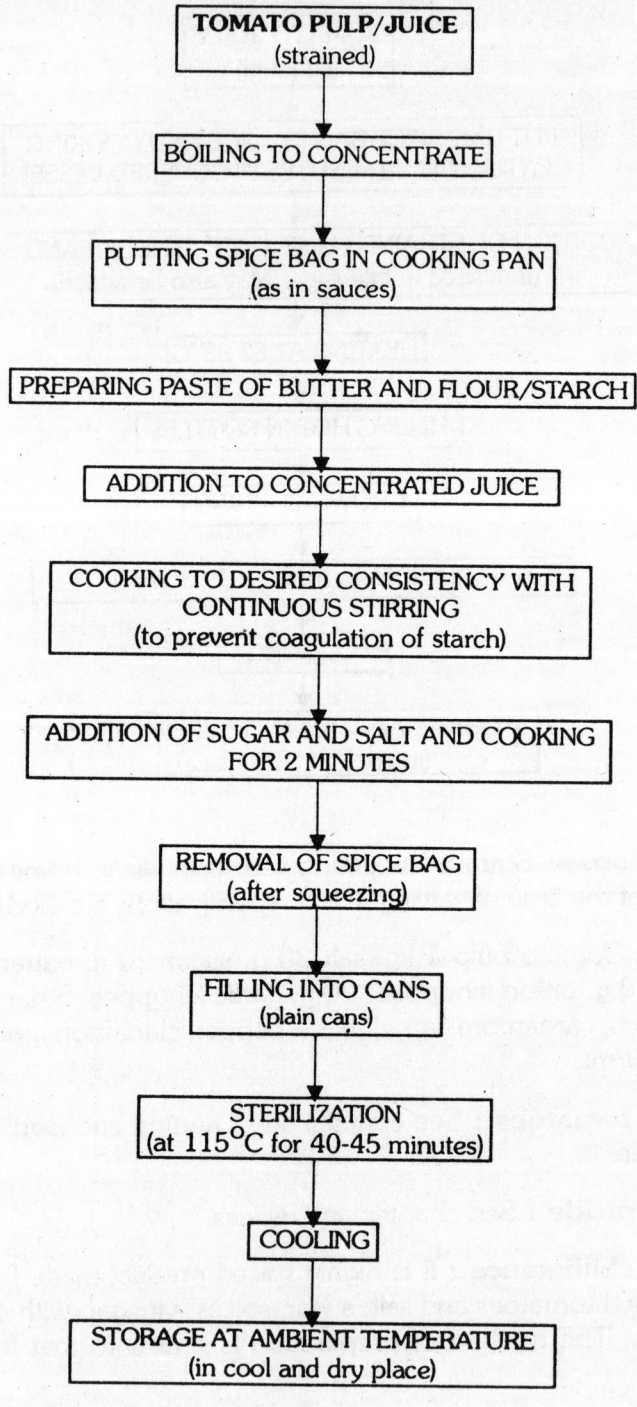

TOMATO PULP/JUICE
(strained)

↓

BOILING TO CONCENTRATE

↓

PUTTING SPICE BAG IN COOKING PAN
(as in sauces)

↓

PREPARING PASTE OF BUTTER AND FLOUR/STARCH

↓

ADDITION TO CONCENTRATED JUICE

↓

COOKING TO DESIRED CONSISTENCY WITH
CONTINUOUS STIRRING
(to prevent coagulation of starch)

↓

ADDITION OF SUGAR AND SALT AND COOKING
FOR 2 MINUTES

↓

REMOVAL OF SPICE BAG
(after squeezing)

↓

FILLING INTO CANS
(plain cans)

↓

STERILIZATION
(at 115°C for 40-45 minutes)

↓

COOLING

↓

STORAGE AT AMBIENT TEMPERATURE
(in cool and dry place)

except that the total unstrained pulp is used and seeds are not removed. Hot product is filled in bottles or cans and processed in water at 85-90°C for 30 minutes.

PROCESSING FLOW-SHEET FOR TOMATO CHILLI SAUCE

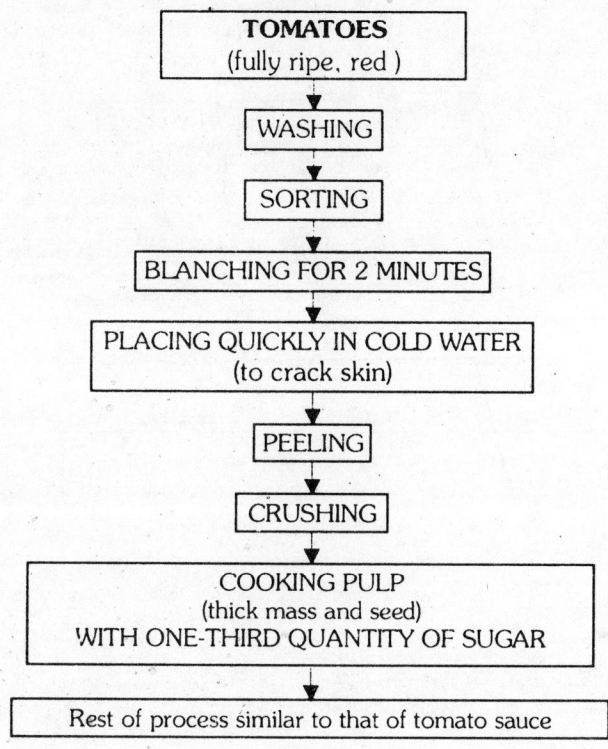

TOMATOES
(fully ripe, red)

↓

WASHING

↓

SORTING

↓

BLANCHING FOR 2 MINUTES

↓

PLACING QUICKLY IN COLD WATER
(to crack skin)

↓

PEELING

↓

CRUSHING

↓

COOKING PULP
(thick mass and seed)
WITH ONE-THIRD QUANTITY OF SUGAR

↓

Rest of process similar to that of tomato sauce

Chapter 23

Potato Processing

P otato is semi-perishable in nature because it contains about 80% water. Therefore, post-production management in potato is as important as the production management. Under tropical and subtropical conditions, 40-50% losses occur due to poor handling and storage. Therefore, it is of utmost importance, to minimize postharvest losses. For successful postharvest management of potato, the farmers should have a better understanding of the production-storage-demand system. Good postharvest management increases returns to the growers. Therefore, the farmers should have access to market information and the ability to take advantage of the market needs. For this access to efficient transport system is very important. Whether to sell the potatoes immediately after harvesting or to store them and, if the potatoes are to be stored, how to store them, and how long to store them are commercial decisions which the potato-growers have to take. Postharvest losses cannot be avoided completely. Good postharvest management minimizes losses, while bad post-harvest management results in high storage losses.

Processing of potatoes is advantageous, because is makes storage easier due to reduction in bulkiness and increase in shelf-life. It adds value to potatoes and, therefore, gives better returns. From the consumer point of view, all processed products should have an attractive colour, acceptable texture and good flavour. Generally, use of high quality potatoes will help to obtain and maintain good quality of the processed products. Potato processing quality, in turn, is dependent on various conditions, including cultivation and environment as well as the time of harvest. The variety of the potatoes used also is an important factor.

Potatoes are processed into many types of products, (i) fried products such as wafers/chips etc.; (ii) dehydrated products such as dice etc.; (iii) frozen products such as French fries, patties, puffs, dice etc.; and (iv) canned. For such diverse forms of products, the raw material requirements are likely to be different. The raw material requirement for some of the processed potato products are given on the next page :

Quality requirements of potatoes for processing[+]

Characteristics	Potato Products			
	Dehydrated	**French fries**	**Chips**	**Canned**
Tuber shape		Long shape	Round to Round-oval	
Tubler size, mm	30	50	40-60	35
Eyes	Shallow	Shallow	Shallow	Shallow
Specific gravity	1.080	1.080	1.085	1.080
Drymatter (%)	22-25	20-24	22-25	18-20
Starch (%)	15-19	14-16	15-18	12-24
*RS (%) after 8°C	2.5	2.5	1.25	2.5
*TS (%) after 6°C storage	5.0	5.0	5.0	5.0
ACD	Slight	Slight	-	Nil
ED	Slight	-	-	-
Texture	Fairly firm to mealy	Fairly firm	Fairly firm to mealy	Firm (waxy

* On dry weight basis, RS = Reducing sugars; TS = Total sugars; ACD = After cooking discolouratio ED = Enzymatic discolouration.

+ Source : Verma (1991).

Perhaps the first attempt at processing of potatoes in India on a commercial scale was made by one Col. Rennick, who established a factory at Narkanda in Himachal Pradesh, to produce potato 'Meal'. Dehydration of potato on commercial scale was also taken up during the second world war to meet the demands of the defence forces. Solar dehydration of potatoes in the form of slices, shreds and 'papads' is carried out in many households for their own use. Recently, however, there has been a lot of interest in India in processing potatoes. The installed capacity in the organized sector for processing of potatoes in India is very very low as compared to the annual production. Thus, there is a considerable scope for an increase in the processing of potatoes in the country.

The situation appears to be ideal for the development of potato processing industry, but there has been hardly any progress in that direction. This is because processing plants can not be operated economically on periodic or seasonal gluts or on unmarketable potatoes. A regular supply of raw material of the desired specific quality has to be available for a greater part of the year. Moreover, processed products will have to be priced so as to compete with fresh foods. Presently potatoes in India, as a raw material, are not cheap, except for a few weeks soon after harvest. And, the cost of the frying medium, processing and packaging etc. adds to the cost of production making the finished product beyond the reach of a common Indian.

The prospects for using potato as an industrial raw material appears to be limited at present to unmarketable potatoes, as cheaper alternative raw materials for the production of starch such as maize and tapioca are available. Similarly molasses from sugar factories is abundantly available for production of industrial and potable alcohol.

Notwithstanding the above, there are some special situations, where potato processing is extremely desirable, e.g., in the Nilgiri hills where cyst forming nematodes occur. The movement of potatoes from this area is a potential hazard. Processing *in situ* will reduce the risk. Similarly, Darjeeling district in West Bengal, where wart disease is prevalent, will benefit from potato processing. Processing is certainly an attractive proposition in areas of high production/productivity as in certain districts of UP, West Bengal and Gujarat. Some form of processing may also help the farmers in the hilly and other regions where lack of transportation is still a major constraint.

Considering that the potato products using sophisticated processing technology are at present very costly, there appears to be a limited scope in the immediate future. The cost of the products such as chips, is pushed up because of the scarcity of frying medium, which is not even sufficient for meeting the requirements of housewives.

In order to make processed potato products available to a common Indian at a reasonable price, it would be desirable to develop appropriate technology and products. In this context products like dehydrated dice (piece), flour may be desirable. Dehydrated dice or pieces can be used in the households for preparation of curries, and also by the fast food outlets for stuffing in the *Masala Dosa* or *Samosas*, while potato flour can be used to prepare '*Tikkis*' and extruded products like '*Papads*' etc.

Important considerations in Potato Processing

The quality required for processing of potatoes has been mentioned in the Table given above. However, for processing potatoes it would be desirable to identify/select/breed long dormancy varieties with round or oval tubers of medium to large size with fleet eyes and free from diseases and peeling losses. The dry matter content of the tubers should be high for greater yield of dehydrated products. The sugar and phenol content should be low and the tubers should be free from after cooking darkening. In addition to the morphological characters, some other factors determining the suitability of potatoes for processing are the specific gravity, or the dry matter content of potatoes and their sugar content.

(A) Specific gravity and dry matter content

Potatoes, high in specific gravity (or dry matter) are preferred for preparation of chips, French fries or dehydrated products, whereas those of lower specific gravity are used for canning or for such other products where a firm piece is desired. Yield of chips and flour etc. is higher from high specific gravity potatoes. Besides high yields of the product, the uptake of fat or oil during frying is lower. Moreover, relatively much less moisture has to be removed per unit of products when high specific gravity potatoes are used. However, potatoes of very high specific gravity may not be suitable for the production of French fries etc. French fries produced from potato with a specific gravity of 1.106 were too hard and biscuit like. It is also of the opinion that very high specific gravity potatoes may yield 'hard chips'.

Dry matter content (specific gravity) is vital in terms of yield, of potato chips or wafers, and the texture of potato chips and reconstituted dehydrated potatoes. Generally even small (marginal) increases in dry weight, will ensure greater yield of the product.

Specific gravity of potatoes can be determined by a number of methods e.g. use of i) brine solution of known specific gravities (Burton 1989), ii) Potato Hydrometer, iii) Archemides principle (Nissen 1967), iv) variable load hydrometer (Sukumaran and Ramdass 1980), and v) ordinary scales (Misra 1983). Dry matter content of fruits and vegetables, including potatoes is determined by oven drying, but a non-destructive method is also available for potatoes and sweet potatoes. Von Schee *et al.* (1937) demonstrated that the specific gravity and dry matter content of potatoes are directly related to each other. Since then relationships have been established in other countries including India.

(B) Sugar content

Sugar content of potatoes influences the colour of the processed products and plays a very important role in determining the acceptability of fried products. Chips and French fries prepared from potatoes containing large amounts of sugars, especially reducing sugars, i.e. glucose and fructose, turn brown and black and become unacceptable to the consumers. This discolouration is ascribed to a reaction, between the reducing sugars and amino acids, which takes place when the moisture content is low and the temperature is high. Generally, freshly harvested mature potatoes contain-acceptable levels of reducing sugars but when stored at low temperatures, the sugar content increases and potatoes become unfit for processing.

For storage of potatoes for the processing industry, the current storage practices followed in India are not suitable, as potatoes stored below 5°C are rendered unfit for processing due to an increase in reducing sugars.

One of the methods of overcoming this problem is to store the potatoes at high temperature. It has been shown that when potatoes were stored at ambient temperatures, there was very little increase in the reducing sugar content of potatoes. But under such conditions sprouting and weight loss were excessive. However, when potatoes were stored in an evaporatively cooled store, similar changes in the sugar content were observed but with a lower weight loss of the potatoes, yet the problem of sprouting remained. To overcome this problem, potatoes were treated with CIPC (Isopropyl-N-chlorophenyl carbamate) and stored in an evaporatively cooled store, and also at lower temperatures recommended for storage of potatoes meant for processing. Even under such conditions of storage, potatoes became unfit for processing within a very short period. Recourse had to be taken to reconditioning another method used to overcome the problem of excess sugar in cold stored potatoes. During reconditioning, cold stored potatoes are stored at 15-20°C for 2-3 weeks. Under such conditions a reduction in the contents of sugars take place. However, in many cases this was also not very effective and dark coloured chips were produced. In an attempt to produce acceptable colour, the chips were fried at lower temperatures. While the colour of chips was acceptable the oil content of the chips so produced was about 30% higher than the oil content of chips produced by frying under the normal conditions.

The discolouration of chips and French fries due to high sugar content of cold stored potatoes is a problem faced by the industry all over the world and attempts have been made to identify varieties which do not accumulate large amount of sugars during the low temperature storage. In UK, a variety Brodick has been released and in India, Kufri Sherpa has been found to accumulate much lower quantities of sugars than many other potato varieties (Kufri Badshah, Kufri Chandramukhi, Kufri Jyoti, and Kufri Sindhuri) examined.

(C) Discolouration

One of the problems affecting appearance and acceptability of any potato product is the tendency for discolouration of the·product or browning to occur. This is generally a result of physiological conditions, and some subsequent chemical reactions. Potato and potato products are prone to three types of discolouration: i) enzymatic discolouration, ii) after cooking discolouration and iii) discolouration of fried products (Chips/Wafers/French fries) and dehydrated potatoes.

(i) Enzymatic discolouration

Discolouration of peeled or cut raw potatoes results from enzymatic oxidation of polyphenolic compounds in the presence of air or oxygen. The problem is encountered in sun-drying of potatoes and is due to the action of polyphenoloxidase enzyme on the phenolic compounds. Similar reaction takes place in the development of black spot in potatoes during harvesting, handling and transport, specially at low temperatures.

Exclusion of oxygen, or preventing contact of the potatoes with air can prevent discolouration. Inactivating the enzyme with heat or lowering the pH also helps to control browning. An alternative way is to treat the whole potato with SO_2 gas. Such potatoes can be stored. High concentrations of CO_2 can also be used to treat whole potatoes to prevent the accumulation of reducing sugar and to improve the colour of wafers.

Storage of potatoes also influences enzymatic browning. Generally, higher temperatures and longer storage periods has been associated with higher levels of tyrosine; thus, such potatoes tend to be more discoloured when peeled or cut.

Enzymatic discolouration and black spot in potatoes can also be prevented by the application of potassium fertilizers specially muriate of potash. But the application of muriate of potash resulted in a decrease of the dry matter content of potatoes. Therefore, the industry uses other methods to overcome the problem of enzymatic discolouration, i.e., the application of chemicals to peeled potatoes. Sulfiting, as the common procedure is known as, helps to reduce or eliminate enzymatic browning but is a potential health hazard, specially to people prone to asthmatic conditions. As such efforts have been made to select varieties which do not show any enzymatic discolouration. It has been reported that varieties D2286 and C2703 did not show much enzymatic discolouration.

(ii) After cooking discolouration (ACD)

As the term suggests, it develops in cooked potatoes and potato products after exposure to air, specially in boiled and steamed potatoes. Discolouration and /or darkening occurs after cooking due to the non enzymatic browning reactions which take place at high temperatures used in preparation of chips/wafers, French fries, canned potatoes or during dehydration. After cooking darkening is, generally, due to the formation of a dark coloured complex of ferric iron and a phenolic compound. Factors such as iron content, presence of organic acid, pH and phenolic compounds are involved in such darkening, which usually, is less in immature than in mature tubers. In solutions more acidic than the normal pH of potatoes, the darkening can be prevented; while, in contrast, it is intensified by reactions which are alkaline.

The organic acid content, aspartic acid, of the tubers affects the discolouration after cooking. This has been attributed due either to the effect of pH, or the ability of the acid to chelate iron and compete with chlorogenic acid for iron, and form a colourless complex. The more the citric acid, the lesser the content of darkening. Thus, darkening is associated with low levels of organic acid, such as citric, oxalic, malic and orthophosphoric acids. It has been suggested, however, that the amount of free organic acid is a greater determinant for discolouration.

Almost all the Indian potato varieties are free from ACD, though it has been observed occasionally in Kufii Jyoti. But ACD develops in gamma irradiated potatoes stored at or below 15°C for 2½ to 3 months. The problem could be overcome by storing potatoes at higher temperature or by reconditioning such potatoes at 30-35°C for 2 weeks.

(iii) Discolouration of fried products and dehydrated potatoes

Products made from potatoes with high sugar content are more likely to be scorched, or discoloured during dehydration and to turn dark during storage. Two methods have been suggested for overcoming the problem. In one of the methods, excess quantity of sugars is fermented to lactic acid by *Lactobacillus plantarum* and it was claimed that "Satisfactory product, with respect of colour, flavour/aroma, texture and general acceptability could be produced by this method". In another method, the reactants were removed by repeated washing of the raw slices in water. It was claimed that about 50% of the reducing sugars and about 40% of the free amino acid were removed by washing the raw slices in water. It may be pointed out that these two reactants are involved in the development of the discolouration of fried products.

(D) Peeling Potatoes for Processing

After selection of raw materials, peeling is an important preliminary step in the manufacture of various potato products, since the effectiveness and efficiency of peeling determine the yield of the finished product, the amount of waste, and the cost of waste disposal.

The ideal peeling operation should only remove a very thin outer layer of the potato, leaving no eyes, blemishes, or other material for later removal by hand trimming. It should not significantly change the physical or chemical characteristics of the remaining tissue.

Preferably peeling should use small amount of water and result in minimal effluent; compromises will have to be made in all of these aspects of peeling.

First, the potatoes are thoroughly washed, not only for sanitary reasons, but also to prevent dirt of grit from abrading the equipment the tubers will later contact. Washing may take place in streams, as the potatoes are being conveyed by water streams, or in equipment provided with means for scrubbing the potato with brushes or rubber rolls.

In barrel-type washers, potatoes are cleaned by being tumbled and rubbed against each other and against the sides of the barrel while they are immersed in, or sprayed with, water.

After washing, the potatoes are allowed to drain, usually on mesh convey-ors, and they travel over an inspection belt where foreign material and defective tubers are removed. The more common peeling methods are abrasion, lye im-mersion, and steam. Various methods used in peeling of potatoes are briefly discussed below:

(i) **Abrasion Peelers :** These are designed to uniformly contact the surface of the tubers with abrasive discs or rollers so that, while peeling, the losses are minimum. Abrasion peelers which may be either batch or continuous, use discs or rollers coated with grit to grind away the potato surface. An impor-tant design feature is to ensure that all surfaces of the tuber are equally exposed to the rasping action. The peel fragments are flushed out of the unit by water sprays. During peeling, potatoes are sprayed with water in order to decrease the tendency for the tubers to darken as a result of enzymatic action.

Abrasion peelers work best with uniform, round, undamaged pota-toes. Non uniform size also results in uneven peeling. Peeling losses are, usually, greater for small than for large potatoes. Some of the advantages of abrasion peelers are their simplicity, compactness, low cost and conven-ience. Abrasion peeling is suitable for potatoes to be used for manufacturing chips/wafers, since other peeling processes which use heat, give a coated layer of tissue, or a visible heat ring. About 10% of the original tuber weight is lost through abrasion peeling prior to chipping.

(ii) **Lye Peeling :** It depends on chemical attack and thermal shock to loosen and soften the skin, eyes and blemishes of potatoes so that they are readily worked off, or rubbed off, by pressure spray and washers. In this method lye (sodium hydroxide) solution is used at a high temperature, i.e., 160°F or a lower temperature, i.e. 120°F to 160°F.

Potatoes may be pre-heated for a short time in water at temperatures ranging from 140 to 190°F. This minimizes the cooling effect and help to maintain a uniform temperature that the potatoes would otherwise have on the lye solution and thus, increase the capacity of the peeler.

The use of low temperatures reduces the heat ring or cooked dena-tured surface layer on the peeled potato. However, the contact time required is longer than with the use of lye at high temperatures. If a heat ring or partially cooked layer of tissue remains on the peeled surface, it can be removed by immersing the potatoes again in a lye solution maintained at a low temperature (usually 70°F, and lye concentrations ranging from 10 to 40 per cent, or at 12°F with concentrations of 15 to 20 per cent).

Different types of lye peeling equipment are available. These are designed such that the potatoes can be submerged in heated lye solution, the temperature of which is maintained for a specific period of time. The equipment used with low or high temperature lye treatment is the same. At low temperatures, the lye is more viscous; hence, there is need for rapid circulation. Further, the viscosity is increased due to the starch, protein and other components, from the potatoes that are dissolved in the solutions. The contact time or dip/immersion time needs to be longer when lye concentrations are higher, probably because of increased viscosity which makes it more difficult to ensure adequate circulation of the peeling medium.

Lye peeling softens the surface of the potato and the colour changes to a deep yellow due to the reaction of the lye with constituents of the potato. After removal from a lye peeler, potatoes are washed to remove the remaining lye. Failure to remove the lye allows it to continue to react with the flavours in the potato, and results in further yellowing of the potato. Sometimes the potatoes may be sprayed with or immersed in dilute solutions of some acid to neutralize the lye.

(iii) Steam Peeling : In this method potatoes are subjected to high pressure steam for a short time. This treatment hydrates the potatoes and cooks their surface tissue, which softens and, consequently, lossens the peel from the underlying tissue. The softened tissue is removed by brushes or water sprays. However, steam peeling leaves a heat ring on the peeled potato surface. In many processed products, this is not objectionable. The exception is potato chips/wafers, in which this ring is visible and has been known to affect consumer acceptance of the product.

(iv) Brine Peeling : Brine solution maintained near boiling and saturation points has been used for peeling potatoes. However, evaporation of water occurs constantly, hence, it is necessary to prevent over saturation and crystallization. Immersion time required for adequate peeling may range from 3 to 10 minutes.

Brine peeling is less expensive than lye peeling, and is also less of a hazard to the operating personnel. Another advantage with brine peeling is that any salt left on the potato surface does not need to be neutralized and may reduce enzymatic discolouration of the peeled potatoes. The only problem is that the brine solution corrodes the equipment it is in contact with.Lye and brine may also be used together.

(v) Flame Peeling : Potatoes are subjected to high temperatures which lead to charring or carbonization of the skin. Potatoes are passed through a flame or a refractory oven which subjects all surfaces of the potato to approximately 2000°F for 15 to 30 seconds. Since the tubers are exposed to such an elevated temperature for a relatively short time, the depth of the heat ring formed is much less.

Peeling losses are usually less by flame peeling than by the use of abrasion peelers. The demerits of this method lie in the difficulties in controlling temperature, and noise; and considerable maintenance of the equipment is required. Flame peelers are used mostly for peeling onions and peppers than potatoes.

(vi) Oil Peeling : Oil heated at 300 to 400°F can be used to remove the peel. Vegetable and mineral oil can be used. If the mineral oil is used, the oil must be completely removed otherwise undesirable oily odours will impair the product.

After peeling and washing, hard trimming is done to remove any residual skin, discoloured areas, disease and insect injured potatoes, black spot as well as parts of potatoes which are green. The amount of trimming required depends on how efficiently the peeling was done. Subsequent to trimming, the tubers may either be sized, or conveyed directly to the next processing operation.

It is desirable, therefore, that the potato varieties used for processing should have following characteristics:

(i)   Potato tubers should have high degree of maturity (fully mature), round or oval shape, medium to large size with fleet eyes, and free from diseases.

(ii)   Potato tubers should have long dormancy.

(iii)   Potato tubers should have high specific gravity or dry matter content.

(iv)   Potato tubers should have low sugar content.

(v)   Potato tubers should be free from after cooking discolouration.

(vi)   Potato tubers should have low peeling losses.

Recently Kufri Chipsona-1 and Kufri Chipsona-2 potato varieties, released from Central Potato Research Institute, Shimla, are free from after cooking discolouration and due to their high dry matter and low reducing sugars and phenols contents these varieties are highly suitable for making chips and French fries.

Potatoes can be processed in a number of ways as follows:

(1) Potato chips/wafers

FLOW-SHEET FOR PROCESSING OF POTATO CHIPS/WAFERS

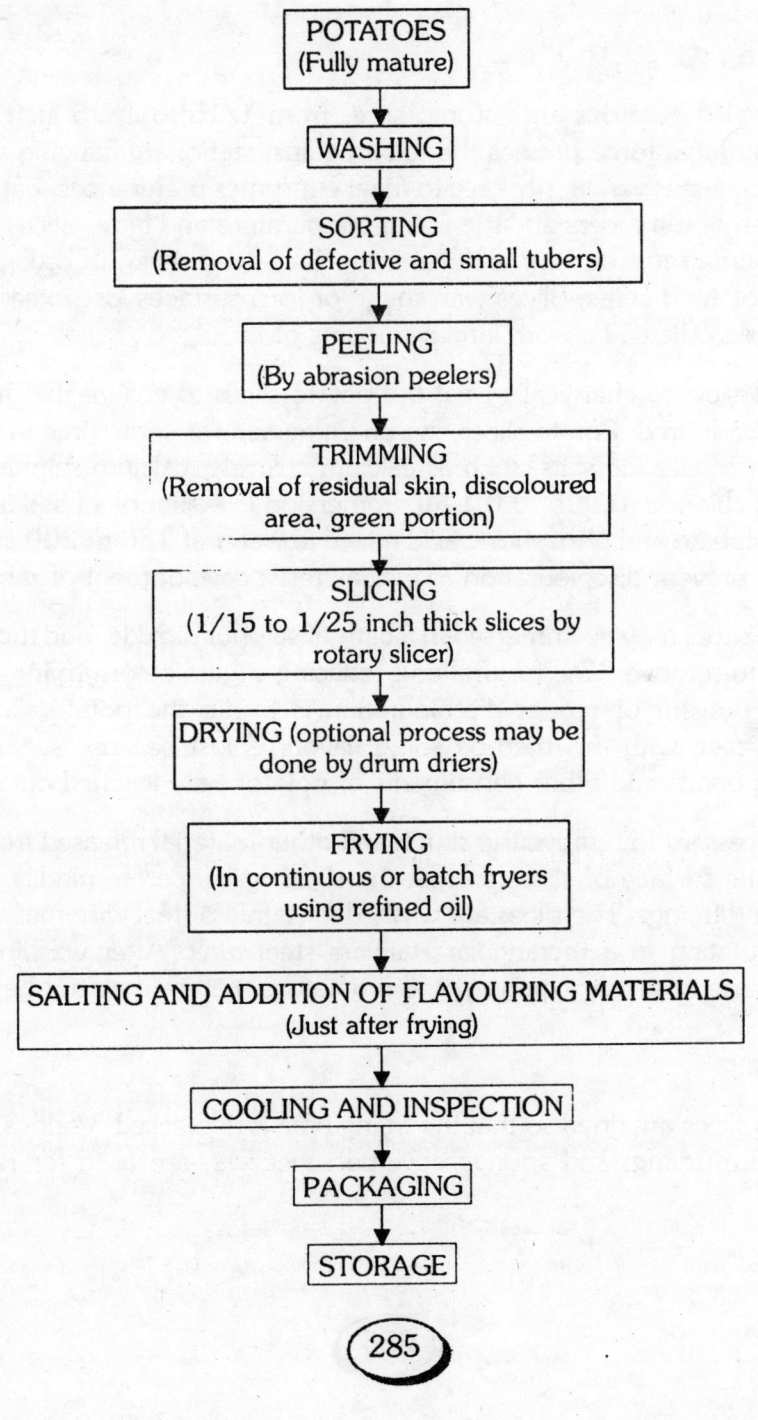

POTATOES
(Fully mature)

↓

WASHING

↓

SORTING
(Removal of defective and small tubers)

↓

PEELING
(By abrasion peelers)

↓

TRIMMING
(Removal of residual skin, discoloured
area, green portion)

↓

SLICING
(1/15 to 1/25 inch thick slices by
rotary slicer)

↓

DRYING (optional process may be
done by drum driers)

↓

FRYING
(In continuous or batch fryers
using refined oil)

↓

SALTING AND ADDITION OF FLAVOURING MATERIALS
(Just after frying)

↓

COOLING AND INSPECTION

↓

PACKAGING

↓

STORAGE

285

Selection of potato varieties/tubers; their washing, sorting, peeling, and trimming; for processing into various products have been described before in detail. The other important steps involved in processing of potato chips/wafers are discussed here:

(i) Slicing

The peeled potatoes are cut into slices from 1/15 to 1/25 inch by rotary slicers. Centrifugal force presses the tuber against stationary gauging shoes and knives. Thickness is varied, not only to meet consumer preferences, but also to fit the condition of the tubers and the frying temperature and time. Slices produced at any one time must be very uniform in thickness, however, in order to obtain uniformly coloured chips. Slices with rough or torn surfaces lose excess solubles from ruptured cells and absorb larger amounts of fat.

It is possible to chemically treat the potato slices to ensure that the wafers will be light coloured. Potato slices can be immersed for some time in hot aqueous solution of alkaline salts, such as calcium chloride, calcium sulphamate and magnesium chloride (0.005 to 0.1 M). Immersion in solutions of sodium citrate, sodium bisulphate and phosphoric acid mixed in water at 180 to 200°F has been reported to prevent discolouration as well as resist development of rancidity.

Potato slices may be immersed in a bath of sulphur dioxide, and then washed with water to remove SO_2, furfural and reducing sugars before frying. A simple method to prevent or reduce discolouration is to dip the potato slices in hot water. However, with this method some flavour is lost because sugars, nitrogenous compounds and other constituents of potatoes are leached out.

It is necessary to remove the starch and other material released from the cut cells from the surface of slices so that the slices will separate readily and completely during frying. The slices are washed in stainless steel wire-mesh cylinders or drums rotating in a rectangular stainless steel tank. After washing and an additional rinse in similar equipment, the potatoes may or may not be dried.

(ii) Drying

Potato slices are dried so that the frying time is decreased. Various methods, such as drum drying, and sponge covered squeezers, are used for removal of water.

286

(iii) Frying

The capacity of the fryer is generally the limiting factor in the process line. Most manufacturers currently use continuous fryers but some batch equipment is still employed. Modern continuous fryers have the following essential elements: (1) a tank of hot oil in which the chips are cooked; (2) a means for heating and circulating the oil; (3) a filter for removing particles from oil; (4) a conveyor to carry chips out of the tank; (5) a reservoir in which oil is heated for adding to the circulating frying oil and (6) vapour-collecting hoods above the tank. Temperatures normally used are from 350 to 375° F at the receiving end and 320 to 345°F at the exit end.

The oil used for deep-fat frying of potato chips has two functions:

(i)   it serves as a medium for transferring heat from a thermal source to the tuber slices;

(ii) it becomes an ingredient of the finished product.

Use of highly refined oil is of great importance in flavour and stability of chips/wafers. Flavour, texture, and appearance are affected both by the amount of oil absorbed and its characteristics as it exists in the chips/wafers. Oils change continuously during the frying process but the heat abuse resulting from the chips/wafers cooking is relatively mild. Temperatures rarely rise above 385°F at any point.

Better control over chips/wafer colour could be obtained if the final stage of moisture removal could be achieved without the browning reaction that always accompanies it in the frying process. It is desirable to maintain a fairly low oil level in the wafers, not only because of the cost but also because excess oil makes the wafers oily and decreases their consumer acceptability. On the other hand, if the oil content is too low, the wafers lack flavour and seem harsh in texture. Oil content of chips is influenced by various factors; viz.

(1) Dry matter content/specific gravity inversely influences the oil content, i.e., the oil content in wafers decreases as the dry matter content of potatoes increases.

(2) Partial drying of potato slices prior to frying lowers the oil content of chips/wafers; the lower the moisture content, the smaller the amount of oil absorbed. Pre drying also reduces the length of frying time.

(3) Leaching the raw slices with hot water or some chemical, e.g., hot brine affects oil absorption. Leaching with hot water is done to remove reducing sugars in order to obtain lighter coloured chips. However, leaching increases oil absorption. In contrast, leaching in hot brine decreases the oil content of the wafers. Another factor to be considered is that leaching in hot brine also ensures that the wafers do not need any additional application of salt.

(4) As the thickness of slice decreases oil absorption increases.

(5) Usually the higher the frying temperature, the less is the oil absorbed.

(6) The longer the frying time, the more is the oil absorption.

Chips/wafers may be sorted for size after frying, with the larger chips/wafers being diverted to the bulk packs and larger pouches and the smaller pieces used for vending machine packs and other individual service containers. Potato chips/wafers sizing is also accomplished by separating the peeled potatoes into large and small sizes, which are then sliced and fried separately.

(iv) Salting and addition of flavouring materials

The chips/wafers are salted immediately after they leave the fryer. It is important that the fat be liquid at this point to cause maximum adherence of the granules. Powders containing other flavour compounds like monosodium glutamate, protein hydrolyzates, various types of cheeses, spice mixture, or other speciality materials may be added at this point. The salt may contain added enrichment materials or antioxidants. Approximately 1.5-2 kg of salt is applied to each 100 kg of chips/wafers.

After salting, the chips/wafers pass on to a conveyor belt where they are visually inspected and off-colour material is removed. If the chips/wafers are allowed to cool before packaging, better adherence of salt and flavour powders is obtained.

Some consumers prefer the hard, curled-up chips/wafers that is characteristics of the hand-kettle type of operation. The special flavour of the hand-kettle chips/wafers is said to be due, at least partly, to the starch retained on the cut surfaces of the potato slices as a result of the omission of a washing process after slicing. Starch-covered slices tend to stick together in the fryer so it is necessary to use devices to prevent clumping.

The principal factors affecting potato chip/wafer acceptability are pieces size, colour, and of course, flavour. These factors are controllable primarily by selection of the raw material, adjustment of processing condition, and packaging.

(v) Packaging and storage

Flexible packaging materials are used. Some packages are stapled, but heat sealing is more desirable. If pouches are used, foil-containing films are preferable, since they not only resist moisture vapour transfer but reflect light.

If the frying oil is stabilized and has not deteriorated through use, and if the packaging is opaque and has a low moisture-vapour transmittance rate (MVTR), a shelf-life of 4-6 weeks should be achieved when chips/wafers are stored at temperatures of about 70°F.

Once potato chips/wafers are in the bag, the three forms of quality loss which have the greatest effect on consumer acceptance are breakage, absorption of moisture with loss of crispiness, and fat oxidation leading to development of rancid odours.

The mechanical abuse causing breaking of the crisps can be partially prevented by using stiff packaging material, making the package "plump" with contained air, and avoiding crushing in the shipping case.

Absorption of moisture is prevented largely by proper choice of packaging material. Cellophane coated with various moisture barriers has proved to be a satisfactory pouch films for the relatively short shelf-life expected (generally) stated to be 4-6 weeks).

Light (especially fluorescent light) accelerates oxidation, so that opaque packaging material must be used to obtain maximum shelf-life.

Potato crisps are considered commercially unacceptable when they have a moisture content above 3%, which is in equilibrium with a relative humidity of about 32%. The containers should have a high degree of resistance to moisture-vapour transfer.

(2) French Fries (Frozen Potato Chips)
FLOW-SHEET FOR PROCESSING OF POTATO FRENCH FRIES

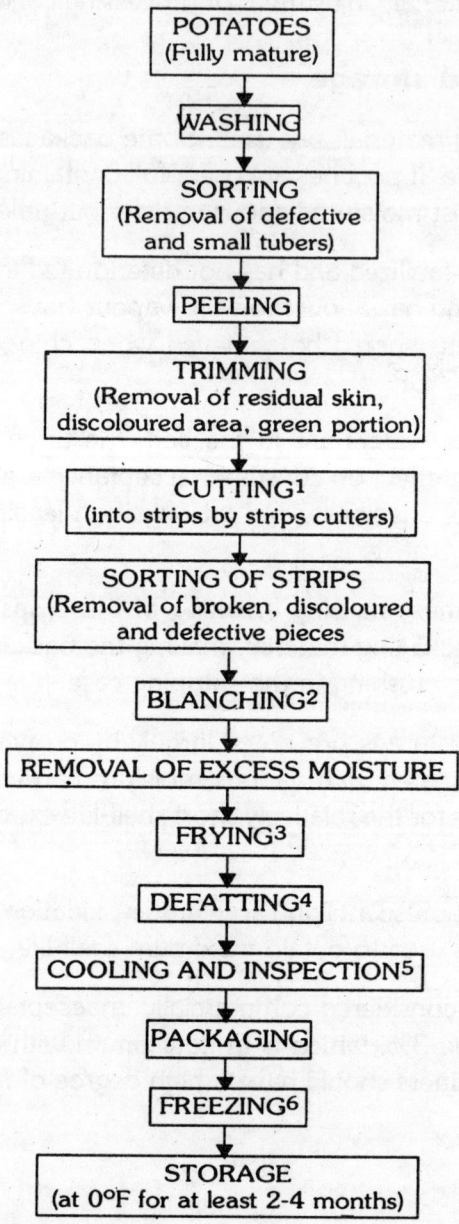

```
                POTATOES
               (Fully mature)
                    │
                    ▼
                 WASHING
                    │
                    ▼
                 SORTING
          (Removal of defective
            and small tubers)
                    │
                    ▼
                 PEELING
                    │
                    ▼
                 TRIMMING
         (Removal of residual skin,
       discoloured area, green portion)
                    │
                    ▼
                CUTTING¹
        (into strips by strips cutters)
                    │
                    ▼
            SORTING OF STRIPS
        (Removal of broken, discoloured
            and defective pieces
                    │
                    ▼
               BLANCHING²
                    │
                    ▼
        REMOVAL OF EXCESS MOISTURE
                    │
                    ▼
                 FRYING³
                    │
                    ▼
                DEFATTING⁴
                    │
                    ▼
          COOLING AND INSPECTION⁵
                    │
                    ▼
                PACKAGING
                    │
                    ▼
                FREEZING⁶
                    │
                    ▼
                 STORAGE
      (at 0°F for at least 2-4 months)
```

1. Peeled and trimmed Potatoes are kept in holding tanks to regulate their flow to the strip cutters in mechanized operations. These tanks are filled with water to reduce discolouration and surface operation. Thin slices, and short or broken pieces, are separated out after the strips have been cut. This may be done by using shaker screens or bean graders, where the diameters of the holes in the screen

correspond to the length of the short pieces to be separated. These pieces can be used to produce other potato products.

At this point, the cut strips may be inspected briefly to remove discoloured, broken or defective pieces.

Yield of French fry cuts is determined by losses incurred during peeling, trimming and cutting. Peeling and trimming losses are usually 15 to 40 per cent. Cutting losses (in the form of slivers and small pieces) usually add another 10 per cent to the losses incurred in the previous processing steps. Thus, the overall yield generally ranges from 50 to 75 per cent of the weight of potatoes. Further loss in the weight occurs during frying due to loss of moisture. The final yield of strips from 100 Kgs of potatoes is usually approximately 30 to 40 Kgs.

2. After cutting, the potato strips are blanched before frying in order to ensure that the fried product will have a more uniform colour, reduced fat absorption due to gelatinization of surface starch, reduced frying time since the potato is partially cooked, and improved texture of the final product. Blanching leaches out the soluble sugars, gives a lighter and more uniform colour on frying. However, blanching does not eliminate the need for conditioning potatoes to reduce the overall reducing sugar content. Blanching is said to help control the texture of frozen chips and for obtaining a more uniformly mealy texture. Compounds such as calcium lactate (for improvement of texture) and sodium acid phyrophosphate (to control after cooking darkening) have been tried and found useful.

After blanching, the excess moisture is removed from the potato to reduce the load on the fryer and to minimize hydrolytic decomposition of fat. Also free surface moisture, if left in contact with the potato strips tends to soften the pieces.

3. The blanched potato strips are fed into fryers at a carefully regulated rate. Various types of conveyors can be used to carry the strips through the hot fat. In one method, the strips are placed in small perforated trays/baskets which are mounted on a chain. These containers are submerged in the fat and conveyed from one end of the fryer to the other, ensuring that the potato is fried in transit along the conveyor chain. Close attention to, and control of, frying conditions are necessary to obtain the desired colour and texture when the pieces are removed from the fryer. Overcooked potatoes will tend to have concave surfaces and collapsed centres. The amount of fat absorption determines whether the product will have a good flavour or whether it will be too oily. Frying can be done in a single stage (one fryer) or two stage systems (two fryers in series).

4. Immediately after the strips emerge from the fryer, excess fat is removed. In the simplest method, defatting can be accomplished by passing the product over a vibrating screen and allowing the free fat to be drawn off.

5. After defatting the strips are air cooled while being conveyed on a wire mesh belt from the frying area to the freezing tunnel. Cooling not only reduces the load on the freezer but also reduces breakage of the chips when they are packed prior to freezing. Before packing, the chips are inspected, and dark, over fried or defective pieces are removed.

6. Sometimes loose chips are frozen in a continuous belt freezer in a freezing tunnel at a very rapid rate (approximately at 40°F). The frozen chips are then packed into poly bags depending upon the unit weight of packing.

Other products such as patties, puffs, mashed potatoes, diced potatoes, etc actually represent a way of utilizing small pieces or slivers of potato that would otherwise be wasted in cutting operations for preparing chips (French fries).

(3) Potato Drying/Dehydration

(i) Sun Drying

A home-drier for fruits and vegetables (including potatoes) was fabricated in which best dried product was obtained when the potatoes were peeled, sliced, and blanched for 3-5 min at 81-100°C; The slices could be dried in 9-11 hr. The dehydrated slices could be rehydrated to normal shape, appearance and flavour if they were soaked for 24 hr in water. Peeling and trimming losses were lower in 'new' potatoes but the yield of the dried product (22-29%) was higher in old potatoes.

(ii) Solar Drying

Solar energy has been used since ancient times to dehydrate potatoes in the Andes mountains to prepare *Chuno*. In India also, sun-drying of potatoes in the form of slices, shreds and *Papads* etc. is practiced by housewives. But quite often the products are varying shades of grey and therefore, unappealing. Investigations were, therefore, conducted at the Central Potato Research Institute and its regional stations to develop a procedure to prepare dehydrated potato slices of acceptable colour. Discolouration of peeled potatoes and the slices is minimized by immersing them in cold water. Blanching of slices inactivates the enzymes) responsible for browning. Use of potassium metabisulphite ensures that such slices have a long shelf life, if stored in air-tight containers or in sealed polythene bags. Such slices could be ground to prepare potato flour for use in the preparation of biscuits etc.

A number of investigations have been conducted to study factors which have a bearing in solar dehydration of potatoes, e.g. thickness of the slice, use of various surfaces for sun-drying, and evaluation of the efficiency of different types of solar dehydrators etc. It was observed that black polythene and nylon mesh was a better surface for dehydration than clear polythene. The thickness of slices affected the rate of dehydration, thinner slices dried in the sun at a faster rate than thicker ones.

A problem related to quality of sundried products is the reported occurrence of dust, and at times dead insects, when dehydration is carried out in open. A number of solar dries have been fabricated and evaluated. These not only ensure better hygenic standards but also generally result in faster drying.

Solar dehydration of partially cooked potatoes

In some parts of our country, particularly in Gujarat and Maharashtra considerable quantities of partially cooked potatoes are dried and are consumed after deep fat frying. Such slices take up much less cooking medium during frying and are, therefore, more economical. The procedure for preparing such slices consists of cooking the potatoes in boiling water for 8 min before peeling and slicing. Slices are then allowed to dry in the sun. Dehydration of such slices take longer time and is usually accomplished in about 8-10 hours.

(iii) Dehydrated Diced Potatoes

At the Central Food Technological Research Institute, Mysore extensive investigations were carried out for evaluating different potato varieties for preparation of dehydrated dice. When all the factors viz., blanching time, cooking time, sulphite content and browning of dice during storage were taken into consideration, the varieties Kufri Chandramukhi, Kufri Kuber, C-990 and VB-8 were found to be the most suitable for processing into conventionally dehydrated dice.

FLOW-SHEET FOR PROCESSING OF DEHYDRATED DICED POTATOES

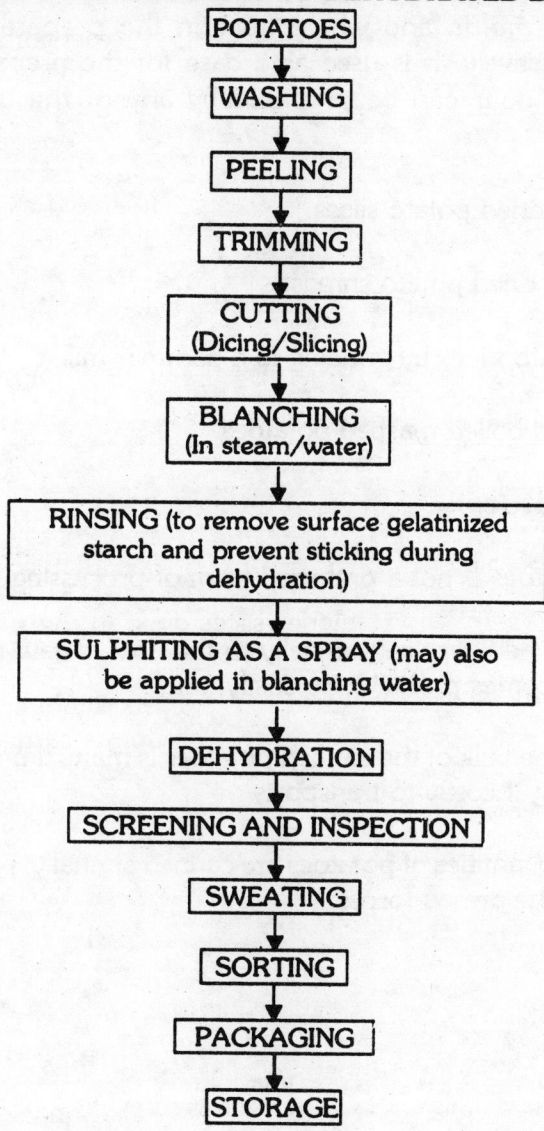

POTATOES
↓
WASHING
↓
PEELING
↓
TRIMMING
↓
CUTTING
(Dicing/Slicing)
↓
BLANCHING
(In steam/water)
↓
RINSING (to remove surface gelatinized starch and prevent sticking during dehydration)
↓
SULPHITING AS A SPRAY (may also be applied in blanching water)
↓
DEHYDRATION
↓
SCREENING AND INSPECTION
↓
SWEATING
↓
SORTING
↓
PACKAGING
↓
STORAGE

Besides above dehydrated potato cubes, vacuum-puffed dried potatoes and instant potato flakes are also being prepared by various drying/dehydration techniques.

(4) Potato Flour

Potato flour is a very important product and is used in the baking industry, mainly to reduce the protein content of the mix, but also to impart softness to bread and for better retention of moisture. Potato flour can also be used to partially replace wheat *maida* and wheat flour in the preparation of biscuits and 'Chaptai'. respectively. It is used as a base for the preparation of many soup mixes. Potato flour can be prepared by any of the undermentioned procedures:

(i) By grinding sun-dried potato slices.

(ii) By grinding Kiln dried potato shreds.

(iii) Dehydrated potato slices by grinding in a hammer mill.

(iv) By grinding dried boiled mashed potatoes.

(5) Canned Potatoes

Canning of potatoes is not a preferred form of processing, because:

(i) the cost of cans add very substantially to the cost of raw material and the final product becomes prohibitively costly, and

(ii) the weight and the bulk of the canned potatoes is many times that of the raw potatoes, making it costly to transports

However, small quantities of potatoes are canned annually, primarily, to meet the requirements of the armed forces.

FLOW -SHEET FOR PROCESSING OF CANNED POTATOES

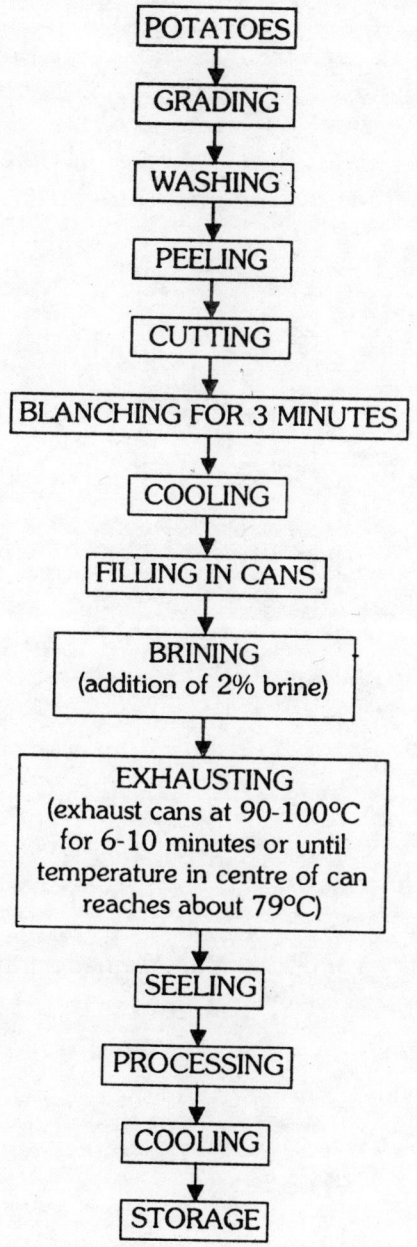

POTATOES

GRADING

WASHING

PEELING

CUTTING

BLANCHING FOR 3 MINUTES

COOLING

FILLING IN CANS

BRINING
(addition of 2% brine)

EXHAUSTING
(exhaust cans at 90-100°C
for 6-10 minutes or until
temperature in centre of can
reaches about 79°C)

SEELING

PROCESSING

COOLING

STORAGE

Chapter 24

Mushroom Processing

Mushrooms are a simple form of plant life which lack chlorophyll and hence cannot produce their own food. They depend upon other living or dead plants and organic matter. Mushrooms are a rich source of proteins, vitamins and minerals. Their low content of carbohydrate and fat makes them an ideal food for diabetics and persons who wish to shed excess fat. They are also a good source of energy, about 454 g of fresh mushrooms providing 120 K-calories.

Most of the edible varieties of mushroom belong to the family Agricaceae of the class Basidiomycetes. However, gucchi (*Morchella esculentii*) belongs to the class Ascomycetes. It grows wild and has not been cultivated under artificial conditions. Commonly cultivated species of mushroom are:

(i)   Button mushrooms (*Agaricus bisporus, A. campestris*),

(ii) Oyster mushroom or dhingree (*Pleurotus sajorcaju, P. columbinus*), and

(iii) Paddy straw mushroom (*Volvariella volvacea*).

Of these, button mushroom is the most important for the preservation industry because products prepared from it are much superior in texture and cooking quality than those from other species. Besides, this species is easily digestible and rich in proteins and vitamins.

Because of the highly perishable nature of fresh mushrooms and poor transportation facilities for marketing, growers do not get a proper return. It is, therefore, essential to consume mushrooms immediately or preserve them in various forms.

Processing

Pickling and sun-drying are economically-viable methods of preserving mushrooms. However, freezing and freeze-drying give them an excellent quality. They can be used commercially for export market. Mushrooms can be processed in a number of ways. Different technologies which have a potential for processing mushrooms are described.

(1) Drying/Dehydration

Drying is done to remove free water to such a level (a_w <0.7) that the bio-chemical and microbial activity are checked due to reduced water activity in the product. Freeze drying yields a product of excellent quality but, the cost of removal of water is 10 times higher than the conventional air-drying. Sun-drying is appropriate technology for our country because of free source of energy and minimum investment in capital cost. Blanching and sulphuring/sulphiting are important treatments given before drying.

PROCESSING FLOW-SHEET FOR MUSHROOM DEHYDRATION

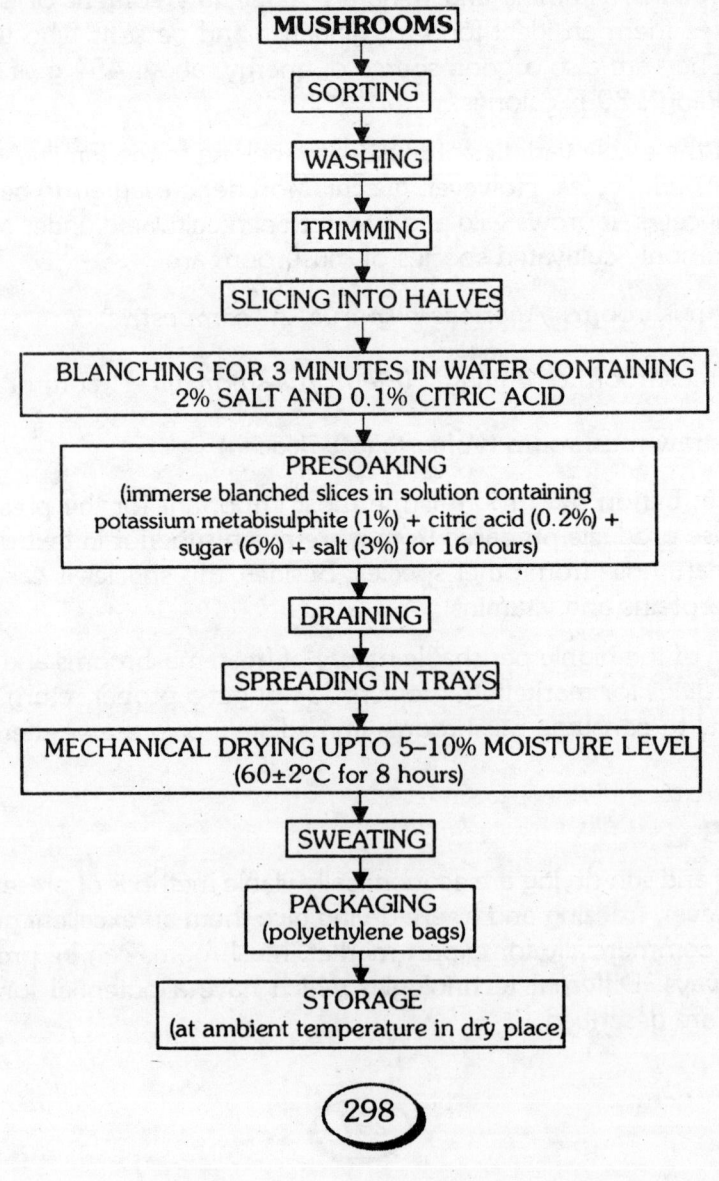

MUSHROOMS

↓

SORTING

↓

WASHING

↓

TRIMMING

↓

SLICING INTO HALVES

↓

BLANCHING FOR 3 MINUTES IN WATER CONTAINING
2% SALT AND 0.1% CITRIC ACID

↓

PRESOAKING
(immerse blanched slices in solution containing
potassium metabisulphite (1%) + citric acid (0.2%) +
sugar (6%) + salt (3%) for 16 hours)

↓

DRAINING

↓

SPREADING IN TRAYS

↓

MECHANICAL DRYING UPTO 5–10% MOISTURE LEVEL
(60±2°C for 8 hours)

↓

SWEATING

↓

PACKAGING
(polyethylene bags)

↓

STORAGE
(at ambient temperature in dry place)

(2) Low temperature

Individual quick freezing technology is employed to yield a product of excellent quality with longer shelf-life. The basic principle of freezing is the speedy removal of heat from mushrooms. Quick freezing is a process where temperature of mushrooms passes through the zone of maximum crystal (0°-3.0°C) in 30 minutes or less. Freezing stops microbial activity. Enzyme activity is only retarded at freezing temperatures. To control their activity, mushrooms prior to freezing are required to be blanched. To obtain the best performance, the storage temperature should be maintained at -35° to -40°C. Repeated freezing and thawing are deterimental and should be avoided.

(3) High temperature

Its main principle is to destroy the microorganisms, and to prevent the recontamination by hermatic sealing. This is a well practised technique all over the world. Recently, retortable glass bottles and flexible pouches are also used due to high cost of cans. Generally, for canning purpose, small-sized buttons are required without stem attached. Ascorbic acid, ethylene diamine tetra acetic acid and citric acid are recommended as useful adjunct for improving colour in canning of mushrooms. Steeping buttons in 0.5% solution of methyl cellulose or carboxy methyl cellulose prior to canning results in increasing the yield by 5-9% without any deleterious effect on their quality. Food additives - agar (0.125%) and pectin (0.5%) – improve the flavour of canned products.

Canning of Mushrooms

See Processing flow-sheet on next page.

(4) Chemicals

There are several chemical additives which are non-nutritive and are added in small quantities in foods to improve their appearance, flavour, texture and storage properties. These additives contribute substantially in preservation. Salt, sugar, acetic acid, vinegar and essential oils from spices are main additives. On the other hand, chemical preservatives maintain nutritional quality and enhance their keeping quality. Potassium metabisulphite is commonly used preservative in mushroom processing.

PROCESSING FLOW-SHEET FOR CANNED MUSHROOMS

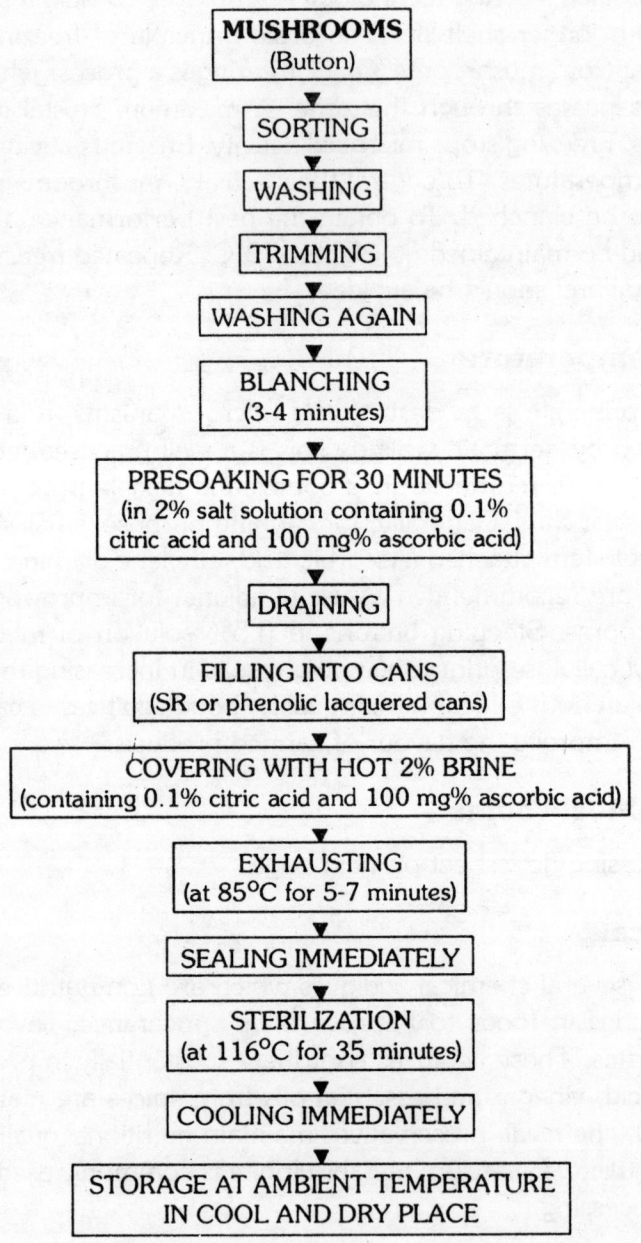

MUSHROOMS
(Button)

▼

SORTING

▼

WASHING

▼

TRIMMING

▼

WASHING AGAIN

▼

BLANCHING
(3-4 minutes)

▼

PRESOAKING FOR 30 MINUTES
(in 2% salt solution containing 0.1%
citric acid and 100 mg% ascorbic acid)

▼

DRAINING

▼

FILLING INTO CANS
(SR or phenolic lacquered cans)

▼

COVERING WITH HOT 2% BRINE
(containing 0.1% citric acid and 100 mg% ascorbic acid)

▼

EXHAUSTING
(at 85°C for 5-7 minutes)

▼

SEALING IMMEDIATELY

▼

STERILIZATION
(at 116°C for 35 minutes)

▼

COOLING IMMEDIATELY

▼

STORAGE AT AMBIENT TEMPERATURE
IN COOL AND DRY PLACE

(i) Preparation of Ketchup

FLOW-SHEET FOR PROCESSING OF MUSHROOM KETCHUP

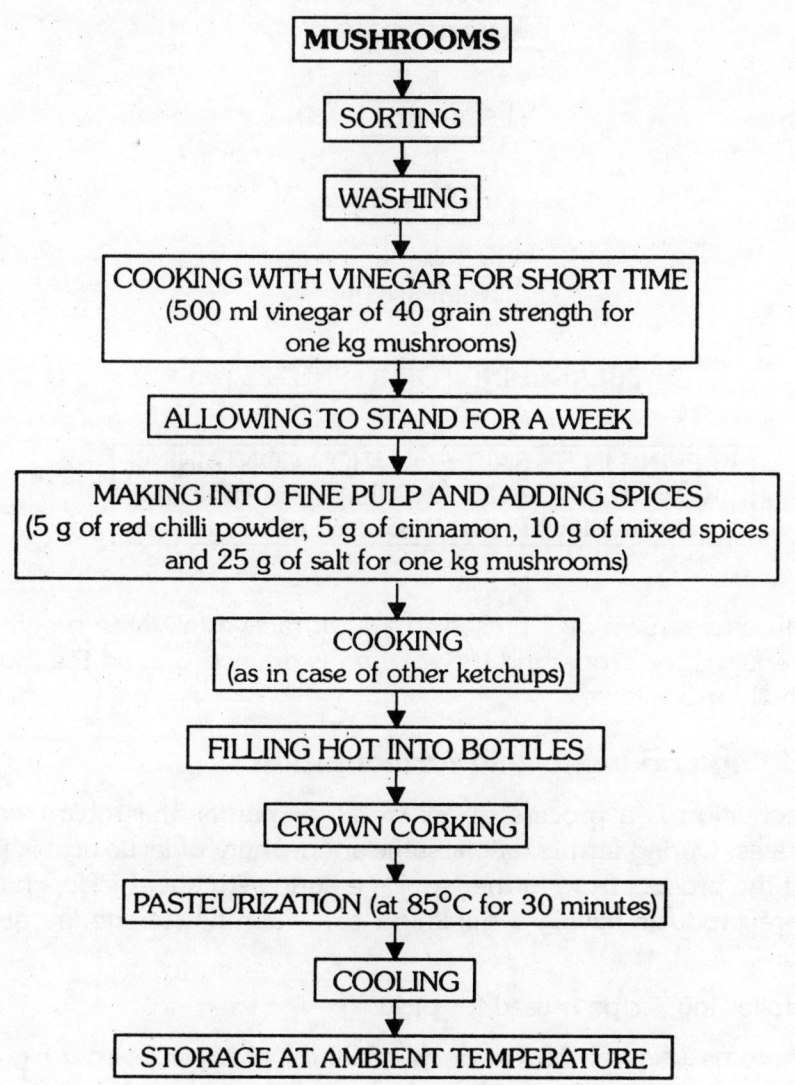

| MUSHROOMS |
| ↓ |
| SORTING |
| ↓ |
| WASHING |
| ↓ |

COOKING WITH VINEGAR FOR SHORT TIME
(500 ml vinegar of 40 grain strength for
one kg mushrooms)

↓

ALLOWING TO STAND FOR A WEEK

↓

MAKING INTO FINE PULP AND ADDING SPICES
(5 g of red chilli powder, 5 g of cinnamon, 10 g of mixed spices
and 25 g of salt for one kg mushrooms)

↓

COOKING
(as in case of other ketchups)

↓

FILLING HOT INTO BOTTLES

↓

CROWN CORKING

↓

PASTEURIZATION (at 85°C for 30 minutes)

↓

COOLING

↓

STORAGE AT AMBIENT TEMPERATURE

(ii) Preservation with salt and acetic acid

TECHNOLOGICAL FLOW-SHEET FOR PRESERVATION OF MUSHROOMS WITH SALT AND ACETIC ACID

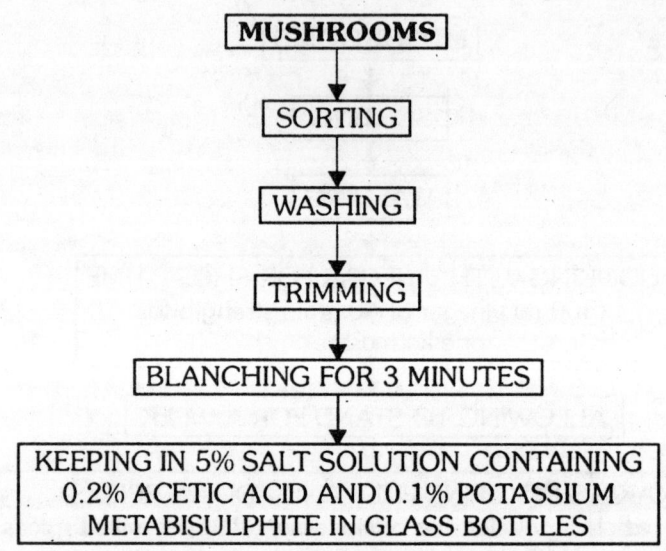

Mushrooms remain well preserved and attractive for three months. When they are required for processing the solution is drained off and the mushrooms are blanched for 3 minutes.

(5) Pickling and lactic acid fermentation

Fermentation is a process of anaerobic or partial anaerobic oxidation of carbohydrates. During fermentation, sufficient quantity of lactic acid is produced to prevent the product from further spoilage during storage. Pickle, chutney and ketchup are products having a minimum of 6 months storage life at ambient temperature.

The following recipe is used for pickling :

Mushrooms 1 kg, salt 100 g, vinegar 100 ml, red chilli powder 5 g, turmeric powder 10 g, coriander powder 15 g, aniseed powder 5 g, cumin powder 5 g, fenugreek powder 2 g, black pepper powder 2 g, cinnamon powder 1 g, clove (headless) 5 numbers, garlic paste 20 g, onion chopped 100 g, tamarind paste 50 g and mustard oil 350 ml.

PROCESSING FLOW-SHEET FOR MUSHROOM PICKLE

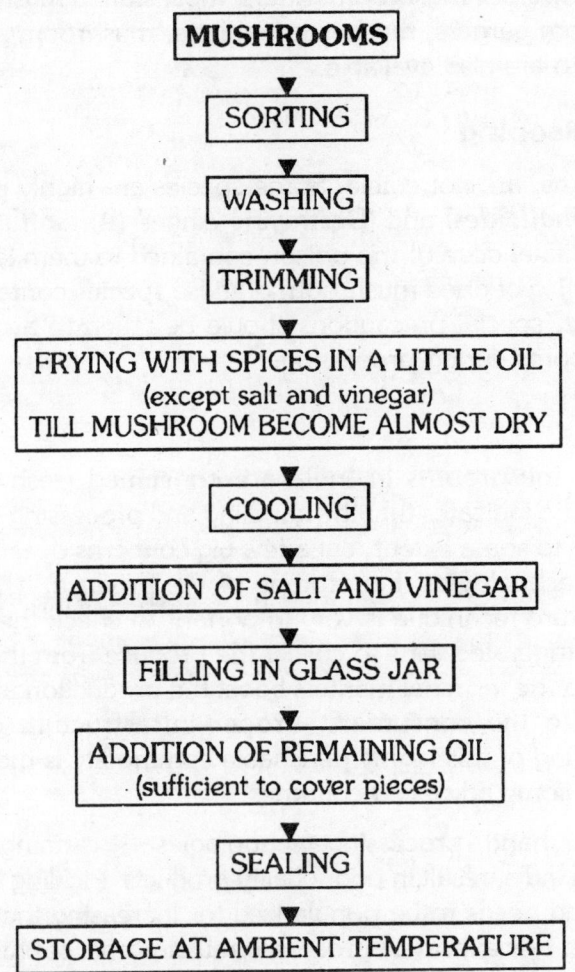

```
┌──────────────────┐
│    MUSHROOMS     │
└──────────────────┘
         ▼
┌──────────────────┐
│     SORTING      │
└──────────────────┘
         ▼
┌──────────────────┐
│     WASHING      │
└──────────────────┘
         ▼
┌──────────────────┐
│     TRIMMING     │
└──────────────────┘
         ▼
┌──────────────────────────────────────┐
│  FRYING WITH SPICES IN A LITTLE OIL   │
│      (except salt and vinegar)        │
│  TILL MUSHROOM BECOME ALMOST DRY      │
└──────────────────────────────────────┘
         ▼
┌──────────────────┐
│     COOLING      │
└──────────────────┘
         ▼
┌──────────────────────────────┐
│  ADDITION OF SALT AND VINEGAR │
└──────────────────────────────┘
         ▼
┌──────────────────────────┐
│   FILLING IN GLASS JAR    │
└──────────────────────────┘
         ▼
┌──────────────────────────────┐
│   ADDITION OF REMAINING OIL   │
│   (sufficient to cover pieces)│
└──────────────────────────────┘
         ▼
┌──────────────────┐
│     SEALING      │
└──────────────────┘
         ▼
┌──────────────────────────────────┐
│  STORAGE AT AMBIENT TEMPERATURE   │
└──────────────────────────────────┘
```

(6) Irradiation

Application of gamma radiation retards the deteriorative processes and helps extend their shelf-life. Doses of 1-2 KGy delays cap opening and stem elongation in button mushrooms, extending their marketability and also increases their storage life for 9-10 days at 15°C.

(7) Other products

Mushrooms can also be utilized in the preparation of weaning foods, biscuits and soup powders. The recipies for preparation of dishes like mushroom kidney fry, mushroom curry, mushroom salads, cheese sandwiches, mushroom stuffed capsicum, stuffed morels, mushroom fritters, meat stuffed mushroom, mushroom hot dog, mushroom burgers, mushroom omlette, mushroom and pouched eggs and, stuffed potato are also available.

Mushroom poisoning

All mushrooms are not edible. Some species are highly poisonous, 'Death Cap' (*Amanita phalloides*) and 'Destroying Angel' (*Amanita virosa*) being the most deadly. The fatal dose of the poison contained in them is just 1 mg per kg body weight, and 1 g of dried mushroom of these species contains about 2 mg of poison. Therefore, special precautions should be taken to avoid contamination with such mushrooms during processing.

Future thrust

Most of the mushrooms in India are consumed fresh. An overview of postharvest scenario indicates that the handling and processing technologies have been standardized to some extent, but a few big concerns dealing with export are employing such technologies. For storage of the produce, it is well established that low temperature technique is very important to check the postharvest loss. Introduction of refrigerated vans to collect the produce from the growers directly and delivering it to the terminal markets boost the production and make available quality produce to the consumers. Proper infrastructure development for postharvest handling of this highly perishable commodity is more or less negligible, compared to some advanced countries.

On the other hand, processing technologies — canning and air-drying – commonly used in India, result in poor quality products. Pickling is a cheap method of preservation and needs to be popularized for increasing the demand of processed mushrooms. For export of processed mushrooms, sophisticated technologies – individual quick freezing, freeze-drying and vacuum drying — are required. Development and introduction of new products with wider acceptability and comparatively at low price further increase the demand and consumption of mushroom products. Wild mushrooms (*Morchella* sp. and *Pleurotus erygnii*) are in great demand for export to Switzerland, France and Germany, but the processed quality of these mushrooms is very poor. After their collection, mainly by local people from the temperate forests, the postharvest handling practices like drying, packing and transportation are not on scientific lines thus delivering a product having dust and smoky smell. Therefore, without employing proper handling and processing techniques such a highly perishable commodity cannot be made available to the common masses at a reasonable cost.

Chapter 25

Some other Valuable Products from Fruits and Vegetables

(1) Sauerkraut

It is highly popular in some countries of Europe and in the U.S.A. Sauerkraut means acid cabbage. It is a clean, wholesome product with a characteristic flavour, obtained by complete fermentation of shredded cabbage in the presence of 2-3 per cent salt. It contains not less than 1.5 per cent acid, expressed as lactic acid. Sauerkraut which has been rebrined in the process of canning or repacking contains not less than 1 per cent acid, expressed as lactic acid. Thus it is the product of lactic acid bacterial fermentation of cabbage under conditions favouring the production of lactic acid, acetic acid, alcohol and carbon dioxide.

Sauerkraut stimulates the peptic glands and has mild laxative property which is due to the esters acetylcholine and lactylcholine formed during fermentation by lactic acid bacteria.

White cabbage because of its low content of polyphenols is more suitable for making sauerkraut than winter cabbage.

Role of microorganisms, temperature, salt and air (oxygen) in sauerkraut production

(i) Microorganisms

Many types of microorganisms are present in raw cabbage, most of which are not involved in fermentation. Cabbage contains substances which are inhibitory to Gram-negative bactéria. Because of inhibitors, salt and an anaerobic environment, lactic acid bacteria predominate. The fermentation is started by *Leuconostoc mesenteroides* which converts sugar to lactic acid, acetic acid, alcohol, carbon dioxide and other products which contribute to the flavour of sauerkraut. The carbon dioxide helps to maintain anaerobic conditions in the fermenting cabbage.

As acid accumulates, *L. mesenteroides* is inhibited, but fermentation is continued by *Lactobacillus brevis. Pediococcus cerevisiae* and finally *Lactobacillus plantarum.*

PROCESSING FLOW-SHEET FOR CABBAGE SAUERKRAUT

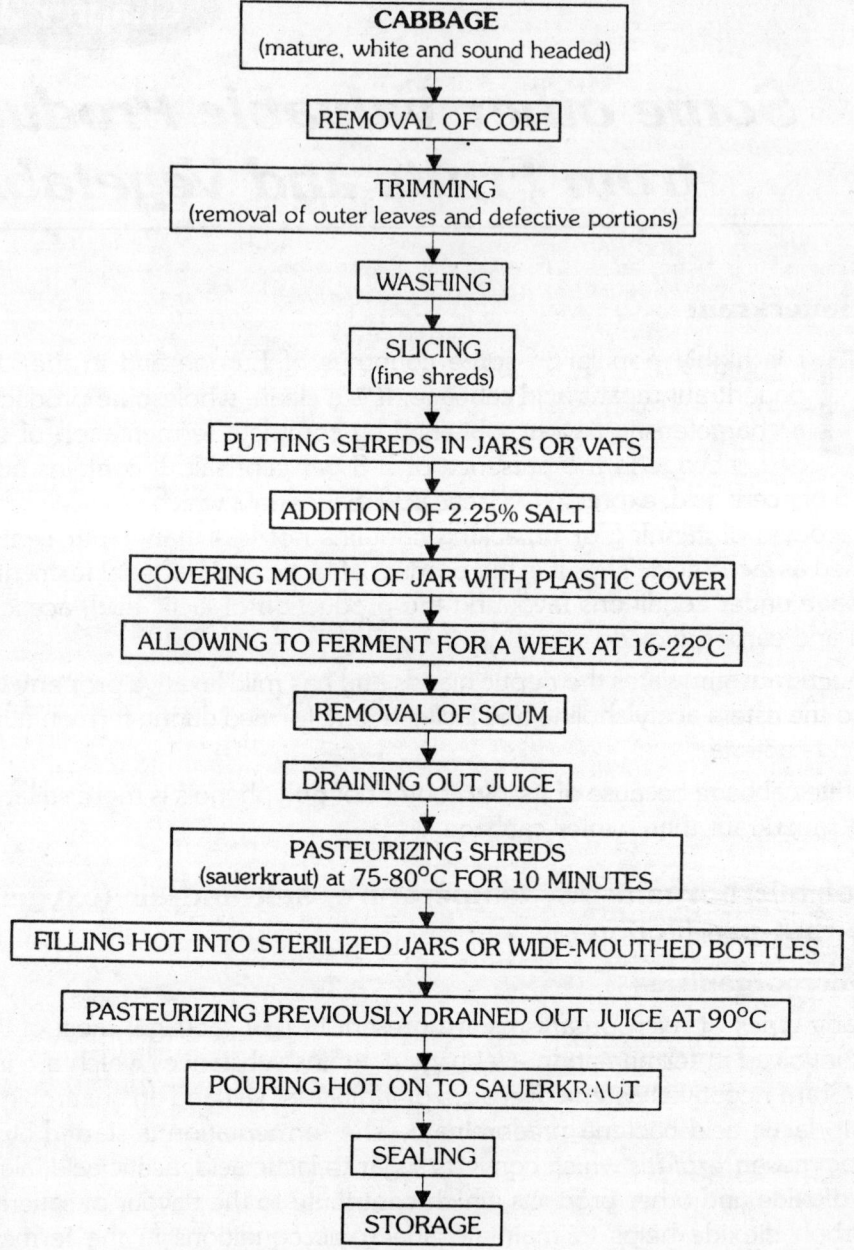

```
                    CABBAGE
        (mature, white and sound headed)
                       ↓
              REMOVAL OF CORE
                       ↓
                    TRIMMING
      (removal of outer leaves and defective portions)
                       ↓
                    WASHING
                       ↓
                    SLICING
                  (fine shreds)
                       ↓
          PUTTING SHREDS IN JARS OR VATS
                       ↓
            ADDITION OF 2.25% SALT
                       ↓
     COVERING MOUTH OF JAR WITH PLASTIC COVER
                       ↓
       ALLOWING TO FERMENT FOR A WEEK AT 16-22°C
                       ↓
              REMOVAL OF SCUM
                       ↓
             DRAINING OUT JUICE
                       ↓
             PASTEURIZING SHREDS
      (sauerkraut) at 75-80°C FOR 10 MINUTES
                       ↓
   FILLING HOT INTO STERILIZED JARS OR WIDE-MOUTHED BOTTLES
                       ↓
   PASTEURIZING PREVIOUSLY DRAINED OUT JUICE AT 90°C
                       ↓
          POURING HOT ON TO SAUERKRAUT
                       ↓
                    SEALING
                       ↓
                    STORAGE
```

Note : *Sauerkraut is generally canned in A 21/2 cans. After filling with sauerkraut, hot juice is poured into cans which are exhausted, sealed hot and processed till the temperature at the centre of the can reaches 82°C.*

(ii) Temperature

A temperature of 18 to 22°C is desirable for good fermentation. Above 22°C the growth of *Lactobacilli* is favoured resulting in rapid fermentation.

(iii) Salt

A proper concentration of salt favours the growth of lactic acid bacteria. Too little salt (less than 1.7%) results in poor flavour and texture and soft kraut while too much (more than 2.5%) inhibits lactic acid bacteria and may result in an acid flavour, darkening and growth of yeasts.

Although salt affects certain organisms, the inhibition of undesirable bacteria is due primarily to the acid produced by the fermentation of sugars.

(iv) Air (oxygen)

Exclusion of air from the fermentation is important for controlling moulds and yeasts whose growth on the cabbage surface can lead to softening, darkening and the development of an undesirable flavour.

(2) Mango slices (Amchur)

FLOW-SHEET FOR PROCESSING OF MANGO SLICES

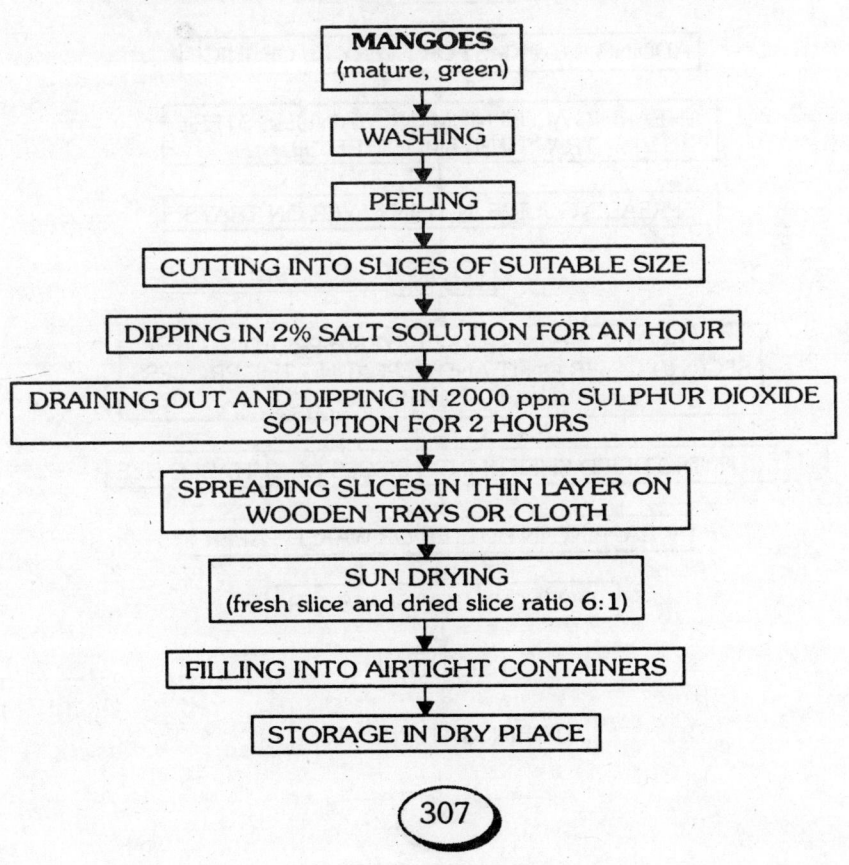

MANGOES
(mature, green)

↓

WASHING

↓

PEELING

↓

CUTTING INTO SLICES OF SUITABLE SIZE

↓

DIPPING IN 2% SALT SOLUTION FOR AN HOUR

↓

DRAINING OUT AND DIPPING IN 2000 ppm SULPHUR DIOXIDE
SOLUTION FOR 2 HOURS

↓

SPREADING SLICES IN THIN LAYER ON
WOODEN TRAYS OR CLOTH

↓

SUN DRYING
(fresh slice and dried slice ratio 6:1)

↓

FILLING INTO AIRTIGHT CONTAINERS

↓

STORAGE IN DRY PLACE

The dried slices should be powdered before the setting in of rains, otherwise the product is spoiled due to high humidity. Slices dried in a dehydrator give a product which is better in colour, flavour and keeping quality than those dried in the sun.

(3) Mango leather

It is also known as mango slab, amawat and ampapar. Ripe fruits are used in its preparation.

FLOW-SHEET FOR PROCESSING OF MANGO LEATHER

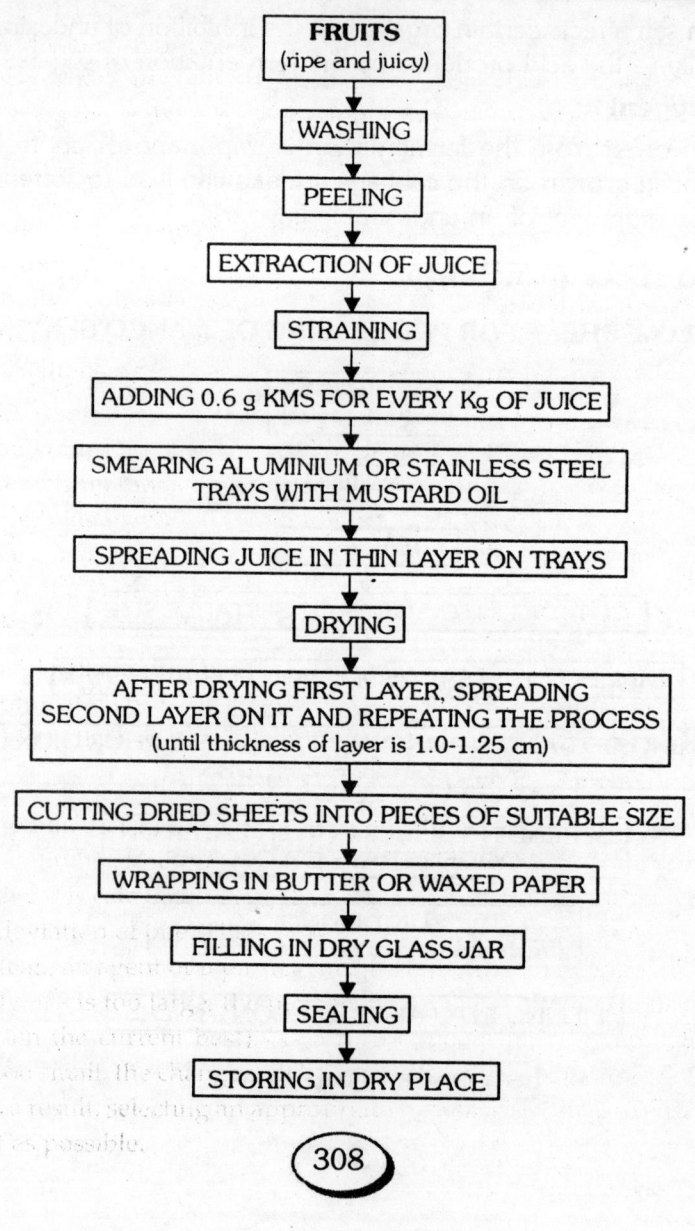

(4) Fruit Cheese

Fruit cheese has recently become very popular. It is a confection of the type of Karachi Halwa and is prepared from fruits like guava, apple, pear and plum. Fruit cheeses have a long shelf-life and are at their best after 3 to 6 months storage. They can be prepared by using fruit pulp 1 kg, sugar 1.25 gk, butter 70 g, citric acid 3 g, salt 2 g and appropriate amount of colour.

FLOW-SHEET FOR PROCESSING OF FRUIT CHEESE

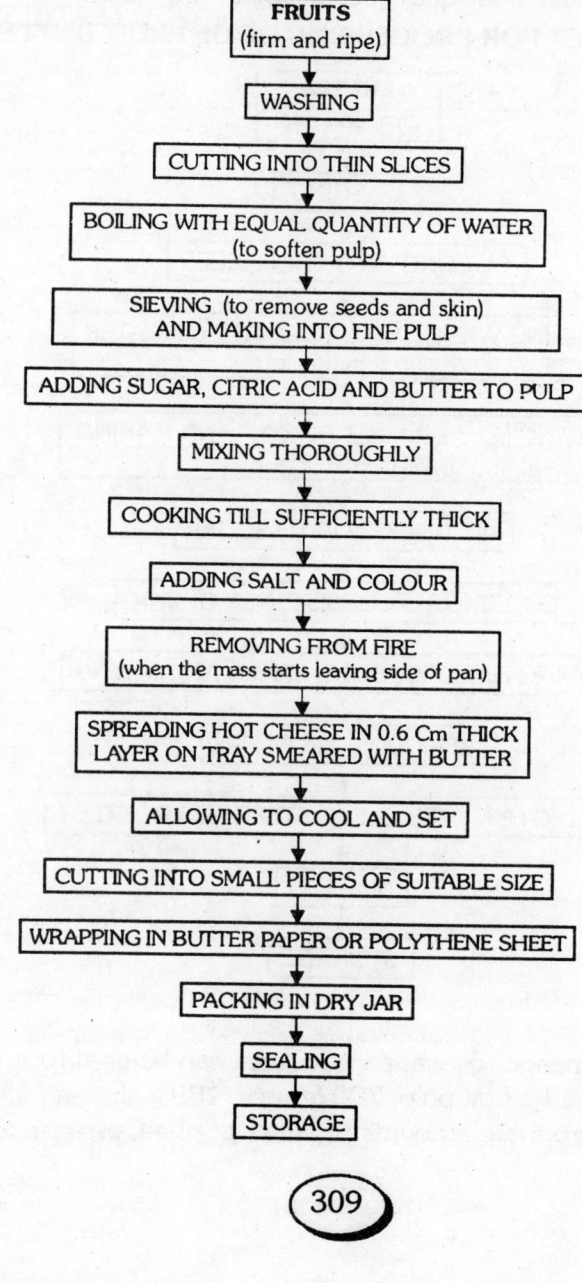

FRUITS
(firm and ripe)

WASHING

CUTTING INTO THIN SLICES

BOILING WITH EQUAL QUANTITY OF WATER
(to soften pulp)

SIEVING (to remove seeds and skin)
AND MAKING INTO FINE PULP

ADDING SUGAR, CITRIC ACID AND BUTTER TO PULP

MIXING THOROUGHLY

COOKING TILL SUFFICIENTLY THICK

ADDING SALT AND COLOUR

REMOVING FROM FIRE
(when the mass starts leaving side of pan)

SPREADING HOT CHEESE IN 0.6 Cm THICK
LAYER ON TRAY SMEARED WITH BUTTER

ALLOWING TO COOL AND SET

CUTTING INTO SMALL PIECES OF SUITABLE SIZE

WRAPPING IN BUTTER PAPER OR POLYTHENE SHEET

PACKING IN DRY JAR

SEALING

STORAGE

(5) Fruit butter

Fruit butters are prepared from apples, peaches, pears, apricots, plums, grapes, etc., or a combination of these fruits. They have a soft butter-like consistency and can be spread easily on breads. They are made by cooking 750 g of sugar with 1 kg of pulp and adding spices like nutmeg, cinnamon, clove, etc. On account of mild spicy taste and flavour fruit butters, specially apple butter, are very popular. The preparation of fruit butter is similar to that of jam except that fine pulp is used to which small quantities of spices are added.

FLOW-SHEET FOR PROCESSING OF OF FRUIT BUTTER

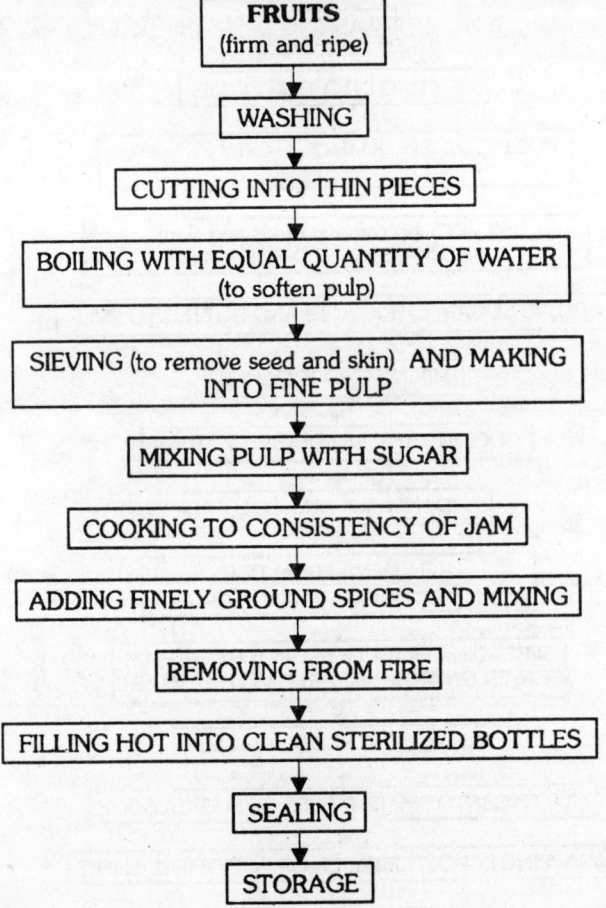

```
          FRUITS
      (firm and ripe)
             │
             ▼
         WASHING
             │
             ▼
   CUTTING INTO THIN PIECES
             │
             ▼
  BOILING WITH EQUAL QUANTITY OF WATER
          (to soften pulp)
             │
             ▼
  SIEVING (to remove seed and skin)  AND MAKING
            INTO FINE PULP
             │
             ▼
   MIXING PULP WITH SUGAR
             │
             ▼
  COOKING TO CONSISTENCY OF JAM
             │
             ▼
  ADDING FINELY GROUND SPICES AND MIXING
             │
             ▼
      REMOVING FROM FIRE
             │
             ▼
  FILLING HOT INTO CLEAN STERILIZED BOTTLES
             │
             ▼
         SEALING
             │
             ▼
         STORAGE
```

(6) Fruit toffee

Pulpy fruits like mango, guava, papaya, etc., can be used for making toffee. It is prepared by using 1 kg fruit pulp, 700 g sugar, 100 g glucose, 150 g skimmed milk powder and appropriate amounts of butter or ghee, essence and colour.

FLOW-SHEET FOR PROCESSING OF FRUIT TOFFEE

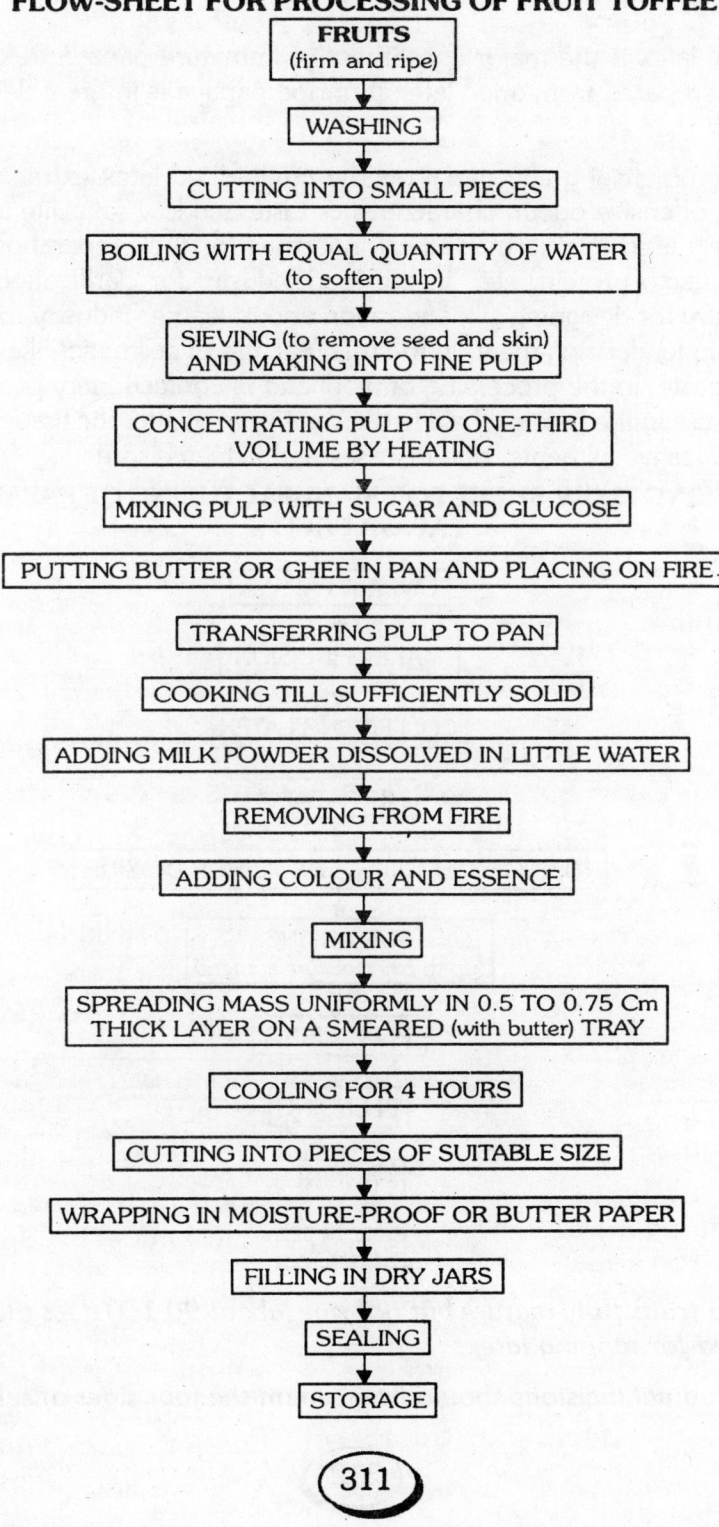

FRUITS
(firm and ripe)

⬇

WASHING

⬇

CUTTING INTO SMALL PIECES

⬇

BOILING WITH EQUAL QUANTITY OF WATER
(to soften pulp)

⬇

SIEVING (to remove seed and skin)
AND MAKING INTO FINE PULP

⬇

CONCENTRATING PULP TO ONE-THIRD
VOLUME BY HEATING

⬇

MIXING PULP WITH SUGAR AND GLUCOSE

⬇

PUTTING BUTTER OR GHEE IN PAN AND PLACING ON FIRE.

⬇

TRANSFERRING PULP TO PAN

⬇

COOKING TILL SUFFICIENTLY SOLID

⬇

ADDING MILK POWDER DISSOLVED IN LITTLE WATER

⬇

REMOVING FROM FIRE

⬇

ADDING COLOUR AND ESSENCE

⬇

MIXING

⬇

SPREADING MASS UNIFORMLY IN 0.5 TO 0.75 Cm
THICK LAYER ON A SMEARED (with butter) TRAY

⬇

COOLING FOR 4 HOURS

⬇

CUTTING INTO PIECES OF SUITABLE SIZE

⬇

WRAPPING IN MOISTURE-PROOF OR BUTTER PAPER

⬇

FILLING IN DRY JARS

⬇

SEALING

⬇

STORAGE

(7) Papain

A milky latex is the major constituent of immature papaya fruits. Papain is an enzyme prepared from dried latex if unripe papaya is in great demand in the international markets.

The Commercial grade papain is the crude dried latex extracted from papaya. It has offensive odour, characteristics taste and low solubility in water. Papain is widely used in pharmaceutical industries for the preparation of protein hydrolyzate, lacto protein, etc., in the food industry for clarification of beer, in textile industry for designing silk and rayon and in leather industry for tanning. It is also used in tenderizing meat, in the manufacture of cosmetics like face creams and dental paste, in the processing of wool and in confectionery products. It has also several use in the medical field in the treatment of necrotic tissues, dyspepsia and other digestive ailments, skin diseases and kidney disorders.

PROCESSING FLOW-SHEET FOR MANUFACTURING OF PAPAIN FROM PAPAYA FRUITS

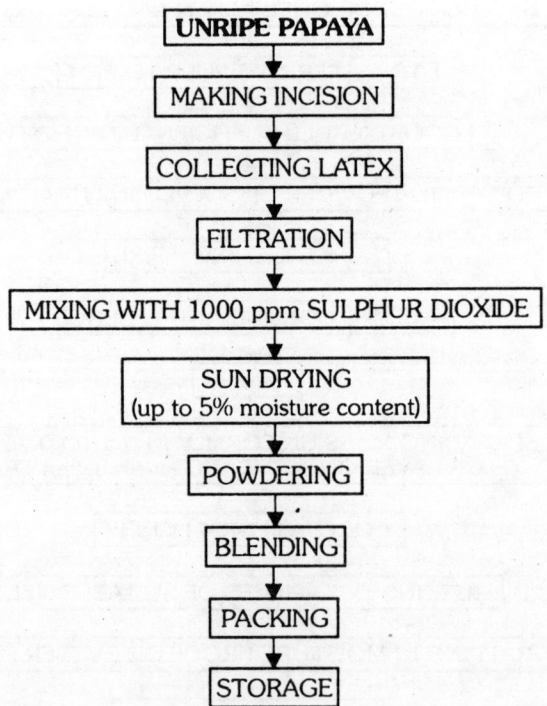

UNRIPE PAPAYA
↓
MAKING INCISION
↓
COLLECTING LATEX
↓
FILTRATION
↓
MIXING WITH 1000 ppm SULPHUR DIOXIDE
↓
SUN DRYING
(up to 5% moisture content)
↓
POWDERING
↓
BLENDING
↓
PACKING
↓
STORAGE

Note

(1) *Papaya fruits fully mature but not ripe (about 90-100 days old) should be selected for tapping latex.*

(2) *Longitudinal incisions should be given on the four sides of selected fruits*

from stalk end to the tip in the morning hours. The depth of incision should be maintained up to about 0.3 cm.

(3) After making longitudinal incisions latex starts flowing which should be collected in a suitable containers. Different containers other than those used for papain collection should not be used. Solidified latex should be scrapped carefully and added to the liquid latex.

(4) Over a period of 12-16 days the process of making four incisions on the untapped fruit surface should be repeated thrice or four times at 3-4 days interval.

(5) Temperature for drying latex in the sun or dryers range between 50-55°C. Before it is dried the potassium metabisulphite (Sulphur dioxide 1000 ppm) is added to the liquid latex. It helps to extend the storage life of papain. The drying of papain is continued until it comes off in flakes having porous structure and moisture content up to 5%.

(6) The dried papain is powdered, sieved in a 10 mesh sieve and stored in polythene bags or other suitable containers.

Chapter 26

Utilization of Fruit and Vegetable Waste

A certain amount of waste products cannot be avoided in the fruit and vegetable processing industry. However, a large amount of waste poses the problem of its disposal without causing environmental pollution. Manufacture of useful by-products from this waste would not only result in reducing the cost of production of the main products but also solve the problem of waste disposal.

The following products may be commercially manufactured from fruit and vegetable waste.

1. **Apple :** The pomace remaining after extraction of juice and removal of cores can be used for preparation of pectin, cider, vinegar, chutney, etc.

2. **Apricot:** Kernels of white apricots are sweet and can be added to the jam after removing the seed coat to improve the colour and appearance. Oil can also be extracted form the kernels, and after refining it is just like almond oil and can be used in pharmaceutical and cosmetic preparations. The oilcake is very rich in protein and can be used as cattlefeed.

3. **Citrus fruits :** Peels are the most important waste product; other wastes are rags, seeds and sludge. Peels can be used for making candy and extraction of essential oil used in confectionery. Pectin can be prepared from the rags of galgal and orange. Rags can also be utilized in the preparation of marmalade, orange toffee and (after drying) as cattlefeed. Orange and lime seeds can be used for the extraction of seed oil used in several industries. Lime sludge is used for distillation of lime oil. Citric acid can also be prepared from sludge. Orange residues can be fermented into fruit vinegar.

4. **Grape :** Stems and pomace are the main waste products. The stems are used for preparing cream of tartar. Oil can be extracted from the seeds and the cake used as cattlefeed. Pomace can be used for making jelly and chutney.

5. **Guava :** The most important product prepared from guava waste is guava cheese. It is prepared from the cores, seeds and peels left after extracting the juice and is just like 'halwa'.

6. **Jackfruit :** The thick rind and inner perigons can be made into high class jelly. Pectin can also be extracted from them. Seeds can be eaten after roasting or ground into flour.

7. **Mango :** 25 to 30 per cent of the fruit is wasted during canning. The peel can be fermented into vinegar. Kernels from the stones can be dried, powdered and utilized for edible purposes.

8. **Passion-fruit :** Pectin can be prepared from the thick rind and oil from seeds.

9. **Peach :** Oil can be extracted from the kernels for industrial use.

10. **Pear :** Peels and cores can be dried and used as an animal feed or can be fermented into perry or vinegar.

11. **Pineapple :** 40 to 50 per cent of the fruit is wasted during canning. Juice extracted from the shell, trimmings and other wastes can be refined and used for canning pineapples. Citric acid can be prepared from this juice as also alcohol and vinegar by fermenting it. The cores can be used for preparing candy or extracting juice and the cake as cattlefeed. Pineapple tops and leaves mixed with molasses (1 per cent) and urea (0.2 per cent) can be used as cattlefeed.

12. **Other fruits :** Pulpy portion of banana peel and pseudostem of banana can be used for making banana cheese and paper pulp, respectively. The latex of green papaya yields papain, a proteolytic enzyme which finds industrial application.

13. **Tomato :** The seeds can be used for extracting an edible oil and the trimmings for preparing juice, sauce or puree.

14. **Other vegetables :** Wastes of potato, cabbage, cauliflower, turnip, sweet potato, carrot, beet, beans, etc., can be used for making cattlefeed.

Chapter 27

Water for Fruit and Vegetable Processing Industries

W ater is one of the important factors in activity of the fruit and vegetable processing industries. Water is needed in the processing plants for generating steam; washing and peeling of raw materials particularly fruits and vegetables; as an ingredient in finished products; as a heat exchange medium in heating and cooling operations; for cleaning plant and equipments; and for protection against fire.

Different sources of water supplies may be classified as surface water (from lakes, streams and reservoirs) and subsurface water (from shallow and deep wells). The characteristics of water from these sources vary with rainfall, the nature of materials with which the water comes in contact, and the time of year.

The general characteristics of water from different sources are shown in the table below:

General characteristics of water from different sources

Type of water	General characteristics		
	Organic matter	**Mineral matter**	**Microbial count**
Surface water	May be high	Ordinarily low	May be contaminated
Shallow well	Variable	Ordinarily low	Variable
Deep well	Usually low	Usually high	Usually low

The suitability of water for use in processing plants depends upon the following:

(1) Physical properties, including colour, odour, flavour and turbidity.

(2) Chemical properties, including dissolved solids and gases, pH and hardness. The presence of excessive amounts of hydrogen sulphide in ground and well waters, and phenols and other organic substances from industrial wastes impart undesirable off-flavours.

(3) Microbiological contaminants, including algae, and pathogenic and non-pathogenic organisms.

317

Most of the functions of fruit and vegetable processing plants call for water of a high degree of purity. An overall quality of water cannot be prescribed as so many specialized requirements prevail, so that characteristics that are objectionable for one use may not necessarily prove detrimental for others. In general, only potable water should be used in the preparation of any food intended for human consumption. Potable water is that water which contains no bacteria capable of causing human intestinal diseases and is aesthetically satisfactory for drinking purposes, i.e., free from undesirable odours and flavours. The public health services of industrialized countries have laid down standards for potable water in terms of their physical, chemical and microbiological characteristics. These characteristics are determined through the physical examination and chemical and microbiological analysis of municipally treated water. Countries that do not have their own acceptable limitations have adopted these limits to safeguard the health of their populations with regard to potable water.

Standards for drinking/potable water

	Water characteristics	Recommended maximum limits (ppm)	Concentrations which constitute grounds for rejection (ppm)
(A) Physical characteristics			
(1)	Turbidity (Silica scale)	<10	-
(2)	Colour (Cobalt scale)	<20	-
(3)	Odour	-	-
(4)	Taste	-	-
(B) Chemical Characteristics			
(5)	Hardness (CaCO$_3$)	<250	-
(6)	Alkyl benzene sulphonate (detergent)	0.5	-
(7)	Arsenic	0.01	0.05
(8)	Barium	-	1.0
(9)	Cadmium	-	0.01
(10)	Carbon (chloroform extract, exotic organic chemicals)	0.2	-
(11)	Chloride	250.0	-
(12)	Chromium	-	0.05
(13)	Copper	1.0	-

318

(14)	Cyanide	0.01	0.2
(15)	Fluoride	1.7	2.2
(16)	Iron	0.3	-
(17)	Lead	-	0.05
(18)	Manganese	0.05	-
(19)	Nitrate	45.0	-
(20)	Phenols	0.001	-
(21)	Selenium	-	0.01
(C) Microbiological characteristics			
(22)	Bacteriological examination *Escherichia coli communis*	Absent in less than 50 ml.	-

The water used in fruit and vegetable processing industries should be free from contamination and should be of potable quality in every respect. Its mineral content should be low, and it should be specially free from sulphate and iron salts. The water used in cannery should not be hard, as this toughens the product. In pickling, the carbonates and bicarbonates of calcium and magnesium combine with the lactic acid produced in the process, thereby lowering the acidity of the pickle and affecting its flavour. If the water used is excessively hard, scales are formed in the boiler and also a white crust is formed on the surface of the cans when they are cooled and dried after processing. Such water will, therefore, have to be softened suitably before use. When iron is present in the water, it combines with the tannins of fruits and vegetables and leads to their darkening. The water used should be colourless, odourless, tasteless, and bacteriologically pure.

Purification of Water

(1) Boiling/Sterilization

Boiling/sterilization is the most satisfactory way of destroying the disease-producing organisms in water. It is equally effective, whether the water is clear or cloudy, and whether relatively pure or heavily contaminated with organic matter. To be safe, the water must be brought to a good boil and kept boiling for about 15 minutes. Boiling drives out gases dissolved in the water, and gives water a flat taste, but if left for a few hours in a partially open container, it absorbs air and loses its flat, boiled taste. Sterilization of water is effected by adding chlorine or bleaching powder. Normally, 0.7 to 1.8 kg of liquid chlorine is mixed with ammonia and used for treating 4540000 litres of water. This corresponds to 0.15-0.40 ppm of chlorine. Water treated with chlorine is not harmful in canning process.

Water can also be sterilized with potassium permanganate, ozone gas, silver ion process, ultra-violet rays, etc. The silver ion process, known as Katadyn process, can also be applied for sterilizing fruit juices such as lime juice, apple juice, grape juice. etc.

Boiling/sterilization can, however, be done only on a small-scale because it consumes a lot of energy, and can be applied to water which is not highly polluted and relatively clear. Alternative methods of purification are thus employed in the treatment of large quantities of water. These include: filtration, distillation, deionization, softening, reverse osmosis using membranes, disinfection with iodine, ultra-violet light or chlorine. But filtration, softening and disinfection are the methods most commonly applied.

(2) Filtration

(a) **Sand filters :** The simplest form of water filtration uses a column of sand, or other porous matter, such as crushed hard coal, diatomaceous earth, or gravel that strains out particles from water. A gravity sand filter removes most of the suspended organic material: clay, silt, colloids and some bacteria, if the pores of the filter are small enough, otherwise bacteria and viruses may pass through it. Slow sand filters are commonly employed for the treatment of pond water because the cost is low, and the effectiveness quite high if they are properly maintained. Sand filters get partially clogged with organic matter which may, under certain conditions, cause bacterial growth in the filter. The column, therefore, has to be cleaned out regularly and replaced with clean sand. If not properly operated and maintained, it adds bacteria to the water being filtered.

If the water passed through the filter is found to be acidic, sodium hydroxide is added to raise the pH. The acid may also be neutralized by using a filter containing limestone or marble chips. As the water passes through the filter bed, the acid is neutralized by the limestone to form carbonates.

Although sand filtration does not make polluted water safe for drinking, the cleansing makes the water clearer and more suitable for further treatment by distillation, filtering by granulated active carbon filter, reverse osmosis, deionization, or boiling.

(b) **Activated Carbon filters :** Filters filled with granular activated carbon are used as extremely effective filters to remove chloroform, chlorine, and any bad taste or odour from polluted water. Activated carbon removes or reduces many other organic chemicals including: pesticides, industrial chemicals, and heavy metals like lead and cadmium. It also reduces the level of trace minerals which are, however, desirable in water. Activated carbon filters do not remove fluorides, nitrates or other salts, nor do they remove asbestos fibres. Water loaded with minute particles, therefore, has to be pre-filtered through a sand filter before it is passed through a carbon filter, otherwise the carbon gets clogged up and quickly loses its effectiveness. Activated carbon filters come in various sizes for use. The most popular but the least effective are the small filters that are attached to the end of a faucet to filter water as it leaves the tap. Larger units perform more effectively.

During the filtering of water with a granular activated carbon column, most of the unwanted organic pollutants are adsorbed in the top layers, and as the water passes downwards it progressively contacts cleaner and cleaner carbon. The in-depth filtering purifies the water as it passes out of the column and provides a good margin of safety.

One disadvantage, however, with granular activated carbon filters is that, like other filters, bacteria and other organisms can grow on the carbon surface. Because of this and the possibility that filtered chemical compounds may drop off a saturated filter to contaminate filtered water, the carbon is replaced every three weeks or after treating 90 litres (about 20 gal.) of water. While in use, the following signs of filter failure may be noticed: a change in the taste of the filtered water; a noticeable reduction in water pressure, resulting in lower than normal output; and the appearance of sediment in the filtered water.

Sometimes, alum is used to coagulate the suspended matter including bacteria. This water is then allowed to settle down before filtration.

(3) Softening

(a) **Temporary hardness :** Temporary hardness is due to the presence of bicarbonates of calcium and magnesium. These are removed by boiling the water, when carbon dioxide is driven out, leaving the insoluble carbonates.

$$Ca(HCO_3) \rightleftharpoons CaCO_3 + H_2O + CO_2\uparrow$$

Calcium bicarbonate   Calcium
(soluble)   carbonate
                      (Insoluble)

Temporary hardness in water can also be removed by *Clark's process*. In this process, the amount of bicarbonate present in the water is determined, and the requisite amount of quick lime is added to remove the excess of carbon dioxide. The bicarbonates are converted into insoluble carbonates and carbon dioxide, which holds them in solution, combines with quick lime, which is added to form a second portion of insoluble carbonate. Quick lime forms $Ca(OH)_2$ when added to water.

$$Ca(OH)_2 + CO_2 \longrightarrow CaCO_3 + H_2O$$

Quick lime   Calcium
(Soluble)   carbonate
                      (Insoluble)

$$Ca(HCO_3)_2 + Ca(OH)_2 \longrightarrow 2CaCO_3 + 2H_2O$$

(Soluble)   (Soluble)   (Insoluble)

Commercially, hardness is expressed as carbonate of lime. For every 1000 litres of water with hardness of 29 milligrams per every one litre about 13 g of quick lime will be required. If magnesium bicarbonate is present, then double the amount of quick lime is added, then the sparingly soluble magnesium hydroxide is formed.

$$Mg(HCO_3)_2 + 2Ca(OH)_2 \longrightarrow Mg(OH)_2 + 2CaCO_3 + 2H_2O$$

Magnesium   Calcium   Magnesium   Calcium
bicarbonate   hydroxide   hydroxide   carbonate
(Soluble)   (Soluble)   (Insoluble)   (Insoluble)

(b) Permanent hardness : Permanent hardness is due to the soluble sulphates or chlorides of calcium and magnesium. This type of hardening cannot be removed by boiling the water. It requires special treatment. By adding sodium carbonate to the water, the chlorides and sulphates are converted into insoluble carbonates.

$$CaSO_4 + Na_2CO_3 \longrightarrow CaCO_3 + Na_2SO_4$$

Calcium   Sodium   Calcium   Sodium
sulphate   carbonate   carbonate   sulphate
(Soluble)   (Soluble)   (Insoluble)   (Soluble)

$$MgSO_4 + Na_2CO_3 \longrightarrow MgCO_3 + Na_2SO_4$$

Magnesium   Magnesium   Sodium
sulphate   carbonate   sulphate
(Soluble)   (Insoluble)   (Soluble)

$$MgCl_2 + Na_2CO_3 \longrightarrow MgCO_3 + 2NaCl$$

Magnesium   Magnesium   Sodium
chloride   carbonate   chloride
(Soluble)   (Insoluble)

If both temporary and permanent hardness are present, they may be removed by the addition of commercial caustic soda and sodium carbonate. Caustic soda neutralizes the bicarbonates of calcium and mag-

322

nesium, precipitating carbonate and forming sodium carbonate which further reacts with the sulphates and decomposes them into insoluble carbonates.

$$Ca(HCO_3)_2 + 2NaOH \longrightarrow CaCO_3 + Na_2CO_3 + 2H_2O$$

| Calcium bicarbonate (Soluble) | Caustic soda (Soluble) | Calcium carbonate (Insoluble) | Sodium carbonate (Soluble) |

$$CaSO_4 + Na_2CO_3 \longrightarrow CaCO_3 + Na_2SO_4$$

Calcium sulphate   Sodium carbonate   Calcium carbonate (Insoluble)

$$H_2CO_3 . CaCO_3 + Na_2CO_3 \longrightarrow CaCO_3 + 2NaHCO_3$$

$$CaSO_4 + Na_2CO_3 \longrightarrow CaCO_3 + Na_2SO_4$$

Calcium carbonate and magnesium carbonate are slightly soluble in water to the extent of 1.3 and 0.93 parts per 100,000 parts respectively. It is, therefore, not possible to produce water of zero hardness. Since 4 to 5 parts per 100,000 does not have any harmful effect upon any material, water of zero hardness is seldom required in a canning factory. Water for canning fruits and vegetables should not have both temporary and permanent hardness in excess of 10 to 12 parts per 100,000. Salts of calcium and magnesium combine with pectin thereby toughening the skin of fruits and vegetables. If the water is of temporary hardness, carbonates of calcium and magnesium settle down during sterilization, thereby making the liquid cloudy, which spoils the appearance of the canned product.

Besides the above techniques, *Permutit process* is also used for softening of hard water. By this process in which an artificial zeolite is used, both types of hard water can be softened. Permutit is a silicate of sodium and alumina ($2SiO_2$, Al_2O_3, Na_2O, $6H_2O$), which is practically insoluble in water. It is ground coarsely and packed in a tube. When water is percolated through this column, double decomposition of the salts present in water and in the zeolite takes place.

$$CaSO_4 + 2NaP \longrightarrow CaP_2 + Na_2SO_4$$

Calcium sulphate   Sodium permutit

323

The exchange is reversible. When the permutit is exhausted, it is reactivated by percolating a strong solution of sodium chloride for 8 to 10 hours.

$$CaP_2 + 2NaCl \longrightarrow CaCl_2 + 2NaP$$

Commercial units based on the Permutit process are readily available for treatment of water. These units are specially useful where boiler feed water is to be treated.

(4) Disinfection

(a) Iodine disinfection : Several treatments are available for the simple disinfection of water. Water may be disinfected using iodine, bromine, silver and ultra-violet light. Iodine is effective in destroying bacteria, viruses cysts, and other contaminants in water. It is, however, not recommended for use in water that is cloudy or muddy, or water that has a noticeable colour even when clear. It is also not recommended for use on water drunk by pregnant women, and not considered safe for long-term use. Preliminary filtering may render the water suitable for iodine treatment.

(b) Chlorination : Chlorination is the most common form of treatment available for water. It is used by municipal water treatment plants to disinfect water before it is pumped into pipes for domestic and industrial use. Chlorine is added to kill germs. Untreated water entering a municipal treatment plant generally contains dissolved minerals, bacteria, heavy metals, humic acids (by-products of dead leaves), trash, humus, and animal wastes. These enter the earth's water systems as run-off from the land, or as treated sewage dumped into rivers and lakes. The water is filtered to remove suspended matter and other organic materials, and chlorine is then added. The chlorine attacks and combines with any suspended organic matter. It combines with humic acids in water to form small amounts of chloroform and related compounds, which have recently been implicated as health hazards, causing chlorination to be suspected a low-level health risk. Where chlorination is used, the ideal situation is to have a system in which applied chlorine kills germs and bacteria, before being removed from the drinking water, so that its benefits are provided without the related risk to health.

The amount of chlorine added to water is often called the *chlorine dosage*, and is independent of the amount of chlorine demanded by the status of the water. When chlorine is added to water other than distilled water (which does not contain impurities), a small amount reacts with the impurities in the water. The amount which reacts depends upon the type and level of impurities, the acidity or alkalinity of the water being treated, the time allowed for contact, and the temperature and the amount of chlorine applied.

When a given amount of chlorine is added to water, the amount that remains after the demands of the water have been satisfied is called *total residual chlorine*. This residual chlorine exists either as free chlorine or loosely combined with other elements. Free chlorine exists mainly as hypochlorous acid which is germicidal. The rate at which bacteria exposed to chlorine are killed is thus proportional to the amount of chlorine present as hypochlorous acid. Residual free chlorine also acts as a safety measure to safeguard against recontamination of the water after treatment. Residual chlorine is thus maintained at permissible levels which are not deemed harmful to health. By contrast, harmful amounts of chlorine are extremely distasteful and easily detectable.

The condition of water that is chlorinated is generally clear with few minerals dissolved in it. Gaseous chlorine is ordinarily applied to water in municipal water treatment plants where the time of contact, the temperature, and the amount of chlorine used are all strictly controlled. The result is the production of potable water.

Water quality for various uses in fruit and vegetable processing industry

(1) **General purposes :** Water used for general purposes in a fruit and vegetable processing industry, such as washing, processing and general sanitation. The total bacterial count of water considerably influences plant sanitation. The purpose of washing fruits and vegetables and cleaning equipment is to reduce contamination. Obviously, water used for this purpose should itself have a low bacterial count. The bacteriological quality of water used throughout the plant should meet the standards required for drinking water. The tolerance limits and standards for water for general purposes are as follows :

Standards for water for general purposes

Water characteristics	Standard	Tolerance
Colour	Should be quite colourless	-
Appearance	Clear, free from insoluble matter and appreciable deposit	-
Odour	-	-
Taste	-	-
Hardness (CaCO$_3$)	100-150 ppm	<250 ppm
Chlorine	None-Trace	< 25 ppm
Free Ammonia	-	< 1.0 ppm
Albuminoid Ammonia	-	< 0.1 ppm
Heavy metals (Iron)	-	< 2.0 ppm
Nitrate nitrogen	-	Nil
Bacteriological examination *E. coli communis*	Absent in 100 ml.	Absent in Less than 50 ml.

(2) **Canning of fruits and vegetables :** The water used in cannery should not be hard, as this toughens the product. When very hard water is used for blanching vegetables some pecto-calcium and pecto-magnesium complexes are formed which starts the hardening of vegetable tissues. This process continues over the pasteurization of the finished product. Soft water has negative consequences associated with minerals and hydrosoluble substances and losses during blanching of vegetables. When fruit is processed in sugar syrup, the use of hard water for the syrup preparation could induce the formation of pectin-sugar-acid gel facilitated by the medium pH and presence of calcium salts. The generally permitted level of hardness in water used for canning should not exceed 85 ppm as CaCO$_3$. Water used in a retort should be free from bicarbonate hardness, otherwise unsightly calcium carbonate deposits will develop on the outside of the filled cans or glass containers during processing. The sodium alkalinity of retort water should also be low, because high sodium alkalinity attacks can and gives them a spangled appearance.

(3) **Soft fruit drinks and carbonated beverages :** Water from municipal supplies sometimes contains mineral residues and organic matter which makes it unsatisfactory for the preparation of carbonated bever-

ages. For bottling carbonated beverages, it is necessary that the water used should be clear, colourless, odourless, and free from water-borne organisms. Its alkalinity must be less than 50 ppm; its total dissolved solid content less than 500 ppm; and its iron or manganese content less than 0.1 ppm. Iron or manganese contents above this level may form a sediment in the beverage and contribute to a poor taste. If the water contains suspended matter, it does not carbonate readily and the beverage made from it rapidly becomes flat. Hardness further influences the degree of carbonation, and in some cases, colour and clarity. Odours found in water alter the flavour of beverages often making them extremely disagreeable. Odours found in water are classified in a number of ways: they are indicated as 'chemical when coming from industrial wastes or chemical treatment plants; as 'fishy' when due to certain water-born organisms; as 'septic' when from sewage contamination; as 'hydrocarbon' when from oil contamination as 'sulphurous' when from hydrogen sulphide; and as 'chlorine' when from the presence of fresh chlorine in the water. For the taste to be acceptable, water must be free from all these objectionable odours and must have no noticeable taste. Chlorinated water has a marked effect on the quality of citrus products, especially orange drinks. Alkalinity in excess of 50 ppm will neutralize sufficient acid in the beverage and destroy much of the zest or the tang, often making it extremely disagreeable. Neutralization of the acid also reduces the keeping quality of the product, because the concentration of acid aids in the preservation of beverages. Total dissolved solid exceeding 500 ppm will give the beverage a brackish taste.

Although water used in beverage manufacture may be potable and free from pathogenic organisms, it may contain microorganisms which are capable of spoiling the product. The microorganisms may give rise to growth which will cause deposits or opalescence and cause the product to spoil during storage. Carbonated beverages usually contain a flavouring extract, sugar, water, and substances to produce foam. Some may even contain a fruit juice base. Algae and other water-borne organisms may find these products favourable to their development and produce a off-taste and sediments. The products may frequently become cloudy and ropy; ropiness being caused by capsulated organisms. Carbonated beverages usually contain yeasts and bacteria. Yeasts frequently cause spoilage. Most of the bacteria seem to remain dormant, but occasionally they may grow and cause spoilage. In addition, water used for beverage manufacture should not contain colloidal matter which, upon standing, may cause precipitation in the product.

Standards of water for various products

Water characteristics	Maximum tolerance limit (ppm)		
	Canning	Carbonated beverages	Beverages
Turbidity	1	1	5
Colour	-	10	-
Taste and odour	None	None	None
Iron and manganese	0.2	0.3	0.1
Sulphates (as SO_4)	-	250	-
Chlorides (as Cl)	-	250	-
Alkalinity (as $CaCO_3$)	-	30-85	50
Hardness (as $CaCO_3$)	85	-	150
Total dissolved solids	-	850	500
Organic matter	-	None	None
Fluorine	1.0	1.0	1.0

(4) **Fruit acids and pectin :** In the manufacture of fruit acids and pectin, it is necessary to have water with a low mineral content. If possible, the ash content must be completely eliminated to avoid interference with the extraction of these products.

(5) **Citrus fruit packaging :** When hard water is used for washing citrus fruit, the dust and dirt tend to cling to the fruit and give a dingy and unattractive appearance. Hard water thus needs to be softened. Soft water used in the washing of fruit has been found to loosen and remove the dirt, thus furnishing a clean and attractive product.

(6) **Bottle washers, keg washers and pasteurizers :** Water used for these purposes should be of almost zero hardness. In pasteurization, waters which are high in bicarbonate hardness, form unsightly deposits on the outside of the bottles. This necessitates polishing operations later. Softening of this water eliminates these defects.

(7) **Boiler feed water :** Water containing appreciable quantities of soluble salts especially those of calcium and magnesium, is not suitable for boilers. As the steam formed evaporates, the soluble salts get concentrated and form compounds which are deposited in the equipment. Hard water forms scale or adherent sludge on the heat-transfer surfaces of the boiler, due to the deposition of insoluble carbonates and sulphates of calcium

and magnesium, with or without silica. Scaling results in a loss of efficiency of heat transfer; a reduction in the capacity of the boiler, and its eventual damage.

A high solid content in feed water, which is alkaline and contains substances that promote foaming, causes these to be carried over in the steam. The steam generated is thus strongly alkaline and will corrode metals such as aluminium and tin. For this reason, maximum permissible limits are provided for boiler feed water and these vary with operating pressures. For operating pressures of 0 to 330 psig, the permissible limits of water solids are 3,500 ppm. For pressures between 1,000 to 1,500 psig, the permissible limits for water solids are 1,000 ppm.

It is important that the quality of water supplied to fruit and vegetable processing plants meets certain maximum tolerance limits ascribed as standard characteristics. Where such tolerance limits are exceeded, undesirable effects may show up in products and equipments. The maximum tolerance of water characteristics and the typical effects when these are exceeded are summarized as under:

General Standards of water for fruit and vegetable processing plants

Water characteristics	Maximum tolerance (ppm)	Typical effect when in excess of maximum tolerance
Turbidity	1 to 10	Deposits on product and equipment
Colour	5 to 10	Possible discolouration from organic matter
Taste and odour	Noticeable	Corresponding or intensified taste or odour in product
Iron and manganese	0.2 to 0.3	Staining, discolouration, off-taste and possible growth of iron bacteria
Alkalinity	30 to 250	Neutralization of acid constituents, possible inhibition of bacterial action, deposits or white butts in ice
Hardness ($CaCO_3$)	10 to 250	Deposits, absorption by some products, precipitation with alkaline constituents
Total dissolved solids	850	Perceptible taste and possible inhibition of chemical reaction
Organic matter	Generally any	Off-taste, sediment, spoilage, undesirable reactions
Fluorine	1.0	Mottling of tooth enamel in children

Chapter 28

Quality Characteristics of Fruits and Vegetables for Processing

The quality of a processed fruit or vegetable product ultimately depends upon the quality of the raw material that is used to make the product. Most of the fruits or vegetables are marketed as they are, without undergoing any further processing. For marketing purposes, the characteristics of primary importance are size, attractiveness, maturity, organoleptic quality and freedom from infection.

When the same vegetable/fruit is to undergo processing, other properties assume more importance; these are colour, flavour and texture. Obviously, fruits or vegetables of poor quality cannot ensure that a good quality processed product will be obtained. In many countries, there are precise specifications of various characteristics for products intended for processing.

Quality characteristics are importance since they are related to the total yield of a finished product, and are, therefore major considerations in processing.

Quality is a measure of the degree of excellence or degree of acceptability by the consumer. Quality characteristics of a product may be divided into three major categories-

(A) Sensory characteristics of quality include appearance (colour, size and shape and defects), texture and flavour (taste and odour) which the consumer can evaluate with his senses.

(B) Hidden characteristics of quality are those which the consumer cannot evaluate with his senses, such as nutritive value, presence of harmless adulterants, and presence of toxic substances.

(C) Quantitative characteristics are also considered as an attribute of food quality, since it forms a part of the total quality evaluation of a product, e.g., the finished product yield of a variety of fruit or vegetable.

(A) Sensory Characteristics

(a) Appearance (Eye appeal judged by sense of light) : The overall eye appeal of a food product is more important than dependence on taste and odour, and may determine acceptance or rejection without a trial tasting. Appearance, therefore, deserves much consideration in food processing. It includes colour, size and shape and defects.

(1) Colour : Colour increases the attractiveness of fruits and vegetables and in most cases, it is used as a maturity index. It is also associated with flavour, texture, nutritive value, and wholesomeness. Surface colour is important for the fresh market and internal colour for the processing. Green colour is indicative of insufficient ripeness in fruits but it is desirable attributes in vegetables.

Coloured fruits, when picked at the firm-ripe stage, should be fully and uniformly coloured. Three major classes of pigments occur in fruits: the carotenoid, the chlorophyll, and the anthocyanin pigments.

Carotenoids play an important part in the colour of canned mangoes, citrus, and pineapple. The red and violet colour in fruits and vegetables is due to anthocyanins, and this has to be accounted for in processing, since the colour gradually passes out into the syrup or brine used in canning. Certain fruits and vegetables — notably guava, litchi, banana, and broad beans — may turn pink during processing due to the presence of leuco-anthocyanin, and this appears to differ with variety.

Non-enzymatic browning or discolouration is also caused by the presence of chlorophyll in certain products. The browning of cooked tomatoes, presumably due to phaeophytin formation, greatly reduces the intensity of the natural red colour. Use of too great a proportion of green fruit during the manufacture of tomato products will give a brown or brownish-red product. The condensation of reducing sugars with amino acids, a process accelerated by heat, is responsible for much of the darkening that occurs during the drying of fruits such as dates and grapes. Potatoes with high sugar content have a tendency to turn dark during dehydration and during subsequent storage as a result of this reaction. Conditioning of potatoes to reduce sugar content and application of SO_2 before processing control non-enzymatic browning.

Many fruits and vegetables undergo rapid browning during peeling and slicing operations. Bananas, potatoes and grapes will turn brown if injured during the preparation, unlike pineapple and tomatoes. The browning reaction is mainly caused by the enzyme(s) polyphenol oxidase acting on a suitable phenolic substrate in the presence of oxygen. Dates and grapes become dark upon drying and are acceptable in this form. With other fruits and vegetables in which darkening is unacceptable, enzyme inhibition is effected partially or totally by heat (blanching), by sulphur dioxide, or by addition of ascorbic acid, sodium chloride, etc. Another solution is to select varieties having less tendency to discolour during preparation for processing.

The colour requirements of fruits and vegetables used for quick-freezing differ markedly from those needed for canning, since in quick-freezing there is little change of chlorophyll to phaeophytin, no marked change in leuco-anthocyanins, and little migration of the anthocyanins from fruit to syrup. Colour and appearance are, however, extremely important quality attributes in unblanched, frozen, cut fruits, because they are subject to enzymatic browning when thawed.

The measurement of surface colour presents many problems. When the unit size is large, such as mango, papaya, guava, apple, melons, tomato, etc., individual units have to be measured. When the unit size is small such as, strawberry, grape berries, phalsa, peas, etc., a representative sample can be measured. The instrument used for colour measurement are Hunter colour-difference meter, Spectronic-20 (reflectance measurement) and Spectrophotometer.

(2) **Size and shape :** Size is of major interest to the grower as it is directly proportional to the yield in certain crops, e.g., pineapple.

The importance of size and shape of fruits and vegetables is often underestimated. They make important contribution to the appearance of fresh produce and processed product. Grading of fruits and vegetables into various size and shape categories is usually one of the first steps in packaging and processing operation. Size grading is done mainly to facilitate succeeding operations such as cutting, peeling or blending, to obtain uniformity in the product, and to provide consumers with the preferred size.

Shape of the raw materials sometimes determines the suitability for processing. The reduce losses during mechanical trimming and handling, the shape of the fruit or vegetable should readily lend itself to such processes. Selection and breeding of raw materials for shape is yet to be attempted in most crops. In fact, many tropical fruits are often of inconvenient shape or size and thus present problems of handling while processing, e.g., mango, papaya, guava, etc.

Size and shape can be measured with manual operation (human judgement), simple scale, vernier calliper, micrometers, planimeters and machine which measures weight, diameter and length.

(3) **Defects :** Most defects or imperfections are still largely evaluated by the consumer's eye, though in some cases instruments may be used. The presence of defects frequently lowers the grade of products which are otherwise of very high quality. Defects may be caused by-

(i) Deformities caused by unfavourable environmental conditions.

(ii) Insects and microorganisms.

(iii) Mechanical injury caused during handling, transportation and processing such as damage, bruising and crushing.

(iv) Specks and sediments.

(v) Foreign material or any other harmful added substance.

(b) **Texture (Hand and mouth feel judged by sense of touch):** Texture characteristics involve touch sensations. It includes hand feel and mouth feel which determine the quality.

(1) **Hand feel :** It is finger feel such as firmness (apple), softness (mango and plum) and juiciness (citrus and grapes).

(2) **Mouth feel :** It include sensory characters such as chewiness, fibrousness, grittiness, mealiness and stickiness.

Instruments developed for measuring the textural qualities of fruits and vegetables are:

(1) **Succulometer :** Instrument developed for measuring the maturity of sweet corn. It is also used to determine the storage life of apples.

(2) **Tenderometer :** Instrument developed for measuring the tenderness of peas. It determines the suitability of raw peas for canning.

(3) **Pressure Tester :** This is a very light and portable instrument used for measuring the maturity of various fruits.

Texture of fruits and vegetables can also be measured by texture meter, puncture meter and fibrometer.

In addition, certain physico-chemical tests are also used successfully for measuring textural properties. These are -

(1) **Moisture content :** Moisture content or the total solids is a useful index for determining the tenderness of vegetables.

(2) **Alcohol-insoluble solids :** It is a measure of texture rather than an index of maturity.

(3) **Fibre content :** In vegetable, such as asparagus, fibrousness of the product is determining the texture.

(4) **Brine flotation :** It is used for grading of maturity of peas for canning. Density of the material is made use of to separate lighter, more tender units from heavier, more mature units.

(c) **Flavour :** Flavour distinguishes one food from another. It is a combination of taste and smell (odour or aroma).

334

(i) **Taste :** It includes sweet, salty, sour and bitter.

(ii) **Smell :** It may be fragrant, acidic and burnt,

(iii) **Off-flavour :** Enzymatic, physiological or chemical.

Feelings such as astringency, bite, pungency are all attributes which are significant to flavour, especially in spices and other foods, such as wine. Basic characteristics of taste like sweetness, saltiness, sourness and bitterness can be determined but odour characteristics are difficult to measure. Odour or aroma is a vastly complex sensation and the most important factor in flavour. It has not yet been successfully measured by an instrument. Estimation of volatile acids, amines and succinic acid provides indications of off-flavour in stored fruits and vegetables. Gas chromatographic technique has been developed for isolating specific volatiles, and spectrometry and nuclear magnetic resonance for their identification in the direct measurement of flavour quality.

(B) Hidden Characteristics

(a) **Nutritive value :** Consumers pay little attention to the nutritive value of the fruits and vegetables. The more nutritious form may incidentally be preferred if it is associated with one or more attractive features. Fruits and vegetables are of high food value. The details regarding nutrients in fruits and vegetables, their functions and sources of availability are given in Appendix IV, while nutritional values are tabulated in Appendix V for further studies.

(b) **Toxicity :** Various chemical compounds are used extensively in fruit and vegetable production. Edible tissues may accumulate amounts of persistent insecticides belonging to chlorinated hydrocarbon group even beyond permissible limits. These residues may lead to bitter or musty flavour in the canned and other processed products and present a health hazard.

(C) Quantitative Characteristics

(a) **Crop yield :** High yields and disease resistance cut costs of production and processing.

(b) **Finished product yield :** Raw material cost per kg of finished product is another important consideration in processing. This is calculated by determining the amount of product yield per kg of raw material. The ratio of the weight of raw material to the weight of pre-packaged finished product is called the overall shrinkage ratio. The higher the ratio for a given product, the greater will be the unit cost of the processed product. Naturally, low shrinkage ratios are to be desired, consonant with the limitations of the particular vegetable and fruit, e.g., in potatoes for dehydration, factors important in determining overall shrinkage ratios include: (a) dry matter content of the raw material, (b) peels, cores, roots, bruises, deep eyes, and other undesirable material that must be removed and discarded, (c) size and shape of tubers (small and irregular shapes have greater peeling, trimming, and sizing losses), and (d) rejects for poor colour, odour, and composition.

In the processing of juice concentrate, the solids content and the yield of juice are equally important and determine the cost of the finished product.

Another important factor which determines the product yield is the loss which occurs in preparing the material for processing, such as smooth shape and shallow eyes eliminate much waste in the preparation of potato tubers for dehydration.

Factors affecting fruit and vegetable quality

Not all varieties of fruits and vegetables are satisfactory for processing. There are many factors involved in selecting fruit and vegetable varieties for processing. Although high visual quality is desirable for most processing methods, the composition of the fruit in relation to flavour, texture, colour, and nutritional value is of paramount importance. In addition, these qualities should be impaired as little as possible during the specified process, e.g., some vegetables cannot be dehydrated or frozen because of their chemical composition or physical structure. Some kinds have a bitter taste when dried, others loose colour and flavour, or do not reconstitute to even near their original form. Varieties suitable for processing must have satisfactory quality both at harvest time and after storage at low temperatures. The factors affecting quality of fruits and vegetables can be classified largely into two groups, i.e., (a) Pre-harvest factors, and (b) Post-harvest factors.

(A) Pre-harvest factors : These factors can be grouped into environmental and cultural.

(a) Environmental factors

	Factors	Quality affected
(1)	Temperature	Maturity, colour, sugar, acidity, etc. High temperature reduces the quality, e.g., citrus, radish, spinach cauliflower, etc., and increased the quality in grapes, melons, tomato, etc. Low temperature cause chilling and freezing injury.

	Factors	Quality affected
(2)	Light	Essential for anthocyanin formation. Exposed fruit to sun light develop lighter weight, thinner peel, lower juice and acids and higher TSS than shaded fruits, e.g., citrus, mango, etc. Exposure of potato to light causes greening (Solanine formation) which has toxic properties. High sun light intensity causes sun scald in citrus and tomatoes and reduces the pure white colour of cauliflower. Low light intensity causes thin and large leaves in leafy vegetables.
(3)	Rains	Causes cracking in grapes, dates, litchi, limes, lemon, tomato, sweet potato, etc. It reduces appearance and sweetness.
(4)	Wind	Causes bruising, scratching and corky scar (citrus fruits) on the fruit and damage leafy vegetables.
(5)	Humidity	High humidity reduces the colour and TSS and increases acidity in citrus, grapes, tomato, etc., but on other hand it is needed for better quality of banana, litchi and pineapple.

(b) Cultural factors

	Factors	Quality affected
(1)	Mineral nutrition	
(i)	Nitrogen	High nitrogen reduces ascorbic acid content, TSS/acid ratio and keeping quality but increases thiamine, riboflavin, carotene, e.g., citrus and spinach. Its deficiency reduces size of fruits.
(ii)	Phosphorus	High phosphorus decreases size, weight, vitamin C, e.g., citrus. Its deficiency causes poor appearance of fruit.
(iii)	Potassium	Increases size, weight and vitamin C, e.g., citrus. Its deficiency causes uneven ripening.
(iv)	Calcium	Increases firmness of many fruits, e.g., apple, mango, guava, tomato, etc.
(v)	Magnesium	Increases size, weight and vitamin C, e.g., citrus fruits.
(vi)	Zinc	Increases size, weight and vitamin C, e.g., citrus. Deficiency causes straggled cluster in grape.
(vii)	Boron	Deficiency causes flesh browning in fruits, e.g., aonla and gummy discolouration of albedo in citrus. Fruits and vegetables become hard and misshapen. Cabbage, turnip and cauliflower are sensitive to boron deficiency.

	Factors	Quality affected
(viii)	Copper	Deficiency causes irregular blotch on citrus fruits and spoils the appearance.
(2)	Growth regulators	
(i)	Auxins	Increases fruit size in loquot (2,4,5-TP), mandarins (NAA) and TSS in mango (2, 4-D).
(ii)	Gibberellic acid	Increases size and weight of grape berries, apricot, strawberry and causes parthenocarpic fruits in fig, guava, grape, tomato, etc. It reduces disorder of fruits, e.g., water spot and corky spot in citrus.
(iii)	Cytokinin	Maintain green colour of leafy vegetables and causes parthenocarpic fruits in fig.
(iv)	Ethylene	Ethephon increases anthocyanin (coloured grape, plum, apple, chillies, brinjal), carotenoids (mango, guava, papaya, citrus, tomato, etc.), ascorbic acid and TSS and reduces tannin (grapes, dates, etc.) and acidity (grape, mango, tomato, etc.).
(v)	Growth retardant	Alar (B$_9$) increases colour in fruits, e.g., apple, cherry, apricot, etc. Malic hydrazide (MH) inhibit sprouting in onion bulbs.
(3)	Rootstock	In citrus Troyer and Carrizo (Citranges) rootstock produce the fruit of excellent quality of oranges, mandarins and lemons. In guava *P. pumilum* rootstock increases sugar and *P. cujavillis* ascorbic acid content of fruits.
(4)	Irrigation	Excess irrigation causes high acidity and deficiency of moisture reduces fruit size, juice content and increases thickness of peel.
(5)	Pruning	It affects the size, colour, acidity and sugar content of grape, phalsa, ber, peach, apple, etc.
(6)	Thinning	Thinning in grapes, dates, peaches, plum, etc., increases size, colour, acidity and sugar content of fruits.
(7)	Girdling	In grapes, it increases, size, colour and sugar content of the berries.
(8)	Variety	Varieties differ in size, shape, colour and chemical composition. High yield, bright appearance and good shipping qualities are most important characters of the varieties.
(9)	Diseases and Pests	Both are harmful to fruits and vegetables.
(10)	Pesticide	Pesticide spray residues may give rise to flavour taints in the processed product. Excessive use of pesticides may even produce harmful metabolites and toxicity not necessarily destroyed during processing.

338

	Factors	Quality affected
(11)	Maturity	In general vegetables with exception of potato and onion are of higher quality when less mature because they are more tender, succulent, less fibrous or starchy. On the other hand fruits when ripe are of higher quality on account of full size, bright colour, sweetness and less acidic.
(12)	Mechanical injury	Fruits and vegetables should be in no case injured or damaged otherwise injury, such as skin abrasion and tissue bruising will reduce appearance and may be source of infection for fungal diseases.

(B) Post-harvest factors

	Factors	Quality affected
1.	Temperature	High temperature causes off-flavour, weight loss and wilting particularly in leafy vegetables and reduces vitamin C content. Low temperature reduces the appearance of fruit by checking the carotenoid development. Temperature lower than the optimum resulting chilling injury.
2.	Heat of respiration	It deteriorates the quality and speed up the growth of microorganisms during storage and transport.
3.	Relative humidity	Low humidity leads to weighloss and wilting whereas high tends to encourage growth of microorganisms.
4.	Cleaning and Washing	Cleaning (Fruits) and Washing (root vegetables) remove dirt and spray residue and provide good appearance or freshness to the produce.
5.	Trimming	Removal of damaged, dead, discoloured parts for improving the appearance of fruits and vegetables.
6.	Grading	Fruits and vegetables must be graded to maintain uniformity in shape, size and quality.
7.	Chemical treatment	Treating fruits and vegetables with oil (groundnut/mustard) and wax emulsion reduces weight loss and maintain freshness. Treating fruits with ethephon and alar increases colour and reduces astringency. Gibberellic acid, cytokinin, malic hydrazide and cycocel (CCC) retard the colour development.
8.	Pro-cooling	Reduces weight loss and maintains the freshness or appearance. It is desirable to harvest the commodity "in the cool of the day" and to allow it to stand in the orchard or field in open boxes during part of the night to cool before it is loaded into trucks.

	Factors	Quality affected
9.	Hot-water treatment	Increases carotene and total sugar in fruits and protects from diseases, e.g., anthracnose in mango.
10.	Packing	Loose packing causes more damage in fruits and vegetables than tight packing. Wrapping of fruits (apple, mango, etc.) in tissue paper reduces weight loss and maintain colour. Similarly packing of fruits and vegetables in ventilated polythene bag reduces weight loss and maintain colour.
11.	Transportation	Besides above, the quality of the finished product is also affected very markedly by the length of time between picking and processing. On this account the raw product should be transferred from the orchard or field to the processing unit in the shortest time possible. Refrigerated transport from field to factory also reduces the incidence of loss of quality in fruits and vegetables.
12.	Storage	Storage is usually required for the following purposes: (a) to ensure continuous supply of raw material to the processing line; (b) to extend the length of processing season; (c) to condition certain commodities such as sweet potatoes, potatoes and onions; (d) to ripen certain fruits such as mangoes and bananas; and (e) to hold raw material obtained during favourable price situations. The temperature during storage affects the length of storage and the quality of the fruit/vegetable.

Chapter 29

Quality Control in Food Processing Industry

Food quality control is generally defined as the regulation by law of food manufacture, distribution and sale, in order to prevent health hazards and fraud to the consumer. Thus, it becomes a criminal offence to sell (deliberately or in any other way), adulterated, filthy or contaminated food. Food is defined under the law as any article used for food or drink by man or animal. This is interpreted to include substances added to food which may have no nutritive value whatsoever, e.g., artificial colouring, condiments, flavour, spices and preservatives. There are three main aspects to the application of food quality control: 1) moral, 2) commercial, and 3) legal. The application of controls on food quality put a moral responsibility on the food manufacturer towards the consumer. The commercial aspect requires that standard quality products are economically produced. And in increasingly competitive markets, it is important that produces exercise a stringent degree of quality control on what they produce. The legal viewpoint demands that the quality of products conforms to national and international standards. Fruit and vegetable processing industries produce very large quantities of products which are intended for consumption, often on a daily basis, by the population at large. Such industries, therefore, have a special responsibility to ensure that their products are both wholesome and safe, as well as successful in the marketplace. The control of food quality by law leads to:

(1) Improved quality of product.

(2) Achievement of greater consumer satisfaction.

(3) The promotion of quality consciousness.

(4) Increased consumption and sales.

(5) Employment opportunities for scientific and technical personnel.

(6) Avoidance of controversy and litigation in marketing at the national and international level.

(7) Promotion of national and international trade.

(8)   Provision of the means for the intelligent comparison of prices in relation to quality and grade.

(9)   Greater confidence in the minds of consumers.

Quality control within a food manufacturing industry demands constant vigilance at all stages in processing, so that any necessary adjustments can be made at the appropriate time. The responsibility for quality control in industrial food manufacture is generally delegated to a person, or a department, depending on the size of the factory.

The specific responsibility of quality control is to ensure that the system used produces a standard product with acceptable quality in respect to nutrition, purity, wholesomeness and palatability. The specific responsibilities of quality control assigned to a department or to an individual include:

(1)   Standardizing procedure for sampling and examining raw materials.

(2)   Development of test procedures.

(3)   Establishment and implementation of quality standards for fresh and processed products.

(4)   Setting up preventive quality control methods for in-plant liaison between manufacturing section and test laboratories.

(5)   Examination of finished products.

(6)   Storage controls.

(7)   Recording and reporting.

(8)   Special problems, including attendance to consumer complaints by locating their cause and eliminating them.

(9)   Research and development into new products and their packaging.

The sequence of operations in quality control is as follows:

(1)   Raw material control.

(2)   Process control, or the control of the manufacturing process.

(3)   Production inspection, including the inspection of the finished product, packaging and storage.

(4)   Sensory evaluation, or evaluation of the acceptability of the final product.

(1) Raw material control

The principal aim in any food industry is to produce standardized products that do not vary significantly. The quality of a food material is judged in terms of its nutritional value, its purity, its wholesomeness and its palatability. If any of these properties is not optimal, the food quality is affected.

The definition given to a 'raw material' in the food industry is anything purchased by the manufacturer for direct or indirect use in food processing. Raw materials include: food ingredients, water, and packaging materials. The quality of raw materials required varies according to the material, the product to be manufactured, and the standard qualities desired in the end-product.

Before buying raw materials in bulk, large food manufacturers generally examine a buying sample to make sure that it conforms to the factory's specifications. This is very important, especially if samples have to be obtained from different sources. It is also necessary to examine the representative samples of any subsequent delivery to make sure that the bulk is up to approved factory specifications. Failure to check conformity to the specifications may lead to the acquisition of unusable qualities of raw materials.

Raw materials examinations generally include tests for genuineness and composition, freedom from contaminants, and conformity with official or factory standards. Once raw material quality standards are established, regular checks are carried out to bring about a uniformity of properties such as colour, clarity, particle size, and other factors which affect palatability.

Examinations carried out vary with the nature and type of ingredient and its expected use. Where fats and oils are included in the ingredients used, they are examined to determine their identity, purity, freshness and keeping qualities because chemical changes or rancidity occur in facts during storage will develop unpleasant taste and odour if the fat is used below the required quality.

In order to achieve desirable specified qualities in raw materials manufacturers demand a certain quality in crops. For these reasons, successful food product manufacturer depends, to a large extent, upon close collaboration between plant breeders, agronomists and food technologists. The food technologist defines the characteristics required in raw materials in order to obtain products with specified qualities and the plant breeder and the agronomist collaborate to provide crops with these qualities.

After their control and selection, a sample batch of raw materials is put through a 'trial run'. The trial run gives a preview of the end-product. All control tests are run on the sample and any adjustments in processing procedure made where necessary. The shelf-life of the end-product is also checked. Equipment used for the trial run is examined for signs of corrosion due to the acidity or alcohol content of the materials used. Approval for processing is only given after all quality specifications on the sample run have been met.

(2) Process control

During the actual processing, careful attention is given to the processing procedure. All treatments given during the processing are standardized, ingredients are used in the correct amounts, accurate methods of preparation and mixing are employed, checks are made on the containers used to make sure that they are sound, and processing times and temperatures are standardized to make sure that the desired results are obtained.

A set of specifications is established by the technical staff in every factory to cover every product that is handled. It is the duty of the laboratory personnel to acquaint the production staff with the quality specifications and to evaluate production samples for compliance with these.

It is vital that quality control tests run continuously and concurrently with a 24 hour production schedule. Failure to maintain a round-the-clock check can mean considerable quantities of material being rejected as substandard, because it does not meet the quality specifications. This can be very costly to the manufacturer, as sometimes a salvage operation is not always practicable. Liaison between the quality control and production department is, therefore, of paramount importance.

Intermediary product samples are taken for routine tests to establish that specific targets of quality are being achieved. The desired composition, consistency, colour and concentration are checked and ensured. Rapid on-the-spot analysis are used to give prompt results so that appropriate information can immediately be fed back to the factory floor, and any necessary modifications made to the original formulation. This rapid communication of information is very important in process control. Where processing controls are not properly employed as, e.g., during dehydration, the quality of the product may be seriously impaired. There may be change in shape or structure: cracks, case hardening, a browning reaction, and the oxidation of unstable components due to physical, chemical or biological processes.

Satisfactory hygienic conditions are also maintained during processing, in order to protect the product from bacterial contamination. For the routine bacteriological control of the plant or factory, counts on utensils, equipment, working surfaces, walls, and floors are regularly carried out and the results tabulated or recorded on charts to give an immediate indication of any change. The counts are used as a check on the sanitary conditions of the plant. If the sanitary conditions of manufacture are to be passed as being 'good', the general bacterial counts must be low. In addition, periodic inspection of the plant is made by a trained inspector to make sure that adequate hygiene standards are maintained.

(3) Inspection of finished product

Inspection or examination of the finished product is carried out to determine to what extent the desired quality specifications have been achieved. Although the purity of individual ingredients was determined earlier on, there may have been some contamination during processing. The ability to withstand storage can only be confirmed on the finished product, e.g., in a cannery, representative samples of the canned product are taken for inspection. Careful inspection is made of the external conditions of the can and distinctive signs looked for. A can where both ends are concave is said to be 'flat', this is considered to be good because it means that the vacuum inside is high enough to maintain the ends in a concave condition. The cans which have the problem of flipper, springer or swell do not pass inspection.

Finally, the seams are inspected for leakage, as contamination is likely to occur along these zones. Acceptable cans are then weighed to determine gross weight.

A gauge is used to check both the vacuum and the pressure within the can. Vacuum and pressure in the can are indicated by deflections of a needle on the dial of the gauge. Only cans which are passed are measured.

In case of canned products a sample of the passed cans is opened and their contents inspected. This is done against a known standard. Underfilling and over-filling can be detected at this stage by head space gauge. Cloudiness in the syrup or brine, or the unsatisfactory appearance of the product is more frequently evident when the colour of the product is observed. Finally, the drained weight is determined to check the net weight of the product.

Where the product is dried, samples are examined for a blemish count. A limited number of minor blemishes are often allowed which will mainly disappear on reconstitution. The dried product is regularly checked for its reconstitution value to enable the correct cooking instructions to be supplied on the package for the ultimate user. A 50 g sample is rehydrated and cooked in the prescribed manner and time. The cooking water is drained off, and the drained weight calculated against the original dry weight to obtain a reconstitution ratio.

At the end of the production line, packets are weighed individually. Manufacturers are expected to supply customers with finished products of the correct weight and volume, as specified.

Chemical analysis are carried out on samples of the finished product to:

(1) determine the general composition of the essential ingredients (to check if there are variations from the limits set), and

(2) to check that the composition conforms to the set legal requirements for contaminants, such as heavy metals.

Tests are also performed to check certain physical properties, such as crispness, colour, viscosity and texture, which are related to the palatability and acceptability of the product. The keeping qualities of foods, which depend upon sugar, salt, or acid for their preservation are checked to ensure that they will keep under the conditions to which they are most likely to be exposed. Both the contents and the containers are examined for faults. rancidity, microorganisms development, loss of colour and flavour, the other attributes.

Microbiological examinations are carried out to check whether proper hygienic procedures have been followed, and whether the finished product is safe to keep and to eat.

(4) Sensory evaluation

After physical, chemical and microbiological examinations have been performed on a finished product with a satisfactory result, the product is considered ready for distribution, but only after its palatability or sensory quality has been assessed. The ultimate criterion for the desirability of a food product to consumer is its eating quality. Palatability or sensory quality is of great importance to both processors and consumers. To the processor, a palatable product ensures sales because palatability attracts consumers; to the consumer, palatability satisfies his aesthetic an gustatory senses. Sensory quality is a combination of different senses of perception which come into play in choosing and eating a food. The principal sensory properties which affect the palatability of food are as follows:

(i) Appearance

(ii) Texture

(iii) Flavour

These properties have already been discussed in the chapter on 'Quality Characteristics of Fruits and Vegetables for Processing'.

Although chemical and physical tests have been devised to measure differences in the sensory qualities of foods, these alone are not adequate to give the required information Human judges, therefore, have to be used. Measurement of the relative palatability of a food product is attempted in two ways: (i) by obtaining the judgement of experts, and (ii) by testing the preferences of a sample of the public for whom the product is intended - this is also known as market testing.

(i) **Expert sensory judgement** : Sensory evaluation (acceptance measurement) is generally performed by a panel. The members are trained in order that their sensitivity and consistency are established by repeated test. These tests determine the significance of variation of average scores and the contribution of individual quality characteristics to the overall quality. A trained panel is generally formed to look after in-line quality, quality of the final product, process development and, to a limited extent, preliminary acceptance testing. This small group of people work in the rigorously controlled environment of the quality control laboratory.

(ii) **Market testing** : Market testing is carried out to obtain the preferences of a sample of the public for whom the food product is intended. An untrained panel, made up of a number of men and women selected to be representative of the population to be surveyed, is used. Their natural emotional reaction to the selected food is ascertained. Such surveys are time consuming and costly. They are, therefore, usually restricted to products selected through a series of laboratory tests and presented in their marketable form to a sample of the public. Data from these surveys, known as consumer surveys, are analyzed statistically to determine the significance of preference and rejection.

Broad demand for the measurement of actual consumer preference has led to the development of three major survey techniques :

(1) Summarizing market data on what consumers buy.

(2) Surveying consumer opinions about products of different quality.

(3) Setting up experiments designed to test preferences on the spot.

Obtaining a representative sample of consumers and the interpretation of market survey data are very difficult.

(5) Packaging

Packaging has multi-purpose functions for food products. The primary purpose of a manufacturer is to protect the food product, to keep it in good condition, and to preserve the flavour until it reaches the consumer. It is essential, therefore, that a suitable form of packaging is chosen for a finished product. The package must be capable of protecting the product from thermal changes, humidity variations, the hazards of rough handling, and infestation and contamination by rodents and insects. It must be kept under hygienic conditions at all times. The material used for packaging must not contaminate the product, and must be effective in preventing the product from deterioration. Such an ideal packaging material, which meets all these requirements, is rare indeed.

Traditionally all sorts of materials such as corn (maize) sheaths, banana leaves, other broad leaves, cane baskets, empty bottles are used as packaging materials. They are all low cost and easily available materials. However, traditional packaging materials cannot withstand rough handling and are not suitable in protecting the product in long distance transportation.

With the Industrial Revolution, the need to package large quantities of the same item for shipping became economically important. Any industrial packaging material needs to provide five basic functions:

(1) Protection of the product from the hazards of handling and environmental conditions.

(2) Containment of the product as a handleable unit.

(3) Compatibility with the machines of mass-production, such as filling machines (whether manual or mechanical).

(4) Ease of communication or identification of the contents to aid in marketing, and to conform to quality control regulations.

(5) Ease of manufacture convenience to everyone concerned with the distribution and use of the product. In addition, disposal of the package must be easy.

A variety of containers have also been designed to handle products that are sensitive to light, temperature, air, moisture, and contact with chemicals.

The industrial use of packaging materials, in order of importance, is as follows: paper and paper board, metal, plastics, glass, wood, textile and others. However, the selection of a packaging material depends intrinsically on the nature and properties of the product.

    (i) Paper and paper board : Paper and paper board are used in a variety of package types and forms. These include paper wrappers, sacks, and labels. Others are fibreboard cases, boxes, folding cartons, paper, and carrier bags. Solid and corrugated fibreboard cases are probably the most widely used, convenient and economical shipping containers for shipping materials lighter than 100 kg of weight. They are light in weight and inexpensive and can be easily manufactured, printed and stored. They may be closed successfully with adhesives, gummed paper tape, self-adhesive plastic tape and stapling.

Folding cartons and paperboard boxes are the most extensively used method of packaging in the food industry. In most cases, where little climatic protection is needed, a carton provides the cheapest and best physical protection against crushing. It can be supplemented with a barrier against moisture by adding an inner film, or an outer wrapper.

(ii) **Metal :** Metal is used for packaging in the form of tin-plated steel cans and boxes. Tin-plate is durable and highly resistant to chemical and mechanical damage. Tin-plate retail containers are divided into two classes: the cylindrical, open-top variety, and the general line cans that have replaceable lids. Some 80 to 90 per cent of the cylindrical open-top type are in use for food packaging.

The modern tin can, composed of 98.5 per cent sheet steel with a thin coating of tin and manufactured on high-speed automatic machinery is the cheapest and most serviceable container for mass production. The development of the sanitary or open-top can eliminated the use of solder in sealing the can — a perfect closure was guaranteed by the double seam, top and bottom. Enamel coatings have also been developed to replace tin as the interior lining of the can for certain foods.

Aluminium on the other hand, is lighter and more malleable but inter-acts more readily with chemical agents particularly to that by alkali. Its application must, therefore, be carefully considered in relation to the properties of the product.

Other forms in which metal is used are aluminium foil, aerosols, col-lapsible tubes, steel drums, boxes, and crates.

(iii) **Plastics :** Of the large number of plastic materials available, only a relatively small number have a substantial impact on packaging. Recent developments in the plastic industry have provided: polyethylene (often referred to as polythene), polystyrene, polyvinyl chloride, and polypropylene as packaging materials.

More than half the polythene used is in the form of film, and much is converted into shrink film, liners, sacks and bags. Some plastics are used in the form of bottles, others are used for larger specialized containers, and the remainder for coatings and laminates. Polyvinyl chloride is used typically for soft drinks, cooking oil and vinegar bottles, and as trays for chocolates. Polystyrene is principally made into tubs for ice cream, packs for eggs and sausages, and small pots or jars for butter, jam and cheese. The use of polypropylene is growing rapidly, especially as a transparent overwrap.

(iv) Glass : Glass is a highly inert material of great cleanliness. Containers made of glass are durable, chemical resistant, and can be kept under highly sanitary conditions. They are, therefore, ideal for the storage of solid and liquid foods.

Glass is easily formed into almost any shape and has exceptional aesthetic potential. Glass containers, both bottles and jars, are easily mass-produced and can be reused. It is widely used to package products which are normally dispensed at intervals over relatively long periods.

(v) Wood : Boxes, crates, casks, kegs, pallets, and a few other types of containers made of wood are used on a limited scale to package food product. Wood is usually used for shipping whenever the package is large or the product of high density. Timber cases and crates are used extensively for weights above 100 kg. Timber is also used for casks for wine and beer. More recently, however, there has been a trend toward its replacement by metal.

(vi) Textiles : Cotton bags, sacks and bales are also used in the shipping of food products. They have limited use in the packaging of larger quantities of some products. They are manufactured in bleached and unbleached quantities and may be printed. Open mesh bags are frequently used to pack products such as fresh vegetables, which require complete ventilation in transport and storage.

(vii) Barrier packages : To maintain a favourable climatic environment around food products which are normally subject to deterioration from moisture, oxygen, light or heat, any of several barrier materials are employed. These include waxed paper, metal foil, plastic film, or any of the flexible materials. Most are good barriers to moisture and moisture vapour; some are good barriers to oxygen and other atmospheric gases. The opaque materials form a barrier to light, and in some instances, for relatively short periods of time, provide a certain degree of heat insulation for some products.

6. Labelling and storage

After packaging, labels are required on finished products intended for distribution and sale. Labelling can reflect on the quality of a product. Effective labelling is clear and informative. The name and address of the manufacturer, the list of important ingredients and additives, and the net weight or volume of the product should be declared on the label. A good and attractive label is an aid to the successful marketing of a product.

High moisture, high storage temperatures, light, and air or oxygen are all detrimental to stored foods in general, and to dehydrated foods in particular. Dehydrated foods are generally hygroscopic in nature or easily pick up moisture from their surroundings during storage. Mould and insect infestation, then follow. It is important that dehydrated foods are stored in a cool, dry and dark place to prevent the deteriorative effects of high storage temperatures, light, air and humidity. Further study may be needed concerning changes in colour, odour, flavour, texture, nutrient content, moisture content, staling, and rancidity.

Since most manufactured foods can be stored for many years under appropriate conditions, it is important to establish the conditions and storage periods that afford the optimum balance between the cost of storage and the changes in quality of stored products. Warehousing facilities are generally provided close to industrial units for the storage both of raw materials and finished products. The unnecessary and careless handling of products is avoided and, when needed, quick and efficient transportation is provided for the distribution of the product to retailers or wholesalers.

Prospects for quality control services

Though quality control is essential to food processing and the successful marketing of the products but small and medium-scale food industries, especially young ones, are not able to set up quality control laboratories. Prospects are quite good for chemists and qualified technical personnel to use their professional training to set up private laboratories providing quality control and other analytical services for local food processing industries. Capital is needed initially to purchase laboratory equipment, glassware and chemicals. But such costs may eventually be recovered as demand for the laboratory services grows. This is likely to happen as food processing enterprises compete, and as quality standards come to be enforced by law.

Chapter 30

Important Methods for Analysis of Fruits/Vegetables and their products

(A) Determination of total soluble solids (TSS)

A mong the various constituents of fresh fruits and vegetables, minerals, acids, sugars, vitamins B and C and some proteins are soluble in water. Sugars constitute 80-85 per cent of the soluble solids. The TSS value is defined as the amount of sugar and soluble minerals present in fruits and vegetables. The method for its determination by means of a hand refractometer is given below.

A hand refractometer is based on the principle of total refraction.

The refractometer should be checked for accuracy before use. This is done by placing a few drops of distilled water on the prism in the specimen chamber of the refractometer with the help of a glass rod after folding back the cover. By looking through the eye-piece with the projection inlet facing towards light the point on the scale is noted when the boundary line of the shaded area intersects with the unshaded area. If necessary, the eyepiece is rotated to either side for clear reading. The distilled water reading should be zero. If it is not so, it should be set to zero with the scale correction knob. The specimen chamber is now cleaned with muslin cloth or tissue paper.

For determining the TSS, a drop of sample (juice, syrup, etc.) is placed on the prism and the percentage of dry substance in it read directly. If determinations are made at temperatures other than 20°C, the readings are corrected to the standard temperature of 20°C using the correction table given on the next page :

Temperature Corrections for Standard Model of Sugar Refractometer calibrated for 20°C

Temp. (°C)	Percentage of dry substance													
	5	10	15	20	25	30	35	40	45	50	55	60	65	70
Subtract from the reading														
15	0.29	0.31	0.33	0.34	0.34	0.35	0.36	0.37	0.37	0.38	0.39	0.39	0.40	0.40
16	0.24	0.25	0.26	0.27	0.28	0.28	0.29	0.30	0.30	0.30	0.31	0.31	0.32	0.32
17	0.18	0.19	0.20	0.21	0.21	0.21	0.22	0.22	0.23	0.23	0.23	0.23	0.24	0.24
18	0.13	0.13	0.14	0.14	0.14	0.14	0.15	0.15	0.15	0.15	0.16	0.16	0.16	0.16
19	0.06	0.06	0.07	0.07	0.07	0.07	0.08	0.08	0.08	0.08	0.08	0.08	0.08	0.08
Add to the reading														
21	0.07	0.07	0.07	0.07	0.08	0.08	0.08	0.08	0.08	0.08	0.08	0.08	0.08	0.08
22	0.13	0.14	0.14	0.15	0.15	0.15	0.15	0.15	0.16	0.16	0.16	0.16	0.16	0.16
23	0.20	0.21	0.22	0.22	0.23	0.23	0.23	0.23	0.24	0.24	0.24	0.24	0.24	0.24
24	0.27	0.28	0.29	0.30	0.30	0.31	0.31	0.31	0.31	0.31	0.32	0.32	0.32	0.32
25	0.35	0.36	0.37	0.38	0.38	0.39	0.40	0.40	0.40	0.40	0.40	0.40	0.40	0.40
26	0.42	0.43	0.44	0.45	0.46	0.47	0.48	0.48	0.48	0.48	0.48	0.48	0.48	0.48
27	0.50	0.52	0.53	0.54	0.55	0.55	0.56	0.56	0.56	0.56	0.56	0.56	0.56	0.56
28	0.57	0.60	0.61	0.62	0.63	0.63	0.64	0.64	0.64	0.64	0.64	0.64	0.64	0.64
29	0.66	0.68	0.69	0.71	0.72	0.72	0.73	0.73	0.73	0.73	0.73	0.73	0.73	0.73
30	0.74	0.77	0.78	0.79	0.80	0.80	0.81	0.81	0.81	0.81	0.81	0.81	0.81	0.81

SOURCE : *Proceedings of the ninth Session of the International Commission for Uniform Methods of Sugar Analysis, London, 1936.*

(B) Determination of acids (citric and acetic acids)

(i) Citric acid

Dissolve a known volume or weight of sample in a known volume of distilled water. From this, take an aliquot and titrate with 0.1 N NaOH using phenolphthalein as indicator. The end-point is denoted by the appearance of pink colour.

(ii) Acetic acid

Dilute 10 ml of sample with water in a porcelain dish (about 5 inches in diameter), add pheonlphthalein as indicator and titrate with 0.5 N NaOH.

Calculation

$$\% \text{ Acid} = \frac{\text{Titre x Normality of alkali x meq wt. of acid* x 100}}{\text{Wt. or volume of sample}}$$

*Note : meq= milliequivlent
meq wt. of citric acid   =   0.06404
meq wt. of acetic acid   =   0.06005

(C) Determination of vitamin C (ascorbic acid) by titration

In the absence of interfering substances that may reduce the dye or oxidize ascorbic acid during sample preparation, the capacity of a sample to reduce a standard dye solution, as determined by titration, is directly proportional to the ascorbic acid content.

Reagents

(i) Metaphosphoric acid (HPO_3) solution (3%)

(ii) Dye solution : Dissolve 50 mg of 2, 6- dichlorpophenol-indophenol in approximately 150 ml of hot distilled water containing 42 mg of sodium bicarbonate. Cool and dilute with distilled water to 200 ml. Store solution in brown bottle in a refrigerator at about 3°C, standardize every day and prepare afresh every week.

(iii) Standard ascorbic acid solution : Dissolve 100 mg of L-ascorbic acid in a small volume of 3% metaphosphoric acid solution and make up to 100 ml with same solution. Dilute 10 ml this of stock solution to 100 ml with 3% metaphosphoric acid (0.1 mg ascorbic acid per ml).

Procedure

(i) **Standardization of dye** : Dilute 5 ml of standard ascorbic acid solution with 5 ml of 3% metaphosphoric acid. Titrate with dye solution till pink colour persists for 10 seconds. Calculate the dye factor (mg of ascorbic acid per ml of dye) as follows:

$$\text{Dye Factor (D.F.)} = \frac{0.5}{\text{Titre}}$$

Preparation of sample and titration

In case of a liquid or juice sample, take 10 ml sample and make upto 100 ml with 3% HPO_3 and filter. In case of a semi-solid or solid product, blend 10 g of sample, with 3% HPO_3 and then make up to 100 ml and filter. Pipette 10 ml of filtrate into a conical flask and titrate with the standard dye to a pink end-point. If a sample contains sulphur dioxide which reduces the dye and thus interferes with the ascorbic acid estimation, the following procedure is followed.

Take 10 ml of filtrate, add 1 ml of 40% formaldehyde and 0.1 ml of HCl, allow to stand for 10 minutes and then titrate.

Calculation

$$\text{Ascorbic acid (mg/100g)} = \frac{\text{Titre x Dye Factor x Volume made up x 100}}{\text{Volume of filtrate taken} \quad x \quad \text{Wt. or volume of sample taken}}$$

355

(D) Estimation of sugars by Shaffer-Somogyi micro method

Reagents

(i)   Copper sulphate solution (10%) : Dissolve 100 g of copper sulphate in water and make upto 1000 ml.

(ii) Potassium iodate solution (0.1 N) : Dissolve 3.567 g of potassium iodate in water and make upto 1000 ml.

(iii) Shaffer-Somogyi carbonate reagent: Dissolve 25 g each of anhydrous sodium carbonate and Rochelle salt (potassium sodium tartrate) in approximately 500 ml of water in a beaker. Add with stirring 75 ml of copper sulphate solution and 20 g of sodium bicarbonate. After dissolving, add 5 g of potassium iodide. Transfer the solution to a 1-litre volumetric flask, add 250 ml of 0.1 N potassium iodate solution. Make upto volume, filter and store overnight before use.

(iv) Iodide-potassium oxalate solution: Dissolve 2.5 g each of potassium iodide and potassium oxalate in water and dilute to 100 ml. Prepare afresh every week.

(v)   Thiosulphate solution (0.005 N): Prepare daily from standard stock of 0.1 N solution.

(vi) Sulphuric acid solution (2 N)

(vii) Potassium oxalate solution (22%)

(viii) Lead acetate solution 45%

Procedure

(1) Preparation of sample

Take 2.5 to 5.0 g sample in a 250 ml of beaker, add about 50 ml of water, heat to boiling, cool and transfer to a 250 ml volumetric flask. Add 2 ml of lead acetate solution, shake and allow to stand for 10 minutes. Precipitate excess lead by adding 2 ml of potassium oxalate solution. Make up the volume with water and filter.

(2) Reducing sugars

Take 5 ml of filtrate in a test tube, add 5 ml of Shaffer-Somogyi reagent and mix well. Simultaneously prepare blank using 5 ml of water and 5 ml of reagent. Place the two tubes in a water bath for 15 minutes. Remove the tubes carefully without disturbing the contents and cool in running water for 4 minutes. Along the side of each tube, add 2 ml of iodide- oxalate solution and then 3 ml of 2 N sulphuric acid and allow both tubes to stand in cold water for 5 minutes. Then titrate against 0.005 N thiosulphate solution using starch as indicator. Subtract the titre value of the test solution from that of a blank and determine the amount of dextrose in 5 ml of solution from the table given below.

Shaffer-Somogyi Dextrose-Thiosulphate Equivalents*
mg Dextrose=(0.1099) (ml 0.005 N Na$_2$S$_2$O$_3$ x 0.048)

Ml of 0.005 N Na$_2$S$_2$O$_3$	Tenths ml 0.005 N thiosulphate									
	0.0	0.1	0.2	0.3	0.4	0.5	0.6	0.7	0.8	0.9
	mg Dextrose in 5 ml of solution									
3	0.378	0.389	0.400	0.411	0.422	0.432	0.444	0.455	0.466	0.477
4	0.488	0.499	0.510	0.521	0.532	0.543	0.554	0.565	0.576	0.587
5	0.598	0.608	0.619	0.630	0.641	0.652	0.663	0.674	0.685	0.696
6	0.707	0.718	0.729	0.740	0.751	0.762	0.773	0.784	0.795	0.806
7	0.817	0.828	0.839	0.850	0.861	0.872	0.883	0.894	0.905	0.916
8.	0.927	0.938	0.949	0.960	0.971	0.982	0.993	1.004	1.015	1.026
9	1.037	1.048	1.059	1.070	1.081	1.092	1.103	1.114	1.125	1.136
10	1.147	1.158	1.169	1.180	1.191	1.202	1.213	1.224	1.235	1.246
11	1.257	1.268	1.279	1.290	1.301	1.312	1.323	1.334	1.345	1.356
12	1.367	1.378	1.389	1.400	1.411	1.422	1.433	1.444	1.455	1.466
13	1.477	1.488	1.499	1.510	1.521	1.532	1.543	1.554	1.565	1.576
14	1.587	1.598	1.609	1.620	1.631	1.642	1.653	1.664	1.675	1.686
15	1.697	1.707	1.718	1.729	1.740	1.751	1.762	1.773	1.784	1.795
16	1.806	1.817	1.828	1.839	1.850	1.861	1.872	1.883	1.894	1.905
17	1.916	1.927	1.938	1.949	1.960	1.971	1.982	1.993	2.004	2.015
18	2.026	2.037	2.048	2.059	2.070	2.081	2.092	2.103	2.114	2.125
19	2.136	2.147	2.158	2.169	2.180	2.191	2.202	2.213	2.224	2.235
20	2.246	2.257	2.268	2.279	2.290	2.301	2.312	2.323	2.334	2.345
21	2.356	2.367	2.378	2.389	2.400	2.411	2.422	2.433	2.444	2.455
22	2.466	2.477	2.488	2.499	2.510	2.521	2.532	2.543	2.554	2.565

* Official Methods of Analysis (1970).

(3) Total sugars

Take 25 ml of filtrate in a 50 ml volumetric flask and add 5 ml of HCl (1:1). Allow to stand for 24 hours at room temperature. Neutralize exactly with NaOH using phenolphthalein as indicator and make upto volume with water. Take an aliquot and determine the total invert sugars as in case of reducing sugars.

Calculation

$$\% \text{ Reducing sugars } = \frac{\text{mg of Dextrose x Volume made up x 100}}{5 \times \text{Wt. of sample taken} \times 1000}$$

$$\% \text{ Total sugars as invert sugar } = \frac{\text{mg of Dextrose x Volume made up x 100}}{\text{Titre x Wt. or volume of sample} \times 100}$$

% Sucrose = (% Total invert sugars - % Reducing sugars originally present) x 0.95

% Total sugars = % Reducing sugars + % Sucrose

(E) Estimation of starch

After the sugars present in the sample have been leached out, starch is hydrolyzed and estimated as invert sugars.

Reagents

(i)   Ethanol (95%)

(ii) Ethanol (50%)

(iii) HCl

(iv) NaOH

Procedure

To a weighed sample (100 g in case of barley water) add a little water and heat to 60°C. Allow to stand for some time, add about 100 ml of 95% ethanol and centrifuge till the precipitate settles at bottom, and filter. Wash the residue with 50% ethanol and transfer to a 500 ml conical flask with about 100 ml of water. Add 20 ml of concentrated HCl and place a funnel in the neck of the flask to prevent evaporation and heat in a boiling water bath for $2^{1/2}$ hours. Cool, neutralize with NaOH using phenolphthalein as indicator and make up to a definite volume with water. Determine the reducing sugars as described earlier.

Calculation

% Starch = % Reducing sugars x 0.90

(F) Determination of pigments

(1) Chlorophyll

Reagent : Acetone (80%)

Procedure

Take 1 g of fresh sample, cut into small pieces, add about 5 ml of water and homogenize in blender. Make up homogenate to 10 ml with water and centrifuge solution. Take 0.5 ml aliquot and add 4.5 ml of 80% acetone to it to extract pigments. Centrifuge, remove the supernatant and record its optical density (O.D.) at 480, 645 and 663 nm, using 80% acetone as a blank.

Calculation

Total chlorophyll (g/litre) = (0.0202) (O.D. at 645) + (0.00802) (O.D. at 663)
Chlorophyll a (g/litre) = (0.0127) (O.D. at 663) – (0.00269) (O.D. at 645)
Chlorophyll b (g/litre) = (0.0229) (O.D. at 645) – (0.00488) (O.D. at 663)
Carotene (g/litre) = (O.D. at 480) – (0.114) (O.D. at 663) – (0.638) (O.D. at 645)

(2) Lycopene

Reagents

Acetone, petroleum ether, anhydrous sodium sulhphate

Procedure

Take 5 to 10 g of sample and crush repeatedly in acetone in a pestle and mortar until the residue is colourless. Transfer the acetone extracts to a separatory funnel containing 10 to 15 ml of petroleum ether. Mix gently to take up the pigments into the petroleum ether phase. Transfer the lower (acetone) phase to a 100 ml volumetric flask and extract it repeatedly with petroleum ether until colourless. Combine the petroleum ether extracts and dry over a small quantity of anhydrous sodium sulphate. Make up to 100 ml with petroleum ether and measure the O.D. of the solution at 503 nm using petroleum ether as blank.

Calculation

O.D. of 1.0 = 3.1206 µg of lycopene/ml

$$\text{Lycopene (mg/100g)} = \frac{3.1206 \times \text{O.D. of sample} \times \text{Volume made up} \times \text{Dilution} \times 100}{1 \times \text{Wt. of sample} \times 1000}$$

(3) Beta-carotene

Reagents

Acetone, anhydrous sodium sulphate, petroleum ether

Procedure

Take 5 g of fresh sample and crush in 10-15 ml acetone, adding a few crystals of anhydrous sodium sulphate, with the help of pestle and mortar. Decant the supernatant into a beaker. Repeat the process twice and transfer the combined supernatant to a separatory funnel, add 10-15 ml petroleum ether and mix thoroughly. Two layers will separate out on standing. Discard the lower layer and collect upper layer in a 100 ml volumetric flask, make up the volume to 100 ml with petroleum ether and record optical density at 452 nm using petroleum ether as blank.

Calculation

$$\beta\text{- Carotene } (\mu g/100 \text{ g}) = \frac{\text{O.D.} \times 13.9 \times 10^4 \times 100}{\text{Wt. of sample} \times 560 \times 1000}$$

$$\text{Vitamin A (I.U.)} = \frac{\text{beta-carotene } (\mu g/100)}{0.6}$$

(4) Anthocyanin

(i)   In skins

Reagents

(i)   Ethanol (95%)

(ii)   HCl

Procedure

10 discs of 5 mm each are taken in a screw cap culture tube containing 20 ml of 95 per cent ethanol to which 0.1 ml of concentrated HCl is added. Tubes are tightly capped, placed in a waterbath for 5 minutes and then kept in the dark for 2 hours. Now record the absorbance at 530 nm as 'O.D./10 discs'.

(ii)   In pulp

Reagents

Ethanolic HCl solution: Prepared by mixing 95% ethanol and 1.5 N HCl in the ratio of 85:15.

Procedure

Blend 10 g of sample with 10 ml of ethanolic HCl and transfer to a 100 ml volumetric flask and make up to volume. Store overnight in a refrigerator at 4°C, filter through Whatman No. 1 filter paper and record optical density (O.D.) of filtrate at 535 nm.

Calculation

$$\text{Total O.D./100 g} = \frac{\text{O.D. x Volume made up x 100}}{\text{Wt. of sample}}$$

$$\text{Total anthocyanin (mg/100 g)} = \frac{\text{Total O.D. / 100 g}}{98.2}$$

(iii) In juice

Reagents

0.1 N HCl

Procedure

Dilute 10 ml of juice to 50 ml with 0.1 N HCl and allow to equilibrate in the dark for 1 hour. Record the absorbance (O.D) at 510 nm.

Calculation

$$\text{Total O.D./100 ml} = \frac{\text{O.D. x Volume made up x 100}}{\text{Ml of juice taken}}$$

$$\text{Total anthocyanin (mg/100 ml)} = \frac{\text{Total O.D./100 ml}}{87.3}$$

(G) Determination of total pectins as calcium pectate

Pectin extracted from the plant material is saponified with alkali and precipitated from an acid solution as calcium pectate by the addition of calcium chloride.

Reagents

(i)   1 N acetic acid: Prepared by dissolving 30 ml of glacial acetic acid in a little water and making up the volume to 500 ml with water.

(ii) 1 N calcium chloride: Prepared by dissolving 27.5 g of anhydrous calcium chloride in water and making upto 500 ml volume.

(iii) 0.05 N HCl

(iv) 1 N NaOH

(v)   Phenolphthalein indicator

Procedure

Take 50 g of blended sample in 1000 ml beaker. Add about 400 ml of 0.05 N HCl and heat the contents for 2 hours at 80-90°C (in case of jam, jelly and marmalade, acid is not added, the sample is boiled in 400 ml of water only with stirring). Replace water lost by evaporation. Cool and transfer to a 500 ml volumetric flask, make up the volume and filter.

Pipette a 100 ml aliquot into a conical flask and add 250 ml of distilled water. Neutralize the acid with 1 N NaOH using phenolphthalein as indicator. Add another 10 ml of 1 N NaOH and allow to stand overnight. Now add 50 ml of 1 N acetic acid followed by 25 ml of 1 N calcium chloride. Allow to stand for 1 hour, boil for 1-2 minutes and filter through a previously weighed filter paper (wet the filter paper in hot water, dry in oven at 100°C for 2 hours, cool in dessicator and weight). Wash the precipitate free of chloride with hot water. Dry the precipitate, cool in dessicator and weigh again.

Calculation

$$\% \text{ Pectin (as calcium pectate)} = \frac{\text{Wt. of precipitate} \times 500 \times 100}{\text{Ml. of filtrate} \quad \times \quad \text{Wt. of sample}}$$

Ml. of filtrate taken for estimation

(H) Total minerals by dry ashing

Procedure

Weigh 2-3 g of sample in a previously weighed silica crucible. Heat crucible first over a low flame to volatilize as much of the organic matter as possible (until no more smoke is given off by the material), and then heat in a muffle furnace (temperature controlled) at about 600°C for 3-4 hours. Cool in dessicator and weigh. To ensure complete ashing, the crucible is again heated in the furnace for 30 minutes, cooled and weighed.

Calculation

$$\% \text{ Ash (total minerals)} = \frac{\text{Wt. of ash}}{\text{Wt. of sample}} \times 100$$

(I) Non-enzymatic browning

Preparation of sample

(i) Liquids and juices : Centrifuge the sample at 4000 rpm for 15 minutes. To 20 ml of centrifugate add 30 ml of 60 per cent alcohol, mix thoroughly and filter.

(ii) Semi-soilds and solids (pulp, jam, etc.) : Blend the sample and to 10 g of blended sample add 10 ml of distilled water and 30 ml of 60 per cent alcohol. Mix thoroughly and filter.

(iii) Dried fruits and vegetables : Soak 5 g of sample in 100 ml of 60 per cent alcohol for 12 hours and filter.

In the case of chlorophyll containing sample, shake filtrate thrice with 50 ml of benzene each time to remove chlorophyll, before measurement.

Observation

Record the absorbance of the filtrate at 440 nm using 60 per cent alcohol as blank and express as optical density (O.D.)

(J) Some other calculations

(i) Calories=[9 x (g fat) + 4 x (g protein) + 4 x (g carbohydrates)]

(ii) Carbohydrates by difference

% Carbohydrate = (100%) — [(%moisture)+ (% fat)

+ (% protein) + (% ash)]

(iii) % Moisture = $\dfrac{\text{loss in wt. of sample on drying}}{\text{wt. of sample taken}}$ x 100

(iv) % Juice = $\dfrac{\text{wt. of extracted juice}}{\text{wt. of fruits taken}}$ x 100

Appendices

MAJOR DIFFERENCES BETWEEN FRUITS AND VEGETABLES

S. No.	Vegetables	Fruits
1.	Most vegetable plants are annuals.	Fruit plants are perennial (except for Cape gooseberry which is an annual).
2.	Mostly sexually propagated.	Mostly asexually propagated.
3.	Cultivation is seasonal and special techniques like pruning and training are generally not required.	Special practices like training and pruning are required seasonally.
4.	Plants generally non-woody.	Plants generally woody.
5.	All parts of the plant are edible.	Only fruit is edible but sometimes false fruit (e.g., fleshy thalamus of apple) also edible.
6.	Generally consumed after cooking.	Mostly consumed fresh.

Note : *Sometimes a fruit is commonly called a vegetable, and a vegetable a fruit.*

FRUITS : COMMON NAME, BOTANICAL NAME AND FAMILY

S. No.	Common name	Botanical name	Family
1.	Cashew nut	*Anacardium occidentale* L.	Anacardiaceae
2.	Amada	*Spondias mangifera* L.	Anacardiaceae
3.	Pistachio nut	*Pistacia vera* L.	Anacardiaceae
4.	Mango	*Mangifera indica* L.	Anacardiaceae
5.	Annonaceous fruits		
	(i) Custard apple	*Annona squamosa* L.	Annonaceae
	(ii) Soursop	*A. muricata* L.	Annonaceae
	(iii) Pond apple	*A. glabra* L.	Annonaceae
	(iv) Bullock's heart	*A. reticulata* L.	Annonaceae
	(v) Cherimoya	*A. cherimola* L.	Annonaceae
	(vi) Ilma	*A. diversifolia* Saff.	Annonaceae
6.	Karonda	*Carissa carandas* L.	Apocynaceae
7.	Natal plum	*C. grandiflora* A.D.C.	Apocynaceae
8.	Pineapple	*Ananas comosus* Merr.	Bromeliaceae
9.	Papaya	*Carica papaya* L.	Caricaceae
10.	Hazelnut	*Corylus avellana* L.	Corylaceae
11.	Persimmon	*Diospyros kaki* L.	Ebenaceae
12.	Aonla	*Emblica officinalis* Gaertn.	Euphorbiaceae
13.	Chestnut	*Castanea sativa* Mill.	Fagaceae
14.	Mangosteen	*Garcinia mangostana* L.	Guttiferae
15.	Pecan nut	*Carya illinoensis* Koch.	Juglandaceae
16.	Walnut	*Juglans regia* L.	Juglandaceae
17.	Avocado	*Persea americana* Mill.	Lauraceae
18.	Tamarind	*Tamarindus indica* L.	Leguminosae
19.	Barbados cherry	*Malpighia glabra* L.	Malpighiaceae
20.	Jackfruit	*Artocarpus heterophyllus* Lamk.	Moraceae
21.	Monkey jack	*A. lakoocha* Roxb.	Moraceae

S. No.	Common name	Botanical name	Family
22.	Breadfruit	*A. altilis* Fosberg.	Moraceae
23.	Fig	*Ficus carica* L.	Moraceae
24.	Mulberry		
	(i) White	*Morus alba* L.	Moraceae
	(ii) Black	*M. nigra* L.	Moraceae
	(iii) Red	*M. rubra* L.	Moraceae
25.	Banana (Table)	*Musa paradisiaca* L.	Musaceae
26.	Banana (Plantain)	*M. sapientum* L.	Musaceae
27.	Jamun	*Syzygium cumini* L. Skeel.	Myrtaceae
28.	Rose apple	*S. jambos* L. Alston.	Myrtaceae
29.	Surinam cherry	*Eugenia uniflora* L.	Myrtaceae
30.	Guava	*Psidium guajava* L.	Myrtaceae
31.	Strawberry guava	*P. cattelianum* L.	Myrtaceae
32.	Guisaro	*P. molle* Sabine.	Myrtaceae
33.	Olive	*Olea europaea* L.	Oleaceae
34.	Carambola	*Averrhoa carambola* L.	Oxalidaceae
35.	Date palm	*Phoenix dactylifera* L.	Palmaceae
36.	Passion-fruit	*Passiflora edulis* Sims.	Passifloraceae
37.	Pomegranate	*Punica granatum* L.	Punicaceae
38.	Ber (Cultivated)	*Zizyphus mauritiana* Lamk.	Rhamnaceae
39.	Ber (Chinese)	*Z. jujuba* Mill.	Rhamnaceae
40.	Apple	*Malus pumila* Mill.	rosaceae
41.	Crab apple	*M. baccata* L. Borkh.	Rosaceae
42.	Pear	*Pyrus communis* L.	Rosaceae
43.	Peach	*Prunus persica* Batsch.	Rosaceae
44.	Sweet cherry	*P. avium* L.	*Rosaceae*
45.	Sour cherry	*P. cerasus* L.	Rosaceae
46.	Plum		
	(i) European	*P. domestica* L.	Rosaceae

S. No.	Common name	Botanical name	Family
	(ii) Japanese	*P. salicina* Lindl.	Rosaceae
47.	Apricot	*P. armeniaca* L.	Rosaceae
48.	Almond	*P. amygdalus* Batsch.	Rosaceae
49.	Strawberry	*Fragaria chiloensis* Duch.	Rosaceae
50.	Blackberry	*Rubus fruticosus* L.	Rosaceae
51.	Quince	*Cydonia oblonga* Mill.	Rosaceae
52.	Raspberry	*Rubus occidentalis* L.	Rosaceae
53.	Loquat	*Eriobotrya japonica* Lindl.	Rosaceae
54.	Citrus fruits		
	(i) Citron	*Citrus medica* L.	Rutaceae
	(ii) Grapefruit	*C. paradisi* Macf.	Rutaceae
	(iii) Hazara	*C. myrtifolia* Raf.	Rutaceae
	(iv) Karna khatta	*C. karna* Raf.	Rutaceae
	(v) Jambhiri (rough lemon)	*C. jambhiri* Lous.	Rutaceae
	(vi) Kumquat (oval)	*Fortunella margarita* Swingle	Rutaceae
	(vii) Kumquat (round)	*F. japonica* Swingle	Rutaceae
	(viii) Lemon	*Citrus limon* Brum.	Rutaceae
	(ix) Lime	*C. aurantifolia* Swingle	Rutaceae
	(x) Mandarin orange (loose skin)	*C. reticulata* Blanco.	Rutaceae
	(xi) Rangpur lime	*C. limonia* Osbeck	Rutaceae
	(xii) Sweet lime	*C. limettoides* Tanaka	Rutaceae
	(xiii) Sour orange	*C. aurantium* L.	Rutaceae
	(xiv) Sweet orange	*C. sinensis* Osbeck	Rutaceae
	(xv) Pummelo	*C. grandis* L.	Rutaceae

S. No.	Common name	Botanical name	Family
55.	Bael	*Aegle marmelos* Correa.	Rutaceae
56.	Wood apple	*Limonia acidissima* L.	Rutaceae
57.	Litchi	*Litchi chinensis* Sonn.	Sapindaceae
58.	Longan	*Euphorbia longana* Lam.	Sapindaceae
59.	Sapota	*Achras sapota* L.	Sapotaceae
60.	Cape gooseberry	*Physalis peruviana* L.	Solanaceae
61.	Phalsa	*Grewia subinaequalis* D.C.	Tiliaceae
62.	Grape		
	(i) European	*Vitis vinifera* L.	Vitaceae
	(ii) American	*Vitis labrusca* L.	Vitaceae
	(iii) Muscadine	*Vitis rotundifolia* L.	Vitaceae

VEGETABLE : COMMON NAME, BOTANICAL NAME AND FAMILY

S. NO.	Common name	Botanical name	Family
1.	Onion	*Allium cepa* L.	Amaryllidaceae
2.	Garlic	*Allium sativum* L.	Amaryllidaceae
3.	Leek	*Allium porrum* L.	Amaryllidaceae
4.	Amaranthus	*Amaranthus tricolor* L.	Amaranthaceae
5.	Colocasia (Arvi)	*Colocasia esculenta* L.	Araceae
6.	Elephant foot	*Amorphophallus campanulatus* Blume.	Araceae
7.	Malabar nightshade (Indian spinach)	*Basella alba* L.	Basellaceae
8.	Spinach (Common palak)	*Beta vulgaris* L. var. *bengalensis*	Chenopodiaceae
9.	Spinach	*Spinacia oleracea* L.	Chenopodiaceae
10.	Beetroot	*Beta vulgaris* L.	Chenopodiaceae
11.	Chicory	*Cichorium intybus* L.	Compositae
12.	Lettuce	*Lactuca sativa* L.	Compositae
13.	Endive	*Cichorium endivia* L.	Compositae
14.	Artichoke (Globe artichoke)	*Cynara scolymus* L.	Compositae
15.	Jerusalem artichoke	*Helianthus tuberosus*	Compositae
16.	Sweet potato	*Ipomoea batatas* Poir.	Convolvulaceae
17.	Cauliflower	*Brassica oleracea* L. var. *botrytis*	Cruciferae
18.	Cabbage	*Brassica oleracea* L. var. *capitata*	Cruciferae
19.	Knol-khol	*Brassica oleracea* L. var. *caulorapa*	Cruciferae
20.	Kale	*Brassica oleracea* L. var. *acephala*	Cruciferae
21.	Brussels sprouts	*Brassica oleracea* L. var. *gemmifera*	Cruciferae
22.	Mustard (Sarson)	*Brassica* spp.	Cruciferae

S. NO.	Common name	Botanical name	Family
23.	Radish	*Raphanus sativus* L.	Cruciferae
24.	Turnip	*Brassica rapa* L.	Cruciferae
25.	Chinese cabbage	*Brassica pekinensis* and *B. chinensis*	Cruciferae
26.	Sprouting broccoli	*Brassica oleracea* var. *italica*	Cruciferae
27.	Horse radish	*Armoracia rusticana*	Cruciferae
28.	Ash gourd (Wax gourd)	*Benincasa hispida* Cogn.	Cucurbitaceae
29.	Long melon (Kakri)	*Cucumis melo* L. var. *utilissimus*	Cucurbitaceae
30.	Cucumber (Kheera)	*Cucumis sativus* L.	Cucurbitaceae
31.	Bitter gourd	*Momordica charantia* L.	Cucurbitaceae
32.	Pumpkin (Sitaphal)	*Cucurbita moschata* Poir.	Cucurbitaceae
33.	Sponge gourd	*Luffa cylindrica* Roem.	Cucurbitaceae
34.	Ridge gourd	*Luffa acutangula* Roxb.	Cucurbitaceae
35.	Water melon (Tarbuz)	*Citrullus lanatus* Mansf.	Cucurbitaceae
36.	Musk melon (Kharbuza)	*Cucumis melo* L.	Cucurbitaceae
37.	Round gourd (Tinda or Squash melon)	*Citrullus vulgaris* var. *fistulosus*	Cucurbitaceae
38.	Bottle gourd (Lauki)	*Lagenaria siceraria* Standl.	Cucurbitaceae
39.	Snake gourd (Chichinda)	*Trichosanthes anguina* L.	Cucurbitaceae
40.	Pointed gourd (Parwal)	*Trichosanthes dioica* Roxb.	Cucurbitaceae
41.	Cho-cho	*Sechium edule*	Cucurbitaceae
42.	Summer squash	*Cucurbita pepo*	Cucurbitaceae
43.	Winter squash	*Cucurbita maxima*	Cucurbitaceae
44.	Yam	*Dioscorea alcta* L.	Dioscoreaceae
45.	Tapioca (Cassava)	*Manihot esculenta*	Euphorbiaceae
46.	Hyacinth bean	*Dolichos lablab* (Roxb.) L.	Leguminosae
47.	Cowpea	*Vigna unguiculata* (L.) Walp.	Leguminosae
48.	Pea	*Pisum sativum* L.	Leguminosae
49.	Kidney or French bean	*Phaseolus vulgaris* L.	Leguminosae

S. NO.	Common name	Botanical name	Family
50.	Fenugreek (Methi)	*Trigonella foenumgraecum* L.	Leguminosae
51.	Lima bean	*Phaseolus lunatus* L.	Leguminosae
52.	Cluster bean	*Cyamopsis tetragonoloba* (L.) Taub.	Leguminosae
53.	Broad bean	*Vicia faba* L.	Leguminosae
54.	Asparagus	*Asparagus officinalis* L.	Liliaceae
55.	Okra (Bhindi)	*Abelmoschus esculentus* L. Moench.	Malvaceae
56.	Rhubarb	*Rheum rhaponticum* L.	Polygonaceae
57.	Portulaca (Kulfa)	*Portulaca oleracea* L.	Portulacaceae
58.	Brinjal (Egg plant)	*Solanum melongena* L.	Solanaceae
59.	Chilli	*Capsicum annuum* L.	Solanaceae
60.	Capsicum (Bell pepper)	*Capsicum frutescens* L.	Solanaceae
61.	Tomato	*Lycopersicon esculentum* Mill.	Solanaceae
62.	Potato	*Solanum tuberosum* L.	Solanaceae
63.	Celery	*Apium graveolens* L.	Umbelliferae
64.	Parsely	*Petroselinum hortense* L.	Umbelliferae
65.	Carrot	*Daucus carota* L.	Umbelliferae
66.	Parsnip	*Pastinaca sativa*	Umbelliferae

NUTRIENTS IN FOODS, THEIR FUNCTIONS, SOURCES OF AVAILABILITY AND DEFICIENCY SYMPTOMS

The physiological function of food may be divided into three general categories: the need for food to supply energy, the need for food to build and maintain the body tissues, and the need for food materials to regulate body processes. These needs are satisfied by substances called nutrients which are found in the food. The foods we consume daily include, rice, wheat, pulses, vegetables, fruits, milk, eggs, fish, meat, sugar, butter, and oils. These foods are made up of one or more of a number of substances called nutrients which are classified into six groups according to their chemical composition.

1. **Carbohydrates** : These constitute one of the three major classes of nutrients (carbohydrates, fats and proteins) which supply energy. Each gram of carbohydrate consumed provides 4 kilocalories of energy to the body. Carbohydrates are formed in plants from carbon dioxide and water by photosynthesis in sunlight. Thus solar energy is stored as chemical energy in the form of carbohydrates (starch, sugar) in the plant. Carbohydrates contain the elements carbon, hydrogen and oxygen. Starch is present mainly in cereals, pulses, roots and tubers. Sugar is found in fruits, sugarcane and sugar beet.

    Carbohydrates which provide a major portion of calories in the human diet are of two kinds: complex carbohydrates like starch and simple sugars like monosaccharides (glucose, fructose) and disaccharides (sucrose). Apart from serving as a source of energy, the intermediary products of carbohydrate metabolism provide substrates for synthesis of a wide range of biocompounds in the body.

    Diabetes is a disease of impaired carbohydrate metabolism manifest as hyperglycemia.

2. **Fats and Oils**: These are esters of glycerol and fatty acids and form the second group of major nutrients. They contain carbon, hydrogen and oxygen, but the proportion of oxygen present is much smaller than in carbohydrates. Each gram of oil or fat supplies 9 kilocalories of energy. Thus these are a more concentrated source of energy than carbohydrates. Oils and fats are obtained from plants and animals.

375

Dietary fat is essential, as a source of essential fatty acids (EFA), as a vehicle for fat soluble vitamins and for providing a certain level of energy density and palatability to diets. Besides cardiovascular diseases, high fat intake is also a risk factor in obesity and diabetes. High fat intakes particularly of the saturated type have been shown to be associated with occurrence of cancer at several sites, especially the breast, prostate and large bowel. Experimental evidence indicates that polyunsaturated fats are tumorigenic. Of all the nutrients the causal relationship between fat intake and occurrence of cancer is most suggestive.

3. **Proteins**: This is the third class of major nutrients. There are thousands of proteins found in nature which vary in their composition and size. All the proteins contain the elements carbon, hydrogen, oxygen and nitrogen. Proteins are made up of smaller compounds known as amino acids. Each gram of protein supplies 4 kilocalories of energy.

Proteins are essential for tissue building and maintaining N equilibrium. Protein in the diet should be derived from different sources and provide at least 10 to 12 per cent energy, and such levels would meet the normal protein requirements of all age groups.

4. **Minerals** : The term mineral refers to inorganic substances present in foods. They include salts and other compounds of calcium, phosphorus, magnesium, sodium, chlorine, potassium, sulphur and other elements. On heating to high temperature (about 550°C) they are converted to ash.

Body needs a wide range of macrominerals (K, Na, Cl, Mg, Ca, P) and trace elements (Cr, Co, Cu, F, I, Fe, Mn, Mo, Ni, Se, Si, Sn, V and Zn) for maintaining body function and health at an optimum level. Quantitative requirements for man of several of these elements have been defined.

5. **Vitamins** : These are organic compounds present in very small amounts in foods, but essential for normal growth of the body and maintenance of health. Vitamins may be fat-soluble such as A,D, E or K or water-soluble such as vitamin C (ascorbic acid), thiamine, riboflavin, niacin and others which belong to the B-complex group.

6. **Water** : Water is an essential part of the body structure as a carrier of nutrients and regulator of a number of body functions. Its importance as a nutrient has been recognized only recently.

Major functions of nutrients

Nutrient	Function		
	Body building	**Energy giving**	**Regulating**
Carbohydrates	AF	MF	-
Proteins	MF	AF	AF
Fat	AF	MF	-
Minerals	MF	MF	-
Vitamins	MF	AF	-
Water	MF	AF	MF

MF = Main Function

AF = Additional Function

Symptoms of deficiency of various nutrients

S. No.	Nutrient	Deficiency Symptoms
1.	Proteins	Retarded growth in children; irritability; apathy and possibly retarded mental development; discolouration of skin and hair; swelling of face and lower part of legs and feet.
2.	Vitamin A	Inability to see in twilight, sensitivity to bright light; foamy white patches on conjunctive, softening of cornea, eventually leading to blindness; frequent respiratory infections.
3.	Vitamin B-Complex	
	(a) Thiramine (B_1)	Beriberi; loss of appetite.
	(b) Riboflavin (B_2)	Cracks at corners of mouth; raw red cracked lips; glossy tongue; ulcers in oral cavity.
	(c) Nicotinic acid (B_5)	Sore tongue (scarlet coloured); pellagra; skin changes in hands, feet, legs and neck; mental changes in severe deficiency.
	(d) Pyridoxine (B_6)	Ulceration in oral cavity; anaemia.
4.	Vitamin C	Scurvy; bleeding gums and mucous membranes; susceptibility to common cold.
5.	Calcium	Important for bones and teeth, blood clotting; osteomalacia in women after repeated pregnancies; rickets, pigeon chest, irritability in children.
6.	Iron	Anaemia; pale smooth tongue, pale lips, eyes and skin; spoon-shaped nails; frequent exhaustion.

Functions and sources of availability of various nutrients

Nutrient	Functions	Sources of availability
Carbohydrates	1. To supply energy 2. To help assimilate other nutrients	Cereal products including rice, chapati, bread; potato, corn, yam, sugar, syrup, jam, honey, jaggery, dried fruits, banana, cashew nut, mango, bael, date, pea, tapioca, arvi, sweet potato, etc.
Proteins	1. To maintain body structure and composition 2. To build and repair tissues 3. To help formation of antibodies to fight infections 4. To form enzymes and hormones to regulate body processes 5. To provide energy	Milk, curd, cheese, pulses, beans, pea, groundnut and other oilseeds, egg, fish, meat, bread, cereals, cashew nut, almond, coconut, green vegetables, etc.
Fats	1. To supply energy in concentrated form 2. To supply essential fatty acids for transport and absorption of fat-soluble vitamins	Edible oils, ghee, butter, cream, vanaspati, cashew nut, almond, etc.
Fibres	1. To improve digestion 2. To prevent constipation 3. To reduce cholestrol	Banana, mango, apple, guava, potato, brinjal, spinach, sweet potato, cabbage, beans, etc.
Minerals		
(i) Calcium	1. To build bones and teeth 2. To help clotting of blood 3. To help normal functioning of muscles and nerves	Milk, curd, cheese, fish, ragi, sesame seeds, tomato, pea, almond, raspberry, coconut, pomegranate, wood apple, banana, guava, amaranth, leaves of colocasia, chaulai, drumstick, fenugreek, radish, etc.
(ii) Iron	1. To form haemoglobin	Egg, shellfish, leafy vegetables, cereal products, ragi, bajra, pulses, beans, banana, date, papaya, mango, guava, karonda, tomato, cabbage, etc.

Nutrient	Functions	Sources of availability
Vitamins		
(i) Vitamin A	1. To help growth 2. To help keep skin and mucous membrane healthy and resistant to infection 3. To protect against night blindness	Leafy vegetables, amaranth, chaulai, radish tops, spinach, fenugreek, carrot, mango, papaya, ghee, butter, vanaspati, egg, etc.
(ii) Thaimine (B_1)	1. To maintain appetite and keep the nervous system healthy 2. To help release energy for the body	Wheat products, pulses, parboiled rice, fresh pea and beans, egg, milk, pomegranate, bael, plum, jamun, pumpkin, cabbage, wood apple, etc.
(iii) Riboflavin (B_2)	1. To help cell respiration; essential for growth 2. To help keep clear vision 3. To help maintain the skin around mouth and nose smooth	Milk, curd, cheese, egg, fish, banana, litchi, cowpea and other pulses, papaya, colocasia, bael, radish tops, pineapple, etc.
(iv) Niacin or Nicotinic acid (B_5)	1. To help growth 2. To help in energy release	Groundnut, meat, prawn, pulses, green vegetables, peach, cherry, banana, strawberry, etc.
(v) Vitamin C	1. To make cementing substance to hold cells together and to strengthen walls of blood vessels to help resist infection 2. To help healing of wounds 3. To help absorption of iron	Aonla, guava, cashew apple, drumstick leaves, cabbages, radish tops, amaranth, orange, grapefruit, pummelo, tomato, Barbados cherry, carrot, green, chillies, etc.
(vi) Vitamin D	1. To help absorption of calcium 2. To help in building strong bones and teeth	Cabbage, carrot, fish, oil, butter, egg, etc.
Water	1. To maintain body structure and composition 2. To help digest and absorb food 3. To regulate body temperature 4. To help regulate body pH	Water and water-based beverages such as tea, coffee, juice, sherbet, coconut water, etc.

Dietary guidelines for prevention of diseases

There are many common features among diseases insofar as the influence of dietary factors on disease prevention is concerned. Based on these observations an integrated or common dietary guidelines for prevention of these groups of diseases (obesity, diabetes, coronary heart diseases, cancer) and for maintaining health can be provided:

1. Excess calorie intake should be avoided and energy balance and constant body weight should be maintained. Excess energy intake can be prevented in several ways: (a) reducing total dietary intake, (b) increasing energy expenditure through exercise, (c) reducing total fat content in the diet, and (d) increasing dietary fibre content. Maintaining of energy balance is essential for prevention of most of these diseases.

2. Protein intake can be maintained to provide 10 to 12 per cent of energy.

3. Energy contribution from carbohydrate should be around 60 per cent and most of it should be in the form of complex carbohydrate (starch) and contribution from simple sugars should be less than 10 per cent of energy.

4. The amount of fat in the diet should contribute less than 30 per cent energy and preferably around 25 per cent. Cholesterol content should be reduced to the minimum.

5. Vitamin and mineral intake should be adequate to meet the normal requirement according to recommended dietary allowances and particular attention should be paid to adequate intake of Ca, Mg, Zn and selenium and vanadium. Sodium intake should be kept low (2 to 3 g/day) and potassium intake should be increased.

6. Diet should contain an adequate level of fibre covering all types of fibres in order to obtain an optimal response.

NUTRITIONAL VALUE OF VEGETABLES, CONDIMENTS, SPICES AND FRUITS
(per 100 g of edible portion)

S. No.	Name of foodstuff	Mois-ture (%)	Prot-ein (%)	Fat (%)	Mine-rals (%)	Fibre (%)	Carbo hyd-rate (%)	Ene-rgy (Kcal.)	Calc-ium (mg)	Phosp -horus (mg)	Iron (mg)	Caro-tene (µg)	Thia-mine (mg)	Ribo-flavin (mg)	Niacin (mg)	Vita-min C (mg)
1	2	3	4	5	6	7	8	9	10	11	12	13	14	15	16	17
(A) LEAFY VEGETABLES																
1.	Amaranth (tender)	85.7	4.0	0.5	2.7	1.0	6.1	45	397	83	25.5	5520	0.03	0.30	1.2	99
2.	Bathua leaves	89.6	3.7	0.4	2.6	0.8	2.9	30	150	80	4.2	1740	0.01	0.14	0.6	35
3.	Beet (greens)	86.4	3.4	0.8	2.2	0.7	6.5	46	380	30	16.2	5862	0.26	0.56	3.3	70
4.	Brussels sprout	85.5	4.7	0.5	1.0	1.2	7.1	52	43	82	1.8	126	0.05	0.16	0.4	72
5.	Cabbage	91.9	1.8	0.1	0.6	1.0	4.6	27	39	44	0.8	1200	0.06	0.09	0.4	124
6.	Celery leaves	88.0	6.3	0.6	2.1	1.4	1.6	37	230	140	6.3	3990	0.00	0.11	1.2	62
7.	Colocasia leaves	82.7	3.9	1.5	2.2	2.9	6.8	56	227	82	10.0	10278	0.22	0.26	1.1	12
8.	Coriander leaves	86.3	3.3	0.6	2.3	1.2	6.3	44	184	71	18.5	6918	0.05	0.06	0.8	135
9.	Fenugreek leaves	86.1	4.4	0.9	1.5	1.1	6.0	49	395	51	16.5	2340	0.04	0.31	0.8	52
10.	Lettuce	93.4	2.1	0.3	1.2	0.5	2.5	21	50	28	2.4	990	0.09	0.13	0.5	10
11.	Mint	84.9	4.8	0.6	1.9	2.0	5.8	48	200	62	15.6	1620	0.05	0.26	1.0	27
12.	Mustard leaves	89.8	4.0	0.6	1.6	0.8	3.2	34	155	26	16.3	2622	0.03	-	-	33
13.	Parsley	74.6	5.9	1.0	3.2	1.8	13.5	87	390	175	17.9	1920	0.04	0.18	0.5	281
14.	Radish leaves	90.8	3.8	0.4	1.6	1.0	2.4	28	265	59	3.6	5295	0.18	0.47	0.8	81
15.	Spinach	92.1	2.0	0.7	1.7	0.6	2.9	26	73	21	10.9	5580	0.03	0.26	0.5	28

1	2	3	4	5	6	7	8	9	10	11	12	13	14	15	16	17
(B) ROOTS AND TUBERS																
16.	Beetroot	87.7	1.7	0.1	0.8	0.9	8.8	43	18.3	55	1.0	0	0.04	0.09	0.4	10
17.	Carrot	86.0	0.9	0.2	1.1	1.2	10.6	48	80	530	2.2	1890	0.04	0.02	0.6	3
18.	Colocasia	73.1	3.0	0.1	1.7	1.0	21.1	97	40	140	1.7	24	0.09	0.03	0.4	0
19.	Onion	86.6	1.2	0.1	0.4	0.6	11.1	50	46.9	50	0.7	0	0.08	0.01	0.4	11
20.	Parsnip	72.4	1.3	0.3	1.1	1.7	23.2	101	50	40	0.5	18	0.06	-	0.4	16
21.	Potato	74.7	1.6	0.1	0.6	0.4	22.6	97	10	40	0.7	24	0.10	0.01	1.2	17
22.	Radish	94.9	0.5	0.1	0.7	0.6	3.2	16	20	20	1.0	4	0.02	0.03	1.4	21
23.	Sweet potato	68.5	1.2	0.3	1.0	0.8	28.2	120	46	50	0.8	6	0.08	0.04	0.7	24
24.	Tapioca	59.4	0.7	0.2	1.0	0.6	38.1	157	50	40	0.9	-	0.05	0.10	0.3	25
25.	Turnip	91.6	0.5	0.2	0.6	0.9	6.2	29	30	40	0.4	0	0.04	0.04	0.5	43
26.	Yam	78.7	1.2	0.1	0.8	0.8	18.4	79	50	34	0.6	260	0.06	0.07	0.7	0
(C) OTHER VEGETABLES																
27.	Artichoke	77.3	3.6	0.1	1.8	1.2	16.0	79	120	100	2.3	37	0.23	0.01	-	0
28.	Ash gourd	96.5	0.4	0.1	0.3	0.8	1.9	10	30	20	0.8	0	0.06	0.01	0.4	1
29.	Banana (green)	83.2	1.4	0.2	0.5	0.7	14.0	64	10	29	0.6	30	0.05	0.02	0.3	24
30.	Bitter gourd	92.4	1.6	0.2	0.8	0.8	4.2	25	20	70	1.8	126	0.07	0.09	0.5	88
31.	Bottle gourd	96.1	0.2	0.1	0.5	0.6	2.5	12	20	10	0.7	0	0.03	0.01	0.2	0
32.	Brinjal	92.7	1.4	0.3	0.3	1.3	4.0	24	18	47	0.9	74	0.04	0.11	0.9	12
33.	Broad bean	85.4	4.5	0.1	0.8	2.0	7.2	48	50	64	1.4	9	0.08	-	0.8	12
34.	Cauliflower	90.8	2.6	0.4	1.0	1.2	4.0	30	33	57	1.5	30	0.04	0.1	1.0	56
35.	Cluster bean	81.0	3.2	0.4	1.4	3.2	10.8	16	130	57	4.5	198	0.09	0.03	49	48
36.	Cowpea (pods)	85.3	3.5	0.2	0.9	2.0	8.1	48	72	59	2.5	564	0.07	0.09	0.9	14
37.	Cucumber	96.3	0.4	0.1	0.3	0.4	2.5	13	10	25	1.5	0	0.03	0	0.2	7
38.	Drumstick	86.9	2.5	0.1	2.0	4.8	3.7	26	30	110	5.3	110	0.05	0.07	0.2	120
39.	Field bean	86.1	3.8	0.7	0.9	1.8	6.7	48	210	68	1.7	187	0.10	0.06	0.7	9
40.	French bean	91.4	1.7	0.1	0.5	1.8	4.5	26	50	28	1.7	132	0.08	0.06	0.3	24
41.	Jackfruit (green)	84.0	2.6	0.3	0.9	2.8	9.4	51	30	40	1.7	0	0.05	0.04	0.2	14

1	2	3	4	5	6	7	8	9	10	11	12	13	14	15	16	17
42.	Knol-khol	92.7	1.1	0.2	0.7	1.5	3.8	21	20	35	0.4	21	0.05	0.09	0.5	85
43.	Ladies finger (okra)	89.6	1.9	0.2	0.7	1.2	6.4	35	66	56	1.5	52	0.07	0.10	0.6	13
44.	Leek	78.9	1.8	0.1	0.7	1.3	17.2	77	50	70	2.3	18	0.23	-	-	11
45.	Musk melon	95.2	0.3	0.2	0.4	0.4	3.5	17	32	14	1.4	169	0.11	0.08	0.3	26
46.	Pea	72.1	7.2	0.1	0.8	4.0	15.9	93	20	139	1.5	83	0.25	0.01	0.8	9
47.	Pointed gourd	92.0	2.0	0.3	0.5	3.0	2.2	20	30	40	1.7	153	0.05	0.06	0.5	29
48.	Pumpkin	92.6	1.4	0.1	0.6	0.7	4.6	25	10	30	0.7	50	0.06	0.04	0.5	2
49.	Ridge gourd	95.2	0.5	0.1	0.3	0.5	3.4	17	18	26	0.5	33	-	0.01	0.2	5
50.	Round melon	93.5	1.4	0.2	0.5	1.0	3.4	21	25	24	0.9	13	0.04	0.08	0.3	18
51.	Snake gourd	94.6	0.5	0.3	0.5	0.8	3.3	18	26	20	0.3	96	0.04	0.06	0.3	0
52.	Tomato (green)	93.1	1.9	0.1	0.6	0.7	3.6	23	20	36	1.8	192	0.07	0.01	0.4	31
53.	Tomato (ripe)	94.0	0.9	0.2	0.5	0.8	3.6	20	48	20	0.4	351	0.12	0.06	0.4	27
54.	Water chestnut	70.0	4.7	0.3	1.1	0.6	23.3	115	20	150	0.8	12	0.05	0.07	0.6	9
55.	Water melon	95.8	0.2	0.2	0.3	0.2	3.3	16	11	12	7.9	0	0.02	0.04	0.1	1
(D) CONDIMENTS AND SPICES																
56.	Asafoetida	16.0	4.0	1.1	7.0	4.1	67.8	297	690	50	22.2	4	0.00	0.04	0.3	0
57.	Cardamom	20.0	10.2	2.2	5.4	20.1	42.1	229	130	160	5.0	0	0.22	0.17	0.8	0
58.	Chilli (dry)	10.0	15.9	6.2	6.1	30.2	31.6	246	160	370	2.3	345	0.93	0.43	9.5	50
59.	Chilli (green)	85.7	2.9	0.6	1.0	6.8	3.0	29	30	80	1.2	175	0.19	0.39	0.9	111
60.	Cloves	25.2	5.2	8.9	5.2	9.5	46.0	286	740	100	4.9	253	0.08	0.13	0	0
61.	Coriander	11.2	14.1	16.1	4.4	32.6	21.6	288	630	393	17.9	942	0.22	0.35	1.1	0
62	Cumin seeds	11.9	18.7	15.0	5.8	12.0	36.6	356	1080	511	31.0	522	0.55	0.36	2.6	3
63	Fenugreek seeds	13.7	26.2	5.8	3.0	7.2	44.1	333	160	370	14.1	96	0.34	0.29	1.1	0
64.	Ginger (fresh)	80.9	2.3	0.9	1.2	2.4	12.3	67	20	60	2.6	3027	0.25	0.42	1.4	0
65.	Mace	15.9	6.5	24.4	1.6	3.8	47.8	437	180	100	12.6	40	0.06	0.03	0.6	6
66.	Nutmeg	14.3	7.5	36.4	1.7	11.6	28.5	472	120	240	4.6	0	0.33	0.01	1.4	0
67.	Turmeric	13.1	6.3	5.1	3.5	2.6	69.4	349	150	282	14.8	30	0.03	0	2.3	0

1	2	3	4	5	6	7	8	9	10	11	12	13	14	15	16	17
(E)	**FRUITS**															
68.	Almond	5.2	20.8	58.9	2.9	1.7	10.5	655	230	490	4.5	0	0.24	0.57	4.4	0
69.	Amada	90.3	0.7	3.0	0.5	1.0	4.5	48	36	11	3.9	270	0.02	0.02	0.3	21
70.	Aonla	81.8	0.5	0.1	0.5	3.4	13.7	58	50	20	1.2	9	0.03	0.01	0.2	600
71.	Apple	84.6	0.2	0.5	0.3	1.0	13.4	59	10	14	1.0	0	-	-	0.0	1
72.	Apricot	85.3	1.0	0.3	0.7	1.1	11.6	53	20	25	2.2	2160	0.04	0.13	0.6	6
73.	Avocado	73.6	1.7	22.8	1.1	-	0.8	215	10	80	0.7	-	-	-	-	-
74.	Bael	61.5	1.8	0.3	1.7	2.9	31.8	137	85	50	0.6	55	0.13	0.03	1.1	8
75.	Banana (ripe)	70.1	1.2	0.3	0.8	0.4	27.2	116	17	36	0.9	78	0.05	0.08	0.5	7
76.	Ber	81.6	0.8	0.3	0.3	-	17.0	74	4	9	1.8	21	0.02	0.05	0.7	76
77.	Blackberry	87.2	1.3	0.5	0.5	3.8	6.7	37	30	20	4.3	7	-	-	2.0	9
78.	Cape gooseberry	82.9	1.8	0.2	0.8	3.2	11.1	53	10	67	2.0	1428	0.05	0.02	0.3	49
79.	Carambola	91.9	0.7	0.1	0.4	0.8	6.1	28	4	11	-	-	-	-	-	-
80.	Cashew apple	86.3	0.2	0.1	0.2	0.9	12.3	51	10	10	0.2	23	0.02	0.05	0.4	180
81.	Cashew nut	5.9	21.2	46.9	2.4	1.3	22.3	596	50	450	5.0	60	0.63	0.19	1.2	0
82.	Cherry	83.4	1.1	0.5	0.8	0.4	13.8	64	24	25	1.3	0	0.08	0.08	0.3	7
83.	Chilgoza	4.0	13.9	49.3	2.8	1.0	29.0	615	91	494	3.6	-	0.32	0.30	3.6	0
84.	Coconut	36.3	4.5	41.6	1.0	3.6	13.0	444	10	240	1.7	0	0.05	0.10	0.8	1
85.	Currant	18.4	2.7	0.5	2.2	1.0	75.2	316	130	110	8.5	21	0.03	0.14	0.4	1
86.	Custard apple	70.5	1.6	0.4	0.9	3.1	23.5	104	17	47	1.5	0	0.07	0.17	1.3	37
87.	Date (fresh)	59.2	1.2	0.4	1.7	3.7	33.8	144	22	38	-	12	-	-	-	-
88.	Durian	58.0	2.8	3.9	1.2	-	34.1	183	10	50	1.0	-	-	-	-	-
89.	Fig	88.1	1.3	0.2	0.6	2.2	7.6	37	80	30	1.0	162	0.06	0.05	0.6	5
90.	Grape (blue variety)	82.2	0.6	0.4	0.9	2.8	13.1	58	20	23	0.5	3	0.04	0.03	0.2	1
91.	Grape (pale green variety)	79.2	0.5	0.3	0.6	2.9	16.5	71	20	30	0.5	0	-	-	0.0	1
92.	Grapefruit	88.5	1.0	0.1	0.4	-	10.0	45	30	30	0.2	-	0.12	0.02	0.3	-
93.	Guava	81.7	0.9	0.3	0.7	5.2	11.2	51	10	28	1.4	0	0.03	0.03	0.4	212

1	2	3	4	5	6	7	8	9	10	11	12	13	14	15	16	17
94.	Jackfruit (ripe)	76.2	1.9	0.1	0.9	1.1	19.8	88	20	41	0.5	175	0.03	0.13	0.4	7
95.	Jamun	83.7	0.7	0.3	0.4	0.9	14.0	62	15	15	1.2	48	0.03	0.01	0.2	18
96.	Karonda	91.0	1.1	2.9	0.6	1.5	2.9	42	21	28	-	-	-	-	-	-
97.	Lemon	85.0	1.0	0.9	0.3	1.7	11.1	57	70	10	2.3	0	0.02	0.01	0.1	39
98.	Lime	84.6	1.5	1.0	0.7	1.3	10.9	59	90	20	0.3	15	0.02	0.03	0.1	63
99.	Loquat	88.2	0.6	0.3	0.5	0.8	9.6	43	30	20	1.3	559	-	-	0.0	0
100.	Mahua (ripe)	73.6	1.4	1.6	0.7	-	22.7	111	45	22	1.1	307	-	-	-	40
101.	Mango (green)	87.5	0.7	0.1	0.4	1.2	10.1	44	10	19	5.4	90	0.04	0.01	0.2	3
102.	Mango (ripe)	81.0	0.6	0.4	0.4	0.7	16.9	74	14	16	1.3	2743	0.08	0.09	0.9	16
103.	Mangosteen	84.9	0.5	0.1	0.2	-	14.3	60	10	20	0.2	-	-	-	-	-
104.	Mulberry	86.5	1.1	0.4	0.6	1.1	10.3	49	70	30	2.3	57	0.04	0.13	0.5	12
105.	Papaya (ripe)	90.8	0.6	0.1	0.5	0.8	7.2	32	17	13	0.5	666	0.04	0.25	0.2	57
106.	Papaya (green)	92.0	0.7	0.2	0.5	0.9	5.7	27	28	40	0.9	0	0.01	0.01	0.1	12
107.	Passion fruit	76.3	0.9	0.1	0.7	9.6	12.4	54	10	60	2.0	54	0.07	0.14	1.6	25
108.	Peach	86.0	1.2	0.3	0.8	1.2	10.5	50	15	41	2.4	0	0.02	0.03	0.5	6
109.	Pear	86.0	0.6	0.2	0.3	1.0	11.9	52	8	15	0.5	28	0.06	0.03	0.2	0
110.	Persimmon	80.0	0.7	0.2	0.3	0.9	17.9	76	15	10	0.3	2268	0.03	0.01	0.0	33
111.	Phalsa	80.8	1.3	0.9	1.1	1.2	14.7	72	129	39	3.1	419	-	-	0.3	22
112.	Pineapple	87.8	0.4	0.1	0.4	0.5	10.8	46	20	9	1.2	18	0.20	0.12	0.1	39
113.	Pistachio nut	5.6	19.8	53.5	2.8	2.1	16.2	626	140	430	7.7	144	0.67	0.28	2.3	-
114.	Plum	86.9	0.7	0.5	0.4	0.4	11.1	52	10	12	0.6	166	0.04	0.10	0.3	5
115.	Pomegranate	78.0	1.6	0.1	0.7	5.1	14.5	65	10	70	0.3	0	0.06	0.10	0.3	16
116.	Pummelo	88.0	0.6	0.1	0.5	0.6	10.2	44	30	30	0.3	120	0.03	0.03	0.2	20
117.	Quince	85.7	0.3	0.1	0.3	1.7	11.9	50	10	20	0.4	-	0.02	0.02	0.2	11
118.	Raisin	20.2	1.8	0.3	2.0	1.1	74.6	308	87	80	7.7	2.4	0.07	0.19	0.7	1
119.	Raspberry	84.8	1.0	0.6	0.9	1.0	11.7	56	40	110	2.3	1248	-	-	0.8	30
120.	Sapota	73.7	0.7	1.1	0.5	2.6	21.4	98	28	27	2.0	97	0.02	0.03	0.2	6
121.	Strawberry	87.8	0.7	0.2	0.4	1.1	9.8	44	30	30	1.8	18	0.03	0.02	0.2	52
122.	Sweet lime	88.4	0.8	0.3	0.7	0.5	9.3	43	40	30	0.7	0	-	-	0.0	50
123.	Walnut	4.5	15.6	64.5	1.8	2.6	11.0	687	100	380	4.8	6	0.45	0.40	1.0	0
124.	Wood apple	64.2	7.1	3.7	1.9	5.0	18.1	134	130	110	0.6	61	0.04	0.17	0.8	3

SOME COMMON PRACTICES FOR REDUCING NUTRIENT LOSSES DURING PROCESSING OF FRUITS AND VEGETABLES

Fruits and vegetables are a source of vitamins, proteins, minerals, carbohydrates and fibres in our diet. The nutritive value is affected by variety, management practices, weather and degree of maturity at harvest. Storage conditions before processing affect vitamins and other nutrients. Washing, trimming, and heat treatments affect nutrient content. Canning, drying, and freezing alter nutritional values, and the choices of times and temperatures in these operations frequently must be balanced between good bacterial destruction and minimum nutrient destruction.

Moreover, packaging and subsequent storage also affect nutrients. One of the most important factors is the final preparation of the food in the home and the restaurant-the steam table can destroy much of what has been preserved through all prior manipulations. Thus the ultimate nutritive value of a food results from the sum total of losses incurred throughout its history-from farmer to consumer.

During fruit and vegetables processing loss of nutrients occur which may be quantitative as well as qualitative.

Quantitative losses occur when edible parts are discarded, e.g., in case of leafy vegetables such as colocasia, fenugreek (methi) and amaranth the stems may be discarded due to ignorance of their use. During canning, dehydration and in preparation of various other products, a part of the raw material is rejected. This rejection may be to the extent of fifty per cent.

Qualitative loss means loss of soluble constituents. Ascorbic acid or vitamin C and thiamine are water-soluble vitamins which are affected by cooking. If fruits/vegetables are cut and then washed, some loss of these vitamins and other soluble constituents may occur from their cut surfaces. When vegetables are boiled in water and the water is discarded the dissolved nutrients are lost. Such loss may amount to 5-10 per cent. About 20 per cent of the thiamine is destroyed in normal cooking and if the food is reheated, there is additional loss. Vitamin C is the most heat-labile vitamin, and its loss is 25 to 35 per cent. Therefore, preparation procedures that reduce loss of vitamin C also conserve all other nutrients. Loss of water soluble vitamins may go up to 60 per cent as a result of leaching and heating. Minerals are also lost by leaching but the loss is smaller (up to 35 per cent).

Stability of nutrients*

Nutrient	Neut-ral pH 7	Acid < pH 7	Alkaline > pH 7	Air or Oxygen	Light	Heat	Cooking losses, Range (%)
(A) Vitamins							
(i) Vitamin A	S	U	S	U	U	U	0-40
(ii) Carotenes (Provitamin A)	S	U	S	U	U	U	0-30
(iii) Thiamine (B$_1$)	U	S	U	U	S	U	0-80
(iv) Riboflavin (B$_2$)	S	S	U	S	U	U	0-75
(v) Folic acid	U	U	S	U	U	U	0-100
(vi) Niacin	S	S	S	S	S	S	0-75
vii) Pantothenic acid	S	U	U	S	S	U	0-50
(viii) Pyridoxine (B$_6$)	S	S	S	S	U	U	0-40
(ix) Biotin	S	S	S	S	S	U	0-60
(x) Cobalamine (B$_{12}$)	S	S	S	U	U	S	0-40
(xi) Choline	S	S	S	S	U	S	0-10
(xii) Inositol	S	S	S	S	S	U	0-95
(xii) Ascorbic acid (Vitamin C)	U	S	U	U	U	U	0-100
(xiv) Vitamin D	S	-	U	U	U	U	0-10
(xv) Tocopherol (Vitamin E)	S	S	S	U	U	U	0-55
(xvi) Vitamin K	S	U	U	S	U	S	0-5
(B) Essential fatty acids	S	S	U	U	U	S	-
(C) Essential amino acids							
(i) Isoleucine	S	S	S	S	S	S	0-10
(ii) Leucine	S	S.	S	S	S	S	0-10
(iii) Lysine	S	S	S	S	S	U	0-40
(iv) Methionine	S	S	S	S	S	S	0-10
(v) Phenylalanine	S	S	S	S	S	S	0-5
(vi) Threonine	S	U	U	S	S	U	0-20
(vii) Tryptophan	S	U	S	S	U	S	0-15
(viii) Valine	S	S	S	S	S	S	0-10
(D) Mineral Salts	S	S	S	S	S	S	0-3

*Source : Harris and Karmas, 1975   (U= Unstable; S= Stable)

From the table it is clear that the cooking losses of some essential nutrients may be in excess of 75%. In modern food processing operations, however, losses are seldom in excess of 25%.

Cooking

It is difficult to define the cooking process in such a way as to satisfy all branches of science; nevertheless, cooking is commonly practised to make food eatable and more palatable. Cooking thus is an essentially classical process of food engineering which can be comprehensively characterized only by combining engineering with other disciplines of science, such as physics, chemistry, mathematics and biology.

Several classifications of the cooking process are possible. Based on time required for cooking, it can be divided into the following three categories.

(A) Quick cooking - Time needed to cook the food is extremely short and is usually less than a minute. Examples are high temperature short time (HTST) and ultra high temperature (UHT) processing of milk, extrusion cooking.

(B) Slow cooking - Domestic and/or industrial cooking comes under this category and the time needed to cook food varies between a few minutes and an hour. Examples are baking, pressure cooking, boiling, canning, roasting.

(C) Very slow cooking -   This process is not at all a common cooking process. Here, food is partially cooked and immediately kept in an insulated box so that the cooking process continues slowly. The whole process takes a few hours at least, but it is economical from the viewpoint of energy conservation.

Paulus (1984) has divided cooking process into dry and moist cooking methods, which are given below in the table with modifications.

Characteristics of some important cooking processes

S. No.		Humid Medium				Dry Medium		
		Boiling	Steaming	Simmering	Baking	Roasting	Frying	Grilling
1.	Cooking/ heating/ medium	Water	Steam	Water	Air	Air/hot/ surface sand	oil/ fat	Infrared
2.	Temp. of heating/ cooking medium (°C)	≥100	≥100	≤100	>>100	>>100	>100	≥100
3	Cooking time	←——Medium - high——→				←—— Low - medium——→		

S. No.		Humid Medium				Dry Medium		
		Boiling	Steaming	Simmering	Baking	Roasting	Frying	Grilling
4.	Pressure during heating	> 1 bar	≥ 1 bar	1 bar	← 1 bar →			
5.	Moisture of product	← Usually increases →				← Decreases →		
6.	Water activity (a_w)	← 1 →				← 1 →		

EFFECT OF COOKING ON VARIOUS NUTRIENTS

Heat affects foods in many ways. Some foods lose their nutritive value through cooking. The loss depends upon the solubility of the particular food in water. Exposure to air during cooking or the addition of baking soda destroys the vitamin content.

Nutrients	Effect of cooking
(1) Proteins	(1) Application of moderate moist heat to proteins causes coagulation and shrinking. (2) Moderately cooked proteins are more easily digested than the raw ones but severe heat processing such as roasting, baking and frying affect adversely the nutritive value of the proteins of certain foods which is mainly due to the reaction of the end amino group of the essential amino acid (lysine) in the intact protein with reducing sugars present in them. This reaction is known as 'Maillard-Reaction'. (3) Not only lysine, but certain other amino acids, e.g. arginine, tryptophan and histidine, also react with reducing sugars when the heat processing is drastic hence the availability of lysine and other amino acids from the heat processed proteins is less than that from the unprocessed proteins due to Maillard-Reaction. (4) The nutritive value of the proteins of legumes is improved to a considerable extent as a result of heat processing, as heat destroys the antinutritional factors.
(2) Carbohydrates	(1) Cooking is essential for proper digestion of starch, which is the main source of calories in the diet. (2) Cooked starch is digested more readily than raw starch. (3) Sugar is converted into a combination of glucose and fructose. (4) Cooking helps the breaking of cell walls in vegetables and, thus, facilitates digestion of proteins present in them.

Nutrients	Effect of cooking
(3) Fat	(1) Cooking under ordinary household conditions has very little effect on fat. (2) Prolonged heating while frying for long periods, a part of essential fatty acids present is destroyed and toxic polymerized products are formed. (3) Fats, which are solid (congeal) at room temperature, soften in heating. (4) When heated beyond its boiling point, a fat smokes (smoke point), then flashes (flash point) and lastly it catches fire (fire point). (5) If the fat is heated for a long time, it browns and thickens. These changes are accompanied by changes in flavour, which may not be acceptable. (6) Fats and oils become rancid by action of air (oxidised), water (hydrolyzed) and enzymes.
(4) Vitamins (i) Vitamin A and Carotene	(1) There is slight destruction of vitamin A and carotene during cooking in water due to oxidation by air. (2) Frying or roasting of vegetables causes considerable losses of vitamin A and carotene. (3) As these vitamins are insoluble in water, no loss occurs by discarding cooking water.
(ii) Thiamine (B_1)	(1) During cooking, thiamine is destroyed by (i) Destruction by heat during cooking; (ii) Dissolution in the cooking water. About 20 per cent of thiamine is destroyed in normal cooking and if the food is reheated, there is additional loss. Discarding the cooking water accounts for a loss of nearly 20-50 per cent depending upon the quantity of water used in cooking. (2) The loss of thiamine during cooking under pressure is greater than that occurring during steaming. (3) Cooking soda or sodium bicarbonate should not be used, as it destroys the most of thiamine present in pulses.
(iii) Riboflavin (B_2)	During cooking, riboflavin is destroyed by - (i) Exposure of the food to strong light. (ii) Destruction by heat during cooking. (iii) Dissolution in the cooking water (due to leaching by discarding excess of cooking water). (iv) Due to the addition of sodium bicarbonate during cooking of vegetables and pulses.
(iv) Ascorbic acid (vitamin C)	Vitamin C is lost by- (i) Oxidation (due to exposure of food to air during cooking). (ii) Leaching in water (when excessive cooking water is discarded). The quantity of ascorbic acid lost during cooking of vegetables may vary widely from 10 to 60 per cent.

Nutrients	Effect of cooking
(5) Minerals	(1) Maximum quantity of Ca and P is lost during cooking when excessive cooking water is discarded.
	(2) Losses of Fe, Na, K and Mg occur by leaching, when excess of water used in cooking is discarded.
	(3) When vegetables are cut with iron knives, appreciable amount of iron are incorporated in the vegetables or when foods are roasted in cast iron pans, appreciable amounts of iron also incorporated in them.
	(4) When vegetables are cooked in hard water, appreciable amounts of calcium present in the water are incorporated with them.
	(5) NaCl used in cooking increases the sodium content of cooked food.
Therefore, some fruits and vegetables must be eaten raw, if we have to get the vitamins and minerals in them. Tomato, radish, cauliflower, cucumber, mango, green chillies, coriander leaves, mint and onion stalks can be eaten raw.	

One of the principal responsibilities of the food scientist and food technologist is to preserve food nutrients through all phases of food acquisition, processing, storage and preparation. Some simple practices which can be followed for retaining the nutritive value of fruits and vegetables are given below-

1. Wash fruits/vegetables before, but not after, cutting.

2. Vegetable salads should be prepared just before serving. Use of acid foods such as lime juice, tomatoes, vinegar or curd (as dressings in salads) prevents loss of vitamin C which is stable in acid medium.

   Fruits such as bananas are best eaten right after peeling, oranges are usually sucked after peeling, grapefruit is usually peeled and eaten, mangoes are sucked to get in the juice. In this manner, no loss of vitamin C occurs, as the fruit is not much exposed before eating.

   Some colour changes, which occur during food preparation, are undesirable and efforts should be made to minimize them. Certain fruits and vegetables such as some varieties of apples and brinjals brown when cut surfaces are exposed to air. Efforts should be made to avoid exposure of the cut surfaces to air. Brinjals should be cut in a pan filled with water, apples should be covered with sugar and/or lime juice, fruit salad can be served with custard.

3. Cut vegetables just before cooking and put into the heated oil used for seasoning and cook until just done.

4. Use a peeler to remove the skin as it removes only a very thin layer. Cut vegetable just before cooking and put into boiling water, if it is to be cooked in water.

5. Use minimum amount water for cooking, if the vegetables are to be served as such.

6. Cook foods until just done and serve immediately.

7. Cook roots and tubers, e.g., potato, sweet potato, beetroot, and colocasia, whole with skin, to retain flavour and nutrients.

8. After the first couple of minutes of cooking to permit volatile plant acids to escape, cover vegetables and cook on a low flame to reduce loss of nutrients. Avoid the use of soda as it increases the loss of vitamin C and B-complex vitamins (thiamine and riboflavin).

9. While preparing soups, cook the slowest cooking ingredient first, then add ingredients, which cook in less time, e.g., meat should be cooked half-way before adding vegetables. This procedure avoids overcooking of the vegetables.

10. Spices and other flavouring ingredients should be added to the oil used for seasoning, as these substances are soluble in fat and are thus easily dispersed in the preparation with the oil or fat.

Colour factors in foods such as anthocyanins, carotenoids chlorophylls, etc. are affected by heat. In addition to heat, the acidity or alkalinity of the cooking medium, oxygen and presence or absence of metals, also contribute to colour changes when heated. In some cases, the colour changes in foods on cooking are desirables (as in baking) while in some other cases the changes may be undesirable (as in prolonged cooking of cabbage). The cooking condition should so organized as to obtain the desired colour qualities in the cooked food.

STORAGE LIFE OF VEGETABLES

S. No.	Vegetable	Temperature (°C)	Relative humidity (%)	Storage life (weeks)
1.	Asparagus	0.0	95	3-4
2.	Beet, bunched	0.0	90	1.5
3.	Beet, topped	0.0-1.7	90-95	8-14
4.	Bitter gourd	0.6-1.7	85-90	4
5.	Brinjal	10.0-11.1	92	2-3
6.	Cabbage (Early)	0.0-1.7	92-95	4-6
	(Late)	0.0-1.7	92-95	12
7.	Carrot, topped	0.0	95	20-24
8.	Cauliflower (Snowball)	0.0-1.7	85-95	7
9.	Celery	0.0-0.6	92-95	8
10.	Colocasia	11.1-12.8	85-90	21
11.	Coriander, leaves	0.0-1.7	90	5
12.	Cucumber	10.0-11.7	92	2
13.	Hyacinth bean, pod	0.6-1.7	90	3
14.	Garlic	0.0	65	28-36
15.	Ginger	7.2-10.0	75	16-24
16.	Lettuce, leaves	0.0	95	1
17.	Lima bean, pod	4.4-7.2	90-95	1.5-2
18.	Musk melon			
	(Cantaloupe)	1.7-3.3	85-90	1.5
	(Honeydew)	7.2	85	4.5
19.	Okra	8.9	90	2
20.	Onion, bulbs	0.0	70-75	20-24
21.	Pea (Green)	0.0	88-92	2-3
22.	Pepper (Green)	7.2	85-90	3-5
	(Ripe)	5.6-7.2	90-95	2
23.	Potato	3.0-4.4	85	34
24.	Pumpkin	1.7-11.6	70-75	24-36

S. No.	Vegetable	Temperature (°C)	Relative humidity (%)	Storage life (weeks)
25.	Radish, topped	0.0	88-92	3-5
26.	Squash (Winter)	12.8-15.6	70-75	24-36
27.	Sweet corn	0.6-1.7	90-95	1
28.	Sweet potato	10.0-12.8	80-90	13-20
29.	Tapioca, root	0.0-1.7	85	23
30.	Tomato (Unripe)	8.9-10.0	85-90	4.5
	(Ripe)	7.2	90	1
31.	Turnip	0.0	90-95	8-16
32.	Water melon	7.2-15.6	80-90	2
33.	Yam	26.7	66-70	3-5

STORAGE LIFE OF FRUITS

S. No.	Fruit	Tempera-ture (°C)	Relative humidity (%)	Storage life (weeks)
	**I. Tropical and sub-tropical fruits**			
1.	Banana (i) Green (for ripening) (ii) Ripe	12-13 12-13	80-85 85-90	1-2 3
2.	Chiku (Sapota)	3-4	85-90	6-8
3.	Citrus fruits			
	(i) Mandarin (a) Coorg orange (b) Nagpur orange	6-8 5-6	85-90 85-90	10-12 10-14
	(ii) Sweet orange (a) Malta Blood Red (b) Malta Common (c) Valencia Late (d) Mosambi (e) Sathgudi	2-5 5-6 5-6 7-8 7-8	85-90 85-90 85-90 85-90 85-90	16 16 20 16 16
	(iii) Pummelo, Lime	8-10	85-90	3-6
	(iv) Lemon	8-9	85-90	8-12
	(v) Grapefruit (Marsh Seedless)	8-9	85-90	12
4.	Custard apple	5-7	85-90	5-6
5.	Dates (Ripe)	7-8	85-90	2
6.	Figs (i) Fresh (ii) Dry	0-2 0-2	85-90 65-70	4 52
7.	Grapes	0-2	80-85	6-8
8.	Guava	9-10	85-90	3
9.	Jackfruit	11-13	85-90	6
10.	Litchi	0-2	85-90	10

S. No.	Fruit	Tempera-ture (°C)	Relative humidity (%)	Storage life (weeks)
11.	Mango	8-9	85-90	4-7
12.	Mangosteen	5-7	85-90	6-7
13.	Papaya	9-10	80-85	1-2
14.	Passion-fruit	7-8	80-85	4-5
15.	Pineapple			
	(i) Mature (green)	11-13	85-90	3-4
	(ii) Ripe	8-9	85-90	4-6
16.	Pomegranate	0-2	80-85	4-6
II. Temperate fruits				
17.	Apple	0-2	85-90	16-32
18.	Apricot	0-2	80-85	2
19.	Cherry	0-2	85-90	2
20.	Peach	0-2	80-85	2-4
21.	Pear	0-1	85-90	12-26
22.	Persimmon	0-2	85-90	7
23.	Plum	0-2	85-90	4-8
24.	Strawberry	0-2	80-85	2-3

F.P.O. SPECIFICATIONS FOR FRUIT AND VEGETABLE PRODUCTS

Specifications for fruit syrup, crush, squash, nectar, cordial, juice, aerated water containing fruit juice or pulp, ready-to-serve beverage, fruit juice concentrate, jam, jelly, marmalade, cheese, preserve, chutney, etc.

Product (Prepared from any suitable fruit and variety)	Specifications	
	Minimum % of total soluble solids in final product (w/w)	Minimum % of fruit juice or prepared fruit in final product (w/w)
Fruit syrup	65	25
Crush	55	25
Squash	40	25
Fruit nectar (excluding orange and pineapple nectars)	15	20
Orange and pineapple nectars	15	40
Mango nectar	15	20
Cordial	30	25
Unsweetened juice	Natural	100
Sweetened juice	10	85
Ready-to-serve fruit beverages including aerated water containing fruit juice	10	10
Barley water	30	25 (minimum % of barley starch 0.25)
Fruit juice concentrate	32	100
Jam and fruit cheese	68	45
Fruit jelly and marmalade	65	45
Fruit preserve	68	55
Fruit chutney	50	40
Synthetic syrup/sharbat (prepared from herbs, flowers or essences)	65	-

Specification for candied and crystallized or glazed fruits

Product	Specifications	
(Prepared from any suitable fruit and variety)	Total sugar (%)	Reducing sugar as % of total sugar
Candied and crystallized or glazed fruit and peel	Not less than 70	Not less than 25

Specifications for bottled or canned fruits and vegetables

Product	Specifications
Bottled or canned fruit	1. Head space in the can shall not be more than 1.6 cm. 2. The drained weight of the fruit shall not be less than 50 per cent and the fruit should be firm. 3. No preservative shall be added. 4. No artificial colour shall be present, except in case of peas where permitted colour may be added. 5. The can shall not show any positive pressure at sea level and shall not show any sign of bacterial growth when incubated at 37°C for a week.
Bottled or canned vegetable	1. Head space in the can shall not be more than 1.6 cm. 2. The drained weight of the vegetable shall not be less than 55 per cent (50% in the case of tomatoes). 3. No preservative shall be added. 4. No artificial colour shall be present, except in case of peas where permitted colour may be added. 5. The can shall not show any positive pressure at sea level and shall not show any sign of bacterial growth when incubated at 37°C for a week.

Specification for tomato products

Product (Prepared from any suitable variety)	Minimum total soluble solids (%)	Mould Count
Tomato juice Tomato soup	5 7	Not in excess of 30 per cent of the field examined.
Tomato puree Tomato paste	9 25	Not in excess of 60 per cent of the field examined.
Tomato ketchup/sauce	25 (Minimum acidity as acetic acid 1.0%)	Not in excess of 40 per cent of the field examined. (Yeast and spores not in excess of 125 per 1/60 c.mm.; Bacteria not in excess of 100 million per c.c.)
Sauces (other than tomato and soybean)	15 (Minimum acidity as acetic acid 1.2%)	Not in excess of 40 per cent of the field examined. (Yeast and spores not in excess of 125 per 1/60 c.mm.; Bacteria not in excess of 100 million per c.c.)

Important considerations

1. In case of RTS containing lime juice the minimum content of juice shall be 5%.

2. The container of synthetic syrup shall not bear any label which leads the consumer into believing that it is a genuine fruit product. In addition the label shall have the word 'Synthetic' distinctly and clearly displayed on it. If the product declared as 'Synthetic' syrup does not contain any fruit juice as prescribed above the product shall be clearly marked as 'Contains no fruit juice'.

3. Peas or any other products which have been dried or otherwise processed before canning must be described as 'Processed' and may not be described as 'Green Fresh' or 'Garden Produce'. It shall be clearly marked as prepared from dried raw material. Dehydrated any dry fruits, if canned, shall be clearly marked as prepared from dried raw material.

4. When dry fruit is used for making jam or cheese, it shall be clearly declared so on the label.

5. Jelly made from sugar and chemical pectin shall be clearly declared as synthetic jelly.

6. When preserves are packed in sanitary top cans, the contents shall not be

less than 85 per cent of the total space of the can.

7. In case of fruit chutney, the names of fruits may not be declared on the label. However, in case of mango chutney or other chutneys the content shall be declared on the label.

8. In case of tomato puree and paste the percentage of total soluble solids shall be declared on the label.

9. In case of sauces other than tomato and soybean, the names of fruits, vegetables or dried fruits used shall be declared on the label.

10. When more than one vegetable is used in vinegar pickle the product shall be labelled as 'mixed pickles'.

11. In case of oil pickles the name of the fruit or vegetable used shall be declared on the label.

PERMISSIBLE LIMITS OF PRESERVATIVES IN FOOD PRODUCTS

S. No.	Food Product	Preservative	Parts per million (ppm)
1	2	3	4
1.	Fruit, fruit pulp or juice (not dried) for conversion into jam or crystallized, glazed or cured fruit or other products		
	(a) Cherries	Sulphur dioxide	3000
	(b) Strawberries and raspberries	- do -	2000
	(c) Other fruits	- do -	1000
2.	Fruit juice concentrate	- do -	1500
3.	Dried fruits	- do -	
	(a) Apricots, peaches, apples, pears and other fruits	- do -	2000
	(b) Raisins and sultanas	- do -	750
4.	Squashes, crushes, fruit syrups, cordials, fruit juices and barley waters	Sulphur dioxide or benzoic acid	350 600
5.	Jam, marmalade, preserve, canned cherry and fruit jelly	Sulphur dioxide or benzoic acid	40 200
6.	Crystallized, glazed or cured fruit (including candied peel)	Sulphur dioxide	150
7.	Fruit and fruit pulp not other-wise specified in the schedule	- do -	350
8.	Sweetened ready-to-serve beverages	Sulphur dioxide or benzoic acid	70 120
9.	Pickles and chutneys made from fruits or vegetables	Benzoic acid or sulphur dioxide	250 100
10.	Tomato and other sauces	Benzoic acid	750
11.	Dehydrated vegetables and dried ginger	Sulphur dioxide	2000
12.	Tomato puree and paste	Benzoic acid	250

1	2	3	4
13.	Syrups and sharbats	Sulphur dioxide or benzoic acid	350 600
14.	Cider	Sulphur dioxide	200
15.	Wines	- do -	450
16.	Beer	- do -	70
17.	Brewed ginger beer	Benzoic acid	120
18.	Sugar, glucose, gur and khandsari	Sulphur dioxide	70
19.	Cornflour and suchlike starches	Sulphur dioxide	100
20.	Corn syrup	Sulphur dioxide	450
21.	Gelatin	- do -	1000
22.	Coffee extract	Sulphur dioxide	450
23.	Cheese or processed cheese	Sorbic acid or its sodium, potassium and calcium salts (calculated as sorbic acid) or Nisin	1000 1000
24.	Flour confectionery	Sorbic acid or its sodium salt	1500
25.	Hard boiled sugar confectionery	Sulphur dioxide	350
26.	Sausages and sausage meat containing raw meat, cereals and condiments	Sulphur dioxide	450
27.	Cooked pickled meat including ham and bacon	Sodium or potassium nitrate or commercial saltpetre (calculated as sodium nitrate)	200 500
28.	Smoked fish (in wrappers)	Sorbic acid	Only wrappers may be impregnated with sorbic acid

FOOD TOXINS

A large majority of the population in developing countries are ignorant and are guided by tradition, superstition and taboos in the use of less familiar foods, some of which may contain toxic compounds. As a result of this, diseases and deaths due to acute or chronic poisoning occur frequently in these countries through the habitual consumption of foodstuffs containing toxic substances. These include natural toxins, microbial toxins, environmental contaminants arising from processing, accidental contaminants, and chemical additives.

(1) Natural toxins: Some plants and animals used as food by man contain substances having toxic properties. Pulses contain a number of toxic substances such as protease inhibitors, lathyrogens, flavism causing agents, cyanogens, haemagglutinins and saponins. Some of these are also present in other foods, e.g., protease inhibitors in cereals and potatoes, saponins in spinach and asparagus, goitrogens (which cause hypothyroidism and thyroid enlargement) in rapeseed, mustard, cabbage and related species. Oxalic acid, a constituent of rhubarb, spinach and beet, may cause oxalic poisoning in certain individuals.

The inhibitor of trypsin which is proteinous in nature suppresses the release of amino acids and thus interferes with the normal growth of animals fed with such pulses. Raw soybean leads to pancreatic hyperplasia in rats and chicks, and increases the production of pancreatic enzymes, leading to substantial removal of endogenous N. Trypsin inhibitors are present in almost all the legumes like kidney beans and navy beans, that are quite rich in cystine, accounting for about 30-40 per cent of the total cystine content of the food. But the inhibitor makes the cystine unavailable. Heat treatment destroys the inhibitor.

Haemagglutinins are proteins in nature, and are sometimes referred to as phytoagglutinins or lectins. They occur widely in leguminous seeds like kidney beans and field beans, and have the ability to agglutinate the red blood cells from various species of animals. They may also combine with the cells lining the intestinal wall, causing an impairment with the absorption of amino acids. But most of these factors are heat-liable, and lose their deleterious effects as a result of heat treatment. Cyanogenic glycosides cause cyanide poisoning. On hydrolysis of the glycoside by the enzyme ß-glucosidase,

405

hydrogen cyanide (hydrocyanic acid) is liberated in the legumes like lima beans and linseed. Cooking inactivates these enzymes. A cyanide content of 10-20 mg per 100 g of pulses is considered safe and many legumes, except lima bean (*Phaseolus lunatus*), contain cyanide within this limit. Saponins are bitter tasting, foam-producing glycosides of high molecular weight. These have been reported in soybean, sword bean (*Canavalia gladiata*) and jackbean (*Canavalia ensiformis*). Not all saponins are poisonous; the poisonous ones are called sapotoxins. They occur in peanuts and soybeans with varying degrees of haemolytic and foam-producing activity. Toxic saponins cause nausea and vomiting and can be removed by soaking the beans prior to cooking. Alkaloids are known to occur in the seeds of many legumes but they are relatively innocuous.

Some compounds present in pulses appear to fix iodine thus producing a state of iodine deficiency in the thyroid, and eventually goitre. Two toxic substances in legumes produce serious pathological conditions. These are a factors in khesari dhal which causes lathyrism and a haemolytic factor in *Vicia faba* causing favism.

Lathyrism is a disease which paralyses the lower limbs. β-*Oxylyl-amino-alanine* (BOAA), a free amino acid compou,d is the factor, present in *Lathyrus sativus* (Khesari dhal), responsible for spastic paralysis with nervous symptoms. Its incidence is higher in males than in females. The disease is associated with consumption of khesari dhal and occurs commonly in poor families. Even when other crops fail, this legume thrives and thus in times of scarcity poor people are forced to eat this dhal. However, lathyrism develops only when the consumption of dhal is high (300 g daily), it is taken for a long time (6 months or more), and the diet does not contain adequate quantities or cereals. In lathyrism, the toxic substance interferes with the formation of normal collagen fibre in the connective tissue. The concentration of the toxin depends upon its stage of development. This toxin is inactivated by heat treatment. BOAA is water soluble and leaches out easily following the steeping process. Soaking the grains in water, steaming for 15-20 minute and sun-drying, remove about 80-90% of the toxin. A genetic approach has also led to a low-toxin strain. The disease can be prevented by ensuring a reasonable balance between intake of khesari dhal and other foodstuffs.

Favism is caused by eating broad beans or by inhaling the pollen of its flower. Divicine and Isouramil are glycosides containing pyrimidine bases, present in broad beans or faba beans (*Vicia faba*). They cause a reduction in glutathione content and glucose 6-phosphate dehydrogenase activity in RBC and, hence, may be responsible for the development of favism, which is a haemolytic anaemia. In severe cases death may occur within 24-48 hours of the onset of the attack. These constituents, in some legumes like soybean protein, interfere with availability of minerals like Zn, Cu, Mn and Fe by binding with these metals.

They are partially eliminated by heat treatment or by chelating agents such as EDTA.

Djenkolic Acid is a substance present in djenkol beans availab.e in Indonesia, Java and Sumatra. In the concentration of 1.2 per cent, it leads to acute kidney trouble.

Mimosine or Leucenine an unusual amino acid that occurs in the seeds and leaves of *Leucaena glauca* causes blindness.

Antivitamin factors: Kidney beans contain anti-vitamin E that produces recrosis of liver and muscular dystrophy. Linseed contains an anti-pyridoxine factor that depresses growth. The factor responsible is L-amino-D-proline that occurs as a peptide linatine in combination with glutamic acid. L-amino-D-proline is about 4 times as active as linatine. The factor could be eliminated by extracting the meal with water. Raw soybean containing lipoxidase, oxidizes Vitamin A and carotene present in foods, resulting in lowered plasma Vitamin A and carotene. Unheated isolated soya protein is found to have an anti-Vitamin D factor producing rickets in experimental animals. Autoclaving the meal destroys the anti-Vitamin D present.

Amylase inhibitors interfere with starch digestion and have been extracted from 12 varieties of beans, but not from cowpeas, chickpeas and lentils. Although the exact biological significance of amylase inhibitors is not known, presence of undigested starch has been reported in the faces of rats fed raw beans containing high amylase inhibitor activity. It may perhaps get destroyed on cooking just as other inhibitors.

Legumes contain considerable amount of phytic acid that may affect the absorption of minerals by forming insoluble salts. In kidney beans, 99% of the total Phytic acid is in water-soluble form, and it is, therefore, easy to decrease or remove its level in the product.

Thiocyanates and isothiocyanates yielded by hydrolysis of thioglycosides present in certain oil seeds, viz. Rapeseed, mustard etc., act as goitrogenic. Phenolic Glycosides present in the red skin of groundnut have been found to possess goitrogenic properties. Possibly, the phenolic metabolites formed are preferentially iodinated and deprive the thyroid of available iodine. Raw soybean results in marked enlargement of thyroid gland. Heat treatment helps in overcoming the problem. Groundnuts are also known to have goitrogenic properties. Direct heat treatment prevents further liberation of goitrogenic agent but it will not destroy any of the goitrogenic substances which have been released prior to heat treatment.

Soaking, heating or fermentation of pulses can reduce or eliminate most of the toxic factors in them. Correct application of heat in cooking can eliminate most toxic factors without impairment of nutritional value. Heat causes denaturation of the proteins responsible for trypsin inhibition and haemagglutination and of the enzyme causing hydrolysis of cyanogenic glycosides. Fermentation also destroys toxic factors and yields more digestible products of high nutritive value.

Tissues of certain marine animals contain toxic substances which cause adverse responses when eaten. These substances are not destroyed by heating. Some algae, e.g., *Gymnodinium* and *Gonyaulax* are toxic.

(2) Microbial toxins

(i) **Mycotoxins:** Mycotoxins are metabolites elaborated by a variety of fungi such as Aspergillus, *Penicillium, Rhizopus* and *Fusarium*. Ingestion of the toxin-containing food causes the syndrome known as 'mycotoxicosis'. The first type of mycotoxicosis recorded was that due to rye ergot (*Claviceps purpurea*). Food grains, especially bajra, rye and jowar, get infected with the ergot fungus, and eating the infected grain causes ergotism. Mycotoxins produced by moulds such as *Aspergillus flavus* and *A. parasiticus* are known as aflatoxins. *Aspergillus* spp. develop in many foods, particularly groundnut and cottonseed, and their cakes and flour. Among 14 chemically related toxins, aflatoxin B is the one most frequently found in food and is a well known carcinogen. Incidence of liver cancer due to aflatoxin is high in our country.

(ii) **Bacterial toxins:** Bacterial spoilage of foods may be of two types, i.e., Food Intoxication and Food Infection. Food intoxication refers to illness caused by the consumption of bacterial toxin formed in the food, while food infection refers to illness caused by the entrance of bacteria into the body through ingestion of contaminated foods. The major types of food-bornn intoxication and infection are given below:

(A) Intoxications

1. **Staphylococcal intoxication** (Staphylococcal enterotoxicosis): caused by an enterotoxin produced by *Staphylococcus aureus*;

2. **Botulism**: caused by a neurotoxin produced by *Clostridium botulinum*.

(B) Infections

1. Salmonellosis: due to endotoxin of *Salmonella* spp.;

2. *Clostridium perfringens* illness: due to an enterotoxin released during sporulation of *Clostridium perfringens* in the intestinal tract;

3. *Bacillus cereus* gastroenteritis: caused by an exoenterotoxin released during lysis of *Bacillus cereus* in the intestinal tract;

4. Enteropathogenic *Escherichia coli* infection: caused by several types of *E. coli* some invasive and some enterotoxigenic;

5. Yersiniosis, Shigellosis, *Vibrio parahaemolyticus* infection, etc.

Staphylococcal food poisoning is perhaps the most commonly occurring food-borne disease, but it is much less serious than botulism. The illness usually starts 2-6 hours after ingestion of the contaminated food and is manifested by the onset of nausea, vomiting, abdominal pain and diarrhoea. In severe cases, dehydration and collapse may occur. Cooking kills the staphylococci but the toxin may still remain. Poisoning can be avoided by preventing the infection of food, destruction of the bacteria by heat and restriction of their growth by refrigeration.

The disease caused by the toxins of *C. botulinum* is known as botulism. The toxins which are produced after an incubation period of 18-36 hours act on the nervous system. They are potent poisons. A dose of less than 1.0 µg is fatal to man and death occurs in 1 or 2 days. The toxins are produced only under anaerobic conditions, such as found in canned products in airtight packages. *C. botulinum* survives at freezing temperature but does not grow. Hence, frozen foods do not present the hazard of botulism. The toxins causing botulism are thermolabile and lose their activity on heating at 80oC for 30 minutes. Hence, canned foods, low in acid, could be hazardous if they have not been sufficiently heated to kill the spores of the organism which might be present.

Food-poisoning bacteria grow in a food and infect the persons eating it. *Salmonella* spp., *Vibrio parahaemolyticus*, *Escherichia coli*, *Yersinia enterocolitica*, *Clostridium perfringens* and *Compylobacter jejuni* belong to this group.

Salmonella spp. are ubiquitous, but they are more common in foods such as pork, poultry and eggs, and products containing them. The illness caused by this organism is known as salmonellosis. It starts 12-36 hours after ingestion of food and continues for 1-7 days. The symptoms are diarrhoea, abdominal pain, vomiting and fever. Infants are more susceptible to this infection than adults. Acids and temperature tend to destroy the microorganism.

Clostridium perfringens grows in the alimentary canal producing the poison some 8-12 hours after the ingestion of contaminated food. The symptoms of illness are diarrhoea, abdominal pain, and nausea, but rarely vomiting, but there is no fever. The spores of the organism can withstand heating at 100°C for one hour, but there are marked variations between strains.

It has been reported that gastroenteritis in humans is caused by food contaminated with the enterococcus, *Streptococcus faecalis*, which is frequently found in the human intestinal tract. Poisoning is caused by inadequately refrigerated food contaminated with the organism.

Bacilius cereus, a Gram-positive, aerobic, spore-forming organism, has been reported to be the etiologic agent in numerous food poisoning outbreaks. The spores are heat-resistant and survive a considerable degree of cooking. The toxin is produced after an incubation period of 8-16 hours and is active for 12-24 hours. Abdominal pain, diarrhoea, vomiting and nausea are the ill-effects of the toxin.

(iii) Viruses: Several viruses are known to be transmitted through food and water and cause infection in humans and animals, e.g., poliomyelitis virus through milk and hepatitis virus (causing jaundice) through consuming sewage-contaminated water and sea foods. The onset of symptoms occurs a long time after intake. Some viruses are known to survive even at low temperature and can cause problems when refrigerated food is used without proper processing.

Some food-borne diseases caused by pathogenic organisms are listed in the table below.

Food-borne diseases and causative organisms

	Organism	Foods infected	Toxic effect/disease
A. Fungi			
(i)	*Aspergillus flavus*	Corn and ground nut	Liver damage and cancer
(ii)	*Claviceps purpurea*	Rye and pearl millet	Ergotism (burning sensation in extremities, peripheral gangrene)
(iii)	*Fusarium sporotrichiodis*	Cereals	Elementary toxic aleukia
(iv)	*Penicillium islandicum*	Rice, aonla	Liver damage
B. Bacteria			
(i)	*Bacillus cereus*	Cereal products	Nausea, vomitting, abdominal pain
(ii)	*Clostridium botulinus*	Defectively processed meat and fish	Botulism (muscular paralysis, death due to respiratory failure)
(iii)	*C. perfringens*	Defectively processed pre-cooked meat	Nausea, abdominal pain and diarrhoea
(iv)	*Salmonella* spp.	Defectively processed meat, fish and egg products, raw vegetables grown on sewage	Salmonellosis (vomiting, diarrhoea and fever)
(v)	*Shigella sonnia*	Foods kept exposed in unhygienic surroundings	Bacillary dysentery

	Organism	Foods infected	Toxic effect/disease
(vi)	*Staphylococcus aureus*	-do-	Increased salivation, vomiting, abdominal pain and diarrhoea
(vii)	*Streptococcus pyogenes*	-do-	Scarlet fever, septic sore throat
C. Parasites			
(i)	*Trichinella spiralis*	Pork and pork products	Nausea, vomiting, diarrhoea, colic and muscular pains (Trichinosis)
(ii)	*Ascaris lumbricoides*	Vegetables grown on sewage	Ascariasis
(iii)	*Entamoeba histolytica*	-do-	Amoebic dysentery
(iv)	*Ancylostoma duodenale* (Hookworm)	-do-	Epigastric pain, loss of blood in stools, anaemia

(3) Contamination during handling and processing

These include residues that become part of food as a result of processing, handling and distribution of food.

Fumigants are used to sterilize food under conditions in which steam heating is impractical. Ethylene oxide is a commonly used fumigant which reacts with food constituents to produce toxic products or destroys essential nutrients. It reacts with inorganic chlorides to form ethylenechlorohydrin which is toxic.

Various solvents are used for the extraction of oil from oilseeds. But solvents like trichloroethylene react with the foodstuff being processed, with the formation of a toxic products and are not used now.

During processing of foods their lipids can undergo a number of changes. On prolonged heating, oxidative and polymerization reactions take place which decrease the nutritive value of the processed product.

Smoking of meat and fish for preservation and flavouring is an old practice.

This processing contaminates the food with polycyclic aromatic hydrocarbons such as benzopyrene, many of which are carcinogenic.

Metals are one of the many unintentional contaminants of food. When present beyond small quantities they are toxic. They find their way into foods through air, water, soil, industrial pollution and other routes. Metals may enter foods from utensils also. Enamelware of poor quality contributes antimony and galvanized utensils zinc. A major source of tin contamination is tin plate which is used for making containers for all types of processed foods. Canned foods, if acidic, and foods stored in tins after opening, change in colour or develop a metallic flavour that is unpalatable. A small quantity of the metal is dissolved when food is cooked in aluminium utensils but this is not harmful. Copper is an essential trace element required by the human body but copper-contaminated food is toxic.

Lubricants, packing material, etc., also contaminate food. Further, a number of chemicals are intentionally added to foods to improve their nutritional value, maintain freshness, impart desirable properties or aid in processing.

Toxic effects in humans of consuming foods contaminated with toxic metals and chemicals are shown in the table below.

Toxicity of some metals and chemicals in food

S. No.	Metal/ Chemical	Food involved	Toxic effect
1.	Arsenic	Fruits sprayed with lead arsenate	Dizziness, chills, cramps, paralysis leading to death
2.	Barium	Foods poison contaminated by rat poison (barium carbonate)	Violent peristalsis, muscular twitching and convulsions
3.	Cadmium	Fruit juices, soft drinks, etc., in contact with cadmium plated vessels	Excessive salivation, liver and kidney damage, prostate cancer, multiple fractures
4.	Cobalt	Water, beer	Cardiac failure

S. No.	Metal/ Chemical	Food involved	Toxic effect
5.	Copper	Acid foods in contact with tranished copperware	Vomiting, diarrhoea, abdominal pain
6.	Lead	Some processed foods	Paralysis, brain damage
7.	Mercury	Mercury fungicide treated seed grains or mercury contaminated fish	Paralysis, brain damage and blindness
8.	Tin	Canned foods	Colic, vomiting, photophobia
9.	Zinc	Foods stored in galvanized ironware	Dizziness, vomiting
10.	Pesticides	All types of foods	Acute or chronic poisoning causing damage to liver, kidney, brain and nerves leading to death
11.	Diethyl-stilbestrol	Meat of stilbestrol-fed animals	Teratogenesis, carcinogenesis
12.	Antibiotics	Meat of animals fed antibiotics	Drug resistance, hardening of arteries, heart disease

Permissible limits of some toxic elements

S. No.	Element	Foodstuff	Parts per million (by weight)
1.	Arsenic	**(i) Milk**	0.1
		(ii) Beverages	
		Soft drinks intended for consumption after dilution (except carbonated water)	0.5
		Carbonated water	0.25
		(iii) Food additives	
		Preservatives, antioxidants, emulsifying and stabilizing agents and synthetic food colours	3.0
		(iv) Other	
		foods Icecream and similar frozen confections	0.5
		Dehydrated onions, edible gelatin, liquid pectin	2.0
		Chicory (dired or roasted)	4.0
		Dried herbs, fining and clearing agents, solid pectin all grades, spices	5.0
		Food colouring other than synthetic colouring	5.0 on dry colouring matter
		Hard boiled sugar confectionery	1.0
		(v) Foods not specified	1.1
2.	Copper	**(i) Beverages**	
		Soft drinks excluding concentrates and carbonated water	7.0
		Carbonated water	1.5
		Concentrates for soft drinks	20.0

S. No.	Element	Foodstuff	Parts per million (by weight)
		(ii) Other foods	
		Chicory (dried or roasted), coffee beans, flavourings, pectin liquid	30.0
		Colouring	30.0 on dry colouring matter
		Edible gelatin	30.0
		Tomato ketchup	50.0 on dried total solids
		Yeast and yeast products	60.0 on dry matter
		Cocoa powder	70.0 on fat-free substance
		Tomato puree, paste, juice powder, and cocktails	100.0 on dried tomato solids
		Tea	150.0
		Pectin, solid	300.0
		Hard boiled sugar confectionery	5.0
		(iii) Foods not specified	30.0
3.	Lead	**(i) Beverages**	
		Concentrated soft drinks (but not including concentrates used in the manufacture of soft drinks)	0.5
		Fruit and vegetable juices (including tomato juice, but not including lime juice and lemon juice)	1.0
		Concentrates used in the manufacture of soft drinks, lime juice and lemon juice	2.0
		Baking powder	1.0

S. No.	Element	Foodstuff	Parts per million (by weight)
		(ii) Other foods	
		Anhydrous dextrose and dextrose monohydrate, edible oils and fats, refined white sugar (sulphated ash not exceeding 0.03%)	0.5
		Ice-cream and similar frozen confections, canned fish, canned meats, edible gelatin, meat extracts and hydrolyzed protein, dried or dehydrated vegetables (other than onion)	1.0
		All types of suar, sugar syrup, invert sugar	5.0
		Cocoa powder	50.0 on dry fat-free substance
		Yeast and yeast products	5.0 on dry matter
		Tea, dehydrated onions, dried herbs and spices, flavourings, alginic acid, alginates, agar and similar products derived from seaweed	10.0 on dry matter
		Liquid pectin, chemicals not otherwise specified, used as ingredients or in the preparation or processing of foods	10.0
		Food colouring other than caramel	10.0 on dry matter
		Solid pectin	50.0
		Hard boiled sugar confectionery	2.0
		(iii) Foods not specified	2.5
4.	Tin	**(i) Processed and canned products**	5.0
		(ii) Hard boiled sugar confectionery	5.0
		(iii) Foods not specified	250.0
5.	Zinc	**(i) Ready to drink beverages**	5.0
		(ii) Edible gelatin	100.0

S. No.	Element	Foodstuff		Parts per million (by weight)
		(iii)	**Fruit products covered under the Fruit Products Order 1955**	50.0
		(iv)	**Hard boiled sugar confectionery**	5.0
		(v)	**Foods not specified**	50.0

Permissible limits of certain insecticides in foods

S. No.	Insecticide	Mode of application	Permissible limit
1.	Aluminium phosphide	As tablets for stored grain	Leaves no residue
2.	BHC	As dust for spraying or impregnation of containers, treatment of storage premises or surface of bagged grain	3 ppm
3.	Carbon tetrachloride :	As fumigant for foodgrains, cereals and pulses	Leaves no residue
4.	DDT	As spray for treatment of storage premises	3 ppm
5.	Ethylene dibromide	As fumigant	Leaves no residue
6.	Ethylene dichloride	As fumigant for cereals and pulses	Leaves no residue
7.	Hydrocyanic acid gas	As fumigant	10 ppm
8.	Malathion	As spray or dust for treatment of storage premises or surface of bagged grain	3 ppm
9.	Methoxychlor	As spray or dust for treatment of storage premises or surface of bagged grain	3 ppm
10.	Methyl bromide	As fumigant	Inorganic residue 50 ppm as bromine
11.	Pyrethrum	As spray on green vegetables	10 ppm

FOOD ADULTERATION

Adulteration of foodstuffs is commonly practised in India by traders. In order to protect the health of the consumer, the Government of India promulgated the Prevention of Food Adulteration Act (P.F.A. Act) in 1954 which prohibits the manufacture, sale and distribution of not only adulterated foods but also foods contaminated with toxicants and misbranded foods. A Central Food Laboratory established under the Act is located at Kolkata for the purpose of testing suspected food products. Besides, the Central Food Technological Research Institute, Mysore has been recognized as another laboratory for the testing of adulterated foods.

According to the Prevention of Food Adulteration Act 1954, an article of food shall be deemed to be adulterated:

1. If the article sold by a vendor is not of the nature, substance or quality demanded by the purchaser and is to his prejudice, or is not of the nature, substance or quality which it purports or is represented to be;

2. If the article contains any other substance which affects, or if the article is so processed as to affect, injuriously the nature, substance or quality thereof;

3. If any inferior or cheaper substance has been substituted wholly or in part for the article, so as to affect injuriously the nature, substance or quality thereof;

4. If any constituent of the article has been wholly or in part abstracted so as to affect injuriously the nature, substance or quality thereof;

5. If the article has been prepared, packed or kept under insanitary conditions whereby it has become contaminated or injurious to health;

6. If the article consists wholly or in part of any filthy, putrid, disgusting, rotten, decomposed or diseased animal or vegetable substance or is insect-infested or otherwise unfit for human consumption;

7. If the article is obtained from a diseased animal;

8. If the article contains any poisonous or other ingredient which renders it injurious to health;

9. If the container of the article is composed, whether wholly or in part, of any

poisonous or deleterious substance which renders its contents injurious to health;

10. If any colouring matter other than that prescribed in respect thereof and in amounts not within the prescribed limits of variability is present in the article;

11. If the article contains any prohibited preservative or permitted preservative in excess of the prescribed limits;

12. If the quality or purity of the article falls below the prescribed standard or its constituents are present in quantities which are in excess of the prescribed limits of variability.

Common food adulterants

Foodstuff		Adulterant
(A)	**Milk and milk products**	
(i)	Milk, liquid	Water refined oil or fat after removal of milk fat, skim milk reconstituted from skim milk powder
(ii)	Milk powder	Starch, dextrins
(iii)	Cream	Other fats
(iv)	Ice cream	Non-permitted colour, artificial sweeteners, other fats and jelling agents
(v)	Butter and ghee	Hydrogenated fats
(B)	**Vegetable oils and fats**	
(i)	Vanaspati	Animal fat and other high melting fats
(ii)	Vegetable oils	Argemone oil, mineral oil, cheap non-edible oils
(C)	**Spices and condiments**	
(i)	Whole turmeric	Coating with lead chromate or coal tar dye
(ii)	Turmeric powder	Coal tar colour, yellow earth, starch or talc coloured yellow with coal tar dye

	Foodstuff	Adulterant
(iii)	Curry powder	Starch coloured brown with coal tar dye
(iv)	Coriander seed	Other seeds coloured green
(v)	Coriander seed powder	Powdered bran or sawdust coloured green with dye
(vi)	Chilli powder	Starch coloured red with coal tar dye
(vii)	Mustard seed	Argemone seeds
(viii)	Cumin seed	Artificial cumin seed-like product
(ix)	Black pepper	Dried papaya seeds
(x)	Asafoetida	Resins and other plant gums
(D)	**Cereals**	
(i)	Wheat and rice	Stones
(ii)	Wheat flour	Tapioca flour, talc, chalk powder
(iii)	Semolina	Tapioca semolina
(E)	**Pulses**	
(i)	Bengal gram dhal	Khesari dhal
(ii)	Red gram dhal	Khesari dhal coloured yellow with dye
(iii)	Bengal gram flour	Topioca flour or starch coloured yellow with dye
(F)	**Sweetening agents and soft drinks**	
(i)	Honey	Coloured invert sugar syrup

	Foodstuff	Adulterant
(ii)	Soft drinks	Artificial sweeteners (saccharin), mineral acid other than phosphoric acid
(G)	**Beverages**	
(i)	Coffee powder	Exhausted coffee powder, starch, roasted dates and tamarind seeds
(ii)	Tea	Other leaves with added colour
(H)	**Miscellaneous**	
(i)	Processed arecanut	Other seeds or nuts broken and coloured

It is evident that according to P.F.A. Act of 1954, food adulteration includes: (a) intentional addition, substitution or abstraction of substances which adversely affect the quality of foods, (b) incidental contamination of foods with deleterious substances such as toxins, insecticides, pathogenic bacteria and fungi, due to ignorance, negligence or lack of proper storage facilities, and (c) contamination of the food with harmful microorganisms during production, storage and handling.

Thus addition of adulterants could either be intentional or incidental. Some adulterants added intentionally to food products so as to increase the margin of profit.

Types of Adulterants

S. No.	Type	Substances added
(1)	Intentional substances	Sand Marble Chips Stones Mud Other filth Talc, Chalk powder, Starch, Salt Water to milk Mineral oil to edible oil Harmful colours
(2)	Incidental adulterants	Pesticide residues Tin from can Dropping of rodents Larvae in foods
(3)	Metallic contamination	Arsenic from pesticides Lead from water Mercury from effluents from chemical industries Tin from cans.

Simple tests for common food adulterants

	Foodstuff	Adulterant	Test
1.	Milk, curd, khoa, ghee, butter	Starch	Add a drop of iodine solution to a little of the sample. Blue colour indicates added starch in any form. (Iodine solution is prepared by dissolving 2.5 g of iodine crystals and 3 g of potassium iodide in sufficient water to make the volume 100 ml.)

	Foodstuff	Adulterant	Test
2.	Milk or curd	Cane sugar	Add 0.1 g of resorcin and 1 ml of concentrated hydrochloric acid to 10 ml of the sample and boil. A rose-red colour indicates sugar.
3.	Ghee or butter	Vanaspati	Dissolve a pinch of cane sugar in 10 ml concentrated hydrochloric acid taken in a glass stoppered test tube. Add 10 ml of the melted ghee, stopper the bottle and shake vigorously for two minutes. Allow to stand till 2 layers separate. If the lower layer turns pink or red, the ghee contains vanaspati.
4.	Edible oils	Argemone oil	Shake 5 ml of filtered oil with 2 ml of concentrated hydrochloric acid in a test tube and warm the mixture for 5 minutes in a water bath with occasional shaking. Decant off the oil from the top and add to the remaining acid layer 1 ml of 10% ferric chloride solution, gently. Rotate the tube between the palms of the hands to mix the solutions and heat the mixture in boiling water bath for 10 minutes. Formation of a reddish brown precipitate or crystals indicates argemone oil.

	Foodstuff	Adulterant	Test
		Mineral oil	Mix 2 ml of oil with 2 ml of 3% alcoholic potassium hydroxide, heat in boiling water bath for 15 minutes, add 10 ml of water. Any turbidity indicates mineral oil.
		Castor oil	Dissolve oil in petroleum ether in a test tube and cool the test tube in ice-salt mixture. Turbidity within 5 minutes indicates castor oil.
5.	Soft drink	Mineral acid other than phosphoric acid	Soak a strip of filter paper in a 0.1% solution of metanil yellow and then dry. Dip one end of paper into the soft drink. Wetted portion turns violet if mineral acid is present.
6.	Coffee powder	Starch (toasted bread crumbs, rye, wheat, peas, etc.)	Make decoction of the coffee, decolourize it by adding potassium permanganate and then add a drop of iodine solution. Blue colour indicates starch.
		Roasted dates and tamarind seeds	Shake powder with 2% sodium hydroxide (or washing soda) solution. Formation of reddish colour indicates tamarind seeds.
7.	Tea (dust/ leaves)	Artificially coloured foreign matter or exhausted tea leaves	Sprinkle the tea on a sheet of wet white paper. Pink or red spots appearing on the paper indicate added colour.

	Foodstuff	Adulterant	Test
8.	Honey	Commercial invert sugar (mixture of glucose and fructose)	Fiehe's test. Mix about 5 g of honey with 10 ml of ether in a mortar, using a pestle. Decant off the ether extract into a china dish. Repeat extraction twice with more ether and collect all the extracts in the same dish. Allow the ether to evaporate off at room temperature. To the residue in the dish, add a large drop of 1% solution of freshly sublimed resorcinol in concentrated hydrochloric acid. Immediate appearance of a cherry-red colour indicates invert sugar.
9.	Foodgrains and nuts (e.g., ground nut)	Mould (infection)	Grains and nuts appear discoloured and shrunken and usually have an off taste and float on water.
10.	Wheat, bajra and other foodgrains	Ergot (a poisonous fungus)	Long irregular black grains indicate ergot. Treat with 2% salt solution. Ergot will float and sound grains will sink.
11.	Foodgrains and pulses (whole and ground)	Insect, larvae (infestation)	Visual examination. Excessive infestation result in unpleasant odour and taste and the grains float on water.
12.	Wheat flour, semolina (suji), Bengal gram flour (beans)	Sand, grit	To a little of the sample in a dry test tube add 5 ml of carbon tetrachloride and shake well. Sand and grit will settle at the bottom, leaving flour on top.

Foodstuff	Adulterant	Test
	Chalk powder	Treat sample with hot dilute hydrochloric acid. Bubbling of gas indicates carbon dioxide from chalk or other carbonates.
13. Whole black masoor and Bengal gram	Khesari pulse (whole)	On visual examination wedge-like-shapes seen. Also gives brown colour with hydrochloric acid in 15 to 30 minutes.
14. Split and dehusked pulses (arhar dhal and Bengal gram)	(a) Khesari pulse	Visual examination.
	(b) Metanil yellow	Shake portion of sample with cold or warm water. The water becomes yellowish and on treatment with a few drops of conc. hydrochloric acid turns magenta red.
15. Turmeric (whole and powdered) and mixed spices (powdered)	Metanil yellow	Shake sample with some water. Dilute water till it is almost colourless and then add a few drops of conc. hydrochloric acid. Magenta red colour seen if dye present.
16. Powdered spices (turmeric, chilli, coriander, garam masala, curry powder, etc.)	Sand, grit, talc	Shake up a little of the sample in a dry test tube with 5 ml of carbon tetrachloride. Allow to settle. Sand, talc and grit will sink to the bottom, leaving spice on top.

	Foodstuff	Adulterant	Test
17.	Mustard and rai seeds	Argemone seeds	Examination under magnifying glass shows small seeds resembling mustard but blacker, more rough and not uniformly smooth and round.
18.	Mustard, rai, cumin seeds, khus-khus, etc.	Stones and foreign matter	Visual examination.

Note: *Adulteration detected as above needs to be confirmed by analysis by a recognized food testing laboratory; the above tests in no way replace the prescribed laboratory tests.*

Statutory Provisions for Quality Control in India

Statutory provisions came into existence for a number of reasons:

(i)   To maintain the quality of food produced in the country;

(ii) To prevent exploitation of the consumer by the sellers;

(iii) To safeguard the health of the consumers;

(iv) To establish criteria for quality of food products, since more and more foods were eaten in processed, rather than in natural forms. This has resulted in the inability of the consumer to identify the quality of the contents that could be identified easily.

1. **Prevention of Food Adulteration Act 1954 and Rules 1955 (PFA Act) -** The Prevention of Food adulteration (PFA) Act was promulgated in 1954 and is primarily intended to check adulteration of foodstuffs available in the country. The rules and regulations that are formulated for operation of this Act are directed to make available pure food materials devoid of adulterants and contaminants to the Indian population at large. Any food not conforming to these standards is said to be adulterated. The rules include, among others, specifications for a large number of raw and processed foods which are of main importance in the trade. The Central Government has appointed to consider all aspects pertaining to PFA including revision and formulation of standards for various articles of foods. The various provisions of PFA Act formulated at Central level have to be implemented at States and local bodie' levels.

2. **Fruit Products Order 1955 (FPO)-** Regulates the manufacture, storage and sale of fruit and vegetable products.

    The Fruit Products Order 1955 was issued by the Department of Food, Ministry of Food Processing Industries under the powers vested in the Government under the Essential Commodities Act to ensure the quality of fruit and vegetable products. This order controls Production, distribution and quality of the Fruit & Vegetable Products manufactured in the country as well as Registration, Licensing and Operation of manufacturing units. Under the FPO, the Central Government has constituted an expert committee called Central Fruit Products Advisory Committee to advise the Government on standards and policy matters pertaining to Fruit & Vegetable Preservation Industry.

The various provisions of the FPO are being Implemented by the Director, Fruit & Vegetable Preservation attached to the Ministry of Food Processing Industries with the assistance of Zonal deputy directors stationed at Chennai, Mumbai, New Delhi and Kolkata and large number of technical staff. 'FPO' Mark is given to each processor, after the grant of licence for manufacturing fruit or vegetable products, after the inspection of the factory for hygiene and sanitation. FPO Mark and licence number is required by law to be exhibited on labels of each processed item along with other information as laid down in the FPO Rules. Continuous inspection scheme and pre shipment inspection scheme are being exercised under the FPO especially regarding export oriented Fruit & Vegetable Products.

The FPO specifications cover methods of preservation, permissible colours in the preparations and also the minimum quality requirements of the final products. Fruit and vegetable products which do not conform to the FPO specifications are considered adulterated.

3. **Agricultural Produce (Grading and Marketing) Act 1937 (AGMARK) -** This is one of the oldest Food Laws promulgated in the country to provide for quality control of agricultural produce through grading and marketing. This Act provides compulsory standards for export and voluntary standards for vegetable oils, ghee, butter, cream, essential oils, guar, egg, groundnuts, potatoes, fruits, pulses, rice, condiments, spices, etc. These standards are formulated on the physical and chemical characteristics of food, both the natural as well as those acquired during processing. This Act is administered by the Directorate of Marketing & Inspection with Agricultural Marketing Advisor to the Government of India, Faridabad, as its Chairman. "Agricultural Produce" includes all produce of Agriculture or Horticulture & all articles of food or drink wholly or partly manufactured from any such produce. A number of grading standards of raw or processed agricultural or Horticultural produce have been brought out by the AGMARK. The AGMARK seal issued by the Directorate of Marketing and Inspection of the Government of India is thus a stamp of good quality. The Directorate of Marketing & Inspection operates a certification scheme under AGMARK for scheduled articles covered under the ACT. Any organization or packer who wants to use 'AGMARK' symbol on the lable of the sample containers can apply to the authorities. The authorities after inspection and ensuring that the necessary facilities like equipment, laboratory, etc., are available, allows them to use AGMARK symbol which ensures that the quality standards laid down for that product under AGMARK have been complied with. This gives a sort

quality assurance to the consumers and at the same time a fair return to the farmers.

4. **Sugar (Control) Order 1956** - Indigenous Production of raw sugar and its quality are controlled primarily under this order. The Directorate of sugar, Ministry of Agriculture and Rural Development is the operating authority of this order. The quality of sugar is specified in terms of its colour and size. Detailed quality standards have been specified under the provisions of PFA Act 1954 and rules thereof.

5. **Vegetable Oil Products (Control) Order 1947; The Solvent Extracted Oil, Deoiled Meal and Edible Flour (Control) Order 1967; Vanaspati Control Order 1975** - These orders have been promulgated under the Essential Commodities Act, 1955, by the Central Government & Covers Commodities like Vanaspati, Margarine, Bakery shortening, edible vegetable oils, edible flour, meal etc. The Directorate of Vanaspati, Ministry of Food and Civil Supplies is the operating authority, Registration, Licensing, manufacture and distribution are all controlled by this Directorate.

6. **Meat Food Products (Control) Order 1975** - This order covers both raw and processed meat and meat products and has been promulgated under Essential Commodities act 1955. This order is operated by the Meat Food Advisory Committee with agricultural Marketing Advisor to the Govt. of India as its Chairman.

7. **Rice Milling Industry (Regulation) Act 1958 and Regulation and Licensing Rules 1976** - Modernization of rice mills and safe preservation of stocks.

8. **Export (Quality Control and Inspection) Act 1963 and Rules 1964**- Certain notified exportable commodities are subjected to compulsory quality control and inspection before shipment. This Act is intended to provide for sound development of export trade from India. Under this Act, the Export Inspection Council of India is exercising Quality Control & preshipment inspection on export oriented commodities including marine products.

9. **Insecticide Act 1968**- provides for compulsory registration of all insecticides. Regulates import, manufacture, transport, storage, sale and use of all pesticides.

10. **Standards of Weights and Measures Act 1976** - It is an Act enacted by the Parliament (No. 60 of 1976) to established standards of Weights and Measures, to regulate inter-state trade or commerce in weights, measures

and other goods which are sold or distributed by weight, measures or number and to provide for matters connected therewith or incidental thereto.

Director of Legal Metrology appointed under Section 28 of the Act, Additional, Joint, Deputy or Assistant Directors and other officers and staff appointed by the Director implements the provisions of the Act. The Central Government in consultation with the State Governments may Controller of Legal Metrology for speedy and strict enforcement of the provisions of the Act and Rules thereof including packaged commodities.

11. **State Licensing Order Governing Grain Dealers**- State Governments control grain dealers so as to protect stock against deterioration through moisture, insects, rodents, etc.

12. **The Consumer Protection Act 1986 -** This Act operated by the Ministry of Food and Civil Supplies is enacted recently where consumers through recognized consumer organizations can play the role of Food Inspector under PFA Act in the case of adulterated food samples. Rules are yet to be formulated for implementation at state levels.

Food Standardization and Regulatory Agencies in India

1. **Central Committee for Food Standards** is concerned with the Prevention of Food Adulteration Act. It specifies standards for food items to check food adulteration and fraudulent practices.

Since 1941, CCFS has been functioning to advise the Central and State Governments on matters arising out of the administration of the PFA Act. The PFA Act, 1954 and the PFA Rules, 1955 amended in 1976, 1980, 1981 and 1985, provide guidelines for the minimum basic requirements of food quality such as handling, storage, preparation and serving of food under sanitary conditions; freedom from extraneous matter, use of approved food additives such as preservatives, flavours, colours, etc.; proper packaging, branding and declaration of net weight as well as the date of manufacture and packing on the package. The guidelines are primarily intended to protect consumers from the health hazards of poisonous food. They also serve to prevent consumer exploitation by malpractices such as misbranding, adulteration, incorrect labelling, false claims, excessive and indiscriminate use of food additives., etc.

There are at present four Central Food Laboratories (CFL) serving as appellate laboratories for the analysis of food. These are : (1) Central Food

Laboratory, Kolkata; (2) Food Research and Standardization Laboratory, Ghaziabad; (3) Public Health Laboratory, Pune; and (4) Central Food Technological Research Institute (CFTRI), Mysore.

2. **Central and State Food Departments,** which come under the Ministry of Food and Civil Supplies, formulate specifications for cereal foodgrains/ pulses and selected foodstuff for purchase and procurement operations.

3. **State Food Laboratories/Food and Drug Administration**, generally under the Department of Health-These are law-enforcing authorities to check food adulteration.

4. **Bureau of Indian Standards**, the then Indian Standards Institution has been constituted under the Act of Parliament which deals with standardization of various articles including food. Agriculture Food Division Council (AFDC) deals with quality standards of various articles of food. This organization prepares National standards for various articles of food in consultation with the experts in the country. The certification scheme under ISI is a voluntary one and any manufacturer who wants to use ISI mark on his food product may apply for the same to the authority. The authorities after inspection and other formalities permit the manufacturer to use ISI Mark on their product. ISI symbol on any product ensures quality to the consumers. Recently, ISI has been renamed as Bureau of Indian Standards (BIS).

5. **Food corporation of India** has laid down specifications for several food commodities for internal purchase and procurement.

   To meet the essential requirements of the people in respect of rice, wheat, other cereals, pulses and gram products, the FCI procures these items in season, stores them and then distributes according to need the stored foodstuffs to the public through fair price shops as well as other outlets. The foodstuffs are stored in godowns, silos and cover and plinth (CAP) storage facilities specially built for the purpose at several places in the country. Modern rice mills, maize mills, soybean processing units and solvent extraction (of oil seeds) plants are maintained by the FCI to help in food processing. Besides, the FCI has provision to make nutritious foods such as fortified atta (wheat flour) and Balahar, on a very limited scale. Portable grain driers and food crop grain purifiers developed by the Corporation serve to furnish clean and dry grain to consumers in addition to ensuring better prices to the farmer.

6. **Army Supply Corps** has stipulated A.S.C. specifications for supply of food commodities to Army purchase organizations.

7. **Central Insecticide Board**, under the Department of Agriculture, controls the use of insecticides as applied to food crops. Under the Insecticide Act, all insecticide are required to be compulsorily registered with the Registration Committee established under section 5 of the Act. Registration certificates are issued after the Committee is satisfied that the insecticide is effective in pest control and at the same time safe to human beings, domestic animals and wild life.

CITRIC ACID AND ITS USES

Citric acid may be considered as "Nature's acidulant". It is found in the tissues of almost all plants and animals, as well as many yeasts and moulds. Commercially citric acid is manufactured under controlled fermentation conditions that produce citric acid as a metabolic intermediate from naturally-occurring yeasts, moulds and nutrients. The recovery process of citric acid is through crystallization from aqueous solutions.

The high water solubility of citric acid (181 g/100 ml) makes it an ideal additive for fountain fruit syrups and beverages concentrates as a flavour enhancer and microbial growth inhibitor (preferably at pH < 4.6).

(A) In beverages	1. As flavour enhancer.
	2. As preservative (microbial growth inhibitor).
	3. Eliminates haze due to trace metals.
	4. Prevents deterioration of colour and flavour and impart a fresh fruit "tanginess".
	5. Reduces heat processing requirements by lowering pH.
	6. Supplement antioxidant potential.
	7. Inactivate undesirable enzymes.
	8. *Wines:* Prevents turbidity, inhibits oxidation and adjusts pH.
	9. *Soft drinks:* Gives a cool taste and maintains carbonation.
	10. Improves palatability.

(B) In food and candy	1.	*Confectionery:* Enhances flavour, inverts sucrose, prevents oxidation, produces dark colours in hard candies, jams and jellies, and adjusts pH.
	2.	*Frozen foods:* Neutralizes residual lye, protects ascorbic acid from oxidation, inactivates trace metals and oxidative enzymes by lowering the pH, prevents changes in colour and flavour.
	3.	*Dairy products:* Acts as an antioxidant and emulsifier in cheese, ice-cream, etc.
	4.	*Canned foods*
		(i) Reduces heat-processing requirements by lowering pH (inhibition of microbial growth is a function of pH and heat treatment. Higher heat exposure and lower pH result in greater inhibition. Thus the use of citric acid to bring pH below 4.6 can reduce the heating requirements. In canned vegetables, citric acid usage is greatest in tomatoes and onions. For tomato packs, the National Canners Association recommends a pH of 4.1 to 4.3. In general, 0.1% citric acid will reduce the pH of canned tomatoes by 0.2 pH units).
		(ii) Optimize flavour (citric acid is added to canned fruits to provide for adequate tartness. Recommended usage level is generally less than 0.15%).

	(iii) Supplement antioxidant potential (citric acid is used in conjunction with antioxidants such as ascorbic acid, to inhibit colour and flavour deterioration caused by metal-catalyzed enzymatic oxidation. Recommended usage levels are generlly 0.1% to 0.3% with the antioxidant at 100 to 200 ppm).
	(iv) Inactivate undesirable enzymes (oxidative browning in most fruits and vegetables is catalyzed by the naturally present polyphenol oxidase. The enzymatic activity is strongly dependent on pH. Addition of citric acid to reduce pH below 3 will result in inactivation of polyphenol oxidase enzyme and prevention of browning reactions).

Sodium citrate is often added to beverages to mellow the tart taste of high acid concentrations. It provides a cool, distinctive smooth taste and masks any bitter aftertaste of artificial sweeteners. In addition, it serves as a buffer to stabilize the pH at the desired level.

HINDI EQUIVALENTS OF ENGLISH NAMES OF RAW MATERIALS COMMONLY USED IN PROCESSING

English name	Hindi Name
Ajma	Ajwain
Almond	Badam
Alum	Phitkari
Amaranthus	Chaulai
Aniseed	Saunf
Apple	Seb
Apricot	Khubani
Asafoetida	Hing
Banana	Kela
Beetroot	Chukander
Bitter gourd	Karela
Black pepper	Kalimirch
Brinjal	Baingan
Cabbage	Bandgobhi
Cane sugar	Chini
Cardamom	Elaychi
Carrot	Gajar
Cashewnut	Kaju

English name	Hindi Name
Cassia leaves	Tejpat
Cauliflower	Phoolgobhi
Chillies (green)	Hari mirch
Chillies (red)	Lal mirch
Cinnamon	Dalchini
Cloves	Laung
Cluster beans	Gwar ki phali
Coriander	Dhania
Coriander seeds	Sukha Dhania
Cumin seeds	Jeera
Date	Khajur
Dried date	Chohara
Drumstick	Sahijan ki phali
Fennel	Saunf
Fenugreek	Methi
Fig	Anjeer
Garlic	Lassan
Ginger (dried)	Sonth
Ginger (fresh)	Adrak
Grape	Angoor
Guava	Amrood
Jackfruit	Kathal
Jaggery	Gur

English name	Hindi Name
Knol-Khol	Ganthgobhi
Lime, Lemon	Nimboo
Mace	Javitri
Mango powder	Amchoor
Mango (ripe)	Aam
Mint	Podina
Musk melon	Kharbooza
Mustard leaves	Sarson ka sag
Mustard seeds	Rai or Sarson
Nigella seeds	Kalaonji
Nutmeg	Jaiphal
Onion	Pyaz
Orange	Santra
Papaya	Papita
Peach	Aru
Pear	Nashpati
Pea	Matar
Pineapple	Annanas
Plum	Alu bukhara
Pomegranate	Anar
Potato	Aloo
Raisin	Kishmish
Saffron	Kesar

English name	Hindi Name
Sago	Sabudana
Salt	Namak
Sapota	Chiku
Spinach	Palak
Tamarind	Imli
Tomato	Tamatar
Turmeric	Haldi
Turnip	Shalgam
Vinegar	Sirka
Water melon	Tarbooz
Yam	Zimikand

SUPPLIERS OF RAW MATERIALS AND EQUIPMENTS/ MACHINERY USED IN FOOD PROCESSING/PRESERVATION

(A) SUPPLIERS OF RAW MATERIALS

(1) Food Chemicals

- M/s. Advance Chemical Sales Corporation, 138, Pul Mithai, Teliwara, Delhi-110006

- M/s. Allied Chemical Corporation, 658, G.I.D.C. Makarpura Road No. 54, Vadodara-390010, Gujarat

- M/s. Amba Chemicals, 35, Western India House, Sir P.M. Road, Fort, Mumbai-400001, Maharashtra

- M/s. Camlin Ltd. (Pharma & Fine Chem. Divn.), Camlin House, J.B. Nagar, Andheri (E), Mumbai-400059, Maharashtra

- M/s. Chemishot, Sunita Bldg., 2nd Floor, Flat No. 9, G.D. Somani Marg, Cuffe Parade, Mumbai-400005, Maharashtra

- M/s. Dungra Chemicals Pvt. Ltd., 3rd Floor, Medows House, Nagindas Master Road, Fort, Mumbai-400023, Maharashtra

- M/s. Essdee Chemocrafts, 46, White Hall, 143, August Kranti Marg, Mumbai-400036, Maharashtra

- M/s. Farmsons Antioxidants, Shanker Bhuvan, Sayaji Gunj, Vadodara-390005, Gujarat

- M/s. Fine Organics, 15/2, Neelkanth Market, M.G. Road, Ghatkopar (E), Mumbai-400077, Maharashtra

- M/s. Ganesh Benzoplast Ltd., Ganesh House, Marol Naka, Andheri (E), Mumbai- 400059, Maharashtra

- M/s. Ganga Chemicals, 124, Naimappanaikken Street, Chennai-600003, Tamil Nadu

- M/s. Gaurav Enterprises, Sarvodaya Charity Trust Bldg., Room No. 33, Gokhale Road (s), Dadar (W), Mumbai-400028, Maharashtra

- M/s. Kushal Chand Sons, Devkaran Mansion, Block No. 1, 2nd Floor, Room No. 07/3, 79, Princess Street, Mumbai-400002, Maharashtra

- M/s. Navyug Pharmachem (P) Ltd., A/10, Avkar Apartment, Near Rachana Flats, Opp. Nilambaug Place, Bhavnagar-364002, Gujarat

- M/s. Pachisia Chemical Works, Rahul Chambers, 2nd Floor, 1172, Gate Telian, Tilak Bazar, Delhi-110006

- M/s. Perfect Chemicals, 1, Navyug House, 14, Dhirubhai Parikh Marg, Princess Street, Mumbai- 400002, Maharashtra

- M/s. Prabhahari Exim Pvt. Ltd., B-3, Nirmal Indl. Estae, Next to V.V.F. Ltd., Sion (E), Mumbai-400022, Maharashtra

- M/s. S.A. Chemicals, 220, Udyog Bhavan, Sonawalla Road, Goregaon (E), Mumbai-400063, Maharashtra

- M/s. S.D. Fine Chemicals, 315-317, T.V. Indl. Estate, 248, Worli Road, Mumbai-400025, Maharashtra

- M/s. Uma Brothers, C-110, Bhaveshwar Plaza, 189, L.B.S. Marg, Ghatkopar, Mumbai-400086, (W), Maharashtra

- M/s. Venkatesh Chemicals, 11/21, Daryasthan Street, 3rd Floor, Mumbai-400003, Maharashtra

(2) Food colours

- M/s. Aarkay Food Products, 35, IIIrd Floor, City Centre, Near Swastik Char Rasta, Navrangpura, Ahmedabad- 380009, Gujarat

- M/s. Ajanta Products Co., 45, West Avenue, Punjabi Bagh, New Delhi-110026

- M/s. Amreli Industrial Aromatics, 301, Royal Plaza, 3rd Floor, Kandaswamy Lane, 4-4-933/35, Sultan Bazar, Hyderabad-500095 (A.P.)

- M/s. Asim Products, 296, Samuel Street, Room No. 29, 2nd Floor, Mumbai-400003, Maharashtra

- M/s. Bush Boake Allen (India) Ltd., 1-5, Seven Wells Street, St. Thomas Mount, Chennai-600016, Tamil Nadu

- M/s. Dadajee Dhackjee & Co., Plot No. 278 (1), Village-Kardej, Bhavnagar, Gujarat-364064

- M/s. Devarsons Industries Ltd., Devarson House, B/h. Jain Temple, Usmanpura Charasta, Usmanpura, Ahmedabad-380014, Gujarat

- M/s. Drytech Process (I) P. Ltd., B-16, Girikunj Ind. Estate, Mahakali Kaves Road, Andheri (E) Mumbai-400093, Maharashtra

- M/s. Fab Flavours & Fragrances, Pvt. Ltd., 70-A, Rama Road, New Delhi-110015

- M/s. Golden Dyes Corporation (India) Pvt. Ltd., Bela Court No. 2, Colaba, Mumbai-400005, Maharashtra

- M/s. Hindustan Drug House, 867/8, Joshi Karol Bagh, New Delhi-110005

- M/s. Howrah Chemical Works, 148, M.G. Road, Kolkata-700001, West Bengal

- M/s. L. Liladhar & Co., 257-259, Samuel Street, Vadgadi, Mumbai-400003, Maharashtra

- M/s. Mansukhlal & Brothers, 1, Benfield Lane, 1st Floor, Kolkata-700001, West Bengal

- M/s. Mittal Associates, 211, Mahesh Market, 2280 Gali Hinga Beg, Tilak Bazar, Delhi-110006

- M/s. Narmada Food Colours Pvt. Ltd., Sanghrajka House, 4th Floor, 431, Dr. Dadasaheb, Bhadkamkar Marg, Opera House, Mumbai-400004, Maharashtra

- M/s. Natvarlal Nathalal & Co., 49, Balahanuman, Above Rangdeep Bangles, M.G. Road, Ahmedabad-380001, Gujarat

- M/s. Olin Chemicals, A-303, Padmavati Nagar, Gen. Arun Kumar Vaidya Marg, Goregaon (E), Mumbai-400063, Maharashtra

- M/s. Roha Dyechem Pvt. Ltd., Suryodaya Mill Compound, M.P. Mill Road, Tardeo, Mumbai-400034, Maharashtra

- M/s. Royal Marketing (Food Products Divn.), No. 11, 1 Cross St. Lest C.I.T. Nagar, Chennai-600035, Tamil Nadu

- M/s. Sun Dye Chem, B-4/3092, Vasant Kunj, Aruna Asaf Ali Marg, New Delhi-110070

(3) Food Flavours/Essences/Oleoresins

- M/s. Aromatik Bangalore Pvt. Ltd., 5, Chikkasandra, Hesarghatta Road, Dasarahalli Post, Bangalore-560057, Karnataka

- M/s. Arun Minerals & Chemicals Co., 10577, Pratap Nagar, Krishna Gali No. 4, Delhi-110007

- M/s. Ashwani Fine Chemicals, M-246, Sector-25, Noida-201301, U.P.

- M/s. Asian Chemical Works (Bombay) Pvt. Ltd., Asian House, 29, Ramkrishna, Mandir Road, Andheri-Kurla Road, Andheri (E), Mumbai-400059, Maharashtra

- M/s. Beeta Chemicals, B-31/33, Nandjyot Industrial Estate, Kurla Andheri Road, Safed Pool, Andheri (E), Mumbai-400072, Maharashtra

- M/s. D.V. Deo, G.C.D.A. Comml. Complex, Office No. 3, 3rd Floor, Marine Drive, Ernakulam, Cochin-682031

- M/s. Devi Industries, 2/174, Subbaih Naidu Indl. Complex, Y. Pudupatti, Arumbanur (P.O.), Madurai North-625107, Tamil Nadu

- M/s. Feroze Foods & Flavours, 6/79, Jahagir Mansion, 2nd Floor, Hughes Road, Chowpatty, Mumbai-400007, Maharashtra

- M/s. Garlico, 9/1, Indl. Estate, Mandsaur-458001, M.P.

- M/s. Gee Kay Sales Corporation, C-15, Hari Nagar Ashram, New Delhi-110014

- M/s. Gogia Chemical Industries Pvt. Ltd., A-127, Okhla Ind. Area, Phase-II, New Delhi-110020

- M/s. Gujarat Essence Mart Pvt. Ltd., Keshav Baug, 124/126 Shamaldas Gandhi Marg (Princess Street), Mumbai-400002, Maharashtra

- M/s. Gupta & Co. (P) Ltd., XIV/294-95, Gali Mandi Pan, Sadar Bazar, Delhi-110006

- M/s. Hajoori & Sons, Udhna Magdalla Road, Surat-395002, Gujarat

- M/s. Harish C. Khosla & Co., Zinat Mahal, Lal Kuan Bazar, P.O. Box-1328, Delhi-110006

- M/s. M.C. Dawar Aromatics Pvt. Ltd., 5/9, Indl. Estate, Gorwa, Vadodara-390016, Gujarat

- M/s. M.N. Hassa Singh & Co., 71, Johri Bazar, Jaipur-302003, Rajasthan
- M/s. Megha Herbal Products, 197/1, Sion (W), Mumbai-400022, Maharashtra
- M/s. Mittal Associates, 211, Mahesh Market, 2280, Gali Hinga Beg, Tilak Bazar, Delhi-110006
- M/s. Natvarlal Nathalal & Co. 49, Balahanuman, Above Rangdeep Bangles, M.G. Road, Ahmedabad-380001, Gujarat
- M/s. R.R. Chemicals, 703, Vishal Tower, Janakpuri, New Delhi-110058
- M/s. Rakesh Sandal Inds. Ptv. Ltd., 7/177 A, Swaroop Nagar, Kanpur-208002, U.P.
- M/s. Royson (Roy Agencies) 34, C.R. Avenue, "Jabkusum House", 2nd Floor, Room No. 4, Kolkata-700012, West Bengal
- M/s. S. Flavour & Fragrances of India, 102/103, Nav Vivek Indl. Estate, Moghul Lane, Mahim, Mumbai-400016, Maharashtra
- M/s. Sanrad Chemicals & Essential Oils, 302, Shiv Darshan Shopping Centre, Opp. Rly. Station, Santacruz (W), Mumbai-400005, Maharashtra
- M/s. Shri Mahila Griha Udyog Papad, Lijjat Bhawan, Wright Town, Jabalpur, M.P.
- M/s. Sonarome Chemical Pvt. Ltd., Peenya Indl. Area, 2nd Stage, Bangalore-560058, Karnataka
- M/s. Spices Board, Sugandha Bhawan, P.O. Box No. 2277, Cochin-682025, Kerala
- M/s. T. Ali Mohammed & Co., 144-146, Sarang Street, Mumbai-400003, Maharashtra
- M/s. The Haryana State Co-op. Supply & Marketing Federation Ltd. (Hafed), SCO 19, Sector 7C, Chandigarh
- M/s. United Aromatics Pvt. Ltd., Post Box No. 2, Kaviyoor P.O., Thiruvalla-689582, Kerala

(4) Sweeteners and Salt

- M/s. Allwyne Brine-Chem Pvt. Ltd., 1-Bileshwar Krupa, Chittaranjandas Road, Ram Nagar, Dombivli-421201, Maharashtra

- M/s. Anzen Exports 55/3D, Ballygunge Circular Road, Ground Floor Kolkata-700019, West Bengal

- M/s. Dhampur Alco-Chem Ltd., 507, Kusul Bazar, 32-33, Nehru Place, New Delhi-110019

- M/s. Dharani Sugar & Chemicals Ltd., 1, Venus Colony, 2nd Street, Alwarpet, Chennai-600018, Tamil Nadu

- M/s. J. Chittaranjan & Co., 864, Dr. Joshi Lane, Karol Bagh, New Delhi-110005

- M/s. Marketing & Material Management Services, 521/B, Narayan Villa, R.P. Masani Road, Matunga, Mumbai-400019, Maharashtra

- M/s. National Chemical Industries, 602, Monalisa, Hari Niwas, Thane-400602, Maharashtra

- M/s. Radix Laboratories Ltd. SCO 845, 1st Floor, Mani Majra, Chandigarh-160101

- M/s. S.A. Chemicals, 220, Udyog Bhavan, Sonawala Road, Goregaon (E), Mumbai-400063, Maharashtra

- M/s. Saboo Sodium Chloro Ltd., D-5, Kalwad Scheme, Behind Gopal Bari, Jaipur-302001, Rajasthan

- M/s. Sunash Chemicals, 143/4298, Kannamwar Nagar 2, Vikhroli (E), Mumbai-400083, Maharashtra

- M/s. Tata Chemicals Ltd., Bombay House, 24, Homi Mody Street, Mumbai-400001, Maharashtra

(5) Enzymes and Yeasts

- M/s. Advance Biochemicals Ltd., Above Navneet Motors, Gokul Nagar, P.O. Box 182, Thane (W)-400601, Maharashtra

- M/s. Bio Con India Pvt. Ltd., 20th K.M. Hosur Road, Hebbagodi, Bangalore-561229, Karnataka

- M/s. Burns Philip India Ltd., D.C. Silk Mills Bldg, Ist Floor, 5, Chunawala Estate, Kandivitta Road, Andheri-Kurla Road, Andheri (E), Mumbai-400059, Maharashtra

- M/s. Kasturi Food & Chemicals Ltd., No.17, Platform Road, Bangalore-560020, Karnataka

- M/s. Kothari Fermentation & Bio Chem Ltd. 16, Community Centre, Saket, New Delhi-110017

- M/s. Kushalchand & Sons, Devkaran Mansion, Block No. 1, Room No. 0713, 2nd Floor, 79, Princess Street, Mumbai 400002, Maharashtra

- M/s. Mixrozyme (India) Pvt. Ltd., Kriplani Estate, Saki Vihar Road, Powai, Mumbai-400072, Maharashtra

- M/s. Monozyme India Ltd., 7-1-58, Amrutha Business Complex, Ameerpet, Hyderabad-500016, A.P.

(6) Packaging Materials

- M/s. Alu Foil Products Pvt. Ltd., 208, Mukti Chambers, 2nd Floor, 4, Clive Row, Kolkata-700001, West Bengal

- M/s. Arora Box & Carton Pvt. Ltd., HR 12, Gali No.10, Anand Parbat Indl. Area, New Delhi-110005

- M/s. Jain. Flexipack Pvt. Ltd., M.A. C-9/9, Sector-8, Rohini, New Delhi-110085

- M/s. Jayco Trading Co., 506, Kakad Market Bldg., 306, Kalbadevi Road, Mumbai-400002, Maharashtra

- M/s. Oriental Containers Ltd., P.O. Box No. 6584, 1076, Dr. E. Moses Road, Worli, Mumbai-400018, Maharashtra

- M/s. Packwell Industries 3746, Netaji Subhash Marg, New Delhi-110002

- M/s. Panchmahal Polypack (P) Ltd., 36, Mithila Society, Opp. Shreyas School, Ambawadi, Ahmedabad-380015, Gujarat

- M/s. Swan Packaging, 53/54, Unique Indl. Estate, Dr. R.P. Road, Mulund (W), Mumbai-400080, Maharashtra

- M/s. Vindhyachal Process Corporation, 116, Malviya Nagar, Bhopal-462003, M.P.

(B) SUPPLIERS OF EQUIPMENTS/MACHINERY

(1) Food and Beverage Processing/Preservation Equipments/ Machinery

- M/s. Adam Fabriwerk Pvt. Ltd., 203, Rajguru Apts., New Nagardas Road, Andheri (E) Mumbai-400069, Maharashtra

- M/s. Akshay Industries, 107, Rajshree Indl. Estate II, Chitalsar Manpada, Ghodbunder Road, Thane-400607, Maharashtra

- M/s. Alok Technical & Marketing Service Pvt. Ltd., P.O. Box-8, Chandra Bldg., Kalkaji Temple, New Delhi-110019

- M/s. Alven Foodpro System (P) Ltd., 24, Goldfield Plaza, 45, Sassoon Road, Pune-411001, Maharashtra

- M/s. Asian Chemical Works (Bombay) Pvt. Ltd., Asian House, 29, Ramakrishna Mandir Road, Andheri-Kurla Road, Andheri (E), Mumbai-400059, Maharashtra

- M/s. B. Sen Barry and Co., 65/11, New Rohtak Road, Karol Bagh, New Delhi-110005

- M/s. Bajaj Maschinen Pvt. Ltd., D-14, Lajpat Nagar-II, New Delhi-110024

- M/s. Baker Enterprises, 23, Bhera Enclave, Near Peera Garhi, New Delhi-110087

- M/s. Cantech Machines, 13, Vora Bhavan, Maheshwari Udyan, King's Circle, Matunga (C. Rly), Mumbai-400019, Maharashtra

- M/s. DSI Industries, C-10, Devatha Plaza, Residency Road, Bangalore-560025, Karnataka

- M/s. Eastend Engineering Co., 173/1, Gopal Lal Thakur Road, Kolkata-700016, West Bengal

- M/s. Filtron Engineers Ltd., 117-A, Vithalwadi Road, Pune-411030, Maharashtra

- M/s. FMC Food Tech, 7, Shivaji Housing Society, Pune-411053, Maharashtra

- M/s. Frigoscandia Winner Food Process System Ltd., Shreesh Chambers, 3rd Floor, 25/1, Yeshwant Niwas Road, Indore-452003, M.P.

- M/s. Gardners Corporation, 6, Doctors Lane, Near Gole Market, Post Box 299, New Delhi- 110001

- M/s. Guru Nanak Engg. & Foundary Works (Regd.), 166, Indl. Focal Point, Mehta Road, Amritsar-143001, Punjab

- M/s. HMT Ltd., (Food Processing M/c Div.), H-2, MIDC, Chikalthana Indl. Area, P.B. No. 720, Aurangabad-431210, Maharashtra

- M/s. K.S. Seetharamiah & Sons Pvt. Ltd., 29/1, Jaraganahalli, 10th Km. Karakapura Road, Bangalore-560078, Karnataka

- M/s. Mather and Platt (India_) Ltd., 805-806, Ansal Bhawan, 16, Kasturba Gandhi Marg, New Delhi-110001

- M/s. Mojj Engg. Systems (P) Ltd., 81-B/15, M.I.D.C., Opp. Morris Electronics, Bhosari, Pune-411026, Maharashtra

- M/s. Mukul Brothers Engg. Works, P.B. No. 325, Kishan Flour Mill Compound, Tirthankar Mahavir Mart (Rly. Road), Meerut-250002, U.P.

- M/s. Pharmalab Engg. India Ltd., Star Metal Compound, L.B.S. Marg, Vikhroli (W), Mumbai-400083, Maharashtra

- M/s. Quasar Engineers, Plot No. 53, Sector 'A' Indl. Area, Sanwer Road, Indore-452003, M.P.

- M/s. Sri Rajalakshmi Industrial Agency, 57(30/1), Silver Jubilee Park Road, Rajalakshmi Corner House, Post Box No. 6690, Bangalore- 560002, Karnataka

- M/s. Raylons Metal works, Ramakrishna Mandir Road, Kondivita Village, opp. Marol Bazar, J.B. Nagar, Andheri (E), Mumbai-400059, Maharashtra

- M/s. Rita Bottling Machines Ltd., 1B & 1C, Suvarna Darshan, 47, 2nd Main Road, Gandhi Nagar, Adyarn, Chennai-600020, Tamil Nadu

- M/s. Veenu Hitech, Plant Manufacturing Pvt. Ltd., F-6 St. Soldier Tower, G-Block, Vikas Puri, New Delhi-110018

(2) Canning Equipments/Machinery

- M/s. Asian Consolidated Industries Ltd., "Asian House", D-193, Okhla Indl. Area, Phase-I, New Delhi-110020

- M/s. Ganga Singh Engg. Works'P. Ltd., No. 1, Vishal Indl. Estate, Village Road, Bhandup (W) Mumbai- 400078, Maharashtra

- M/s. Quality Equipment Co., 89, Mahavira Street, Haiderpur Indl. Area Delhi-110052

- M/s. Recon Machine Tools Pvt. Ltd., 37, Sarvodaya Indl. Estate, Mahakali Caves Road, Andheri (E), Mumbai-400093, Maharashtra

- M/s. Sangram Engg. Ltd., B-5, Super Con, Opp. I.T.I., Aundh, Pune-411007, Maharashtra

- M/s. Thakar Equipment Co., 66, Okhla Indl. Estate, New Delhi-110020

(3)   Drying/Dehydration Equipments/Machinery

- M/s. Admir Enterprises, Plot No. 1/E, 4, Shivaji Nagar Govandi, Mumbai-400043.

- M/s. Aifso Industrial Equipment Co., B/13, Veena Beena Apts, P. Thakrey Marg, Sewri (W), Mumbai-400015, Maharashtra

- M/s. Aratic India Engg. Pvt. Ltd., 20, Rajpur Road, Delhi-110054

- M/s. Bombay Industrial Engineers, 430, Hind Rajasthan Chambers, D.S. Phalke Road, Dadar (C. Rly.), Mumbai-400014, Maharashtra

- M/s. Bry-Air India Pvt. Ltd., 419-420, Udyog Vihar, Phase-III, Gurgaon, Haryana

- M/s. Burman Plant & Machinery Co. Pvt. Ltd., 36, Sarkar Lane, Kolkata-700007, West Bengal

- M/s. C.M. Equipments & Instruments (India) Pvt. Ltd., B-194, 5th Main Road, P.B. No. 5847, Peenya 2nd Stage, Bangalore-560058, Karnataka

- M/s. Eec Cee & Co., 1, Anant Indl. Estate, Opp. Cemet Fruit & Chemicals, Rakhial Ahmedabad-380023, Gujarat

- M/s. Orbit International Technologies (P) Ltd., 404, Taramandal Complex, Secretariat Road, Hyderabad -500004, A.P.

- M/s. Ratan Equipments 69, Lake View Road, Kamakati St., West Mambalam, Chennai-600003, Tamil Nadu

- M/s. Raylon Engg. Works, 31 A, Ghanshyam Indl. Estate., Near Veera Desai Road, Andheri (W), Mumbai-400058, Maharashtra

- M/s. Wintech Taparia Ltd., 25/1, Yeshwant Niwas Road, Shreesh Chambers, III Floor, Indore-452003, M.P.

(4)   Product Specific Equipments/Machinery

(a)   Jam Making

- M/s. Foram Foods Pvt. Ltd., 397, Swami Vivekanand road, Vile Parle (W), Mumbai-400056, Maharashtra

- M/s. Inventure India BV, 24, Gold Field Plaza, 45, Sassoon road, Pune-

411001, Maharashtra

(b) Pickle and Chutney Making

- M/s. Geeta Food Engineering, Plot C-7/1 TTC Area, Pawana M.I.D.C., Thane-Belapur Road, Behind Savita Chemical Ltd., Navi, Mumbai-400705, Maharashtra

- M/s. Techno Equipments, Saraswati Sadan, Girgaum Court, Girgaum, Mumbai-400004, Maharashtra

(c) Tomato Processing

- M/s. Goma Engineering Pvt. Ltd., Majiwada, Behind Universal Pertol Pump, Thane-400601, Maharashtra

- M/s. K.S. Seetharamiah & Sons. Pvt. Ltd., 29/1, Jaraganahalli, 10th Km. Kanakapura Road, Bangalore-560078, Karnataka

- M/s. Penwalt India Ltd., 507, Kakad Chambers, 32, Dr. Annie Besant Road, Worli, Mumbai-400018, Maharashtra

(d) Mushroom Processing

- M/s. Jwala Engg. Co., 12, Surve Indl. Estate, Sonawala Cross Road No.1, Goregaon (E), Mumbai-400063, Maharashtra

- M/s. Wintech Taparia Ltd., 25/1, Yeshwant Niwas Road, IIIrd Floor, Shreesh Chambers, Indore-452003, M.P.

(5) Wrapping/Filling/Packaging Equipments/Machinery

- M/s. Aarkay Wrapping Machines Pvt. Ltd., 1, Hormurz, 131, August Kranti Marg, Mumbai-400036, Maharashtra

- M/s. Abhay & Abhay Pvt. Ltd., B-84-1, Okhla Indl. Area, Phase-II, New Delhi-110020

- M/s. APT Packaging, 184/5007, Pantnagar Ghatkopar (E), Mumbai-400075, Maharashtra

- M/s. Bombay Engineering Industry, R. No. 6 (Estns.), Sevanthibhai Bhavan, Chimatpada, Marol Naka, Andheri (E), Mumbai-400059, Maharashtra

- M/s. Compack Systems, E-211, F.F. Complex, Okhla III, New Delhi-110020

- M/s. Debes Industries, 11, Govt. Place East, Kolkata-700069, West Bengal

- M/s. E.C. Packaging Pvt. Ltd., 14/7 Mile Stone, Mathura Road Faridabad-121003, Haryana

- M/s. Europack Machines (I) Pvt. Ltd., Akash Business Centre, CST Road, Kurla (W), Mumbai-400070, Maharashtra

- M/s. Multipack Systems Pvt. Ltd., 2nd Floor, Patrict Complex, Ellora Park, Vadodara-390007, Gujarat

- M/s. Packaging Machines of India, 8-3-229/5/3/7, Jai Bharani Nagar, Yusufguda Check Post, Hyderabad, A.P.

- M/s. Reliance Packaging, 155-A, Ekta Enclave, Peeragarhi, Main Rohtak Road, New Delhi - 110041

(6) Refrigeration /Cold Storage Equipments/Machinery

- Airtech Engineers, B-19, Okhala Indl. Area, Phase-II, New Delhi-110020

- M/s. Anand Refrigeration Co. Pvt. Ltd., D-Lajpat Nagar-I, New Delhi-110024

- M/s. Blue Star Ltd., Kasturi Bldg., Mahan T. Advani Chowk, Jamshedji Tata Road, Mumbai-400020, Maharashtra

- M/s. Carrier Refrigeration (P) Ltd., 700/701 A, Lado Sarai, Aurobindo Marg, Mehrauli, New Delhi-110030

- M/s. Greenfield Agencies Shop No. 6, Anuradha, Opp. Golf Club, Rest House, Tidke Colony, Nasik-422002, Maharashtra

- M/s. Industrial Refrigeration Pvt. Ltd., 901, Maker Chambers-V, Nariman Point, Mumbai-400021, Maharashtra

- M/s. Kooling System, 35, Mannar Reddy Street, T. Nagar, Chennai- 600017, Tamil Nadu

- M/s. Western Refrigeration Ltd., 4, Ready Money Terrace, Dr. A.B. Road, Worli, Mumbai-400018, Maharashtra

CONVERSION DATA

Mass

1 gram (g)	=	1000 milligrams (mg)
1 mg	=	1000 micrograms (µg)
1 µg	=	1000 millimicrograms (mµg) or nanogram (ng)
1 mµg	=	1000 micromicrograms (µµg) or picogram (pg)
1 ounce (oz)	=	28.4 g
1 pound (lb)	=	16 oz =453.6 g
1 g	=	15.4 grains
1 grain	=	65 mg

Volume

1 litre (l)	=	1000 millilitres (ml)
1 millilitre (ml)	=	1000 microlitres (µl)
1 litre	=	1.76 pint
	=	35.196 fluid ounces (fl.oz.)
1 pint	=	568 ml
1 pint	=	20 fluid ounces
1 quart	=	2 pints
1 fluid ounce	=	28.4 ml
1 gallon	=	4.55 litres
1 cubic inch (cu. in.)	=	16.39 cubic centimetres
1 cubic centimetre (c.c.)	=	1000 cubic millimetres
	=	0.061 cubic inches
1 cubic metre (cu. m.)	=	35.31 cubic feet
1 cubic foot (cu. ft.)	=	1728 cubic inches
	=	0.083 cubic metre

Length

1 metre (m)	=	1000 millimetres (mm)
1 millimetre (mm)	=	1000 microns (µ)
1 micron	=	1000 millimicrons (mµ)
1 mµ	=	1000 micromicrons (µµ)

1 mµ	=	10 Angstrom units (A)
1 inch	=	2.54 centimetres
1 foot	=	0.305 metre

Area

1 square inch	=	6.451 square centimetres
1 acre	=	4840 square yards
1 hectare	=	2.47 acre
1 acre	=	0.405 hectare
1 square foot	=	0.093 square metre

Weight - Volume Relationship

1000 ml (1 litre)	=	1000 ppm	=	0.1%
10000 ml (10 litres)	=	100 ppm	=	0.01%
100000 ml (100 litres)	=	10 ppm	=	0.001%
1000000 ml (1000 litres)	=	1 ppm	=	0.0001%

Conversion of Feet and Inches to Centimetres
(1 inch = 2.54 cms)   (1 cm = 0.39 inch)

Ft.-In.	Cm	Ft.-In.	Cm
0-6	15.2	2-7	78.7
1-0	30.5	2-8	81.2
1-6	45.7	2-9	83.8
1-7	48.3	2-10	86.3
1-8	50.8	2-11	88.8
1-9	53.3	3-0	91.4
1-10	55.9	3-1	93.9
1-11	58.4	3-2	96.4
2-0	61.0	3-3	99.0
2-1	63.5	3-4	101.6
2-2	66.0	3-5	104.1
2-3	68.6	3-6	106.6
2-4	71.1	3-7	109.2
2-5	73.6	3-8	111.7
2-6	76.1	3-9	114.2

Ft.-In.	Cm	Ft.-In.	Cm
3-10	116.8	5-1	154.9
3-11	119.3	5-2	157.5
4-0	121.9	5-3	160.0
4-1	124.4	5-4	162.6
4-2	127.0	5-5	165.1
4-3	129.5	5-6	167.6
4-4	132.0	5-7	170.2
4-5	134.6	5-8	172.7
4-6	137.1	5-9	175.3
4-7	139.6	5-10	177.8
4-8	142.2	5-11	180.3
4-9	144.7	6-0	182.9
4-10	147.3	6-1	185.4
4-11	149.8	6-2	188.0
5-0	152.4	6-3	190.5

Conversion of Pounds (lb) to Kilograms (kg)

lb	kg	lb	kg	lb	kg
1	0.454	13	5.90	25	11.34
2	0.91	14	6.35	26	11.79
3	1.36	15	6.80	27	12.25
4	1.81	16	7.26	28	12.70
5	2.27	17	7.71	29	13.15
6	2.72	18	8.17	30	13.60
7	3.18	19	8.62	31	14.06
8	3.63	20	9.07	32	14.52
9	4.08	21	9.52	33	14.97
10	4.54	22	9.98	34	15.42
11	4.99	23	10.43	35	15.88
12	5.44	24	10.89	36	16.33

lb	kg	lb	kg	lb	kg
37	16.78	49	22.23	80	36.28
38	17.24	50	22.68	100	45.36
39	17.69	51	23.13	120	54.44
40	18.14	52	23.59	140	63.50
41	18.60	53	24.04	160	72.56
42	19.05	54	24.49	180	81.54
43	19.50	55	24.95	200	90.72
44	19.96	56	25.40	220	99.80
45	20.41	57	25.86	240	108.86
46	20.87	58	26.31	260	117.92
47	21.32	59	26.76	280	126.90
48	21.77	60	27.22	300	136.08

Conversion of Ounces (oz) to Gram (g)

oz	g	oz	g
1	28.35	9	255.15
2	56.70	10	283.50
3	85.05	11	311.85
4	113.40	12	340.20
5	141.75	13	368.55
6	170.10	14	396.90
7	198.45	15	425.25
8	226.80	16	453.60

Temperature

Thermometer scale	Freezing point degree	Boiling point degree
Celsius (Centigrade)	0	100
Fahrenheit	32	212
Reaumur	0	80

4 Reaumur (r) scale divisions = 5 Celsius (C) divisions = 9 Fahrenheit (F) divisions

$$\frac{F-32}{9} = \frac{C}{5} = \frac{r}{4}$$

Hence, to convert degrees C into degrees F, multiply by 9, divide by 5 and add 32.

To convert degrees F into degrees C, subtract 32, multiply by 5 and divide by 9.

Domestic Measures

Liquids

1 teaspoonful	= 1/8 fluid ounce
1 dessertspoonful	= 1/4 fluid ounce
1 tablespoonful	= 1/2 fluid ounce
1 tumblerful	= 10 fluid ounce

Solids

1 level tablespoonful	= 1/2 ounce

IMPERIAL TO METRIC CONVERSION

Multiply by	of ⟶ to to ⟵ of		Multiply by
LINEAR MEASURES			
0.394	Inches	Centimetres	2.54
33.281	Feet	Metres	0.305
1.094	Yards	Metres	0.914
0.621	Miles	Kilometres	1.609
SQUARE MEASURES			
0.155	Square inches	Square centimetres	6.452
10.764	Square feet	Square metres	0.093
1.196	Square yards	Square metres	0.836
2.471	Acres	Hectares	0.405
0.386	Square miles	Square kilometres	2.590
CUBIC MEASURES			
0.061	Cubic inches	Cubic centimetres	16.387
35.315	Cubic feet	Cubic metres	0.028
1.308	Cubic yards	Cubic metres	0.765
WEIGHTS			
15.432	Grains	Grams	0.065
0.035	Avoirdupois ounces	Grams	28.3350
0.032	Troy ounces	Grams	31.104

Multiply by	of ———————→ to ←——————— of	to	Multiply by
2.205	Avoirdupois pounds	Kilograms	0.454
1.968	Hundred weight	Quintals	0.508

CONCENTRATION

0.160	Ounces per Imp. gallon	Grams per litre	6.236
0.134	Ounces per U.S. gallon	Grams per litre	7.490

YIELDS

0.892	Pounds per acre	Kilograms per hectare	1.121
89.218	Pounds per acre	Quintals per hectare	0.011
0.008	Hundred weight per acre	Kilograms per hectare	125.54
0.796	Hundred weight per acre	Quaintals per hectare	1.255
0.089	Gallons per acre	Litres per hectare	11.21

Suggested Reading

Arya, P.R. and Rastogi, P.P. (1984). **Fruit-Vegetable Preservation at Home** (In Hindi). Directorate of Translation and Publication, G.B. Pant University of Agriculture and Technology, Pantnagar, Nainital.

Athalye (1992). **Plastics in Packaging**. Tata McGraw-Hill Publishing Company Limited, New Delhi.

Banwart, G.J. (1979). **Basic Food Microbiology**. The AVI Publishing Company, Inc., Westport, Connecticut.

Bhat, C.M., Sharma, R.N. and Sehgal, S. (1982). **A Manual on Food Preservation at Home**. Directorate of Publication, Haryana Agricultural University, Hissar.

Board, P.W. (1988). **Quality Control in Fruit and Vegetable Processing.** FAO Food and Nutrition Paper 39. Food and Agriculture Organisation of the United Nations, Rome.

Burton, W.G. (1989). Specific gravity as a guide to the content of dry matter and of starch in potato tubers. In **'The Potato'**. 3rd Ed. Longman Scientific and Technical. Essex, England.

C.F.T.R.I. (1981). **Home-Scale Processing and Preservation of Fruits and Vegetables**. Central Food Technological Research Institute, Mysore.

Dauthy, M.E. (1995). **Fruit and Vegetable Processing.** FAO Agricultural Services Bulletin 119. Food and Agriculture Organisation of the United Nations, Rome.

Desrosier, N.W. and Desrosier, J.N. (1987). **The Technology of Food Preservation**. CBS Publishers and Distributors, New Delhi.

Desrosier, N.W. and Tressler, D.K. (1977). **Fundamentals of Food Freezing**. The AVI Publishing Company, Inc., Westport, Connecticut.

Frazier, W.C. and Westhoff, D.C. (1983). **Food Microbiology**. Tata McGraw-Hill Publishing Company Limited, New Delhi.

Gauri Shanker (1984). **Practical Manual in Horticulture**. Kitabistan, Allahabad.

Girdhari Lal, Siddappa, G.S. and Tondon, G.L. (1986). **Preservation of Fruits and Vegetables**. Publications and Information Division, Indian Council of Agricultural Research, New Delhi.

Gopalan, C., Rama Sastri, B.V. and Bala Subramanian, S.C. (1982). **Nutritive Value of Indian Foods.** National Institute of Nutrition, I.C.M.R., Hyderabad.

Harris, R.S. and Karmas, E. (1975). **Nutritional Evaluation of Food Processing**. 2nd Edition. AVI Publishing Co. Westport, Connecticut.

Jacob, T. (1987). **Poisons in our Food**. Publications Division, Ministry of Information and Broadcasting, Government of India, New Delhi.

Jayaraman, J. (1981). **Laboratory Manual in Biochemistry**. Wiley Eastern Limited, New Delhi.

Kordylas, J.M. (1991). **Processing and Preservation of Tropical and Subtropical Foods**. Macmillan Education Ltd., Houndmills, Basingstoke, Hampshire.

Meena, R.K. and Yadav, J.S. (2001). **Horticulture Marketing and Post Harvest Management**. Pointer Publishers Jaipur (Raj.).

Misra, J.B. (1983). A simple arrangement for the accurate determination of the specific gravity of potato tubers. *J. Indian Potato Assoc.* 10: 121-128.

Mudambi, S.R. and Rao, S. (1986). **Food Science**. Wiley Eastern Limited, New Delhi.

Negi, J.P., Singh, B. and Dagar, K.S. (2000). **Indian Horticulture Database-2000**. National Horticulture Board, Ministry of Agriculture, Government of India, Gurgaon (Haryana).

Nissen, M. (1967). The weight of potatoes in water. Further studies on the relation between the dry matter and starch content. *Eur. Potato J.* 10: 85-99.

Pandey, P.H. (1997). **Post-harvest Technology of fruits and Vegetables (Principles and Practices)**. Saroj Prakashan, 646-47, Katra, Allahabad.

Pantastico, Er. B. (1975). **Postharvest Physiology, Handling and Utilization of Tropical and Subtropical Fruits and Vegetables**. The AVI Publishing Company, Inc., Westport, Connecticut.

Paulus, K.O. (1984). Modelling in Industrial Cooking. In: *Thermal Processing and Quality of Foods*. Zeuthen *et al.* (eds.), Elsevier Applied Science Publishers, London.

Potter, N. N. (1984). **Food Science**. 3rd Edition. The AVI Publishing Company, Inc., Westport, Connecticut.

Potter, N.N. (1973). **Food Science**. The AVI Publishing Company, Inc., Westport Connecticut.

Potter, N.N. and Hotchkiss, J.H. (1996). **Food Science**. 5th Edition. CBS Publishers and Distributors, New Delhi.

Potty, V.H. (1988). **Horticultural Industry in India**. UNIDO Consultation Meeting, Beijing, Nov. 22-24.

Powar, C.B. and Daginawala, H.F. (1986). **General Microbiology** Vol II Himalaya Publishing Company, Bombay.

Ranganna, S. (1979). **Manual of Analysis of Fruit and Vegetable Products**. Tata McGraw-Hill Publishing Company Limited, New Delhi.

Shakuntala Manay, N. and Shadaksharaswamy, M. (1987). **Foods : Facts and Principles.** Wiley Eastern Limited, New Delhi.

Singh, A. (1986). **Fruit Physiology and Production**. Kalyani Publishers, New Delhi.

Srivastasva, M (1985). **Essentials of Food and Nutrition** Vol. II (Applied Aspects). The Bangalore Printing and Publishing Company Limited, Bangalore.

Srivastava, R.K. and Singh, S. (1987). **Utilization of Mushrooms for Preparation of Different Types of Preserved Products**. Government Fruit Preservation and Canning Institute, U.P., Lucknow.

Srivastava, R.P. (1992). **Preservation of Fruit and Vegetable Products**. Bishen Singh Mahendra Pal Singh, New Connaught Place, Dehra Dun.

Sukumaran, N.P. and Ramdass, C. (1980). A simple variable load potato hydrometer. *J. Indian Potato Assoc.* 7: 32-37.

Tauro, P., Kapoor, K.K. and Yadav, K.S. (1986). **An Introduction to Microbiology**. Wiley Eastern Limited, New Delhi.

Tressler, D.K. and Joslyn, M.A. (1971). **Fruit and Vegetable Juice Processing Technology.** The AVI Publishing Company, Inc., Westport, Connecticut.

Verma, S.C. (1991). **Potato Processing in India-An Appraisal**. Central Potato Research Institute, Shimla

Woodroof, J.G. and Luh, B.S. (1975). **Commercial Fruit Processing**. The AVI Publishing Company, Inc., Westport, Connecticut.

Woods, A.E. and Aurand, L.W. (1977). **Laboratory Manual in Food Chemistry**. The AVI Publishing Company, Inc., Westport, Connecticut.

Subject Index